On The Hills Of God

On the Hills of God

A Novel

By Ibrahim Fawal

NewSouth Books
MONTGOMERY

NewSouth Books
P.O. Box 1588
Montgomery, AL 36102

This book is a work of fiction. Names, characters, places, and incidents are either products of the author's imagination or are used fictitiously. Any resemblance to actual events or locales or persons, living or dead, is entirely coincidental.

 Published in the United States by NewSouth Books, a division of NewSouth, Inc., Montgomery, Alabama.

ISBN 1-58838-075-0

This book was originally published in 1998 by Black Belt Press with the ISBN 1-57966-002-9. An Arabic edition was published by the Jordan Book Centre, Amman, Jordan. A German edition is forthcoming.

Design by Randall Williams
Printed in the United States of America

To Rose

On The Hills Of God

1

In Palestine's last summer of happiness, seventeen-year-old Yousif Safi was awakened by the familiar voice of the muezzin calling man to prayer. It was not six o'clock yet and he lay warm and comfortable in his bed, but the moment he opened his eyes he was fully awake. He could hear the chirping and twittering of his birds in the aviary in the next room. On this day early in June 1947, the new house was to get its roof. His parents and relatives and all their friends had been waiting for this occasion. He could hear the workers gearing up for the mixing and pouring of cement on top of the house. The iron grill, which would hold the roof together, had been fastened atop the nearly finished villa a week or two earlier.

He stretched in bed thinking of the ten years his parents had spent waiting to build such a house. Thank God it was nearly finished. He admired them for their foresight and determination. They had divided and landscaped the whole mountaintop long ago. Trees needed years to grow and his parents had wanted the house and gardens to be ready at the same time. And while the trees were growing, they were saving the money to build their villa. Not satisfied with a good income from his medical practice, his enterprising father had invested wisely over the years, buying and selling real estate at a good profit.

Luck must have been with Dr. Jamil Safi. Young as Yousif was, he could tell that scheming and making money were against his father's natural instincts. What did interest the doctor was building things and making them grow. It was he who had thought of developing the only real estate agency in Ardallah. It was he who had invested in the first cinema. It was he who had advised the Chamber of Commerce to send men on a public relations tour of the surrounding Arab countries to promote Ardallah as a summer resort. It was he who had conceived the idea that Ardallah needed a hospital and had started raising money for it. No wonder, Yousif thought, the townspeople had wanted his father to be their mayor.

In every municipal council election he had entered, Dr. Safi had always come out on top. The British, who effectively ruled Palestine and with whom he was on relatively good terms, had offered him the position of mayor several times. But the doctor had always declined, satisfied with being just a council member. After all, the major decisions for the city were subject to approval of the British authorities, and they consulted him on important issues such as zoning and opening new roads. Anyway, from the doctor's point of view, who needed a job of worrying about paying garbage collectors and inspectors and a dozen or so policemen, or threatening with legal action people who were delinquent in paying their local taxes, or issuing building permits, or listening to citizens' complaints about the need for light posts on dark street corners? No, the doctor felt he had better things to do than be a bureaucrat, no matter how exalted. And now, in the summer of 1947, Yousif's parents were realizing their dream of building their own villa and Yousif, their only son, was happy for them.

Yousif shaved, took a quick shower, and stood by the window tucking in his shirt. It was a beautiful morning, without a cloud to mar the blue summer sky. He could see the maid, Fatima, spreading white tablecloths on the fifteen long tables that had been set under the trees the night before. Fatima's husband and two teenage sons were bringing in dozens of chairs borrowed from relatives and friends or rented from cafes. Two or three workers were picking up odd pieces of wood or scrap metal off the ground. Others were inside the house, hammering at the scaffolding.

A large pile of cement was already on the ground and another big truck was being unloaded, raising a cloud of dust. The builder, a stout man with a grayish beard, was on top of the roof for a last-minute inspection. The two workers with him were bent down, welding. The gravel-voiced blacksmith and a couple of helpers were at the far end of the driveway installing the huge wrought-iron gate before the crowds arrived. Only Abu Amin and his six stonecutters were relaxed. Their job done, they looked awkward in their clean ankle-length robes. They had done a beautiful job on the house, Yousif observed, and he was glad to see them with no dust clinging to their clothes. It would be nice, he mused, to see drinks in their hands rather than hammers and chisels.

By the time Yousif finished eating breakfast and feeding his birds, the old house had begun to fill up. Aunt Hilaneh, Uncle Boulus's wife, and other women were already stuffing three large lambs with rice, chunks of meat, pine nuts, and spices. Two or three of these women took great pride in their cooking, and Yousif wondered which one would appoint herself as supervisor. At other occasions he had seen them make faces behind each other's back and bicker about too much cinnamon or not enough nutmeg. But not today. Today, everyone was working in harmony.

Maha, cousin Basim's wife, was hard at work with a crew of women on the balcony. Aunt Sarah, Isaac's mother, was helping to chop parsley, mint, lettuce, tomatoes, and to fry meats and mash garbanzo beans. One and all, they were preparing *maza* for the guests to nibble on while drinking. *Kabab, falafel,* fried kidneys and dips—*hummus* and eggplant—cheeses, pickles and olives were piled up in dozens of small dishes to be placed on the tables throughout the yard.

Yousif was in charge of drinks: whiskey, beer, *arak, kazoze,* lemonade, and water. By ten o'clock, his best friends, Amin and Isaac, were with him. They helped him crush the large ice block which had been laid in the bathtub, and they helped pass around drinks as the guests began to arrive.

Yousif's father was in constant motion, giving last-minute instructions and greeting well-wishers. Around 10:30, Father Mikhail and Father Yacoub of the Roman Catholic Church joined the small knot of guests under the trees. Soon scores of men were in the garden. Some sat around on chairs with high backs or small short backs with straw bottoms; the younger ones stood watching by the sparkling-white, colonnaded house. Yousif and his two friends brought out the drinks and the *maza.* The rest of the clergy followed each other, as if by plan. Then came two more priests: one Melkite Catholic, the other Greek Orthodox. Five minutes later they were joined by an Arab Anglican minister and two Muslim *shaykhs.* Then came the suppliers and sub-contractors. They were followed by the mayor of Ardallah, the entire municipal council, attorneys Fouad Jubran and Zuhdi Muftah, Dr. Fareed Afifi and his wife, Jihan. Even Moshe Sha'lan had closed his shop for the occasion.

Half an hour later the moment of excitement was at hand. The grayish builder wove his way through the crowd until he found the doctor. Yousif saw him signal with his forefinger that the ceremony was about to begin. The doctor in turn signaled Father Mikhail.

Suddenly there was a flurry of activity. Everyone stood up, silent. A laborer was ready to haul the first leather bucket full of cement up one of the many ladders placed against the exterior of the house. But before he would start, the crowd waited expectantly for the Roman Catholic priests to say a prayer.

As everyone watched, Fathers Mikhail and Yacoub put their vestments around their necks and smoothed them down their chests, looking resplendent with their large crosses. The priests alternated saying short prayers, giving thanks to God for all his blessings and exhorting all the saints and angels to look after the Safi family and make their home free of jealous eyes or evil spirits. Their prayers were augmented with a profusion of incense from the two large censers they kept swinging back and forth over Yousif's head, over the heads of his parents, the guests, over the cement mixers, the hands of the laborers, over the balconies and doorsteps, and throughout the finished but unplastered, unpartitioned house itself.

The last to be blessed was the laborer at the bottom of the ladder who was poised to haul the first bucket. No sooner had the priests stopped praying than the laborer lifted the leather bucket to his side and began to ascend. The moment his sole touched the first rung, a woman's voice burst out in a ululation halfway between a yodel and an aria. She had a powerful voice that managed to startle quite a few. Yousif turned to look. An unsuspecting man standing by the singing woman had both of his hands over his ears. His mouth puckered. His eyes closed. At the end of the customary four verses, the woman began trilling. She pursed her lips as if she were about to whistle, while the tip of her tongue darted left and right like a piston. She electrified the crowd; they burst into applause.

Other women now broke out in song. The men atop the walls of the building and those mixing and transporting the cement started a chant that Yousif knew from experience would last for hours. The eighteen or twenty workers, reminiscent of those who had toiled to build the great Pyramids, were divided into two groups: those on the ground and those on top. One would start a verse and the other would repeat it, and so on and so forth until more than a hundred verses had been exhausted. But the robust, rhythmic, joyous singing was uplifting to Yousif.

Yousif stood by his parents and put his arm around his mother. Well-wishers approached them and shook their hands.

"Mabrook," they all said, smiling. "Congratulations."

There were hugs and kisses. The guests were full of compliments and good sayings.

"It's a beautiful house."

"May you see nothing but happiness in it."

"Mabrook. May we visit you next at your son's wedding."

"May your son fill your house with grandchildren."

Yousif broke away to tend to his duties. He rushed inside to be with Amin and Isaac. The three were soon joined by Salman and other young relatives who helped carry out trays of drinks. Glasses were touched and the guests moved about, sampling the variety of *maza* laid out on the tables.

The maid, Fatima, came out of the old house carrying on her head a large tray of stuffed lamb. She was followed by two women carrying two more lambs. All three were headed toward the neighborhood bakery to have them cooked and browned. At the sight of the lambs the men on top of the house cheered louder—and within moments the festivities increased to a new level of gaiety.

By 11:30, no less than forty or fifty women began to arrive from all directions carrying *manasef* on their heads. This substantial meal, Yousif knew, was most appropriate on such occasions. All his life he had seen some of the town's women carry such large wooden bowls filled with layers of thin sheets of bread soaked in delicious *maraka,* topped with heaps of rice and fried pine nuts, all covered with chunks of spiced lamb meat.

This was the meal to be proud of—the one to serve a multitude of honored guests. Normally eleven or twelve such bowls would arrive on similar occasions. Today, Yousif counted up to thirty and stopped. They were so many, half the town could have been fed. They were brought by Christian families and Muslim families; by rich and poor; and by quite a few patients of Dr. Safi's, grateful to be alive. Of the three Jewish families in town, the family of Moshe and Sarah Sha'lan, Isaac's parents, was the closest to the doctor and his family, and they too chose to participate in the celebration. Instead of contributing the usual *mansaf,* they had ordered two large trays of *kinafeh* from Nablus—a town twenty miles to the northeast and famous for its pastries—and paid a taxi driver an outrageous fare to drive all the way and pick them up. The arrival of the two reddish trays was met with more cheers.

For Yousif the bacchanal was incomplete until he saw Salwa Taweel arrive with her tall, handsome parents. In her yellow dress, she stood out like a goddess. Yousif had been in love with her ever since she came to his house, almost two years ago. She and her mother had been attending a women's meeting. That day Salwa wore a white cashmere sweater and a brown pleated skirt, her hair tied in a bun behind her head. She was only fifteen then, but was as tall and mature looking as a girl of eighteen. From that moment her image had not left his mind. One day he would move heaven and earth to marry her, of this he was certain; but until then he knew he would have to endure all the agonies and obstacles of a romance in a sheltered society.

Yousif had been carrying a tray of cold beer around the garden when he spied Salwa. He stood frozen, unable to take his eyes off her. He could not move until she looked around. Then he beamed, causing Amin and Isaac and some of the men to laugh at him. Embarrassed, he moved on but his foot got caught in the leg of a chair and he almost stumbled. The beer bottles on the tray began to bang and rattle.

At noon, a black limousine arrived, escorted by two jeeps full of British soldiers. Yousif watched many of the older men in the garden rise and line up to receive the dignitaries. He saw his father also weave his way through the crowd to welcome them. A very tall, uniformed man, with cap and baton in hand, stepped out of the limousine, which had been opened for him by a slender chauffeur with a birthmark the color of raw liver on his right cheek.

Yousif recognized the distinguished man with the matted hair as Captain Malloy, the British chief-of-police for the entire district, which consisted of Ardallah and thirty villages. The smallish, bespectacled man who got out next was the Appellate Court Judge Hamdi Azzam. The rest of the retinue was made up of British first and second lieutenants, who stood out like gold statues compared to the dark Arabs.

These men had been to Yousif's house before on religious holidays. Still, he felt conflicting emotions at seeing the Britishmen again. He knew the troubles brewing between the Arabs and the Jews would not be there had Britain not acquiesced to the Zionist demands. Should a representative of that colonial power be welcome at an Arab home? On the other hand, could a hospitable Arab turn a guest away?

"I'm sorry we're late," Captain Malloy said to Yousif's father.

"You're welcome any time," the doctor answered, shaking his hand.

"The District Commissioner planned to be here," Malloy explained. "But at the last minute something came up and he couldn't make it. He asked me to convey to you his regrets and his congratulations. *Mabrook.*"

"Thank you," the doctor said.

"The house is truly magnificent."

"You're very kind."

Yousif did not care for his father's politeness, even though he knew it was no more than formal good manners. At least his father was not kissing Britain's ring, nor was he fawning around her representative as others were doing. What was wrong with these Arab men? Where was their dignity?

It bothered Yousif that many of the women also seemed impressed. They raised their voices and the men atop the building waved their hands in salute, without ever stopping their chant. Captain Malloy smiled broadly and attempted a few words in Arabic, his pink complexion turning red. He even stopped and watched the singing and dancing, tilted his neck backward, and nodded his head to greet the men above. The town's elders, including the mayor and his council, lined up to shake hands with the British guest who towered almost a foot above them.

Cousin Salman walked toward Yousif, frowning. Yousif read his thoughts. Ardallah's bluest sky could not conceal from these two the troubles that were gathering over Palestine in 1947. Nor did they miss hearing the rumbling of conflict between Arabs and Jews over whose ancestral land was Palestine.

"Good thing Basim isn't around," Salman whispered. "Look at them scrambling to meet that Englishman."

"Can you believe it?" Yousif asked. "And I don't care if he's the chief-of-police. He's still an Englishman. Look how we receive him. Like royalty. It's disgusting."

Salman nodded. "No one hates the English as much as Basim," he said. "He thinks they are the root of all evil."

"He's right," Yousif said. "Where is Basim anyway?"

"Who knows," Salman said. "Just don't tell him how some of these men behaved."

"Thank God my father kept his *karameh*—his dignity."

THREE WEEKS later the family moved into their new five-bedroom house. Ever since they had settled in their new residence, there had been an uninterrupted stream of visitors bearing gifts. They received enough sets of ornate coffee cups and ceramic ashtrays and crystal vases and silver trays and imported table lamps to fill a small shop.

One night Yousif stood with his parents on the balcony. In the prized aviary the birds were singing themselves to sleep. "The one word I keep hearing from people when they talk about the house," Yousif said, "is magnificent. And I really believe it is."

Colonnaded and well-lit all around, it brought to mind the Dome of the Rock when viewed from the Mount of Olives. It thrilled Yousif to know that people actually drove long distances just to see it.

"There's one more thing for me to do in this life," his father said, puffing on his pipe and pressing his wife to his side.

"To see Yousif married?" his wife guessed.

Yousif was taken aback, and the three exchanged glances.

"No," the doctor said, smiling. "We have plenty of time for that. Yousif still has a lot of studying to do."

His father was referring, Yousif knew, not only to his last year in high school, but also to medical school, which the doctor hoped his son would attend.

"I wish I had a brother," Yousif said, "so he could carry on in your footsteps, father."

"We do too," Yasmin said, sighing. "But we have no right to question God's will. If He wanted us to have another child, we would've."

Yousif could sense that his parents were disappointed but resigned to the fact that life had denied them other children. Living in a world that exalted big families, they too would have welcomed and enjoyed a bigger brood.

"When I think of all those who don't have any children," Yasmin said, "I'm thankful we have you. Look at Dr. Afifi and Jihan. Look at my brother Boulus and Hilaneh. What wouldn't they give for someone to carry on their names?"

"That's true," Yousif said. "Nevertheless, you *are* disappointed, are you not?"

Yasmin put her arm around her son's waist. "We'd be both lying if we said we weren't. There were times when I was bitter. All my life I looked forward to a house full of children and grandchildren. I wanted to cook for them. I wanted to open my arms for them when they returned from schools. I wanted to knit sweaters and scarfs and gloves for them. I wanted to shower them with gifts and love. But . . ."

"Don't forget," his father said, chuckling, "it took five years for your 'majesty' to arrive."

"But you made up for all that we may have missed," Yasmin told her son, giving him an affectionate squeeze. "You brought us joy that wiped out all our sadness."

"Even if I don't become a doctor?" Yousif teased.

"No matter," she told him. "We've always been and we'll always be proud of you."

Should the troubles escalate into war, Yousif thought, it would be impossible for him to even contemplate leaving for school. He would stay and defend his country from the Zionists. How he would serve he still did not know. And if the threat of war was removed, he would rather be a lawyer than a doctor. He hated to disappoint his father, but he had no interest in medicine whatsoever; he was squeamish at the sight of blood.

"I guess," Yousif said to his father, "the one thing left for you to do now is build the hospital."

"Yes, that indeed," the doctor agreed. "But construction work being so expensive nowadays, I don't see how this town could afford it. Yet we can't afford not to have it either."

His wife snuggled against him. "It doesn't have to be big. If you wait too long you may never be able to build it."

The doctor nodded. "It needs to be at least five times the size of this house, and you know how much this cost."

"How much?" Yousif asked, holding the railing and looking at the opposite mountain. From a distance he could hear an orchestra playing at the Rowda Hotel's garden. He could imagine vacationers dancing under the full moon.

"Nearly ten thousand pounds," the doctor answered. Then, turning to his wife, he added, "What do you think? You keep up with the figures more than I do."

His wife shrugged her shoulder. "I don't care. It's worth every bit of it."

"That we know," her husband agreed. "In any case, today I contributed another hundred pounds to the hospital fund."

"Again!" his wife protested.

Her husband looked at her reproachfully. "I should've given more, but right now that's all we can afford."

"It's enough," his wife assured him.

"I wouldn't say that," the doctor replied, stroking her back. "Some paid as much on lesser occasions."

Yousif knew what his parents were saying. Ever since his father started the community fund to build a hospital, people had contributed at all happy occasions: weddings, childbirths, baptisms, the building of a new house, returning from abroad. Weddings had always been a good source of income, but of late people had learned to make donations in the loving memory of their deceased. How many times had Yousif seen his father take out his small black book to register five pounds here or ten pounds there?

What would the political troubles ahead do to all these plans? The thought nagged at the back of Yousif's mind. Was there a solution that could satisfy Arabs and Jews? He would not bring up the subject tonight with his parents; there was no need to spoil their happiness.

2

Wearing well-pressed pants and short-sleeved sport shirts, Yousif and his friends, Amin and Isaac, were out for their ritual Sunday afternoon stroll. Yousif was Christian, Amin Muslim, Isaac Jewish. They were born within a few blocks of each other. They had gone through elementary and secondary school together. Together they had switched from short to long pants, learned to appreciate girls, enjoyed catching birds, suffered over acne, and, because they were all Semites, wondered who among them would have the biggest nose. They were so often together that the whole town began to accept them as inseparable.

Yousif, considered by many to be the leader of the three, was tall and had a thick black head of hair. He was first in his class, many considered him handsome, and no one doubted that he was relatively rich, being the only son of the most popular doctor in town. Amin was short and compact, with a perfect set of gleaming white teeth and skin that was a shade darker than the other two. He was the oldest of nine children and the poorest of the three companions: for his father was a stonecutter and all his family lived in a one-room house in the oldest district in town. Isaac was of medium height, with high cheekbones, sunken cheeks, and a shy, winsome smile. His father was a merchant who sold fabrics, mostly to the villagers who came to shop in the "big" city, in a store he had inherited from *his* father.

None of the three boys wanted to follow in his father's footsteps. Yousif wanted to be a lawyer; Amin a doctor; Isaac a musician. Such were the dreams that fluttered in their hearts as they walked together, like birds awaiting the full development of their wings to fly.

That afternoon these three were enjoying a favorite Ardallah pastime: tourist watching. Ardallah was a town thirty miles northwest of Jerusalem and fifteen miles east of Jaffa. Tourists made the population of this summer resort swell from ten thousand in the off season to nearly double that during the summer, and to perhaps twenty-two thousand over the weekends. Ardallah swarmed with automobiles and pedestrians. There were occasional camels and mules, which, however archaic, were still viable means for moving goods. Pushcart vendors weaved from one sidewalk to another, undaunted by the heavy traffic or by the angry, sometimes rhythmic honking from drivers who were not above coupling their blasts with a few choice words or obscene gestures. The many little shops—and the few big ones—did a thriving business. Shoppers coming out of the Muslim and Jewish stores had their arms laden with packages. But to the Christian shopkeepers of this predominantly Christian town, Sunday was truly a day of rest.

On that particular Sunday, the three boys nudged each other in anticipation as they saw a group of nine tourists descend from the Jerusalem-Ardallah bus, which stopped at the *saha,* the main clearing at the entrance of town.

Normally such an arrival would have drawn little or no attention, for the sidewalks were crowded with strangers and the outdoor cafe across the street was jammed with locals and chic tourists luxuriating under red, yellow, and blue umbrellas sparkling in the bright Mediterranean sun. But the newcomers who had just stepped off the shining yellow bus were noticeable for their conspicuous good looks and identical khaki clothes. A couple of the men had cameras strapped to their shoulders; a third had what seemed like a flask of water strapped around his neck. The attractive young women wore shorts that displayed legs and thighs, clashing sharply with Muslim women, who hid their faces behind black veils. For although the great majority of the Arab women in town did wear modern western dresses, most were on the conservative side, and quite a few still wore the traditional ankle-length and heavily embroidered native costumes. The most stylish, even daring, of the Arab women wore short sleeves, or knee-length skirts, or low-cut dresses. Any spirited female dressing in this fashion invited tongue wagging and faced the possibility of a fight with her husband or father or brothers. Such was the society into which these nine tourists entered. Their bronze-deep tans and the generous exposure of female flesh drew some lecherous looks and good-natured whistles. Even the four tall handsome men accompanying them, who carried duffle bags on their backs, wore shorts, and had their sleeves rolled up on their brown muscular arms. The group became self-conscious and laughed, and the spectators laughed with them. So did Yousif and his two friends.

"I think they're Jewish," Yousif said.

"Who cares?" Amin glowed. "Seeing them here is better than taking a half-hour ride to Jaffa to watch them swimming on the beach."

"They're Jews, I tell you," Yousif insisted, as if Isaac were not there.

"They could be English," Amin told him. "We have a lot of them around."

"I don't think so," Yousif argued. "Only the Jews speak Arabic with that guttural sound. I heard one of them say *khabibi* instead of *habibi.*" He knew that the mispronunciation of the *h* was the shibboleth that most quickly set Arab and Jew apart.

Isaac laughed. "The Jews I know don't have that sound. I say *habibi* just as well as you do."

Yousif looked surprised. "I meant Jews who were not born and raised here, the recent immigrants—"

"I know what you mean," Isaac said, his eyes following the scantily clad arrivals. "But I think it's Yiddish."

"You think? Don't you know?"

"I speak Hebrew—but the few words I caught sounded Yiddish to me."

The three boys trailed the exotic group down a sidewalk crowded not only with pedestrians but with men playing dominos or backgammon in front of shops. Passing magazine stands and tables laden with leather and brass goods, the boys followed the strangers all the way from the Sha'b Pharmacy right up to Karawan Travel Agency, the only travel agency in town. Arm in arm, the men and women looked like close friends.

Yousif envied them. He bit his lip as he saw one of them hug the waist of the girl walking next to him. He wished he could put his arm around Salwa.

Three blocks from the bus stop, two of the tourists stopped and bought multi-colored ice cream cones from a pushcart at the corner of one of the busiest intersections in town.

"Are you thinking what I'm thinking?" Amin asked, rubbing his hands.

"What are you thinking?" Yousif asked.

"That we're not trailing just boyfriends and girlfriends on a Sunday stroll?"

Isaac looked at him and scratched his chin. "Who are we trailing then?"

"Lovers," Amin grinned. "Lovers intent on serious business."

"You're crazy," Isaac told him, disinterested.

"You'll see," Amin said. "Before long they're going to be on top of each other. And I'm going to be there watching. Yousif, what do you think?"

All his life Yousif had heard that Jewish girls were promiscuous, and these women seemed even more loving than most. Were the stories he had always heard about them true? Was it true that the girls of Tel Aviv had seduced many an Arab man? Supposedly they would romance them for a weekend and leave them dry.

Bearing this in mind, Yousif found it entirely possible that these attractive and healthy-looking men and women were lovers looking for a place to camp and make love, that they had come to consummate their passion in the seclusion of Ardallah's wooded hills.

"It's hard to say what they are," Yousif answered finally.

"Look what they're carrying," Amin replied with conviction. "What do you think they have in those canvas bags on their backs?"

"You tell us," Yousif said.

"It's obvious," Amin said, bumping into a pedestrian but not losing his thought. "They're carrying blankets. That's what they need for outdoor sex, isn't it?"

Isaac shook his head. "I think your parents had better find you a wife before you embarrass them."

They all laughed and continued walking, jostling others so as not to lose sight of those they were trailing.

The strangers were heading toward Cinema Firyal. There was a chance Salwa might be attending the matinee. If she were, Yousif would try to convince his friends to go in, and while they watched the screen, he would content himself with watching Salwa, even from a distance. Damn it, he thought; why couldn't Arab society allow those in love to walk or sit together in public?

BECAUSE HE WAS in love, Yousif suspected that the whole world was in love: either secretly or publicly, as in the case before him. He looked for a touch, a glance, a word and construed them as definite signs of an affair. To him, summer was the season for love, and Ardallah was the ideal place.

Only Ramallah, a town fifteen miles to the east and a better-known resort, surpassed Ardallah in the number of vacationers who arrived every summer. They came to either town from every corner of Palestine, sometimes from as far as Egypt and Iraq. The affluent stayed at hotels, but most rented homes for the long duration. From the north they came from Acre; from the south from Gaza. They came to Ardallah from the seashores of Jaffa and Haifa, and from the fertile fields and orchards of Lydda and Ramleh. They came with their children and grandchildren. They came wealthy or simply well off. But they never came poor.

Summer in Ardallah, Yousif knew, was meant for the elite who could afford it. It was meant for those who preferred it to Lebanon, or were not lucky enough to find a room in Ramallah, those who wanted to slip away for the weekend from the sweltering weather on the Mediterranean coast, or had not yet discovered Europe.

Ardallah sat as a crown on seven hills from which could be seen a spectacular panorama of rolling hills and, on a clear day, a glimpse of the blue Mediterranean waters. Ardallah was close enough to the big cities, but small enough to have its own charm. It was not exactly a playground for the rich, but an oasis for the young and the aged and all those in between who cared for the cool fresh air and the soft invigorating breeze.

Ardallah had over ten schools (different ones for boys and girls); five churches (one big Greek Orthodox, one big Roman Catholic, one small Greek Catholic, two tiny Anglican); one mosque; five hotels (renowned for their spacious wooded gardens); and three cinemas. The highest building was three stories, built of chiseled white stone, as were all the houses that were scattered over the mountain slopes. Some of the new homes had all the conveniences of the modern world. Such luxuries were important not only because the new owners desired them and could afford them, but because most of these homes were let during the summer months to the vacationers who insisted on hotel-type accommodations.

Except for fruit trees in private gardens, the trees around Ardallah were primarily cypress and pine. Perhaps it was these trees that had conspired with the geographic location to give the town its glory. But they said it was the Ardallah breeze that most attracted tourists—the gentle caressing breeze that blew against one's skin like a mother's breath. Built 2500 feet above sea level, Ardallah was a natural landmark. Between Ardallah and the Mediterranean Sea lay Jaffa, Lydda, and Ramleh, which were surrounded by hundreds of orange groves; between Ardallah and the highlands lay hundreds of Arab villages surrounded by fig and olive groves and pasture lands, where shepherds could still be seen sitting atop a hill playing the flute or herding their flock as in biblical times.

Ardallah had always welcomed her guests. Yousif himself waited nine months a year for their return. He loved the change and the excitement that resulted from their appearance. They brought their fashions, their gaiety, their dialects, the glamour of their women in their latest fashions or fancy cars, and their money, which made everyone in town walk around with a smile. The tourists slept in the morning, drank tea and ate fruits on their verandas, and played backgammon or bridge in the afternoon. And, yes, they danced at night.

Often Yousif would go with his parents to these hotels and meet the rich families and powerful men his parents knew. How lovely the women and their daughters were, Yousif remembered. The women of this upper class did not abide by old-fashioned restrictions; they swayed under the moonlight to the tango and foxtrot and waltz tunes played by orchestras—often imported from places as distant as Athens and Rome.

Often Yousif would dance with their daughters. The colored lights which had been hung outdoors over the dance floor would shimmer, the dresses of the elegant women would rustle, and Yousif, dressed in the conservative manner of his father, would wish Salwa and not his mother or some stranger's daughter were in his arms.

On two occasions the previous summer he had been fortunate enough to have danced with Salwa herself, and to have given her a peck on the cheek when the dance floor was overcrowded and no one was looking. The smell of her hair and the feel of her body burned in him for weeks and still lingered in his mind. This year luck might smile on him again; at least he hoped.

BY THE TIME the conspicuous strangers reached Bata, the famous shoe store, Yousif was jolted out of his daydreaming. What triggered his suspicion was the large amount of equipment they were carrying. What did they need all the canvas bags and the cameras and binoculars for? And what about that tripod under the tall man's arm?

It struck Yousif that they were carrying surveying equipment. This new perception was anchored in the depth of his being and born out of many nights of listening to his father and his father's friends discuss the mounting tension between the Arabs and Jews. Should hostilities break out, as some expected, what these outsiders were doing could prove detrimental to the Arabs. Such preparation, he reasoned, could mean the difference between victory and defeat.

"My favorite is the tall blonde," Amin said, his brown eyes dancing. "The one with the long shapely legs."

"I bet you wish she had her arms around your waist," Isaac taunted.

"Do I!" Amin swooned.

"How far are we going to follow them?" Isaac asked, elbowing his way through the crowd.

"Until we find out what they're up to," Yousif said, his mood changing. "They could be Zionists."

"So what?" Amin asked, impatient. "What's a Zionist anyway? Some kind of a weird Jew, isn't he? Isaac, are you a Zionist?"

"You're crazy," Isaac said. "Of course I'm not a Zionist."

"Don't get angry, I'm just asking. Well, is your father a Zionist?"

"No one in my family is a Zionist," Isaac explained, wiping his glasses with his handkerchief.

"Well, do you know what a Zionist is?" Amin pressed.

Isaac looked around. "He's a member of a political party. Most Zionists are Jews, but not necessarily. They're just members of a party, like any other political party. They have their aims and goals and ideology. Isn't that right, Yousif?"

"That's what I've heard."

"Okay," Amin said, keeping his eyes on the tourists. "They are members of a party. But what do they want?"

"To take over Palestine," Yousif told him. "They think it's theirs. They think God promised it to them."

"And what about us? We're Abraham's children too. Just like them."

"They want us out," Yousif told him.

"Out where?" Amin inquired.

"I don't know. Just out."

Amin looked at Isaac, grinning. "Now you tell me who's crazy. Me or them. Well, if they're that cuckoo, let's follow them for sure."

Yousif kept his eyes on the strangers, who were stopping now to look at the variety of sweets and pastries. He restrained Amin and Isaac from walking any closer lest anyone become aware that they were being followed. The tall dark man with the sinewy arms who was accompanying the blonde with the bluest eyes bought two portions of red-colored cheese-filled *kinafeh* wrapped in waxed paper. Three others, including the statuesque brunette in her thirties who reminded Yousif of Salwa, bought dark roasted peanuts from a tall, thin, Ethiopian woman selling from a portable stand that emanated smoke.

"Where do you think they're going?" Amin inquired.

"I have a feeling they're headed for the woods, but not for what you're thinking," Yousif said, stepping off the curb and holding back his friends to let a car make a right turn.

"They're heading west," Yousif explained. "There's nothing in that direction except the olive and fig orchards. There must be more comfortable places to make love than a rocky field. Besides, I just don't believe they'd screw in broad daylight with everyone watching."

"Well I hope you're wrong and I'm right," Amin said, again rubbing his hands. "If I catch them in the act, I think I'll go crazy."

"Don't worry, you're not about to," Yousif told him, leaning against a wall to count the strangers ahead of him. "Look, there are nine of them. Who's going to make love to the odd number? I tell you they're not lovers."

The new suspicion seemed to destroy Amin's confidence in his own theory. "What a bore," he said, "but I still would like to know for sure."

The strangers were half a block away from the entrance to Rowda Hotel's garden. Maybe, Yousif thought, they would turn to go in and bask in the shade of the ancient trees. But the strangers passed the entrance without even turning their heads and proceeded to descend the hill, going west. The three boys looked at each other again, then began to follow them in earnest. They maintained a respectable distance from the strangers and, to avoid suspicion, chose to walk on the other side of the street.

On the outskirts of town, the group paused at a main fork in the road. One of them looked back and saw Yousif and his friends. Then all of them turned around and looked in the direction of the three boys. Yousif quickly bent down to tie his shoelaces, and Isaac and Amin stopped and waited for him to finish.

"They saw us," Yousif muttered as he tightened the lace through every hole.

When he looked again the group had split up and gone in two different directions. Yousif rose and the three boys resumed their walking. They agreed to stay together, but didn't know which group to follow. By the time they reached the fork they decided to follow the group of five that had turned right and taken the dirt road.

The group ahead of Yousif and his friends moved briskly, doubling the hundred meters between the two groups. They had to walk much faster to keep up with them.

As the straight road ended and dipped into the valley Yousif could see the Roman arch, a landmark two-thirds of a mile away. Beyond it was a steep hill, a narrow road, and vast fields of olive and fig trees which stretched over several mountains. Yousif was alarmed.

"If they get to that arch before us," he told his two friends, "they could disappear very easily and we'd never find them."

Isaac frowned. "I'll be damned," he said, kicking a stone.

"I know a short cut," Amin suggested. "But we'll have to run. Are you willing?"

"Yes," Yousif and Isaac said together.

"Let's go then," Amin said, starting to run across the field to his left.

Yousif and Isaac ran behind him, leaping over small stone walls and ducking under tree branches. A bush tore a small hole in Isaac's trousers and a pebble caused Yousif's ankle to twist under him as they tried to catch up with Amin, who had struck out ahead of them and was now racing down the hill like a gazelle chased by two foxes. Five minutes later, they reached the Roman arch, confident that they had beaten the strangers. They hid behind the thick columns and waited, wiping sweat from their faces and around their necks.

Yousif could soon hear thudding footsteps. He had to take a chance and look. He raised himself up and checked the road. He saw a farmer walking behind a burdened mule and heading toward town, singing.

> They have erected mountains between you and me.
> But what could stop the souls from reaching out across the mountains.

The three friends had to suppress a giggle. Did the sight of the handsome couples put the farmer in such a romantic mood? Then Yousif was distracted. He focused on the "lovers." One of the men raised the binoculars to his eyes and inspected the mountain. Another took out a map which he and the striking blonde at his side hunched over.

"I tell you they're up to no good," Yousif said, turning toward Amin and Isaac.

Suddenly, Yousif's eyes fell on a shiny round object lying on the ground. The sun hit it at the right angle and made the silver gleam. He was sure it was a watch. He picked it up and rolled it in his hand, disappointed. "It's a compass," he said.

"A compass!" Isaac exclaimed. "Let me see it."

Yousif handed it to Isaac, knowing that it had fallen from the strangers they were following. His earlier suspicions deepened; he was now convinced that they were surveying the hills. He turned around to tell Amin. To his surprise Amin was standing on the edge of a large rock. In his white shirt, Yousif thought, Amin might as well have waved a flag.

"Get off that rock," Yousif told him, his voice hushed.

In answer, Amin stepped closer to the edge and craned his neck to see where the couples went.

"Get down," Isaac warned, his hands cupping his mouth.

Amin did not seem to pay attention, but stood looking for a better spot. He stepped down on an adjacent wall, and it gave under him. The stones toppled, creating a roaring sound that could have been heard from a distance. Yousif and Isaac leaped to catch Amin, but it was too late. He rolled down the hill with large and small boulders crashing around him. His friends gasped and then ran after him. When the avalanche stopped, Amin lay sprawled at the bottom of a field, one huge rock on top of his left arm.

"Jesus!" Yousif said, frightened.

Yousif looked at Amin, then at the strangers. His loyalty was divided. He didn't want to see Amin hurt but he also didn't want to lose the strangers. Had they been regular tourists, he thought, they would have come back to help. Surely they must have heard the sound of the stone wall collapsing. He watched in frustration as they hurried around a bend in the valley and disappeared.

3

Amin opened his eyes, grimacing. His two friends were towering over him. "I broke my arm," he informed them. "I actually heard it snap."

"Good God!" Yousif said, kneeling.

"What rotten luck!" Isaac agonized, joining them on the ground.

Amin bit his lip and did not answer. Very carefully, Yousif and Isaac pushed back the huge rock and freed Amin's arm. A sharp-edged bone, broken like a dry piece of wood, was sticking out just above the elbow. Yousif flinched. The side of Amin's white shirt was smeared with blood. Isaac shut his eyes. Yousif felt sick but kept staring at Amin, wondering what to do to help him.

"Don't worry, we'll take care of you," Yousif said. "I bet it hurts like hell."

Amin shook his head. "Not yet. Right now my arm is just hot."

The bone was sticking out in such a way that Yousif wasn't sure that Amin could see it.

"Would you let me," Yousif asked, "straighten your arm a bit? There's a bone sticking out that I don't like."

"Actually it wouldn't be smart to leave it exposed," Isaac added.

Amin craned his neck to see around his elbow. "Go ahead. So far I feel no pain."

As Yousif reached for Amin's arm, Isaac interrupted. "Why don't we stand him up first?" he asked. "That way the bones might settle in place by themselves. Don't you think?"

"A good idea," Yousif agreed. "Come on, let's get him on his feet."

They lifted him up, and Amin's left arm hung limply at his side. Isaac rolled Amin's short sleeve all the way to the shoulder to give Yousif a better view. Most of the bone seemed to disappear.

"Only the tip is showing," Yousif told Amin. "I think if I pull it a bit I'd get it all in. Let me know if it hurts too much."

"Go ahead," Amin said.

Holding the injured arm by the elbow and forearm, Yousif pulled gently, keeping his eyes on the broken bone. It began to slide under. Amin gritted his teeth.

"Don't you faint on us," Yousif said.

"Just do it, please," Amin said, turning his head away.

With a bit more luck, Yousif thought, he might get it in all the way. He tugged at it somewhat forcefully, until the wound swallowed the bone.

"Wonderful!" Isaac said. "And it didn't hurt, did it?"

"Like hell it didn't," Amin answered. "But I can bear it."

"Now we need to bandage it," Yousif said. "The broken skin shouldn't be left uncovered."

"I have a clean handkerchief," Amin told him. "It's in my hip pocket."

Yousif reached for it, then looked around for a comfortable place for Amin to rest. There was a smooth rock not too far to the left. Slowly the two friends sat Amin on it. Isaac held the injured arm, and Yousif tied the handkerchief around it. The arm seemed broken in more than one place.

"Tell me if it's too tight," Yousif said to Amin. "We just need to stop the bleeding."

"It's okay," Amin said, taking a deep breath. "The sooner we get home the better."

Both friends put their arms around Amin. He in turn put his right arm around Yousif's neck. Blood, which smelled like rust, was spreading on Amin's torn shirt. Isaac's shirt was stained from contact. The hill was steep and the road above it was several fields away. Not for a second, though, did Yousif stop thinking of the strangers they had left behind. What they were doing there preyed on his mind. He wished Amin had not fallen; he wished he had a chance to track them.

"Your timing is lousy," Yousif said to Amin, walking beside him. "Next time you decide to break an arm, make sure we're not following spies."

"I'll remember," he said, wincing.

BY THE TIME they reached the main road, the three were out of breath. Amin looked wan. There was no sense in wishing for a car, Yousif thought, for rarely did vehicles travel that deep in the countryside. But he did wish for a mule or a camel. None was in sight. Things were always plentiful until they were needed, Yousif reflected. But he dismissed the possibility too soon; a rider on a horse was coming their way. It was obvious from the rising column of dust that he was in a big hurry.

"We'll ask him to take us back," Yousif suggested.

"I wish he would," Amin replied, his face contorted.

Upon reaching them, the rider pulled upon the reins. He looked familiar, but Yousif could not place him. The horse whinnied, slowed down, circled, and then came to a full stop.

"What happened?" the rider asked, addressing Amin.

"I fell and broke my arm," Amin answered, clutching his injured arm.

"Let me see," the rider said, dismounting. He handed Yousif the reins to his horse, saying, "My name is Fayez Hamdan."

The rider, Yousif observed, wore the traditional *fellaheen* robe, which folded around his body like a kimono and was tied with a black sash. A corner of the hem was raised and tucked under the sash, exposing the long baggy off-white *sirwal.*

Yousif noticed that the rider had a dagger attached to his right side. He also had one front tooth missing and two others covered with gold. Yousif wondered what the man might have done with that dagger if he had discovered the spies.

"An injured arm needs attention," Fayez Hamdan said, pulling out a large red and white scarf and tying it around Amin's neck like a sling. Slowly but deftly he lifted Amin's arm and put it through the loop.

"Thank you," Amin said.

"Where do you live?" the rider asked, looking at the setting sun as though to tell time.

"This side of town," Amin answered. "But I can't ask you—"

"You didn't ask me, I asked you," the rider interrupted. "I'll take you home."

Yousif and Isaac helped him put Amin up on the horse. Fayez held the reins and turned the horse around and gave it a gentle slap. They headed toward home, all walking except Amin.

AMIN'S HOUSE was part of a compound in Ardallah's oldest and poorest section, where women washed their clothes on their doorsteps and dumped the dirty water beside the unpaved road. This part of town was hundreds of years old. The compound of connected "homes" was like a ghetto. The thick muddy-looking walls had grass growing on them and looked as old as the Roman arch the boys had seen earlier that afternoon. Today some women sat in knots on the flat rooftops or against walls. They gossiped and darned clothes or combed and braided their waist-length hair. Smoke rose from behind an enclosure where a woman crouched to bake her bread.

Yousif stepped over a dog's dropping. He could smell the pungent stench of goats a woman kept in her small corral. Children jumped rope and played hopscotch.

Amin's mother, whom both Yousif and Isaac called Aunt Tamam, came running to meet them. She was a tall thin woman in her late fifties, wearing the traditional ankle-length dress with little or no embroidery—a sign of their poverty. Her hair was covered with a rust-colored scarf, and her face had a hundred wrinkles. Yousif could sense and understand her great anxiety. Some of the children must have run and told her about Amin. From the look on her face, Yousif knew she had not believed it was only a broken arm and had come out to see for herself.

"Habibi, Amin," she said, wringing her hands. "How did it happen?"

Amin, still mounted on the horse, reached out with his good hand and took hers. "I fell off a stone wall."

"Where were you?"

Amin glanced at his two friends and then at his mother. "I'll be all right," he told her. "Don't worry."

The horse entered the narrowest path leading to the house, followed by a group of curious children.

"Does it hurt a lot?" his mother wanted to know. "I wish it were my arm instead of yours."

The rider held the reins and stopped the horse in front of Amin's house. Yousif and Isaac helped Amin dismount. The sight of blood made Aunt Tamam purse her lips and beat on her chest. Then she bent down, touched the ground, and kissed her fingertips, an expression of humility and gratitude Yousif had seen his mother make many a time.

"Allah be praised," she said, "it wasn't more serious. Here we are worried sick about your Uncle Hassan—"

"What about Uncle Hassan?"

"It looks like he had another heart attack."

"Did father go to Gaza? Is that why he isn't here?"

"No, not yet. But I know he's checking to see if he he should leave now or wait."

A wall of silence descended among them.

"That's the way it is," Fayez Hamdan said, turning his horse around. "Trouble comes in groups." The horseman left them standing in front of the house, taking with him all the blessings of a grateful mother.

"I sent one of the children after Abu Khalil," Aunt Tamam said as they entered the house.

"Who?" Yousif asked.

"The one who mends bones," she told him.

"But why?" Yousif asked, surprised. "Why not my father? You know he's a doctor. Why didn't you send after him?"

For the first time the old woman's face wrinkled with a genuine smile. "You don't have to tell me who your father is. Dr. Jamil Safi is the best doctor there is, but this is too small a job for him. Abu Khalil has been mending bones all his adult life—and he's nearly seventy."

Yousif shook his head. "My father will be disappointed. He loves Amin like a son."

"Believe me there's no need to trouble the doctor with something as simple as a broken arm," she assured him. "He's too busy for this sort of thing."

Yousif was not convinced; he suspected she did it to save money. The poor, he knew, carried their pride like open wounds. But the old woman disappeared inside the dark cave of a house, and he could not talk to her.

"I'm going to get my father," Yousif insisted, walking away.

"Please don't," Amin entreated, clutching his arm.

Yousif couldn't understand. "He would want to look after you."

"No doubt," Amin said, biting his lip. "But like mother said, mending bones is not a big deal."

Pride. Yousif knew it in the silence that lingered.

Aunt Tamam held a kerosene lamp atop the stairs they were about to climb. Although he had been to Amin's house several times, Yousif still marveled at its simplicity. It was basically a spacious room that served as a bedroom, living room, and kitchen, plus a low-ceilinged basement used to raise chickens. Amin's father, Abu Amin, was not only the town's best stonecutter, but was also in charge of several men working on the villa Yousif's parents were building. Why couldn't such a man afford a better dwelling, Yousif wondered? Then he remembered that Abu Amin, a Muslim, at one time had two wives and two sets of nine children. He was lucky he could feed them, much less build them a house.

As they ascended to the main floor, Yousif was struck by the darkness. Even in daytime three oil lamps were lit, since light from the one curved window that ran to the floor and from the two holes high in the opposite wall was hardly sufficient. Shadows hovered in every corner. A large mirror was hung at an angle facing the front door. It magnified the size of the room and made the shadows twice as ominous.

Amin's mother brought a mattress and laid it on the floor next to the window. There he sat, propped by a couple of pillows, apologizing all the time for the trouble he had caused his friends.

Within minutes, Abu Khalil was at the door. Yousif glimpsed him in the mirror and watched him walk up the six or seven steps. Yousif and Isaac rose and made room for the sprightly old man who was dressed in plain, ankle-length, black *dimaya*. What impressed Yousif most was the matching rust color of the turban, the sash, and the ankle-length *'aba*. It contrasted well with black. For a few seconds, the tidiness of the diminutive old man seemed promising.

Having removed his outer garment, Abu Khalil was even smaller than he looked. He knelt by Amin's side and began inspecting the injured arm. It was broken in three places, he grimly announced: once above the elbow and twice below. Amin groaned.

"It's a bad accident," Abu Khalil muttered, smoking a hand-rolled cigarette down to a butt he could hardly hold, "but I've seen a lot worse."

There was no ashtray around, so Abu Khalil ended up giving the butt to Yousif, who passed it on in turn to one of Amin's little brothers. Yousif laughed as the little boy took a drag on the cigarette before pitching it outside through the open window.

"Where's that old mother of yours," Abu Khalil complained, scratching his white beard.

"Don't you call me an old woman, you old goat," Amin's mother rebutted from one of the shadowy corners.

"Hurry up and bring me what I need then," he told her, blowing his nose boisterously, wiping his whiskers with a flourish, and then unwrapping Amin's arm. The unsanitary way Abu Khalil went about doing things belied his tidiness and disturbed Yousif.

"Aren't you going to wash your hands?" Yousif asked.

The old man glared at him, his small blue eyes clear as crystal. "Young man, I was mending bones long before you were born. You dare tell me what to do?"

"I'm sorry, but—"

"Aren't you Dr. Safi's son?"

"Well, yes."

"I even mended *his* bones when he was knee-high."

"Medicine has changed."

The old man shook his head and, under his breath, cursed the new generation.

But the exchange soon ended, for when Aunt Tamam came up with the ingredients and utensils, the old man rolled up his sleeves and went to work. He cracked a dozen eggs in a large wooden bowl and began to whip them with a large wooden spoon. Then he reached for a dish covered with white hair from a horse's tail, took out a bunch, and placed them over the whipped eggs. Over this he sprinkled a cup of pulverized fenugreek they called *hilbeh*. Then he proceeded to mix and batter everything with the same spoon.

Yousif was fascinated. "What's that for?" He looked at Isaac and Amin; both shrugged their shoulders.

"That's how we make our plaster cast," the old man grunted, without looking up. "It will soon get hard as a piece of wood."

Within minutes everything was ready for the old man to begin. He removed Amin's shirt and untied the bloodied handkerchief over the broken skin. The mother tore a bed sheet and handed rectangular pieces to Abu Khalil. The old man spread the pieces of cloth on the floor, covered them with a thick layer of horse and black sheep hair, then poured on it the mix of eggs and fenugreek. Then he applied the plaster to the arm.

In his own primitive way the old man was an expert, Yousif begrudgingly admitted. He worked deftly and without wasted motion. His bony and yellowed fingertips were sensitive to the slightest imperfection. He massaged the arm and pulled at it from the wrist and tried to set the shattered bones in place—one at a time.

"Aaaah . . ." Amin screamed, closing his eyes and gnashing his teeth.

The scream jolted Yousif and made him turn his head away. Isaac looked about to faint. But the old man and Amin's mother took the agony in stride. The old man broke an empty sugar box into long narrow pieces and made a splint out of them. He wrapped more cloth and mix around the supportive wood, then put the mended arm through a sling he had tied around Amin's neck.

At the end of the operation, which had taken no more than fifteen minutes, Amin's mother brought a pot of Turkish coffee for the old man. Abu Khalil seemed satisfied with a job well done and was now rolling another cigarette. He chuckled at the sight of Amin's mother holding the coffee tray and looked around the room as if to tell the young boys, "she must be crazy." Everyone laughed, even Amin, whose pain seemed to be easing. Yousif liked the old man's sense of humor, his long white beard, and his impish blue eyes.

"If I had known that's all I was going to get for my effort," the old man chided the mother, "I would've stayed at the coffeehouse."

"What on earth do you mean, Abu Khalil?" the mother asked, setting the coffee tray on a small straw chair before him. "It's good fresh coffee. Let it rest a minute before you pour it."

"Mama," Amin said, impatient. "He wants a drink. A glass of *arak,* not a cup of coffee."

"I see," she said, catching on and smiling. "A drink, here? In a Muslim home?"

No one answered. Yousif knew that some Muslims drank and sneaked bottles of liquor to their homes as much as the Christians did, if not more. Abu Khalil himself was a Muslim, and he had been known to polish off many a glass.

Finally, she turned to the old man and shook her head. "You drink too much," she reproached him. "It's not good for you."

"You *talk* too much," Abu Khalil told her, his small eyes twinkling. "It's not good for *you.*"

They all laughed and the old man's chuckle was the loudest.

Four days later Amin's arm had to be amputated.

4

It was getting fairly dark when Yousif and Isaac left Amin's home on the day of the accident. Yousif couldn't wait to get home and tell his parents what had happened. After parting from Isaac at the wheat presser, Yousif ran the last two blocks home. At the wrought-iron gate, he paused and took a deep breath. The scent of the roses in the garden permeated the air. He was glad to see his father's green Chrysler parked in the driveway.

Yousif sprang up the steps two at a time. While still on the balcony he could hear the radio blaring an Abd al-Wahhab song, "Ya Jarat al-Wadi", one of his favorites. But the first thing he did when he burst into the house was head for the living room on his left and turn the radio off.

He found his mother in the kitchen getting supper ready. Fatima was with her. The noisy primus, a portable one-eyed stove, was flaming red, and the tiny kitchen was so hot that he could see sweat running down his mother's neck. But she seemed happy enough—even in her faded, blue, short-sleeved dress. With the sleeves of her black ankle-length dress rolled up and pot holders in both hands, Fatima was about to produce one of his favorite dishes, *makloubeh*.

"You wouldn't believe what happened," he began, breathless.

Fatima got too close to the primus and jerked away from the heat.

"Mother . . ." he said.

"Step back, son," his mother cautioned, concentrating on what she was doing. "I'll be with you in just a minute."

He flattened himself against the wall to make room for their maneuvering between the sink and the cooking counter.

"Amin broke his arm," he blurted, kicking himself for his poor timing. He didn't want his mother and Fatima to drop the pot between them or to get scorched. But they did not seem to have heard him.

"In the name of the Cross," his mother prayed, as she always did at the start of anything remotely serious. She covered the deep pot Fatima was holding with a large aluminum baking tray. Then both women entangled four arms to turn the whole thing upside down. They were both relieved that it didn't spill. His mother tapped the bottom and the sides of the pot and waited for a few seconds before lifting it slowly. To their satisfaction and Yousif's utter amazement, all the contents of the pot, to the last grain of rice, were now on the tray. Standing about a foot and a half high, with a circumference of about thirty inches, the *makloubeh* looked delicious. Yousif loved the aroma of its rice, cubed lamb meat, potatoes, cauliflower, and an assortment of spices. The pungent steam that arose filled his nostrils and made him ravenous.

"Now, what were you saying?" his mother asked, turning the faucet on and washing her hands. "I couldn't hear a word you said."

He waited for her to turn the water off and look at him.

"What is it?" she asked, her eyes narrowing.

"Amin broke his arm," he told her.

"Oh, my God!" she exclaimed, her fingers touching her lips.

"Haraam," Fatima said. "What a pity!"

"Where's father?"

"In the bathroom," his mother answered, her crimson face turning pale.

He left them stunned and went to look for his father. The bathroom door was open and the doctor was shaving. He was wearing a purplish robe and his thin, receding hair was wet. He had just taken a shower.

"Father, Amin had a terrible accident," Yousif told him.

His father, whose old-fashioned razor was poised to slide down his lathered chin, stopped and stared. "What kind of accident?"

"He broke his arm. I tried to get them to let you set it, but they called old man Abu Khalil instead."

"Hmmmm!" the doctor said, pouting. "Was the skin broken? Did he bleed at all?"

"See," Yousif answered, pointing to a spot of blood on his shirt.

"That's no good," the doctor said, stirring his stubby brush in a fancy cup of scented shaving soap.

"And that old fool Abu Khalil kept blowing his nose and working on Amin's arm without washing his hands."

"I'll have to stop by and give him a shot," the doctor said, lathering his face.

Five minutes later the three-member family sat in the small dining room for dinner. The gloom was palpable.

"How did Amin break his arm?" his father finally asked, wiping his glasses with a linen napkin.

"A stone wall collapsed under him."

"Where were you?" his mother wanted to know.

"In the woods. By the Roman arch."

Both parents looked at each other and then at Yousif.

"What were you doing there?" his father inquired.

"Following some tourists. At first they looked like lovers. Amin, Isaac, and I thought it would be fun to see what they were up to."

His mother looked flabbergasted. "It would be fun?" she asked.

"We thought we might catch them kissing or—" he admitted.

His father eyed him sternly. "I'm dismayed. Didn't it occur to you that you might've been intruding?"

Yousif felt embarrassed, but he was too excited to let them reprimand him.

"But wait," he said. "What these tourists were really up to was espionage."

Again his parents looked at him in amazement. "You certainly are full of news today," his mother told him, passing a small basket of bread.

"I'm convinced they were Zionist spies," Yousif insisted. "Why did they need cameras and binoculars and tripods and duffle bags if they were just on a romantic outing?"

"What did you think they needed them for?" his father asked, chewing.

"I thought they were surveying these hills for military purposes," Yousif said. "But Amin fell and we lost them. I wish to God he hadn't."

Throughout the meal Yousif told them about the compass and where he had found it. To him, it was conclusive evidence that those who dropped it were more than just ordinary Jewish tourists.

His mother shook her head at his seemingly incredible theories. "You need to take a shower and get dressed quickly. It's a quarter to seven already."

"Dressed for what?" Yousif asked, glancing at his wrist watch.

"The special show at Al-Andalus Hotel. Have you forgotten?"

"It totally slipped my mind," Yousif said. "Isaac mentioned it this morning."

He had meant to go back and be with Amin, but the thought of joining his parents at the hotel garden seemed irresistible. Besides, there was a good chance

Salwa might be there. He would be able to tell her about Amin and his afternoon adventure. He might even get a chance to dance with her. For the last two weeks he had been tutoring her ten- and twelve-year old brothers, Akram and Zuhair. Every time he went to their house, he had been able to see her. But seeing her was nothing compared to their dancing together.

Yousif finished showering and dressing long before his parents. He sat in the living room worrying about Amin, trying to listen to the news, and wondering where the spies had gone.

Why had they come to survey hills and valleys so close to his home? Certainly there was no big Jewish community in Ardallah that warranted protection. He had never thought of his hometown in military terms. Now that his imagination was ignited, he began to find all kinds of reasons why Ardallah would be considered a natural target for the enemy. It overlooked many towns and villages. It was only ten or twelve miles to the airport in Lydda. It was close to the Sarafand Military Camp. Above all, it towered over the highway connecting Jaffa and Tel Aviv to Jerusalem. The more he thought about it the more convinced he was that sooner or later his hometown would be in imminent danger. Ardallah was not only strategic—it was essential to whoever wanted to dominate the region.

He saw Fatima clearing up the dishes in the dining room. He heard his father fussing about a silk tie he wanted to wear.

"Ask Yousif if he wore it last," his mother was saying. "Or let him help you find it. I can't be bothered now."

Over strains of music drifting from the radio, Yousif heard his father sliding back the hangers in his closet. He knew from experience that his father would not settle until he found what he was looking for. Although generally easy-going and congenial, in some respects his father was a difficult man. He had a strong streak of vanity. Twelve years older than his wife, he was quite particular about the way he looked. And if he had a vice, it was his inordinate spending on clothes. He had dozens of suits, all tailored. He had dozens of shirts, all silk. He had dozens of ties, all imported. Every time a friend traveled abroad or to some Arab capital, especially Beirut or Cairo, the doctor would ask him to bring him the finest of ties or shirts. British wool was a fetish with him.

When they were ready to leave they looked to Yousif like a handsome family, elegantly scented and immaculately dressed. He himself wore a gray suit and a solid blue tie he had borrowed from his father's collection. His father wore a blue suit with striped tie and a puffed-up white handkerchief in his small pocket. In his hand was his favorite pipe, a golden meerschaum he smoked on special occasions. His mother wore a knee-length, violet chiffon dress, a diamond watch, and a diamond necklace. Her slim body seemed to complement her husband's slightly bulging stomach. Her pitch-black hair, fair complexion, large hazel eyes, delicate features, and sweet disposition made her one of the loveliest women ever to have left Jerusalem. Even her twin sister, Aunt Widad, did not begin to compare with her in looks or temperament. They were hardly identical.

"You look terrific," Yousif complimented both parents. "But I wish," he added with a glint in his eyes, "father would worry about his health as much as he does about his clothes."

"What do you mean?" his father said in a huff. "There's nothing wrong with my health."

"I meant this," Yousif laughed, tapping his father on the stomach.

The normally reserved doctor smiled. "It's your mother's cooking," he said.

"They call it *kersh el-wajaha,"* his wife teased, stepping on the front balcony. "The bulge of the rich."

"Only we're not that rich," Yousif said, waiting for his father to follow his mother.

"We have a lot to be thankful for," she said, growing somber.

"Yes, indeed," her husband concurred, joining her on the balcony.

Yousif shut the iron front door and locked it with a small key. Then he followed his parents to the Chrysler, which was parked in the driveway.

Instead of driving straight to the hotel garden, the doctor swung by the old district to give Amin a shot. But neither Amin nor his father was there. They had gone to Gaza to see about Uncle Hassan, whose condition they had learned was rapidly deteriorating.

"But why did Amin have to go?" the doctor asked the mother who had rushed out of the house to greet him. "A broken arm needs rest while it's setting. I don't like all that jarring on a bus."

"Abu Khalil said it would be all right," she replied anxiously.

"Abu Khalil, hell," the doctor said. "Listen, the minute they return tell Amin to come and see me. I need to give him a shot."

THE MOON WAS full, the night perfect for an outdoor event. And from what Yousif could observe, Al-Andalus Hotel was ready for it. Tables were covered with white cloths. The crystal glasses and silverware glistened. The entire garden, on both sides of the canopied dance floor, glittered with colored lights strung between the big, tall, hundred-year-old trees.

The crowd was already there by the hundreds and still coming in droves. Never had Yousif seen so much gaiety, so much splendor. The flat rooftops and the balconies of nearby homes crowded with those who wanted to be entertained without having to pay. Children had climbed pine trees outside the gate and in neighbors' front yards, so they too wouldn't miss the fun. Waiters in black pants, white jackets, and black bow ties were bringing out trays laden with food and drinks. The Greek band played with gusto.

A big round table had been reserved for Dr. Jamil Safi and his family, right by the dance floor.

"Is this whole table for us?" Yousif asked, as he held the chair for his mother.

"No," she answered. "We've invited a few friends."

Yousif did not have to wait long to see who they were, although he had a pretty good idea whom to expect. The two couples joining them were Dr. Fareed Afifi and Attorney Fouad Jubran and their wives. They were as smartly dressed as Yousif's parents. In general, Yousif observed, men were just as vain as their wives, for they spared no money on their clothes.

Dr. Afifi was short and full of fire, positively radiating energy. His wife, Jihan, was lovely in a slender European sort of way, a brunette with hair that was always brushed to the back and tied in a bun. Her green eyes were beautiful to a fault—they were too distracting. But there was always about Jihan, despite her laughter, a tinge of sadness. She and her husband of twenty-two years were childless, and Yousif knew she yearned and ached for children more than anything else.

Attorney Fouad Jubran was tall and stout, with the deep, strong voice of an orator. His clothes were just as expensive as his two friends', but somehow he never looked polished no matter what he wore. The touch of the peasant was in him, even though he was born and raised in the city. His wife was also hefty but in a most likable way. In fifteen years she had given her husband six sons and three daughters. No wonder, Yousif thought, the poor fellow's skin was coarse and his eyes cunning. The man was exhausted.

While his parents and friends were chatting and ordering drinks, Yousif scanned the garden for Salwa. She was nowhere in sight, and he felt disappointed. Restless, he rose and walked around looking for her. Isaac was across the terrace with his parents, who seemed to be enjoying themselves with their neighbors for the summer, the Haddad family from Haifa. Isaac, wearing a sports jacket but no tie, rose from his chair, glad to see his friend. But before the two boys could talk, Isaac's father drew their attention.

"What's this I hear about Amin?" Moshe said, smoking a *nergileh.*

"He broke his arm," Yousif said.

"I know," Moshe said, pain registering on his long dark face. "You boys need to be more careful."

Isaac's mother and the other guests showed the same concern.

"Pull up a chair and sit down, Yousif," Moshe said. "Have something to drink."

"No, thank you," Yousif said. "I should be getting back to our table."

Moshe would have none of it. "Isaac, call up that waiter," he said.

Yousif loved the whole Sha'lan family, not just Isaac. He had known them all his life. In looks and manners and customs they blended so well in Ardallah that no one thought about whether they were Jewish. In his late forties, Moshe was so tall and strong of build that he could pass for a brother or a cousin of the Arab near him; three or four years younger than he, his wife was short and chubby. She looked like all the middle-aged Arab women who abandoned all pretense at youth and became plump from rice, bread, and potatoes. At home, Yousif remembered, the Sha'lans ate like Arabs and sang like Arabs. They were so different from the blond, blue-eyed Zionists from that afternoon.

From Basim Yousif had learned about the difference among the Orthodox Jews and Reformed Jews and Ashkenazi Jews and Sephardic Jews. Although this might be the wrong time to ask, he wanted to know who among the Jews leaned toward Zionism and who didn't? And why? He had heard that some of the Jews who clamored the most "to return home" were only converts and not real Jews. Was that true?

"What do you call the Jews from south Russia?" Yousif whispered. "Khazars?"

"I've heard of them," Isaac answered, surprised. "But what are you getting at?"

"Some say they aren't even Jews."

Isaac shook his head. "Tell me something. Are you still thinking about the tourists we followed this afternoon?"

"They weren't tourists," Yousif insisted, careful not to use the word spies.

"Whatever. What do they have to do with the Jews from south Russia?"

"I'm just curious. Would Jews who aren't originally from here—would they be claiming Palestine is theirs and not ours?"

Isaac paused. "If they're Zionists they would," he answered.

A couple wanted to pass behind Yousif and he had to pull up his chair to let them squeeze by. "Do you know what I think?" he asked, under his breath.

"What?" Isaac said, humoring him.

"Zionists are bad news for all of us."

"My parents are afraid of them," Isaac agreed.

"Do they say why?"

"They think they'd bring nothing but trouble to all of us who live here."

"I agree."

"Fine. But let's have fun tonight, will you? Amin's accident was sad enough."

"I'm sorry."

A waiter stopped by and they ordered two beers. The band had stopped playing. The garden looked overcrowded.

"Have you seen Salwa?" Yousif whispered.

"Sure," Isaac answered.

"She's here?"

"She made a double take when she saw me. I guess she expected you to be around."

Yousif looked for her. "Where's she sitting?"

"On the other side," Isaac motioned with his head.

Suddenly Yousif heard a roll of drums. Those standing began to clear the aisles so those sitting could get a better view. The floor show was about to begin, and Yousif returned to his table. A man and a woman dressed in white costumes covered with sequins were walking briskly down the aisle, closely followed by a boy, who looked no more than ten years old, and five musicians. As soon as they reached the dance floor and took their places, the hotel's assistant manager, Adel Farhat, a young man about thirty years old with his hand at his waist as if his side were hurting him, tapped the microphone for attention.

"Ladies and gentlemen," he said, "Al-Andalus Hotel takes pleasure to present the best act this town has ever seen. The trio you are about to enjoy has performed not only in Palestine, but in Cairo, Beirut, and Baghdad. Here they are, the famous father and mother and son, the singing and dancing Saad, Saada, and Masoud."

Yousif laughed at the funny names, for they were variations on "happy" and "lucky."

The band began to play, and the entertainers stepped forward. The bright lights made their costumes dazzle. Husband and wife looked more like brother and sister. Their round faces, ruddy complexions, and blue eyes disproved the theory that opposites attract. The husband reached for an accordion, his wife for a tambourine. In a moment, they joined the band in playing, their eyes fixed on the trees, not on the crowd. They seemed exhilarated, but in a dream world of their own.

Their son reminded Yousif of little Shirley Temple. To the women at Yousif's table, he was embraceable. His parents had dressed him up as a circus ringmaster, except for the red hat with a rubber band under the chin, which looked like a bellboy's cap. But a midget ringmaster he was, complete with a crackling whip. He began to sing:

If I could only have a wishing ring
And rule over the ladies for one day.

The tune was light and catchy. The lyrics poked fun at modern marriages. The women, the boy sang, were mistreating their men and getting out of hand. They needed to be put back in place. And if they did not know what was good for them, then the men had better straighten them out with the whip. To demonstrate, Little Masoud pranced around the floor, rendered the song with gusto, and cracked the whip on the floor—both left and right. The sound of the lashes and the energy with which he cracked the whip made the women in the audience howl with laughter.

"How cute!" Jihan Afifi said.

"Adorable!" Yousif's mother concurred. "He ought to be in films."

"Cairo should snap him up. That boy is going places."

Yousif could not wait for the song to be over. He wanted to dance with Salwa and tell her about Amin, about the spies.

Half an hour later, she appeared from behind the bandstand like a star making her first entrance. Yousif was transfixed. Tall, erect, dressed in white, followed by a girlfriend who came to her shoulder, Salwa strode through the garden. All eyes were on her, but her own eyes seemed to be searching. Yousif knew that she was looking for him, and he was thrilled. The instant their eyes met, she headed in his direction, they stood facing each other quietly, and then began to dance.

"What would you do if you had a wishing ring?" Salwa asked him, as they stepped to the rhythmic music amidst the big crowd.

Yousif hesitated. Salwa was the best-looking woman in the whole garden; of this he had no doubt. He loved her height, her big almond-shaped eyes, her curved eyelashes, her long neck. He loved her auburn, shoulder-length hair, and the expensive perfume she was wearing. He loved her smile. Her full red lips tantalized him and made his blood rush. Even her teeth were perfect.

"I'm still waiting," she told him, swaying in his arms.

"What would I do if I had a wishing ring?" he repeated, enraptured by the warmth of her body. "I'd wish you to be my wife."

She laughed and tilted her head backward.

"Can't you be serious?" she flirted.

"I am serious," he told her.

"Well, what's your second wish?" she asked, smiling.

His eyes scanned the garden. "I'd wish to have the heads of all the men around here examined."

"Why?"

He told her about the afternoon adventure, about the trip through the woods, about Amin's accident, and especially about the Zionist spies.

"You think they were spies?"

"I'm sure of it. They walked as if they were on a mission. And all that gear they were carrying."

"How can you prove it?"

"They might come back. When and if they do, I'm going to track them no matter who falls and breaks his arm." He turned around and surveyed the scene before him. "Look at all these men drinking scotch and soda, even champagne, as if the world is safe for them. Look at that table . . . and that . . . ."

At one table were young men known to be playboys. They hardly worked, but dressed well, gambled, and chased women. How could these grown men live off their parents? Yousif could not understand. Where was their pride? He would never be like them. He himself was only seventeen, still in high school, and still living at home. Yet he felt bad, even guilty, every time his parents handed him his weekly allowance from their hard-earned money. He couldn't wait to finish school and be on his own.

One day he would take care of his parents and repay them for all the good things they had done for him. That any man as old as these playboys—who had to be in their late twenties or early thirties—would want to be in their position was incomprehensible. Looking at them, one would think they were movie stars or gangsters in American films. If the truth were known, he thought to himself, they probably had to borrow money to buy the tickets for this show.

"Would you trust the future of Palestine to such idlers?" Yousif asked.

Salwa looked puzzled. "What do you mean?" she inquired.

"They look so carefree," Yousif whispered. "They don't know what's happening in their own backyards. They don't know that these hills are being mapped by the enemy."

They moved their feet, but they did not dance. Tension lingered between them in spite of the gaiety around them.

The assistant manager, Adel Farhat, was dancing next to them. But to the apparent distress of the young woman in his arms, he was staring at Salwa.

"May I have the rest of this dance?" Farhat asked, ready to dump his partner.

Yousif looked at him unkindly. "No way," he said, swinging Salwa away from him.

Salwa grew pensive, though the intrusion didn't seem to bother her.

"Guess what I would wish for if I had a wishing ring?" she asked.

"Let me guess. You'd wish for a whip to crack on these men's backs."

She shook her head. "Worse than that. I'd wish for a well to dump them all in."

The lively music stopped and Yousif looked at Salwa.

"Are you coming tomorrow to tutor my brothers?" she asked as they walked on the gravel between the crowded tables.

"I only come on Thursdays."

"I wish you could come tomorrow, too," she admitted, blushing.

This unexpected remark was enough to lift Yousif's spirits. He walked her back to the table to pay his respects to her parents. Her father was like his own father in many ways: reserved, bespectacled, well-dressed. In other ways they were different. His father was of medium height, his mustache about an inch wide like Charlie Chaplin's. Her father was tall, his mustache pencil-thin like Ronald Coleman's. Yousif did not know her father well. The man was humorless, icy, often grave. His mouth was almost always drawn at the corners. It was her cheery mother who charmed Yousif. A tall, buxom woman, she was always in good spirits, always laughing. Her dark red hair contrasted well with her green satin dress and milky complexion. Yousif liked her and had a feeling that she liked him.

At the table with them were men and women who were strangers to Yousif. The two youngest men earned his instant suspicion. One was about twenty-five years old, with a short haircut, a striped bow tie, and a high thin voice. The other was a couple of years older, had a big nose, and wore a tie with so many flowers on it that Yousif thought he ought to stick it in a vase. Both men seemed unattached and this bothered Yousif. Who were they? What did they want?

Salwa was bubbling with conversation. Yousif could tell that she did not mean to ignore him but was waiting for a pause to introduce him to everyone at the table. He looked around for a chair. He would not leave until he had an opportunity to watch the young men's glances and determine the drift of their intentions. Salwa's mother noticed that he was still there and told her two young boys, Akram and Zuhair, to get up and give him one of their chairs. At that point Salwa's father stopped talking long enough to introduce him.

"Oh, Yousif, I'd like you to meet a couple of my friends," he began. "We work together at the office. This is Ahmad Jum'a and this is Jowdat Muhyiddin."

A relieved smile crossed Yousif's face and he shook their hands. From their names he could tell they were both Muslims. There was no longer any reason for him to be worried. Salwa would never marry outside her Christian faith.

Then a bottle of champagne arrived—compliments of Adel Farhat. Yousif didn't know what to think. Was the assistant manager a friend of the family? Did he have designs on Salwa? Yousif hated himself for being so suspicious. The poor guy might already be married. He might have been dancing with his wife when he'd tried to cut in. While Salwa chatted with her mother, Yousif watched her father turn and wave to Farhat, who was standing on top of the stairs. Adel waved back—grinning. Yousif felt a strange, sinking feeling.

5

Amin's uncle Hassan died on Monday morning and was buried in Gaza late that afternoon. But Amin and his father didn't return to Ardallah till Wednesday. When Yousif happened to run into Amin in the *souk,* talking to Isaac in front of his father's shop, he was alarmed to see that Amin's left hand, particularly the fingernails, had turned bluish.

"Amin," Yousif gasped, "you shouldn't be walking around like this. Father needs to take a look at you. We'll go together."

Amin refused, saying that he had some errands to run for his mother. But if his hand didn't improve for another day, he'd certainly have it checked.

"Nonsense," Yousif said. "Come on, let's go."

Isaac and his father urged Amin to go along with Yousif, convinced that his hand required immediate attention.

"It must be worse than I thought," he said, inspecting his unsightly hand.

"I wouldn't be surprised if you're running a fever," Yousif said, leading him through the crowd.

The doctor was not at his clinic, and Nurse Laila didn't know where he was. All she knew was that he was making house calls, and she didn't know how to reach him. Most of the people didn't have telephones, she explained. Besides, she didn't know in which order he'd be seeing his patients.

"Listen, Laila," Yousif said, with authority, "you keep on trying to reach

Father. Tell him what's going on. Tell him Amin's hand looks awful. And you Amin, run along to the house. And don't stop anywhere, please. In the meantime, I'll fetch your father. Just tell me exactly where he's working."

Following Amin's directions, Yousif came upon weather-beaten, dusty-looking men chiseling rectangular stones. He followed the sound of hammers until he found Abu Amin supervising a man marking a rock for cutting.

"Abu Amin," Yousif said, his voice catching. "I don't mean to alarm you but I think you ought to go home."

Abu Amin, wearing the traditional robe, and dusty from head to toe, studied his face. "What's wrong?" he asked, his beady eyes frightened.

"What's wrong?" Yousif asked, furious. "Couldn't you tell? Couldn't you see Amin's hand was turning bluish?"

"We had enough worries," Abu Amin explained, dropping his tools and shaking the dust off his clothes.

"I'm sorry about your brother. I'm also sorry you didn't let a doctor in Gaza take a look at Amin's arm. They do have doctors in Gaza, don't they?"

"What is that supposed to mean?" the old man asked, glaring at him.

"Well, damn it, Amin's hand is looking awful. And it must've looked awful yesterday and the day before that. Didn't it occur to anyone to—. Oh, forget it."

Both rushed down the hill, consumed with anxiety. Yousif's heart went out to the old man.

"I'm sorry, Abu Amin," Yousif said, putting his arm around his shoulders. "I didn't mean to raise my voice. I'm just worried."

"Of course you are," the old man said, taking long strides.

They arrived at Amin's house before the doctor. The inside of the house was not just dark—it was gloomy. Amin's mother and several neighbors had been waiting anxiously. When the doctor finally showed up, they all stood up out of respect. His bag in his hand, the doctor motioned for them to sit down, and headed straight for Amin, who was lying by the window.

Breathing heavily, the doctor took Amin's hand in his own. Yousif and the others hovered at a discreet distance.

"I need more light," the doctor said.

Aunt Tamam rushed to bring the kerosene lamp from the dresser under the huge mirror. Large shadows moved across the walls and low ceiling.

"How long has it been like this?" the doctor asked.

"It started yesterday," Amin answered.

"You didn't tell me," Abu Amin said, defending himself. "Really, I had no idea—"

"Couldn't you see for yourself?" the doctor asked without looking at the tormented old man.

"We were busy . . ."

"Busy, hell," the doctor said.

Even from where he was standing, Yousif could see that Amin's whole hand looked bruised now. It had gotten worse. He felt nauseated just looking at it.

The doctor reached for his handbag and took out a syringe and a small bottle of medicine. He filled the syringe and rolled up the sleeve of Amin's good arm. The whole room grew quiet as he made the i njection.

"Get his pajamas," the doctor said to the mother, closing his handbag. "I'm taking him to the hospital."

The mother gasped and her fingers went to her lips.

"Hospital?" Abu Amin said, incredulous.

"Yes, hospital. Let's not waste time, please."

The mother was opening and closing drawers. "Here's a pair," she said. "But I don't have a bag or a newspaper to put them in."

"He'll carry them under his arm," the doctor said. "Let's go."

"I'm going with you," Abu Amin said.

"Me too," Aunt Tamam added. "I can't sit here and wait until you come back. Where will you be taking him?"

"To the Government Hospital in Jaffa," the doctor said, already at the top of the stairs. "That's the nearest one."

The neighbors muttered blessings on the "good" doctor whom one old woman called an angel of mercy. Yousif heard someone remark that Ardallah should have its own hospital, his father's pet project. Normally the doctor would welcome such support and address it at length. But now he was too engrossed, too upset, to comment.

Within minutes the doctor was behind his steering wheel ready to chauffeur Amin and his parents to the hospital. Yousif wanted to go but his father shook his head.

"Too crowded," he said, starting the ignition.

"No it's not," Yousif said, opening one of the doors and squeezing himself inside.

He watched his father shift gears and tear off like a policeman chasing a robber. Normally a cautious driver, the doctor sped through the main street, sending pedestrians and pushcart vendors scampering to the sidewalk. He drove through the old district's dusty alleys, honking at every turn. Yousif sucked his breath as a boy on a bicycle came flying out from a side street, but luckily his father had applied the brakes just in time.

An hour later Yousif called home from the hospital in Jaffa.

"We're going to be late coming home," Yousif told his mother.

"How late?" she asked.

"I have no idea. Father just said I'd better call you and tell you not to wait for us."

"I'm glad you did. Isaac has been by twice to see if I heard from you. How is Amin?"

Yousif expelled his breath. "Pretty bad. He has developed gangrene."

"Oh, I'm so sorry. Is his arm in real danger?"

"Absolutely. Maybe even his life. Father says if they can't stop the gangrene from spreading it might kill him. Mother, can you believe all this?"

"No, I can't. It happened so fast."

"It's that Abu Khalil. Every time I remember his blowing his damn nose while working on Amin's hand . . ."

"It's just meant to be, son," his mother said. "The death of the uncle, the trip to Gaza. None of this helped. It just piled up on poor Amin."

"If anything happens to him I don't know what I'll do."

"God forbid, nothing is going to happen to him. I'll keep him in my prayers. And call me whenever you can. I'll be right here."

"Mother, will you send a word to Isaac?"

"No need to. I'm sure he'll be back. He said he would."

After he hung up the receiver, Yousif sat in the hospital administrator's office, thinking. The bright summer day began to grow dusky in his eyes. How quickly and mercilessly, he thought, could life turn on the least suspecting. A few days ago Amin was in pink condition, eager to catch lovers in the act. Now his arm was broken and his hand black and blue. Who would have thought this could happen overnight? Who would have thought one's own life could be threatened when least expected? No wonder people did not trust happiness.

They spent the night in Jaffa. But Yousif did not sleep. Early the next morning he called his mother again, sounding more and more depressed. The gangrene, he said, could be stopped only by amputation. That was in the morning. By late afternoon, Amin's left arm had been cut off above the elbow.

A CURTAIN of gloom descended on the doctor and his family when they sat that night on the balcony. Yousif's heart and mind throbbed with sorrow for Amin, as he looked around the circle of friends and relatives. Several neighbors were there. One was a barber who catered to the villagers. He was big enough to be a wrestler and his mustache was as thick as the Kaiser's. His wife wore the traditional ankle-length costume, took snuff, and cackled like a hen. Another visitor was a man who had spent most of his life in Brazil. Now that he was nearsighted and his mouth was slightly twisted from the ravages of Bell's palsy, he had come to retire in Palestine. He struck Yousif as pathetic, for he seemed an outsider—a stranger—in both "homes." His wife was Spanish, had big dimples, and spoke the few Arabic phrases she knew with such a heavy accent that she was almost unintelligible.

Cousin Salman, the bald-headed shopkeeper, looked smaller than usual, for he sat with his arms folded and his eyes glued to the floor. Salman specialized in potions for the lovesick and was known as the druggist for the superstitious. Of all their relatives, the doctor enjoyed this nephew's company the most. Salman amused him with stories about customers who'd come for potions to stop their husbands from cheating or to make a certain man or woman fall in love with them. But tonight, Salman was as sorrowful as one of his jilted lovers.

Sixty-year-old Uncle Boulus, Yousif's mother's only brother, was also deep in thought. A prosperous grain merchant who lived a few doors away, Uncle Boulus was known for his sharp business nose and considerable common sense. This intelligent and respectable man loved to sit at his doorstep, where people from all walks of life would stop and chat with him, sometimes unloading their most intimate burdens. If Uncle Boulus had something to say tonight, Yousif reflected, he was keeping it to himself. Uncle Boulus sat in silence, flicking thirty or forty yellow beads as though they were a rosary. Those worry beads were his trademark, for Yousif never saw his uncle without them.

But of all the night visitors, none impressed Yousif as much as cousin Basim, who happened to be in town. Basim was visiting this evening with his wife, Maha, and their two young boys, ages three and one. Basim was forty-two years old, his black hair and mustache hardly touched by gray. For all Basim had been through, Yousif thought, they should have already turned white. Here was a veteran who had fought both the British and the Zionists in 1936 and 1937 and had been exiled from Palestine from 1939 till the end of 1944.

Yousif eyed him with admiration and respect. Basim was handsome, manly, and powerful looking, with broad shoulders, a wide forehead, big hands, and long limbs. Men respected him, even those who did not agree with his radical political views. Women loved him for his strong profile and deep smoky eyes. Basim could sit brooding for hours, but when he talked, everyone listened. Tonight, Basim too was in a quiet mood. Even he who had seen many die in battle seemed touched by what had happened to Amin.

"Yes, I believe bones can be set by a layman," Dr. Safi explained, tapping his armrest with the bowl of his black curved pipe. "But not every case is simple. When the skin is broken it becomes a serious matter. It needs antibiotics which only a doctor can prescribe. So Amin didn't have any when he needed it."

Basim turned to Yousif. "How did Amin break his arm?" he asked.

"A stone wall collapsed under him," Yousif answered. "We were following a Jewish group—"

His mother gave him a restraining look.

"First we thought they were out for some romancing in the woods. Then I thought they weren't."

Silence lingered for a moment too long.

"Yousif was suspicious from the start," his mother said. "He thinks they weren't just tourists."

Basim pouted, the tips of his ten fingers touching. "You thought they were out for some fun," he said. "Then you changed your mind. Why?"

Yousif knew all eyes were on him. "It struck me that they might actually be involved in espionage," he explained.

Not a breath could be heard.

"How did you know they were Jewish?" Basim asked quietly.

"Isaac thought they were speaking Yiddish," Yousif answered.

Basim nodded and wiped his mouth. "You were right," he said. "They were spies."

The word "spies" fell in their midst like a hand grenade. Yousif was the only one who felt a sense of elation. Here was someone who believed him.

"Yes, Jewish spies," Basim repeated, fixing his stare on his astonished audience. "Probably here to survey the hills and valleys. So that when the time comes they can occupy them and quickly seize strategic points. While we're sitting on our haunches, they're planning for war."

"War!" Yousif's mother said. "Do you think there's going to be war?"

"No doubt about it," Basim told her.

"When?" the mother interrogated him, sitting on the edge of her chair.

"It's already started. But if you want an official declaration, you'll have to wait another year."

"When the British Mandate ends?" she asked.

"More or less."

Cousin Salman, who had not cracked a single joke all evening, folded his arms and seemed to double up. He smiled wryly and his first word seemed to hover on his lips. "Why do you always see the dark side of things?" he asked. "The story of innocent young boys who are curious about lovers was sweet. Why did you have to ruin it?"

"Ruin it?" Basim shot back, pulling out a cigarette from a half-empty pack. "What are you saying? Even young Yousif didn't believe it. The Zionists were doing this sort of thing in 1936, and they're doing it now. It's their system, their style. Last month we caught a group near Hebron; a week ago some Zionist map-makers were caught in the hills overlooking Nablus. It's nothing new. And for every group we accidentally discover there are dozens more. It's a pattern the Zionists have been following all over Palestine for years, no doubt in my mind. They're getting ready for a big offensive. As soon as all the pieces fall in place they're going to come at us with a vengeance."

Maha sighed deeply, which attracted everyone's attention. "It's 1936 all over again," she said, leaning her head against the wall behind her and holding her one-year-old close to her bosom.

There was something sad about the curve of her neck, Yousif felt.

"There's no comparison," her husband corrected her. "We are on the verge of something catastrophic—either for them or for us."

"Or for both," Uncle Boulus added, his thin lips drawn tight.

"Could be," Basim agreed. "All the troubles we've had with the Jews and the British are nothing but a prelude—a rehearsal—for what's to come. Believe me."

The mention of 1936 seemed to throw everyone into memories of those hard times. Yousif had grown up hearing stories about Basim and his bravery in 1936. Shocked by Britain's treacherous merry-go-round policies toward the Arabs, Basim had abandoned a flourishing law practice and at the age of thirty joined the Arab revolt that had broken out against the British and the Zionists. Basim had distinguished himself as a brave man. Eyewitnesses swore they had seen him run after armed British soldiers with an empty revolver, a bayonet, or just a pocket knife. He had killed so many that the British government had once sent a whole battalion to capture him. But he had eluded them.

When the revolt ended in 1939, the British had insisted on exiling him—and Basim would have remained in exile had it not been for petitions and pleas sent by his family to the British High Commissioner in Jerusalem. The Commissioner had refused time and again, until finally, and after five years of roaming the earth, Basim had sent his word that he would stop his anti-government activities.

"If we catch you doing anything wrong," the British officials had warned him, "we'll hang you from the highest minaret."

Basim had accepted their terms, for the sake of his aging parents, knowing very well that he could serve the Arab cause much better from inside the country.

Following his return, he reopened his law office, married Maha, the sister of a comrade-in-arms who had been killed during the Revolt, and settled down. But his fire remained ablaze. His family and intimate friends had known that he would never rest until the Palestinians achieved their complete independence and eradicated the new Zionist threat.

"If the Zionists are that active in preparing for war," Yousif asked, waking up everyone from the doldrums, "what are we doing about it?"

His cousin's jaws tightened. "Very little," Basim replied. "It would take a concerted effort on the part of a large number of our people to stop such things from happening. Unfortunately we don't have an Arab government in Palestine."

"What about the Arab Higher Commission?" Yousif pressed. "What about the Mufti? He led the 1936 Revolt. Why can't he lead it now?"

All eyes were on Yousif, who seemed to surprise everyone by his questions. Then they looked at Basim, who seemed reluctant to talk about the Mufti or the Arab Higher Commission. Yousif knew that Basim had more or less broken off with the old resistance movement, but he did not know to what extent. From Basim's reaction, he thought perhaps the timing of his question was wrong.

Basim stretched his legs before him. "The Mufti and the Arab Higher Commission are still there," he replied, his low voice full of hurt and disappointment.

Yousif studied his cousin's words, tone, and gesture. Yousif felt a dark and mysterious bond forming between him and his revolutionary cousin. Their eyes met and held.

"As I said," Basim continued, "we don't have the organizations or the money or the manpower to 'police' the countryside. The British authorities who are still running the country don't care. So the Zionists are left free to roam our mountains and valleys as they wish. The payoff for them will come when they jump us from every cave and nook and cranny they've been mapping all these years."

Silence, as thick as fog, enveloped all those present. The doctor puffed on his black pipe and said nothing. Uncle Boulus opened his gold vest watch and closed it indifferently. Yousif got the impression that not everyone agreed with Basim; some seemed to regard him an alarmist.

"Why don't we organize?" Yousif asked, impatient. Again the eyes focused on him. "That's what we should all do," he added, almost in defiance of their stares.

"'And a child shall lead them . . .'" Uncle Boulus quoted, smiling.

Yousif bristled. "How old do I have to be to be called an adult?"

"I apologize, Yousif, you are not a child," his uncle told him, his tone respectful. "In fact, you impress me as being more grown up than most."

Yousif nodded in his uncle's direction and then turned to Basim. "And what do you do with the spies you catch?" he asked, surprising his parents by his persistence.

"We take their maps," Basim replied, "and we interrogate each and every one separately."

Yousif waited for more. When Basim did not volunteer any further information, Yousif asked, "Who's 'we'?"

"A few associates of mine here and there, that's all," Basim said, smoke billowing all around him.

"I see," Yousif muttered, thinking. "And what do you do with them afterwards?"

"We beat them," Basim said. "Some we shoot."

By gesture and word they all seemed horrified. The barber's plump old wife sneezed, causing the baby in Maha's arms to cry. Even the Spanish woman looked confused until her husband explained to her what was going on in her own language. Visibly rattled, she reached for a pinch of snuff from the barber's wife.

"Without trial?" said Yousif's mother.

"Just like that?" asked the barber.

"What if the Zionists begin shooting our boys at random," asked the retiree, resting on a cane with an ivory handle.

"I didn't say we shoot them at random," Basim defended himself. "We shoot the ones we catch spying on us."

"Is that wise?"

"Why not?" Basim wanted to know.

"It could start the violence all over again," Uncle Boulus predicted.

"Sooner or later we're going to have open war," Basim argued, taking his crying baby from his wife. "No sense pretending otherwise."

Shooting was a grave mistake, Yousif thought. But who among them, their silence seemed to say, could argue with a hero who had actually fought in battle against the British and the Zionists? Basim's patriotism was beyond reproach—and so were all his political and military actions, it seemed.

"What do you think, Father?" Yousif asked. "Do you think they should kill the ones they suspect of spying?"

"No, I don't," the doctor answered, drawing on his pipe.

"And why not?" Basim snapped. "What do you want us to do? Accuse them of trespassing?"

"You can do more than that," Yousif argued. "You can interrogate them, learn all about their secret cells, lock them up—but you don't have to kill them. For one thing, you might use them in the future for an exchange."

"A trade for what?" Basim insisted. "For whom?"

"One day they'll probably hold some of our people," Yousif protested. "There could be an exchange of prisoners."

"Who has the time or the money to feed and look after them?" Basim asked. "They are our enemies, and they are working overtime to throw us out."

The clicking of Uncle Boulus's worry beads was the only thing that could be heard.

"I can tell you we're facing hardened people," Basim continued. They're coming at us with full force. Or have we forgotten the bombing of the King David Hotel?"

"And that was a year ago," Uncle Boulus agreed.

"Their terrorists," Basim added, "blew up that hotel at the height of the rush hour. Over a hundred people were killed—all of them innocent. They didn't blink an eye. And you tell us to restrain ourselves? War is hell and we might as well face it—we *are* at war."

"Then take these spies as prisoners of war," Yousif suggested. "Wouldn't that be the decent thing to do?"

Disappointment flashed on Basim's face. "So far I've been impressed with you, Yousif. I hope I don't change my mind."

Suddenly Yousif remembered the compass he had stumbled on that fateful day. He had hidden it in a drawer full of socks. He rushed into his bedroom and returned within a minute.

"I found this in the fields, just before Amin broke his arm," Yousif explained.

"Let me see it."

Yousif handed him the compass. He felt alone with Basim, remote from the rest. The muttering and the whispering around him did not seem to matter. Basim turned the compass over and over in his hand and was now directing his eyes at those around him.

"Salman, what do you think of this?" Basim said to the frail shopkeeper beside him. "Made in Brooklyn. Hardly an object for lovers, don't you think?"

Basim's mild sarcasm made Salman's lips twitch. Again there was silence.

So they were spies, Yousif thought. There were plans for war. On the one hand, he felt vindicated; on the other, he felt initiated to a world he did not like, a world of insecurity, mistrust, and suffering. Everything around him began to look and sound different. The crickets began to chatter. The moon grimaced like a one-eyed god. The lights of Jaffa, twenty miles to the west, looked aflame. Some of his caged birds inside the house twittered in disharmony. He sat next to the railing, toying with the compass, the omen of mysterious and threatening things to come.

Yousif could read fear on the faces around him.

6

"Can you believe this!" Yousif's mother exclaimed next morning on the balcony, as she watched two men unload a pickup truck packed with boxes of oranges.

Yousif shook his head. The truckload was a gift from the family friend who bought the orange grove his parents had visited a few days earlier. The stack of boxes was now getting taller than the men. Yousif was overcome with disbelief. He loved oranges, but what could one do with two thousand of them?

"That's the Arabs for you," his mother said, bemused. "No sense of moderation."

"We're generous people, that's all," Yousif said. Taking his knife, he made a precise incision around the top of one orange. He took pride in the art of peeling. Whereas most people peeled and ate a whole orange in a couple of minutes, he spent far longer. For him the trick was to strip the fruit naked without injuring the flesh. The pleasure was in the ritual as much as it was in the fruit itself.

"What are we going to do with all these oranges?" his mother now asked, wiping her hands with her apron.

"I'll take a few with me to Salwa," he said, offering her half of the orange he had just peeled. "I'm late already."

"Don't take a few, I'll send a box with Fatima sometime today. We need to distribute all these before they rot. Let me see, a box to Basim's house, a box to brother Boulus's house, a box to Salman's house, a box to . . ."

"Don't forget Amin and Isaac," Yousif reminded her.

"Of course not."

"Do you think Father will take me and Isaac when he goes to visit Amin?"

"I don't see why not. Poor Amin," she said and resumed counting on her fingers the names of those to whom she would send a box of oranges.

ON HIS WAY to see Salwa that morning, Yousif carried the compass in his pocket. Amin's amputation broke his heart; Basim's talk of war rang in his ears. The thought of war and the taste of oranges reminded him that the big, juicy, fragrant Jaffa orange was Winston Churchill's favorite fruit. Yousif's father once told him that during World War II Churchill always had special oranges shipped to him from Palestine. Yousif could picture Churchill pacing and plotting his strategy against Hitler while savoring the flavor and delicacy of a Jaffa orange.

Yousif admired the British for their role in defeating the Axis powers, but their continued presence in Palestine was an injustice he couldn't accept. To his mind, the Arabs had not fought with the Allies during World War I in hopes of throwing out the Turks only to be saddled with the British in Palestine, Jordan, and Iraq, and with the French in Syria and Lebanon. But that was exactly what had happened.

Yousif wished he knew more about how and why Britain ended up in Palestine for a thirty-year mandate. That was part of the peace agreement, he had been told, which had brought no peace to his people. It irked him not to know what part Churchill had played in the formulation of the infamous Balfour Declaration of 1917. In one brief, ambiguous paragraph, Britain had ignored the Palestinians and promised the Zionists a national home in Palestine. What a dilemma, Yousif thought. First the Turks, then the British, now the Zionists. And that was only in recent history. In ancient times it was even worse. Were the Palestinians to be subjugated forever?

Now, in 1947, what mattered most to him was the fact that a foreigner—be it Balfour or Churchill or anyone else—could sit thousands of miles away from Palestine and dictate to the Palestinians what would or would not happen to them and their country. The arrogance!

Yousif walked up and down two hills on his way to Salwa's house, paying no attention to those he was passing. He was preoccupied with Britain's duplicity. First the Balfour declaration in 1917. Then the White Paper of 1939, with which Britain had tried to modify the Balfour Declaration. This, in turn, infuriated the Zionists. Yousif shook his head as he thought of Britain's chicanery, and pitied Arabs and Jews who were her victims. Once Churchill had declared, "The cause of unrest in Palestine, and the only cause, arises from the Zionist movement and our promises and pledges to it." Yet, his government, like all British governments before it, had either vacillated or been brutally supportive of everything Zionist. Still, that British Bear received special shipments of Jaffa oranges, even when the world was aflame, when the Mediterranean sea and sky were impassable. The nerve! Yousif wondered what Churchill was thinking now, and whether he had any remorse.

There was so much to tell Salwa. Yousif marveled at how lucky he was to have the opportunity to visit her house every Thursday. Ever since the beginning of summer vacation two weeks earlier, he and Salwa's bothers, Akram and Zuhair, would hold their class in the family garden. They would carry their stubby chairs with the straw bottoms and walk around until they found a suitable spot. On both Thursdays Yousif chose a spot that afforded him a perfect view of Salwa's room.

Today Akram and Zuhair were waiting for him on the balcony, but Salwa was not in sight. They had their books in their hands and behind them were the familiar stubby chairs.

"Good morning," Yousif said, as he approached them.

"Good morning," the two boys answered.

"Where would you like to sit today?" Yousif asked.

The two boys looked at each other. "I don't care," Akram said.

"Why not inside for a change?" Zuhair added.

Yousif frowned. "It's too pretty to be inside. Come on, I'll show you where."

They went down two narrow fields and again sat under a huge fig tree. Yousif wanted to be away from the house for a measure of privacy, just in case he was able to talk to Salwa.

He reviewed the boys' homework. "Did you help each other?" he asked, looking at the arithmetic problems.

"No," they both said.

"It's okay if you did. Both of you did well. I'm proud of you."

"You're a good teacher," Akram said, smiling.

"That's nice of you to say, Akram. Today we're going to study Arabic. Do you have your books with you?"

"I do but I hate grammar," Zuhair complained.

"But it's very important," Yousif emphasized. "You can't speak or write well without it."

"It's hard and boring," Zuhair insisted, his lips twisting.

"Look at it this way. When you play soccer, don't you follow certain rules?"

"Yes," Zuhair answered, uncertain.

"Without the rules the game would be a mess. We wouldn't be able to tell the winner from the loser. Am I right? It's the same thing in reading and writing. The fun is knowing your opportunities and your limitations."

As Yousif explained the intricacies of Arabic grammar to his young pupils, his eyes constantly watched Salwa's windows and balcony. He hoped she would come down to hang her mother's washing on the backyard clothes line, or shake a rug over the balcony railing. Finally, he heard her footsteps and then was able to see her through a curtain of fig leaves. She was wearing a red skirt and a white blouse. In her right hand was a plate of white berries. Yousif decided it was an excuse for her to see him. He smiled with that knowledge.

He heard her murmur good morning.

"Good morning," he replied. He was so happy he could only stare at her.

"I picked them this morning," she said. "I thought you might like some."

He nodded. "I'll be with you in just a minute," he said.

"Can't stay long," she demurred. "Mother is waiting."

"Please," he said, fixing her with a meaningful look.

He gave her brothers a long assignment and walked from under the leafy tree to where Salwa was standing.

"I'd rather help you pick them off the tree," he told her, taking the plate of white berries from her hand.

"What would the neighbors say if they saw us together?" she laughed, her thin gold bracelets tinkling around her wrist.

"Can't they see us now?" he asked, putting a couple of berries in his mouth.

She looked around, worried. "I am taking a chance. Maybe I should leave. The last thing I need is their gossip."

She started to walk away, and he reached out to stop her. "Please don't go. Sooner or later they'll have to know."

His confidence seemed to surprise her. "That day will never come," she teased him and swung away, her round white earrings reflecting the morning sun.

"That day will come," he insisted, taking and eating a few more berries.

For a moment both seemed to be held in suspension.

"You've heard about the amputation," he said, leaning against the trunk of an apple tree.

"It's terrible," she said, nodding.

He pulled out the compass and showed it to her. "Here's what I found that day," he said, looking grim.

"What is it?"

"A compass. It must've fallen out of their pockets. I just knew they were spies.

Basim agrees with me. He also thinks that for all practical purposes the war between us and the Jews has already started."

She took the compass from him, pouting. "I wish I were a man."

Yousif looked at her, surprised. "Why?"

"Then I'd be able to fight. Girls can't do much except hope and pray. I wouldn't like that."

A plane swished over their heads. Apparently it had taken off from nearby Lydda airport only a few minutes earlier, for it was still ascending. He could read the airline markings on it. Yousif watched it streak against the blue sky; Salwa kept her eyes glued to the ground. The mood grew somber.

"I want to find a way to help," Yousif told her.

"There's only one way."

He scrutinized her face. "Fighting?"

"What else?"

"It's not that simple. Oh, Salwa, there's so much we don't know."

When she did not respond, he looked at her. She seemed unmoved.

"Right now it's like watching a film after the fifth reel," he explained.

"It's clear to me," she said. "All I know is that I'm standing on land my father inherited from his father and he from *his* father. This berry tree is our berry tree. That house is our house. Everything we own we either inherited or bought and paid for. And if the Zionists want some strangers from Europe to settle here, they'll have to fight us first."

"And if they succeed? If they take it all away?"

"We'll never rest until we get everything back. The thing to do is to make sure nothing falls into their hands. That's what my father says. And I agree with him."

They heard her mother calling her from inside the house.

Salwa handed him back the compass and started to leave. Then she turned around and took a good hard look at him. "Relax," she said. "Our cause is as clear as this glaring sun."

Yousif glanced at his two young pupils under the fig tree. Finding them busy with their work, he took several steps behind Salwa. "When will I see you again?" he asked, hating to see her go.

"Next Thursday."

"Not before?"

She smiled and moved away from him. "We'll see," she answered, walking in earnest.

As she departed, his heart sank. He held her tall figure in his eyes until she stopped at the top of the stairs, waved her hand, and went inside. Momentarily he returned to the task at hand, finding pleasure in the presence of her two younger brothers.

"Will you bring me a bird next time?" twelve-year-old Akram asked at the end of the morning session. "I did well, didn't I?"

Yousif smiled and made a mental note to stop at Salman's shop and buy cannabis for his birds. Aside from going to the movies, his favorite hobby was buying, catching, and trading birds. But his collection of more than two hundred birds was costing him all his allowance. He really needed to sell some of them, but his heart would not let him. He loved them so much that he had a room in both houses designated just for them. Before the end of the summer he would probably catch more. How was he going to cope with that many?

"You deserve the best," Yousif finally told Akram. "Next time I come I'll bring you my red canary."

"What about me?" said eleven-year-old Zuhair. "I did just as well."

"You know I won't forget you," Yousif told him, rising and keeping his eyes on Salwa's room. "How about a blue cage?"

"YEEEES," Zuhair responded, shutting the book with a bang.

"That's not fair," Akram whimpered. "I'm older and I want the cage."

Yousif laughed and ruffled their hair, wishing their sister would favor him with one more look.

BY THE MIDDLE of August, most of the vacationers were leaving Ardallah to prepare their children for school. Those from outside Palestine were returning home without a worry in their head. The Palestinians themselves were going away less certain about the future of their country. Even the people of Ardallah had been transformed during the summer months. The future looked worrisome.

Like many of his generation, Yousif was developing a new passion—politics. Day after day he would read newspapers, listen to the radio, and participate in discussions with his father and their night visitors.

One night they had many important guests, including the Appellate Court Judge Hamdi Azzam and his wife. Fouad Jubran and Fareed Afifi and their wives were frequent visitors, but the respectable judge came over only two or three times a year, and each occasion took on a special significance. Yousif's parents became a bit more formal, and their hospitality a bit more lavish. Instead of sitting on the balcony, as they normally would on summer evenings, tonight they sat in the living room. Yasmin and Fatima were busy in the kitchen sending out dish after dish of maza. While serving the guests drinks and dishes of cheeses and pickles and *hummus* and, later on, coffee and sweets, Yousif listened to every word they said.

Of particular interest to the men and women that night was what Britain was going to do in Palestine. Her mandate was about to end. For a while, it was generally believed that Britain would choose to stay. Some Arabs were of two minds about that prospect. They wanted Britain to leave, but they did not want the Zionists to replace her.

"Frankly," Dr. Afifi said, "I prefer Britain's staying to an open war with the Zionists."

"I agree," Fouad Jubran said, lighting a cigarette. "It's the lesser of two evils. What do you think, Judge?"

"Hard to tell," the judge answered, resting on his left elbow, his legs crossed at the ankles. His right hand was toying with the ivory head of a cane that was his trademark. A smallish man, he wore glasses and cultivated a well-trimmed mustache. As many times as he had seen him, Yousif could put everything the judge had uttered on one page.

"Is there the slightest chance a war can be avoided?" Dr. Afifi pressed.

"No," the judge answered, shaking his head. "But the British are determined to get out."

"And leave us with the mess they created?" Yousif asked, emptying one ashtray into another.

"True, true," the judge said, sipping on his Arabic coffee. "But now they want to dump the whole affair in the United Nations' lap."

Uncle Boulus's worry beads ticked like a bomb.

"Imagine the vacationers who came to Ardallah a couple of months ago," said Jihan Afifi, biting on a piece of baklava. "They came in one mood and left in another."

The regional problem, they all feared, would be internationalized and the world powers would have a field-day playing football with tiny Palestine. Who could predict the outcome, especially when the Zionists start bringing up the Holocaust?

That night Yousif fell asleep knowing that Palestinians had every reason to be worried.

7

On the first Monday morning in September, Yousif woke up earlier than usual. The darkness still filled his window, but he knew there was nothing else to do but rise and face the day. It was time to go back to school.

Yousif felt too old for school. He had been jolted more than once during the three-month vacation. But there was a time for everything, he said to himself. As he yawned and stretched in his big warm bed, he realized that in spite of the political rumbling and the talk of war, life still seemed normal in Ardallah.

He got up and took a shower in the spacious new bathroom with its pale blue ceramic tile. Then he shaved, looking at himself in a mirror that also functioned as a door for the built-in medicine cabinet. All the while he was thinking of the road before him: passing the London Matriculation which was given to all high school seniors throughout the British colonies; graduating; and going on to a university. Brushing his teeth, he wondered if he should make such long-range plans when the country might be ravaged by war.

The thought of all these years of schooling also troubled him: one more year in high school, four more years in college, maybe three years in law school. My God! He'd be twenty-five before he was through. In any case, which university should he select? Many seemed attractive, but they were all outside Palestine. He splashed his face with cold, invigorating water. The Palestinian Arabs did not have a single university, while the Jewish minority had at least two. It simply did not make sense.

That morning, books under their arms, Yousif, Isaac, and Amin met at the flour mill. All public and private schools were opening today. Students of all ages were dressed in clean clothes and headed in different directions. Some were eager, walking briskly, their neatly covered books under their arms. Then there were the six-year-olds on their first day to school. Yousif and his two friends grinned as they saw one boy crying and holding his mother's hand. Memories rushed to Yousif's mind. He remembered his first day, when his mother had had to bribe him by filling his pockets with British toffee. He also remembered meeting two other youngsters, Amin and Isaac, who were to become his two best friends.

How long had that been! Nearly eleven years, he recalled. They had been inseparable ever since. Nothing in their relationship seemed to change. They had shot up in height, Isaac began to wear glasses, and the three learned to shave. But the most obvious physical change in them that morning was Amin's amputated arm.

Yousif was still uncomfortable seeing Amin with the sleeve of his jacket tucked and pinned under his armpit. Walking with his two friends, Yousif remembered how much Amin loved to play soccer. Amin would certainly have to give up his position as the school's goalkeeper.

Yousif just hoped his fellow students would be kind enough not to make Amin more self-conscious. When they reached school, however, most of them acted true to form. They stared at Amin, their mouths gaping. Even those who knew of the accident seemed to look at him with shock and hesitation in their eyes.

Sitting in the last row next to the back wall, Yousif looked around the room and wondered where they would all be next year. He felt too old to be confined to the desk on which he'd carved Salwa's initials next to his own, during the first throes of infatuation two years ago. He felt too old to go back to studying and memorizing and trying to compete for the top grades.

Soon he would be waiting for Salwa on the road. He longed to see her, to gaze at her eyes and face. He hungered to be near her, to touch her, to kiss her. But all he could do now was hope to see her during the one-hour lunch break or certainly at the end of the day. It was Salwa's last year in school, too. He had no idea what her plans were after graduation. Not too many girls from this small town could afford or were even allowed to seek higher education. He would soon know whether she would be one of the lucky ones. On second thought, the matter of her future began to worry him. Most girls got married and started having babies soon after graduation from secondary school, for even work outside the house was unacceptable to most families. What would he do if someone asked for her hand? More important, what would she do?

TWO MONTHS later, there was a flock of birds in the carob tree, but none drinking at the shallow creek where Yousif had cast his net. The net itself was made up of three rectangular pieces bounded by long thin strips of wood and connected by hinges. It looked like three window shutters floating in a most unlikely place. The idea was to throw bread on the net to attract the birds. As soon as they landed, the bird catcher would pull a string or two and trap them.

That afternoon, Amin and Isaac had already caught two birds each, Yousif but one. Yousif reached for a medium-sized stone and threw it at the ancient tree, causing the leaves to rustle and the birds to fly away. They flew against the gray sky, then returned to their haven.

"Why don't you face it? It's not your day," Amin said, laughing at Yousif's eagerness to match their catch.

Yousif threw a bigger stone and heard it thud against a big branch. The birds flew again, and the leaves rustled, but he waited in vain. Soon raindrops began to fall.

"Let's go," Isaac said. "It's time to leave."

They folded their nets and strings, picked up their cages, and started down the hill.

Descending the hill had often brought pleasure to Yousif. He tried to time it so they could watch the magnificent blending of colors as the sun set on the far horizon. This view of Ardallah, resting leisurely on the crests and slopes of seven hills, inspired in him a sense of joy. He often paused to offer a silent prayer. Looking at the town, he felt touched by its serenity. Perhaps the trees gave it splendor and warmth. They seemed to sheathe the little houses, hovering over them protectively. Yousif saw the women carrying their fruit baskets on their heads after an arduous day in the fields, the shepherd playing his flute, silhouetted behind his sheep. He heard the murmur of the brooks, the fields with hundreds of birds over them noisily flapping their wings and singing, the steeples and the one minaret, the melodious haunting voice of the *muezzin* chanting a praise to Allah and calling Man to prayer.

At such times Yousif would often be so saturated with nature and its glory that he'd walk silently, thoughtfully. At other times, however, life would seem too wonderful to contain. He would burst out singing or shouting—then hear the hills echo his youthful voice.

The three friends would swing the bird cages in their hands or start throwing stones to see who could throw farthest. They would climb an apricot tree to fill their pockets and the insides of their shirts with fruit. They would pick ripe black or white sour grapes and stuff their mouths to see who could eat the most. Passing a brook they would stop and stretch flat on their stomachs and dip their mouths to drink. Sometimes one would dunk the head of another and they'd all start splashing. Then they might persuade a farmer to let them ride his donkey or his horse. If he had a camel, each competed for the first ride.

On this day late in November, however, the sunset was missing, the sky was solid gray. Even beautiful Ardallah seemed more depressing than tranquil or inspiring. Everything was the same, yet it seemed like a painting by an artist whose touch was as heavy as his heart. Yousif felt the difference. He looked for the farmers and the shepherds and saw nothing but black crows circling far above their heads. He descended the hill with his friends, not leaping, not singing, not laughing, but restrained.

Soon the rugged dirt road ended and the paved street began. Turning the corner, they came upon a crowd of sixty or more men in front of Fardous Cafe.

"My God, I almost forgot," Yousif said. "You two. Do you know what day it is?"

"What?" Amin asked, swinging a bird cage in his right hand.

"You really don't know?" Yousif asked him, feeling a bit superior.

"Oh, yes," Amin finally said. "It's the day the United Nations votes on the partition. Not such a big deal, though."

"Why not?" Yousif asked.

"We know they'll turn it down. Except for a few western countries, the world isn't for it. From what I hear no one gives the plan a chance."

"Maybe so," Yousif said. "But I still want us to make a pledge."

"A pledge? What kind of a pledge?" Amin wanted to know.

Yousif ignored Amin and looked straight at Isaac. Isaac seemed to read his mind. They had stopped walking and faced each other.

"Let's make a pledge," Yousif repeated, "that no matter which way the vote goes we'll always be friends."

"Friends!" Amin exclaimed. "What's the matter with you? Of course we'll always be friends. Is it because Isaac is Jewish? Is that it? My God, he's one of us."

Isaac smiled and Amin motioned with his head for them to keep on walking.

"Just the same," Yousif persisted. "It will be good that we—"

"Why not?" Isaac spoke for the first time. "Let's shake hands."

They stopped in the middle of the road and shook hands. Yousif and Isaac were a bit solemn, while Amin made light of the fact that their arms crossed as each reached to shake hands with the other two.

"When arms cross like this," Amin remarked, "it means someone is going to get engaged. I wonder which of us will be first."

A middle-aged woman came out of Abul Banat's bakery wearing a native dress and carrying a tray of freshly baked bread on her head. Yousif thought he had seen her once or twice at his house, but he was not sure. She became flustered asking about Amin's accident and, by way of apology, lowered the tray on her head and handed him a whole loaf of bread.

After she'd left, Amin looked at his friends, grinning. "Perfect," he said. "Now we can break bread to go along with our pledge. A handshake on a full stomach will make our vows last forever."

"What a clown!" Yousif said.

"It's soooooo good," Amin said, chewing the crusty bread.

"Delicious," Isaac agreed. "But I wish we had some white cheese."

The Fardous Cafe was made up of two parts: a large hall and a tiny kitchen in a building as old as Ardallah, with a separate yard across a narrow street. The yard was covered with a canopy of straw, under which were about fifteen tables where old men wearing turbans and indolent youth sat and killed time playing cards or smoking a *nergileh.*

On one of the posts holding up the straw canopy was a speaker wired to the radio set inside the cafe itself. The cafe was jammed on both sides of the street and the radio turned on full volume. The motley crowd, even some women with shopping baskets on their heads, seemed to be listening attentively. Yousif traded looks with Amin and Isaac. The moment of decision was approaching. They walked up and stood unnoticed at the edge of the crowd.

Suddenly the music stopped and the announcer broke in saying: "A news bulletin of historic importance is about to be broadcast. The public is urged to stay tuned to this station."

Again there was music. The listeners remained riveted in their seats. Yousif surveyed those around him. It was so quiet he could hear the dice rattling inside a backgammon box, and the water gurgling in someone's *nergileh*. The liquor store, the barber shop, and all the businesses between the Greek Orthodox Church and the sidewalk vegetable stalls were left open and unattended.

The stillness had invaded the liquor store. Yousif turned and saw his cousin Salman approaching. Salman stood by Yousif and his friends, then reached inside his pants pocket and drew out a handful of roasted watermelon seeds. He poured a few in each one's palm. Quietly the four split the seeds with their front teeth, ate the pulp, and delicately spat the shell on the street.

Again, the music stopped and the announcer returned to the microphone. Standing between Amin and Isaac, Yousif placed the bird cage on the ground and put his arms around his friends. Unwittingly, he touched the stump of Amin's amputated arm, and both cringed. But the announcer's voice distracted them.

"The United Nations has passed a resolution to partition Palestine . . ."

The crowd gasped as if someone had jerked a big noose around its neck.

"The holy city of Jerusalem and its environs," the announcer continued, *"are to be internationalized. The British mandate in Palestine is to end and the British are to evacuate not later than next August."*

"That's crazy!" Yousif heard Salman cry out behind him.

"Of great significance is the way the unexpected vote was reached. Thirty-three members voted for the resolution, thirteen against it, and ten abstained. Among those who voted for it were the United States and the Soviet Union. Among those who abstained was Great Britain."

"The bastards!" Yousif said.

"Arab delegates at the United Nations were shocked," the announcer went on, *"to observe the extent to which the United States had gone to coerce nations to vote for the partition. Even a large country such as France was threatened with the cut-off of American foreign aid unless it toed the line and voted for the partition plan. But the most stunning reversal in voting position came from the Philippines. The 'yes' vote the Philippines cast illustrates the kind of pressure the Americans applied on the members of the United Nations."*

The crowd stirred.

"Why should the Americans hate us?" Yousif whispered to his cousin. "What have we done to them?"

Salman shrugged his shoulders.

"Arab diplomats," the announcer went on, *"recalled with great dismay the eloquence with which the Philippines' delegate, General Carlos Romulo, had argued against the partitioning of Palestine. Only a few days ago he stood behind the podium of the United Nations and declared, 'We cannot believe that the United Nations would sanction such a resolution to the problem of Palestine that would turn us back on the road to the dangerous principles of racial exclusiveness and the archaic documents of theocratic governments.' Incredibly, this same General Romulo today cast a vote in* favor *of the partition plan."*

The crowd gasped in unison.

"Arabs everywhere should conclude for themselves," the announcer continued, *"what pressure must have been put to bear in the dark corridors of the United Nations to effect such a dramatic reversal. They should also come to realize the depth of undeserved hostility we Arabs, as a nation, are encountering from the so-called leader of the free world, the United States."*

A player threw a deck of cards across the table, knocking off a glass of water.

A waiter, carrying a brass tray high above the crowd, lost his balance and dropped the cups of hot demitasse coffee over several people's heads and shoulders. A backgammon box was upset, its chips scattering by Yousif's feet. Salman's hand froze, a watermelon seed clenched in his front teeth. Yousif's grip around his friends' waists tightened, but their eyes never met.

No Arab in his wildest imagination, Yousif knew, had expected this outcome. Palestine was theirs. Telling them otherwise was like trying to hide the sun with a forefinger. They had expected the United Nations to sympathize with the Zionists but not to give them other people's homes.

"Never!" someone shouted.

"Never!" another seconded.

"Never!" the crowd repeated.

People began to move, agitated. Yousif watched men shake their heads, twist their mustaches, and bite their lips.

"Crazy, don't you think?" Salman muttered. "Crazy, eh? Crazy."

Isaac began to pull away from his two friends. "I ought to go," he said.

Salman seemed dazed. "Isaac," he said, "don't you think it's crazy? They can't do that, it's crazy. Don't you think?"

"Incredible!" Isaac replied, his eyes wandering.

Yousif heard a familiar voice addressing the crowd. He saw his cousin, Basim, standing atop a flight of stairs that led to a dentist's clinic above the cafe. As the crowd heard Basim, they stopped their milling and focused on him.

"Remember this day," Basim shouted, his arms gesturing for the crowd to settle down, "as a day of shame. Remember November 29, 1947, as the day the world lost its senses and demanded a catastrophe. Remember it as the day the world leaders held hands and jumped off a suicidal rock."

Basim, Yousif knew, was not supposed to get involved in politics. This was a condition of the British government for his return from exile. Yousif worried about what might happen to his cousin.

"The world which persecuted the Jews for so many centuries," Basim thundered, "decided today to erase its guilt, and in its attempt to right the wrong, it committed another wrong. Remember this day of shame when the world closed its ears to the people who own and inhabit Palestine. We, the majority who have been here from time immemorial. Why did the world leaders deny us the right to self-determination?"

The crowd was spellbound by Basim's fiery oration. But Yousif noticed that Isaac was growing fidgety.

"We'll leave soon," Yousif whispered. "I want to hear what Basim has to say."

"It's getting late," Isaac whispered back, his face turning pale.

"A few more minutes," Yousif urged. Isaac stayed.

"Remember this black day," Basim exhorted, "as the day the world declared that you have no right to live in your own homes, or to plough your own fields. They're telling you that you must move out and make room for the Zionists of the world, as if *you* were responsible for their dispersion. As if *you* were the Hitler who thirsted for their blood. Remember this day as the day the world decided that our living in this country for thousands of years isn't long enough to call it a home. Raise your voices and let the conscience of the world be awakened. How long, how long does one have to be rooted in a country before he can call it a home?"

The people roared their approval, shouting, "How long? How long?"

Basim held his arms up and the crowd quieted. "You may wonder what will happen now that the UN has approved the resolution. You can be sure that its consequences for us, if they go unchecked, will be disastrous. One look at the map they have devised for a divided Palestine would tell you that it was the work of demented minds. The jagged borders look like the rough edges of a jigsaw puzzle. Arab villages and towns and Jewish colonies and kibbutzes would be enmeshed so as to foster hatred and violence between the two peoples forever. This particular town, Ardallah, is to remain Arab. But who would guarantee it? And who cares? Who would want a Palestine without Haifa and Acre and Nazareth? Would *you?*"

"NOOOOO!" the crowd screamed.

"Our concern is not this or that town," Basim told them. "Our concern is the whole country."

"YEEEEES!" the crowd roared.

"For the last thirty years Britain has been allowing Jewish immigrants to come in by the shipload, and yet we Arabs are still the overwhelming majority. You'd think our numbers would mean something. You'd think our opinion would count when it comes down to how we should run our affairs. But no! Now the United Nations wants to divide the country and give the best half to the Zionists. No one in his right mind would say this is fair, and no Arab would accept it."

"Down with Zionism," a farmer shouted, his white mustache bobbing up and down.

"Down with Zionism," the crowd echoed.

"Bad as it is," Basim went on, "this is just the tip of the iceberg of what's to come. What we should all fear is this: the Zionists will never settle for the half they're being offered, even if they accept the UN resolution and sign a hundred documents. Sooner or later they'll be asking for the other half. Why do I say this? Because I read what they're saying and I follow what they're doing. Because

Palestine is too small for Arabs and Jews, especially if they're going to gather the ten million Jews in the world and settle them right in our midst. That's exactly what they have in mind."

"Boooo!" the crowd shouted.

"What this shameful UN resolution means," Basim explained, his arms flailing, "is that when the British leave here by next August, the small minority of Zionists will get the fertile and cultivated seashore of Palestine and we the great majority of Arabs will get the rocky mountains where men and goats will have to graze for a living."

"No!" a fruit merchant shouted.

"No!" again the crowd echoed.

"Listen carefully to what I'm saying," Basim exhorted. "Go home and tell your relatives, friends and neighbors. Unless we stop them now—and I mean *now*—we as Palestinians have no future whatsoever in this country. We'll either have to pack up and leave or they'll drive us out. They want to build an empire stretching from the Euphrates in Iraq to the Nile in Egypt. Their strategy is this: take what you can get and then ask for more. Today half of Palestine, tomorrow the second half, and the day after tomorrow most of the Middle East."

"Let them dream," shouted a cab driver, gesturing and dropping ashes from his half-chewed cigar.

"If we don't send the Zionists a message loud and clear," Basim cried, "if they think we're bluffing or inept, then we might as well lie down and die, because Palestine will be lost and *we* will be lost."

A multitude of clenched fists were raised and a thunderous cheer shook the square. Yousif and his two friends looked at each other, recognizing each other's fears. Because they were standing at the edge of the crowd, they were the first to notice the British soldiers arrive in two jeeps. They saw them park their vehicles and scramble out, their hands on their rifles. Amin and Isaac wanted to leave, and began to move away.

"Wait," Yousif said.

"What do these bastards want?" Amin asked.

"I'm leaving," Isaac answered, his voice shaking. "They're telling the people to go home. Can't you hear them?"

The crowd eyed the soldiers with anger and hate. The men in the street seemed to form a human wall to block their way. As the eight soldiers tried to push through, the people pushed back. Yousif stood on a nearby chair and watched. He saw a thin soldier squeeze by and run up the steps toward Basim. Basim and the soldier seemed to have an argument and then began to push and shove each other.

Freeing himself from Basim's grip, the soldier turned around and blew a whistle. Two more soldiers, their rifles in both hands, dashed up the steps and the three tried to arrest Basim. Arabs chased them up the stairs and were clutching at their feet. One soldier kicked a man and he fell back. Other men reached Basim and began to create a wall between him and the British soldiers.

Yousif became worried. He jumped in and rushed through the crowd, urging for calm. Seeing Basim struggling to defend himself, he was afraid that the soldiers might know Basim's identity and have him arrested. He wished his cousin would try to escape.

Two shots were fired. The crowd gasped; Yousif froze. His heart fluttering, he hoped the shots were just a warning. For a second the crowd grew calm; Yousif prayed that no one was hurt. Anxious and afraid, he stood on his toes and craned his neck. Basim stood still on top of the stairs, gesturing. A wall of men separated him from the soldiers. Slowly the crowd recovered. They were urging Basim to resist.

"We're with you, Basim!" one man shouted.

"We're all with you!" another seconded.

Basim raised his arm, and the crowd hushed. "They want to take me to jail," he told them. "What would you say to that?"

"Hell no, they won't," Yousif yelled. "Tell them we're all with you."

The crowd roared, "YEEESSS! We're all with you!"

Basim looked at the police, defiant. A moment later one of the soldiers who tried to arrest Basim turned and faced the hundred or so people below.

"Clear out—all of you," he shouted, waving his arm. "If you'll calm down and go home there will be no trouble."

"We won't go until Basim tells us to leave," Yousif shouted back. "You cannot order us around anymore."

"Not anymore," the crowd again roared.

Before Yousif knew it, he was being lifted up on somebody's shoulders.

"Tell them, Yousif, tell them," a woman cried.

"This trouble," Yousif went on, "was started by the UN, not us. Leave us alone or we'll turn this peaceful gathering into a demonstration against you."

There was a dramatic pause. Yousif also wished the man who had lifted him on his shoulders would put him down. His neck was crushing Yousif's balls. And Yousif hadn't planned on getting involved. But someone had to support Basim and stand up for what was right.

"What should we do, Basim?" Yousif asked his cousin, as though speaking for the crowd.

Basim raised both his hands in triumph, his smile broad and his eyes fixed on Yousif. "We will choose the time and place for a confrontation. We won't fight until we're ready. Today let us be satisfied that we have raised our voice and that the British government has heard it. Tomorrow is another day. For now, let's all go home and start preparing for war."

Before he was put down, Yousif saw a group of men turn one of the jeeps upside down. The way they lifted it, swung it around, and tossed it aside, it seemed no more than a toy. Then someone doused it with lighter fluid and touched a match to it.

The sight of fire and black smoke and the smell of burning plastic and rubber made all those in the street disperse. By the time the crowd thinned out Basim had vanished and Yousif couldn't find Amin or Isaac. What he did find broke his heart. Crushed on the street was the blue cage with the birds they had caught that afternoon—flattened in the stampede. Why hadn't his friends picked up the cage and taken it with them? But this was no time to worry about birds. Human lives were at stake. The fate of Palestine itself was hanging in the balance.

Then, as if on cue, a drizzling rain began to fall.

By the time Yousif had run as far as the blacksmith's shop, the jeep's gas tank exploded. Would it be the first blast of war?

APPROACHING the hilltop on his way home, Yousif found his neighborhood in an uproar. Many had poured out of their houses and were standing in the streets despite the drizzle, too shocked to discuss their new dilemma. The gloom was palpable. Some kitchen windows were lit, but most of the street was wrapped up in shadow. Those gathered seemed already touched by the memory of a simple good life that was about to be snatched away from them for reasons they could not understand. Some of the women wore house slippers and their arms were folded. The men looked stung, paralyzed. Yousif greeted several people he knew. No one even nodded back.

"What was that explosion?" the wife of a mattress maker asked.

Yousif told her what he had seen.

"Was it the British soldiers who did the shooting?" asked the bosomy wife of a bus driver.

Yousif looked at her. "Who did you think?" he asked.

"I was hoping it was one of our men," the same woman answered.

A quiet moment of understanding passed between them. Suddenly the crowd perked up, showering him with questions.

"Tell us what happened. Was anyone hurt?"

Yousif briefed them, skipping the part about himself. No one was hurt as far as he knew, he told them as they clustered around. Soon they themselves passed on the news: from the wife of the bus driver in the street to the seamstress standing at her doorway, to a widow on the balcony above, to a spinster school teacher at the window across the courtyard, to an endless chain of women at other doorways, windows, and balconies.

His father was home early, standing with his mother on the steps in front of their house, talking to some men and women from their neighborhood. Only his mother acknowledged his arrival with a nod.

"When they postponed the voting two days ago," a neighbor said, "I was afraid it would come down to this."

Yousif understood what the man was saying. The United Nations had been scheduled to vote on the resolution Wednesday, November 27. At the last minute, however, the voting was postponed till after the Thanksgiving holiday in the United States. Many feared that the postponement was meant to give the U.S. enough time to coerce countries that received foreign aid from Washington to vote in favor of partition.

"Huh," Uncle Boulus scoffed. "I knew it thirty years ago, when that damn Balfour promised this country to the Zionists. And I knew it again in 1936 when Britain really tried to test our resolve. What do you think, doctor?"

"It's unfortunate . . . most unfortunate," answered the doctor. He seemed to be listening and not listening, paying attention yet preoccupied.

"In 1917 when Balfour promised the Jews a home here they were no more than three percent of the population," Uncle Boulus said. "Even now they are no more than fifteen or twenty percent. Yet, look what they get. It's unfair."

The drizzle changed to a heavy rain, and the people quickly moved inside their houses or sheltered themselves on their balconies. Yousif and his parents were left alone. They stood outside for a minute looking down at the town and the people scurrying in the streets.

All the pieces were falling in place, Yousif thought. Basim was right. War was inevitable. "What happens next?" Yousif asked his father, who was looking west, in the direction of Jaffa.

"The only thing that can happen in a situation like this—war," his father answered, biting the stem of his black pipe. "Tonight they'll put a match to the dynamite which Balfour unwisely, unnecessarily, and stupidly planted."

"Do you see any way out of it?" Yousif asked his father.

It was his mother who answered. "Only by a miracle," she said, putting her arm around Yousif's waist. "But if they try to take you away from me," she said,

"I'll go with you." She seemed frightened by the prospect.

"Take me where?" Yousif asked.

"If they draft you I'll join the army. I'll do something. I don't care what."

"What army?" her husband asked, tamping out his pipe. "You know we have no army. This is an occupied country. The British are still here, remember?"

"Who knows," she said. "Now that things are serious, the Arabs might start one. If they do and take Yousif away—"

"I'm no different from anyone else," Yousif objected.

"—I won't wait and die slowly," his mother added.

"Don't worry," the doctor assured her, "you'll have plenty of work to help me with at the clinic. There'll be many wounds to patch."

His words made her shiver. "You speak like a prophet of doom," she reproached him.

"I'm no prophet, but we are doomed," the doctor answered with conviction.

The street lights were soon turned on and Yousif's parents went inside. Yousif walked slowly around the veranda. His eyes traveled from the top of the hills before him to the bottom of the valleys, exploring the town street by street.

It was unnaturally quiet. Not a human being moved; not even a car or a bicycle or a stray cat. His eyes focused on a little house a few acres below him. He could imagine what was going on inside, for he had been there often. In the house was the Sha'lan family, Isaac's family. Yousif could also imagine how they must be agonizing over their future.

At the dinner table Yousif stirred the lentil soup before him. "What's going to happen to Isaac and his family?" he asked, as if trying to read their fortune at the bottom of his bowl.

"Nothing, of course," his mother answered, and looked at her husband for assurance.

Her husband drank his soup in silence, as if, Yousif felt, his wife's naiveté sometimes were too much to bear.

"Mama, you surprise me," Yousif said, looking at her. "They live in an Arab town, don't they? There's going to be war. Will they be safe?"

His tone upset her and color rose to her cheeks. "Well, they're not involved. It's a conflict between us and the outside agitators, the Zionists. The Sha'lan family are just like the rest of us—getting sick over what might happen."

"That's not the way your average Arab is going to look at it," her imperturbable husband predicted, without raising his eyes from his plate.

Yousif broke off a piece of bread. "Don't be surprised if the police come after me," he said.

Both parents were startled. "After you?" his father asked.

"Yes," Yousif replied.

"What on earth for?" his mother wanted to know.

Yousif told them what had happened after Basim's oration.

"What did you tell them?" his father asked.

"That they can't order us around anymore."

"That's all?"

"I also threatened them with a demonstration."

His mother gasped. "You threatened them?"

"Yes, I did."

"That's the least of their worries," his father said. "They just don't want you to throw bombs or go around shooting people."

"Then why did they try to stop Basim from making a speech? Wasn't that what a demonstration is all about?"

"Right now they're nervous. They're afraid things might get out of hand."

His mother reached out to touch Yousif's hand. "Please, son, stay out of it."

"One way or another, we're all going to get involved," her husband said, as he stopped eating, pushed back his chair, and rose slowly from the table.

AFTER DINNER, Dr. Safi went out to make his nightly house calls. He had a number of very sick patients, he said, and might be out for a while. His wife helped him put on his jacket and heavy black topcoat and told him that she and Yousif would be waiting for him at her brother's house.

Five or six people were already hovering around a portable heater and discussing politics with Uncle Boulus. Soon other people from the neighborhood arrived. The living room—with its plush mahogany furniture and thick Persian rug—was almost full of bewildered men and women who had reached a crossroad in their lives and had no idea which way to turn. Some were dressed in native robes and red fezes. Others, like Uncle Boulus, were in modern suits with nothing on their heads. Some were rolling cigarettes; others were fingering worry beads. Most were staring at the medallion in the middle of the Tabriez rug as though it were an open casket. Abu Nassri wore large tinted glasses, like a movie star traveling incognito, and chain-smoked his cigarettes until the fire scorched the tips of his yellowed fingers. One old bearded man had only one tooth. They all wanted to know what had happened that afternoon, and Yousif tried to answer all their questions, finding himself slowly but surely slipping into the vortex.

"Who fired the two shots?" Uncle Boulus asked. "Did anyone find out?"

"One of the soldiers, I'm sure," Yousif said. "Who else?"

"If I had a gun I would've been proud to empty it in their skulls," the old man fumed. "The sons of dogs! They shaft us and then expect us to like it. Dare we open our mouths?"

"I bet they won't stop the Zionists from celebrating all over Palestine," Yousif predicted.

"Hell no," someone said. "They're already dancing in the streets of Jerusalem."

"I bet the British soldiers are dancing with them," Yousif said.

"Well, of course," said Abu Nassri. "You think they'd try to muzzle them as they tried to muzzle us? Hell no."

Then, Yousif heard the heavy iron door open and footsteps cross the long marble corridor. Salman appeared and sat on the sofa nearest the door, followed by Yacoub Khoury, a man in his late twenties whose hair was parted in the middle and slicked down. Yacoub was a house painter who was ashamed of his trade. At sunset, he would throw away his work clothes and dress up like a civil servant. He was also a high school drop-out; to compensate for his lack of education, he would read all the magazines, listen to all the news, and try to engage in serious discussions. He lived with his mother and two older sisters and refused to get married lest his wife mistreat them. Poor Yacoub, people said. He was misery personified. But Yousif liked him.

"What do you think of the Philippines?" Yacoub asked as soon as he sat down, pulling up his sharply creased trousers at the knees.

"That's Truman for you," Uncle Boulus answered, crossing his legs.

"But General Romulo was so eloquent, so positive," Yacoub persisted.

"He wasn't the only one who had to swallow his pride and buckle under American pressure," Abu Nassri said. "Truman probably told him, either come across with the vote or there will be no more foreign aid to the Philippines."

"Sure," Salman commented. "Washington dealt us a dirty hand."

"Not Washington, only Truman," someone corrected him.

"Same thing," Yousif said.

Silence enveloped them like steam in a hot shower. Yousif wondered what happened to Basim. Did he leave, did he stay in town? Did the police know who he was? Were they now searching for him? He needed to find out, so he got up suddenly and headed for the door without an explanation. A few doors down he ran into Maha, carrying one child in her arms and walking another beside her. She too was on her way to spend the evening at Uncle Boulus's house to catch up with the latest news.

"Where's Basim?" Yousif asked her, standing under the street light.

Maha shook her head. "You should know more than I do. Is it true that he made a speech and you both defied the police?"

Yousif nodded. "Haven't you seen him?"

"No. Don't look so surprised. I'm used to it by now."

Her pretty face was long that night, and Yousif could detect the sadness in her voice. He wondered what kind of a family life someone like Basim had; he wondered also what kind of a life he himself would have with Salwa if he were lucky enough to marry her. Salwa, he knew, would not settle for just being a housewife waiting for him to show up whenever he could.

Yousif walked Maha back to Uncle Boulus's house, with Yousif carrying the baby. An hour later his father came in from his nightly visits and the conversation again gained momentum. All those present wanted to hear the good doctor's views.

"Only a few weeks ago, Truman came out against the partition plan," he reminded them, his eyebrows knitted. "Twenty-four hours later he changed his mind. Someone must've sat him down and said, 'Do you want the election or don't you?' Now you can see what his answer must've been."

"Then it's not a matter of conviction, is it, doctor?" the grizzled old man with the single tooth asked. Yousif looked at him, surprised by his probing.

"Expedience is more like it," the doctor replied, smiling benevolently and reaching for a cup of coffee. "At least Truman was honest. He said he didn't give a damn where they put Israel so long as they didn't put it in Missouri."

"What's Missouri?" the old man asked, flicking his ivory worry beads with his bony fingers.

"His home state," Yacoub answered, proud that he could recognize the name.

"That's it," Salman concluded, smacking his lips and folding his hands like an old woman. "It's the Jewish vote."

"No question about it," Abu Nassri added, his big abdomen resting almost on his knees. "Money and votes talk—especially in America."

Yousif sat and listened, impatient with the men's calm frustration. He wanted them to be angry, restless—even in their probing of what had brought them to this point.

"How should we have handled it?" Yousif asked his father.

Everyone in the room turned and looked at him.

"Handled what?" his father asked.

Yousif's eyes met his father's. "What should we have done to prevent this from happening?"

There was silence. Men exchanged looks. Some expelled streams of breath.

"I'm not sure we could've," Uncle Boulus offered. "The West seems set on paying old debts to the Jews. Nothing we could've done would've mattered."

"Do you agree, father?" Yousif asked. "We did all we could?"

"I don't know about that," the doctor replied, reaching for his pipe. "I guess we could have tried to reason with the Zionists."

"How?" Yousif pressed.

"I guess," his father reflected, unzipping his black tobacco pouch, "we could've sat with some of their moderate leaders and said something like, Is this the way to come home again? Look, it's unfortunate that you've been gone all these years, but it was the Romans who pushed you out, not us. Now that some of you want to come back, we want you to know that you're welcome. Come and live with us and share with us what we have like so many of you have done before over the centuries. We can build the country together, run it together, live in it in peace together. But we can't let you carve a state for yourselves in our midst, because that would be at our expense. The law of survival will tell you we can't let that happen. One thing for sure, you can't possibly love the land more than we do—"

"That's for sure," Yacoub interjected.

"—and if you think you can just come back and take it from us—some of us might get unhappy or downright angry."

There was a long pause.

"Do you think they would have been persuaded?" Yousif wanted to know.

"It would've been worth a try," his father said. "I don't know whether it would've worked, but I certainly would've tried it."

The sadness of all those in the living room seemed to deepen. They looked, Yousif thought, as though every one of them either had seen a ghost or at least was suffering from a terrible heartburn.

"What now?" Yousif again asked. "What if they try to implement the resolution? How can we stop it?"

"By war," Yacoub said. "What else is there to do?"

"Who's going to do the fighting?" Yousif questioned him, thinking of the spies who had mapped Ardallah's countryside.

A long discussion ensued. It was clear to most that the security of Palestine depended on the defense provided by the surrounding Arab states.

"You mean Lebanon, Syria, Jordan, and Egypt?" Yousif asked.

His father nodded. "That's what's usually meant by the confrontation states. They are the ones that have borders with Palestine. They are the ones who would come to help us save it."

"What about Iraq and Saudi Arabia?" Yousif inquired. "What about Arab countries in north Africa? Won't they come to our aid?"

Uncle Boulus smiled. "I guess they might if we need them. But they're too far away. Besides, unless the West intervenes directly or indirectly, this Jewish state, whatever they might call it, would prove no problem for us. History would record it as an aberration, as a futile attempt on the part of the misguided Zionists. Nothing else."

Yousif could not believe his ears. "You mean we have no problem?"

"We do," Uncle Boulus admitted, "but it's nothing we can't control."

"I'm surprised you say that."

"The Jews are not stupid," Uncle Boulus explained, flicking his worry beads. "When they know the crunch is on, they'll negotiate. They'd settle for a lot less than they're asking for now."

Stunned, Yousif pursued the argument. "But will a Jewish state be created?"

"They're going to give it a try, that's for sure. But nothing will come of it."

"Uncle, how can you say that? We didn't think the UN would pass the silly resolution. But it did."

"It's not the same thing. Nothing will come of it, I'm telling you."

"What if they declare a state the minute the British pull out?"

"They can do that, for sure. And probably will. So what? The state will be stillborn. Take my word for it. It will die at birth as sure as I'm sitting here."

All those in the room grumbled. Yacoub was so upset his face turned white.

"I hope you're right," Yousif said, not convinced. "What do you think, Father?"

The doctor leaned on his elbow and puffed on his pipe. "It will be a miracle if they don't get their state," he said, deep in thought.

Again Yousif heard the iron front door clang. Someone was walking down the marble hall. The steps got closer, and Yousif looked up. The sight of the new arrival made him gasp. Everyone turned and looked. Jamal, the blind musician, stood like an apparition at the door, his right hand resting rigidly on his cane. His black robe was wet, his sunken eyes and grim expression further electrified an already charged scene. For a moment no one said a word.

"I was so upset when I heard the news," Jamal said finally, "I hated to stay home alone. I knew I'd find someone here."

"I'm glad you came," said Uncle Boulus, rising to greet him.

Everyone in the room, even the old man with the one tooth, stood up in deference to Jamal. They seemed disturbed by the sudden appearance of his ominous black figure and touched by his shaky voice. Yousif led him to a seat. Jamal seemed pleased to learn of Yousif's presence. His cold hand clutched Yousif's arm a bit tightly, and Yousif was certain that Jamal's twitching lips were suppressing a cry gnawing at his heart.

If anyone in the room could feel pain in the depth of his heart and soul, it was Jamal. He lived alone and made a living weaving baskets. How many times had Yousif and his two friends been touched and inspired by him. About ten o'clock every night, Jamal would play the violin for an hour before he went to sleep. During that hour, many neighbors would open their windows or sit on their doorsteps, listening to his disquieting, haunting music, unlike any other they had ever heard. They were grateful.

If anyone loved the land of Palestine and its people, Yousif knew it was Jamal. It had taken Isaac months to convince Jamal to teach him how to play the *'oud*. Yousif recalled when Jamal, who had become comfortable after a while with Isaac and his two friends, actually picked up the violin and played for them. It was a rare privilege none of the three friends was likely to forget. But it wasn't only the music nor the manner of playing that stuck in Yousif's mind. It was the words Jamal used to describe the music that swelled within him but which he felt he could not express—a failure, he said, that frustrated him to the point where he had "destroyed four violins—and my life."

Yousif looked now at the small, pale, piteous man sitting beside him. His eyes seemed to have been sealed by a surgeon. He dressed in total black like a man in mourning. Yousif recalled the exact words Jamal had used: "Did you ever hear a shepherd on top of a mountain play his flute to his sheep? Or the farmers sing when harvesting their wheat and plowing their fields? Have you ever heard the women sing when their men return from across the ocean? Or the men and women sing at weddings? Did you ever hear women wail and chant their death songs?"

"When I was young, before I lost my eyesight," Jamal had added, "I used to sit among them and cry. I wanted to write a symphony of these hills—the hills of God. I wanted to write about their glory and everlasting meaning. I wanted to write about the people who lived and still live on them. I wanted to write about their deaths, for here a divine human conquered death with death."

It was this kind of love for the land and its people that gave Yousif hope. No one in the room, he knew, could express himself as well as Jamal, but deep in their hearts they all felt the same. If a blind man, Yousif thought, could fall in love with these hills and valleys, what about those who grew up looking at them everyday?

Let the UN pass resolutions. Let the Zionists dream of taking Palestine from its rightful owners. None of it would come to pass. This Yousif resolved—as he watched and pitied the men in the room who only sighed and complained. His generation would put up a fight and he, Yousif, would be a part of it.

8

By ten o'clock the next morning, Isaac had not shown up at Yousif's house for their regular weekly study, so Yousif and Amin walked down the hill to find out why. Isaac's modest stone house with its yellow window shutters looked like all the houses around it. They stepped onto the porch and Yousif rang the bell.

After a minute, Isaac's mother opened the door. She was short and plump and her graying hair was wrapped in a white scarf. Her round, kindly face was pale and she looked hesitant. She held the door only slightly ajar. Then, seeing who they were, she let them in.

"What's wrong, Aunt Sarah?" Yousif asked, surprised at her hesitation.

"I didn't think you'd come today," she said, still holding the door open.

"Why not?" Amin asked, looking at Yousif.

"I just wasn't sure," she said, embracing them. She looked outside, shook her head, and shut the door.

Yousif could read her mind. "We've got nothing to do with what's happening."

After an awkward pause, she led them to the living room and motioned them to sit down. On the far wall Yousif could see several pictures of old women and men, one of whom looked like a rabbi. On a table in the corner was Isaac's *'oud*, covered in a maroon velvet jacket. It reminded Yousif of Jamal's agony the night before.

"Do you think there's going to be war?" Amin asked.

Aunt Sarah wrung her hands and remained standing. "I'm afraid so," she answered. "You're too young to know what real suffering means. If war does break out we'll all suffer."

"But why war?" Amin pressed. "You're happy here, aren't you?"

"It's not the native Jews, Amin. You know as much as we do who's starting the troubles."

Isaac came out of his room carrying his books. His friends involuntarily stood up as if they were about to meet a stranger. Aunt Sarah looked at them, biting her knuckles.

"What's for breakfast?" Isaac asked, trying to sound cheerful.

Aunt Sarah stared at him and his two friends. "The three of you could split up," she said. "Before it's over you could be fighting on opposite sides."

As when Yousif had suggested the pledge, Amin looked shocked. "We won't," he told her.

"But you will," she said, nodding. Tears began to fill her eyes. She hastened out of the room.

After a short pause, the three friends sat down.

"We waited for you," Yousif told Isaac. "Why didn't you come?"

"Studying was the last thing on my mind," Isaac answered, his voice low. "Last night, mother was so worried she couldn't sleep. In her lifetime she cried a lot for the Jews. Now she's crying for the Jews and the Arabs." He waited a moment and then added, "She's going to ask you to have breakfast. Please agree."

"I've already had breakfast," Amin said.

"Have another one."

Ten minutes later, Aunt Sarah came in and announced that breakfast was ready. She seemed to take it for granted that they would eat together. The three boys exchanged glances, and followed her to the small dining room without saying a word. She had made a special dish of chick peas with fried lamb meat and pine nuts, and served large rings of bread with sesame seeds. There were black olives, sliced tomatoes, white cheese, and irresistible olive oil and thyme. Of all the breakfast foods, the last two items were Yousif's favorites.

The three broke pieces of bread, dunked the tips in the olive oil, and then dipped them in the small bowl of thyme. They chewed heartily, as though relishing a gourmet meal.

"How do you like your eggs?" Aunt Sarah asked no one in particular.

"I pass," Yousif told her. "This is more than enough."

"I'd be disappointed," she said. "Do you like them scrambled or sunny side up? Tell the truth now. Don't be bashful. You're like Isaac to me."

"I know that," Yousif said. "But honestly I don't care for any."

"How about you, Amin? How do you like your eggs?"

"None for me, please. Oil and thyme is all I want."

"Come on now," she said, bringing out a wicker basket full of eggs.

"Mama!" Isaac implored.

She seemed to remember something. "Just run out," she told her son, "and get me a handful of mint and parsley from the yard. I'll make you omelets."

She reached for a white bowl and began to crack some eggs. Isaac's rolled his eyes. Then he got up and went out, resigned to let her have her way.

Minutes later, she hovered around them, breaking more bread, filling their cups with hot tea, and telling them to eat more. In her loving care she looked flustered. They ate and talked, and pretended to enjoy the meal. Yousif felt such a lump in his throat, he could not swallow. Sitting at one table and breaking bread together was good, but the world would not leave them alone. A steady roar filled his ears, from which he knew they could not escape. From now on, he said to himself, things would never be the same.

After breakfast they went back to Yousif's house to attend to their studies. All their books were there and there were no children to disturb them. They had vowed not to allow politics or anything else distract them. The cause of their seriousness was the London Matriculation. That crucial international examination would be held next March or April, and it was never too early to start preparing for it. It was a great honor to pass it and a greater shame to fail it. The names of those who passed would be published in the national newspapers, and the morning the announcements hit the stands, the whole town would read the list.

The thought of failure filled Yousif, Amin, and Isaac with apprehension. Unless they passed, all their achievements over the last eleven years would be forgotten. Moreover, in the eyes of their parents the "Matric" was the yardstick by which their fitness for college was measured. All three boys wanted to continue their education. Amin, in particular, was hoping for a scholarship. Without one he wouldn't be able to afford college, but with the "Matric" to his credit he stood a chance.

For that reason, Yousif and his two friends had obtained published copies of old tests on the six subjects (Arabic, British, History, Mathematics, Chemistry, Physics) out of which every senior had to sit for five. They had set aside every Saturday morning to study for the "Matric" and nothing else. They resolved to answer every question, memorize every equation, and solve every problem. And they were making good progress.

Today was no exception. At one point, Yousif's mother brought them a pot of

Arabic coffee. Half an hour later Fatima tiptoed in with a plate of peeled oranges. The three boys read, discussed, and reviewed. But on the hour, Yousif would interrupt his studies to fiddle with the radio set. He was anxious to hear the latest news. Or he would glance at the morning newspaper, which his father had left in his armchair.

The headline, in bold red letters, screamed, THE SHOCK OF THE AGES. On the front page was a large map of the recommended division. To Yousif's chagrin, northern and southern Palestine and most of its coastline would be allotted to the Zionists. A corridor would connect Arab Palestine with Jaffa and Gaza.

"This is bizaare," Yousif said, shaking his head and picking up the newspaper.

Both Isaac and Amin looked up, frowning.

"Are you going to study or not?" Amin asked.

"I can't help it," Yousif answered, the paper rustling in his hands.

Isaac bit his lower lip and stared at his friend. "Maybe it won't come to pass. Now that both sides know that the threat of war is real, maybe they'll come to their senses. No one wants war. Not really."

For the rest of the review session, the three read in silence.

They had lunch at Yousif's. They ate sardines, *tabouleh,* and fried potatoes cut like small moons. Then they went out.

They passed the market place and saw the damage done by the explosion late yesterday afternoon. Scores of windows had been shattered, several corrugated iron doors mangled, and the nearest wall charred. The mutilated jeep, however, had been removed, and the streets had been cleared of glass.

"Amazing no one was hurt," Yousif said.

"Someone will get hurt if they don't fix that balcony," Isaac said, pointing his finger.

Yousif looked up. The balcony right above the street was still hanging—but teetering, on the verge of collapse.

They backed off to the other sidewalk.

A woman carrying her shopping in a wicker basket on her head stopped, gaping at the damage. She murmured something and made the sign of the cross.

The three boys resumed their walking. The shops were mostly empty, with the owners sitting behind their counters wrapped up in scarfs or wool sweaters. On the wall between the site of the explosion and the nearest grocery store, the slogan "Down with Zionism" was painted in black. Not far from it was painted another one. It read, "Down with Britain." On the green wrought-iron gate of the Greek Orthodox Church was a third. It said, "Down with Truman."

"Somebody must've been up all night," Yousif commented.

"Where did they get all that black paint?" Amin asked.

"Look," Yousif said, pointing his finger. "It's not all black."

Across the wall of the public lavatory was a huge arrow painted in red, pointing toward the edge of the door. Above it were words, also in red: "Herzl Lives Here."

Yousif had no love for the Austrian Jew who had founded Zionism at the end of the last century, but the vulgar slogan embarrassed him.

"Whoever wrote that doesn't know history," Yousif said. "Herzl died years ago. Like Moses, he never set foot on Palestinian soil."

"This scares me," Isaac said, turning pale.

"It's shitty," Yousif apologized.

Amin jerked his neck. "Words don't kill, though," he said. "It's the bullets and bombs that worry me."

"Words are powerful enough," Isaac said. "They could lead to real violence."

Amin's face reddened. "I guess you're right."

They were nearing the Fardous Cafe where Basim had made his speech the day before. Yousif was worried for Isaac. Would the Arabs remember that he was Jewish? Would any of them make a snide remark or try to hurt him?

As usual, the cafe was crowded. Some customers were reading newspapers, or staring blankly. Several, however, had gone back to old habits: playing pinochle or checkers, gambling for a cup of coffee, and smoking *nergileh.* It was an overcast day, but it was warm and dry enough for many to sit in the yard under the canopy.

There was nothing abnormal about the way the Arabs looked at Isaac or talked to him. They accepted him as though nothing had happened the day before. To them he continued to be an inseparable part of the trio. Yousif was relieved.

"Let's go to the movies," Yousif suggested, rubbing his hands.

"What's playing?" Amin wanted to know.

"I don't care," Yousif replied. "We haven't seen a film in two weeks."

Isaac slowed down. "You go ahead. I can't."

"And why not?" Yousif asked, waving to someone across the street.

"I need to be with my father," Isaac explained. "He can't even go to the rest room unless someone minds the store for him."

His two friends did not seem convinced. They exchanged looks but did not argue with him.

"I'll see you later," Isaac said, leaving.

Yousif and Amin stood motionless, each wrapped up in his own thoughts. Then they began to walk again and ended up at the movies. Salwa usually came to Saturday or Sunday matinees, so Yousif spent more time looking for her than watching the screen. Today she never showed up, and Yousif made Amin walk out of the theater with him, even before John Wayne finished kissing Maureen O'Hara. How could he sit through an American film? No more would he like anything from the land of Truman.

Yousif would never again dream of going to the United States. Nor would he let his father speak so fondly of his years at Columbia University. The America his father had known in the 1920s might have been great, but since then she must have changed. How could she call herself the leader of the free world when she was conspiring to deny him and his people their freedom? Yousif would never watch another cowboy defend *his* West, when that same cowboy was insisting on giving Palestine away to the Zionists.

The plaza in front of the cinema was full of peddlers: one selling *falafel* sandwiches, and another *shish kabab.* A third one, a ragged-looking old man, was waving a newspaper.

"Long live Arab Palestine," he shouted. "Read all about it."

Men on both sidewalks headed in the old man's direction. Yousif was afraid the big bundle under the peddler's arm would be gone before he got to him. Yousif squeezed through the crowd and managed to purchase three papers. The Egyptian and Lebanese tabloids were very popular and Yousif wanted to read what the Arabs' reaction was to the UN vote. "TIME FOR HOLY WAR," shouted *Falastin.* "ONCE AGAIN THE CRUSADES," shouted *Ad-Difaa.* "THE WEST GANGS UP ON ARABS," shouted *Al-Ahram.*

As soon as they were away from the heavy traffic, Yousif handed Amin one newspaper, put one under his arm, and began to read the third. Both read in silence, then aloud to each other.

Everything in the papers stirred their blood. The reports of the Jews singing and dancing throughout Palestine the night before infuriated them. Then there was the battle cry. It had been sounded from Yemen to Iraq, from Kuwait to Morocco. Much of it was Arab rhetoric; that Yousif knew. But the neighboring Arab states did seem eager to deliver on their promise to save Palestine from the aggressors who were converging on them like waves of locusts bent on swallowing everything in sight.

On top of a high hill that overlooked Jaffa and the Jaffa-Jerusalem road, Yousif stopped and stared. The distant, brown, rolling hills were clustered and elongated. They looked like a basket full of Easter eggs, dyed the color of onion skin. To his left was the hill on which they had often caught birds; to his right was the slope where they had followed the Jewish spies and Amin had fallen. Below them was a deep valley already engulfed in darkness.

"We're not too far from the Zionists," Yousif said, thoughtful. "Tel Aviv itself is less than twenty-five miles away. They just might make a grab at Ardallah."

Amin stared at him, shaking his head. "Not a chance," he said.

"I wouldn't put it past them," Yousif said.

"They could try but they would fail."

"What if they didn't? What if Ardallah fell into their hands."

In his wildest dreams, Amin had never considered the possibility. "If that happened," he said, looking astonished, "then it's something bigger than all of us. Something we couldn't help."

"But we can stop it."

"If it can be stopped, it's going to take Arab armies to do it."

"But you and I can help."

"How?"

"That's what I'm trying to figure out," Yousif said, kicking a pebble with his foot. "Who are the people making decisions on our behalf? Where do they come from? Who elected them? No one I know has ever been consulted about what's going on. You and I don't want war. Isaac and his parents don't want war. So why are we all being ignored? I feel trapped, left out, condemned without a trial. The destiny of Palestine belongs—or should belong—to the people. So why—"

"It's politics," Amin interrupted. "That's how it's done."

"Well, look where it's taking us. We need to get involved. There must be thousands of Arabs and Jews living beyond these hills who share our feelings. Why can't we all get together and tell the politicians to go to hell?"

They walked in silence. "Everyone we passed today had a long face," Yousif said. "Well, damn it, long faces don't save the country."

"What do you expect them to do?"

Yousif got angry. "They can get off their butts for a change. The country is going to be torn apart while they're swatting flies."

"Oh, Yousif, the Arab regimes are not going to sit back and let a bunch of Zionists steal our land. If that ever happens there'll be hell to pay. Every Arab king and president would be scared to death of his own people. The masses would turn on every one of them. I wouldn't be surprised if there was a revolution."

From the depth of his heart, Yousif wanted to believe Amin. But he couldn't. It sounded like wishful thinking more than anything else.

"I don't care what happens afterwards," Yousif said. "The main thing is to prevent the Jewish state from getting established. They must not get a foothold here at all. If we lose one Arab village now, it will take us a generation to get it back.

Father says we Arabs have too many so-called governments, too many factions within each country. The West can play us one against the other. For them it would be like splitting wood. It's true."

Amin looked at him quizzically. "Since when are you so cynical?"

"Basim is right," Yousif answered. "Now is the time to stop the Zionist takeover or we'll be lost."

A shepherd passed behind them with his flock of sheep. Again Yousif was reminded of the simple life on these hills that Jamal had called the hills of God. But now Yousif was worried about the future. When they reached the flour-mill, they parted. It was already dusk.

ON MONDAY, Arab Palestine went on strike. The doctor stayed home as did Yousif. They read newspapers, listened to the news, and spoke of nothing except the impending crisis.

While the Jews danced and blew their shofars in the streets, the Arabs rioted, especially in large cities such as Jerusalem, Jaffa, and Haifa. Multitudes of angry citizens rioted in the Arab capitals of Damascus, Beirut, Baghdad, and Cairo. They turned their vengeance on foreign embassies, especially those of the United States. They shouted "Down with America" and "Down with Truman." They burned British vehicles and looted Jewish stores.

What was more important, from Yousif's perspective, was not knowing Isaac's whereabouts.

Next morning, Yousif and Amin did not find Isaac waiting for them by the flour-mill. Nor was he at school when Yousif, as the prefect of the senior class, rang the bell at 10:15 to end the recess. Teachers and students hurried from the playground toward the building. It was a chilly, cloudy December morning, and all were bundled in topcoats or woolen scarves. Yousif rang the bell again and again for the benefit of the tardy and those at the far end of the field.

Knowing what the country had gone through the last few days, Yousif's class of twenty-two students did not really expect to be tested in the next period. The history test had originally been scheduled for the day before, but the school had been shut down on account of the strike. Most of the students were still cold, and sat now rubbing their hands, wondering what their teacher would do. Some buttoned their sweaters and leafed through their textbooks for a last-minute review, but most thought he would postpone the test. As prefect, Yousif stood at the head of the class and tried to keep it quiet.

Then the teacher, ustaz Rashad Hakim, opened the door briskly and closed it behind him. He moved toward his desk, energizing the whole class with his mere presence. He was short, compact, sleeveless even in the dead of winter. His gum shoes gave him an extra bounce.

"Are you ready?" Hakim asked, his clear brown eyes expecting rebellion.

"No!" several students responded.

"I didn't think so," Hakim said, grinning behind his desk. "By the way, where's Isaac?"

"We don't know," Yousif volunteered.

There was a moment of silence.

"You don't suppose . . ." asked Khalil, a handsome boy with short curly hair.

"There's nothing to suppose," the teacher said, cutting him short.

Ustaz Hakim looked at the blackboard, found it full of algebraic formulae from the previous class, then admonished Yousif with a look for having neglected one of his duties as a prefect. Yousif started to get up, but the teacher motioned for him to keep his seat.

He cleaned the blackboard meticulously. Then he opened the window to dust off the eraser on the outside wall.

"This morning," he began, "I intend to depart from our text and speak on the crisis at hand."

The students breathed satisfaction and seemed eager to hear him out.

"The Manchurian War of 1905 is good to know about," ustaz Hakim said, "but the UN resolution to partition Palestine is more urgent, more relevant. It's imperative that you should be well-informed."

Silence filled the room.

"If you read the newspapers and listen to the news," the ustaz added, sitting on the edge of his desk and wiping his hands off with his handkerchief, "you'd know that the situation here in Palestine is rapidly deteriorating. Both sides are stubbornly opposed to a compromise, and the world's attempted help seems to be nothing but an irresponsible meddling that will help hasten the eruption."

The students cleared the tops of their desks, folded their arms, and sat soaking up every word uttered by their favorite ustaz.

"Because man has not yet learned how to live with his fellow man," ustaz Hakim continued, "wars are usually expected to occur, but the world never knows when or where. *The Arab-Zionist clash is different.*"

"How different?" Yousif asked.

"As soon as the partition plan was passed," the teacher explained, "the whole world knew not only that war was going to happen, but the exact day. That day is steadily approaching and no one is able to stop it."

"The UN could've stopped it last Friday when it passed that damn resolution," Amin blurted.

"Watch your language," the teacher said.

"I'm sorry," Amin apologized.

"But you're right," ustaz Hakim agreed. "The UN could've, but it didn't. And now we have to deal with a new set of realities. I predict the war will start one minute after the British officially pull out of Palestine and thereby end their thirty-year mandate. This they have repeatedly promised to do. According to the UN resolution, they must leave not later than next August. That's only nine months from now. And for once the Arabs and the Zionists agree that *that* promise isn't going to be broken like so many promises before. The historic moment, then, will take place at midnight when the British leave and the Zionists create their Jewish state in a land owned and inhabited overwhelmingly by Arabs. Ever since 1917, when Britain—"

Mustapha interrupted. "How did the British get involved? What I don't understand is why they're here in the first place."

Ustaz Hakim waited for a signal from the class to see if the rest wanted him to go that far back. Several students agreed with Mustapha; they, too, didn't know.

"Well," Ustaz Hakim said, seemingly shifting gears. "I'll tell you, but remind me, Mustapha, to drop your 'B' to a 'C' for the course. You do well on world history but you don't know your own."

"It's not my fault," Mustapha protested.

The fog descending outside the window caught the teacher's eyes. He stared at it, trying to sort out his thoughts. "I presume you all know," he began, "that at one time the Arabs ruled most of the known world—from Asia in the east to Spain in the west—from the seventh century till the end of the fifteenth. Their empire-building began with the Prophet Muhammad, who in the seventh century led his followers and gave spark to the most brilliant series of conquests the world had ever seen."

Although Yousif was a Christian Arab, he was proud of all Arab history, even when it was dominated by Islam. Like most Christian Arabs, he considered himself Arab first and Christian second. He had been raised to believe that the Arabs of old were heroes, giants, supermen. And he had the highest admiration for their accomplishments. Sitting in class now, he wondered if the spirit of old would return and save the day for his generation.

"The Arab Empire, which reached its zenith around the tenth century A. D., was the center of civilization," ustaz Hakim continued. "Knowledge in every field flourished as never before. All history books will attest to that. But then the empire began to collapse. It was too big, too fat; both rulers and citizens grew apathetic, corrupt. It crumbled. Like everything else in life, it had a beginning, a middle, and an end. The end came in 1492—the same year Columbus discovered America—when the Arabs were finally driven out of Spain."

Yousif raised his hand and waited for the teacher's permission to speak.

"Didn't Ferdinand and Isabella of Spain expel the Jews too?" Yousif asked.

"You're right, Yousif," ustaz Hakim added, smiling. "Ferdinand and Isabella did throw the Jews out. But that's another story—really. It has to do with how abominably the West has always treated the Jews. The West, mind you—not the Arabs. The truth is, the Jews never fared better than they did under the Arabs, in Spain or anywhere else. In Spain they actually flourished, and more than a few rose to the highest ranks of government."

"Some of them became *wazirs,"* Mustapha said. "Isn't that true?"

"That's true," the teacher said. "But to get back to the events that led directly to the current crisis, let me say this: by the year 1492, when the Arabs were expelled from Spain, the Ottoman Empire—with its seat of power in Constantinople, Turkey—was rising. Soon it was able to occupy most of the Arab world and to dominate it for four hundred years."

Here, Yousif thought, was a chance for Ustaz Hakim to answer a question that had always nagged him.

"How did that happen?" Yousif asked. "It seems incredible that those who ruled the world for eight hundred years would fall apart so quickly. Why didn't they revolt? Didn't they crave freedom?"

Ustaz Hakim got off the table and walked to the window. "That's still another story. But don't ever forget that the Ottomans were the worst thing that could've happened to us or to any people. They were unenlightened to say the least. Whereas the Arabs spread knowledge and light wherever they went—look at the advances they made in medicine, astronomy, philosophy, algebra, architecture, poetry—the Ottomans did the very opposite. They ruled by setting libraries on fire, closing schools, spreading fear, and creating an atmosphere of darkness and terror."

He slid his watch with the silver elastic band off his wrist and began to wind it. "Around the turn of this century, when the Ottoman Empire was reaching its end, it allied itself with Germany for security reasons. At the same time, Britain and France were eyeing it with interest—wanting to carve it up for themselves. That's when the British sent in an inconspicuous little officer who was stationed in Cairo. This fellow knew archaeology and some Arabic. He tried to interest the Arabs in revolting against the Turks and helping the Allies—Britain and France—win the upcoming war against the Axis—Turkey and Germany. That was around

1915. The war to come was, of course, World War I. The officer was T. E. Lawrence, better known as Lawrence of Arabia."

"Well, then," Yousif said, "did we help the Allies because we hated the Turks? Or was there more to it than that?"

"We did it because we hated the Turks and loved what the British promised," the ustaz said, again sitting on the edge of his desk, his hands under him. "We sacrificed thousands of men because the British dangled before us the promise of freedom and independence. They told Sharif Hussein—spiritual leader of Mecca and the father of Jordan's present King Abdullah—that if he would rally his people to fight on the side of the Allies against the Turks, he would be rewarded at the end of the war by being crowned king and having all the Arabs in the Middle East free and united under him. You can only imagine what his response was. Sharif Hussein put the men of his tribes under the command of his son Faisal and the British Lawrence. Together they stormed over the desert, from the Arabian peninsula all the way to Damascus, defeating the Turks at every turn."

The students were sitting on the edge of their seats and clutching their desks. Yousif felt his blood race with excitement.

"Those poor Bedouins thought they were going to get independence at the end of the war," the teacher explained. "Little did they know that the British were also going to promise the Jews a national home in Palestine. That came in 1917, only two years after the Arabs had entered the war on the side of the Allies. But obviously negotiations between the British and the Zionists must have been going on for some time—behind the Arabs' back.

"The British made their promise to the Zionists in the form of what's known as the Balfour Declaration. Some say the British double-crossed the Arabs because they wanted the rich Jews to help them finance the war. Some say it was because a Jewish scientist had developed poisonous gas as a weapon and the Allies needed it to win the war. Others say it was because the Allies wanted the American Jews to put pressure on Washington to enter the war on their side."

Khalil tapped his desk with the eraser of his yellow pencil. "What do you think the reason was?"

"Personally," the teacher said, "I think there were two other reasons. One, the British wanted a European outpost here to make sure that the Arabs would never rise again and be able to rebuild their empire. Two, they were already smelling oil under the Arabian sands and they wanted to corner it all for themselves."

"Then colonialism," Yousif said, "was the root of the problem."

"Absolutely," the teacher agreed. "That one word explains it all. Both Britain and France were colonial powers and they wanted to subjugate other peoples to their will. Why is France in Far East Asia, for God's sake, if it weren't for their greed for other countries' resources? Why is Britain ruling India for that matter? Why is it in Ireland? Britain and France are two major colonial powers and they want to drain the wealth and resources of all countries for their own benefit. Anyway, what's interesting is that while Britain was telling the Arabs one thing and the Jews another, she was conspiring with France behind the scenes to triple-cross both."

"Fine fellows these British," Khalil said.

Some students sneered; others shook their heads. The pimpled student to Yousif's left muttered, "Sons of dogs."

"How did they triple-cross them?" Mustapha asked, chewing his lip.

Again, ustaz Hakim smiled. "By reaching a secret agreement—known as the Sykes-Picot Agreement—according to which terms these two colonial powers would divide the region between themselves. Britain would take Palestine and Iraq; France would take Lebanon and Syria."

"What about Jordan?" Amin asked, shifting in his seat. "Weren't the British there until three years ago when Emir Abdullah became king?"

The teacher nodded, amused. "Jordan was carved out of the wild desert—in 1922, or three years after the Peace Conference in Paris—to appease Emir Abdullah, one of Sharif Hussein's sons who is now King of Jordan. Abdullah had felt left out and was threatening to start another war of sorts. But that's yet another story we don't have time for now."

History was full of interesting drama, Yousif reflected, along with much bloodshed and misery. The British, the French, the Turks, the Arabs, the Romans, the Greeks, the Persians, the Mongols—they had all coveted other peoples' lands. They had all been greedy, selfish, and unconscionable. And now the Palestinians were to pay the price.

"In the thirties," the teacher said, pacing the floor, "Britain almost went back on its promise to the Zionists."

"How?" Amin wanted to know, hugging his amputated arm.

"It never expected our violent reaction to her Balfour Declaration. During the late twenties and throughout all the thirties—especially 1936 and 1937—we Palestinians waged guerrilla warfare against the British and the new Zionist settlers to the point that Britain was willing to renege on her promise to the Zionists. It issued what's known as the White Paper, which aimed at curtailing the Jewish immigration into Palestine. And then external events—completely out of our control—took a sharp turn to the worse. In 1939 World War II broke out, and you know the rest."

The town's clock, which was located on top of the Roman Catholic Church across the yard, chimed on the hour. Ustaz Hakim waited for the eleventh strike to be completed before he would continue.

"War is man's worst crime," ustaz Hakim said finally, "but if there's one war that can be condoned it's World War II. Hitler needed to be stopped. He wasn't only mad, he was evil. I'm not saying this because he was indirectly responsible for the predicament we're in now. I'm saying it because anybody who could kill twelve million human beings—six million of them Jews—is evil. When the concentration camps were discovered and the extent of Hitler's atrocities became known, there was a great swell of sympathy for the Jews and a feeling that they deserved a place of their own. Hence, we now have the UN resolution to partition Palestine."

"But we had nothing to do with what happened in Germany," Yousif said.

Ustaz Hakim nodded. He looked tired. His voice had gotten softer and more strained. Again he glanced at his watch and went back to his desk as though ready to pick up his books and papers to leave. "That's where we are now," he added, "and that's why the stage is set for another war—right here, right before our eyes. The Zionists are determined to carve a state for themselves out of Palestine, and we Arabs are equally determined to stop them. So when the British leave by next August, blood will flow down the street."

Ustaz Hakim picked up his books and waited for the bell to ring.

"My father says," Khalil said, "that the Zionists have raised enough money to get all the weapons and manpower they need. What do we have?"

"The support of the Arab regimes, ostensibly."

There was a long pause.

"Why 'ostensibly'?" Nadim asked.

"Because it may or may not materialize," ustaz Hakim answered.

"Let's assume it did materialize," Nadim pressed. "Would it be enough?"

"We'd have to wait and see," the ustaz answered. "Frankly I think we'll be outmatched. Our man on the street thinks we could stand up to all the Zionists, but I have my doubts. You see, we won't be fighting the Zionists by themselves. When big powers such as Britain and France and the United States throw their weight behind our enemies, what chance do we have? You know they're going to do whatever it takes to make the Zionists come out on top."

"So you're predicting our defeat?" another boy behind Yousif asked.

"In a way. But don't go around saying I said that. Listen, unless we shut down all the coffeehouses and kick everybody's ass and make them train and smuggle arms and get massive help from outside and get the whole Arab world on war footing—I'm afraid it's going to be too late."

"Why don't you start a movement?" Mustapha asked. "We'll all join you. I know I will."

"Me too," several voices echoed.

Yousif watched and listened, having resolved to work with Basim. An idea occurred to him. Shouldn't ustaz Hakim and Basim get together? Perhaps he should arrange it.

"It's going to take a lot more than a few of us," ustaz Hakim said, already at the door. "Just remember this: he who has the gun has the upper hand."

THAT NIGHT, in the middle of dinner, the phone rang at Yousif's house. His mother, who was sitting closest to the foyer where the telephone was placed, got up to answer it. Yousif could not see her, but he could hear every word she spoke.

"Hello, Rasheed," she said. "How's the family? Oh! Widad? Oh, dear! When did it happen?"

The doctor and Yousif stopped eating and perked their ears. Yousif could tell she was talking to her brother-in-law, Rasheed Ghattas. He got up and went to the door between the dining room and the foyer.

"What is it, Mama?" he asked, holding the napkin.

She cupped the receiver and told him that her sister Widad had had a gallbladder operation. "Now you tell us?" she complained to her brother-in-law. "What if something had happened to her during surgery? You know I would've come to see her before she went in for the operation. Poor girl! How's she now? Is she all right? What pathology test? Why? Do they suspect something else, God forbid? Well, here's Jamil. You tell him and he'll explain it to me. In any case, I'll be there tomorrow."

Father and son looked at each other, skeptical. Then the doctor spoke on the phone for a few minutes. When he returned to the table, he was optimistic. The likelihood of a malignancy was very small. Normally cancer would develop in the gallbladder only after a long illness. But Widad had never had any problem with hers. So there was nothing to worry about.

"I hope so," his wife answered, suddenly drained of energy.

"But, my God, Yasmin," her husband chided her, picking up a drum-stick, "you berated Rasheed as though he intended to keep your sister's surgery from you."

"All he had to do was pick up the phone," she said.

"And?" Yousif said.

"I would've taken a taxi and gotten to the hospital before they wheeled her into the operating room. Jerusalem is a forty-minute drive, you know."

Husband and son stared at her.

"What are you looking at me for? I haven't lost my mind, have I?"

"No," her husband answered, chewing. "You just seem to forget there was a curfew."

She did not answer; nor did she pick up her knife and fork.

"And I presume you were serious," her husband said, "when you told him you'd be there tomorrow."

"I was serious," she said, her eyes widening. "What of it?"

"Tomorrow I'm busy. Why not wait until we could go together? I'd like to check on her myself."

"We'll go again," she said, still not touching her food.

No argument was strong enough to dissuade her. The doctor looked to his son for help.

"When mother makes up her mind," Yousif said, "there's no sense trying to change her mind. I'll skip school tomorrow and go with her."

"You don't have to," his mother said.

"I know I don't have to," her son told her. "But you might need protection."

9

Yousif took a day off from school to accompany his mother to see Aunt Widad in Jerusalem. As Makram drove them in his dusty black Mercedes taxi across the thirty-five-mile stretch southeast, his mother voiced concern about her sister. But Yousif was preoccupied with other matters.

Passing Sarafand, the British military camp, he wondered what the British were going to do with all those arms. Couldn't the Arabs find a way of getting any of them? Couldn't some of the officers be bought? Couldn't they look the other way as the Arabs helped themselves? It would be a shame if all these acres of guns and ammunition were taken out of the country or if they fell in the hands of the Zionists. He should speak to Basim about that.

A few miles later, he could see the outlines of Lydda and Ramleh, two large Arab towns. They were known for their fertile fields of vegetables. Lydda was also famous for the bravery of her men. Yousif was curious what these brave men were doing now, on the eve of war. Were they thinking of attacking the Sarafand camp, for example? Or were they, like everyone else, wasting their time daydreaming or playing dominos at coffeehouses? Lydda was also the birthplace of Saint George, the dragon slayer, his favorite saint.

When they reached Latrun, Yousif thought of the Trappist monks who lived in the monastery. Were there Arab monks among them? Were they all Europeans? Where were their earthly loyalties—if they had any? Could their monastery be available to the Arabs to defend themselves? There was no doubt in his mind that Zionist agents had already made their "arrangements."

But Yousif's thoughts were soon interrupted. Across the narrow road from the monastery was a British police station, heavily barb-wired. Two young M.P.s, with cheeks pink from the December weather, stopped the car. Their guns were at the ready. They flanked the Mercedes on both sides. Makram was quick to roll down the window. A gust of raw wind blew inside the car. Yousif saw his mother wrap her beige wool scarf around her neck.

"Let me see your I.D.," one M. P. ordered the driver.

Makram had his hand already at his hip pocket. Within seconds he was showing him a small card with his picture on it. The policeman studied it and then returned it to the driver. He looked at Yousif and his mother.

"Let me have yours," the Britisher said.

"We don't have any," Yousif replied, lowering the window on his side.

"Why not?"

"Is this a new law?"

"It's not a new law," the policeman answered. "It's always been a requirement. Get one as soon as you can and make sure you have it on you at all times. And that goes for the lady in the back seat. Lady, do you understand English?"

She nodded.

In the meantime, the other M.P. had Makram open his trunk for inspection. Shortly, Makram returned to his seat and they were winding their way up to Jerusalem.

"If it's like this here, I can imagine how it is in Jerusalem," his mother said, tight-jawed.

The road wound itself around the hills like a snake. Soon they were entering Bab al-Wad, a narrow passageway between high cliffs. It was obvious to Yousif that whoever controlled this strategic point would control the entire highway and be able to cut off Jerusalem from Jaffa and Tel Aviv.

Such twists and turns in the road seemed to parallel the twists and turns in Yousif's mind. Palestine must be protected; Arabs must survive—Jews too if he could help it. He would quit school and join whatever resistance group there was and do his share. But where was such a group?

The Grand Mufti, who had led the revolt in the 1930s, was still a leader around whom some rallied. But not many. Most people, Yousif now remembered, had no qualms with the Mufti's patriotism. But to others, he had become obsolete. They had little faith in his band of villagers and their outmoded tactics. Even Basim, one of the Mufti's closest aides, was striking out on his own. Yousif watched the road as they passed two more Arab towns well perched above high hills. Kastal and Abu Ghoush were on the outskirts of Jerusalem.

A sense of foreboding seemed to grip Yousif as they crossed the city limits. The atmosphere in this city of churches, mosques, and synagogues seemed funereal. The sights and sounds of bustle were gone. The usually clean roads were littered with yesterday's debris. Were the sweepers on strike, Yousif wondered, or were they afraid to do their work? There were few shoppers on the sidewalks. Some of the stores were even closed. Posters bearing the star of David were plastered on walls and over movie billboards. The writing on them was in Hebrew. Yousif could tell they were urging Jewish men and women to join the Hagana, the Jewish underground. Blue and white banners, some of them ripped, were hanging from telephone posts.

"Get us out of here," Yousif's mother said to the driver.

Yousif looked at his mother. Her face was as yellow as a lemon.

"You'd think you're in Tel Aviv," Makram remarked, shaking his head. "Look at all the Hebrew signs."

"It's not that," the mother complained. "I feel uneasy . . ."

They passed a number of rabbis and orthodox Jews, all clad in black. Some huddled in groups; many walked along the sidewalks, their elbows and fur-trimmed hats touching the wall. Several blocks later Yousif saw a fist fight.

"Where did you say you're going?" Makram asked, looking in the rear-view mirror. "The French Hospital?"

"That's right," she answered, clutching her purse. "But don't take us there. Stop us at Jaffa Gate and we'll walk up the couple of blocks. I need to buy something for Widad."

Yousif was surprised. "Like what?" he asked.

"I don't know," she replied. "A robe, a bottle of perfume. Something."

"I wish you wouldn't. It's too dangerous."

His mother frowned. "You don't expect me to visit her empty-handed?"

"This is no time for formalities between sisters," he answered. "Look, why don't we let Makram drop us off at Barclays Bank. You can buy a box of chocolate from the delicatessen next door. It'll save us time."

His mother would have none of it. She was not coming to Jerusalem every day. Now that she was here, there were a few things she needed to do. This was her hometown. She wanted to light a candle at the *Qiyameh,* Holy Sepulchre. And she wanted to see her parents.

"You wouldn't come all the way to Jerusalem and not see your grandparents, would you?" she asked, looking him in the eye.

She succeeded in making him feel guilty. He turned around and faced the road ahead of him. A city in mourning zipped by. He felt a lump in his throat. Some of his happiest recollections resonated around this sacred and blessed city of shrines, temples, belfries, minarets, and domes. From childhood, he had loved everything about Jerusalem: the old and the new, the visits with his grandparents in the old district of Musrara and with his cousins up at modern Qatamon. He had loved the exotic and appetizing smells of herbs and foods drifting from restaurants and sidewalk cafes, the sounds of church bells and muezzins, the voices of vendors and heavy traffic, the sight of silks and leather goods hanging in the middle of the streets and touching the pedestrians' heads, the bazaars in *souk* Khan iz-Zait and the modern shops at Al-Manshiyyeh, the skullcap and the fez, the priest and the rabbi and the shaykh, the chic and the dowdy, the marble of new Jerusalem and the mud huts of old, the cobblestoned labyrinth of old Jerusalem within the ancient, imposing, wind- and sun-beaten stonewall.

Maneuvering his way through the heavy traffic, Makram seemed to know his way around the holy city. Staying on Jaffa Road, he cut through Jerusalem from almost one end to the other. Strangely, there were no checkpoints along the way, mainly grim soldiers patrolling the jittery, empty metropolis. Government buildings looked like fortresses.

Makram honked and sped around a stalled truck. "Just tell me when and where to pick you up," he said. "I'm at your service all day."

"Let me think," the mother said, checking her make-up in the small mirror she was holding.

Yousif turned to Makram. "Why don't you pick us up where you're going to drop us off. In front of Barclays Bank. It has a canopy we could stand under if it rains. Is that okay with you, Mother?"

"What time?" she wanted to know.

"How about three o'clock? That'll give you nearly five hours to do all your errands."

She thought for a second, then nodded.

"Look at these sand bags," Yousif remarked, as they passed the main Post Office.

"Look at the barbed wire."

Yousif's imagination ran wild, and his concern mounted.

CARRYING A LARGE box of imported biscuits and a brown bag of apples and bananas, Yousif and his mother followed a beautiful young nun in a white habit as she moved silently down the sparkling marble floor of the huge French Hospital.

They were the first visitors to be admitted. Because of the quiet, Yousif found himself tiptoeing. The nun stopped in front of room 26 and waited for them to enter, her kindly face turning crimson.

"Thank you, Sister," the mother said, bowing her head.

"You're welcome," the nun answered, smiling. "I hope you'll find your patient doing well."

They stepped into a semi-private room with a large window. The outdoor view was blocked by a curtain drawn between the two beds. Aunt Widad was asleep, her long neck bent on the high pillow. Although she was his mother's twin sister, she looked older. The resemblance between the two sisters was slight. His mother was fair-complexioned, but his aunt was olive-skinned. Aunt Widad must have sensed their presence. She opened her eyes—glad to see them. The two sisters embraced and kissed. Then it was Yousif's turn.

Aunt Widad told them all about the sharp pain from the gallbladder attack and her subsequent surgery. God must have listened to her prayers, she said. She had felt the pain all that weekend, but she did not have to be rushed to the hospital until after the curfew had been lifted. The first night and the following day after the resolution was passed, the Jews were dancing right under the Widads' window. Then something strange happened. Their next-door neighbors, Jews they had known for years, stopped talking to them.

"The UN resolution seems to make it illegal or immoral for Arabs and Jews to have any contacts with each other," she said, frowning.

"Did you try to speak to them?" Yousif asked, standing by her bed.

Aunt Widad nodded. "They mumbled something," she said. "But you could tell they didn't want to talk. After that, kindly old Jewish men started walking around wearing black arm bands and carrying guns. We could see them parading through the neighborhood. Then we began to hear firing going on in every direction. Bombs exploding . . . ambulances screaming. It was awful." She sighed and pointed her finger toward the curtain. "The lady in the next bed is one of the first victims. A sniper's bullet hit her in the jaw. They had to operate on her for five hours. Look behind that curtain—she doesn't mind."

Both Yousif and his mother got up from their seats and walked to see the patient in the next bed. She was up, peering at them from behind a white mask but unable to speak. Her bandaged head looked like a mummy's. They nodded in her direction. Yousif bit his lower lip; his mother covered her mouth with her hand.

They returned to stand around Aunt Widad's bed.

"We saw nothing like this in Ardallah," Yousif's mother said, her eyes glistening with tears.

"Any place is safer than Jerusalem," Widad explained, her fingers folding and unfolding the bed sheet. "We're afraid the worst is yet to come."

They stayed with her for the next half hour. By 10:30, they hugged her, kissed her goodbye, and wished her a speedy recovery.

"Have a safe trip back home," Aunt Widad said.

At the door both Yousif and his mother stood silent, absorbing her words. Yousif wondered if they would ever see Aunt Widad other again.

YOUSIF AND HIS mother walked downhill past Notre Dame until they reached Bab el-Amood, two long blocks away. Like the new Jerusalem, the old city within the ancient wall was distressing. People were shopping and going about their business, but they seemed dispirited. Yousif and his mother walked through the narrow, congested streets, not stopping at any shop but heading for the *Qiyameh,* the Holy Sepulchre. Suddenly, there was excitement in the street. People began to push each other as if to make room for someone on the run. In a chain reaction, people were elbowing each other or stepping on each other's feet down the narrow, crowded street. Yousif saw a young man running and a British soldier following him. As they ran, they toppled pushcarts and knocked over fruit stands. The street was strewn with apples, bananas—and crucifixes and crosses from a small showcase that had been knocked over.

"Catch him! Catch him!" the British soldier shouted, unable to shoot lest he hit someone else. But the people would not cooperate. Most of them were Arabs and the fugitive was one of them.

"Don't listen to him," screamed the man running.

"Catch him," insisted the soldier, "he's carrying a bomb. Catch him before it explodes."

"He's lying," shouted the Arab, merging with the crowd.

Nevertheless, the word "bomb" brought more alarm to the scene.

"A bomb!" said Yousif's mother, horrified.

"Don't be afraid, Mother. He's too far from us now."

"But there are others to be afraid for," she said, reproachful. "How could you say a thing like that? Look at them, like ants. If the bomb goes off God knows how many will be killed."

"Let's hope not."

Angry shouts flew from store owners whose goods had been knocked over. Someone picked up a huge ripe melon and threw it at the soldier. It hit him in the back of the head and he stumbled and fell on the cobblestone pavement. Before he could get up, the Arabs converged on him and held him to the ground.

"There's a bomb on that man," the soldier pleaded.

"He says you're lying."

"I'm telling you the God's truth."

"Shove it up your ass."

Just then down the street the bomb went off with a horrible, deafening blast. But the screaming was even louder than the sound of the explosion.

"Oh no . . . oh no!" said Yousif's mother.

The roof of the arcade was blown away. Soon the pedestrians were showered with rubble. A dozen men and women were piled up in the middle of the narrow street, rendering it impassable. Dust particles danced in the sun rays like those in the beam of a motion picture projector. Goods were now the color of dry clay. Blood oozed from the arm of one man nearby, and Yousif rushed to help. Images of Amin flashed in his mind and he envisioned an amputation.

"You need to cover it from all the dust," Yousif warned the injured man, offering him a handkerchief.

"Aaaaaahhh . . ." the man cried, not heeding Yousif.

It was a cry among many. Here was a ten-year old girl yelling for help and squeezing her right eye. When Yousif tried to help her she pushed him away, groping for whomever had been with her. There was a crying woman with her headdress knocked off. A wound as wide as a pencil ran from her right ear to below her chin. Mothers were calling for their children. Children were lost and hurt. Silk scarfs, leather hassocks, embroidered vests were scattered everywhere. Earthen jars full of honey, molasses, and sesame oil had broken open. Sweet and tangy smells filled the air.

Yousif slipped over a box of *halkum* and a jar of pistachio nuts, catching himself in time. He was pulling a bald-headed old man up, when he heard his own mother calling.

"Yousif, what are you doing?" she reproached. "Let's get out of here. I'm about to die."

She did look crimson, but Yousif knew she was prone to exaggeration. He wanted to stay and help out, yet he couldn't abandon his own mother. After all, her blood pressure was a problem. He pushed his way toward her.

"Come on," he obliged, putting his arm around her and hurrying her away.

IN THE RUSH to escape, they failed to turn on *souk* Khan iz-Zait, which would have taken them to the *Qiyameh,* where Yousif's mother had wanted to light a candle. Instead they were on Via Dolorosa and then al-Wad Road, stopping every now and then to catch their breath. When they reached the Khalidiyeh Library, at the corner of the Jewish Quarter, they slowed down so as not to arouse suspicion. On the top of a few roofs Yousif could see Jewish men looking at them down the barrel of a gun. He kept it to himself lest his mother become alarmed.

They turned right on Bab al-Silsilah Road, crossing several streets until they got to Omar Square, just inside Jaffa Gate. It was not twelve o'clock yet but she was too tired to go any further. To the right, less than a block from the Tourist Information Center, was a small restaurant in a dark alcove. She wanted to stop there and freshen up and have a glass of water. She needed to take the pills for her high blood pressure. But the restaurant was closed.

"Let's go to Al-Amad just outside the gate," Yousif told her, remembering a place famous for its kabab. He could almost smell the appetizing aroma drifting from the popular restaurant.

"No, let's stay in the old city for a while," she told him, leaning against a wall. "We're not far from the Qiyameh. Now that we're here we might as well visit."

Yousif stared at her. "I don't think we should. This town is terrifying. If we get stuck here we might not be able to make it home tonight."

"What about Makram? We told him to meet us at three o'clock. It's not twelve yet."

"Knowing him I bet he's waiting for us already."

But getting out of the old city was not as easy as they had thought. The British police had blocked Jaffa Gate.

"What now?" his mother asked, still frightened.

"They're not letting anybody out."

"What for?"

"There may be others carrying bombs."

"Talk to that soldier. Tell him I have high blood pressure. I can't stand this."

"It wouldn't do any good. We've got to wait in line."

"I wonder how many people were killed."

"Who knows."

"I should've listened to your father. We chose the wrong day to come."

"From now on every day will be the wrong day."

The soldiers began to search the line, one by one. There was lightning in the sky and then shattering thunder in the heavens. Most people looked startled, suspecting another explosion.

While his mother leaned on his shoulder, Yousif inspected the scene. In front of him was the Citadel, which the Jews liked to call the Citadel of David, although it was built centuries after David was dead and buried. The Jews wanted the whole thing whether it was theirs or not, he mused, and that was the root of the whole problem. The citadel itself was an imposing fortress that had defied many conquerors. Next to it was a minaret. Beyond it were the Armenian and Jewish Quarters with more churches and synagogues than the rest of Jerusalem.

Behind him was the Christian Quarter and the old Terra Sancta, where his father had gone to school before going to Columbia. Next to Terra Sancta was the Greek Orthodox Patriarchate, which was only two blocks from the Freres School. He had been enough times to Jerusalem, especially the old city, to know it like the back of his hand. And his mother was even more familiar with every brick and every cobblestone.

The multi-faceted character of Jerusalem had always fascinated Yousif. Within that ancient wall were the Holy Sepulchre, the Wailing Wall, and the Dome of the Rock—holy monuments of Christianity, Judaism, and Islam—all proclaiming the same God. No wonder even the misguided United Nations had insisted on internationalizing Jerusalem. Truly, it was a legacy for all mankind. Yet, Yousif's heart ached. He knew that for this Holy City doomsday had come.

"I wonder who that man was?" Yousif whispered.

"What man?" his mother said, her eyes searching the crowd.

"The one with the bomb. What was he up to? Where was he taking it? Who's behind him?"

"Who knows. I feel sorry for his mother."

"Not for him? Not for his father?"

"For them too. But mainly for his mother."

Soon, Yousif thought, the man who had carried the bomb would be called a martyr. What a euphemism for ugly death! Thousands of martyrs would follow. Mothers of Jerusalem, you might as well start crying. Your sons may be snuffed in their prime. Yousif took a deep breath. At that very moment, he thought, men on both sides were already stalking each other. Who were the Arab groups? Did Basim know them? Who was their leader? What plans did they have? What were the enemy's plans? The word enemy sounded harsh. But, El-Quds, the holy city of Jerusalem, was rapidly becoming a battleground. Who would be the victim? Who the victor? His heart ached for both.

Again, Yousif wondered what had happened to Isaac. He had not seen him in a few days. Could he be in Jerusalem right now? With whom . . . doing what? Yousif wanted to know. Above all, he wanted to know that he was safe. He also wanted to know if this was a precursor of a longer separation. Was their friendship doomed to be one of the casualties of war? Aunt Sarah had predicted it. And old people seemed to know.

After about an hour, Yousif and his mother were frisked and allowed to go.

Outside the gate, the mother, looking wan, thanked God they were still alive. The labyrinth of Old Jerusalem had been so claustrophobic and gloomy, they were glad to breathe the fresh outdoor air. She leaned against the wall for a moment of rest, her face ashen and her breathing heavy.

Looking at new Jerusalem from where they were standing, Yousif could see Mamilla Street. Far above it, in the middle of the slope, was Mea Shearim. Every time he had come here with his mother to visit his grandparents or his aunt, she would buy him something from the Jewish shops on these streets. The best football he had ever owned came from one of them. So did the velvety yellow suit with the brown leather buttons he had loved so much.

Those streets were now off limits for him and his mother, simply because they were Arabs. Only a fool would dare set foot in the enemy's neighborhood. His eyes sweeping over the hills before him, Yousif could see a reminder of the violence to come. Right next to the YMCA was the King David Hotel, which the Zionist underground terrorist organization, the Irgun, had bombed fourteen months earlier, killing ninety-six innocent people, wounding many more, and shocking the whole civilized world.

In front of Jaffa Gate were three dilapidated buses with great numbers of people waiting in line to go to Jaffa or Bethlehem or Hebron. Every time a taxi appeared, men, anxious to get their wives and children out of the city, ran to meet it. There was no sense fighting the crowd, Yousif decided. After all, the walk to Barclays Bank should not be too difficult. They would rest at Al-Amad Restaurant, then go on to meet Makram.

"You don't mind walking up the hill?" Yousif asked his mother.

She looked dismayed. "I do, but there's no sense waiting. Let's go."

They started up the incline, walking parallel to the Old City's wall. Just before they went around the bend, Yousif saw a van on Mamilla Street make a left. It stopped in the middle of the street—about a hundred yards in front of them. Two men opened the back of the truck: one stayed on top and the other got down. They seemed to be in a big hurry. Together they lowered a ramp, easing out two large oil barrels. Then the one already on the ground pushed them down the street, one after the other. Instinctively, Yousif pulled his mother to his side.

"Something terrible is about to happen," he predicted. "Look at these barrels rushing toward the bus stop."

"What do you suppose is in them?" she asked.

"Dynamite! What else."

"Oh, God!" she said, clinging to him.

As the barrels rumbled on the wet asphalt, Yousif panicked. Pedestrians were going about their business, unaware of what had taken place. Yousif screamed for them to watch out. Then he turned around to take down the tag number of the van that had deposited the barrels, but it had vanished. Men and women stopped to watch. Many more rushed inside buildings to hide. Customers from Al-Amad restaurant stepped out, napkins in hand. Shoppers coming out of Spenny's with packages under their arms, looked bewildered.

"What did you see?" they all wanted to know.

Yousif pointed to the two barrels still rolling down the street between two lines of curiosity seekers who had gathered on the sidewalks.

"They're booby-trapped," he said, excited.

Fear spread like brush fire. People began to run.

"If they are booby-trapped," said a sullen man wearing a loose neck-tie, "they'll explode on impact."

One barrel careened toward the sidewalk. They all gasped. Yousif saw some men put their hands to their ears and back away, expecting an explosion. Miraculously, the barrel straightened itself out and kept heading toward the unsuspecting crowd at the bus stop. The other barrel got caught between two vehicles trying to pass each other in order to avoid it. Crushed between the two cars, the dynamite within exploded with a deafening roar. The two cars were now pieces of metal flying in all directions. Spilled gas and oil quickly burst into flames. A bearded photographer who had been standing on the sidewalk snapping pictures was among the first victims. With the camera's black, old-fashioned sleeve over his head, he was flattened against a wall. He had no idea what had hit him. When he finally removed the cloth from his eyes, he was aghast. Besides the mayhem in the street, he saw his camera twisted and felt tongues of fire lapping up his legs. An artist to the end, the old photographer tried to snap his last picture. Touched and horrified, Yousif shut his eyes and said a quick prayer. When he found the courage to open his eyes again, he saw that the man had already been charred. Fire was consuming him like a bag of bones. Tears flowed out of Yousif's eyes. Where was the camera to photograph the cameraman for the whole world to see!

"Oh, no!" Yousif yelled, running to the middle of the street to snatch up a little girl from the spreading flames. A wave of hot air enveloped him as he bent down to pick her up. She filled his ears with screams. Where were her parents? She was no more than two or three and beyond herself, beating on him with hands and arms, and kicking him with her knees and feet. What if her parents were already dead? he thought. He didn't know for whom to cry. There were so many injured people. Both sides of the street were littered with bodies. Finally a young man in his late twenties yelled at them from a few yards away.

"Lamia!" the man cried, weaving his way toward her with open arms.

"Daddy!" the girl shrieked, throwing herself at her father.

Yousif was relieved. But only for a fraction of a second. The stink of gas, rubber, cordite, and flesh filled the air. A human arm was lodged on the wrought-iron of a balcony on the second floor. Every window Yousif could see was shattered. People who had frozen in their places were now running.

At his mother's urging, Yousif and his mother hid in a nearby camera shop. Cameras, lenses, and light meters were scattered all over the floor. They watched the frantic proprietor trying to pick up his precious merchandise. It seemed almost indecent to worry about such things when hell had broken loose. People going in and out collided with each other. This time there was no doubt in Yousif's mind that they had chosen the wrong day to come to Jerusalem. He agonized over not having thrown himself on the barrel before it got to the bus stop. But there had been two barrels. He might have been able to stop one; what about the other? No, there was nothing he could have done.

He left his mother inside the store and stepped out. Cars were jammed as far as his eyes could see. He wondered whatever happened to the second barrel. The damage from the first one was bad enough. He could see fire in stores and apartment buildings, and black thick smoke rising from both sides of the street. A whole wall of an office building had been blown away. The stone, red marble, and steel had fallen to the pavement, reducing that part of al-Quds, the holy city of Jerusalem, to rubble.

He rushed back in to take his mother out. But before they could escape, they heard the second barrel explode somewhere out of sight beyond the bus stop. It shook the whole area near Jaffa Gate. Of the two explosions it was the louder. Yousif knew it had to be the most damaging. He closed his eyes, wondering how many innocent people had lost their lives. This time he could hear screams. When he opened his eyes, he could see more billowing clouds of black smoke. A fire blazed above the Citadel.

Ten minutes later, Yousif and his mother stood in front of Barclays Bank waiting for Makram to come and take them home. Both felt tired and dizzy. The two bombings had been so violent they must have shaken every window and broken every pane of glass within a one-mile radius. Crushing glass under their feet, the bank's customers were rushing to do last-minute transactions. A heavy-set man wearing a white apron came out of the nearby delicatessen and began to close the tall iron door. His action spurred another stampede. People began to run and buy everything they could find in his store. Within minutes all the fruits displayed on racks up front were gone. Yousif was among those who were grabbing.

"I'd like a couple of sandwiches," Yousif said.

"You'd better get them somewhere else," the shopkeeper told him, ringing the cash register.

Yousif had to settle for a sack full of apples and bananas. Then he joined his mother.

"Who can eat at a time like this?" she asked, refusing to share any of it.

Fifteen minutes later Makram arrived, famished. He ate a banana and was reaching for a red apple before they could get in his cab.

"Where were you?" Yousif asked the driver. "We were worried about you."

"I was worried about you," Makram answered, circling in front of the Municipality and going down by the French hospital toward Bab al-Amood. To their right were a Convent, the New Gate, and Terra Sancta.

"Why are you going this way?" the mother asked, sitting on edge.

"Better to get out of town through Arab neighborhoods," Makram explained, munching on the apple. "It might take us an hour longer but it's a lot safer, believe me."

He explained to them that going back the same way they had come, down Jaffa Road, was risky. It was much better to go by way of Ramallah—nine miles to the north.

"This way we'll run into only one Jewish colony, Nebi Yacoub, near Qalandia," Makram said. "God willing, we'll manage it."

"Inshallah," the mother said.

Makram turned the car left, passing Schmidt School, the British Consulate, and a cemetery believed by some to be where Jesus was buried. The American Consulate was a block away.

They left al-Quds, the Holy City, with sirens screaming in their ears. Yousif's mother, who was usually terrified of speed, urged Makram to drive fast. Just below Shaykh Jarrah, they were stopped by soldiers.

"Here we go again . . ." Makram said.

"They're searching people," Yousif observed.

"Relax," the driver added, turning his motor off. "We'd be lucky to get home in three or four hours."

"Get us home soon, and I'll give you *bakhshish.*"

"I wish I could. The one thing I can't do is rush soldiers. They take their time. But they always do their searching after the damage has been done."

"I wish we could call father."

"He must be worried sick," his mother answered.

About a hundred cars were ahead of them, and the search was slow. It began to rain. Because of the fog, it began to look like night. His mother leaned her head against the window, drained of all energy. It distressed her to realize how close they were at that point to her parents' house.

"Let's go back and see them," she suggested to her son. "They live less than five minutes from here. If it gets bad we'll spend the night with them."

Yousif was sympathetic, but Makram would have none of it. He was sorry but he needed to get home. He had family to worry about, and if they stayed he would have to go and leave them on their own.

"It could be days before we get home," Yousif explained.

"Days!" she said. "Impossible!"

"Don't say impossible," Makram told her, looking at her in the rear view mirror. "What if there's a rash of incidents? What if they slam on a strict curfew?"

None of them said anything. They just sat and waited for their turn to come, for someone to let them go. It was a long wait. But four searches later, they were on their way to Ardallah.

At the outskirts of their hometown, they ran into a raging storm. Those trees that had given the town a reputation for the gentle breeze were now swaying and threatening to fall down. The rain was so heavy, the windshield wipers couldn't keep up. Makram had a terrible time navigating them through the last few miles.

They finally arrived at five minutes after eight. Half the neighborhood was with the doctor in their living room, waiting for their return.

"Why didn't you call?" the doctor asked, hugging wife and son at the same time.

"Call how?" his wife asked, wiping her face. "From a taxi?"

The nine o'clock news gave the first grim details. The radical underground Jewish group, Irgun, which had bombed the King David Hotel fourteen months earlier, claimed responsibility for the two big bombings at the bus stop. There were sixteen known dead and fifty injured. And the searchers could still hear voices under the rubble.

10

Next morning, half of Ardallah was awakened to the terrible news from Jerusalem. The number of victims had risen from sixteen to twenty-seven dead and sixty-two injured. One of Ardallah's own sons, George Mutran, was among the fatalities.

Yousif knew of George Mutran but did not know him personally. His mother, however, knew him well, having at one time tried to match him with one of her old classmates in Jerusalem. The two had come close to getting engaged and then the whole thing was called off because he had accused his intended of eating too much. At the time of his tragic death he was forty-five years old and still unmarried. He was known for wearing suede shoes, attending church regularly with his mother, and falling asleep during the sermon.

As eye-witnesses to the bombing, Yousif and his mother understood why it had taken so long for the town to hear of the tragedy. Bad news traveled fast, but first the facts had to be established and next of kin notified. Clearing the rubble, uncovering the bodies, and identifying the mutilated victims must have been a horrible job. It was remarkable that it had been accomplished in such a short time.

Yousif spent all morning at school corroborating and embellishing on what was in the morning papers. It was still pouring outside. Teachers and students huddled in classrooms and corridors, waiting for a break in the weather so they could go to the funeral.

"With my own eyes I saw a human arm stuck on a second-story balcony," Yousif said, still unable to shake himself of the previous day's horror.

"Whoever did it must've packed tons of TNT into those two barrels," Amin said.

"It was awful," Yousif agreed.

They were all gripped by fear and wintry bleakness.

AS A RULE, Yousif knew, the dead were buried the same day they died. This time was no exception, even though it was rumored that some people favored postponing the funeral at least another day to give it more significance. Nevertheless, the town converged on the victim's house to share the sorrow with the bereaved family. In spite of the bad weather and short notice, Ardallah witnessed one of the most spectacular funerals in its history.

By one o'clock, it had stopped raining. There appeared long patches of blue sky and several bursts of sunshine. Hundreds of people poured in from the neighboring villages so that Ardallah began to look as it had during summer. Wave after wave of mourners had come from all directions. United in sorrow, they came to pay tribute to the district's first victim—even though many of the mourners had never known him. His death sparked their fears and brought home the darker reality of the conflict. Most shops in town closed, all schools shut down, and the town stood still—except for the long, slow cortege that meandered from the western part of town to the Greek Orthodox Church in the heart of the old district, and to the cemetery overlooking the Jerusalem-Jaffa Road. The distance was nearly three miles, all traveled on foot.

At the Greek Orthodox Church, Yousif chose to remain outside. He did not wish to go in to be squeezed into the midst of an overflowing humanity.

As expected, women formed circles outside the old church and chanted their haunting lamentations. They moved and stepped rhythmically. Some twirled their handkerchiefs, tore their dresses, and beat their breasts. The pageant consisted of several circles in motion at once. At one point, there were circles within circles. Death united the people, Yousif noted, and the gods heard them cry.

"I hear they didn't open the casket," Amin whispered.

"I'm not surprised," Isaac whispered back.

"The poor fellow was probably torn to bits," Yousif said. "It's possible they couldn't find all of him."

"Just think, it could've been me or my father," Isaac said. "We were near the Citadel less than half an hour before the explosion."

"You were?" Yousif said. "Mother and I were there too. I remember wondering at the time where you were."

"Father and I had just dropped mother and the children at a friend's house in the old Jewish Quarter and were on our way to do some shopping for the store. Then the sky split."

"Mother and I saw the barrels rolling down the street. Imagine!"

The sky darkened and it began to drizzle. What if it rained all the way to the cemetery? Yousif thought. It was a long walk, at least two hours at the speed they'd be going. But the women did not seem to mind. They continued with their painful chant, their headdresses falling and their cheeks bathed with tears.

Heading the procession to the cemetery were religious leaders. There were Muslim shaykhs, even though the victim was Christian. There were altar boys dressed in black and white tunics, even though he was not a Catholic. There were at least six priests and a bishop who chanted and prayed and filled the streets with fragrant incense. The men followed in silence; the women wailed.

"It's an honor to be the first victim from this town," Yousif heard an old man in traditional clothes say to another.

"I know what you mean," said the man walking beside him.

"You'll never see another funeral like this one. When you and I die, we'll be lucky if we get buried."

"You think it's going to be that bad?"

"Worse."

"By God I'll fight, and I'm sixty-four years old."

"Who wouldn't fight?" an older man said.

The priest was sprinkling the closed casket with a handful of dirt, intoning the lines "from dust to dust." Once the service had been completed, Yousif realized that the moment belonged to the orators and poets. He was amazed at the speed of some poets. What inspiration! What talent! When did they have time to write all this? Yousif thought. Some of it was even good. He was less impressed by the orators, even though their rhetoric was stirring. Scores cried and hundreds remained deadly silent. War was their theme, revenge their message.

One of the speakers was ustaz Hakim.

"Even if the Irgun had not claimed responsibility," ustaz Hakim said, his tone measured, "one could see the fingerprints of its leaders. Every vicious act so far seems to have sprung from that fountainhead of evil."

Yousif stood by his two friends and listened. Salwa's parents were among the mourners, looking ashen. But where was Salwa? Why hadn't she come? He hadn't seen her in a few days and he had so much to tell her. Half listening to his teacher eulogizing George Mutran, Yousif turned around, still hoping to see her. He saw his father, dressed in black topcoat, standing with Dr. Afifi, away from the open grave. His face was taut and gray.

Standing at the graveside was the victim's mother, supported by two grim men: her brother and one of her cousins. Her black dress contrasted sharply with her pale, waxen skin. She was so frail that when Yousif had first seen her spindly legs stumbling toward the grave, he had felt a sharp pain in his chest. They should have spared her and left her home, he had said to himself. Now she was leaning against her brother's shoulder, her wispy gray hair and sunken glazed eyes making her look like a ghost. The poor woman needed a chair, Yousif thought, checking the tears in his own eyes.

"You made a mistake with me, God," the bereaved mother cried. "You picked the wrong man. My son is too good to die a vicious death. And now they won't even let me see his face. I want to see him one more time. I just want to see him." She started to throw herself over the casket, but her brother and cousin held her back.

Her pathetic outburst caused many women to shriek. Even men couldn't help but reach for their handkerchiefs.

Again Yousif's eyes fell on his father. During the commotion, the doctor was stealthily receding into the background. Yousif saw him move toward Moshe Sha'lan. Moshe was on the outer fringe of the mourners, standing with Selim Rihani, who owned a store next to his. Yousif did not know what to make of it, but he intended to find out.

Yousif made his way to where the doctor and Moshe were now whispering. Moshe was nodding when barrel-chested Shukri Mutran, a relative of the victim, spotted him and walked over.

"You've got the nerve," Shukri said, his small eyes boring into Moshe.

"Why do you say that?" Moshe said, slightly shaken.

"What are you doing here?"

Moshe looked first at the relative, then at the doctor, bewildered. The doctor walked between the two men in an attempt to stop anything from starting.

"I said what are you doing here?" the relative repeated.

"Why not? Like everyone else, I'm—"

"Don't tell me you're sorry for the dead."

"Of course I am."

"The hell you are. Your people killed him, didn't they? And now you come to bury him. You kill a person and then walk in his funeral, is that it?"

The merchant Selim Rihani and Yousif tried to quiet the angry relative. But the more they tried, the louder and angrier Shukri became. "Get out of here, Moshe," the relative said. "Get out. And take your dirty son with you."

Shocked, Yousif had a hard time restraining himself. "What's the matter with you, Shukri?" he said, gently laying his hand on the relative's shoulder. "These are the nicest people."

"The hell with that," Shukri interrupted, ready to fight. "They're *all* dirty."

Yousif knew that if anything started, Shukri would become uncontrollable. Someone could get hurt. Luckily old man Rihani and Amin were able to walk the angry relative away.

"Moshe, listen to me," Dr. Safi said under his breath. "This man is a brute. You've heard of him. And the dead man is his first cousin. If I were you I'd slip out of here while he's still calm. Go home and I'll see you later."

"My God," Moshe said, shaking his head. "You'd think I killed his cousin."

"Just do as I tell you," the doctor advised. "Go on as if nothing has happened. Don't let others see that you're leaving. Don't attract any attention."

"I understand. Come on, Isaac. We're not wanted here."

Grim, the doctor squeezed Moshe's arm. Isaac pulled away from his two friends and followed his father.

"I'd better go with them, don't you think?" Yousif asked his father.

"Good idea," the doctor answered. "Take Amin with you."

The four left the cemetery unnoticed, and hardly spoke all the way home. The streets were deserted. They could have spoken without fear of being heard but were too stunned to talk. When they reached the Sha'lans' house, thirty minutes later, Yousif and Amin followed them in without being invited. Both felt it was the proper thing to do. They sat in the living room, lost for words.

Only ten-year-old Alex was there, baby-sitting for four-year-old Leah. Their mother was still at the cemetery.

"Why aren't you at the store, Papa?" Alex asked.

Moshe picked up Leah and hugged her. "I have a headache," he pretended.

Alex seemed not convinced. "Are all the stores closed?"

"If they're not they ought to be," his father answered, pressing Leah's cheek to his. "This is a day of mourning."

Thirty minutes later, a car stopped in front of the house. Yousif looked out the window. It was his father's Chrysler, out of which came Aunt Sarah, Isaac's mother. She looked agitated and walked in briskly. At her heels was his father, looking somber.

When they entered the living room, Moshe asked Isaac to take away his young brother and sister. Sarah sat by her husband, her hands in her lap. As soon as the children were gone, she burst out crying. Yousif felt as if someone gripped him by the throat. Blood seemed congested in his father's face.

"What's the use?" the wife sobbed. "If that's the way it's going to be . . ."

The doctor gritted his teeth and his lips twitched. "In a moment of anger anything can be said," he reasoned. "We shouldn't blow it out of proportion. Don't misunderstand me, four-year-old Leah has more brains than Shukri."

Moshe crossed his legs and kept his arm around his wife. "I'm not holding it against him. If one of my relatives had been killed I'd be upset too. Shukri was angry at the killers—not me personally. They happened to be Jewish and I happened to be the first Jewish man he ran into."

The room was electrified with tension. Amin excused himself and left. The doctor wanted to leave too, but Sarah was making coffee and Moshe asked him to stay. When the coffee was served, five minutes later, they dismissed Shukri as inconsequential and concentrated on the victim's mother. They agreed that all her life she had been an unfortunate woman.

"With her only son gone," the doctor said, knitting his forehead, "I don't think she'll live much longer."

"A broken heart is hard to heal," Sarah said.

They grieved for the old lady. Soon, Yousif felt numbed by a long sustained stillness. The rising wind caused the shutters to rattle and a whistle to pass through a broken windowpane.

Unnerved, Sarah tidied the already neat living room. She moved from one sofa to another. She went to the kitchen and worked in spurts. She sent the children back to the bedroom against their wishes. Once, Yousif heard her speak to Isaac in the hallway, her voice low. Immediately, Isaac opened the door and left.

Minutes later Isaac returned with a sack full of *falafel* sandwiches. He served the guests first, then his father. His mother was soon to follow with a tray of hot tea. Suddenly, the room became alive.

"Before you sit down, Isaac," his father said, "turn that damn thing off."

"The news will be on in five minutes," Isaac said, unwrapping his food.

"I don't want to hear any news. I've got a headache already." Then he turned and looked at the doctor. "I'm sorry. Perhaps you want to . . ."

The doctor shook his head, taking a bite. "That's all right. I'll listen to it later. Let's eat in peace."

Isaac walked to the radio set and turned it off. Then he went back to his seat. The four men ate and sipped tea in silence. The mother sat with her hands folded in her lap.

Suddenly the room was showered with exploding bullets. Their cups, saucers, and plates crashed to the floor. The half-dressed children ran out of their bedroom screaming. All of them, including Yousif, found themselves stretched flat on the floor, hiding under tables and behind sofas.

"Papa . . ." Alex cried.

Little Leah was hysterical. She clung to her father, the bottom half of her pajama in her hand.

"Get down, lie on the floor," their father warned.

Mother and father held the two children protectively, crouched in corners, and waited for the danger to end. Glass, plaster, and food were all over the wet floor. There was a row of pockmarks on the wall facing them. Yousif felt a sharp pain in his knee. Bending over, he saw a large shrapnel lodged in his kneecap. Slowly he pulled it out, cringing. His eyes fell on his father. There he was on his hands and knees, his eyeglasses ready to fall off the tip of his nose. And there were the Sha'lans, prostrated at the other end of the room.

"Get out of town, Moshe," a man outside shouted. "This time we came to warn you, next time we'll come to kill you."

Yousif strained his ears to recognize the man's gruff voice.

"I can't place him," Yousif whispered to his father.

"Sshhhh," the doctor cautioned. "Let him talk."

But the man on the street did not speak again. Instead, he underscored his threat with another bullet. It hit a picture of Moshe's bearded father, which was hanging on the left wall. More glass flew everywhere. Moshe's hand cupped Leah's mouth, for she seemed about to scream.

They waited for the attacker to speak again, but he didn't. Nor did he fire any more bullets. They did not know whether he was still there or not.

"Whoever you are, you ought to be ashamed of yourself," the doctor goaded him.

"How would you like to have your tires slashed, Doctor?" the man answered. "First the tires, then your neck, if you keep their company."

"I recognize your voice," the doctor bluffed, exchanging glances with Yousif. "If I were you I'd go away."

Two more bullets whizzed into the room, grazing the top of a sofa and knocking off a lamp stand. The shade fell on top of Leah and she filled the room with a terrified scream. Yousif was glad the lamp had not been lit when it was broken in half.

"Next time that baby won't be able to open her mouth," the attacker warned.

Crouching under the table, Yousif knew the full meaning of helplessness. What could he do now? he asked himself. Could he stand up to that armed man in the street and tell him he was firing at the wrong house? Of course not. He felt humiliated.

After ten minutes more of silence, they got up. The doctor felt a cramp in his right leg, and had a difficult time straightening his back. Isaac went inside and Yousif could hear him groping in the dark. He returned with a kerosene lamp whose bluish light shed ominous shadows in the room. Isaac placed the light on a small table in the foyer, then picked up little Leah from his mother's lap. She began to cry again.

Moshe inhaled a lungful of breath, expelling it in a deep sigh. In spite of his age and strong physique, he seemed as terrified as the baby Leah who was afraid of the dark.

"I think you ought to go home with us tonight," the doctor suggested.

All eyes fell on him, not comprehending.

"I'm not going to leave you here alone," the doctor added. "Come and spend the night with us."

The suggestion seemed to deepen Sarah's anguish. Her hand went up to her mouth. If the doctor was frightened for them, her look seemed to say, then perhaps they were in bigger danger than she had imagined.

"There's no need," Moshe said.

"I think it's a great idea," Yousif agreed, wishing he had thought of it first.

Moshe shook his head. "I don't think so," he said, looking at his wife.

The doctor rose to his feet, confident. "It's a big house. We'd enjoy each other's company. What do you think, Isaac?"

"It's okay with me," Isaac replied, rocking Leah.

"Good," the doctor said. "Get your pajamas, all of you. And let's go."

Yousif was delighted. He looked at Isaac's parents. They looked relieved. Perhaps, their expression seemed to say, spending the night at the doctor's house might not be a bad idea after all.

FIFTEEN MINUTES later, the doctor and his son returned home with their guests. They were all bundled in their winter clothes. Yousif's mother, who met them at the door, was surprised to see them all come together. What seemed strange to her wasn't so much that they had come unannounced, but that Isaac was carrying a suitcase.

"We came to spend the night with you," Aunt Sarah said, her round face flushed.

"Ahlan wa sahlan," Yasmin said, extending a welcoming hand. The two women kissed.

Yasmin took Leah from her father's arms. "You came to spend the night with Aunt Yasmin?" she asked, her face brightening. She kissed the children and greeted Moshe and Isaac with a warm handshake.

While everybody was settling in, the doctor walked to the phone and began dialing. Moments later, Yousif heard him talking to the mayor.

"First Shukri acting smart at the cemetery, and then the shooting," the doctor said, outraged. "Yes, I was at their house when it happened. So was my son. He even got a cut on his knee."

Yousif was surprised that he had to be reminded of that. The cut was so small he didn't think his father would even mention it.

They were still standing in the living room. Yasmin had to put little Leah down and then look at her son's knee.

"You didn't tell me," she said, worried.

Yousif felt embarrassed. "It's nothing," he said.

"You ought to call an emergency meeting," the doctor continued on the phone. "I doubt that Shukri was involved in tonight's shooting, but I can't swear to it. The man who spoke didn't sound like him. Whether or not he put somebody else up to do his dirty work is something for us to look into. In any case, we cannot allow this sort of thing to happen. The word must go out that such bullying will not be tolerated. Otherwise we'll have bloodshed on our hands long before the real war starts. And they certainly picked on the wrong man. I don't know about the rest of the Jews in Palestine, but if any of them is half as good as Moshe Sha'lan and his family then by God no one had better go near them."

Isaac and his parents sat in the living room. The doctor's words seemed to deepen their sorrow, for they looked at each other, their faces clouded.

"No, I don't think we ought to wait till tomorrow. See if you can hold one tonight. You know where to find them. They'll all be at the victim's house. Send your chauffeur and round them up. No, I'm not going. I have Moshe and his family with us. They're with us right now. I wasn't about to leave them all alone when a thug is roaming the streets. By the way, do you want to call Captain Malloy or shall I do it? It'll be better coming from you. Good. Let me hear from you. I'm going nowhere."

THE SHA'LANS felt at home, for Yousif and his parents tried their best to make them feel welcome. It was natural for the mothers to help each other in the kitchen. It was natural for the doctor, in his own reserved way, to be hospitable. But Yousif had never seen his father fill up two glasses of whiskey without asking his guest whether he wanted to drink. Nor had Yousif ever seen his father pick up a child and play with her, as he picked up round-faced Leah that night and sat her on his knee.

"He must've been a hoodlum," the doctor said, reaching for the glass of whiskey. "No one in his right mind would think of you as a Zionist."

"I certainly thought so," Moshe replied, lighting a cigarette. "And I'm not the only Jew who feels this way. Many of us are anti-Zionist—including the most pious Jews in Jerusalem."

"Why is that?" Yousif asked, curious. "Why are they opposed to the Zionists? On what grounds?"

"On *Jewish* grounds," Moshe answered, taking a sip.

Yousif was fascinated. "I don't understand," he said.

"Zionism is a form of nationalism."

"Not a religious movement?" Yousif pressed.

"Not really. At least it wasn't at the beginning. It's based on politics and economics and so on. The Zionists want a state like everybody else and they want a flag like everybody else and they want an army like everybody else. The pious Jews think this is contrary to prophesy. They don't think the Messiah is going to come to a state with an air force and a prime minister. He's going to come to a community of believers . . . a community of the faithful."

This was news to Yousif. "Do these Orthodox Jews believe a Jewish state would prevent the Messiah's coming?" he asked.

"Something like that," Moshe answered.

The next question preyed on Yousif's mind. "Do you consider yourself a pious Jew?"

The doctor put Leah down and looked at his son, irritated. "What kind of a question is that?"

"I'm sorry, I didn't mean . . ." Yousif said, embarrassed.

"I don't mind," Moshe interrupted. And then turning to Yousif, he said: "To tell the truth, I don't know. I believe in the ten commandments, because I believe in God and I don't steal and I don't covet anybody's wife. You know the rest. My philosophy in life is simple. It's entirely based on the principle of live and let live. Oh, I observe certain holidays and I go through certain rituals but this seems to be out of upbringing . . . out of tradition, if you know what I mean."

"The same with us," the doctor said, as a way of apologizing for his son's impoliteness.

"Whether this makes me pious or unpious, I don't know," Moshe added, smiling. "That's up to God to decide."

Fatima entered the room, announced in advance by the rustling of her ankle-length dress. She placed before them a bowl of *hummus,* a dish of turnipgreen pickles, and a basket full of freshly baked bread.

Yousif picked up Leah and put her in his lap. She clasped her arms around his neck. He hugged her back, and continued to listen.

"There's something you may not know," the doctor said to Isaac. "Did you know that you and Yousif nursed from the same breast?"

Isaac nodded his head. "You mean Aunt Yasmin's?" he asked.

"Yes," the doctor replied. "She nursed both of you. Not once or twice, but for over a month. So in a sense you're brothers."

"Brothers, indeed!" Moshe said, clasping his hands as if to bemoan the changing tide.

At the dinner table, where spaghetti, salad, white cheese, and bread were served, they talked about the two unfortunate incidents. There were long pauses, quivering sighs, and a collective hope for peace. Eventually the subject of nursing came up again. The two mothers, the men recalled, had had their babies a few days apart and had breastfed them. Two weeks after Isaac was born his maternal grandmother was murdered.

"Murdered how?" Yousif asked, his fork in mid-air.

The parents did not seem eager to discuss the subject, lest it offend Sarah, Isaac's mother. They all waited for a signal from her.

"No one knew," Sarah said, her hands under the table. "Seventeen years later and we still don't know. It could've been a number of things."

"Did you suspect an Arab extremist?" Yousif inquired.

"We did," she admitted, nodding. "We even suspected a Zionist."

"A Zionist! Murdering one of his own people?"

"In those days," she said, "political troubles were just stirring. A hot-headed Zionist could've done it as a warning for the rest of us. Those who came from Europe looked for ways to stop us from mixing with the Arabs."

Her husband nodded. "They looked for any kind of provocation. That's how they attracted attention to their cause. That's how they stayed in the news. It was mainly for publicity. And for fund raising. They kept the pot boiling to further their political aims."

Yousif turned to Aunt Sarah. "Obviously they didn't scare you."

"Nor did they scare my mother, God rest her soul. The more they pushed us the more we resisted."

There was a pause.

"In any case," Yousif's mother said, anxious to relieve her guest from telling the rest of the story, "because Sarah's whole body—her whole system—was so terribly upset, her milk soured. Isaac threw up constantly. The midwife and the other older women in the neighborhood advised her not to nurse him for a while. That was when I offered to nurse him along with you." She reached for Isaac's hand and squeezed it affectionately.

"For nearly two months," Sarah remembered.

Were those days gone forever? Yousif thought. All signs pointed to a drastic change. He looked at Isaac, wondering what he was thinking.

"In Jerusalem," the doctor said, reaching for a piece of white cheese, "there used to be a tradition among Jews and Muslims. Children of both faiths who were born on the same day were breastfed by both mothers. And they used to take this relationship very seriously. They exchanged gifts and so on."

"But in the late twenties," Moshe explained, "that was the first thing the Zionists stopped. They didn't want the two communities to mingle."

The conversation centered on the past as though memories were balsam to their wounds. They recalled the good and bad times in Ardallah. In the old days, however, bad times had always been borne in stride. Now survival was at stake. Like a man digging and sifting through his tangled life to find himself, Moshe recalled his father's emigration to Palestine.

Again, Yousif was the interrogator. "Where did he come from?"

"Originally my family came out of Spain," Moshe reminisced, putting his fork down and reaching for a pack of cigarettes. "They migrated to Turkey during the Inquisition."

The women began to clear the table and Moshe sent his son Alex for an ashtray.

"But the Sultan who ruled at the time," Moshe continued, "was no less cruel than the Spanish Catholics. He killed at whim."

"Only Jews?" Isaac asked, chewing.

"Oh, no," Moshe said. "He killed anybody he didn't like or who happened to disagree with him. But I guess he had a special hatred for Jews because he killed a great number of them. One boatload of Jewish immigrants would be slaughtered on arrival, another would be left alone."

"It depended on how the Sultan felt that day," the doctor added.

"More or less," Moshe agreed. "My family happened to be among the lucky ones. Whether or not our luck will continue remains to be seen."

"It's dangerous for us, too," Yousif said. "Wouldn't you say, Father?"

The doctor leaned on his elbow, nodding. "It bodes ill for all of us."

The room relapsed into silence.

"The trouble is," Yousif said, crossing his arms, "nothing is being done to stop the disaster from happening."

All those in the room looked at him, surprised.

"It's true," Yousif added. "Ordinary people like us are abdicating their power."

"What power?" his father asked incredulously. "This country is not independent. You know that. It hasn't been for centuries. Real power is in the hands of foreigners: first the Turks, then the British, then—who knows! There's no autonomy in sight for Palestine."

"It's about time there should be," Yousif argued.

"Fine," his father agreed, "but first let's get the British out and stop the partition plan from being implemented. *Then* we can talk about self-government, maybe even democracy."

"I disagree," Yousif said. "People must assert themselves *now* and become involved *now,* otherwise it will be too late to save the country."

Curious silence fell all over them.

"What do you have in mind?" Moshe said, puffing on his cigarette.

"Moderate Arabs and Jews," Yousif began, "should band together and let their voices be heard."

"How? By shouting it from the highest steeple?" his father asked.

"Not exactly. But something like that."

"It won't work."

"How do you know it won't work? Here we are six months away from war and all we do is worry."

Yousif realized that he knew nothing about theories and ideologies and political machinations. Yet from the depth of his soul he was convinced that the Arabs and Jews who had been friendly neighbors for centuries would *not* want to disrupt their lives and see their country in shreds.

The doctor seemed deep in thought. "I admire your zeal," he said, holding a glass of water. "But you're very young, and I'm afraid it's more complex than you think."

Yousif was not ready to be dismissed. "By myself I can do nothing," he explained, pushing his dirty plate away. "One hand cannot clap, I know that much. But two hands can clap. Thousands of hands can create a roar. All of us together can prevent the chopping up of our country."

The two fathers exchanged glances, their brows lifted.

"Let's start now," Yousif resumed. "Let's stage hunger strikes. Exercise civil disobedience. Let's charter a plane and fly a hundred children to the United Nations. Let the world hear it from the mouths of these children: that the decent, average citizens of this country, both Arabs and Jews, don't wish to have their country divided. "

"Behold! A sage!" said Moshe, forcing a smile. Then turning to the doctor, he added, "I think we have another Gandhi."

The two fathers seemed desperate for a bright moment. A tremor of shock swept through Yousif as he heard them chuckle. In that chuckle he could hear the crack of doom.

"Why not another Gandhi?" Isaac said, defending his friend. "Yousif has good ideas. Don't make fun of him."

"I apologize, Yousif." Moshe said, still smiling.

"Gandhi himself was once a teenager," Isaac said. "And he was foresighted enough to take on mighty Britain."

The doctor shook his head, struck a match, and applied it to his pipe. "Not in his teens," he said, his pipe clenched between his teeth.

"I wasn't suggesting . . ." Yousif huffed.

"In any case," the doctor continued, "there's no turning around now."

"Father!" Yousif protested. "Will you stop being such a pessimist?"

Genuine concern flickered on the doctor's face. "The die is cast, son, believe me."

The telephone rang, cutting the silence like a razor blade. Yousif started to answer it, but the doctor said it was for him.

Momentarily, they heard the doctor speaking to the mayor again. "All right. I'll be there."

The doctor returned to the dining room, his coat in hand. It had stopped raining but his wife was standing behind him, ready to hand him an umbrella.

"Feel at home," the doctor said, buttoning himself. "I'll be back as soon as I can."

Moshe expelled his breath. "We've caused you too much trouble."

"Had the shoe been on the other foot," the doctor said, "you would've done the same for us."

Yousif walked his father to the door. A gust of cold December wind blew in, yet he knew it was going to be a hot winter.

YASMIN AND FATIMA were busy changing the bed sheets and making last-minute arrangements for the Sha'lans' comfort.

"Come on, Alex," Isaac said. "Time to go to bed."

"Promise you won't leave us," Alex whimpered.

"I promise," Isaac assured him.

"But you will leave us," Leah said, sniffling. "I know you will."

"I promise I won't."

For several minutes, Yousif and the parents sat in thickening gloom, expecting another danger to spring at them.

"Strange," Sarah seemed to remember, brushing back her hair. "Didn't the neighbors hear the shots? I baked bread with Imm Ribhi this afternoon. You'd think she or her husband would ask if any of us got hurt."

"Maybe their windows were closed," Moshe said through lips that seemed glued together.

"My God!" his wife exclaimed. "They live next door. They'd have to be deaf not to have heard. Have we come to this?"

A Jew, Yousif reflected, was supposed to be wily, crafty, even cunning. So the story went. Instead, the two human beings who sat in his living room were no more capable of scheming than were his parents. Moshe had his fingers spread on his knees, and Sarah was massaging the back of her neck. In the next room their children were frightened to death. At that moment, he felt particularly proud of what his father was doing on their behalf.

"What are we going to do, Moshe?" Sarah asked, hugging a pillow.

"I don't know," her husband answered, gritting his teeth. "We'll have to wait and see. We might have to move out."

"Out where?" she demanded.

"Just out," Moshe told her. "The world is wide. There must be room for us somewhere."

"We've been here for years, Moshe. We belong here."

"So do the Arabs."

"There's room for both of us. Don't you think, Yousif?"

"Of course," Yousif answered.

"Unfortunately," Moshe said, "it's not up to you two."

Their uneasiness deepened. Yousif could only imagine what was going on in their minds. Sarah got up and moved to the sofa and sat next to Yousif, the small white handkerchief in her nervous hand fluttering. "You're a sensible young man. Tell us. What would you do if you were in our place?"

Yousif recoiled from the question.

"Nothing makes sense anymore," he finally said, wishing he had a better answer. "Maybe in the future . . ."

"Future? I'm talking about right now."

It hurt Yousif to say what he was thinking. "Would you consider . . ."

"What?" she interrupted, with a flicker of veiled suspicion.

". . . going away? At least until the hostilities blow over."

"Go where?" she asked, her eyes focused on him.

Yousif felt awful, and wished he hadn't opened his mouth. "I only meant . . ."

"You meant well, I know," she told him, touching his hand. "But these are not hostilities. This is war—declared or undeclared, I don't care. It could drag on for months."

She put her head in her hands and began to sob.

"Shhhh," Moshe said, moving next to her and putting his arm around her waist. "The children might hear you, remember?"

With a lump in his throat, Yousif turned his head away as he saw Moshe taste the salt of his wife's tears.

11

The following evening, Yousif stood on the western veranda and tried to start the brazier. But as soon as he added several new pieces of charcoal, doused them all with kerosene, and struck a light—it started to drizzle. It took six matches to get the fire going. For the next fifteen minutes, he fanned the brazier with a piece of cardboard. Then he spent another five minutes waiting for the smell to go away before he could take the *kanoon* inside.

All the while, Yousif tightened the wool scarf around his neck, listened to the rising wind, and thought about Isaac and his family, who had gone home that morning to repair their house. He doubted that they would be harassed again, now that his father had persuaded the mayor and the entire city council to look after them. But who could tell what would happen down the road? Would they end up leaving Ardallah? Where would they go? And for how long?

He carried the *kanoon* inside and handed it to Fatima at the door. Then he turned toward the kitchen. He was so hungry he couldn't wait for his father to come home for supper. He took the lid off the pot on the stove and sampled a few steaming grape leaves.

The dinner table was set as soon as the doctor arrived, dripping wet. It was unusual for him to come home so late, but it seemed he had had a rough day and he looked gloomy. His wife helped him take off his black top coat. She reminded him that he owned two umbrellas and should always keep one in the office and one at home. Her husband did not seem to hear her. On his way to the dining room, the doctor complained about a house-call he had made shortly after five o'clock on a dying baby.

"Fools!" he muttered, spreading the linen napkin in his lap. "The baby had pneumonia. And what do you think they did? Instead of rushing him to a hospital, they resorted to old wives' remedies. Instead of giving him medicine, they applied a hot rod to the baby's body and burned holes in his flesh. Imagine that!"

Yousif had heard of such remedies, especially in the case of adults who desperately needed some kind of relief from back pain or wanted to drain some puss buried deep in their legs. Oddly enough, such primitive methods had been known to work. But placing a red-hot piece of metal on a baby's flesh was cruel beyond explanation. Yousif was shocked. Who had the heart to do such a thing!

"Well, did you save the baby?" Yousif asked, his hands clutching the edge of the table.

"Unfortunately, no," the doctor replied. "They called me much too late. But I gave them a piece of my mind."

"What good would that do?" Yousif grumbled.

"It might stop other fools from making the same mistake," his father answered, pushing his plate away from him.

Yasmin poured red homemade wine into her husband's glass. "Their thinking will change after you build the hospital," she said.

"Sometimes I wonder," her husband said, tasting the wine.

They ate in silence, except for the wind blowing outside and some heavy rain tapping on the window.

After dinner, the doctor retired to the living room, having first asked his son to prepare him a *nergileh.* Without hesitation, Yousif walked to the kitchen where the *nergileh* was sitting on a marble counter between the sink and the dish cabinet.

The *nergileh* consisted of three main parts: a two-foot flask which he half-filled with water; a four- or five-foot tube, at the end of which was attached a mouth piece; and a metallic "head" on which the tobacco and burning charcoal would be placed. When the smoker pulled, the smoke traveled through the water and was purified of nicotine long before reaching the lips. The leisure with which the *nergileh* was smoked appealed to him, and the gurgling sound it produced as the water bubbled inside the flask was pleasant to his ears. He had been raised listening to that sound and had learned the ritual of preparing the apparatus for his father at the age of ten.

Now, he crumbled a handful of tobacco in both hands and turned on the faucet and let the water run over his hands, squeezing the tobacco and watching the water turn into a yellow stream. He then piled up the tobacco on top of the "head" and proceeded to smooth it into the shape of an egg. Normally he would have started a few chips of charcoal a bit earlier so that they would be ready when he was through soaking and sculpting the tobacco. But because it was winter and every day someone prepared the *kanoon,* he had counted on using a few pieces of charcoal from the brazier to place on top of the *nergileh.*

His father was sitting in his favorite armchair next to the radio console, his belt characteristically loosened and the top of his pants unbuttoned as if from overeating. In his hand was an old book of poetry, which Yousif knew was that of Al-Ma'arri, for the doctor was an avid admirer of this great eleventh-century mystic. To his father's left was a huge bookcase full of Arabic and English books, mostly history and literature. The radio was on low. A new song was being introduced. Yousif could tell from the announcer's hard "g" that the dials were set on Cairo.

Yousif placed the *nergileh* on the floor and handed him the mouthpiece at the end of the long cord.

"Thank you," said his father, putting the book aside. He then bent down and picked up a couple of small well-kindled pieces of charcoal from the *kanoon* and put them on top of the tobacco. He pulled on the tube with great satisfaction.

"I know you've read some of Al-Ma'arri's poetry in school," his father said, picking up the book again, "but you should take time and read all of it. He is really a great poet. And a remarkable man as well—so unaffected and so wise. To him matter was worthless, but reason and conscience were important. He placed these two attributes above tradition and authority."

The last thing Yousif wanted to hear now was a lecture on poetry or virtues. The political convulsion of the moment was a lot more pressing. He even looked at all the books behind his father and doubted their usefulness. Apparently all the poets and artists and thinkers had not taught man to live with his fellow man. His father, he felt, should be more involved with what was going on at present instead of wasting his time reading what one blind man had written nine centuries earlier.

"How do you compare him to Omar Khayyam?" Yousif asked out of politeness.

"No comparison," his father said. "Khayyam was a hedonist. Al-Ma'arri was the very opposite. He was a poet of austerity, of total abstinence. A true Sufist. He was a hermit, but a man of conviction. Listen to this:

> The body which gives you during life a form
> Is but the vase: be not deceived my soul.
> Cheap is the bowl thou storest honey in,
> But precious for the contents of the bowl.

"Don't you think his resignation is a form of bitterness?" Yousif asked, looking at his watch and anxious to hear the latest news.

"Bitterness?" the doctor reflected. "I don't think so. I'm sure he was hurt and disappointed when he first lost his eyesight, but I can't believe he was bitter. Bitterness is the quality of the small. Al-Ma'arri was a much grander man. For one thing he believed our fates are pre-determined. He did not judge, and he didn't complain. Such attributes were alien to his nature."

Luckily for Yousif the song on the radio stopped, and there was the usual fanfare announcing the news. Topping the broadcast was a report of Arabs having killed six Jews in Tel Aviv late that afternoon in retaliation for the attacks on Khayyat Street in Haifa the day before in which four Arabs had been mutilated.

Yousif glanced at his father, who, out of sadness, closed the book of poetry and set it aside. For ten minutes they listened in total quiet.

"The cycle of violence has begun," his father said, drawing on his *nergileh*.

Yousif was sitting by the half-moon window, his face turned toward the hills. "What a shame," he said. "Could your poet have guessed that the Holy Land would see more wars than anywhere else?"

His father looked at him reproachfully. "My poet?" he asked.

"Yes, your poet."

"There would be no wars, son," the doctor digressed, expending smoke from his mouth, "if man were not so foolish as to think he actually owns this earth."

"Jamal calls our land the hills of God."

His father shifted the burning charcoal with the brass tongs. "Every generation must learn for itself. It's like discovering fire all over again."

The doctor seemed suddenly withdrawn. On many occasions Yousif had heard his father wonder about the circumstances that shaped the course of a man's life, the drama of one's fate.

"Where would you like to go to school?" the doctor asked. "I mean after graduation."

"I used to think of Columbia, where you went. Not anymore."

"You shouldn't let politics bother you. Columbia is a great school. On the other hand there are fine universities in this region. Why not Beirut or Cairo?"

They fell silent. The prospect of separation seemed to pull them closer to each other. Yousif had never been away from home. It was fashionable for students his age to attend foreign universities, and he had looked forward to that day. But with the impending war, he wasn't so sure.

The doorbell sounded. They were startled by the first long buzz and the many short incessant ones that followed.

By the time Yousif got to the door, he found that his mother had opened it and his cousin Basim was already in the foyer. The door was still open and Yousif could see that the rain and wind had stopped.

"I saw your lights on and thought, Why not disturb them a little," Basim said, kissing his uncle's wife, who was almost his age but whom he called "auntie," just to tease her.

"Basim," she said, "I told you a hundred times not to scare us like this."

"Scare you how? Why should you be scared with Yousif around. He'd look after you. Is Uncle up?"

"As if you care," Yousif chided him, smiling.

"Of course I care," Basim said, slapping him on the back. "You haven't picked up any more compasses, have you?"

Yousif shook his head and followed him to the living room. Basim stopped at the magnificent *Tabriez* rug covering the floor, and hesitated to come in. He looked again at his shoes to make sure they were clean.

"Ah, Basim, welcome," the doctor said, extending his hand.

"Good evening," Basim said, taking long steps toward his uncle. "It's stuffy in here."

"Take off your coat," the doctor said, pulling on his *nergileh.*

"No, let's open the window," Basim suggested, walking to the window and opening it. His eyes roamed over the town below him and at the steep road which led to the cemetery atop the opposite mountain. "It's a hell of a night," he said, his voice low. "No thunder, no lightning, no storm—and yet so ominous. It's the quiet, I guess. The soft pouring of the rain. It's almost afraid to make a noise."

What an amazing fellow, Yousif thought, looking at Basim standing with his broad shoulders turned to them. A tall, powerful man, often capable of violence, yet sensitive enough to feel the strength of quietude. Wearing a trenchcoat with the belt fastened tightly around his waist, and pulling the two ends of a blue wool scarf around his neck, he seemed as strong as a mountain and almost as defiant. Yet, there was a slight stoop in his back, so slight as to be almost imperceptible.

"We had a meeting tonight," Basim said, closing the window and remaining standing. He took a package of Lucky Strikes out of his deep trenchcoat pocket. "Before it was over I could feel Palestine slipping out of our hands."

Yousif and his father held their breath. Basim lit his cigarette and sat down.

"Who's *we?"* the doctor asked.

"A few men from the old days," Basim answered, "but mostly new ones."

"How many were there?" Yousif wanted to know, anxious.

"Fifteen," Basim said, glancing at his young cousin. "We met at one of the hotels in Haifa to see what we could do."

Yousif frowned. "Isn't it kind of late?" he asked.

Basim's eyes flashed. "I don't blame you. Maybe your generation will start making fun of us."

"I'm sorry. I didn't mean . . ."

"That's OK. We deserve worse. It is kind of late."

"But you did your share," Yousif apologized.

"Not enough. Anyway. The Zionists are determined to occupy as much of the land as they can while the British are still here. Incidents are breaking out everywhere. More than you hear on the radio or read in the newspapers. They're bringing in a shipload a day of European Jews. Before you know it every one of these new arrivals will be carrying a gun to blast us away."

Silence fell over them.

"We can't wait until the Arab governments move in," Basim continued. "By then it will be too late for sure. What they'll be coming to save will already be lost."

"What are you going to do then?" Yousif pressed.

"We're going to try to hold them off," Basim answered.

His uncle held the ivory mouthpiece an inch from his lips. "Until when?"

"Until the Arab armies arrive," Basim replied.

Doctor and son exchanged glances, which did not go unnoticed by Basim.

"I don't have faith in these armies any more than you do," Basim admitted. "But that's all we have to fight with. What else can we do? Listen, do you know what I heard today? This is strictly confidential. Yousif, I don't want you to breathe it to a soul. I heard from someone who should know that the British estimate all the arms we Palestinians have in our possession are seventy-two, puny, Goddamn, lousy guns. Just think! Seventy-two old, rusty guns with which we're supposed to fight the Zionists. The Zionists have Tommy guns, Bren guns, Sten guns, Mauser guns, armored cars—even planes."

His words flew around like sparks.

"And here's something else for you," Basim continued. "In all of Ardallah and the thirty villages around it, there are no more than half a dozen guns. Six guns and ammunition for one day. Six guns which I'd like to turn on the Arabs themselves and blow their brains out for waiting until now to prepare. God, if the Zionists only knew. They could come and take us over without a fight."

Basim crushed his cigarette and clutched an orange as though it were a grenade.

"From what father tells me you gave them hell in 1936," Yousif said, reaching for the poker by the *kanoon*.

"It was different then," Basim replied. "Shortly after the revolt of 1936, the British managed to strip us of all arms, except the seventy-two guns which some of us had sense enough to hide. In the meantime they tripled the number of Zionists in this country and allowed them to form a government within a government, with a fully-trained, fully-equipped underground army."

Suddenly the doctor seemed to get tired of smoking. "The British Mandate here has paved the road for the establishment of a Jewish state," he said, curling the tube around the *nergileh.*

Yasmin entered the room carrying a tray of coffee. Fatima, she said, was not feeling well and had gone to bed. Also on the tray were two small glasses of cognac for Basim and her husband.

"You should've brought the whole bottle," Basim said, reaching for the liqueur. "Since when is a thimbleful enough for me?"

"I'm sorry," she said, blushing. "Yousif, will you please get it?"

"Why didn't you bring me a glass?" Yousif asked, rising to his feet and heading for the liquor cabinet in another room.

"Bring the chestnuts with you," his mother said. "I forgot them on the dining room table."

When Yousif returned, he found his mother brewing the coffee on the edge of the *kanoon.* That was one of the reasons his father preferred the *kanoon* to the portable heaters. The making of the coffee was special to him. He enjoyed it most when it was slowly brewed before his eyes, the way his wife was doing.

"After your meeting in Haifa, what are you going to do?" Yousif asked, placing the cognac bottle in front of Basim.

"I'm going to join Abd al-Qadir in Jerusalem," Basim told him, his right foot jerking.

"Abd al-Qadir?" Yousif asked, puzzled.

"The Mufti's cousin," his father explained.

"And the best military leader we've ever had," Basim hastened. "He needs men, arms—everything. The Zionists are pushing to capture most of Jerusalem before we get any outside help, and I must join him. I know how to mix dynamite."

"You're not afraid of the British?" Yousif's mother asked, her eyes widening.

"To hell with the British," Basim snapped.

"You could wait until they leave," she insisted.

"No, I can't. The earlier I can step on their necks, the better I'd like it. If it weren't for their double-crossing we wouldn't be in this holy mess."

The mother left the room, as though remembering something. Lightning flashed through the window, followed by rolling thunder.

"Jerusalem is supposed to be internationalized," Yousif said, making small incisions on the side of the chestnuts before burying them in the ashes.

"True," Basim said, "but the Zionists want to grab it before the British leave. And they, the damn British, are giving them arms to do it with."

"Britain isn't the only country helping them," the doctor said, sipping on his cognac. "There are others."

"Sure there are others," Basim admitted, pouring himself another glass. "But mark my word, the Zionists are biting off more than they can chew and I don't care who's on their side. Britain is devious, France is fickle, and America is still young. Give America time to grow up and mature in foreign affairs and she'll soon learn where her real interests are."

"What about the Russians?" Yousif asked. "They too voted for the partitioning plan."

Basim nodded, his large black eyes squinting. "If you ask me, they're just as bad. There seems to be an international conspiracy against us. But we'll show them. The Zionists must be naive to think we'll let them walk in and steal our land before our eyes. And that's exactly what they're planning to do: *steal* it from us. We're not going to let them do it—even if we have to fight them with our bare hands."

Basim reached for another cigarette. He seemed to pause for one of them to disagree with him. But they remained silent. They had heard him ventilate like this before, and knew that there was no sense in trying to calm him.

"So you came to say goodbye," the doctor said.

Basim nodded.

"Where will it all end?" the doctor wondered, looking for his pipe.

Yousif got up and fetched him a curved one from the collection in the corner.

"I'm almost convinced this region is cursed," the doctor said, striking a match. "Must it always be a crossroads for traveling armies, a battleground for ambitious men? One nation leaves and immediately another fills the void. There's no end to the vicious cycle."

Apparently, something in what the doctor had said displeased Basim. "What are you saying, Uncle?" he asked, his eyes narrowing.

The doctor seemed to float within himself. "I don't have stomach for this war."

"Nor do I," Basim told him.

"Still, you and I are different. You thrive on combat; I cringe from it. In the back of my mind is the spectacle of a barbaric world war that ended only two years ago."

"You sound like a hermit, Uncle," Basim said, pouring himself another liqueur. "As long as I can remember you've always been preaching platitudes I could never understand. Your illusions of grandeur and peace and beauty are absolutely wonderful . . . nevertheless, illusions. Your ideals are honorable, but for a different world. Certainly not for this one. I reject them, Uncle, because they're not practical. I reject them because I simply cannot afford to accept them."

The doctor shook his head. "Believe me," he said, "peace is won by peace and nothing else. So forgive me if I don't get excited over your plans. Besides, if we're going to go to war, why not be smart about it? Why must we fumble everything? The plans we now have to save the country will most likely backfire on us."

Basim glanced at Yousif as if to check if he were as weird as his father. Yousif was noncommittal. He wanted to hear the rest of the argument.

"The only sensible suggestion I heard regarding military action," the doctor said, pushing down the tobacco of his pipe with his finger, "came from King Abdel Aziz of Saudi Arabia. He believed in containing the problem and warned against letting it get out of hand. Instead of letting six or seven armies march on Palestine to save it from the enemy, he thought the Arab governments should satisfy themselves with supplying the Palestinians with arms and money the same way the West is supplying the Jews with arms and money. Then it will be a fight the world could understand—a local fight between two, small, relatively-equal groups. But when you march in six Arab armies against the Jews who had just been mauled by Hitler, the world is going to be horrified. The world doesn't know that these puffed-up Arab armies are made up of tin soldiers—all it could envision is another holocaust. You can imagine where their sympathy is going to be. I can hear them howling, 'Poor Jews! Poor Jews!'"

For a change, Basim nodded in agreement with his uncle. "We're going to look like the aggressors."

"Of course," the doctor said, blowing his match in anguish.

"The armies haven't arrived yet," Yousif said. "Couldn't the Arab governments start sending us supplies instead?"

"Too late now," Basim answered, shaking his head. "We should've been doing that over the years, not overnight. On the other hand, the British wouldn't have sat still and let us get armed. Now we have to face the situation head on." He dug deep into one of his trenchcoat pockets and took out a small bundle wrapped in a linen napkin. Slowly he began to unwrap it in his lap.

"What's that?" Yousif asked, curious.

Basim did not answer. He just laid the contents on the coffee table. It was a collection of jewelry: rings, bracelets, necklaces, and a watch. Most of it was in gold, except the diamond wedding ring, which Yousif immediately recognized. Now Yousif could see why Basim had not taken off his trenchcoat.

"You can have all of it for the price of a gun," Basim said, looking at his uncle straight in the eye. Everything about him was cold and firm.

Yousif was stunned.

"Is it that bad?" the doctor asked, lowering the pipe to his lap.

Basim's reply came in the form of a stare.

"Does Maha know you're doing this?" Yousif wanted to know.

"I told her what it was for and she understood."

The doctor's face was grim. "She gave you her wedding ring to sell for the price of a gun?"

"Other women have done it before her. Guns are being sold at black market prices. Very few could afford to buy them without selling or pawning some of what they have."

"You could've asked to borrow the money without all this."

"I wanted you to see the seriousness of the situation."

Gloom descended on them.

"Who's selling the arms?" Yousif asked, heaping warm ashes around the chestnuts.

"British soldiers who pretend they were robbed," Basim explained. "Mostly smugglers. Their guns, though, come from North Africa. They're rusty, broken guns which were dumped in the desert by the armies of World War II. Some of them are defective. Last week the British caught a smuggler selling weapons to some Arabs in Gaza and they hanged him the same day. Without even a hearing."

"The bastards!" Yousif said.

Yasmin returned with her knitting bag.

The three stared at her, then her eyes caught the sparkle of the jewelry.

"All for the price of a gun," her husband told her.

She almost dropped what she was carrying. "Basim!" she exclaimed. "You want to sell the gold your mother saved to give your wife? The bracelet which was a gift from her father? You want to sell your own wedding band? Take them back before I think you're crazy."

"Maha knows," Yousif informed her.

She looked at Basim quizzically. "What did you do to make her give them to you?"

"Nothing," Basim assured her. "She's not as sentimental as you. Besides, what's a piece of gold at a time like this?"

A pause lingered.

"How much money do you need?" his uncle asked, rising reluctantly.

"Two hundred and fifty pounds," Basim replied, lighting another cigarette.

"That much?"

"If you don't have it I'll get it somewhere else."

"That's not what I meant," his uncle told him, buttoning his pants and buckling his belt.

"Then let me have it, please."

The doctor left the room. The rest sat down in silence. Yasmin did not touch her knitting. Yousif pulled some of the roasted chestnuts out of the *kanoon*. Outside, the trees began to whistle and there was thunder and lightning.

"I think we're going to have a storm," Yasmin said, crossing herself.

"More than one," Basim replied, getting up and stretching his legs. "Wait until he hears about the hospital money."

"What about it?" Yousif asked.

Basim looked at him and then at his mother. "Because we Palestinians have no army," he explained, "each town from now on is going to take care of itself. Some people think Uncle ought to use his hospital money to buy arms."

"Good luck," Yasmin huffed, reaching for her knitting.

"You think he'd refuse?"

"I know he would."

Within a minute the doctor returned carrying a check in his hand. "The additional hundred is for you to *live* on," he said, handing it to him.

"In the name of the cause I thank you," Basim said, accepting the check and slipping it quickly into his wallet. "One day I'll repay you."

"Come back alive and you don't have to repay me," the doctor said, taking back his seat. "I'll keep the jewelry, though, so you won't squander it."

The coffee boiled over. Some of it spilled on the charcoal, making a loud hiss and causing ashes to rise. Quickly, Yasmin raised the pot and then wiped its outside with an orange peel. She let the coffee settle for a few seconds and then poured it into small, ornate demitasse cups. Yousif picked up the tray and served.

Basim sat at the edge of a sofa, holding the tiny cup like a small bird. "Soon," he said, "we're going to start a big fund-raising campaign for arms. Some people think you ought to put up the hospital money . . ."

His uncle shot him a horrified look.

". . . to build watch towers and buy arms."

Nothing Basim could have said would have angered the doctor as much. "Don't make me regret giving you that check."

Basim chuckled. "It's not my idea," he said.

"But you go along with it?" the doctor wanted to know.

"We've lived long enough without a hospital, we can live without it a few more years."

"You are all insane," the doctor glared.

"Without arms we might all be dead."

"Tell them not to try. Because if they do they're going to be awfully disappointed."

Basim took a deep breath. "I have already told them that, but they were not convinced. Someone will approach you."

"Who will dare?"

"It's not a matter of daring. There are priorities. Don't be shocked if those who gave you the money to start with, come back and ask for it to protect themselves. That's all."

The doctor looked around, and Yousif knew that he wanted a cigarette to calm his nerves. Once he had seen him finish a whole pack in one sitting. The doctor now looked as upset as he had ever been that day—if not more. He seemed equally irritated with the message and the messenger. Even when Basim offered him a cigarette, he hesitated.

"Ever since I was a boy, I've been haunted by the idea of a hospital," the doctor said. "I used to see Dr. Mitri galloping on a horse from one house to another all day and all night, winter and summer, year in and year out. He was the only doctor in town and had more patients than he was able to take care of. Even today there are many rural areas that don't even have a doctor to look after them. There are thirty villages around Ardallah but not a single hospital. Even Ramallah—our finest summer resort—doesn't have one. We need clinics, we need health centers, we need hospitals, we need schools. That's what we need, not arms—not guns and ammunition."

Basim's look at his uncle was full of pity. "But we need arms to protect the land you want to build these things on. We need arms to *save* the people you love so much."

"Then get the money from someone else," the doctor insisted, looking truly worried that someone might try to wrestle the money out of him.

"We need arms," Basim repeated.

"I'm telling you," the doctor interrupted, "don't expect it from me."

The doctor rose, agitated. He walked to the window, pulled the ecru curtain aside, wiped the frosty glass with the tips of his fingers, and gazed into the night.

Basim emptied his coffee cup, put it down, and stood up to leave, picking up his blue scarf.

Dr. Safi turned and faced Basim, his face suffused with anger.

"Two months ago," he said, "Amin lost his arm because some old fool set it for him without washing his hands. Today a baby died because his parents burned holes in his flesh to treat pneumonia. Such conditions are intolerable. We need hospitals to take care of people."

"No one can argue with that," Yousif said. "But when I suggested a peaceful solution, you and Moshe laughed at me."

Father and son looked at each other as if no one else were in the room.

"You know better than that," the doctor said, consoling. "I never laugh at you or at anything you say. Maybe it was the way you said it. Maybe the timing was wrong."

"In any case," Yousif said, "if diplomacy is out of the question now, what's wrong with protecting ourselves?"

"Nothing . . ." his father began.

"Well," Yousif jumped in, "we can't depend on Egypt's playboy King Farouk. Nor on Jordan's Glubb Pasha."

"Sir John Glubb," Basim corrected with a smirk. He seemed pleased with Yousif's apparent inclination.

The doctor pouted. "Are you suggesting that I should give up the hospital money to buy arms?"

Yousif was not intimidated. "All I'm saying is that should a demand be made—"

"Demand?" his father asked, offended.

"Sorry, request. Should a *request* be made, one has to be realistic."

His father's face turned purple. "Listen, son, don't talk above your head. If these are dangerous times, and if you want me to be realistic, then answer two questions: what the hell is fifteen thousand pounds going to do? And, how long will it last? In terms of wars, this is kid stuff. If you want to fight a war, you need millions. Do you understand? Millions. There's no sense asking a country doctor like me for a small fund he raised over the years for a humanitarian purpose to blow it in a day or two. It's madness."

Standing by the window, the doctor looked pathetically alone. When he took off his glasses he seemed to have aged five years.

"Good night, Uncle," Basim said, his expression severe.

The doctor simply nodded, the muscles of his jaws tightening.

Yousif saw Basim to the door, but before he opened it Basim signaled that he had something to tell him.

"Let's talk on the balcony," Basim suggested.

Yousif opened the door. Both stepped outside and stood in the dark. The weather was terrible. Trees swayed and the rain blew erratically.

"I'm glad you said we need to protect ourselves," Basim said, tightening his belt. "But tell me, what are you going to do when the war starts?"

Salwa's same question echoed in Yousif's ears. "I don't know," he wavered. "Actually I was thinking of finishing my education."

Basim's forehead became creased. "We have no Arab universities here," he said. "That means . . . Oh, I see. You wouldn't be going away because you're afraid, now would you?"

"Afraid? I'm not afraid."

"Then who's going to do the protecting? You're going to leave it up to others."

"I didn't say that."

"Then why would you want to go? Could you live with yourself if we lost the war and you hadn't done your share?"

Suddenly, Basim turned and was descending the stairs, walking on the long tree-lined driveway. But before he reached the wrought-iron gate, the rain got heavier. Lightning seemed to split the sky, painting the whole scene with silver. Yousif stood in awe. The lightning bolts looked like arrows intent on pinning Basim to the ground. But Basim walked on, his head high. Standing still, Yousif watched him disappear into total darkness.

12

Despite the new worries of the night before, Yousif spent the morning trying to be a good student: listening to lectures and taking notes. But he couldn't concentrate.

At the ten o'clock recess he listened to Amin's worries about money. Winter was very hard on Amin's father. Home construction virtually ceased, and stonecutters did not work. And if Amin's father did not work, the whole family, which depended entirely on his wages from week to week, was left deprived.

"What I can't understand," Amin grumbled, "is why a grown man would settle for a seasonal job for all these years. He might as well be temporary help."

Isaac, who had stopped to talk to some fellow students, joined them. "What are you talking about?" he asked.

"I'm talking about my father," Amin replied, shaking his head. "For nearly forty years he's sat in people's yards chiseling rocks and inhaling dust so *they* would have fine homes. And every time it rains or snows he doesn't work and our whole family has a hard time coping."

Never before had Yousif heard Amin complain so openly about poverty. With the war looming on the horizon, construction would come to a virtual halt and Amin's worries would be compounded. Yousif saw that Amin was already feeling the burden of having to help care for his family.

"Sometimes I feel so angry with him that I want to shake him by the shoulders," Amin confessed. "But when I see him looking so helpless I feel ashamed of myself because I know he's tried his best."

They strolled by several teachers. The tall thin mathematics ustaz from Acre looked comical with his long hook nose. Yousif did not know whether the ustaz seemed pinched because of the cold or because he was smelling disaster.

"I wish money were our only problem," Isaac said, throwing the end of his blue wool scarf around his neck. "Ever since the night of shooting we haven't been the same. Our house looks more and more like a morgue."

It was cold, though the December sun was shining. They were supposed to be enjoying a ten-minute break, but Amin and Isaac sounded so morbid. Yousif felt sorry for both of them. On the school ground, just off the street, dozens of students were swarming around a vendor selling crusty sesame rings and hard boiled eggs. Yousif had a taste for what the man was selling but knew there was no chance he could buy any of it today. Instead, he walked around the football field, carrying a brass bell by the ball-on-chain to stop it from ringing.

Yousif himself was not in the best of spirits. The question of the hospital money still gnawed at him. He felt caught between his father and his cousin. Each one had a point. But he was uncertain how far he could go in opposing his father. Ardallah needed to be protected, no doubt. If the hospital money could buy arms that could save one family or even one child it would be worth it. On the other hand, wouldn't it be awful to lose the war and the money at the same time, especially if you knew in advance that the money would have absolutely no bearing on the outcome?

But Yousif could not tell his friends of these concerns that morning. The argument in his house the night before had to be kept a secret. A more pressing concern was his possible separation from Salwa. Weren't wars unpredictable? Couldn't the most unlikely occur?

"I guess each of us has something to gripe about," Yousif said, swinging the bell without letting it ring.

"You too?" Isaac said, not believing him. "At least people are not shooting at your house. Your parents are rich. You have a girl."

"That's just it," Yousif said. "I'm worried about Salwa."

"Worried how?" Amin asked, sarcastic.

"What if the Zionists invade Ardallah?" Yousif asked. "What if they drive us out to make room for the Jews in Europe? Will she and I end up in the same place? Will I be able to find her?"

Isaac rolled his eyes upward and Amin shook his head.

"Okay," Yousif said. "What if her parents pack up and leave for Lebanon until the war is over? What then? Don't tell me that can't happen."

"You're breaking my heart," Amin said.

"I'm serious. I wish I could marry her now and avoid taking that risk."

"Why can't you?" Isaac said, wiping his glasses. "You're smart and some people think you're good looking. You come from a good family with money and status. I'm sure Salwa's father would love to have a doctor's son as a son-in-law. Don't you think so, Amin?"

"I suppose so," Amin said, again looking withdrawn.

"They'd say I was too young for marriage," Yousif argued. "Boys don't marry at seventeen. We have a lot of growing up and settling down to do first. Both of our parents would agree on that."

Isaac didn't seem convinced. "But this is an emergency. If it weren't for the war you'd be glad to wait."

Amin nodded, his face grim. "What would Salwa say if you were to ask?"

Yousif smiled at the notion. "She'd probably think I was crazy and laugh it off."

"Why?" Isaac asked.

"That's her way of putting off serious matters until she has time to think them through," Yousif answered.

"Later," Amin pressed, "would she consider the idea of marriage silly?"

Yousif pondered the question. "I don't know," he finally said.

Even if Salwa consented, Yousif himself would not be allowed to propose. Elders would carry out the ritual after the negotiations had been completed between the two families and the marriage had already been arranged. But now he wondered if he could circumvent the system.

A minute later he rang the first bell. Many of the students, especially those around the vendor, grumbled and started to head back to class. A few of them passed Yousif and his two friends, looking at them in a strange way. How odd! Yousif thought. Were they objecting to Isaac, the only Jewish boy in their midst? Surely not. In any event, Yousif had more important things on his mind.

THAT AFTERNOON Yousif's mother was in the kitchen making finely chopped salad. From the looks of it he knew they would be having *mujaddarah* for supper. He put his hands around her small waist and gave her a peck. She seemed startled.

"I didn't hear you come in," she said, kissing him back.

"Don't forget to brown lots of onions, please," he said, lifting the lid of the pot on the primus. The sight of rice and lentil and the smell of cumin made him hungry. He opened a drawer, took out a tablespoon, and sampled one of his favorite meals.

"Put some in a dish," his mother chided.

"I love to eat out of the pot."

Yousif put the spoon down and went inside to remove his jacket. On his way back to the kitchen he heard the doorbell ring. He looked out the window and saw Salwa and her short, tomboyish friend, Huda, standing on the balcony. His heart skipped. Astonishment, pleasure and surprise filled him as he quickly turned on the lights and swung the door wide open.

"Hello," he said, smiling and stepping aside.

"Hello," Salwa said. "Is my mother here?"

"Your mother?" Yousif asked, surprised. "Is she supposed to be?"

"I thought so," Salwa said, her wind-kissed cheeks turning rosier.

Still unable to contain himself, Yousif motioned for them to come in.

The two girls looked at each other, uncertain.

"Thank you but we'd better not," Huda said, ready to leave.

"What's the matter," Yousif said, anxious. "Come on in."

Salwa thought for a second. "I'd like to say hello to Aunt Yasmin," Salwa explained to Huda. Then turning to Yousif, she added, "She's here, isn't she?"

"Of course," Yousif replied, letting them both in and shutting the door.

By that time his mother had joined them in the foyer, wiping her hand with a towel flung over her shoulder. She kissed the two girls and made them feel welcome. She wanted them to stay and visit for a while, but Huda complained that it was getting dark and they ought to be getting home. Nevertheless, they lingered on. Bubbly as usual, Salwa explained that she and Huda had been to a Christmas play at their school. Since they were so close by, they took a chance and dropped in to see if her mother were there attending the ladies' meeting.

"That's tomorrow, dear," Yousif's mother said, trying to lead them toward the living room.

"How silly of me," Salwa said, blushing. "I should've remembered."

Yousif studied Salwa's face, delighted in his assumption that she had really come to see him. She knew that the ladies had always met on Saturday afternoon. But he loved her excuse and accepted it as the best Christmas gift she could give him. All the while he agonized that she might be leaving soon. So he questioned Huda about the play they had seen: who was in it, was it in English or Arabic, was it good, was it well attended, would the performance be repeated? Anything just to keep looking at Salwa, who was talking to his mother. He loved the warm way the two behaved toward each other. If his mother had a daughter, she would've wanted her to be like Salwa. Well, he thought, if she couldn't have her as a daughter, one day she will have her as a daughter-in-law.

"We really need to go," Huda said, sidling toward the door.

"Stay until Father comes," he suggested, looking Salwa in the eye, "then I'll drive you both home."

Huda shook her head. "I don't mind walking."

To Yousif's dismay the two girls took a step toward the door.

"Let me call a taxi for you then," he offered, hoping to gain a few more minutes. "It's cold and foggy outside."

Salwa shrugged but Huda insisted that there was no need.

"I like this kind of weather," Huda said, her eyes apologizing to Yousif.

When the two girls left, Yousif and his mother watched them through the open door. Yousif felt his heart walking away from him in Salwa's green coat.

"You'd better snatch that girl," Yousif heard a voice tell him.

Both he and his mother turned around. Fatima was standing behind them, holding a freshly made *kanoon*. The kindled charcoal was giving her clean face a natural glow.

"What did you say?" Yousif asked, shutting the door.

"You heard me," Fatima answered, walking toward the living room.

Yousif watched her place the *kanoon* near the radio console, where they would all be sitting to hear the news.

"That girl is too beautiful to remain unmarried for long," Fatima continued, wiping her ruddy face with her long sleeve. "Somebody is bound to come along and steal her from you. Then you'll be sorry."

Those were Yousif's exact sentiments. That they were uttered by Fatima was uncanny. He smiled, but his mother was frowning.

"Yousif has a lot of schooling ahead of him," his mother snapped. "Don't you give him any ideas."

Yousif wiped the steam off the window pane to take one more look. "Don't worry, Mother," he said. "I already know what I want."

He could hear the two women walking away, chattering. His mother was reprimanding Fatima for making such a foolish suggestion.

"There's more to life than marriage," he could hear his mother saying. "First comes education . . . then career . . . and then . . ."

He followed them to the kitchen, filled a dish with *mujaddarah,* leaned against the wall, and started to eat.

"This house is too big for just the three of you," Fatima went on, grinning and revealing the big gap between her two front teeth. "And the doctor is not getting any younger. He needs little bare feet running around to brighten his old age."

"*Your* husband is old—not mine," Yasmin said, turning off the primus.

"Psshhhh," Fatima smirked, shrugging her shoulder and wiping the counter with a wet rag. "Last week when you sent me to pick up the lamb meat, I saw the butcher Abu Mazen drop his big sharp knife and swear under his breath. His eyes bulged and he kept staring at something in the street. The shop was crowded and everybody turned around to see what made him come so close to chopping off his own fingers. And what do you think he was looking at? Salwa of course. She was wearing a navy-blue outfit. One man standing by me said to his friend, 'Look at the wind blowing her hair and loving her body. It's wrapping the dress around her like on a piece of sculpture.'"

Yousif felt jealous. "Who was that man?" he wanted to know.

"He meant no harm," Fatima said, her voice soft.

Yousif stopped eating. "It must've been embarrassing for her."

There was a pause.

"She's charming," Yasmin admitted, folding her arms. "What's more important, she's good."

"No girl in town is more suitable for Yousif than her," Fatima said. "But listen to this. I turned around and saw two women whispering to each other. I just knew what they were thinking."

"What?" Yousif said, eager for details.

"I just knew they were trying to match her up with one of their sons or brothers," Fatima said. "So as soon as I picked up the package from the butcher and paid my money, I stepped right between these women and I said, 'Excuse me, ladies. But if I were you I wouldn't waste my breath. That girl is already spoken for.' And I walked out with my head high like I'd been insulted."

Both Yousif and his mother laughed. "You did not," he said.

"The Prophet be my witness," Fatima said, raising her right hand.

Yousif thought Fatima was wickedly funny. He ate one more spoonful and handed her the half-full dish. "When I marry her I'm going to buy you the prettiest dress in town," he said.

"Now you're talking," Fatima grinned. "Embroidered at the hem and at the sleeves . . . and bodice . . ."

"You bet," Yousif told her, rushing out.

"Finish your food," his mother called after him.

"Let him go," Fatima said.

Putting on his jacket, he could hear the two women laughing. He opened the door, ready to face the wind.

YOUSIF WALKED through the *souk,* past Salman's 'apothecary', past Moshe Sha'lan's shop, past the bus terminal, and started up the incline toward the new district. By the time he got to the Rowda Hotel, Salwa's green coat flashed through the fog before him that had covered Ardallah like a gray shroud.

Yousif doubled his speed and began to whistle a tune just to let her know he was behind her. Luckily the fog was enveloping them in waves: one second he could see the two girls clearly and the next he couldn't. At one of those splendid moments when the fog lifted, Yousif saw Salwa turn to look behind her and . . . she saw him!

The two girls turned left and Yousif followed suit, about fifty yards behind them. Then Salwa and Huda parted. Salwa continued on a secluded short cut that Yousif had seen her take many a time, especially whenever she wanted to exchange a few words with him.

He caught up with her on a dirt road that ran through a sparsely populated area.

"I hope nobody sees us," Salwa muttered, slowing down.

"When I saw you at the door—I couldn't believe my eyes," Yousif confessed, his breathing heavy. "I looked for you all afternoon."

"We ought to be careful," Salwa said, without looking at him.

They walked in silence.

"Salwa . . ." Yousif said.

"Yes."

"You knew your mother wasn't at our house, didn't you?"

"What do you think?" she replied. Even in the dark Yousif could tell she was blushing.

"I thought so," Yousif said, happy.

"I try to see you whenever I can. But it's not always easy."

He reached for her hand but she pulled it away.

"I missed you, Salwa," he said.

Yellow headlights suddenly appeared, penetrating the fog. As if by reflex, the two split and walked on opposite sides of the street. They remained apart until the car crawled by and was gone. Then Yousif crossed the street to rejoin her.

She walked beside him. "I'm worried," she said, gently swinging her purse.

"About what?" Yousif asked.

"The war."

"We all are," he told her. "Father says if we lose the war we might even be kicked out. That means you and I might get separated. I'd go crazy."

The thud of their heels on the dirt road was the only sound he could hear.

"If all of us do our share," she said, looking ahead, "there's no reason to lose. We'll win." Then she turned around and looked at him. "But I don't see how we can be separated."

"Suppose they drive us out and you end up in Lebanon and I end up in Syria . . . or Jordan . . . What then?"

"You must be joking," she answered. "They can't do that."

"They can if they have the power. We know they want the land without the people."

She did not seem convinced. "Well, if all of you men fight—no such thing will happen."

Yousif was not persuaded. "Suppose your parents ," he said, "decide to take a long vacation and wait out the war in Lebanon. Suppose the Jews win and don't let you come back."

"Not likely," she told him. "One, my parents can't afford such a trip. Two, we're going to win. You really have a fertile imagination."

"I'm always thinking . . ."

"Don't worry. If we get separated you'll find me. But if you haven't fought, don't even try."

Yousif was silent for a long time.

"Don't get upset," she told him. "Just do your share in the fighting and everything will be okay."

He stopped walking. "Doing one's share and fighting are not the same thing," he said.

"What do you mean?" she asked.

"I know we need to protect ourselves. But picking up the gun could be our undoing. We are too small, too unprepared. And we can't depend on outside help. I still think we ought to negotiate a settlement."

"It's much too late for that," she said.

"That's what everybody says. And yet I keep hoping . . ."

"Action, Yousif, not hope. Hope alone is useless."

They were approaching the end of the side street. The right turn would bring them out of seclusion. He stopped in the shadow of a new building, for he knew she would not speak to him once they reached the five-point Saha.

"What are you going to do during the holiday?" he asked.

She looked at him. For the first time she seemed to soften. A moment passed before she replied.

"I'll be thinking about you," she finally admitted.

He was pleased. "Will you be going shopping?"

"I will if you want me to."

"You know I do. That's the only way I can see you. Unless Zuhair and Akram need more tutoring."

She smiled. "I'd better go now."

He leaned forward to kiss her. But she stepped back.

"Please don't embarrass me," she said.

"I love you," he argued.

"I know. But not here. Not now. Please."

As she began to walk away, he wanted to follow her. But he knew he mustn't. Should anyone see them walking behind each other in the fog, rumors would fly all over town. Their reputations would be tarnished, especially hers. Why must Arab society be so hard on lovers? he wondered again.

In a moment he saw Salwa's lovely figure turn the corner and disappear.

MONDAY AFTERNOON, Yousif and his two friends stopped at Arif's bookstore for a look at the magazine rack. The place was crowded with Christmas shoppers buying toys that Arif had begun to import.

"Hey, Yousif," bald-headed Arif said, raising his voice above the hubbub. "Let me see you before you leave."

"Sure," Yousif said, waving his hand.

Five minutes later, between customers, Arif drew Yousif to a corner.

"Salwa has been here five times already," Arif confided, leaning toward the counter and his eyes all over the place. "The first time was about eleven o'clock. She asked if I had seen you today. I said no. And every time she came since then she'd stick her head through the door, look around, and then look at me for a yes or no. I'd shake my head and she'd go on her way."

Yousif became worried. "It's not like her to be so open."

"I think you ought to try and find her."

"When was the last time she was here?"

"About ten minutes ago."

"Thanks," Yousif said, elbowing through the crowd.

With his two friends at heel, Yousif walked out of Arif's bookstore forgetting to pay for the *al-Musawwar* magazine he was now rolling and unrolling. They walked through Kilani's Novelty Shop, but she wasn't there. They peeped inside Bata shoe store and inside Carmen's beauty salon, but no luck. Ten minutes later, Yousif found her sitting with Huda at Nashwan's eating ice cream. The two exchanged glances as he spotted a marble-topped table near hers. A group of school girls joined her unexpectedly and she looked at Yousif, disappointed. She seemed restless and distracted. Her smile was forced.

Within ten minutes Yousif followed her back to Arif's bookstore. In the corner by the magazine stand, looking nervous, she slipped him a note. He moved to another corner before opening it. Scribbled, it read: "Meet me at the cinema. Left balcony. Four o'clock." He glanced at his watch. It was twenty minutes till four.

Precisely at four, he went to the cinema with Amin and Isaac. The two friends sat down in the third row to their right, but Yousif walked around looking for Salwa. The maroon curtain was still hiding the silver screen and the sound system was blaring an Esmahan song. In a slow haunting voice, the female singer was describing a lovesick woman's visit to a rose garden. She had gone there to console herself—to smell the roses and hear the birds singing. She saw two nightingales perched on a tree branch and imagined them in love. In their fancied romance the male was vowing his devotion, calling his paramour an angel and begging her never to leave him. After a long moment of happiness, the uncaring paramour fluttered her wings and flew away—leaving him, his heart melted. It was one of Yousif's favorite songs. But today it stung him.

He found Salwa rubbing her temples, Huda at her side. When they saw him approaching, Huda got up and moved several seats away. Luckily the theater was almost empty and they were able to sit in relative seclusion.

Nothing had prepared him for Salwa's tense mood. He looked at her keenly and reached for her hand. Surprisingly, she clutched his fingertips.

He stiffened. "What is it?"

"Adel Farhat is planning to ask for my hand," she whispered, her eyes steady.

Yousif flinched. "What?" he said.

"You heard me," she answered, uncoiling her hand out of his.

"Adel Farhat?"

"The assistant manager at Al-Andalus Hotel," she said, nodding. "He and his parents visited us twice already. Tonight we're supposed to return the visit."

Yousif had to swallow hard. "Are you sure that's what they have in mind?"

"What else? We don't know these people. We've never visited them before nor have they visited us. We see their son at the hotel, but that's all."

Yousif remembered how Adel Farhat had tried to cut in on him while dancing with Salwa. He remembered the champagne bottle Adel Farhat had sent to her parents' table that same night. Now the pieces were beginning to fall in place.

"You should've seen how his mother looked me over. She made me feel uncomfortable."

"Well don't go."

"Go where?"

"To their house. They'd get the message."

"These visits are prearranged. My father would be very upset with me if I make him break his promise. "

"Has he checked with you to see if you're interested?"

"He hasn't. But mother keeps talking about how nice they are. Adel is an only child. Worked ten years for the Passport Department in Jerusalem, then switched to hotel management because he has a rich uncle in America who wants to buy him a hotel. Father says Adel is negotiating to buy Al-Andalus Hotel itself. His three aunts own a lot of property, which he'll inherit because none of them is married. Even his wealthy uncle in America is childless."

"Did your mother tell you if you married him you'd be sleeping in a bed made of gold?" he sneered.

"Be serious. Mother knows about you and me. But she says you won't be ready for years."

"Pray tell," Yousif said, his head crackling with anxiety, "why is Ardallah's most eligible bachelor getting married at this time?"

"It seems he wants to join the fighting any way he can. But his family wants him to get married instead. They think a bride would make him change his mind. They don't realize they're choosing the wrong girl for that."

The fact that Salwa had allowed the discussion with Adel Farhat's family to get this far made Yousif extremely uneasy.

"I'm not trying to put you on the spot," she hesitated.

Her words woke him up. "Yes . . ."

"I was just thinking . . ."

"Go on."

"If you'd intervene . . . make a counter proposal . . ."

Yousif stared at her in the dark. "You mean ask for your hand?"

"I'm afraid it may be the only way to stop this marriage."

Sheer joy engulfed Yousif. He squeezed her hand, his heart thumping. He couldn't believe his ears. His dream girl was actually telling him to ask for her hand—that she was willing to marry him. Wow! He felt flattered, proud, thrilled, inspired, determined, ecstatic that she wanted him to do this.

"If Adel Farhat asks for my hand we are undone," she warned. "My parents are impressed with him. Mother keeps saying good opportunities don't knock on a girl's door everyday."

He felt his happiness ooze away. Her parents could ruin their future.

"I thought your mother liked me," he complained.

"She still does. But she also says you're too young, not ready for marriage. He's about twelve years older than you. Your mother keeps talking about your wanting to go to America and study at Columbia University like your father. That could be several years. Do you think my family would want me to wait that long? Also, we're facing war. Fathers are worried about what might happen to their daughters. My father keeps saying it's better for a girl to be with a husband at a time like this."

For a second Yousif did not realize what she was talking about. Then it dawned on him that her father was worried that she might get raped during the war. To an Arab, Yousif remembered, there could be no greater shame.

He kicked the back of the seat in front of him. "I don't understand . . ."

"What?"

"One minute you're telling me to ask for your hand," he told her, "and the next minute you're making a case for Adel Farhat."

"Making a case!!! Is that what you think?" She bit her lip and began to cry.

He hated himself for being so tactless. He turned around and found Huda staring at them. When she stopped looking, he took Salwa in his arms and kissed her eyelids.

"Listen," he said. "If they ask you to marry him simply say no."

She pushed him away, her face congested. "And if they don't?"

"Don't what?"

"Don't ask me."

"Throw a tantrum. Rebel. Revolt. Kick and fight. Simply don't accept."

She shook her head. "It won't work."

"Why not?"

"It might be too late. Father might've already given his word."

"Warn him not to."

"He might not listen. You know how Arab fathers are."

"Don't be silly. It's your decision. It's your life."

"Oh, Yousif. I wish it were that easy."

"Why isn't it?"

"Because that's not the way marriages are conducted around here. Wake up. You're in the Middle East, remember? Girls are rarely asked."

"Be that rarity. You're Salwa. Someone special. Put your foot down."

"And if I don't succeed? Don't blame me . . ."

Yousif considered what she just said. Damn it, she was right. Things might not be left up to her. He had better think of something else. Fast.

"Let's think together for a minute," he said. "I guess the thing for me to do is to inform my parents of our plan and let them officially ask your parents for your hand."

Salwa opened her purse to get out a handkerchief. "What if your parents think you're too young?" she asked, dabbing her eyes.

"I'll raise all kinds of hell until they see it my way," he answered. "Meanwhile fight them off as long as you can. And let me know what's going on. Send me a word. Do you know the blind man Jamal, the basket weaver?"

"The one who plays the violin?"

"Do you know where he lives?"

"No, but I can find out."

"He's a good friend of mine. Pretend you want to buy a basket or a tray or something. If things begin to move fast, meet me there. It'll be safe. And Salwa . . ."

"Yes?"

"Remember that I love you."

"You think I'd be here if I didn't know that?"

"Do you love me?"

"You know I do."

He put his arm around her shoulder and squeezed her tight. She whispered that she was afraid, and he reassured her with a tender kiss.

"How will I know you'll be at Jamal's when I need to see you?" she asked.

"When you go out wear something that will give me a signal," he answered. "A yellow blouse, or a blue dress. Or put your hair up."

"What about a red scarf?"

"That'll be fine."

"What if Jamal isn't there when I get there?"

"Don't worry. We'll meet in the arcade, under the steps. It's dark and secluded enough."

"That's it then. The red scarf."

"The red scarf."

She squeezed his hand and he didn't want to let go of her. But she begged him with her eyes, then got up and left. He remained in his seat, mystified. Nothing on the screen interested him. Soon the images began to blur.

What if it really happened? What if she married Adel Farhat? She was not eighteen yet—too young to stand up to a domineering father. He himself was only a month older—too young to propose himself. But Salwa had asked him and he couldn't let her down. Most likely her father would be more receptive if the formality were carried out according to tradition. The problem was, he, Yousif, hadn't told his parents yet about this turn of events. He needed time to hone all the arguments he would marshall to win their approval.

At a time like this? they would surely ask. Let them ask all they wanted.

Imbued with Salwa's love and desire to marry him, he felt nothing could stand in his way. He would rise to the occasion and answer her challenge for an act of intervention.

He thought of the gold-toothed suitor. Prior to returning to Ardallah two summers ago, Adel Farhat had worked in Jerusalem. Yousif knew of him, particularly for being a splendid soccer player on Jerusalem's YMCA team. He was almost as good as Rassass, who played on the Greek Orthodox team in Jaffa. These two teams were the finest in Palestine, and Adel was mentioned after every match. Before joining the Al-Andalus Hotel, Adel used to hang around Arif's bookstore and sometimes at a pool hall playing billiards. A thoroughbred athlete, he attracted many admirers, including Yousif. Sinewy and poised, Adel made the billiards zing in place with the same skill that had made him famous on the football field.

This same Adel was now Yousif's opponent. But marrying Salwa was not a soccer game. A lifetime of happiness would depend on the outcome. At seventeen, Yousif did not want to be a loser.

13

On his way home, Yousif felt deep apprehension. Salwa had asked him to intervene and he mustn't fail her. He had better act fast.

But marriages were arranged by families, not by individuals. He would have to speak to his parents. They might think the whole idea absurd and refuse to help. Then what? Basim was out of the question: either he couldn't be reached or he would be angry at the timing. We are at war, Basim would say, and pound the table. But to Yousif, the two fights went hand in hand: each was about protecting one's own. He would fight for Salwa as he would for Palestine. The idea of losing either one outraged him.

That night his parents were jolted by his announcement. They listened to him in the living room like two judges presiding at a murder trial.

"I knew you cared for Salwa," his father said, loosening his belt and unbuttoning the top button of his pants, "but I had no idea you were that serious. You're only seventeen."

"I'll be eighteen in April."

"That's too young for marriage. Especially for a man."

Yasmin pursed her lips and rested her cheek on her hand. She seemed anxious.

"Under different circumstances Salwa would be ideal," she said, thinking.

Yousif re-crossed his legs to stop them from jerking. "Time is running out."

The doctor poked his pipe with his tamper and emptied the ashes. "I think," he said, "the sooner you get her out of your mind the better."

Yousif stomped his foot. "Never."

His parents stared at him, incredulous.

"All I'm asking you to do is talk to her father," Yousif pleaded.

"And tell him what?" his father asked, dejected.

"That I want to marry his daughter," Yousif said.

"I don't relish getting turned down?" the doctor said, puffing on his pipe. "I know exactly what he would say. And he's right."

"Right about what?"

"Your age."

"Is age everything in a marriage? What about my other assets? I come from a good family. A comfortable . . . decent family with whom they've been friends for years. Also, I'm a good student with a bright future—even if I have to say so myself. Above all, Salwa and I are in love."

His father raised his eyebrows. "That love bit could be a liability."

Yousif ignored the remark. "Don't all these qualities count?"

Fatima walked in with a tray of coffee and rice pudding covered with cinnamon and ground nuts. She pushed aside a large onyx ashtray on an end table to make room for what she was carrying. The doctor reached for a small bowl and a teaspoon and began to eat.

"You're still too young," the doctor said, enjoying the pudding.

"Salwa doesn't think so. She told me that herself."

His mother looked surprised, then reached for the brass coffee pot. "*She* did?"

"Yes. Only three hours ago."

"Where did she tell you that?" his mother inquired.

Up till now Yousif had not told them the whole story. He only said that he had heard that Adel Farhat was getting ready to ask for Salwa's hand, without mentioning the source. But now, with his two parents grilling him with their eyes, he had no choice but to tell them all he knew.

The doctor looked at his wife. "What do you make of a girl—especially one about to get married—who meets a boy behind her father's back?" he asked.

Yousif resented the insinuation and said so. But the doctor kept his eyes on his wife.

"Any other girl might be doubted," she said. "Not Salwa. She's a wonderful girl."

The doctor finished eating, placed the bowl on the tray, leaned back, and unbuttoned one more button in his pants.

Yousif clasped both hands between his knees. "You don't think love is a crime, do you?"

His father shook his head, biting on the stem of his pipe. "In my day a girl wouldn't dare . . ."

His wife poured the coffee, seemingly vexed by her husband. "What's the matter with you? You know better than to malign Salwa. My God, Jamil. Times have changed. This is 1948."

"I know," her husband lamented, reaching for the demitasse cup she was handing him. "The year of the disaster."

"Not on our account," Yousif bristled, refusing the rice pudding and the coffee his mother was offering him. "If you're talking about Palestine and her troubles, you certainly can't say it's our generation's fault. If anyone is to blame . . . well, it's not us."

Yousif couldn't figure his father out. The doctor seemed indifferent, sarcastic, cantankerous. The kindest of all men, normally he would never criticize anyone. Nor would he cast a shadow of doubt on the character of someone who was beyond reproach like Salwa. Why was he being so old-fashioned, so unresponsive? It was certainly the wrong night to talk to him about marriage, Yousif thought. But what other option was there? Hadn't Adel Farhat fallen in their midst out of the blue? Hadn't Salwa asked him to make a counter proposal? He would move heaven and earth to prevent losing her.

"How did you two get married?" Yousif asked, his fingertips touching. "Were you in love? Was there a go-between?"

Yousif could tell that the wheels in his parents' heads were turning. There was a shine in their eyes.

"When your father started visiting us in Jerusalem," Yasmin remembered, smiling, "he was always accompanied by my brother Boulus—who was already living in Ardallah."

"Why?" Yousif asked. "Couldn't he have come alone?"

"I could've," the doctor said, "but I needed moral support. I had already ingratiated myself to Boulus—so why not take him along?"

Yasmin's expression grew soft. "I'll never forget how my girlfriends called him Dr. Pipe," she said, folding her hands in her lap. "Every time they saw him he'd have a pipe in his mouth. Every time I saw him or smelled his aromatic tobacco, I'd run and hide."

"Don't listen to her," the doctor said, pulling smugly on his pipe. "She was smitten from the first day."

Yousif was curious. "When and where was that?"

The doctor eyed his son suspiciously. "You've heard it a hundred—"

"In bits and pieces," Yousif agreed. "But not from start to finish." He wanted to hear the whole story one more time, hoping to unearth anything that might strengthen his bid for Salwa.

The doctor looked at his wife, who shrugged her shoulder. He then turned the radio off, sipped on his coffee, pulled out his tobacco pouch, and began refilling his pipe.

"That was back in 1925," the doctor recalled, leaning on his elbow. "I happened to be standing on the balcony of my brand new clinic. Suddenly I saw a gorgeous girl crossing the street below. I felt a rush in my blood—even though I had never seen her before. So I ran inside and told the nurse to follow her and find out who she was. Ten minutes later I knew her name and that she was from Jerusalem visiting her brother—a grain merchant down the street from me."

"That was all he needed to know," Yasmin said, amused.

"From then on," the doctor continued, "I made it a point to befriend her brother—Uncle Boulus. It was easy. He was about my age and luckily we hit it off. A few of his friends would come to his store to play backgammon. On sunny days they'd sit on the sidewalk just outside the door. So I learned the game and joined the group whenever I could. It was a lot of fun. Sometimes we'd have a dozen spectators hovering over us—some of whom were taking bets. Little by little Boulus and I became close. But all the while, mind you, I didn't lose sight of my mission: to give a good impression of myself and to learn all I could about his sister. A couple of times she came to see him, and that was a big bonus."

Yasmin smiled and looked younger, prettier. "Don't let his reserved ways fool you," she told her son. "In his youth your father was a romantic schemer. When he found out that I worked in my father's souvenir shop in old Jerusalem, he started coming every week."

"Why not?" the doctor asked, lighting his pipe, "especially when I heard you weren't engaged or spoken for?"

Yasmin touched her son's knee, her eyes twinkling. "He bought enough mother-of-pearl crosses and Last Supper pieces to make one think he was holy."

Yousif chewed on his lower lip. "How old were you?"

"I was nineteen and he was thirty-one," his mother told him.

The parallel between them and Salwa and Adel Farhat was disturbing.

"Why weren't you engaged?" Yousif probed. "You were beautiful. And old enough."

"Not for a lack of suitors, let me assure you," she boasted. "But no one was good enough for me or my parents."

"I suppose," Yousif said, his smile twisted, "you were holding out for the highest bidder."

His mother's eyes widened. "If you mean in terms of family, education, money, looks—yes."

"But not love?" Yousif accused.

"Love he says," Yasmin retorted. "It was taboo. Still is. No, I didn't love him. Not at first. But within a few months after marriage I gave him the kind of love he gave me: the kind built on trust and respect and admiration. The kind that grows and deepens and matures with the years."

Yousif was still sifting, weighing, trying to gauge his own chances.

"If you weren't interested in him," he went on, "what changed your mind?"

"They talked me into it," Yasmin admitted. "Boulus thought I'd be a fool to turn him down. Father said I'd be the envy of all the girls my age. Mother said I should thank my lucky stars he asked for my hand."

"And they all said the truth and nothing but the truth," the doctor bragged, puffing on his pipe and ready to change the subject.

Chafing, Yousif recrossed his legs. "Well," he blurted, "those days are gone. Our generation believes in love. No one is going to talk Salwa or me into marrying someone neither of us wants."

The legacy they had just handed him was something he could do without. There was a long pause. The mood became charged.

"Let's suppose," the doctor mused, his chin wrinkled, "that Anton Taweel has for some time been negotiating marriage between his daughter and Adel Farhat. Suppose they have already agreed and only the formalities are left. Do you think he'd go back on his word? Not even if you were an Arabian prince with an oil well in your backyard."

Yousif thought of flattering his father. "I'm a lot better than that. I'm the son of Dr. and Mrs. Jamil Safi."

The doctor smiled. "I'm impressed—but will it impress others?"

Yousif shifted in his seat and looked at his mother for help. "Maybe things haven't progressed too far. Why are you throwing blocks in my way?"

"Because come to think of it, Anton Taweel and Adel Farhat are always seen together," the doctor remembered. "Probably what they're doing now is tying the final knot. Believe me, Anton will not change his mind."

"He's got to," Yousif insisted. "I don't know Adel Farhat and I certainly mean him no harm. But he happened to choose the wrong girl. My girl."

"But you're not ready to get married," his father argued. "You have years of schooling ahead of you. Don't you want to go to Columbia University? Salwa is a modern girl. She wouldn't let you marry her and leave her with us until you've finished and come back."

"Then I'll take her with me."

"Be serious. You can't afford it."

"You can. And I'm your only son."

"You are and I'm proud of it. If you were ready . . . and if we weren't going into war . . . it'd be different. I don't know what's going to happen. No one does. Anything can go wrong. What if something should happen to me? If I go, my income goes. Then what? What would you and your mother and your wife live on? It doesn't make sense. Traveling overseas, living abroad, university tuition—it all costs money."

"Then I won't go. I'll stay here and work."

"And blow away your future?"

"I don't want a future without her. I'll do anything not to lose her."

"Then I feel sorry for you."

"All I'm asking you to do is ask them."

"There's no sense asking for something I don't approve of myself. Don't you understand? We shouldn't even be discussing this. It's way too soon."

The rapid exchange stopped. The doctor lit his pipe, without taking his eyes off his son. The three sat subdued. And for the next hour, the doctor wouldn't budge.

TWO DAYS LATER, the red scarf around Salwa's neck loomed as a summons to judgement. Ever since the meeting at Cinema Firyal, Yousif had roamed Ardallah hoping to see her or hear from her. She had not been going to school and that worried him. Now he was dreading what she might tell him.

On that day, Wednesday, he had cut school himself and spent the morning at Arif's bookstore: alternating between standing inside around the portable heater and shivering in the cold just outside the door. Then she appeared across the street, walking with her father—and wearing the red scarf with her green coat. The minute she stepped out of Kilani's Novelty Shop, her eyes searched for him. Their eyes locked and he saw her head bend in an imperceptible nod. He responded in kind, feeling his body temperature rising.

He watched her and her father walk past a dry cleaner and a beauty salon, tall and erect and in step. But there was no sense standing there, he thought. He needed to find Jamal and arrange for a three o'clock meeting at his place.

Yousif crisscrossed the town looking for Jamal. He went to his room three times, but could not find him. He searched every coffeehouse to no avail. He stopped at the bus terminal and checked with the conductors, relieved no one told him Jamal had gone out of town. But by noon, Yousif became despondent. If he couldn't find Jamal his meeting with Salwa could be jeopardized. Hiding in the arcade would be unbecoming. Just as he was about to despair, luck smiled on him. He happened to look inside a small eatery across from Cinema Firyal. At the far end of the narrow cafe was Jamal.

"I've been looking all over for you," Yousif said, pulling up a chair.

Jamal nodded, holding a *falafel* sandwich with both hands. "Have something to eat, then tell me all about it," he said. Then he cocked his head and raised his voice, calling out to the proprietor. "Fouad, bring him *falafel*."

"No . . . no," Yousif said. "No food for me. Listen, Jamal. I have a big favor to ask of you."

"I'm listening."

"I'm in love."

Jamal smiled and chewed lustily, a spot of *tahini* at the corner of his mouth.

"I'm serious," Yousif continued, handing him a paper napkin. "Please, listen to me. I'm madly in love with a beautiful girl. And she loves me, too. Suddenly her family wants her to marry somebody else. Some kind of fever is sweeping people. They're all scared. They all want to put their personal things in order before it's too late."

"Typical wartime attitude," Jamal said, finishing eating and vigorously wiping his mouth and hands. "How can I help you?" he asked, his brow furrowed.

"All I want of you is a chance to meet her at your place. There's nowhere else we can talk."

Jamal nodded and then reached for his cane that hung on the back of his chair. Jamal paid a shilling to a proprietor with a gravel voice, and he and Yousif left. It was already drizzling.

At the one-room apartment, Yousif looked at his wristwatch constantly, wishing for three o'clock. In the meantime, he poured out his heart to Jamal, telling him again and again how much he loved Salwa. He paced the small low-ceilinged room. Jamal sat in a corner, weaving a basket and listening.

"Have you ever been in love, Jamal?" Yousif asked. "Don't answer if you don't want to."

"I don't mind," Jamal answered, his deft fingers busy with long slivers of cane. "Yes, Yousif, I've been in love. As a matter of fact I still am. And always will be—even though she's been married for twenty years and has three children. They say time heals all wounds. Maybe so. But this wound has never healed."

Sadness hovered over them. But soon Jamal's face brightened.

"I'll tell you what you should do, Yousif."

"What?" Yousif asked, surprised at the change of tone.

"Let cousin Salman prepare you a potion to stop the marriage."

"I thought you were serious."

"They say he's good at it."

The minutes crept by. Jamal lit the primus and put on a pot of Arabic coffee. Yousif watched in disbelief. How could a blind mind manage so well? Ten minutes later, they drank in silence.

"You haven't told me the girl's name," Jamal remarked, resuming his weaving.

"I'm sorry, I didn't think—"

"No, no. Perhaps it's better this way."

They heard footsteps and both perked their ears. The sound of high heels clicking stopped. Yousif rushed and opened the door. But Salwa was not there—only her friend, Huda. His heart sank. He motioned for her to come in, looking right and left to make sure they were not being watched.

"Where is she?" Yousif asked, his voice choked.

"She couldn't come," Huda answered, toying with the strap of her purse.

He stepped aside to let her in. The minute she saw Jamal's back hunched over his basket, she backed away.

"Don't worry," Yousif said.

Reluctantly, Huda remained standing by the door.

"Where is she?" Yousif asked.

"I'm afraid I have bad news. I didn't want to be the one to tell you, but she begged me."

Yousif fixed his stare on her. "Go on," he muttered.

"She's getting engaged to Adel Farhat."

"It's not true."

"Listen, Yousif. I'm sorry for both of you. Now let me out, please."

"Where is she?"

"At home."

"Can't she come out? Can't she see me?"

"The engagement is Sunday."

"This coming Sunday?"

Huda nodded. "I'm sorry," she said. She started to leave, then stopped and looked back at him. "One more thing," she added. "She wants you to know that she still loves you."

Dazed, Yousif hardly noticed Huda slip out of the room. He heard the door open and close but did not see her go out. He pressed his head against the wall and pounded his fist without stopping. He felt robbed, amputated. He kicked and cursed and began to sob. Jamal's outstretched arms found him, and led him back to a seat. But Yousif could not remain in one place. He was inconsolable. He brushed his tears and left without saying a word.

To whom should he turn? Suddenly he was furious with his own parents. They had better come across and ask for her hand. His mind raced as he walked through the old dirty streets. What next? he asked himself over and over again. Salwa engaged to marry Adel Farhat? No . . . no. Never.

YOUSIF KNEW he had to find Salwa's father and convince him that Salwa's impending marriage was a serious mistake. Her father must be warned that his daughter's happiness was at stake. He couldn't force her to marry someone she did not want.

As Yousif left Jamal's district and climbed his way to the upper part of town, arguments tumbled in his head. He would tell her father this and he would tell him that, and if the old bastard would not listen, he'd punch him in the nose. By God, he'd elope with her. But he quickly dismissed the thought. True, she was the one who suggested the counter proposal, yet she might oppose the idea of elopement. That was too radical a step—tantamount to a scandal. No, he couldn't take her for granted on that score. She wouldn't go along. Besides, he had no money. The only option left for him was to take a stand and try his best to put some sense into her father's head.

HE LOOKED FOR her father at several coffeehouses, to no avail. Finally he went to Zahrawi's cafe, a big hall built on a slope with two terraced gardens in front. The place was jammed with customers amusing themselves by playing cards and dominoes or simply smoking, drinking, and trying to solve the problems of the world. There he ran into a bookkeeper with liver-spotted hands whom he had often seen with Salwa's father. The middle-aged, nattily-dressed bookkeeper, with a cigarette dangling from a corner of his mouth, seemed jovial, playing cards.

"Do you know where I can find Mr. Taweel?" Yousif asked.

The bookkeeper looked up and took a drag. "Probably with his future son-in-law," he said, resting the cigarette in an ashtray full of butts.

"Where else would he be?" another player added, slapping a card on the table.

"As the proverb says," the bookkeeper continued, pulling a card from the deck, "being an in-law is better than being a relative." With that he put down a winning hand.

Some of the men laughed at the old joke; others cursed their own luck. Yousif felt his cheeks redden.

He found Salwa's father, Anton Taweel, at the bar inside Al-Andalus Hotel, where Adel Farhat was the assistant manager. Anton was sitting on a bar stool in a small, dark, smoke-filled room with four or five men. Yousif had never seen him in such a happy mood. From the number of glasses and half-empty dishes and bottles of Keo and Barbaross cognac on the counter, and particularly from the loudness of the men's voices, Yousif could tell that the party had been going on for a while. I bet they're celebrating, Yousif thought, as he approached the room and stood stiffly at the door. A moment passed as he surveyed the scene. He knew the others only by name. Adel Farhat, the groom-to-be, was sitting at the counter, his back to the door.

"Ah, Yousif," the father said, recognizing him. "Come and have a drink."

His tone was happy and friendly, but Yousif looked and did not move.

"Come on," the father continued. "What will it be, my boy? Tell me."

Yousif walked up to him. "I'd like to talk to you," he said.

"Sure you would," the father said, motioning to the bartender for a drink. "We're all friends, are we not? Your father is a fine man, let me tell you. And my wife thinks the world of your mother."

"I'd like to talk to you—alone," Yousif repeated, his voice low and his arms hanging by his side.

"Talk, talk, my boy. But first have a drink. Do you know all these gentlemen?" Then turning to the other men he said, "This is Yousif, the son of Dr. Jamil Safi."

One by one, the men quieted and turned to look at Yousif. Adel Farhat's big grin disappeared as he saw Yousif standing behind him.

The father handed Yousif a shot of cognac but Yousif refused to accept it. The father would have none of it, and pushed it in his hand. Yousif finally gave in and held it, with no intention of drinking.

"Salwa and Adel here are getting engaged," the father said. "You two know each other."

Yousif nodded, trying to ignore Adel's extended hand. Because many men were looking at him, he finally shook it, the finger tips barely touching. Then one of the men raised a toast to the two getting engaged.

All except Yousif held up their glasses.

"Why aren't you drinking?" Adel asked, his voice level and his eyes focused on Yousif.

"I don't drink," Yousif said, returning his stare.

"Not even to congratulate me?"

"I never touch it," Yousif lied.

The two stared at each other like enemies.

"I'd like to talk to you," Yousif said again to Salwa's father.

The older man seemed not to have heard him. "It's going to be a small party," he said, "just the two immediate families. You know what I mean. Otherwise my wife and I would love to invite all of you."

"But right now there are more important things to talk about," Yousif said, his lips twitching.

The father gazed hard at Yousif and saw for the first time the serious look on his face. He took another sip from his glass, brushed his mustache thoughtfully, and followed Yousif out.

They stood on the balcony. The trees looked naked, for all their leaves had fallen on the terraced garden.

"I don't know how to say this," Yousif said, "but Salwa and I are in love. We wish you had taken our feelings into consideration before—"

The father's face turned ashen. "What did you say?" he asked.

This was the real man, Yousif thought, watching the father's pleasantness vanish.

"We wish you had considered your daughter's happiness."

"Don't talk so fast, boy, let me hear you right."

Apparently concerned about being overheard, the father glanced at the hotel's door and windows, then grasped Yousif by the elbow, leading him down the steps. The two walked down the tree-lined pathway and around the dance floor, which divided the garden.

"What were you saying, boy?" the father asked, stopping about fifty yards away from the hotel balcony.

"Salwa and I hoped to get married someday. And now—"

"You and my daughter hoped to do *what?*"

"Get married."

The father stared at him. "How did you meet? Where did you discuss this?"

"Never mind."

"Don't tell *me* never mind," the father glowered, his hazel eyes enlarged. "Have you been jeopardizing my daughter's reputation by telling her about your puppy love?"

"It's not puppy love."

"Have you dared to touch her? Say it, boy. Have you?"

"It's pure, honest, decent love. Don't make it sound dirty."

"It doesn't exist."

"It does."

"Don't you dare mention it."

"What if I do?"

"I'd break your neck. If my daughter was naive enough to give you a second look, that doesn't mean you have a right to upset her life."

"I . . . I . . ."

"Listen to me, boy, and know what's good for you. Clear out of her life, now and forever. She has a chance to marry a good man, and I will not allow you to interfere. It's none of your damn business. She's my daughter and I know what's best for her better than you'll ever know."

"But we love each other."

"Keep going, boy, and don't ever associate that word with my daughter. You hear? A silly remark could mark her for life."

Yousif stood erect, his hands clasped behind his back, the skin of his face and the back of his neck tightened. "I don't want us to be enemies," he said. "I'm here to ask you for your daughter's hand. You will honor me if you'd accept."

The father eyed him as though he were looking at something ridiculous. "Don't make me laugh," he said, pulling a pack of Players out of his pocket.

"Salwa and I wish to have your approval . . . your blessing."

The father's eyes bulged as he tilted his head menacingly. "Don't you dare mention her name," he said, lighting a cigarette. He crushed and threw the empty pack on the ground—without taking his eyes off Yousif.

They heard a voice calling them from the main building. It was Adel Farhat standing on the balcony. "Anything wrong?" he shouted.

"No," the father answered, waving his hand and feigning a smile. "I'll be there in a minute." Then he turned to Yousif, threatening. "Go away, boy. Go on."

"I hope none of us will live to regret this day," Yousif said. "I came to you full of respect and good intentions. I thought it was the honorable thing to—"

"The only honorable thing for you to do," the father commanded, "is to forget that you and Salwa have ever met."

The two men glared at each other, then the father walked away. Yousif stood still, his head high. He watched the spoiler of his dreams turn the corner of the dance floor, and felt the afternoon darken.

FULL OF CONSTERNATION, Yousif approached his parents one more time, begging for intervention. He even dared to turn off the radio a few minutes before the 6:00 o'clock evening news. The whole world could burn; he must have Salwa.

His mother took a deep breath. "Maybe they'll accept a ring for now," she said.

Yousif was delighted. Even this mild consent was enough to lift his spirits. But the doctor shot his wife a look that told her she was insane like her son.

"I'd rather Yousif wait a few more years," she added, "but they've rushed him. So why not—if they'd let us put a ring on her finger for now? After the war we'd plan things together, rationally. Right now we're all so edgy, so tense."

His mother went on wondering, her hand touching her chin. "Maybe they'd settle for a private engagement," she said. "Jamil, what do you think?"

The doctor puffed on his pipe without saying a word. Even his silence was a form of consent; Yousif was thrilled.

"Really, Jamil," his wife said. "We've both seen young men get married."

"Not at seventeen," the doctor objected, spires of aromatic smoke billowing around him.

"I'm almost eighteen," Yousif retorted. "Besides, I didn't say I want to get married tomorrow. I just don't want to lose Salwa. That's all."

Yasmin looked at her son, gently biting her lower lip. She seemed to want him to leave the persuading to her.

"We can't find a girl like Salwa every day," she said, her voice not more than a whisper. "I'd love to have her for a daughter. What do you think, Jamil? Say something."

"You already know what I think," her husband told her, striking another match.

"We could use something to dispel the gloom around this place," she insisted. "If they'd settle for a ring now and a wedding a little later, I'm all for it."

Yousif's hopes soared. He wondered if Fatima's encouragement a few days earlier were ringing in his mother's ears. He wondered if the undeniable appeal of little bare feet running around the house was the clincher. No matter, he thought. Wasn't his father's silence a prelude to consent? Yet, the doctor would not commit himself one way or the other.

Hours later, Yousif went to sleep, convinced that no nightmare could match the horror of reality.

IN THE MORNING, the doctor seemed less rigid. They were at the breakfast table, and Yousif could sense that the mood had changed. He wondered what his parents had said to each other in bed. He would not ask. He would just let them tell him.

"For your sake," the doctor said, addressing his wife, "and for the sake of your stubborn son I guess I'll have a talk with Anton."

"Don't talk to him . . . convince him," Yousif pleaded, his voice catching.

His father cracked a hard-boiled egg on the edge of his plate. "I don't think it'll do any good. Not after the damage you've done."

Yousif swallowed hard. "I'm sorry," he said. "But do your best, Father. Please."

The doctor promised, and began shelling the egg.

"I'll try, too," the mother said, her features slackening. "Around ten o'clock I'll drop by their house for a cup of coffee and see what her mother thinks."

They ate in grave silence that the chirping of the birds next door could not improve.

THAT EVENING both parents gave Yousif a report that was so definite, so final—it was devastating. Salwa would be engaged to Adel Farhat. The wedding would not be till June or July—after she graduated from secondary school. This was a promise her father had already made to Adel and his family—a hammerlock promise accompanied by a handshake.

Yousif sat glassy-eyed, dizzy, drained, his mind blank. They might as well have read him the rejection of his last reprieve. He did not raise a single objection. The floor under his feet seemed to shift like quicksand, and he felt he was sinking . . . sinking. He stuck out his lower lip and brooded, feeling dejected, betrayed. But when he realized that they were waiting for him to react, he licked his wounds, jutted his chin, and braved a smile.

"Did you say the wedding will be in June or July?" he asked, clutching the armrests with both hands.

His mother nodded, visibly holding her tears. "They want to wait till after she finishes school."

It didn't make sense to Yousif. "The war might be over by then," he said. "I thought Adel's family wanted him to get married right away, so he won't want to fight."

Both parents looked equally puzzled. "You're right," the mother said. "It does seem strange. Jamil, what do you think?"

The doctor exhaled. "Who knows," he said. "It's probably a compromise."

There was a long, awkward pause. The doctor wiped his misty glasses, a jet of smoke billowing from his pipe.

"July is a long way off," Yousif said, his voice thickening. "We'll have to wait and see."

The doctor frowned, put his glasses back on, and took the pipe out of his mouth. "I trust you'll not do anything foolish. Wish them luck and get her out of your mind. The world is full of wonderful girls."

"But there's only one Salwa," Yousif answered, his head throbbing with anger and despair. What pressure were they exerting on her?

He staggered out of the room. Then a glimmer of hope—an electric charge—seemed to revive his soul. Could it be, he thought, that Salwa was only stalling? Could she have agreed to an immediate engagement, provided they won't rush her into marriage? Surely Adel's family didn't like the idea of waiting.

Sitting on the edge of his bed and staring at the wall before him, Yousif breathed easier. His imagination sprouted; his chest heaved. All might not be lost. Oh, Salwa! The heavens must have listened to his silent prayers. He hoped against hope that what he was feeling now was true—that his girl was resisting. Just as quickly, though, doubt possessed him. He felt weak-kneed. Could she ultimately stand up to her tyrannical father? Could she make him go back on his ironclad promise? Yousif didn't think so—unless he could help her. Which he must do.

Deep in his heart he vowed that Salwa's wedding to Adel Farhat would never—never—happen. He would stop it, so help him God.

14

Salwa's engagement landed Yousif in a dark pit. He did not think he would ever get his wind back. Salwa mattered to him, and she seemed now like a fragrant rose that had turned suddenly into a prickly cactus.

But other disturbing events interceded. A few days after that fateful Sunday when Salwa's engagement was announced, the town woke up to discover that its Jewish residents had disappeared. Isaac's family were among those who had vanished. At first, rumor had it that they'd met their fate at the hands of some extremists. But later the same day it was learned they'd followed the course adopted by other Arabs and Jews all over Palestine. Those who lived in towns and districts highly populated by the enemy left to seek refuge among their own. They quit their jobs, closed their shops, moved to safer areas, and waited for the storm to blow over. Some left even before they could turn off the lights in their homes or lock the front doors.

In some quarters, the news of the sudden disappearance was met with satisfaction. Several Arab women remembered Raheel, the Jewess who had been married to an Arab for more than eight years. Now she had left him and their three children to join her people. How any mother could forsake her children they could not understand. Were the Jews her people, while her own offspring, her own flesh and blood, were not? Some said good riddance. Those who felt differently were afraid to speak.

For Yousif and Amin, Isaac's disappearance was not only sad, but bewildering.

They had never thought he would leave town without telling them, his best friends, goodbye. Yet, they had faith in his friendship.

A week after the Jews had left, Yousif received a letter from Isaac.

Dear Yousif,

I can't blame you if you felt my behavior was strange and unfriendly. I do hope, however, that you'll give me a chance to explain. The decision to leave came as a complete surprise. Even my parents didn't plan for it. That night a "nice" group of men told all of us Jews in Ardallah that we either leave town before midnight or risk our lives. Father wanted to consult with your father and the mayor but they wouldn't let him. He even asked for permission to let him come by and leave the keys to the house and store with your parents, but again they said no.

Just before midnight a taxi stopped in front of our house. Father and I carried the few suitcases while my mother carried Leah and then went back to get Alex. Yousif, you should have seen Mother trying to be cheerful, telling Leah we were going on a trip . . . a lovely, lovely trip. Tears were glistening in her eyes.

So now we are in Tel Aviv. Barbed wires and sandbags are everywhere. Young men and women are being drafted into the Jewish underground. Families are storing food for the days ahead. People are jittery, and don't know what to expect. Everybody is certain that war will break out, and that it's going to be nothing short of hell.

Write soon, please, and let me know how you are. Give my best regards to Amin and tell him I'll write. Good luck to both of you—and I mean it with all my heart.

Sincerely,

Isaac

The letter was heartening. It made clear that the poisonous atmosphere had not begun to touch the goodness of Isaac's love. On the same day, Yousif sat down and answered:

Dear Isaac,

What a relief it was to hear from you, and to know that you're still alive. Being alive these days isn't to be taken for granted, for the 'incidents' are turning into guerrilla war, and one never knows who'll be the next victim.

I hope all is well with you and your family. Every time I pass your house or your store I stop and wonder whatever happened to you. What I know now saddens me. Please give our best regards to your parents and hug Leah for me. And may you all return to us in good health—soon.

Meanwhile, Isaac, I'm losing my mind. Salwa is engaged to be married to Adel Farhat. Can you believe it? It happened so suddenly, I'm still reeling from the shock. They say the wedding is going to be next June or July—but I pray she'll come to her senses and break it off before then. I don't know what I'm going to do to win her back. But I can tell you this much: a bride to Adel Farhat she will never be.

Sometimes I sit with my parents on our balcony at night and listen to the bombing and shelling in Jerusalem and Jaffa. We lapse into these tight silences . . . and I see on my parents' faces shadows of pity and distress. There's so much hate, so much pain around us.

Jamal asked about you the other day. He has been wondering, poor fellow, why you haven't been to your music lessons. Next time I see him, I'll tell him about your letter.

Write soon and tell us more about life in Tel Aviv. Somehow I expected you to write from Jerusalem. Will you remain in Tel Aviv until after the war? How do you spend your time? Have you enrolled in school? Tell us everything. In the meantime, be assured that Amin and I miss you.

Your friend, always.
Yousif

TWO DAYS LATER, Yousif decided to go to the clinic after school and then return home with his father. Before he could leave the school ground, it began to thunder and rain. The shopkeepers came out to roll down their canopies. All the domino players on the sidewalks folded up their games and rushed inside with their chairs in their hands. By the time Yousif reached the clinic he was drenched. The floor of offices that his father shared with a dentist and an accountant was dark and empty, as if everybody had taken the day off.

Nurse Laila was dusting up for the day. Her hair parted in the middle, she told Yousif that his father had gone next door to Zahrawi's cafe for his afternoon *nergileh.* It was almost five o'clock but they had been very busy, she said, and he couldn't take his break any earlier. She gave him a towel to dry himself as he waited a few minutes for the rain to stop. When it didn't, he went out anyway.

Zahrawi's cafe was packed. Entering it was like entering a new world. The happy sounds were deafening. The customers seemed shielded from troubles. Were these people real? Yousif thought. Why were they so happy, so boisterous, when they were about to be wolfed up by the enemy?

His father was sitting near a huge window overlooking the main street, smoking *nergileh* and playing backgammon with Abu Hamed, the *fellah* whose faded, traditional, ankle-length outfit contrasted sharply with his father's fine gray suit and red striped tie.

Abu Hamed was the man who had planted all of the trees around their house and who had mended stone walls for them for years.

"I came to see about pain in my chest," the beady-eyed Abu Hamed explained to Yousif, "and the good doctor insisted on bringing me to this fancy place."

"Why not?" Yousif said, smiling and laying his hand affectionately on the old man's shoulder.

"He even refused to let me pay," Abu Hamed complained. "Why should he be so nice to me when I have been overcharging him for years? I ought to be ashamed of myself."

The doctor rolled the dice and snapped his fingers, gloating. "You're going to be really ashamed of yourself when you lose this game. Keep talking and I'll beat you for sure."

A waiter arrived with a few pieces of charcoal for their *nergilehs*. Yousif asked for a glass of minted hot tea.

Just then two of Palestine's most famous athletes walked in, unruffled by the rain. Yousif, a soccer fan, recognized them at once. They were an Arab and an Irishman: two of the country's best soccer players and also good friends, although they played on opposing teams. Suhail Shammas was a short bouncy little fellow who had been nicknamed "Rassass" as a tribute to his solid physique, quick movement, and bullet-like deliveries. He played on the Greek Orthodox team in Jaffa. George Pinkley was at least five inches taller. He was the left wing on the Army's team and a marvel to watch for all soccer fans. Whenever George got hold of the ball, his team felt relieved, and the other team surrounded him to no avail. He would hold the ball under his foot for a second and then shoot right between his opponents or zip through them as if they were not there.

Yousif knew that George's popularity among the Arabs was due to more than his athletic prowess. An Irishman with a grudge of his own against the British, George was on the Arabs' side. Rumors had it that he had engaged in fist fights over his government's policy in Palestine. It was no secret that he had often disobeyed his superiors' orders not to mix with the natives. From the smiles and handshakes he saw, Yousif could tell how greatly the people in the cafe admired George. Many offered to buy him and Rassass a drink. George declined, but a bottle of *arak* was placed on his table, compliments of someone at the other end of the room. Giver and receiver waved their hands and smiled.

"I wish it would stop raining," the doctor said, glancing at his watch. "It's almost five-thirty, Yousif. You'd better call up your mother and tell her where we are, don't you think?"

Yousif went up to the cafe's proprietor, Nicola Zahrawi, and asked him to use the house phone. His mother was glad for the delay, she said, and they could take their time coming home. She hadn't had time to prepare supper on account of some unexpected afternoon visitors. That suited Yousif just fine. He hung up and went to the restroom.

Returning to his seat, Yousif was astonished by how much liquor the two soccer players had already consumed. *Arak* was potent.

"I want you to know," he heard George saying to his friend, his glass held in front of his pinkish face, "you're just about the best camel rider I've ever seen. And I've seen more of you people than I care to admit."

Yousif smiled. Then he looked around, hoping that no one else had heard it. Some people, he feared, had no sense of humor.

"You're not bad yourself," Rassass retorted, pouring more *arak* in George's glass.

"Well, here's 'Down with the Arabs,'" George toasted, his tongue heavy.

"And here's 'To hell with the British,'" Rassass responded, holding his glass and touching his friend's glass.

George and Rassass laughed as two drunks, two friends. Yousif was happy for them. He wished all Arabs and Englishmen were as friendly as these two. Here were two men who were basically alike, he said to himself, regardless of their background or the color of their hair. He sat in his chair and continued to watch with interest.

"And I also want you to know," George continued, "that even though we gave away your country to the Jews, and expect a damn lot of you to be killed before it's all over, I hope when you get shot you'd find enough goodness in your heart to think of me as your friend."

Rassass grinned. "And when we chase Britain out of the whole Arab world, and by God we will," he said, raising a toast, "I pray you may think of me as your bosom pal."

They laughed again and clanked their glasses. All the while, the cafe was filling up with civilians and soldiers. The doctor and Abu Hamed finished the game, shut the game-box, and puffed on their *nergilehs.*

"We'll leave as soon as I finish this smoke," the doctor said to Yousif.

The soccer players began singing an Irish song with which Yousif was familiar and which of late had become popular among some Arabs. They sang:

> The British came and tried to teach us their ways,
> And mocked us just for being what we are.
> But they might as well go chasing after moonbeams
> Or light a penny candle from a star.

Then Rassass stopped singing, an angry look in his eyes. Yousif noticed the abrupt change in his facial expression. Sitting on the other side of the two soccer players was a British soldier, also drunk. In front of him stood a little frail Arab shoeshine boy, clothed in torn rags. Apparently the boy was shivering for reasons other than lack of heat inside the cafe.

"Not enough, Mister," the shoeshine boy was saying, his palm open.

"Fuck off," growled the lanky, blond, drunk soldier.

"Shoes, two piasters. Boots, three piasters. Please, Mister, one more piaster. Please, Mister, one more piaster."

"Fuck off," repeated the soldier gruffly, kicking the boy's bottom.

Rassass rose from his chair, throwing back George's arm, which had been stretched out to restrain him. He staggered toward the soldier.

"Give that boy his piaster," Rassass demanded, "and quit telling him to fuck off."

"Fuck off yourself," the soldier said, his eyes half shut.

"Stop saying that word, you bastard, or I'll kill you," Rassass threatened.

George stood between the two, sober like a judge. "Don't get hot," he told his pal.

"George, leave us alone," Rassass replied.

"Do it for me, please," George entreated. "Don't start anything."

"Then tell him to stop saying that word, and make him pay the piaster."

"I'll pay the piaster," George said, digging in his pocket.

"No, *he's* going to," Rassass insisted.

George leaned forward and tried to get the soldier to pay the piaster, but was told to fuck off. He tried again and got the same answer. He lost his patience and slapped his fellow soldier, then watched him rub his burning cheek and grin stupidly.

Nicola Zahrawi, the enormous, slightly deaf owner of the cafe, came to the scene and tried to cool things off with smiles and pats on the shoulder. But Rassass shoved him aside and told him he was going to handle this.

"You want to do what?" Zahrawi asked again, cupping his ear.

"I said I'm going to handle this," Rassass shouted.

The doctor circled the tube around his *nergileh,* hooked it in place, stepped forward and tried to mediate. But Rassass would not listen. He wouldn't sit down, he said, unless the soldier paid the piaster. It wasn't the piaster, he explained; it was the principle.

"You can see he's drunk," the doctor said.

"If he can ask for a shoeshine, he can pay for it."

Yousif took out a shilling and gave it to the boy. "Run along now," he told him.

The boy took the money quickly. He bowed several times, lifted the shoeshine box off the floor, and strapped it to his shoulder.

"You shouldn't have," Rassass told Yousif, glaring at him.

"That's all right," Yousif said.

"It's not all right."

"That soldier doesn't know what he's doing," Yousif answered. "There's no sense keeping a ten-year-old waiting."

The crowd pushed, each one trying to disperse the other.

But Rassass resisted. "If the boy is too young to get what's his, I'll get it for him," he muttered. He grabbed the soldier's collar, pulling at it. "Give me that piaster, you lousy cheat," he said, his teeth clenched.

The drunk soldier nonchalantly pushed his hand away. He finished drinking his beer, banged his glass on the table, and stood up to meet the challenge. He was shaky and could barely stand.

"I guess I'll have to lock you up for speaking like this to a British soldier in His Majesty's Army," he said, grinning broadly and trying to smooth his wrinkled khaki shirt.

Someone must have alerted the military police, for at that moment two came rushing into the bar. Their dramatic entrance created more excitement and caused a crowd to grow.

"Push off before I get mad," the drunk soldier demanded.

"You're drunk," said the first M.P.

"You're disturbing the peace," said the second.

The drunk soldier shook his head and curled his lower lip. "And he insulted me—a British soldier—and threatened my life," he said, now less afraid.

"Well, I beg your pardon, your honor," said Rassass, bowing and mimicking the soldier's accent and pomposity, then slugging him in the stomach.

The M.P.s rushed and hand-cuffed Rassass.

"Why don't you arrest *him?"* someone in the crowd shouted, pointing at the drunk. "He's guilty too."

"None of your business," an M.P. told him.

"You're damn right it's our business," answered another Arab.

The M.P.s whistled; one man hurled a bottle at them, hitting one between the shoulder blades; men gasped; waiters dropped trays on the floor; an old man stood on a chair and hit the drunk soldier with his cane. George Pinkley argued with his fellow soldiers and they handcuffed him, too. The drunk was now fully awake. He hurled a chair from the middle of the room. Yousif ducked as it flew by his head. He couldn't see where it landed, but he could hear a window crashing.

"This is crazy," Yousif shouted.

Abu Hamed was now without his headdress, swinging the black *iqal* as a whip. The doctor was trying to restrain him, but Abu Hamed was like the rest—beside himself.

As the police poured in, Yousif stood on a table, waving his hand for everyone to quiet down. "Stop it . . . stop it," he begged.

But one of the arrivals must have misunderstood his motive and clubbed him on the legs, knocking him to his knees. His father reached out for him but was squashed by the pressing crowd.

"Blood . . . blood," cried one Arab, pointing at the drunk soldier who had caused the outbreak. Yousif saw the soldier dropping to the floor.

"They stabbed him," cried an M.P.

"The dogs!"

"The bloody bastards."

The word "blood" frightened many inside the cafe. Some began to run for the door. His legs still in pain, Yousif could see the entrance was now jammed with the police trying to get in and customers trying to get out. His father's glasses had been knocked off his face. He had picked them up and was looking now at the crushed lenses.

"Lock all doors," one M.P. commanded, pushing the people away from the fallen soldier.

A large circle of the military was instantly formed. Crouching on the table, Yousif could see the drunken soldier lying on the floor in the middle, bleeding profusely. But who did it? No matter, the man was dying and people were fleeing. The stampede at the entrance became worse. One man busted the rest of the glass out of the window pane and made an exit through the jagged edges. Others rushed behind him.

"Make way for the doctor," Yousif shouted, motioning toward his father.

The crowd parted and his father was allowed to pass through. Yousif watched him kneel and inspect the victim. He turned him on his back, and more blood oozed out of him. Yousif was surprised to see so much blood come out of one human being.

The cafe grew quiet. The doctor took the man's pulse and then reached for the stethoscope in his pocket. Yousif could tell his father was alarmed.

The doctor slowly rose to his feet, looking strange without his glasses. The crowd waited for his opinion.

"Allah yirhamu," the doctor said, his hands smeared with blood. "May God have mercy on his soul."

The crowd was aghast. Then the stillness was broken. People began to move. The soldiers began to swing at everyone in the room. Yousif jumped off the table and hovered around his father. Abu Hamed picked up an empty bottle and vowed to break it over a soldier's head. The senior M.P. blew his whistle again.

"Block all exits," the M.P. ordered his troops.

Soldiers made their way to the door and the broken window. Both Rassass and George Pinkley looked angry, their arms handcuffed behind their backs.

Gun in hand, a policeman stood by the corpse. "No one leaves until we identify the killer," he shouted, his blue eyes clear as crystal. "Anyone who has a weapon must step forward and drop it in front of me. Everyone must be searched. We will fire at anyone who makes the slightest disturbance."

The customers began to whisper and to exchange glances. When a secondary school teacher tried to move, an M.P. fired a warning shot. The bullet ricocheted off the whitewashed ceiling and nicked someone's head. Everyone froze in place. But no one came forth with any weapons.

"O.K." the M.P. said. "Everyone must be frisked. Raise your hands above your heads. We'll start with you."

The doctor was shocked. "With me? You think I killed that man?"

"It makes no difference. Everyone must be frisked. You're no exception."

Reluctantly, the doctor stepped forward.

"Hands above the head," the M.P. commanded.

Yousif jumped off the table. Instantly he knew he had made a mistake. By reflex a nervous soldier fired another bullet blasting another window pane. Shattered glass flew everywhere. Men raised their arms for protection. Yousif stood still, his mouth gaping.

The search continued for over an hour. But no trace of the knife could be found. Frantic, the soldiers threatened to haul everyone off in their wagons.

"Send these bloody two to jail," the M.P. with the angry blue eyes told his colleagues, pointing to Rassass and George. "The rest will be kept here until one of them produces the murder weapon."

Quickly, the handcuffed prisoners were hustled out. Several hours after the dead soldier had been removed on a stretcher, everyone else was still there. No food or drinks were allowed. No one could smoke or sit down. No one could call his family or lawyer. Yousif looked at his father and wished they would at least let him go home. But there was no sense asking. Even his wish to be near his father was summarily denied. The prohibition of smoking, however, was what frayed the nerves of most detainees.

"I've got to have a cigarette," hollered a middle-aged man with a bulging stomach. He looked ready to kill.

A billy club fell on the man's shoulder, and he screamed.

A soldier interrogated them one by one in the proprietor's small office till about midnight, demanding that the killer be identified. As the interrogation dragged on, it was obvious to Yousif that the police were getting no satisfaction. It pleased him to see the solidarity of his people. If they were to succeed against the outsider, he thought, they had better stay united.

He was next in line. He waited impatiently, for he was exhausted and at the same time anxious to know what went on behind the closed door.

Moments later he was in. The interrogating officer had a long face and long teeth. He was about ten years older than Yousif and Yousif could see meanness in his eyes. He had always heard that people with close eyes were either dim-witted or mean. This man filled the bill on both counts.

Two or three minutes passed before the soldier gave him permission to sit down.

"Haven't you ever seen a damn chair before?" the officer barked when he finally looked up. "Or are you stupid like the rest of them."

"I was afraid you might object . . ." Yousif muttered.

"The only thing I object to is living on the same planet with trash like you."

"This is uncalled for."

"Shut your mouth and—"

"I tried to stop the fight."

"Answer the questions and don't waste my time. What's your name?"

"Yousif Safi."

"What kind of a name is that?"

The man's incivility hardened Yousif's resolve.

"Yousif is a biblical name," he explained, feigning humility. "In your language you call him Joseph. He's the one sold by his seven brothers."

The officer stopped writing and looked at him, his eyebrows raised. "How funny!"

"And Safi is an Arabic word which means pure."

"Pure as shit no doubt. How in hell do you spell it?"

"S-H-I-T."

"I meant your bloody name."

Yousif spelled it out for him. Over the next five minutes Yousif told him who his parents were, where he lived, where he went to school, who were his friends, why he came to this cafe, how often did he come, and with whom.

"Who killed the officer?"

"I don't have the slightest idea," Yousif answered.

"You're a liar. Tell us now and spare yourself a lot of agony."

"I'm telling you the truth, I don't know."

"If you knew, would you tell us?"

"Oh, sure," Yousif lied.

The officer lit a cigarette and blew the smoke in Yousif's face. "You know that I know that you're a lying bastard."

Yousif crossed his legs and remained silent.

"Who do you think might have done it? Or let me put it this way: of all the people, who was the most likely to pull out a knife and use it?"

"What do you mean 'use it'?"

"Stab with it. Kill with it. As one of you bastards did this afternoon."

"There were a lot of people I didn't know. People I've never heard of or seen before."

Again, the soldier pulled on his cigarette. Again he blew the smoke in Yousif's face. "Of the ones you've known or heard of or seen, which one has the killer's instinct."

"I'll have to think about it," Yousif said, pretending to be serious. "You see, Officer, I've known and I've heard of and I've seen a lot of people in my life. I'd have to go over a long list and check them all out, one by one."

The man jumped to his feet and grabbed Yousif by the collar. "I meant of all the people who were here *this* fucking afternoon—at *this* fucking cafe."

"I'm sorry, I misunderstood you. I thought you meant . . ."

The officer glared at him. "Get your fucking ass out of here before I kill you," he said, pointing his finger toward the door.

Yousif stepped out of the room, relieved. But when he saw his father leaning against the wall, his knees buckling, he became angry again. Another group of soldiers arrived. One of them was a first lieutenant he had seen with Captain Malloy the day the roof on their house was raised. Yousif looked at his father, as if to say here's hope. But the lieutenant looked grim and ignored everyone.

"We're going to let you go home," he said, walking between the tables in the middle of the room.

The crowd sighed in unison. Yousif saw his father straighten his aching back and take another breath. Abu Hamed, next to him, adjusted his headdress.

"Thirty minutes from now," the lieutenant continued, hitting his pants legs with his billy club, "strict curfew will be imposed all over Ardallah. Once you get inside your homes, stay there till tomorrow morning. At six o'clock, everyone in town will go to the nearest church or mosque or to Cinema Firyal. Every home and dwelling place must be vacated. There will be no exceptions."

It did not require a college degree, Yousif thought, to realize that they were going to turn Ardallah upside down in search of weapons, or that they were going to harass the citizenry until the killer was apprehended. But would they be able to put ten thousand people in one mosque, eight small churches, and a theater auditorium? Most of all, what would they do if the killer were never found?

"You *must* be at one of the designated places not later than seven o'clock," the lieutenant said.

"Does that include women and children?" Yousif asked, mainly for the benefit of those who might not have understood him properly.

"I said everyone—men, women and children," the lieutenant reiterated, "including pregnant women and the sick who are on their death beds. Understand? And be sure to leave all doors unlocked. I repeat: leave all doors unlocked: closets, cupboards, drawers. Everything. Maybe that will teach you not to hide criminals."

They left the cafe like a herd of sheep, guns pointed at their heads. In the streets, military jeeps were circulating throughout the neighborhoods, booming on loudspeakers the lieutenant's message.

"Should you fail to unlock your doors," a soldier's voice warned in the dark, "you can be sure the lock will be busted. To avoid damage to your property, do as you're told: leave everything open. Repeat: leave everything open."

Enveloped in darkness, walking home by his father's side, Yousif had an inkling of the powerful troubles yet to come.

15

Early next morning, people headed toward the "prisons." Mothers and fathers carried or dragged their sleepy children. British soldiers pushed and ordered them to move on. Yousif and his parents were no exception.

"Get going," a soldier said to Yousif's mother.

"You don't have to push," the doctor said to the officer. "We're walking as fast as we can."

"Shut up and keep moving," the soldier ordered, jabbing his ribs with the butt of his gun.

"There are children," the doctor complained. "They can't walk faster. The parents' arms are loaded, can't you see? If you're in such a hurry, why don't you provide some transportation?"

"That's your problem. We didn't tell you to have so many pigs."

Then the doctor became incensed. "Don't call our children pigs," he demanded.

The soldier turned angry. He smashed down the butt of his gun on the doctor's shoulders so brutally that Yousif was afraid he might have broken his bones. Had it not been for so many people jammed against each other, his father would have fallen to the ground. The doctor closed his eyes, bit his lower lip, and leaned against his wife.

Yousif clenched his fist. "How dare you!" he shouted at the soldier.

Another soldier, sitting in a jeep barely crawling amidst thousands of marchers, slapped Yousif twice, once on each cheek. Yousif's face turned red as he looked around for help.

Some of the marchers exchanged furtive looks. Then, as if on cue, several husky men lifted up the jeep about a foot off the ground. Quickly, a dozen billy clubs fell on their heads and backs from all directions. One soldier fired a round of bullets in the air. The marchers panicked, and the men finally dropped the jeep to the ground.

The officer in the jeep stood and faced the crowd. "Next time we won't use billy clubs. We'll bring tanks and crush you like bloody cockroaches. March on and keep your eyes to the ground."

The crowd grumbled. One man refused to be silenced.

"Why don't you lock up the Zionists?" he shouted. "They hanged three of your fellow soldiers in Nethania."

The soldier pointed his gun at the crowd. "Who said that?"

No one answered. The crowd resumed walking.

Even children, Yousif noticed, were gripped by fear. Their faces were pale; their quiet unusual.

"What did he say, Mama?" a little boy asked his mother who was carrying him on her shoulder. "What did he say?"

"He said," his mother answered, "when a foreign nation occupies your country, kick and fight and never stop. Because when you do, then it's time to lie down and die."

"We're not going to die, are we? Are we, Mama?"

"No son. We're just going to practice living in hell."

Yousif felt his spine tingle. The rest of the crowd mumbled, groaned, and muttered their grievances.

THE ROMAN Catholic Church in which Yousif and his family were imprisoned was by far the largest in town. It had a seating capacity of about three hundred, but was so overcrowded today that Yousif estimated two thousand must have been packed inside it.

"Do they think we are sardines?" Yousif asked.

"Shhh," his mother admonished him.

"The hell with quiet," Yousif said, sitting in the middle of an aisle.

Yousif searched about for Salwa but could not find her. People sat everywhere: on the choir balcony, around the altar, in the pews, on each other's laps, wherever they could squeeze themselves. Some seemed to enjoy the warmth of cuddling and nestling so close together on a cold winter day in a church without a heating system. But soon it became suffocating. The church was as foul smelling as a barn.

"Why couldn't they search our homes when we're there?" Yasmin asked her husband. "No one would've stopped them. Not when they have these awful guns pointed at us."

"We'd be too comfortable," the doctor said, feeling his bruised left shoulder.

"Remember what the officer said?" Yousif reminded her. "We're here to pay for the death of that policeman."

The doctor exhaled. "Just pray they don't hang that fellow Rassass. The only thing that might save him is that an Englishman was arrested, too. If they hang one they'd feel obliged to hang the other. So Rassass might be safe after all."

"Don't bet on it," Yousif said. "Most likely they'd hang the Arab and let their own go free."

A baby began to cry. The baby's mother held him close, covered herself with her orange shawl, and took out her breast to feed him.

Yousif looked around the church with some nostalgia. This was his church, the one with which his school was affiliated. Here he had spent every Sunday and religious holiday, not only kneeling and praying, but singing in the choir or serving as an altar boy.

"I can still hear Father Saliba," Yousif said to his parents, "standing in that corner telling us about the meaning of Communion—how to open our hearts and accept Christ."

"If Father Saliba were alive," his mother said, "he'd have a heart attack to see his church today."

"I remember this church differently," the doctor said, taking out his pipe and looking around to see if others were smoking. They were, so he opened his pouch to fill it.

"You're not going to smoke, are you?" Yousif asked, shocked.

"God will forgive me," his father said.

"I don't think you should," his wife admonished.

"I need something for my nerves," her husband insisted. "As I was saying, back in World War I, the Turks used this place as a hospital. Their casualties were mounting, so they demanded from us mattresses, pillows, and blankets. But who had such things to spare? One was lucky to have a couple of mattresses for a whole family of six. People were poor. But what could we do? When the occupying power says do something, you do it. A week later, a British plane circled above this church, suspecting that it was being used for other purposes and dropped a couple of bombs. They went through the roof and blew the whole thing up—wounded and all."

"Are you serious?" Yousif asked, fascinated. "I've never heard that."

"The whole thing," the doctor repeated, opening his right hand and blowing at his palm to show how the church-hospital had gone up in smoke.

"Oh," his mother remembered. "I had forgotten about that."

"They rebuilt it in 1922," the doctor continued, striking a match and applying it to his pipe.

Yousif had to find Salwa. He had not seen her since the announcement of her engagement. He wondered what his reaction would be should they come face-to-face. Should he speak to her, ignore her, or tell her off? Could he find out why the wedding was postponed till next July? A suspicion lingered in his mind that she was stalling. He needed to know the truth so he could plan his next move. Would he ever see her—alone? He stood up and looked around. Too many people were standing and the church was packed.

Finally he spotted her by the right side door, not too far from the organ. She must have seen him first, for she was up on her feet looking at him. Taller than anyone around her, she scanned the scene and fiddled with her earrings. Yousif felt she was nervous . . . eager . . . anxious to know how he felt. She stood with her parents and a few relatives, including her barrel-chested cousin Shafiq who braved the January weather in a short-sleeved white shirt. Luckily, Adel Farhat was not at her side.

Yousif felt a lump in his throat. God, how much he loved her! He glared at her, trying desperately to stop his hand from waving. Seconds later she smiled like an aggrieved Madonna. But before her smile faded, her father must have grown suspicious, for he turned around and ordered her to sit down. Yousif watched her obey in quiet resignation.

Father Mikhail was holding Mass. To keep his mind off Salwa, Yousif watched worshipers make the sign of the cross and close their eyes piously. But the temptation to have a better look at her was too strong for him to stay still. A marble column was obstructing his line of vision. He rose to find a more suitable spot.

By chance Yousif was sitting in the back, near the main door. Salwa was sitting in the middle, on the other side of the aisle. To see her better, he'd have to walk down the middle aisle, go past her, and join someone as a pretext. Then he could turn around and look at her all he wanted—her father be damned.

Salwa was now talking to her mother, her back to him, having shifted in her seat in deference to her father. The pews and aisles were so crowded that Yousif had to be careful as he made his way across the church not to step on those squatting on the floor. He brushed against a man's cigarette and knocked off its ashes. He looked behind him to make sure he hadn't burned a hole in his pants. Before he reached the aisle that crossed the church from right to left, he was no more than ten feet from her and her family. He felt the back of his neck tighten as he was determined to look straight at her—in explicit defiance of her father.

"Yousif," a young voice shouted from her side of the aisle.

Yousif turned around, surprised. It was Akram, her twelve-year old brother.

"Hi," Yousif said, making sure that Salwa saw him.

"I did well in school," Akram told him, beaming. "The teachers can't believe the change in me. I didn't tell them you were my tutor."

"You're a good student," Yousif said, smiling. "Keep it up."

"My report card was just as good," ten-year-old Zuhair volunteered.

"I'm not surprised," Yousif said. "I'm proud of both of you."

Salwa fidgeted, her face crimson. Her father's eyebrows were knit. Salwa's mother was deliciously uncomfortable: glad to see him, but definitely aware of her husband's restraining look.

"How are you enjoying this ordeal?" Yousif asked, eyeing them one by one, including cousin Shafiq, who looked too dim-witted to be a relative of theirs.

All eyes were on Yousif—except Salwa's. She looked at her hands, her neck bent, reminding him of paintings of the Virgin Mary at the foot of the Cross.

"Can't say we're enjoying it," her mother said, exploring his eyes for a hint of how badly he had been hurt. "Where are your parents?"

"Over there," Yousif answered, pointing his finger.

"Well, how are they taking all this?" Salwa's mother asked.

Yousif hesitated, hoping Salwa would look up.

"As well as can be expected," Yousif answered. "With all this going on, who knows what will happen next. The best-laid plans can turn topsy-turvy."

His veiled threat did not escape the father, whose face turned pale and eyelids appeared to stretch. Yousif's ears seemed to filter out all the hubbub around him. It seemed as if he and Salwa and her parents were alone in the room. The rest of the church began to look unreal, almost a vacuum. During the long pause, Salwa looked up—her eyes sending shivers down Yousif's spine. She looked disturbed.

Then Yousif moved on, unable to speak further. What words, what poetry, he thought, could express the hopes, the pain, the hungering that were mounting dizzily in his heart and mind.

Near the vestry, he came upon Dr. Fareed Afifi and his wife, Jihan, her hair tied back in a bun. With them were Uncle Boulus and Aunt Hilaneh, both looking dour. Next to them were their neighbors: the massive barber with the handlebar mustache and his snuff-snorting wife who cackled like a hen. Yousif had a strong feeling Jihan was bored stiff with her company.

"Aunt Jihan," he said, standing behind her.

Jihan was startled, then delighted. "Yousif, can you believe this? We're all prisoners. Fareed, look who's here."

"Well, hello," Dr. Fareed said, extending his hand.

Yousif shook hands all around. Aunt Hilaneh motioned for him to bend down and give her a kiss. Jihan's eyes were moist and her lids red, apparently from crying. But the tension had also made her giggly. Uncle Boulus went on clicking his *masbaha*, faster and louder than ever.

The barber's wife, whom he called Aunt Imm Marshood, took out her snuff box and asked about his parents.

"They're over there," he pointed with his finger, casting an eye in Salwa's direction. They were on opposite sides of the aisle, but at least they could still see each other. Her father was huddling with Shafiq.

"I heard about your bravery last night," Dr. Afifi told Yousif.

"How?" Jihan asked, curious. "What did he do?"

"He tried to stop the fight at Zahrawi's cafe," her husband explained, "and all he got for it was a bang on the leg."

"It still hurts too," Yousif said, hiking his pants leg to show them the bruise.

"Aaaah!" Jihan exclaimed.

"You should've heard the interrogating officer," he told them.

"What did he say?" Jihan asked.

"He was an idiot," Yousif replied, watching Salwa watching him. "But what's the use. Here we are like sheep obeying their commands."

"It burns me up to know they're getting away with it," Jihan said, looking at the soldiers with contempt.

"Astonishing," Yousif said.

They seemed to run out of anything to say. Yousif took the opportunity to watch the speaker at the pulpit and steal another look at Salwa. To his surprise her big almond-shaped eyes were darting from him to her father, then back to him.

To break the silence, Yousif told them about the church having been bombed to the ground during World War I. Painful memories seemed to catapult the older men and women to three decades earlier.

"I remember something else," Dr. Afifi said, lighting a cigarette. "One winter, the Turkish soldiers tore down our wooden doors and window frames and burned them in the middle of our floors to make fire."

"Fire?" Jihan asked, surprised.

"Yes, to warm themselves," her husband continued. "In the middle of our floors. There were no chimneys, and no ventilation of any kind. The smoke filled the rooms. The walls and the ceilings were covered with soot. It was heartless. They burned the wood but kept the hinges and bolts."

"What for?" Yousif asked, keeping an eye on Salwa.

"Iron was scarce then, and they could sell it," Dr. Afifi explained, putting the burned-out match in the cuff of his pants. "They even tried to sell it back to us. Imagine!"

Yousif shifted on his feet again, but his posture was getting awkward. Even at a distance, Salwa seemed delighted by his discomfort. To please her further, he sat on the floor.

"The Mutran house," Dr. Afifi continued, "the one on top of the hill—not too far from your house, Yousif—was used as a school. It was one of the biggest homes in town at that time. Six spacious rooms and a magnificent corridor that could hold a hundred people. You can still see where the Turks had their fire. In the middle of that beautiful marble floor there's a black spot this big," he said, motioning with both arms to indicate the enormous circle.

"That's what happens when your country is occupied," said Yousif.

Yousif walked off, uncertain. Jihan must've noticed him staring in Salwa's direction. Perhaps it was foolish of him to show his emotions so openly. And Salwa herself was a puzzle. How should he read the way she looked at him? She seemed ambivalent about her father. Was she regretting what she had done? Was she miserable because the unwanted engagement had taken place, or because he had failed to prevent it? He was worried that she perhaps thought less of him now.

But she wasn't married yet, he told himself. There was still time to salvage the situation—to rescue both of them from a lifetime of disappointment. Could she help him out? Could he count on her to break off the engagement?

He waved a general goodbye to Jihan and the rest, and exchanged one more glance with Salwa.

BY MID-MORNING, the church was like a carnival. People were eating, laughing, coughing, and, Yousif was willing to wager, farting. Babies cried, and men smoked while the priest delivered a homily.

Sitting in the aisle next to Yousif and his parents were a woman and her five-year-old boy. Suddenly the boy got up and threw his arms around his mother's neck. He whispered in her ear something that must have been shocking, for the expression on her face was mock horror.

"Now?" she asked, her eyes widening.

"Yes, Mama. I've got to . . ."

"Oh, dear . . . oh, dear," said the mother, then turned around and told the others. "Hold your stomach," his mother told him. "Control yourself."

"I can't, Mama. My stomach hurts."

"Yes, you can," his mother snapped, looking agitated.

A soldier appeared and she waved for him, indicating that she had something important to ask him. The soldier ignored her. A minute later, another soldier passed by.

"Mister," the mother pleaded, "my son is ill. Please let me take him out. Please, mister."

"Everybody's son is ill," the soldier replied and walked away.

Yousif saw the pitiful look in the boy's eyes, and felt sorry for his mother, who was on the verge of tears.

"This is an emergency," Yousif pleaded with the soldier. "Let her take him out."

"Sit down," the soldier ordered him.

"Common decency . . ."

"I said sit down," the soldier insisted, raising the butt of his rifle.

Yousif felt his mother's hand pulling him down, and heard her remind him how they had hit his father.

"Where is your friend Captain Malloy?" Yousif asked. "Only a month ago he came to wish us Merry Christmas."

His father faltered. "He may be out of town."

"May he rot in hell," Yousif said.

The little boy began to cry. A few seconds later nature had its way. Yousif saw fingers go up to tighten noses. Some laughed, some frowned. The boy's tears began to fall. He didn't seem to like being the center of attention.

"Did someone break a bottle of perfume?" an old lady jested, holding her nose and laughing.

To Yousif's amazement, Father Mikhail was still preaching. He was speaking of Heaven and Hell. His words sounded hollow.

"Stop the singsong, Father," one man shouted.

"Don't waste your breath," a second interrupted.

When the priest finished his sermon, a young man went up to the pulpit and began to recite a long, stirring political poem. Yousif knew him as a good student, but hadn't realized that he was a poet. Yousif listened carefully. The words were melodious, the imagery provocative. People applauded several times and asked the poet to repeat a certain line. He obliged with a flourish.

"What do you think?" Yousif asked his father.

The doctor looked grim. "It will not defeat the Zionists," he answered.

"But is he another Al-Ma'arri?"

The doctor raised his brows.

Soon another speaker was addressing the crowd. This one was a young attorney who had not been in practice for more than five months.

"When our capitals—Cairo, Damascus, and Baghdad—were the centers of knowledge and enlightenment," the wiry speaker shouted, "the kings of Europe couldn't read or write. When Europe was in the Dark Ages, our libraries contained millions of volumes and our scientists were making gigantic strides in all branches of science. When our people were taking luxurious baths, Oxford University considered such customs dangerous."

The speaker had the audience in his palm. He was followed by ustaz Hakim.

Yousif nudged his father. "He's good," he said.

The short bouncy teacher clutched the pulpit with both hands. "All my life," Hakim said, "I've been hearing too much talk, too much poetry, too much oration. I'm sick of it."

Yousif led the applause. Hundreds of people joined.

"How long," ustaz Hakim asked, "will all the poetry you've read and heard last in the face of the enemy's guns?"

As usual, Yousif found ustaz Hakim articulate, sincere, and less sentimental than the poet who'd painted the same rosy picture other poets had painted a thousand times before—and less infatuated with a past that was a thousand years old. Ustaz Hakim was a man of his time—with both feet on the ground. The crowd seemed to listen with respect.

"Why should the British," ustaz Hakim demanded, "imprison an entire Arab town and search its every corner for a pocketknife when at the same time they are allowing the Zionists to train a whole army right here under our noses? Is this fair?"

"No," the crowd responded.

"Why don't they do something to the Zionists who hanged three of their policemen in Nathania only last week?"

"Yes," the crowd shouted.

"These soldiers with guns in their hands must learn that no matter what they say or do we will defend our land, our homes, and our freedom. And we will not rest until Suhail Shammas—our own Rassass—and his friend George Pinkley are released from jail, the jail they went to because they dared to ask a soldier to pay the piaster he owed for a shoeshine."

Before ustaz Hakim could go any further, two British soldiers pointed their guns at him and ordered him to step down. The crowd tensed. Soon the whole church was quiet. Ustaz Hakim seemed at a loss. Two soldiers stepped closer to him, motioning for him to step down. The teacher didn't budge. One of the soldiers cocked his gun. Yousif waited. So did the whole crowd.

"Long live Palestine," someone shouted, as ustaz Hakim stepped down from the pulpit.

Others echoed the cry.

A third man began singing "Mowtini," one of Yousif's favorite patriotic songs. Hundreds joined in. Faces were red and taut, eyes exhilarated, voices strong and compelling. Yousif joined the singing.

> We, young men, will never get tired,
> Our concern is to be either independent or annihilated.
> We would rather drink death,
> Than be slaves to our enemy.

A shot rang out above the voices. Then another. Yousif looked around to see who was firing. It was a soldier standing by the organ. The soldier cocked his gun again, but the crowd kept on singing. He fired a third shot, shattering a statue of the Virgin Mary into a thousand pieces. Still no one listened.

All the soldiers in the church scurried around, unslinging their rifles and pointing them at the people near the front door. Yousif did not know what that meant. Others looked confused. The women hid their faces, begging the soldiers to turn their guns away.

"Out, I said," the soldier commanded, motioning with his gun.

Reluctantly, people began to exit. Yousif and his parents were among the first to breathe the fresh air. Several soldiers were already waiting to search them. The ninth or tenth to be searched was a woman named Miriam, whom Yousif did not know personally but had seen many times. She was in her late thirties, with silky black hair and marble-like neck. She crossed her arms against her chest as a tall thin soldier tried to search her. Her husband, whose wavy hair was parted in the middle, pulled her back.

"Don't you dare," the husband said to the soldier.

"All women are going to be searched," the soldier told him.

"Not by you," the husband insisted.

Another soldier walked up. His name was Swindle and he was known around town for his cruelty. There were many stories about him, all bad. It seemed he had a roving eye—for boys rather than girls. Consequently he had been beaten up by many fathers and transferred a number of times. The stigma followed him wherever he went.

"What's going on?" officer Swindle asked.

Before the first soldier could answer, the husband interrupted. "Who's going to search the women?"

"These soldiers," Swindle replied.

"No they're not."

"Don't be so brave," the officer threatened him.

The husband wrapped his arm around his wife. "If they must be searched, then bring women to do the job. No man is going to touch them."

Yousif admired the husband. So did all those around. The two men stood up to each other, eyeball to eyeball. But Miriam seemed frightened. She was pulling at her husband's hand to restrain him.

"Lock him up," officer Swindle said, flashing a contemptuous smile before walking away.

Instantly, two soldiers complied with the order. A third one tried to frisk Miriam. He put his hand on her chest and tried to explore her bosom. But she slapped him so hard he staggered and almost fell. But the soldier was determined. He tried to frisk her again. This time she buried her face in her hands, protecting her bosom with her elbows. She wailed so loudly that people began pushing their way out of the church to see what was happening.

The commotion seemed to displease the soldiers. They began to push away those who pressed around. The soldier tried to search Miriam again, though the imprint of her fingers was still on his face. But before he reached her, her husband grabbed him by the collar. Another Arab came to the husband's aid and tried with both hands to yank the gun from the soldier.

Yousif could not believe that unarmed men could be so brave. The threat to the soldier brought back officer Swindle. With two quick cracks of his whip, he made the husband and his friend let go of the collar and the gun. Then Swindle hit the husband again on the side of his face and neck. But suddenly, in a flash of black fury the likes of which Yousif had never seen in his life, the hundred or so Arabs around pounced on the six soldiers in sight, until Yousif could only see a big pile of entangled bodies. Yousif was certain that the soldiers underneath would be buried alive.

"Stop, stop," Yousif screamed, trying to hold back another man from jumping on top of the others.

The doctor was worried. "They've gone berserk," he said.

Father and son began to untangle the pile of flesh. Even the women got involved. Yousif could hear some of them urge the men on as they tried to tear the soldiers limb from limb.

"If they kill one more soldier, may God help us," Yasmin said.

"Enough, please, enough!" Miriam cried.

Other soldiers rushed out of the church. One blew a whistle. Another fired several shots in the air. A minute later the fight was over. Those who had been buried underneath were visibly shaken. Swindle looked like a sick dog.

"Lucky they didn't suffocate," Yousif said to his mother.

The doctor moved to the middle of the circle. He looked around, letting the Arabs know he had something to say. There was silence.

"Listen, Captain . . ." the doctor began, addressing officer Swindle.

The husband again put his arm around his wife. "Go ahead, Doctor. If I could speak better English I'd tell the heathens off myself."

"Tell them," urged a man in Arabic, "they'd have to kill every one of us before they can go through with this."

Yousif motioned with both hands for the men to be quiet and give his father a chance to present their case.

"You've been in this country thirty years," the doctor said, looking around at all the soldiers, "and one would think you'd know by now how we feel about our women. About their honor. You either bring women to frsik the women, or I'm afraid there's going to be more violence."

"Imbeciles," the husband shouted in Arabic.

Again, Yousif moved to restrain the man. "Keep calm, please," he urged.

"Nothing could inflame us more than dishonoring our women," the doctor warned in his own reserved way.

There was dead silence. The angry soldiers waited for Swindle to give them the signal to resume their search. The Arabs waited for a single move to renew their attack. Yousif stood still, apprehensive. Would the cornered officer swallow his pride, acknowledge defeat, and reverse the order? Would he ignite another riot?

"The search will continue," Swindle finally said, "but the women will be excused."

The Arabs sighed with relief. Some of the soldiers looked disappointed. Yousif reached for his father's hand and squeezed it. The women returned to their places inside the church and the frisking of the men continued. But now everything was calm and the soldiers' search seemed perfunctory. Within ten minutes Yousif was back in the crowded church.

ABOUT THREE o'clock in the afternoon the soldiers set the people free. It was raining and many wanted to wait until the downpour had stopped. But the soldiers would not let them. They pushed them into the street as further punishment. By the time Yousif stepped out into the square before the church, the rain was torrential. He offered his mother his arm, and his father suggested they stop at his clinic because it was so close. But his wife said no. They were already drenched, and she was anxious to see what the searchers had done to her house.

As she opened the door of their home, she let out a scream. Both her husband and her son were right behind her. Muddy footsteps were all over the Persian rug in the foyer. They walked in, afraid to look. To their left, the living room was in complete disarray. Armchairs were turned over. Cushions were slashed and emptied. To their right, the dining room was also demolished. The fine linen tablecloth was piled up on the floor with the flower vase spilled over it. The drawers in her china cabinet were open and emptied on the bare dining room table. They were stunned. They stood still, tongue-tied. Then she began to cry.

The doctor trembled. Yousif ran to check on the rest of the house. The bedrooms were chaotic. Mattresses were ripped open, closets emptied onto the floors, clothes trampled on. Every mirror was smashed. He ran from his bedroom to his parents' and then to the kitchen. He felt sick in the pit of his stomach. Flour and rice sacks were spilled onto the floor. Porcelain jugs of oil and glass jars of butter were broken on top of each other.

He could hear his parents' footsteps.

"Oh, my God!" his mother shrieked, biting her knuckles. She sobbed, tears streaming down her face. He embraced her, letting her lean against his chest and cry again.

"What in hell were they trying to do?" Yousif said, in disbelief.

"They wanted you to know they were here," his father replied, disgusted.

"Who would hide a gun in a jar of oil?" Yousif asked.

"It's a thorough search," the doctor muttered.

"May all their life be a nightmare," the mother prayed, raising her arms in an appeal to God.

His father led his mother out of the kitchen. Yousif stayed behind, gazing at the mess. After a long moment, he made his way out, stepping over the wet spots, brushing his back against the wall. He headed for the bathroom, took off his pants and shorts and sat down. When he flushed the toilet two minutes later, Yousif was convinced that the world was as filthy as the swirling contents of the commode.

His parents were in the living room. His mother looked like someone who had escaped from the crypt. His father was pacing the floor, looking ashen. Yousif felt anger and pity. They had been caught in an ever-widening tragedy.

It had stopped raining. Yousif opened the front door and walked to the front veranda. Other neighbors opened their doors, stepped outside, and stood motionless. Then everyone, including Yousif, was pulled as if by a magnet to the clearing in front of Uncle Boulus's house. The neighbors were drawn together, as if in a dreamy slow motion. They gathered and stared. Yousif knew that their hushed silence was not natural. But then, gutting a whole town—every house, every room, every drawer—was not a natural act.

16

Death came again to Ardallah at dawn a few days later. It struck two men riding a bus on their way to Jaffa, even before the roosters crowed. One was a Christian from Ardallah proper, the other a Muslim resident of Ardallah who was originally from Jindas, a village five miles northwest. A couple of miles out of the city limit, bullets ripped into the bus, riddling windows and shattering glass. The twenty-one passengers threw themselves into the aisle or into each others' laps.

Mitry Freij, the shoemaker from Ardallah, was carrying a large box of custom-made shoes for delivery. The box trapped him in his seat and a bullet exploded in his head. Hani Mahmoud, from Jindas, was a tall man in his fifties, lived alone, and was known to be somewhat retarded. When the ambushers sprang out of nowhere in front of the bus, the driver shouted for the passengers to hit the floor. Not comprehending, poor Hani said he wasn't sleepy. He was the only one sitting up when he got a bullet in the neck.

How the bus driver, the diminutive Abu Ziad, managed to escape with the rest of the passengers astounded Yousif and the rest of the townspeople. Some called it sheer luck. Others called it an act of courage. But on the hills of God, many preferred to call it a miracle.

That same day there were two funerals, and half the municipality council went to each. At two o'clock, Yousif walked in the funeral of Mitry Freij. As a gesture of community and respect, Yousif's father was among those who went to Jindas to attend the funeral of Hani Mahmoud.

The procession to Ardallah's cemetery was again a spectacle. Most of the merchants had closed their shops and joined the thousands of mourners. The march itself was orderly, save for the women's high-pitched lamentations that only the Boy Scouts' band could surpass in volume. Heading the Scouts was their leader: an accountant in his late forties—short, solidly built, and sporting a formidable mustache. Behind him were two men hoisting the Scouts' flag and the Palestinian flag. The band itself consisted of young civil servants and artisans, who marched in four rows of fives. Then came the hundred or so teenagers who marched in unison, their chins jutting and their expression grim. The entire group was dressed in khaki shorts, white shirts, red scarfs, and the traditional Arab headgear of *hatta* and *iqal*. The band players beat their enormous drums and blew their shiny horns with gusto, as though they were in a triumphant procession. The casket was carried on men's shoulders. Yousif could see the draped white-green-black-red Palestinian flag bobbing above the marchers' heads as patriotic villagers scurried to share the honor of accompanying the corpse to its grave.

Schools had shut down, and students—from the third grade up—were also marching, as though in an Easter parade. Nuns with fresh-scrubbed, smooth-skinned faces walked beside the fifty or sixty young girls in blue tunics. Yousif would've joined his teachers and classmates, but he was escorting Jamal. He could see Amin assisting ustaz Hakim and the principal, ustaz Sa'adeh, in keeping order among the nearly two hundred students, who marched as if they had all lost brothers.

The crowds at the Christian cemetery flowed on both sides of the narrow dirt road. They spilled over the three sections: Greek Orthodox, Catholic, and Protestant. Yousif and Jamal stayed with hundreds outside the gate, where the old yellow bus, riddled with bullets on both sides, was on display. For two hours, he watched mourners surround Abu Ziad, the driver, and question him about the tragic incident. Yousif smelled incense, heard women crying and priests praying for the souls of the departed, and listened to speakers calling them martyrs destined to heaven. He heard strangers weep, watched men scratch their chins, and saw women tear the fronts of their dresses and beat their bosoms. Feeling a lump in his throat, he wondered who would be the next victim.

"Half the town is here," Yousif said to Jamal. He was craning his neck to see if Salwa was with Adel Farhat, whom he saw no more than a hundred feet ahead. Happily, she wasn't.

"That's no good," Jamal said, tapping his cane.

"Right now," Yousif whispered, "the Jews could walk in and capture Ardallah with no trouble."

Jamal seemed absorbed, his sealed eyes twitching. "I hope we'll learn to use our heads and not just our hearts."

Yousif thought of Basim and his plan to protect Ardallah. Could the doctor now, in good conscience, say no to the demand for the hospital money? All around him, men were huddling and talking about one thing—the need for protection.

"We can't go on like this," said Yacoub, the house painter.

"I agree," a choir leader answered. "It's getting to be too dangerous."

Yacoub smacked his thin lips. "Something must be done," he said.

A round of bullets ripped the air. For a moment everyone was startled. Then they all realized that the shots were fired at the graveside—as a gesture of farewell to the victim.

"They'd better save their ammunition," Jamal said.

Yousif could sense worry and the desire for revenge casting a long shadow over a sea of grim faces. As he mulled over the ugly incident, he realized that the floodgates of pain and sorrow were beginning to burst open.

"I have a feeling," Yousif said, "that Palestine is falling apart."

A WEEK LATER, Yousif lay in bed at six o'clock in the morning. His first thoughts were of Salwa. He had seen her in a kaleidoscopic dream which was nothing but torture. Like the Grecian Urn lovers, like Tantalus and the dangling bunch of grapes, he and Salwa were inches apart yet could never touch. What should he do, Yousif thought, to win her back? Should he unload his problem on her Greek Orthodox priest, Father Samaan, and ask for help? Should he beseech her favorite teacher? He thrashed about, wondering.

He looked outside, thinking what a glorious day it was. Early spring had arrived. Despite the torturous dream, he was glad he had slept with the window open. Ardallah's air was cool and invigorating. The sky was bluer than Salwa's silk dress and the tree tops were as motionless as unlit candles.

He wished his thoughts were as calm, as peaceful. He had gone to bed troubled by his mother's fretting over the expense and time it was taking to replace all in their house that had been damaged by the British soldiers. Night visitors were still shocked by the attack on the bus. But where was Basim? they all asked. With all the fighting at Bab al-Wad, Yousif knew, it wasn't likely that Basim would spend any nights at home.

In five weeks the British would be gone—completely evacuated. Instead of moving out in August, as the UN resolution had stipulated, they decided to step up their withdrawal and be gone by May 15th. And the battle for the control of Jerusalem was already raging. For weeks the Zionists had been trying to secure a safe passage for their military convoys to Jerusalem. But the Palestinians, led by their ablest commander, Abd al-Qadir, had repeatedly pinned them down at the bottleneck at Bab al-Wad.

Yousif did not believe in military heroes, but if he had to name one it had to be Abd al-Qadir—an honest man doing honest work. The Grand Mufti's cousin, Abd al-Qadir was a seasoned soldier with an impeccable reputation. Basim and his late father-in-law, Maha's father, had served with him during the Revolt of 1936 and had come to love him for his courage, patriotism, and determination. Yousif grew up linking Basim's name to Abd al-Qadir's, knowing that they represented Palestine's finest fighting spirit. Of late, Yousif had often seen Abd al-Qadir's picture in the newspapers. Handsome, stout, and with bandoleer criss-crossing his chest, he looked like the Palestinians' best hope to thwart the Zionists' pipe dream. A week earlier Abd al-Qadir had gone to Damascus pleading to the Arab leaders meeting there for immediate help. When they balked at his urgent request and condescended to give him only a few guns and a few rounds of ammunition—not nearly enough for his few hundred volunteers—he reportedly stormed out of the room, shouting: "The blood of Palestine is on your heads."

A fresh wave of morning slumber caressed Yousif's eyes. Then he heard the muffled ringing of the phone. Another sick call for the doctor, he thought, turning over on his side, wondering how he could help, surrendering to another moment of sleep . . . With all the fighting at Bab al-Wad, only twenty miles away, surely he could run food supplies . . . medications . . .

"Wake up, Yousif, wake up," his mother said, banging on this bedroom door. "The Zionists are back, the Zionists are back!"

Yousif jumped out of his bed, thinking it was a bad dream. But the banging on the door was persistent, his mother's voice real. He opened the door, expecting the Zionists to be running through the corridor.

"What are you saying?" he asked, pulling up his pajama pants.

"The Zionists . . . they're here," she answered, gesturing for him to hurry.

He followed her to her bedroom. His father was sitting on the edge of the bed talking on the phone.

"It's true," the doctor said, hanging up. "That was the mayor."

His mother told him what she had heard from the milkwoman. What had happened to Abu Ziad's bus a week earlier happened again this morning.

"You mean the terrorists killed more passengers?" Yousif wanted to know.

"No one has been killed—yet," the doctor said, rising. "This time we were ready for them."

Yousif hesitated, surprised. "Ready? How?"

"According to the mayor," his father said, wiping his glasses with the edge of his pajama top, "Basim and few others have been waiting nights at the same spot for the terrorists to return. This morning they did."

"I thought Basim was at Bab al-Wad," Yousif said.

"So did I," his father said. "But apparently we're in firm control there and at the village of Kastal overlooking it. So Basim took a few of the men to guard the Ardallah-Jaffa road."

They walked out of the room, with Yousif pressing for concrete details. But his parents knew very little.

They ended up on the front balcony, facing Uncle Boulus's house. The roosters were crowing, and the *muezzin* was chanting the Qur'an. Yousif looked at his watch. It was only 6:30, but the neighborhood was already humming with people. Men and women were outside, jabbering and gesturing across their yards. A few men hurried past the Safis' gate. Yousif rushed to question them. Men of all ages, even some children, were approaching from the direction of the flour-mill. Some were in slippers, others in pajamas. Some carried broomsticks and axe handles.

"Aren't you coming, Yousif?" a boy from school asked, his tone cheerful.

"Where?" Yousif asked, bewildered.

"To catch the terrorists," Ribhi said. "They're trapped in a field not too far from here. We're all going to catch them."

"Basim is already there."

"He needs help."

It sounded bizarre. Yet Yousif did not want to miss out on whatever was happening. He ran back to the house, slipped on his clothes, and hurried out. His parents tried to stop him, but he wouldn't listen. Outside the gate, he headed against the flow.

"Wrong way," a sixty-year-old shepherd told him, pointing west.

"I'm going to get a friend," Yousif answered.

Minutes later he ran into Amin and his father. They were rushing along with the crowd.

"I was coming to get you," Yousif said.

"Hell, the whole town is up in arms," the stonecutter said.

"How did they find out?" Yousif asked.

"From the bus driver, Abu Ziad," Amin said. "At the sound of the first bullet he turned around and came back to alert the rest of us."

Yousif was impressed. "But the terrorists and Basim's men are armed. What are we going to do with bare hands?"

"Not every morning do we get our hands on some real terrorists," the old man answered, with relish. "I want to see us have a go at them."

Yousif and Amin exchanged looks.

As they walked along with the crowd, Yousif had a hard time reconciling the seriousness of the matter and the unorthodox approach of the townspeople. So many people were in the posse—almost two hundred. What struck him most was their festive mood. The sticks and brooms and pipes and crow bars they were carrying belied the unnatural glow on their faces. What was going on? Was this a celebration? Even Raouf, the town's only deaf-mute, was walking along with his parents. Even women were in the stampede: young and old, in modern dresses, in native garments, in curlers, some with housecoats thrown on their backs.

The procession reminded Yousif of picking season, when the villagers and landowners would rush to the fields to pick figs or olives. It reminded him of the Saturday before Easter when the burning "light" would be brought from the Holy Sepulchre, when the multitudes would rush to the outskirts of town with their candles. It reminded him of 1946, when many of Ardallah's men had returned from America and families had rushed to the harbors in Haifa and Jaffa to welcome their loved ones. The same kind of exhilaration was in the people's walk that morning. He looked around and saw Sami Awad walking fast, dabs of shaving-cream on his face and ear lobe, a towel around his neck and a cane in his hand.

At the outskirts of Ardallah, hundreds more people were already there, mainly watching. Yousif could hear gunshots in the distance. The battle scene was no bigger than fifteen football fields, cut up in squares and rectangles and—more often than not—terraced. On the right he could see two local men chasing an ambusher who had abandoned half of his Arab guise and was running for his life. On the right were men swinging at each other with all their might and tumbling over bushes or piles of stone. The new arrivals dispersed on both sides of the road. The hills seemed dotted with men and women from the other villages. Everyone seemed determined to block every conceivable path the enemy might take. Yousif and Amin did not know which way to go. They turned left and crossed several rocky vine groves. They jumped over stone walls and stood on a low hill to watch.

A hundred yards in front of them were two men hiding behind two crumbling stone walls and firing at each other like cowboys in American Westerns. The boooooom would soon turn into a zzzzzing as a bullet chipped a rock above one of the combatants' heads. Yousif could hear loud gasps mingled with shouts and see men leaping and chasing each other. A retreating man fell and kept rolling down a steep hill. Some of the housewives in curlers and robes split the sky with their trilling and cheered on those after him.

Yousif's reverie was shattered by a burst of applause and shouts of joy. He turned to look, nudging Amin. Short and mustachioed Aziz Malouf, the town's best known hunter, was passing by, flush with excitement, his sleek-looking hound lolling its tongue and panting at his side. How many times, Yousif recalled, he had seen Aziz with quails or pheasants or rabbits attached to his belt, pulling it down to his hips. That was the way he had swaggered after a successful hunt. As Aziz crossed the field below with his shotgun slung over his shoulder, Yousif noticed the same look about him. He trembled.

"Anyone killed?" Yousif asked the bare-chested Aziz.

"If not, there soon will be," Aziz boasted.

"It's better than hunting rabbits, eh, Aziz?" the baker, Abul-Banat, asked.

"You bet," Aziz said, taking longer strides.

Yousif could see a jeep speeding on a dirt road, a column of dust rising behind it. Suddenly there was a movement close to the stone wall on which Yousif was standing. It sounded like an animal squeezing its way between the wall and the bushes. Yousif looked down but saw nothing. Moments later, he heard a rustle in the dry leaves. Again he looked, but couldn't detect the source. This time, however, he noticed a bulging curve in the wall and decided to look beyond it. He stepped off the wall and walked around.

A small man was crouching between the wall and the wild overgrowth. Instinctively, Yousif wanted to pounce. But then, what would he do with him? Uncertain, he hesitated a second too long. Sensing his presence, the man started running.

"Here's one . . . here's one!" Yousif yelled, going after him.

The terrorist ran up the hill, where the field was full of olive trees.

Yousif chased him full tilt, but the man was faster. Afraid of losing him, Yousif looked back for help. Several men had jumped off the stone wall and were now joining the chase. Mehdi, a lean fellow of about thirty, passed Yousif and gained on the fugitive. They zigzagged behind each other, and circled around a tree. The terrorist tricked Mehdi and ran off again. But to Yousif's surprise he climbed a dark, silvery olive tree. What a mistake, Yousif thought.

Within seconds, several Arabs were under the tree waiting for the terrorist to come down. Middle-aged Jubran, the quilt maker, tried to climb after him. But the fellow stomped on his hand, forcing him to release the branch. Yousif shook the tree but the frightened man wrapped his arms around the tree trunk. Hanania, the jeweler, broke off a long, thin limb and started switching him on the leg. The man climbed another notch until he became unreachable. More people gathered around, knowing that the enemy was as good as caught. A pretty young girl in a blue tunic picked up a pebble and threw it. She gave the men an idea, and they started pelting him. The terrorist began to cry, but clung to the tree.

"You'll get hurt a lot worse if you stay up there," Yousif cautioned. "It's safer for you to come down."

Instead of answering, the terrorist climbed one more notch.

Yousif saw Abul Banat jump and get a good hold on a branch. The jeweler and a bricklayer helped him bend it down. Now the terrorist was exposed and within reach. A toothless old woman tried to hit him with a long broom. But she was too short. A stranger, a thin, pockmarked man, took the broom from her and did the same. Still the terrorist—whom they could now see was no more than a teenager—would not surrender. The thickset bricklayer lifted to his shoulder another man who grabbed the boy, forcing him down.

THE SKY WAS velvety blue. The sun was shining brightly when all the terrorists who had been captured were rounded up and brought back to town. First they were toured around in a truck. Basim and his men led an awesome two-mile parade. It stopped at every major intersection. It stopped in front of the mosque where a *muezzin* circled the minaret and chanted from the Qur'an. Church bells were rung in triumph. In front of the Municipality, the rotund mayor stood on the balcony and delivered his impromptu congratulations to all the captors.

"People of Ardallah," the mayor declared at the top of his voice, "I'm proud of every single one of you. With this kind of spirit, Ardallah is safe, Palestine is safe . . . Death to the enemy."

The crowd roared with approval. After the speech, it began to move again, winding itself through narrow streets. Hundreds stood on their terraces and balconies, or leaned against their windows, gazing at the spectacle.

An hour later, the sea of relieved but angry demonstrators stopped at the five-point *saha.* Many gloated over their victory; others bristled from insult. How dare these Zionists, they all said.

"They don't worry me," one cobbler said to another. "Even with a gun in his hand, a Jew is nothing but a chicken."

Yousif wondered about the fate of the terrorists after the "show" was over. Who would take charge of them? The British were too busy packing to bother. The Zionist underground would ask for them. The British might act as intermediaries and hand back all the prisoners—living or dead. Damn the British! They caused all this.

"Power to the masses," Basim shouted, both his hands forming "V" signs. "Glory to those who seek freedom. Glory to those who rise and defend themselves.

Glory to every man, woman, and child who has participated in this victorious morning."

Men cheered, shaking their fists at the terrorists. The sidewalks and rooftops were congested. Children stood on top of parked cars or window sills. A mother balanced her baby on her hip, looking stunned. A shriveled old man leaned on his cane.

"Brave people of Ardallah," Basim continued, scanning the attentive crowd. "And brave brethren from the surrounding villages. Last week they came and killed two of us—and they became emboldened. They thought we were easy picking. They thought by hitting the villages on either side of the highway, they could stop our recruits from joining Abd al-Qadir, who's heroically defending our sacred land."

The roar was deafening. "Long live Abd al-Qadir," someone shouted, waving the Palestinian flag.

"Long live Abd al-Qadir," someone added, his voice hoarse. "Long live Basim."

"Long live *Palestine,"* Basim corrected, motioning with his arms for them to quiet down. "But, dear brothers and sisters, not every time will we be this lucky. Today we managed to stop them. Tomorrow we might not be able to. Unless we stay alert, unless we remain united, unless we become strong, we will face threat after threat from a relentless enemy bent on usurping our land. Today let us be satisfied that we can send the enemy this message: woe to him who will trespass against us, for he will not be forgiven or forgotten. Woe to him who will dare provoke our ire—dare provoke our wrath."

"Woe to him," the crowd shouted.

Yousif counted fifteen terrorists on the truck, but he had been told there were seventeen. Two terrorists had been killed and thrown on the floor. He saw men climb on the truck and strip the terrorists of their Arab disguise. As the unveiling proceeded, Yousif heard the mob gasp and fall silent. All the invaders were teenagers, shaking with fear. The demonstrators became motionless. They thought they had seized a band of fearless fighters. What they had captured were mere boys. The victory was now hollow. Looking at the pale, smooth, pimpled faces of the raiders, Yousif felt sorry for them. They did not seem anything but helpless.

"Look at them," Basim thundered. "Kids who should be home with their mothers are already killers. Don't let their young looks deceive you. Don't let their innocent eyes mislead you. Look what they've done. *They've killed Mitry Freij and Hani Mahmoud—"*

"—and blinded Suha Badran," Shafiq, Salwa's cousin, shouted.

"—and wounded Taher Khalifeh," added Shukri, who had once picked on Moshe Sha'alan at the cemetery.

"And God knows what else they would've done if we had given them half a chance," Basim thundered again. "They have come to kill and they have killed. They have come to maim and they have maimed. If we let them, they'll kill and maim again. Again and again until we and our children are all *dead.* And what's our crime? Our crime is that we were *born here."*

With a few words Basim canceled any sympathy the crowd might have had toward the young raiders.

"Kill them!" somone shouted.

"Kill them!" the crowd echoed.

Yousif was terrified. "No," he begged. "Basim, please, listen . . ."

"Kill the bastards," shouted Aziz, the famed hunter, unslinging his rifle.

"No . . ." Yousif pleaded, his arms stretched toward Aziz.

"YEEEES!" the crowd shouted.

One of the invaders attracted attention to himself by trying desperately to hide. Yousif noticed that every time a man reached to remove the Arabic headdress, the boy would get on his knees and double up. He had tied the *hatta* around his neck and face and secured it further by pressing the *iqal* around the top of his head. His eyes only showing, he stood behind the others and never looked directly at the crowd. Maurice, a lisping hairdresser, climbed on the hood of the truck, then lay flat on his stomach on the roof above the driver's seat. From there Maurice reached for the camouflaged boy's head and uncovered it. The crowd gasped again. It was Isaac without his glasses.

"Look!" Salman exclaimed, pointing his finger.

"Can you believe it!" Abla, Salman's wife, added.

"Isaac? My God—" said midwife Hanneh, who had delivered him.

Saadallah, a waiter at Zahrawi's cafe, jumped on top of the truck. At the urging of the crowd, he pulled Isaac to stand at the back of the truck where everyone could see him. Yousif was shocked. He sensed Isaac's humiliation and feared for his life. Looking around, he found Amin wide-eyed and gaping. People stared at Isaac with hate in their eyes. Isaac raised his two hands to hide his face. But Maurice forced them down.

"Isaac, you came to kill us?" seamstress Zahiyyeh said, her hand going up to her lips.

"Shame, shame on you," a rosy-cheeked woman blasted.

Yousif felt a lump in his throat. This same woman had given the three boys a loaf of bread on the last day of bird hunting—the day Yousif wanted the three of them to make a pledge of friendship.

"You dirty dog."

They cursed him. They spat on him. They chewed him with their eyes.

"Isaac, this can't be true," rang Yousif's voice.

Isaac raised his eyes to seek out Yousif standing in the middle of the street next to Amin. Their eyes met, and Isaac's lips trembled. Yousif and Amin waved their hands and tried to move forward. Isaac couldn't face his friends and began to cry.

The crowd waited for Isaac to speak. To Yousif's surprise, Isaac's voice was strangely calm. It was not the voice of a young boy but of a man prematurely old and weary.

"It would be foolish of me to plead innocence," Isaac continued, "and to think that you would set me free. This I know. But I also know that in your hearts you don't want to kill me, just as in my heart I didn't want to come back to you with a gun. I was *forced* to come and you'll be *forced* to kill me. Alive or dead, we're all victims—we're caught in a war from which we can't escape. But before you kill me, I want you to know that I bear you no grudge."

A tremor of hope stirred in Yousif's heart. Isaac's words were touching; people were plunged in deep silence. They might spare Isaac; they just might. But their sympathy could swing like a pendulum. A few minutes earlier they had shouted for death. Now they were full of compassion. As he pondered Isaac's fate, Yousif heard the postman Costa demanding punishment. Again Yousif's heart sank.

"They blow with the wind," Yousif whispered to Amin.

The two friends pushed their way toward Isaac. They wanted to tell him not to give up. But before they actually reached him, they heard a wild, woeful cry. Everyone stopped and listened. Again a woman's cry electrified the scene. The mass of humanity parted, as if her voice had sliced it. Yousif saw her running down the narrow human path, wailing hysterically. Her ankle-length dress was beltless and torn to the waist, her long gray hair blowing, her face scratched and bleeding.

Yousif recognized her. She was the mother of Mitry Freij.

Her frightful appearance and wailing brought tears to the people's eyes. Yousif's heart ached for her and for Isaac. But her son was already dead. Isaac was still alive.

Other women joined the bereaved mother in her crying. They threw off the native head coverings, untied their hair and let it blow. They tore the fronts of their dresses, and wrapped their handkerchiefs or colored scarfs around their foreheads. Then they began to jump in a rhythmic dance of death. Yousif knew that the tide was turning against Isaac and he became frantic. He snaked his way toward the pick-up truck and climbed up to be with Isaac. When Isaac saw the effort Yousif had gone through to be with him he began to cry. Yousif wanted to hug him like a lost brother, but satisified himself with throwing his arm around his shoulders lest a greater intimacy offend someone in the mob.

"I didn't come on my own," Isaac said again and again. "They made me. I swear to God they made me."

"Of course you didn't come on your own," Yousif told him.

"You and Amin must believe me. You must."

"Are you crazy? Of course we believe you. Just stay calm and let me work it out with Basim."

"I'm afraid," Isaac confessed, gripping his friend's hand with all his might.

"Just calm down, will you? Everything is going to be all right."

Yousif's last remark was to reassure himself more than Isaac. The way the two huddled together, one would think they were alone on another planet.

"Goodbye, Yousif," Isaac said, tears streaming down his cheeks.

"Don't say that," Yousif entreated, the roar of the crowd filling his ears.

"What the hell are you two doing?" the waiter standing on the truck with them asked. "You'd better watch out, Yousif, before you get your head blown off."

Yousif grabbed the waiter by the throat. "No more violence, do you hear me?"

"Suit yourself. But if I were you I'd get lost."

"No harm must come to Isaac, understand?" Yousif repeated. Then looking around, he appealed to his own cousin who had inflamed the crowd. "Basim, please help. For the love of God don't let them hurt him."

"It's not up to me," Basim said, motioning for him to get off.

"Get off, you idiot," another man screamed. "Move away from that *yahudi.*"

Yousif was incensed. "Isaac is innocent," he pleaded with the angry crowd. "Have you forgotten who he is? Don't you remember what a fine friend and neighbor he's always been? It's *Isaac*—Isaac Sha'lan—we're talking about. Not a stranger who's come from overseas to steal our land. It makes a big difference. Isaac is one of us."

"It doesn't look like it," the waiter said, pushing Yousif away from Isaac.

"Don't touch me," Yousif said, fighting him back and hoping that the scuffle would not generate another surge of emotion.

Then the lisping hairdresser joined in the pushing and shoving until Yousif was several feet separated from his friend. Suddenly shots fired. Yousif didn't have to look to know what had happened. Some gasped . . . some sighed in unison . . . and for a moment neither Yousif's mind nor heart could take in the certain outcome of Isaac's death. Poor Isaac was dangling off the edge of the truck, blood oozing from his back.

"Damn you!" Yousif screamed, flailing his arms and punching all those who were pulling him off the truck.

Some, including Amin, tried to hold him back. But he was uncontrollable.

"They killed the best boy in the world," Yousif shrieked, his tears pouring.

"Calm down," Amin begged, holding him tight. "Please, Yousif."

"They killed him. Killed him."

A blacksmith, twice Yousif's size, pulled him by the hair. "Damn right we did. We killed the whole lot of them. Maybe we should kill traitors like you, too."

"I'm not a traitor," Yousif screamed, clawing at the man's face with his ten fingers.

"You act like one," the blacksmith said, pushing him away and then slugging him on the jaw. It was a powerful blow and Yousif shook his head to recover from it. He felt sure some of his bones were broken. He reached for his teeth, certain they had been loosened. They were all there, but his fingers were stained with blood. His knees buckled . . . his lips thickened . . . he felt dizzy. The rest was darkness . . .

YOUSIF STAYED in bed for the rest of the day, his mind in a turmoil. His mother feared he was having a nervous breakdown. When his father rushed home to see about his condition, Yousif was too exhausted, too sad, to talk. The two stared at each other, saying nothing. Then the doctor sat on the edge of the bed, and opened his bag to give his son a sedative. Yousif shook his head.

"It's no time to be squeamish," his father told him.

"I don't want a shot."

"It will ease the pain."

"I want to *feel* the pain."

The doctor pouted. "Get hold of yourself, son," he said, holding the medicine and syringe in both hands.

The moment of silence seemed eternal.

"Now I can see why you never talked about grandmother's death all those years," Yousif said, crossing his arms under his head. "Death is painful, isn't it? Especially murder."

The doctor's eyes widened. All his life Yousif had heard about his paternal grandmother's death at the hands of the Turks. They had shot her for hiding a British soldier in the *'unbar,* where wheat was stored. He had never been able to get his father to talk about it. His father seemed to carry his sorrow as a secret disease.

The doctor took a deep breath, put the medicine and syringe back. "You know better than to bring up her death," he said, shutting his black bag.

"Thirty years haven't healed the wound?"

"That's different."

"How different? She's your own blood and Isaac isn't? Is that it? Wounds of the heart are all serious, don't you think? You're the doctor."

The doctor put the black bag on the floor and took out his pipe. "See, son," he said, lighting a match. "Life is full of tragedies. Isaac's death is a tragedy, no question about it. And we're going to see a lot more tragedies. Remember, this war hasn't officially started yet. Heinous crimes are yet to come. I remember crying so hard when I heard about my mother's death—I thought I was losing my mind."

A sad smile crossed Yousif's lips, but he kept quiet. This was the closest his father had ever come to broaching the subject.

"Like a fool," the doctor reflected, puffing on his pipe, "I kept wondering what they did with all that wheat in the *'unbar*. I guess I thought of it because wheat was scarce—like everything else in those days—and people were literally starving. Then I decided they must've have thrown it away. What else could they have done with it, soaked with blood?"

"Everything in this country seems to be soaked with blood," Yousif said, his face grim.

The two sat alone—each wrapped in his own misery.

After his father had left, Yousif's mind traveled distant slopes, sifting memories and feelings. Like a millstone, his world turned round and round and round. He remembered something he had read in the Bible: "They are all gone insane, they are altogether become filthy; there is none that doth good, no not one."

WHEN HE OPENED his eyes next morning Yousif found Jamal standing at the door holding a musical instrument. From its shape and maroon color, Yousif knew it was Isaac's *'oud*.

"Come in, Jamal," Yousif said.

The blind musician followed the voice, and stood by the bed. He held the *'oud*, beckoning Yousif to take it. "Isaac would want you to have it," he said, his voice choking.

The moment lingered on. The *'oud* rested on Jamal's stretched arms like an injured baby.

"This is the nicest gift anyone could give me," Yousif said, taking it from him.

Jamal picked up the cane off his arm and stood still for a moment. "You and I wish there were no need for you to have it," he finally said. "But life must go on."

Yousif could tell that Jamal was anguished.

There was a long pause.

"Jamal," Yousif whispered.

"Yes?"

"Will you play for me?"

Jamal's lips tightened as he reached for the *'oud* Yousif was holding out for him. He uncovered it and sat on the edge of Yousif's bed. Yousif crossed his arms under his head and waited. When Jamal began to finger the strings, filling the room with a soft slow tune, Yousif remembered his slain friend—and his eyes welled up with tears of sadness and anger.

After a long pause, Yousif broke the silence. "What's going to happen?" he asked.

"What always happens in wars—death and destruction."

"Is there no way out? To use your own words, these are the hills of God."

"True," Jamal said, the muscles of his eye sockets working. "But like the rest of the world, they are inhabited by weak, flawed, pitiable human beings. Maybe the priests are right. Maybe there'll never be true peace until the Messiah returns and redresses all wrong."

"Do you believe that?"

"What else is there to believe in? Certainly you can't put your trust in people."

Yousif thought of Isaac's family. He wondered who had broken the news to his mother, and how his father had reacted. He could imagine their agony, their despair. Poor Alex, poor Leah!

IN THE AFTERNOON, Yousif busied himself with his birds. The special room was partitioned into four mesh-walled, walk-in cages, each of which contained no less than fifty of the colorful noisy creatures. He had already serviced two of these cages, preoccupied. His curiosity ran rampant—about Basim, about the war, about the consequences of victory or defeat. But his curiosity about Salwa was answered in person.

He was inside the left back cage, pouring water in a shallow container. As he turned around he saw her standing at the door. She was wearing a light-olive dress with a red belt that accentuated her small waist and full bosom. Her height almost filled the door opening. Her expression was uncertain.

Confusion assaulted him. This was the first time they were alone since her engagement. It hurt him to look at her, knowing that she was wearing Adel Farhat's diamond ring.

"I'm sorry about Isaac," she said, her voice low.

"I'm sorry you came," he answered, turning his back.

She did not leave. And he was glad. His heart was not fluttering for nothing.

He wished he could run his fingers through her hair . . . could kiss her. He wished he weren't trapped by his mixed emotions.

"Our mothers are meeting in the salon. So I took a chance to come and see you. God knows what the other women will say. But I wanted you to know how sorry I am about Isaac."

Yousif faced her, a pitcher of water in his hand. "Did you check with your fiancé first? Did you get father's permission? They might disapprove of your coming to see me as much as I do."

"If they find out I'll be in trouble."

He put the pitcher down on the floor and picked up a newspaper which he began to unfold and tear into small squares. Birds chirped all around him, with a couple alighting on his shoulder.

"One thing I am curious about," Yousif said. "Why was the wedding postponed till June or July? I thought Adel Farhat's family wanted him to get married immediately so he won't go to war. What happened?"

Somewhat of a cynical smile flashed on her lips. "Maybe the postponement will give you an idea how much I didn't want to get married. I wouldn't even have gotten engaged if it weren't for my father. We're so close I couldn't say no to him. It would've broken his heart."

Yousif half-smiled. "What about now? Wouldn't he object to your being here? Why are you doing it?"

She fiddled with the straps of her purse. "Because I want us to be friends."

"Oh, really. You used to tell me you loved me."

"Maybe I still do. But I can't marry you."

"Well, I'm not interested. Take your friendship and leave."

"Anger becomes you, Yousif," she muttered, leaning against the door's frame.

Yousif got out of the cage. "One more thing," he said, his hand still on the handle. "I didn't see your Adel Farhat out rounding up the terrorists. I assumed he'd be the first one to fire his gun—just to please you. You're the militant, remember?"

She stepped closer to him, seemingly undaunted by his rebuffs. "Maybe he doesn't want to get killed before he marries me," she said. "Maybe he thinks I'm worth living for."

They were standing in the narrow passageway separating the partitions. Yousif couldn't stand being near her, feeling the urge to put his arms around her waist. He could smell her perfume and feel the warmth of her vibrations.

"Go away," he said, getting inside the left front cage.

"I haven't seen him in a week."

Yousif eyed her carefully. "I wonder why," he said.

Salwa touched the mesh wire between them. "Listen, Yousif. I don't know what's going to happen. But if I do marry him, please don't hold it against me. It only means that the obstacle was bigger than my ability to remove it."

They were only a couple of feet apart. The two-karat diamond ring on her long, shapely, manicured finger sparkled between them like the eye of a serpent. But now Yousif could look past it. Hope was boiling in his veins.

"Salwa, is there a chance?" he asked, scrutinizing her face. "Can I do anything to help? You know I confronted your father, and sent my parents—"

She nodded.

"I was impetuous," he said, moving closer. "Your father didn't realize how serious we are about each other. Do you think he has cooled off by now, should I try again?"

Her face became flushed. "I'm not sure."

"Would he want you to spend your life in misery? I don't think so. Tell him you're my age . . . we share the same ideals . . . we love each other."

She smiled. "You want me to get killed?"

"Maybe not in those words. But you know what I mean. Tell him Adel Farhat is a stranger to you. That you don't feel comfortable around him."

Salwa opened her purse and took out a linen kerchief. "He knows that."

"And he still wants you to marry him? What kind of a father is he?"

"The very best," she insisted, her look stern. "That's the way he was raised. That's what he believes in. He and mother hardly knew each other when they got married. Look at them now. Inseparable."

"But those days are gone. We are a new generation. We live in a different world. And we're facing a war. You and I can be partners. We can be a team . . ."

She took a deep sigh. "I know," she said.

"How can you be full of fervor, full of revolutionary ideas, and then let him arrange your marriage? It's unthinkable."

Her big eyes flashed. "Look who's talking. Our hero is in a cage—feeding the birds. Some revolutionary."

Yousif felt stung, but he wouldn't show it. "Then let's both change."

"I'm sorry," she said. "I didn't mean to deride you."

"That's okay," he told her. "I probably deserve it."

"All I can tell you is I'm trying to get out of this engagement. But it hurts me to see father hurt. I don't want to fail him."

He dropped the newspaper in his hand and shot out of the cage, rejuvenated. His sudden move startled Salwa.

"Don't get near me, please," she begged. "And don't build up your hopes. All I'm saying—"

"What are you saying, Salwa?" her mother said, standing behind her. "I smell a conspiracy. But let me tell you two: it won't work. My husband is a proud man. He'll never go back on his word."

"Go back on his word?" Yousif protested. "Can't he trade a promise for his daughter's lifetime happiness?"

The father's hold on his family soon became more evident. Salwa seemed mystified. And gone was the laughter in her mother's eyes. Her expression dampened Yousif's enthusiasm.

"You used to like me," he pleaded. "Why did you give Salwa to someone else? You knew we loved each other."

"Stop that kind of talk," the mother advised, touching her daughter at the elbow. "Come on, Salwa. Let's go. Your father would be furious if he knew of this. He'd blame me for letting you come. I thought Yousif had gotten over it by now."

"Gotten over it?" Yousif said, appalled.

"We never get all we want in life," she lectured him. "Believe me, what happened has nothing to do with you. If I had my way I would've given you two my blessing. But it's too late now."

"It's not too late until she gets married. She's only engaged."

"The same thing," she said, her face blanched. "You should forget about—"

"Forget about her?"

"—and get on with your life. Many mothers would give their right arms for you to be interested in their daughters."

"But I don't want anyone else."

"Bye, Yousif," the mother said, walking away with her hand in her daughter's.

He followed them out into the corridor. "Is that how it's going to be, Salwa?" Yousif asked, shocked. "You're going to let them drag you about for the rest of your life?"

Before the two women turned around the corner, Yousif saw Salwa look back and shake her head. For a moment he didn't understand what that meant. Was she telling him it was hopeless? Was she telling him not to pay attention to what her mother had said? Every fiber and every cell and every drop of blood in him prayed that from now on she would put her foot down, assert her individuality.

Though seized with wonderment and overcome by emotion and uncertainty, he allowed himself the luxury to hope.

Back in the bird cage, he shut the mesh door, absorbed in thought. What about eloping to Lebanon? No, she won't agree. What about telling Adel Farhat that Salwa did not love him? No, that would only muddy the water. What about seeking the help of the teacher, the priest? Would that be enough? Damn it, maybe not. But it sure as hell beats doing nothing. Then he was seized by new doubts. Was it proper to have love and happiness on his mind—so soon after Isaac's murder? What would the people say? Maybe after a week or so—a decent mourning period—he could . . .

17

The song of spring that year was jarred by the nervous sound of gunfire. Early in April, the breeze blew unusually hot. The orange blossoms around Jaffa seemed less fragrant than they used to be. School girls did not make their annual field trips to pick tulips and daisies. Jamal stopped playing his violin.

Yousif and Amin, who were still in school, ended their preparation for the matriculation examination. It wasn't certain that it would be held that year anyway. And if it were to be held, it would be in Jerusalem, which was becoming impossible to visit. Yousif was aware that many of his classmates had been busy applying to American universities. But neither he nor Amin had any intention of doing so. Amin was too poor to think of higher education. Yousif hadn't applied on account of the political situation and the threat of war. His patriotic impulse wouldn't let him. He would avoid fighting, but he would do his duty—whatever that might be. Besides, how could he leave when Salwa's wedding plans were not resolved? He wasn't about to let her marry Adel Farhat.

To occupy himself, Yousif became a news addict. Although explosions were ripping the country, all eyes and ears were on Jerusalem. The battle for its control was on. The Zionists were dismissing the UN resolution that called for its internationalization. The Arabs were adamant about keeping it from falling into Zionist hands.

Yousif devoured the news like a hungry prisoner. Not satisfied with Arabic newspapers and magazines, he read English publications when he could get them.

He listened to every station he could tune in on his short-wave radio. When the electricity was out, he hurried to the nearest cafe to hear the broadcasts on portable sets. Then he'd run back home and repeat what he'd heard to his father and his guests, almost verbatim. Many marveled at his powers of retention, while he wished he were a bearer of happier news.

To his chagrin, fighting was enveloping the Jaffa-Jerusalem road like a heat wave. Arabs and Jews fought at Latrun, where the Trappist monks were caught in the crossfire. They also fought at Bab al-Wad, the narrowest point on the same road.

Situated between high cliffs, Bab al-Wad was both vulnerable and crucial. Controlling it was like clamping a main artery. Press hard and your life would be endangered. The Arabs rode the high terrain and hunted the Zionists passing below with deadly accuracy. The Zionists panicked but didn't give up. Their convoys were halted and smashed, only to appear again with greater force and fiercer determination. Sometimes they succeeded in getting through; often they did not. All hearts and minds were riveted to what was happening on that highway. Emotions swung. For both sides, "control the highway" became April's battle cry.

What amazed Yousif was that a few hundred disorganized Arab volunteers could hold off the well-organized Jewish stampede on the eternal city. Incredible, he felt, that those Arabs—mostly villagers unskilled in war—could face highly-motivated, well-trained, European-educated Zionists parading before their eyes like one of the armies in World War II. "Imagine!" the Arabs said, their hearts and souls with these brave fighters. It was enough to send goose bumps up Yousif's arms.

On the one hand he was proud, on the other he was angry. Instinct told him that violence was the law of the jungle. People were dying every day—the soldiers and the innocent. Violence begot violence, this he knew from the depth of his soul. But, again, he was not immune to the joys of victory. Pockets of Arab volunteers, armed with puny guns and a lot of spirit, were dealing the Zionists blow after blow. Wagons and pick-ups and trucks and tanks and all the weapons in the Zionists' arsenal were not enough to shake the Arabs' faith in their cause.

But questions flew everywhere. All Arabs, including Yousif, wanted to know where the Zionists had been stockpiling such heavy equipment all those years. Reading and hearing about the Zionists' astonishing supply of arms caused Yousif's heart to sink. Often he would find his father and his nightly visitors wondering how long the brave Arabs would last in the face of all that machinery. Even with Abd al-Qadir al-Husseini as their commander, how could they resist the nightly and daily Zionist assaults?

"One on one, the Jew is no match for the Arab," his father said.

"Oh, yes," Uncle Boulus agreed, clicking his *masbaha.* "But this is the twentieth century. It's modern weaponry that counts."

"And the Zionists have plenty of it," Yousif added.

"That's for sure," Uncle Boulus agreed.

Cousin Salman rested his elbows on his knees. "And all these years we've been told the poor Jews in all those colonies were farmers."

"No one told us to believe it," Yousif snapped.

"We were naive," Salman admitted.

Yousif looked at his uncle who had predicted not too long ago that nothing would come out of the UN resolution. "Do you still think," he asked, "that a Jewish state would be stillborn?"

Uncle Boulus puckered his lips. "I'm afraid I was wrong," he said.

"You wrong?" the doctor chided him.

"I'm not denying it, am I?" Uncle Boulus said, crossing his legs.

Yousif thought of Salwa. Even though she was still engaged to Adel Farhat, he felt sure that he was uppermost on her mind. She would want him to fight. But deep in his heart he knew violence would only prevent peace by exacerbating the hatred and revenge. Luckily none of his peers were flocking to join any fighting group. What would he do if they did? Would he let them get killed while he watched? On the other hand, how could he persuade them not to join? What alternatives could he offer?

And when he looked up to ponder his moral dilemma, he thought the crescent moon was mocking him.

DOOMSDAY WAS fast approaching. The British would be out of Palestine by May 15, several months ahead of the UN deadline.

My God, Yousif thought, six more weeks and the British would be gone. Six more weeks and the war would be officially declared. He had no idea how that was to be done. Would the sleepy Arab kings and presidents wake up one morning, rub their eyes, and decide it was time to get out of bed? Time to meet the Zionist threat, time to salvage Palestine? Would they make ringing speeches on radio? Give fiery statements to the press? Would the parliaments thunder and roar? Would the head of the Arab League speak for all of them? Or would the newly appointed commander-in-chief, Jordan's King Abdullah, scratch his royal beard and nod to the Arab "armies"—which so far had been waiting on ceremony—to start shooting? How theatrical wars were, Yousif thought. If only they weren't so bloody!

Meanwhile, the Palestinians and the Zionists were jockeying for better positions on the ground.

One storm of battle raged in and around Kastal, a small village perched above the hills overlooking the vital Jerusalem-Jaffa road. Its strategic importance was equal to Bab al-Wad's. To control it was to seal the fate of Jerusalem itself. Within a week, the suddenly prominent little village exchanged hands no less than four times. One day the sun rose and set on two different occupiers.

Yousif wavered between excitement and concern. Victory was going to be costly for either side. The more blood got spilled the harder would be reconciliation. He sat in class, not his usual self, his dilemma gnawing at him. Couldn't Arabs and Jews, he thought, have legal and moral claims on the same piece of land? After all, they were both the sons of Abraham. Was God partial to one against the other? Was He playing the role of a real estate agent or probate judge—dividing the land inequitably? The Bible didn't offer Yousif a satisfactory answer. Besides, he didn't think religion should enter into the equation lest the adversaries start shouting, "My God is better than your God."

He sought to find a solution on human terms. Couldn't two men, his mind pushed, fall in love with the same woman? It happened all the time. Like he and Adel Farhat. They could—but only one could have her. One could be the husband, one the lover. Or both could be her lovers—without the benefit of wedding rites. The thought made him smile, and he looked around the class to see if anyone noticed. In the Middle East *that* was forbidden.

Bouncy, short-sleeved ustaz Hakim rolled down a map of Palestine and pinpointed Kastal. Yousif watched him move to the blackboard and draw a road map to familiarize his students with the exact location of this once-sleepy village.

"The Zionists are sending their men from Jaffa and Tel-Aviv," Hakim lectured, a piece of chalk in his hand. "We should hit them at the source—long before they get to Kastal. But we can't. Do you know why?"

"We don't have enough volunteers," Adnan guessed.

"No," the teacher said, "we have plenty of those."

"Not enough arms," Amin suggested.

The teacher nodded. "What's worse," he said, "we don't have the money to buy arms should they become available. Meanwhile, this waiting on Arab armies is absurd."

"What about Fawzi al-Kawiqji?" Nadim asked, sitting in the back of the room. "Isn't his Liberation Army strong enough to have an impact?"

From the expression on the teacher's face, Yousif deduced ustaz Hakim's lack of confidence in the ostentatious Syrian commander who had recently arrived with a few hundred volunteers picked up along the way from Syria and northern Palestine.

"We are thankful for any help," the teacher observed diplomatically. "But saving Palestine is going to require more than a rag-tag army."

Several hands went up. Ustaz Hakim recognized Karam, a quiet, fat boy who hoped to become an electrical engineer.

"Do you think Britain will leave?" Karam asked.

"I really do," the teacher answered. "She wants to wash her hands of the mess she created."

"Good riddance," Mustapha said.

The teacher took a deep breath. "Listen, boys, our biggest problem is not Britain or the Jews—it's ourselves. It's our rulers who are holding the armies back. The masses want a fight but the Arab regimes lack either the heart or the will or the nerve. Not to help immediately is a sin . . . an unforgivable crime."

While the students questioned the teacher, Yousif thought of his father. The doctor's unwillingness to part with the hospital money was becoming very awkward. Before long Basim would be back—with both hands open.

A solemn mood descended upon the students. Yousif studied their faces, his heart full of pity. Before it was over, he was certain, some of them would be killed. Which ones, he did not know. Isaac sprang to mind.

Yousif was so lost in thought that he forgot to ring the bell for ten o'clock recess. When Raja reached for the brass bell on the sill and rang it through the open window, it sounded like church bells tolling for the dead.

THAT AFTERNOON Yousif was walking with Amin near the *saha,* engrossed in a newspaper. Since the attack on the bus, Amin seemed to have hardened. He blamed the Zionists for bringing the war to his doorstep and no longer had any pity for them.

"Yousif," Salwa called from across the street.

Yousif was taken aback by her double daring. This was the first time she had ever called out his name in public. And she was still engaged to Adel Farhat.

"Salwa, what is it?" he shouted back, glad to see her.

She and Huda crossed the street. Staccato bursts from automobile horns and angry looks from drivers didn't faze her.

"Basim is in town. He's looking for volunteers," she said, her face flushed. "We just saw him in front of the municipal building. Men were clamoring to get on his truck."

Yousif almost asked her if her fiancé Adel Farhat had joined. But he didn't wish to betray his hurt feelings in front of the others. At the same time he didn't know what to make of her stopping him in the middle of the street. Why was she so brazen? Was she that confident of her hold on him?

"You ought to go before Basim's truck fills up," she pleaded, their eyes locked.

"Oh, really?" Yousif said, sarcastically. "How sweet of you to tell me."

His heart pounded. She was asking him the impossible. He didn't wish to volunteer. How could he tell her (on the street for Godsake!) to mind her own business? How could he convince her that since the days of Cain and Abel—violence had settled absolutely nothing? Was there nothing to be gained from the experience? The silence among the four stilled the sounds of traffic. Looks crossed and re-crossed.

"The Zionists are making a bloody push to retake Kastal," Salwa pressed. "But it mustn't fall. Take Amin with you."

"I'm ready," Amin said, rubbing his stomach.

Without saying another word, both Yousif and Amin headed quickly toward the *souk*. But by the time they got there Basim was already gone.

Yousif was relieved. Basim, he was told, had taken about thirty volunteers and was on his way to Lydda and Ramleh, where he was sure to fill up several more trucks. Standing in the midst of men who were sorry they hadn't had the chance to go, Yousif wondered if he was truly different from the rest of his generation. Maybe one day he'd find something he could do without having to carry a gun. Yet at the moment it was the thing to do. He felt guilty.

"You would've jumped on that truck, wouldn't you?" Yousif asked.

Amin looked surprised. "Absolutely."

"Not me," Yousif confessed. "I would've found a way to back out at the last minute."

The sidewalk was congested. Amin looked around, being careful. "Don't you want to stop the Zionist takeover?"

"I do," Yousif replied, the din of the *souk* filling his ears. "But I still think that before things get any bloodier, both sides should sit down and talk. Face to face. Heart to heart. Arabs and Jews are the oldest and sharpest traders in the world. Let them drive a hard bargain. Let us drive a hard bargain. Let the negotiators lock horns for months, for years, if need be. But around a peace table—not on a battle field."

Amin studied his face. "I'm beginning to think you really believe all this?"

"With all my heart. I only wish I knew how to make it happen. You think I'm crazy, don't you?"

"No, not crazy. Just touched," Amin answered, pointing to his own temple.

The few afternoon shoppers were milling around. Several peddlers were poised at various street corners, their trays and carts full of piping-hot sweets and polished fruits. Right in front of a wholesale warehouse stood a clean-faced boy selling boiled lupini and fava beans. Yousif and Amin ambled toward him, stopping to buy two piasters' worth. Then they continued their stroll, eating out of newspaper cones.

"Tell me something, Amin," Yousif said, peeling the lupini bean between his front teeth.

"What?" Amin asked, chewing.

"Joshua is gone but Jericho is still here . . ."

Amin looked confused. "I don't get it."

"Samson is gone but Gaza is still here. Nebuchadnezzar is gone but Jerusalem is still here."

"I changed my mind," Amin said, smiling. "You *are* crazy."

"Maybe I am. But please listen. Where is Alexander the Great? Where is Richard the Lion Heart? Where is Salah id-Din? Where are their conquests?"

"Gone to dust—I guess."

"Exactly. And you'd think man would've learned something by now. Either history is useless or we are too dumb. We seem to be taking the same test over and over and over again—and never passing."

Amin shook his head and tipped the newspaper cone over his mouth. "Eat your lupini beans," he said. "It's better for you than all this gibberish."

"It's not gibberish," Yousif insisted, trying to work out his own thoughts. "We are all sojourners, I tell you. We play rich and we play poor. We play merchant and soldier and tailor and housewife and playboy and we think we're here to stay. How foolish of us . . . and how pathetic."

"'Tis a tale told by an idiot / Full of sound and fury / Signifying nothing," Amin quoted, in jest.

"Touché," Yousif said. "Only the meadows, the valleys, the seas and stars are permanent. And we can't own those, can we? What makes us think we can own the land? These hills belong to neither Arab nor Jew, believe me. And we must behave like guests. Not just you and me, but the whole creation."

"Pray tell, wise man," Amin said, popping more beans in his mouth. "What should man do? Kneel and worship the sun?"

"No, just bask in it. And ponder the mystery of existence. Marvel at the butterfly and the giraffe. Make love. Harvest the field. Write poetry. Drink wine. Say a prayer. Heal wounds. Smell the roses, if you will. But for God's sake—don't shoot."

They passed a blacksmith shop, full of soot and noise. The fire in the furnace was two feet high. At the anvil the short but powerful blacksmith was hammering and shaping a pointed fence.

"If I only could see Salwa and talk to her," Yousif lamented.

"Not when you're in this mood, I hope," Amin told him.

"She should know how I feel. There are so many things we should be doing instead of killing each other. Isaac would've been a good musician. You should have the opportunity to complete your medical studies. Salwa and I should get married, have children, build a future—"

"First," Amin reminded him, light-heartedly, "you need to get Salwa out of that engagement. You start talking to her about Nebuchadnezzar and Richard the Lion Heart at a time like this and you might as well be kissing her goodbye forever."

"True," Yousif agreed, nodding.

"Then you can join the seminary in Bethlehem and become a monk. Or you can kill yourself."

By the time they reached the flour-mill, the sun was setting over Jaffa and the Mediterranean Sea. Yousif looked in awe. It was a tableaux of magnificent colors—a feast for the eye, the soul, and the mind. He stood silent for a long moment like a man in a cathedral, letting the stillness wash all over him, drinking the sunburst as though it were the elixir of life. But reality wasn't far off. Children were riding bicycles and filling the narrow street with laughter. Lights were being turned on in windows. A mother was calling her son to come home. A shepherd was returning with his huge flock, bells tinkling around their necks.

Suddenly an idea occurred to Yousif that could perhaps assuage his conscience.

"Do you know what I'm going to do?" Yousif asked his friend.

"What?" Amin said.

"I'm going to borrow father's car and put it to some good use. Maybe you and I can get some food to our fighters. Who's feeding them? Who's looking after their needs?"

Amin stopped walking. "That's a good idea," he said. "Let's do it."

"We'll go to different shops and bakeries," Yousif said, "and fill up the trunk with breads and fresh vegetables."

Enthusiasm brightened Amin's dark face. "We could drive to where the men are fighting. Maybe get in on some action."

That prospect didn't appeal to Yousif, but he didn't show it. "At least," he said, "we can take the wounded to hospitals."

"What hospitals?"

"Jaffa or Jerusalem. And if we have to, we can take them to father's clinic or to Dr. Afifi's."

"I bet there are a lot of casualties already," Amin said.

THAT NIGHT Yousif convinced his father to let him use the Chrysler. He and Amin would start at Salman's shop in the morning and make the rounds until he had his trunk and back seat filled.

"Then what?" his father told him, sitting on the balcony.

"What do you mean?" Yousif asked.

His father eyed him skeptically. "Do you know how to get to Kastal?"

Yousif didn't, and he thought Amin didn't either. But he refused to be discouraged. He turned around and looked at Salman, whose arms were folded in his lap. "Maybe Salman will show us the way. Will you go with us?"

Salman looked thunderstruck. "Who me? You must be kidding."

"Why not?"

"What about the shop? I can't close it."

"Just for a few hours."

Salman's face turned red. "I've never been to Kastal in all my life. I don't even know where it is."

Yousif looked disappointed. "You're not afraid, are you?" he asked, aware that he was beginning to sound like Basim.

"Don't be silly," Salman answered, his lips twitching. "I'm not afraid. I just don't know the way. Let Amin ask his father to go with you. He can probably take you through the back roads blindfolded."

YOUSIF WOKE EARLY with every intention of cutting classes to proceed with his plan. But before he could get started, a curtain of doom fell upon the Arabs. During the night Kastal had fallen again. The fighting men would probably be scattered until they regrouped somewhere else. It was a major setback and Yousif felt battered. Besides, he was uncertain what the day would bring. How would such a defeat affect his immediate plans? Would his father change his mind about the car? Yousif would just have to wait and see.

At seven o'clock, Kol-Yisrael, the Zionist radio station, claimed that Abd al-Qadir himself had been killed. Dream on, Yousif scoffed, slipping on his pants. He dismissed it as Zionist propaganda, yet frantically switched the dials to Arab stations for confirmation or denial. The Palestinians' Sowt Falastin, a new underground station, spoke of a fierce battle the night before. It admitted a major setback but said nothing of Abd al-Qadir's fate.

But by the time Yousif drove his father to his clinic, the rumor was spreading like a gust of yellow fever. Men on the sidewalk were shaking their heads. Faces were etched with fear.

"Have you heard?" nurse Laila said, meeting them at the curb.

"Don't believe it," Yousif told her, his elbow resting on the open window.

"I bet it's true," she said, alarmed. "My brother was one of the men who went with Basim yesterday. He came back early this morning after they had been driven out. He said all the Arab fighters were worried about Abd al-Qadir. They hadn't seen him all night."

"He probably slipped away to recruit more men," Yousif offered, uneasy.

The doctor pursed his lips and shook his head. "Abd al-Qadir wouldn't leave the battle scene. If it's true he's been killed or captured, God help us."

"Were there a lot of casualties?" Yousif asked. "Did your brother say?"

Laila nodded, her eyes moist. "He says both sides lost plenty."

"You might not need the car after all," the doctor told his son, stepping out.

"I could help pick up the wounded," Yousif suggested.

"And take them where?" the doctor asked, dismayed.

"Jaffa or Jerusalem," Yousif answered. "Where else? Unless you want me to bring them to your clinic."

The doctor shook his head, his brows furrowed. "That's exactly why we need a hospital in Ardallah. No, leave it parked here until we see what's going on."

"I'd like to keep it, if you don't mind," Yousif insisted. That his father could brush him off made his skin tighten.

The doctor looked surprised. "Not after all this. Anyway, I need it more than you do."

"Laila just said there were lots of casualties," Yousif argued.

"That was last night," his father explained. "Do you think they're still lying on the ground waiting for you to pick them up?"

"I'd like to find out," Yousif insisted.

"No," the doctor said. "Hand me the key."

The fact that Laila was still on the sidewalk listening to this exchange made Yousif angry.

"You promised I could have it today," Yousif said, frustrated.

"Listen, Yousif, I don't have time for this."

"Then let's go together. They need medical help."

The doctor towered over his son. "Have you heard the saying, The road to hell is paved with good intentions? What you want to do is good, honorable. But it's too dangerous. Too late. The Jaffa-Jerusalem road is impassable with all the caravans trying to go through. The Kastal area is probably swarming with Zionist soldiers now that it's under their control. You'll be shot on sight. You want to help, fine. You'll have plenty of opportunities, believe me. But right now it's too hopeless. So give me the key and go on to school."

Yousif's anger nearly overwhelmed him. He rolled up the window, locked the car, and handed the keys back to his father. They parted without saying a word.

Crushed and humiliated, Yousif continued his walk, stopping here and there to hear what men were saying. They were all wearing mournful looks and whispering the same thing. Abd al-Qadir was missing! By the time he got to school, the rumor was chiseled in rock. Teachers hit the walls with their fists. Students cried. Yousif felt his head spinning.

Within minutes, the church bells were tolling—not only for the distinguished martyr, Yousif thought, but for the Palestinians' best hope.

NEXT MORNING, Palestine was rocked by another tragedy. Again the seven o'clock broadcast crackled with bad news. Still in his pajamas, Yousif tried to shake the sleep from his head. He couldn't be hearing right.

"Deir Yasin," the Arab announcer was saying, his voice choking, "a village four miles south of Jerusalem, seems to have been invaded last night . . ."

Yousif motioned for his father to hurry up, but kept his ears glued to the radio set. The doctor crossed the room, stepping in and out of the bright morning sun that had slashed the floor.

". . . Residents of Lifta and Karyet Abu Ghoush, two neighboring Arab villages," the announcer continued, "report extraordinarily heavy shelling and bombing, coming from the direction of Deir Yasin. The British army would neither deny nor confirm the reports. But they promised to investigate immediately. So did the Red Cross. For further details, stay tuned to this station."

The doctor pouted and knit his eyebrows. Yousif watched him nervously switch the dial from Damascus to Cairo to London and back to Jerusalem. The two were soon joined by his mother, who must have heard snatches of the broadcast and tiptoed into the room, her face white. The three sat enveloped in gloom.

YOUSIF RAN TO school. Students and teachers were in the schoolyard talking about Deir Yasin. The radio set from the faculty lounge was placed on the window sill for everyone to hear. A big crowd gathered to await the latest news. All morning reports were sketchy, but ominous.

By noon, new editions of the newspaper were sold and devoured. Yousif and Amin ran out to the street to get a copy. The square around the bus terminal was crowded with people rushing to buy the few left. Yousif elbowed his way through and purchased one. He unfolded it and was immediately surrounded by many onlookers. The headlines were big and screaming red: MASSACRE AT DEIR YASIN.

"Read," commanded a hunchbacked old man wearing a fez.

"Read, read," others echoed.

Yousif began reading aloud. His voice was low, shaking. He felt someone touch his arm. When he looked up he saw a villager, with delicate features and a well-trimmed beard, begging him with his eyes to raise his voice. Yousif read loud enough for the man to hear. The crowd grew bigger.

"According to the residents of Lifta and Kiryat Abu Ghoushe," Yousif read, "something terrible must have happened last night in nearby Deir Yasin, a village four miles south of Jerusalem. For four hours they could hear shelling of unprecedented intensity. A sixty-year-old man, Ali Abu Ridda, who rushed out of bed and stood on the roof of his house to see what was going on, said, 'It sounded like a gigantic invasion. In the quiet of the night I could hear explosions and I could see the sky ablaze. It was glowing so red I've never seen anything like it.'"

Men and women pushed around Yousif, wanting to see as well as hear him.

"Fear is mounting," Yousif continued, "that of the population of about five hundred, no one was spared to tell the tale. So far the British police have been barred from entering. It is generally believed that the Zionist invaders were, in the words of a high official, 'still mopping up.' They needed time to remove the litter and wreckage they have wrought for this peaceful, defenseless Arab village.

"What gives rise to genuine concern is the fact that all hospitals in Jerusalem reported that no casualties were brought in during the night. Obviously there was too much shelling, too much military activity for no one to be hurt. Where are the wounded, who must be in desperate need of immediate medical treatment?

"The question everyone is asking is this: What exactly has happened? It may be sometime before we find out. One can only hope and pray that Deir Yasin has not been turned into a graveyard—literally overnight."

Yousif looked up at the sea of red eyes, feeling whipped by his own emotions. The cessation of all sound and all movement was unnatural. Nobody seemed capable of breathing. Then commotion started, like a trickle that led to a flood.

"May they never enter the gate of Heaven," the midwife Najla cursed, her voice shrill.

"May they never see the face of God," the widow Martha responded.

"May all their children be orphans," the dressmaker Julia echoed.

Yousif decided to go home and listen to the news on the radio. There he could have control over the dials and switch them as he pleased. Besides, his mother shouldn't be left alone at a time like this.

But by the time he reached Zahrawi's cafe, the radio was blaring more ominous news. The crowd in the terraced garden numbered over a hundred. All looked mesmerized. Yousif stood at the outer edge, listening.

"Slaughtering a whole Arab village must not have been satisfying enough to the invaders," the announcer was saying. Hushed silence enveloped the men and women present. The unmistakable voice of Abu Walid, of the radio station, was distraught.

"Women's torn underclothing and naked sprawled bodies," the announcer added, "bespoke of the terrible shame and suffering to which the residents of Deir Yasin must have been subjected before they were disfigured and ultimately murdered."

"Allahu Akbar," shouted Arif, the bookstore owner.

"Virgins were raped in the presence of their parents," the announcer continued, his voice hoarse, strident. "Pregnant women were slit open and embryos were scattered on the floor. One woman was cut by a bayonet from her womb to her mouth. Babies' heads were crushed like chestnuts. Eyes were knocked out and left hanging like large marbles. One man was burned to ashes in his sleep. His bones and right foot were the only parts which had escaped the blaze. Children were dissected and their young flesh mercilessly scraped off their tender bones."

A waiter smashed a glass against the building. But the eyes and ears of the crowd remained riveted on the radio set.

"The Red Cross observers," the announcer said, "were shocked . . . mortified. Some cried unabashedly. Others recalled the holocaust. According to eye-witnesses, the ghost of Nazism could be found in every street of Deir Yasin, nay, in every home. Shocking evidence is there for the whole world to see. Hitler's victims have turned into victimizers. At their hand Deir Yasin has become a crematory, a cemetery, and a blot on the Jewish conscience forever."

The earth moved under Yousif's feet. He could see women in the crowd shutting their ears with their palms. Others were leaning against their husbands, crying. Men were chewing their lips. All stared. All seemed visited by a nightmare.

The announcer returned. "God," he agonized, "what is the meaning of this cruelty? When, when, O God, are the Arabs going to wake up and face the horrible facts? Save us, O Lord, from our heartless enemy. Save us from ourselves."

A woman with a big wicker basket on her head and a baby in her arms began to cry. She sobbed so fitfully that the baby slipped out of her arms and fell to the ground. The crowd rushed to pick up the infant. Yousif saw a man leaning against a wall, retching.

At the end of the broadcast, Yousif's taut fingers crumbled the paper he was holding. His chin trembled; his teeth cut a wound in his lower lip. Through his blurred eyes he now saw the cafe garden and the street below swarming with people. The atmosphere was electrified. Live wires hummed. Wild angry voices rose from the crowd. Shrieks punctuated the air.

Yousif knew they felt helpless in this new dilemma. The scope of the catastrophe awaiting them deepened their fears. To whom could they turn now? What should they do? How could they meet the Zionist ferocity that threatened their very existence? Yousif trembled with them. Again he was awakened to the true and shocking meaning of real danger.

The throng seemed strung on one cord, pulled by one force. Yousif heard all kinds of cries, all stressing one point: something must be done before it was too late. The Zionists had set Deir Yasin as an example of the terror the Arabs should expect. It would be disastrous if they were not checked in time. One man called for a general strike, others for reprisals.

"This is a *jihad,"* cried a vegetable vendor. "The gates of heaven await those who defend themselves."

ARDALLAH SHUT down. People walked aimlessly, lurched drunkenly. Others poured out from everywhere. Hundreds of students carrying their books under their arms hurried to ask questions. From the other side of the street ran a large group of schoolgirls, all donned in blue. From around every corner, every street, every alley, Yousif saw individuals and groups arriving.

"Dear God!" Yousif thought. "Not another demonstration."

Everywhere he saw people beating their chests, slapping their cheeks, biting their own fingers. Anger, bitterness, frustration gripped them. Not in their wildest dreams, some muttered, did they expect anything so cruel, so blasphemous.

"Where is this Deir Yasin?" Yousif asked Elias Kanaan, a habitual gambler. He was leaning against the wall, holding his black suspenders with both hands, and viewing the scene with the sobered look of a man who had bet on life and lost.

"Never heard of it," the gambler answered, shaking his head.

"Why do you think they did it?"

"A war of nerves," the gambler muttered and walked away.

Church bells began to toll mournful tunes. The *muezzin,* atop a minaret a mile away, could be heard reciting from the Qur'an.

"We need arms," shouted someone Yousif couldn't see.

"YEEEEES," the crowd echoed.

"To hell with the aggressors," screamed Fouad, a cinema usher.

"May God send them the plague," another shouted.

"Damn the British!"

"Damn the butchers of Deir Yasin!"

"Damn the Arab regimes!"

"Yes, down with the Arab regimes. Down with the eunuchs who call themselves kings and presidents."

Not far from where they were gathered was a pharmacy owned by a Jew. Now it was closed, for the thin bespectacled pharmacist had left Ardallah with the Sha'lans. This small well-stocked apothecary became the crowd's first target. Yousif saw several men step back and then charge its corrugated iron door. They tried it again and again until they broke its lock. Then they became wildly destructive. Hands went up to shelves and bottles were swept to the floor. Showcases were shattered by the men outside.

"Why waste all this good medicine?" Yousif pleaded, grabbing a man's arm. "At least take it and use it."

An angry man swung around and held Yousif by the collar. "If you don't like it it's just too bad," he told him, pinning him against the wall.

"Get your hands off me," Yousif demanded, pulling free.

A moment later Yousif saw that Amin was among those who had gone berserk.

"Amin, what are you doing?" Yousif asked, pulling his friend aside.

"Leave me alone," Amin screamed, knocking the fragile contents of a showcase to the ground. "What do you think I'm doing? I'm going crazy. CRAAAAAAAZY, do you hear?"

Yousif let a moment of anger pass then approached Amin again.

"That's enough now," Yousif said to Amin. "Come on, let's go."

"You leave me alone," Amin said. "The dirty sons of bitches."

"Come on, now. Come on."

Slowly, Yousif led Amin away from the shelves he was destroying. Slowly he walked him to the door, glass crunching under their feet. Five blocks later they saw the same thing happen to Moshe Sha'lan's store. The enraged crowd forced the door open and began looting everything on the the racks.

"You're going home with me," Yousif told his friend, his arm around his waist.

"No I'm not," Amin said, calm but drained.

"Why not? We should stay together at a time like this."

"I'd better go home. But thanks anyway."

"Thanks for what? Since when have you become so formal."

"You know what I mean. You go home, and I'll see you later."

Yousif walked away in a stupor. The words of the announcer rang in his ears. The images flashed before his eyes. What madness! What heinous crimes! Was this the Wandering Jew's way of returning to the Promised Land? Was this the fulfillment of biblical prophecy? How inhumane! How immoral!

As he reached the bottom of the hill which led to his house, he saw a small crowd of excited men and women in Isaac's front yard. Yousif stood in the middle of the street and watched the burning of his old friend's house. Other people were rushing to join in, but he remained in his place. Memories of Isaac and his parents flooded his mind. Now Isaac was dead. According to Amin, things were different. Heavy black smoke rose from the doors and windows of Isaac's house.

He climbed the hill, crossing deserted streets. The town's clock struck two as he opened the wrought-iron gate. His mother must have seen him coming. She opened the door and came out to meet him, her face pale, her hair disheveled. They met in the driveway, near the pear tree. He told her all he knew. She hugged him and began to weep.

"What are we going to do?" she asked, sobbing.

He put his arm around her waist and walked toward the house. Sharp wails came to him from near and far. The town was still going through convulsions. Cars sped by at eighty miles an hour. Children plastered themselves against walls to escape getting hurt. A mule got so frightened it took off through the narrow streets.

"Why didn't you bring the paper with you?" she asked, her eyes red.

"I was so angry I tore it up," he told her.

They stood on the balcony to stay in touch with neighbors and passersby. An hour later the doctor arrived, bringing with him a bundle of the latest edition of the newspapers. Yousif and his mother grabbed two and began reading, their faces pale. Momentarily they were joined by Fatima and her elderly husband, Abu Taher. Trailing them were three of their children. Their youngest was Sabha, a three-year-old girl.

"Listen to this," Yousif said. "'A single baby was found among the hundreds of corpses in the slaughtered village.'" A touching picture was printed in the middle of the page. It gripped Yousif's attention. He moved closer to show it to his parents. His father nodded knowingly.

The baby was a few months old, found suckling on his dead mother's breast. He was lying next to her, its mouth clinging to her nipple. The gunners, Yousif thought, obviously had not noticed him; otherwise, he would not have escaped. Younger infants had been slaughtered and tossed in a well. Only as the investigators had passed from house to house did the baby's crying reach a human ear. The baby must have been hungry, but the warm flow in his mother's milk had ceased.

Tears filled Yousif's and his mother's eyes. Yousif looked at the baby's picture again with mixed feeling. He showed it to Fatima and Abu Taher. He also showed it to the neighbors, the barber and his wife, who were climbing the steps, huffing and puffing.

"Look," Yousif said, showing them the picture of the baby. "The only survivor."

The barber's wife burst out crying. Her huge husband wiped his tears and blew his nose.

"Not true," the doctor said.

"What's not true?" Yousif asked.

"According to one report," the doctor informed him, "the Zionists are parading the ones they captured but did not kill."

"You mean some were spared?" Yousif wanted to know.

"Apparently a few," his father told him.

"All in all," the barber asked, "how many did they kill?"

"Hard to tell," the doctor said, "but the figures I heard range from three hundred to five hundred."

"Killed?" his wife shrieked.

"No," her husband said, putting his arm around her, "first raped, mutilated, burned, and *then* killed."

"Aaaaaah!" his wife wailed.

The other two women joined her, moaning and crying. Little Sabha tugged at her mother's ankle-length dress, her face contorted.

Yousif's attention returned to the Deir Yasin baby. Its large, frightened eyes seemed to fill the picture.

"The poor thing is heartbreaking," Yasmin said, tears streaming down her face. "What's to become of it?"

"Can we adopt him?" Yousif asked, clutching the paper with both hands.

The doctor, to whom the remarks were mainly directed, looked up from his newspaper.

"It would be nice, wouldn't it?" Yasmin asked. "To give this precious baby the care and love he needs. Maybe it's not practical, but there must be someone we can call and ask."

"You sound as serious as your son," the doctor chided her, folding the paper and then rolling it.

"Why not?" she asked.

"If it's possible we ought to do it," Yousif urged.

Her husband eyed them skeptically. "He'd be better off adopted by someone who can take him out of the country. Safety is the main thing, isn't it?"

They entered the house in silence, followed by the others. Soon they were joined by Uncle Boulus and Aunt Hilaneh. After them came Rizik Attallah, with his Brazilian wife, who seemed tongue-tied worse than before. His Spanish-looking wife again seemed disoriented.

"You can have this country," the Brazilian emigrant said, the ravages of Bell's palsy still twisting his mouth. "I'm leaving."

"Where are you going?" the barber's wife asked, sniffling.

"Back to where I came from," Rizik said, tapping his cane. "Back to Brazil."

"Si," his wife said, nodding apologetically.

Other women began to weep.

The doctor took out his pipe and tobacco pouch. "What a shame," he finally said, "Deir Yasin is our own Auschwitz."

Silence wrapped them like a black shroud.

"I just wonder," Uncle Boulus said, crossing his knee and clicking his *masbaha.*

When the uncle got lost in his thought, Yousif said: "You wonder what?"

"If it was wise to release the gruesome details of the massacre," Uncle Boulus explained. "It might backfire. Our people are defenseless. They're going to be traumatized. And I won't blame them."

"You've got a point," the doctor agreed, his face grim.

"Especially those surrounded by Jewish strongholds," uncle continued.

Yousif gulped. "What do you think might happen?" he asked.

"I hope they don't start fleeing," his uncle told him. "If someone told you a tornado was headed your way, what would you do? Would you go about your business, or would you run for your life?"

LATE IN THE afternoon Yousif was alone in the living room. Exhausted, he lay on the sofa, his head resting on his folded arms. Just before he dozed off, he heard his mother tiptoe out of the room and return with a blanket to cover him.

When he woke up, two hours later, he couldn't rise. Every muscle in his body seemed paralyzed; his feet felt as though they had been chained. Strange! Frantic, he tried to move his hands and legs but couldn't. His apprehension lasted for a few seconds but seemed much longer. Finally, he unshackled himself and sat up, looking ruffled. He reached for the radio dial. He was moving the needle back and forth when he realized that his mother was in the room ironing.

"Did you listen to the news?" he asked.

"Yes," she said, splashing water on a white shirt. "The Irgun were responsibile."

"Menachem Begin. Again. He also blew up the King David Hotel in 1946. I could've guessed it."

"The Arabs are outraged," she said, moving the iron back and forth.

"Oh, really."

"The whole world is condemning the massacre—even those who voted with the Jews at the United Nations."

"The Zionists themselves are celebrating, no doubt."

"Apparently Ben Gurion isn't. They say he's furious."

"I bet."

Silence fell between them. Yousif looked out the window, wondering if these homes would one day be invaded and their inhabitants brutalized like the people of Deir Yasin. Only yesterday he was crying over the death of one friend. Soon he would have to cry over the deaths of hundreds. And the war had not started—yet. Not officially anyway. But wars, he reminded himself, were nothing new to the Holy Land. They were new to each generation. He would never get used to them, no matter how long he lived.

A thought struck him. He hurried out of the room, without telling his mother where he was going. He headed toward his school-church compound, looking for Father Mikhail. He found him in the church dressed in full vestment, kneeling at the altar and praying the rosary. Six nuns were also kneeling in the front pew. Behind them knelt a dozen or so worshipers, all scattered throughout the church.

Father Mikhail prayed in a deep monotone: "Hail Mary, full of grace, the Lord is with thee. Blessed art thou among women and blessed is the fruit of thy womb, Jesus."

And the somber, black-clad nuns and everyone else in the church murmured, "Holy Mary, Mother of God, pray for us sinners. Now and at the hour of our death. Amen."

Circumstances made the prayers sound hollow—as useless as another demonstration, as empty as another political speech. A true god would not permit his people to sink so low. A true god was, is, a loving god. Yousif couldn't help how he felt. Deir Yasin had knocked all religion and faith out of him.

The recitation droned on and on for the next half hour. Yousif fell into a trance until the service was over, then he approached the priest in the vestry.

"Father, may I ask you a favor?" he began.

"Sure, Yousif," Father said, removing part of his vestment and kissing it before putting it away.

"Is it possible to get all the Catholic churches in Palestine to toll the bells for the next twenty-four hours?"

The priest's hands seemed to freeze. "What a strange request! What do you have in mind?"

Yousif moved closer, standing erect. "The bells have a sweet, melancholy sound. Ringing them all night long throughout the country will send a message. It might make an impression on the foreign press and all the embassies. I want them to know the depth of our revulsion at the massacre."

Father Mikhail took a deep breath. "Also—as an appeal to God for mercy?" he whispered.

Yousif hesitated, not feeling a bit spiritual. "More as an announcement to the world of our sadness, our anger," he said. "We're so helpless, so inept. I feel sorry for our people, and disgusted with myself in particular for being so . . . so paralyzed. No leadership, no army, no money, no friends, no initiative. Palestine is going to be lost and I can't stand it. I want to do something but I don't know what or where or how."

"I see," the priest said, his beard looking grayer than ever.

The tall kindly priest seemed genuinely moved. He stood in the middle of the room, his eyes moist.

"I don't know about the rest of Palestine, or about all the catholic churches," Father Mikhail told him. "But you have my permission to ring the bells of this church from now till tomorrow morning."

"What about the rest? Will you ask the Bishop or the Patriarch?"

"I'll try. In the meantime go ahead and do it here. We'll see what happens."

"Thanks, Father."

"But let me warn you. You need a lot of help. It's not an easy job."

"Don't worry, Father. I can do it."

Yousif rushed out to find Amin and look for other classmates. Within an hour he managed to come up with a crew of six bell-ringers, including Jamal.

And so from dusk to dawn they sat on the tiny stairwell taking turns pulling the heavy ropes connected to the belfry. There were two bells to ring: one large and one small. It took two men to ring the big bell, one to ring the other. Every fifteen seconds Yousif and Khalil, or Adeeb and Karam, or Hassan and Isa would pull down on a two-inch-thick rope, feeling the muscles stretched from their shoulders to their fingertips. The huge metallic ball, a hundred feet above their heads, would give one deep resonant clang. Five seconds later, Jamal or Nadim (a medical technician still wearing a lab coat) would answer with a softer ring that sounded like a distant echo. The effect was like a heart crying.

One-armed Amin couldn't participate in the ringing. Yet he had plenty to do. Yousif could hear him explaining to the curious gathering outside what the constant ringing was all about. Once, Yousif thought he heard Salwa's voice. He handed the rope to Isa and went out, his arms sore and his hands blistered. There was no Salwa—only men and women and children standing in the impenetrable silence of the moonlight.

Throughout the night, the bells of St. George Catholic Church in Ardallah tolled for the hundreds of victims at Deir Yasin.

18

Many of the men at Yousif's house two nights later had been by at Christmas or played poker with his father on New Year's Eve. But tonight there were others—old men in flowing robes and *abayas,* young and middle-aged men in western suits. In addition to the mayor and his entire city council were Uncle Boulus; ustaz Sa'adeh, a former mayor who was so emaciated Yousif feared he might expire every time he spoke; an elderly councilman with a wooden leg he had lost in a car accident in America; old man Abu Khalil, who had mended Amin's arm; and Abu Nassri, with his ubiquitous dark glasses.

But tonight there were no drinks and no laughs. Tonight they were yelling all at once. They hushed for a moment, then started all over again. Led by the corpulent, ruddy, and ill-tempered mayor, the group had come to fulfill Basim's prediction a few weeks earlier: they wanted Dr. Safi to turn over the hospital money so they could buy arms. Ardallah, they all insisted, desperately needed protection. Deir Yasin had made it obvious that they could not wait any longer for outside help. If they wanted to save their town then they would have to do it themselves.

When Basim had predicted such confrontation, Yousif recalled, his father had sounded indignant. Now Yousif feared that a similar posture on his father's part would be labeled nothing short of treason. These men were out for blood. Should his father, so soon after the recent massacre, recite his opposition to violence of any kind, should he proclaim brotherly love for all mankind—including the enemy—

the roof could certainly come tumbling down over their heads.

The salon was now full of fifteen anxious men. The situation was grave; his father had better be careful. The wrong sentiment, the wrong gesture, could be damaging.

"For God's sake, Jamil, what's the matter with you?" the mayor asked, the ashes of his cigar an inch long.

"Nothing is the matter with me," the doctor answered, frowning.

"Since when are you this stubborn?" the mayor continued, gesturing and causing the ashes to fall in his lap. "After all, it's not your money. It's the people's money. And they want it back."

Dr. Safi shook his head. "I'm sorry but I can't do it. I never claimed it was mine. But I was entrusted with it to do one thing and that's what I intend to do."

Affable ustaz Sa'adeh crossed his legs, leaned on the arm of his chair, and rolled the English newspaper he was carrying. "First things first, Doctor. Without some protection we'd be as good as dead."

Dr. Safi's smile was enigmatic. "I can appreciate your fear, Ustaz, believe me. But please answer this: what good would a meager fourteen thousand pounds do?"

"They'd buy sixty or seventy guns on the black market," ustaz Sa'adeh was quick to answer.

"If they save one family from being butchered," the mayor added, "it's good enough for me."

"The hospital will save dozens of families," Dr. Safi countered. "To protect ourselves we need fourteen *million,* not thousand. We need a *hundred* and fourteen million, in fact. That's the kind of armament we'd be facing."

They all wanted to pounce on the doctor at once. But old man Abu Khalil, the bone fixer, held the floor.

"You've got to start with something," he objected, his white beard trembling. "That's all we've got. And it will have to do for the time being. As the proverb says, you stretch your legs according to the size of your mattress."

The doctor glared at the old man. Yousif suspected that his father wanted to remind this old goat that they needed the hospital for the express purpose of stopping the likes of him from costing the Amins of Ardallah their arms. Luckily, his father kept quiet.

"Common sense will tell you that," Uncle Boulus agreed.

"Boulus!" the doctor said, annoyed. "Are you suggesting I lack common sense?"

"That's not what I meant," Uncle Boulus apologized.

"It's a waste of time, Abu Khalil," the doctor said. "And a waste of money, if I may add."

"Money, he says," the emaciated former mayor said, shocked. "Who cares about money at a time like this? We're talking about lives, Doctor. *Lives.*"

"It will take money to save lives," the doctor pressed. "If all the Arab armies combined don't pitch in now, the little money we have will go down the drain."

"Hell, we agree with you a hundred percent," said a chainsmoking Abu Nassri. "But we must get out of the hole we're in. We've got families to protect."

"We should've thought of that long ago."

"It's never too late," ustaz Sa'adeh said.

"It will be worse tomorrow," the feisty Abu Khalil warned. "Even at my age I'll fight. Just hand me a gun."

No one laughed. Fatima appeared at the door with a large tray of Arabic coffee. Yousif got up to take it from her. Tradition dictated that coffee should be served according to age, but Yousif was in no mood to guess who was older. He served the emaciated former mayor, then the incumbent mayor and then went around the room. Gloom seemed to descend on them, as they all sipped their demitasse cups without speaking.

It was the doctor who broke the silence. "I'll tell you what we should do."

Everybody looked up, curious.

"Let's leave the hospital money alone and start another fund," the doctor suggested. "And I'll put up the first hundred pounds." He reached for his hip pocket and took out his wallet.

"That's a good idea," said Badr Khalifeh, the youngest councilman.

"Hell no, it's not," said Jiryes Abdu, removing his thick, horn-rimmed glasses. "We don't have time."

"People are terrified," objected the lame councilman, Ayoub Salameh.

"I have another idea," Yousif offered, raising his voice above the rest.

They all perked their ears. Before speaking, Yousif got up and cracked the window to let the cigarette smoke out.

"Why not form a delegation and start a dialogue with the Jews?" Yousif asked. "We have intelligent people. They have intelligent people. Why not talk? Words are better than bullets."

Some men shifted in their chairs, unimpressed. A woman could be heard yelling at her child and then spanking him. The child's scream filled the air.

The house painter, Yacoub, smacked his lips. "I thought you had something to say."

But Yousif stood his ground. "One can always fight. But first let's try talking to them. I don't think the average Jew likes what's happening. We lived together like good neighbors. They were happy. We were happy. Why can't we go on just like before?"

Yousif could tell his father was proud of him. But the two avoided each other's eyes.

"You seem to have a short memory," said Lutfi Khayyat, a round-faced bank manager. "Didn't your friend Isaac come back with a gun? The outsiders have gotten to the local Jews. They've changed. We can't talk to them now."

"But we haven't tried," Yousif said. "Have we?"

"What do you want us to do," the bank manager asked, "put a full-page ad in all the newspapers here and abroad—in New York, London, Paris—and ask for a PEACE conference?"

"Maybe we'll be surprised."

Most of the men shrugged their shoulders. Several turned their backs on him and started talking to each other.

"If a war breaks out," Yousif argued, "both sides—"

"If a war breaks out?" the lame councilman mocked. "Hell, what do you think this is? A soccer game? Grow up, boy."

The doctor sat at the edge of his chair, his back stiff. "Yousif is not a boy," he insisted. "We'll all be a whole lot better off if we listen to what he has to say."

"It's juvenile," someone blasted.

"It's not juvenile," the doctor defended.

There was a short but tense pause.

"Much, much too late," Yacoub said. "The enemy is baring his teeth. We need arms. Now."

The doctor pursed his lips. "Then you'd better get you a war chest. Fighting them with the hospital money is like treating cerebral hemorrhage with aspirin."

"Agreed," said left-handed Nicola Awad, the cabinet maker. "But time is running out."

Yousif pulled his chair forward and raised his voice. "Let's be honest. Have we exhausted all peaceful means? Frankly, I don't think so."

"Sure we have," said Jiryes Abdu. "We offered to live in one country, but they said no. They want a separate *Jewish* state. Where will that be if not on your land and my land and his land?"

"I'm talking people-to-people," Yousif insisted. "Have we tried to work with the tens of thousands of Jews like the Sha'lans? I'm sure they don't want war any more than we do."

Their looks froze him in place.

"What is it with him?" Jiryes asked, leaning toward Yacoub.

"He's dreaming," Yacoub answered, shaking his head.

Some of the men began to shift in their seats. Finding no solace in the grim faces around him, Yousif's eyes fell on the two-layered curtains before him. The ecru-colored sheer behind the white, hand-made lace—which his mother had commissioned the nuns of the Sacred Heart to crochet for her—displayed a scene that for a moment caught his attention. Silhouetted against the window were gracefully-winged cherubim playing the trumpets.

"There are fifteen men in this room," the doctor said, winding his wrist watch. "I offered to put up a hundred pounds to start a new fund. I raise it to two hundred. Come on, match it. There are at least three thousand families in this town. If every family would come up with twenty pounds, we'd have a lot more money than we're arguing about."

"Some people can't afford it," someone protested.

"Okay, let them come up with whatever they can afford. And don't forget that there are many who can give a lot more. That will solve the problem."

"But that's not the issue," the mayor insisted, his face flushed. "The hospital money doesn't belong to you."

Yousif was surprised at his Uncle Boulus, expecting him to come to his father's defense. Uncle Boulus must've read his mind. He put his *masbaha* away and accepted a cigarette from a packet Yacoub was passing around.

"In all fairness," Uncle Boulus said. "The doctor isn't exactly pocketing the money. He's safeguarding it for the good of the community."

"Still," the mayor argued. "We made a mistake when we didn't elect a board of directors."

Soon they were engulfed in a fresh round of arguments.

Before long Uncle Boulus threw up his hands. "Give them the money, for Christsake, and be done with it. After the war, we'll see—."

"That's just it," the doctor interjected. "I'm not going to wait and see. After the war people will have all kinds of excuses not to pay. Then I won't be able to raise a shilling."

"If we lose the war, who cares?" ustaz Sa'adeh asked, slapping his own knee with the rolled English newspaper.

"I care," the doctor told him, his wallet still in hand. "People will get sick then just as they do now—only worse."

Again, a heavy silence filled the room.

"Put your wallet back in your pocket, Doctor, we don't need your money," councilman Ayoub Salameh, with the wooden leg, said very slowly. "But wait until every woman in town comes knocking on your door. I'm going to organize a demonstration against you, so help me God."

All eyes looked at the handicapped man and then at the doctor.

The doctor looked tired. "Don't threaten me."

"And if that doesn't work," Ayoub Salameh continued, his small black eyes unblinking and his voice raspy, "we're going to drag you to court and smear your name with mud."

"You're still threatening," the doctor said.

"Damn right, I'm threatening, and I'm going to threaten more," the man shouted, reaching for his cane. "This is war, Doctor, not a crisis. Keep your filthy money and your Goddamn wisdom and I'll show you."

The salon was now in an uproar. Someone inadvertently knocked a small serving table. Cups and saucers tumbled to the floor, spilling coffee on the Tabriez rug. The men began to leave, some reticent, some vocal—but all unhappy.

"Read this," ustaz Sa'adeh said to Yousif, handing him the English newspaper. "And then give it to your father."

"Anything in particular?" Yousif asked, still reeling from the commotion.

"You'll know," the principal said and left.

Like a good host, Yousif walked out with the guests. On the veranda he felt a hand tapping his shoulder. It was the mayor.

"Do you know where Basim is?" the mayor asked, unwrapping a new cigar.

"No, sir," Yousif said.

"He's the only who can convince your father."

"Probably."

The mayor squinted his eyes. "I admire a boy who's true to his blood. But if you really love your father you ought to work on him. He's got to change his mind."

Yousif appreciated the mayor's speaking to him as an adult. But because they were standing a few inches from each other, and because the man was reeking with the smell of cigars, Yousif found himself backing away.

"I still think he has a valid point," Yousif said.

"People are scared. That massacre woke them up."

Yousif nodded.

"There's no reason to split Ardallah at a time like this," the mayor pressed.

The other men at the bottom of the steps seemed impatient. By look and gesture they were telling the mayor to hurry up. But Yousif wanted to have one more word with him.

"Have you thought about—"

"What?" the mayor interrupted.

"—getting together with Arab and Jewish mayors to see what could be done?"

The mayor's large hazel eyes became moored. "What Jewish mayors?" he asked. "There aren't any—except the one in Tel Aviv. Their colonies don't have mayors, per se. Damn it, that's the whole point. We're the overwhelming majority and they want to take over."

In reply, Yousif tried to be diplomatic. "Wouldn't you like to go down in history as a man who tried? As a man of peace?"

The mayor scrutinized his face. "You know, I really think you're serious about all this drivel."

"It is *not* drivel."

Someone blew his horn for the mayor to hurry up. But the mayor took his time. Yousif could tell the man's facial muscles and hazel eyes were suddenly relaxed.

"When I heard about your tantrum after that boy Isaac was killed," the mayor said, "I wondered what kind of a milksop you'd turn out to be. I judged you wrong. Now you strike me as a sincere young man. I disagree with you—but I admire your courage."

Yousif stood on the veranda until he saw the mayor's car backing all the way out. Then he went inside, heading toward his bedroom. He threw himself on his bed and opened the newspaper ustaz Sa'adeh had given him. It was the *New York Times,* dated April 10, 1948. One of the headlines read:

> 200 ARABS KILLED, STRONGHOLD TAKEN
>
> JERUSALEM, April 9—A combined force of the Irgun Zvai Leumi and the Stern group, Jewish extremist underground forces, captured the Arab village of Deir Yasin in the western outskirts of Jerusalem today. In house-to-house fighting the Jews killed more than 200 Arabs, half of them women and children.
>
> At the same time a Haganah counter-attack three miles away drove an Arab force, estimated by the Haganah at 2,500 men, out of the strategic village of Kastal on a hill overlooking the Jerusalem-Tel Aviv convoy road. This village was captured after a six-hour fight during which it repeatedly changed hands. The Jews, who first seized Kastal last Saturday, had been forced out yesterday.

The battle at Kastal was old news by now. Yousif's eyes scanned the newspaper column looking for more information about the massacre.

> The capture of Deir Yasin, situated on a hill overlooking the birthplace of John the Baptist, marked the first cooperative effort since 1942 between the Irgun and Stern groups, although the Jewish Agency for Palestine does not recognize these terrorist groups. Twenty men of the Agency's Haganah militia reinforced fifty-five Irgunists and forty-five Sternists who seized the village.
>
> The engagement marked the formal entry of the Irgunists and Sternists into the battle against the Arabs. Previously both groups had concentrated against the British.
>
> In addition to killing more than 200 Arabs, they took forty prisoners.
>
> The Jews carried off some seventy women and children who were turned over later to the British Army in Jerusalem.
>
> Victors Describe Battle
>
> The Irgunists and Sternists escorted a party of United States correspondents to a house at Givat Shaul, near Deir Yasin, tonight and offered them tea and cookies and amplified the details of the operation.

Yousif was mortified. "*. . . and offered them tea and cookies . . .*" he read again, incredulous. Had man sunk this low! Tea and cookies after such an atrocity? But he read on:

> The spokesman said that the village had become a concentration point for the Arabs, including Syrians and Iraqis, planning to attack the western suburbs of Jerusalem. If, as he expected, the Haganah took over occupation of the village, it would help to cover the convoy route from the coast.
>
> The spokesman said he regretted the casualties among the women and children at Deir Yasin but asserted that they were inevitable because almost every house had to be reduced by force. Ten houses were blown up. At others the attackers blew open the doors and threw in hand grenades.
>
> One hundred men in four groups attacked at 4:30 in the morning, the spokesman said. The Irgunists wore uniforms of secret design and they used automatic weapons and rifles.
>
> An Arabic-speaking Jew, the spokesman said, shouted over a loudspeaker from an armored car used in the attack, that the Arab women and children should take refuge in the caves. Some of them, he said, did so.

Yousif closed his eyes, unable to read further. His heart was wrenched. How could he be a pacifist after reading such an account? Still, he didn't believe war was the answer. What in God's name should he do? Suddenly he jumped up and rushed to the living room, where his father was still fiddling with the radio dials.

"Read this," Yousif said, handing him the newspaper.

The doctor seemed startled. "What's it about?" he asked, his tie loosened.

"Tea and cookies," Yousif answered, sitting in the opposite armchair.

The doctor eyed him suspiciously. Ten minutes later, their eyes met. Yousif kept his eyes on his father, but the doctor turned his head away, absorbed.

"Premeditated mass murder," the doctor finally said, the newspaper rustling in his hands.

"The details aren't nearly as graphic as those we heard from the Red Cross and British observers," Yousif said.

"What do you expect from the Western press?" the doctor said. "I'm surprised they wrote that much."

"Nothing about the rapes and mutilations. Nothing about the wells they dumped the victims in."

The doctor nodded, pouting. "Nothing is new under the sun and nothing will remain hidden under the sun. Sooner or later it will all come out."

"Sooner or later you'll have to give up the hospital money," Yousif said.

"I will not."

"It would be a pity if you did, but I'm afraid fear is mounting."

"Mark my word," the doctor said, the stem of his pipe resting on his cheek, "if I gave them the money they'd go bang-bang-bang for about a week and nothing would be accomplished. I'm sorry to say this, but it's true. I know our people. What this country needs is schools, hospitals, roads—not another war. Of course the Jews aren't helping matters any with their insistence on a separate Jewish state. If you ask me, both sides are foolish. The winner will be a loser."

"That's beside the point," Yousif said, his right leg jerking.

The doctor remained stern. "Can you forget Isaac's murder?

"No I can't."

"And you never will," his father told him. "What you see with your own eyes stays with you. Do you understand? It stays with you. Well, there's a scene I'll never forget . . ."

It was going to be a long story, Yousif could tell. But he was willing to listen.

"As you know," the doctor said, "when I was your age I was drafted into the Turkish army. I fought in World War I against the English. Toward the end of the war—about a year after my mother was brutally—"

The doctor seemed unable to finish the sentence. Then he got up, motioning for Yousif to follow. They walked through the house and Yousif could hear his mother talking on the phone to his grandparents in Jerusalem. Yousif and his father finally stood on the western veranda. It was a balmy night. The lights of Jaffa were like a million jewels scattered by the sea. In the distance they could hear muffled sounds of guns. But from the garden immediately below they could smell the roses.

"See that hill?" the doctor said, pointing his finger. "Just beyond it there's a huge field that becomes swampy during winter. In the summer of 1917, the British were winning but the Turks refused to surrender. And in that open field the two sides pitched a fierce battle: face to face, hand to hand. Luckily, I was fighting on the other side of Jaffa at the time, but they brought us here to bury the dead. What I saw there with my own eyes I'll never forget as long as I live."

Never had Yousif heard his father unburden himself as he was now. He was grieving as though it had happened yesterday. The doctor removed his glasses and began to wipe them with his white handkerchief. As always, he looked myopic without them.

"The whole field was littered with bodies," the doctor remembered, making a wide sweep with his right hand. "I got sick seeing so many corpses. Torn-off limbs, decapitated bodies, broken arms, frozen eyes, wide-open mouths."

"Another Deir Yasin," Yousif interjected.

"It was awful, just awful," his father continued. "Our job was to dig up ditches and bury the dead. But I didn't have the heart or the strength. I just stood there—sad, angry, devastated. I was so sick in my stomach I wanted to scream. But I was afraid of the Turkish officer: he was in a nasty mood. I bit my lip and prayed to God to keep me from fainting. Then I felt someone push me down. It was the officer himself. His name was Heidar Bey—I'll never forget it. He rattled some Turkish which we couldn't understand. But his tone told us everything."

Yousif could hear some of his birds in the next room twittering.

"Heidar Bey himself," the doctor continued, "went around inspecting the endless carpet of casualties, firing off his pistol at all those who were still breathing."

"How long did it take you to bury all those people?" Yousif asked, touched by his father's memories.

"We didn't actually bury them," the doctor answered, taking a deep breath. "They were so many, Heidar Bey finally decided it would take too long. So we just piled them up in several heaps, covered them with wood and brush and set them on fire."

"How awful!" Yousif said.

"You should've seen the tall flames, the black smoke. Every few minutes you would hear human skulls popping like chestnuts. It was a nightmare. The stench was nauseating. Can you imagine lifting up bodies and having all their intestines spill out on your hands and feet?"

"My God!" Yousif said.

"For months," the doctor resumed, clutching the railing, "bodies were scattered all over these mountains. Animals didn't eat them because there were no animals left. The heavy fighting—especially the bombings for three years—had taken its toll on the animals. They either were killed or simply vanished. The farmers wouldn't touch the human carcasses because they were afraid of disease. So they just sat there and rotted. Some of them became solid as a rock and black as a burnt tree trunk. It wasn't unusual to find one or two such corpses scattered here and there among grapevines in one's own field. This land is tragic I tell you. It wouldn't surprise me if every inch of it has been part of a grave at one time or another. You know the human skull I have in my office?"

"Yes," Yousif answered.

"It came out of our own front yard when we were building the old house."

Yousif recalled the eerie-looking skull with the elongated chin and black sockets.

"It's true," the doctor continued. "Ploughmen find them all the time. As much as I love this country, it's nothing but a big cemetery. More wars have been fought here than any other place in the world. From time immemorial, here more than anywhere else, man has been at his brother's throat."

Yousif listened intently.

"I have an idea that might sound crazy to most people, maybe even to you," the doctor said, walking around the veranda until they faced east. "But you're my son and you're entitled to know how your father thinks."

"Go ahead," Yousif said.

"Listen," the doctor said, leaning against a marble column.

Yousif perked his ear. All he could hear were normal city sounds, especially the rolling of cars. Every now and then he could hear a volley of bullets in the distance.

"Some nights when you sit here and listen carefully, especially on a quiet night, you can almost hear a kind of current murmuring underground. Some think it's water that needs to be discovered. Others think it's oil which will one day make us all rich. Personally, I think it's Mother Earth groaning from the weight of our sins. It's her bowels churning from the *filth* we've dumped into her throughout the ages."

The doctor's pipe glowed in the darkness.

"People will forget everything I've done for this town," he said, his eyes shining. "But I don't care. I honestly believe the meek *will* inherit the earth. Arabs and Jews belong to the only three monotheistic religions. They should forget about their differences and try to build on what's common to all of them. Why can't they live according to the Sermon on the Mount? Muslims and Jews should love it as much as we Christians do. It's simple—yet so compassionate."

The doctor's decency was contagious. Yousif could hear his mother turning lights off around the house and calling their names. He wanted to tell her that they were on the veranda, enveloped in darkness. That they were alone—but not afraid.

19

Yousif soon discovered that his support for his father was going to cause him trouble. Everywhere he turned in school, someone made a nasty remark. Except for Amin, no one would talk to him. Today, right after the ten o'clock recess, he sensed the atmosphere in the class was particularly charged. Why, he didn't know. Good thing it was ustaz Hakim and no one else was coming to teach. The other teachers were just like the students—unfriendly, derisive. But ustaz Hakim had better hurry up, Yousif thought, if he cared to stave off a fight.

"Did you hear about the doctor who's a fraud?" Anees was telling Nabeeh, the school's best runner.

"No," Nabeeh answered, carving his name on the desk with a pocketknife.

"Well, they say there's a doctor who won't leave a room even if a bomb's exploded next door."

"Why?" Nabeeh asked, feigning surprise. "Is he dumb?"

"No, he's deaf *and* dumb," Anees replied. "They should take his license away from him."

A chubby-faced cross-eyed student, Amjad, sat on top of his desk and chimed in. "They say his son is just as awful—if not worse. And he wants to be a doctor. I feel sorry for his patients, don't you?"

Yousif wiped the blackboard and tried to laugh it off.

"Your act stinks," he said, turning to face them. "You need someone else to write your lines. But if you want to cut out the comedy routine and debate the issue of the hospital money—I'm willing."

There were giggles.

"Only if you invite us on the pages of the *New York Times,"* Anees said. "Fellows, would you go to a Peace Conference uninvited?"

"No," the class answered like a chorus in the Greek Orthodox church.

Yousif knew what to expect. The crippled councilman, Ayoub Salameh, had started his smear campaign. There was no telling what vicious rumors he had spread around about his father. Amin looked at Yousif, then turned around and faced the three jokers—unamused.

"Perhaps we should keep in mind what Dr. Safi means to this town," Amin reminded them.

"Who, the Jew lover?" Nabeeh asked.

Yousif was startled.

"Some people are liable to get their tongues pulled out," Amin said, "unless they shut up."

"Big words from a one-armed midget," Adeeb said, chewing gum and leaning on his side. "Aren't you afraid someone might cut off this stump of yours and stick it up your ass?"

Suddenly, Amin and Adeeb were like two tightly wound coils that had been let loose. They sprang at each other with full force. Students flew away from them, banging their desk tops in the process.

"Stop it, stop it," Yousif pleaded, reaching for the bell.

Someone flicked the light off and on several times. Yousif looked up, trying to pull the combatants apart. Ustaz Hakim was at the door, his hand on the switch. He kept flicking the lights on and off to get everyone's attention.

"What's going on?" the ustaz asked, walking into the room.

As Amin turned and looked at the teacher, Adeeb punched him right on the jaw. Blood squirted from Amin's mouth. Amin became furious and began kicking the bigger boy, catching Adeeb squarely on the crotch. Everyone in the room gasped. Adeeb howled. Yousif thought Adeeb would keel over any second.

"Aaaaaaaoooooowwwwww!" Adeeb howled again, clutching his testicles.

Yousif looked at the door, expecting ustaz Saadeh to dash in any minute. The principal did not show up. Others did. Yousif could see their faces peering in through the small glass rectangle. And ustaz Hakim, his face ruddy, found it necessary to go out and explain to the other teachers what had happened. In the meantime, the fury within the classroom seemed to subside. But Adeeb's face looked bleached.

"Unbecoming," Ustaz Hakim said, returning to his desk. "Especially of seniors graduating in a few weeks."

"Amin started it," Nabeeh accused.

"You're lying," Amin defended himself.

Ustaz Hakim picked up his books nervously. "I don't *care,* "he said, dropping the books on the desk with a bang. "All of you are to blame. What a terrible example you're setting for the rest of the school. You sound like the rest of the Arab countries—bickering at a time when we need unity in the worst way. Shame on you."

At lunch time Yousif didn't go home. His stomach was knotted and he couldn't eat anyway. Besides, he wanted to be with his father and tell him about the incident.

His father's waiting room was crowded as usual. Nurse Laila was on the phone, her hair parted in the middle and her black eyes sparkling. Children were crying or jumping on empty seats or getting between their parents' legs. Many of the patients were villagers Yousif didn't know. But there were a few from Ardallah, whom he was glad to see.

A young couple, married for less than three months, was there together. Osama Attiyeh, the handsome groom, stood up and shook Yousif's hand and spoke to him briefly. But the attractive bride averted her eyes, color rising to her cheeks. The way she blushed and cast her eyes down let Yousif know that they were there to see his father about having children. How embarrassing, Yousif thought, feeling sorry for the young bride. How Arabs loved offspring! Probably her mother-in-law, Yousif thought, was behind this visit to the doctor's office. Probably the women at the baker's shop had aroused her concern, having asked her, "Is your daughter-in-law pregnant? She's *not?*Anything wrong? Three months is long enough."

Yousif walked in on his father and Basim, who were apparently having another argument. Sunlight was flooding half the room from the big rectangular window. It highlighted the doctor's wispy gray hair and made the chrome of the stethoscope sparkle around his neck. The doctor was seated in his swivel chair, both hands at the armrests. Basim was standing in the shaded area, his fist pounding a pile of medical books on the desk. Yousif might as well not have entered, the little attention either paid him.

"How can a man be like this?" Basim asked, about to explode.

On a bookcase, catty-cornered behind his father, was the human skull that the doctor had talked about the night before. For some reason Yousif thought it was staring at him. He moved around to get it out of his peripheral vision.

Basim straightened up, looking grim. "There's going to be a public meeting this afternoon at al-Rowda Hotel's garden," he said, reaching for a pack of Players. "We're starting a fund-raising campaign to buy arms."

"That was my idea," the doctor said, leaning back. "When I suggested it they all thought I was crazy. Yousif can tell you."

Up till now, Yousif didn't think they were aware of his presence.

"They still prefer using the hospital money," Basim continued. "In fact, they were planning to demonstrate in front of your house. I managed to stop them but I don't know for how long. If I walk out of this room empty-handed, there's no telling what will happen. Things can get out of control." He leaned forward and rested his hands on the book. "Surprise them, Uncle. Give them the money and let them do whatever they want with it. If not the fourteen thousand, give them ten. If not ten—seven. Let them know you're on their side. You'll become an instant hero."

Looking like the Sphinx, the doctor lit his pipe. "What side do you think I'm on?"

"The side of the Holy Spirit, I guess," Basim answered, his voice without edge. "Whatever it is, I don't understand it."

"Yousif understands it," the doctor said, proud.

Yousif tightened his lips and watched. There was a long pause. What seemed to infuriate Basim most, Yousif noticed, was the doctor's impervious attitude, his sense of superiority, his apparent immodesty. Yousif observed his father leaf through a book on his desk, his pipe in his mouth. He seemed absorbed.

"It took me over fifteen years to raise that money," the doctor said, shutting the book, "and I'm not about to let them buy firecrackers."

Nurse Laila opened the sliding door. Before she could say anything the doctor told her to hold off all patients for a few more minutes. She left and closed the door.

"You're probably still smarting from the death of your friend Isaac," Basim said to Yousif. "I can understand that. But remember, not all Jews are as innocent as Isaac."

"Nor are all Arabs as good as my father," Yousif rebutted.

"But your father is not the issue," Basim argued, flicking his ashes angrily. "Unless he chooses to become one. There are people out there yelling for his blood."

"Let them yell," Yousif said, defiant. "I'm no soldier."

"That's for sure," Basim sneered, starting toward the sliding door. But before he went out he turned around and looked at Yousif.

"Deir Yasin," he said, his lips pursed, "is scaring everybody. How would you feel if there's another massacre right here in Ardallah? Wouldn't your conscience bother you?"

Basim slammed the sliding door so hard behind him that it closed and then bounced open about three inches. When Yousif got up to close it he discovered that it had jumped off the track. He had a hard time pulling it up and putting it back in place.

Father and son sat for a long time in deep silence. Even the nurse must have sensed that the two needed to be alone. Yousif picked up a metallic letter opener from his father's desk and toyed with it, wondering what Salwa would think of all this. A bird dipped sweetly before his eyes, perched itself on the window sill for a brief moment, then alighted on a power line.

Slowly the doctor, looking wary, opened his desk. He pulled out his checkbook and started writing. When he finished he tore the check out and handed it to Yousif.

"Go to the meeting and give them this," the doctor said. "That is, if you don't mind taking the heat and abuse for your father. I don't feel up to facing the uproar today. Some other time yes, but not now. I'm too tired."

"I don't mind," Yousif said, looking at the five hundred-pound check in his hands. "It's pretty generous, but I doubt it will appease them."

"I'm sure Ayoub Salameh would take me to task," the doctor said, smiling for the first time. "How people do change!"

Yousif waited for an explanation.

"When that man returned from America," the doctor recalled, "I took him under my wings, so to speak. His leg was still bothering him, and I looked after it. I started him in business, I loaned him money to pay for his son's wedding, and I helped him get elected to the city council. Now he's leading a campaign to smear my name with mud."

"But why?" Yousif asked, shocked.

"It's not uncommon," the doctor told his son, rising out of his chair. "He was pushing for a zoning policy that would've netted him some money. I opposed it because it would've cost the city tens of thousands, ruined many a choice piece of land, and ended up being a crooked road in more ways than one. Anyway you looked at it, it just didn't make sense. I thought he got over it, but it looks like he's still holding a grudge."

"Ittaqi sharra man ahsanta ilaih," Yousif quoted a popular proverb.

"Exactly," his father agreed. "Beware of the one you've been good to."

Yousif's mind drifted. A mist seemed to rise before his eyes, revealing new truths. Nations, it was clear to him now, behaved like individuals.

"The Arabs have always been good to the Jews," Yousif said, with genuine consternation on his face. "The West has mistreated them and we've given them a haven."

The doctor walked around his desk and put his hand on his son's shoulders, nodding like a man accustomed to twists and ironies. "That's why we have to fear them most," he said, smiling knowingly.

Uncertainty filled the silence. Again, Yousif became uncomfortably conscious of the human skull on the bookcase behind his father. It looked sinister. The darkness in the steady gaze of those sockets was insensibly seductive. A keen chill shot through his spine.

THE PUBLIC meeting was held at one o'clock in the garden of Al-Rowda Hotel. Although he was an early arrival, Yousif took a back seat. He did not tell anyone about the check in his pocket, wanting to keep people in suspense. Here was an opportunity for him to study mob psychology firsthand.

The garden looked stripped naked. Tables were stacked up on the balcony and chairs were arranged in classroom fashion. Except for the fifteen or twenty people scattered here and there, the garden looked deserted, almost depressing. There was no gentle breeze to blow the scraps of paper off the ground. The midday sun cast ominous shadows under the solemn rows of gigantic cypress trees.

Only a summer ago, Yousif remembered, the moon had shone through the branches and shimmered over the dancing couples. Some danced cheek-to-cheek; others stepped and swayed to the rhythmic beat of the tango, the rhumba, and the foxtrot. He recalled dancing with Salwa, and ached to see her again. Would she be coming to the meeting? He hoped she wouldn't come with Adel Farhat.

The crowd began to arrive in groups of twos and threes. Ustaz Sa'adeh and Rashad Hakim came together. Yousif did not join them lest they question him about his father. The new arrivals were mostly men, Yousif noticed, except for a few high school girls and a couple of women he had seen around town. Spring had shed the coats off most men, and they came in short sleeves and open collars. The women looked lovely in their yellow and red spring dresses.

The few hundred seats were soon occupied, and a few hundred more people were standing. Everyone was busy looking around, either to be seen or to see who was not present. The mayor and a few prominent citizens, including Lutfi Khayyat, the bank manager, sat at the front row. Basim was among them, looking restless. The mayor walked up to the makeshift podium.

"Let's all stand and bow our heads for a minute of silence in memory of the victims of Deir Yasin," the mayor said.

The crowd rose and remained standing, all heads bowed. A minute later everyone sat down.

"I need not tell you why we're here," the mayor said, clutching the podium with both hands. "But I can tell you that we are approaching a watershed in our destiny. We need money and we need arms. It's as simple as that. And we need them now. If there ever was a time for us to dig deep in our pockets—this is it. If there ever was a time for us to sacrifice—this is it. So let me open this fund-raising drive by pitching in two hundred pounds."

The audience applauded. The humming began. A short, slightly cross-eyed clerk from the municipality was seated behind a small table. People walked up to him with money in their hands. Each pushed forward to be next. Each contribution was announced with fanfare. Yousif folded his arms and watched. The bank manager contributed one thousand pounds from the bank and three hundred from him personally. Deafening applause followed. Yousif then saw both Dr. Afifi and Attorney Fouad Jubran contribute two hundred pounds each. The tailor Shibli Mubarak, who was melting with diabetes, huddled with his hefty wife for a minute and then stood like a ghost. Yousif watched him shuffle his feet, weave his way to the podium, and hand the clerk twenty pounds. Some applauded, others said it was too much. But the tailor stood erect, his head high. Even Abu Amin, as poor as he was, contributed ten pounds.

Basim was pacing the floor, his eyes at the main gate. Yousif knew whom he was looking for. When their eyes met, Basim motioned for Yousif to follow him inside the building. They met just before entering the lobby.

Basim narrowed his eyes. "I want to check one more time and see if Uncle would come."

Yousif hesitated. "I doubt it, but you can try."

"All hell will break loose if he doesn't," Basim warned.

Behind the registration desk stood a tall eager clerk, his mustache pencil-thin. Basim asked him to use his private telephone and the clerk was only happy to oblige. But the doctor was not at his clinic. Nurse Laila did not know where he was. Basim was disappointed; Yousif was not sure how he felt. Both withheld their emotions from each other and walked out. But when they reached the balcony they did not like what they were hearing.

"Who does he think he is, refusing to give us the hospital money?" Ayoub Salameh was asking. "Again and again I propose that we, as a body, move against him now. Let's all—everyone of us—walk out of here and head in one direction. Let's all go to his clinic. If he's not there, then let's go to his house. Let's hound him until he realizes that it's not his money."

It was the mean tone, more than anything else, that offended Yousif.

Beautiful Jihan Afifi, her pitch-black hair combed in a bun, rose to her feet. "Let's not get carried away," she said, her voice trembling. "Dr. Safi isn't the kind of man one demonstrates against. Have we forgotten who he is? Have we forgotten his thirty years of dedicated service? He *should* give us the money, but my God! We shouldn't treat him as we would an enemy. Whatever reasons he might have, I'm sure they are well-intentioned, moral reasons. If one thing we can be sure of in these tormented times it's his kindness, his decency. So let's remember the good things about him and not rush to an unfair judgement which we will, for sure, come to regret."

Yousif was so pleased he wanted to run and hug her. Instead, he remained in his place, anxious to see how the others reacted. To his surprise Jihan's words were met with sporadic clapping. Most men, however, remained unmoved.

"He's a pacifist," Ali Ramadan said, wearing his chef hat.

"He's a lot worse than that," Nael, a waiter at Zaharawi's cafe, blasted.

Jihan shook her head. "You can't find a nobler human being in this town or anywhere else."

The crippled councilman sneered. "You should've been with us when we went to see him. He treated us like we were beggars. The Zionists are terrorizing our villagers, threatening other Deir Yasins, and our holier-than-thou doctor won't even show up at a meeting like this. What do you think of that?"

Yousif and Basim, still on the balcony, looked at each other.

"We shouldn't let him get away with it," Yousif muttered.

"It won't be easy," Basim said, walking away.

Yousif returned to his seat. But Basim went straight to the podium, nudging the mayor aside. In a surge of excitement, the mayor motioned with both arms for everyone to quiet down.

"For the sake of time and harmony," Basim cautioned, "let us stick to the matter at hand. We are gathered here today to raise money for arms. Let us do so without further delay. In the meantime I promise you this: no one will sweep the issue of the hospital fund under the rug. And now, with the permission of our good mayor, I urge you to continue with your contributions so that we may defend our beloved Ardallah. I already have my gun. And by the way, it was Uncle Jamil, Dr. Safi, who gave me the money to buy it with months ago. Let us at least remember *this* about him and be kind."

Many hands were raised, but Basim scanned the audience until his eyes fell on Yousif.

"Yousif," Basim said, giving him the floor.

Yousif stood up. "Before I make my father's contribution, I'd like to say a few words."

Some men turned around and looked. Others hissed.

"Words!" the crippled councilman growled. "We need money, not words."

"Yes," the crowd responded. Some even laughed.

The mayor motioned for Yousif to step forward.

Yousif made his way up to the front, aware of the derisive stares of those around him.

The crowd waited. Yousif pushed them to the edge of patience. His love and respect for his father were such that he wanted them to squirm.

"First I'd like to thank the gracious Mrs. Fareed Afifi for what she said about my father," he said, looking straight at Jihan. "He will be honored that she has come to his defense. Also, I'd like to thank those brave souls who dared to applaud Mrs. Afifi's kind words."

"Get to the point," Yacoub said.

"How much money do you have?" a stranger wearing a fez asked.

Yousif reached in his pocket and pulled out the check. "From my father—a check for five hundred pounds." He handed it to the mayor, who looked at it, dismayed.

Dr. and Mrs. Afifi and Attorney Fouad Jubran led a vigorous applause, participated in by at least a third of those attending.

When Yousif started to return to his seat, the audience stirred.

"Is that all?" asked Nicola Awad, the cabinet maker.

"Yes," Yousif answered.

"What about the hospital money?" the barber, Maurice, asked. "That's what we want."

"Basim explained—" Yousif began.

"Not everybody is willing to wait," Abu Nassri said, hostility lurking behind his dark glasses.

Ignoring the two who had just spoken, Yousif returned to his seat and looked around, still hoping to see Salwa. She wasn't there, but he could see her father and Adel Farhat standing under a tree, both looking as though they had swallowed lye.

Ayoub Salameh was on his feet, leaning on his cane. "I move that we conclude this drive shortly and then descend on the doctor wherever he may be."

Ghanem Jadallah stood up. A sickly man in his late sixties who had suffered a couple of heart attacks, he looked ashen. Also, he had a tendency to stutter, especially when he was emotional. From the way he was now mouthing his first words, Ghanem seemed very upset.

"I aggggree with ccccouncilman Salammmmmeh," Ghanem stuttered. "But before we go I'd llllike to aaaask Yousif a qqquestion. Is it tttrue that your father isn't ccccoming forth with the hhhhhospital money because he uuuuused it to build his bbbbig house?"

Those near Ghanem gasped. Others wanted the question repeated. The mayor obliged.

"That's a lie," Yousif snapped, truly outraged.

"PPPProve it," Ghanem said, sitting down.

The mayor was frantic. The purpose of the whole enterprise was derailed and he was trying hard to get it back on track.

"We haven't raised three thousand pounds yet," the mayor shouted, "and here we are already fighting. Why can't we conduct our business in an orderly manner?"

Everyone spoke at the same time. Many converged up front. Others stood on their chairs.

"Wait a minute . . . wait a minute," the mayor was saying, flailing his arms. "I have a suggestion. We have with us right here Mr. Lutfi Khayyat, the manager of Al-Wattan Bank, where I presume the doctor is still keeping the hospital account."

The mayor looked at Lutfi Khayyat, the bank manager, for confirmation. "Just before I came to this meeting," Khayyat said, "I checked the hospital fund account. I'm happy to report that it's all intact."

"That's good to know," the mayor continued, looking around.

Many applauded. Ghanem looked embarrassed and was gesturing in self-defense.

"What I'm trying to say is this," the mayor continued, looking around. "Now we know for sure that the hospital money is all there, and that's good. But we also have with us today several lawyers. Maybe all of them—including the bank manager—could answer a question. Is it feasible for us as citizens of Ardallah to sue Dr. Jamil Safi for the hospital money and collect it?"

Yousif's back stiffened. How dare they challenge and revile his father!

"In other words," the mayor explained, "could we take him to court, win the case, withdraw the money from the bank, and buy arms with it? After all, we gave it to him and we want it back. Is that possible?"

Lutfi Khayyat, Fouad Jubran, and a few others looked at each other and seemed to agree that it was.

The bank manager hesitated. "It can be done," he said, looking around for legal support. "Whether I'd advise it or not is another matter."

Yousif was so disgusted he wished he hadn't given them the check. But it was too late. The fervor was rising. Basim had disappeared into the lobby.

Yousif rested his foot on one of the chairs, contemplating the immediate future. There was no question the city would conspire to rob his father of his hospital account. They would take him to court. What court? There was no law in the land. Anarchy—only anarchy!

In the meantime, he noticed that Salwa's father and Adel Farhat were already gone. He couldn't care less. Had Salwa been with them it would have been different.

As he stared toward the podium, he felt Jihan nudge him.

"Look who's coming," she said.

At first Yousif didn't understand. Then he saw it was Salwa herself. Coming in among other stragglers, Salwa was dressed in red, her hair tied back with a white ribbon. With her was Huda, in a sleeveless polka-dot dress. Both were walking briskly. He wondered why Salwa was coming so late. Did she wait until her father and Adel had left?

"You still love her?" Jihan whispered.

What a superfluous question, Yousif thought. But coming from Jihan he had to respect it.

"Does a bird like to fly?" he answered.

Jihan smiled, as though eager for a moment of relief. "It likes to sing too," she said, teasing.

"So do I," Yousif told her.

On her way into the garden Salwa stopped to talk to an old couple. The three of them seemed to be having an animated conversation. Yousif could only guess what they were saying. But when Salwa shot him a dirty look, he knew.

"She knows," Jihan whispered.

"I think so," Yousif said.

A moment later, Salwa headed toward Yousif, looking angry. He braced himself but wasn't about to let her belittle him.

"Tell me it's not true," Salwa said to Yousif, her lips twitching.

"What's not true?" Yousif asked.

"You know what I'm talking about," she said, her gaze steady.

"Let's not—"

"Let me tell you something," she blurted. "They say the town is going to file a lawsuit against your father to collect the hospital money. Are you defending his position? If it's true then something must be wrong with you."

Suddenly an airplane zoomed over the trees, drowning the uproar of the crowd. Like others, Yousif tilted up his head, startled. The plane looked hawk-headed, antiquated. He could see four propellers and two sets of wings.

"A Jewish plane," Yousif cried, reaching for Salwa's waist.

Salwa pushed him away and looked up. The bi-plane cleared the treetops, made a circle, and returned. Yousif threw himself on the ground, motioning frantically for everyone else to do the same.

"Get down, Salwa," he implored her.

As though to defy him, Salwa turned her back and went on talking to Huda. The plane was diving toward them, the blue-and-white Star of David painted on its tail.

Jihan screamed and rushed into her husband's arms. Huda pulled Salwa's hand and both started to run. While the crowd scrambled and screamed, the plane continued to dip lower and lower. It dropped a cylinder that seemed to be three feet long. Then it nosed up into a steep climb.

This time there was panic, men and women bumping and tripping each other.

"Salwaaaaaaaaaa!!" Yousif cried, hoping she would listen.

The bomb exploded, shaking the ground, tearing the hotel's front balcony, twisting wrought iron, scattering glass, blackening the pinkish stone walls. Yousif pivoted to make sure Salwa was still near him. But the portly agent, Abu Nassri, was running backward. Before he could warn her, Yousif saw Abu Nassri plow his hundred kilos into her, knocking her down on her face. At the same moment a huge tree limb started to fall right over her head. In a split second Yousif fell on his knees by her and raised his hands to push the limb back. As it crashed down, he saw that it was too big to handle and threw himself between her and the limb, letting the many branches poke his back, rip his shirt, cut his arms, and bruise his neck.

"What are you doing?" she screamed under him, her dress hiked half-way up her thigh.

"You were about to be crushed," he told her, trying to ease the limb off his back.

"You're crushing me now," she complained, her voice muffled. "I'm about to suffocate."

She felt wonderful under him. Touching her flesh was enough to make him crave her forever. He could hear people talking around him. Some were trying to roll the limb off his back.

"Ouch," he said, pine needles and sharp wood spars sticking in his ears and scratching his face.

"What will people say?" Salwa protested, trying to get on her knees.

Her movements brought her body closer to his. He reveled in the warmth that was generated between them. If he could only make her see the futility of everything except love.

"I love you, Salwa," he whispered, his lips an inch away from her ear. Smelling the delicious fragrance of her hair, he wanted to cover her nape and supple arms with kisses.

"I love you, too," she confessed. "But please hurry up and move. I'm embarrassed."

He pulled his knees up and hunched his back, giving those who were trying to help a better chance of lifting off the branch. By the time they were freed, a group of men and women were marvelling that neither of them had been really hurt.

"He saved you in the nick of time," Abu Nassri told her, the buttons of his shirt popping off. "That branch could have broken your back. And it was all my fault. I'm sorry."

Salwa seemed confused. "I don't understand."

"I knocked you down. Yousif saw the branch falling on top of you. But he threw himself just in time."

Yousif took off his torn shirt and wiped the blood off his cheeks and neck. But he was more concerned about the bumps and scrapes on Salwa's leg and arms.

"I'm sorry if I embarrassed you," he told her, tearing part of his shirt to let her wipe the dirt off her face.

She blushed. "I didn't realize what was going on."

"I'll try to do better next time," he said, the memory of her under him stirring his blood.

"Let's hope there isn't going to be another time," she said, giving him a tender look.

There was a long pause. Yousif was oblivious to the whole world around him.

But his reverie was short lived. The black smoke rising above the hotel building paralleled the cries rising from the women who were present. Apparently several men and women had been injured. A stone had fallen on a boy, fracturing his skull. Dr. Afifi was rushing him to his clinic for some stitches. The tall thin choir director was cradling his right elbow in his left palm and biting his lip. The baker's wife, Imm Farah, was clutching her eye with her handkerchief, screaming that she would never be able to use it again.

Worst of all, the proprietress's fiancé, Kamal Malouf, had met his fate at the front door. When they picked him up from under the rubble his face had been smashed beyond recognition.

20

Another bead on a layered necklace of tragedies, Yousif thought as he stood with his parents at the edge of a crowd at Kamal Malouf's graveside. The cemetery was overflowing with over a thousand mourners who had come to bid farewell to Ardallah's latest victim.

As never before, Yousif and his parents felt like strangers among their own people. Squeezing the bandaged gash under his rib cage to stop it from throbbing, Yousif chafed at what he was seeing and hearing. While his father stood courtly calm, his wife at his side, people turned sideways, their brows knit and their eyes full of curt distrust. From the way these people looked, Yousif knew that the aftermath of the hotel garden meeting was still festering like an open wound.

The funeral service had not started. A few feet away from where Yousif was standing, several men were discussing the air raid of the day before. Yousif perked his ears, although his father seemed to feign indifference.

"I never thought they'd send their planes in broad daylight," Jiryes Abdu was saying.

"Why?" asked the cabinet maker, Nicola Awad. "Are they afraid of our anti-aircraft? The whole idea is to scare us. To drive home the fact that they have military superiority."

"I bet they know," Nicola said, casting a furtive look in the doctor's direction, "that some of us are fainthearted."

"You mean ready to raise the white flag," Jiryes Abdu said, smirking.

Yousif saw the whole group look at his father, as though to make sure he had heard them. The insolence in that look infuriated him. But his father looked ahead, his hands clasped before him and his face wearing a melancholy mask. Yousif nudged both parents to move on.

"What's the matter, Yousif?" Badr Khalifeh asked. "Is your head still in the sand?"

Yousif looked at him, surprised. "My head has never been in the sand," he answered.

"Maybe in the clouds then."

Yousif stiffened. "Have respect for the dead," he said, walking away.

As the plain casket was being brought to the open grave, Yousif saw Salwa with her parents. Her left cheek bone looked bluish despite the heavy make-up. That shadow of a bruise hurt him more than his own wounds. He wished to God she hadn't even been scratched. He thanked God he had been able to save her from that falling tree limb. But what about her father, Yousif wondered. Did he know that he had lain flat on top of his daughter—in public? Yousif shuddered. Admiring Salwa at a distance, he forgot for a moment the townspeople's hostility toward him and his father.

ABANDONMENT and loss rode with them as the doctor drove his family home after the funeral. Silence filled the automobile. Yousif couldn't hear the Chrysler's engine, as though they were weightless in space. Normally they would go to the dead man's home for a mercy meal after a funeral. But today his father decided to skip it. The way the doctor's hands rested on the steering wheel and the way he pouted, Yousif could tell he wished he were driving them out of town forever.

"Are they going ahead with the lawsuit?" his mother finally asked, wiping the sweat on her forehead and neck.

The doctor nodded. His lower lip overlapped the upper one.

"I hope you don't plan to let them run all over you," she said, facing her husband.

"What do you want him to do?" Yousif asked, remembering Badr Khalifeh's belligerence.

"The least we should do is get a lawyer," she suggested.

"What good will that do?" Yousif asked. "We have enough headaches already."

"One more headache won't kill us," she insisted. "The way they behaved at the cemetery you'd think we bombed the town. Not one said good morning to me. And the ones I spoke to didn't even bother to answer. The nerve!"

The doctor honked his horn before turning around a corner. "At least Fouad Jubran, the town's attorney, is refusing to handle the case for them," he said.

"Good for him," Yousif said.

"What about the other lawyers?" the wife wanted to know. "Would they put you on the stand and quiz you like a common criminal?"

"They would if I let them," the doctor said. "I don't plan to be in court."

"You're not going to contest it?" his wife asked, livid.

"No, I'm not," the doctor answered, with the voice of a man with a skewed dream. "There are no real courts anymore, nor any justice. They'll ram a decision through before you can blink an eye, and I'm not going to give them a chance to claim another victory. They want the money, let them have it."

Nothing, Yousif knew, was dearer to his father's heart than the dream of a hospital. He felt so sorry for the loss of that dream and for the town's grievous insult to her noblest citizen. Now the doctor was acting nonchalant. But Yousif knew better.

"You don't mean that, I know," Yousif said.

"Mean it or not, that's the way it is."

Yasmin would have none of it. She spun sideways, curling her left leg under her. "Then why didn't you give in to them to start with? Why did you let it go this far?"

"I hoped to spare them some foolishness," the doctor said.

"Then I say back up your conviction to the limit."

The doctor's tongue moved around his closed mouth, as though licking his wounds.

"Mother!" Yousif said. "You sound like somebody else I know."

"Salwa? I've always liked that girl. She's got spunk."

"I hated to see that bruise on her face," Yousif said, wishing to change the subject.

"Your face will be bruised a lot worse," his mother said, "if her father hears you topped his daughter."

"I didn't top his daughter!"

"They tell me she was under you for quite a while."

For the rest of the ride home Yousif could think of nothing short of his secular and spiritual salvation. Salwa and Palestine completed the trinity of his soul.

WHILE WAITING for a trial date to be set, the same undertow of coldness they had experienced at the cemetery spilled even into the women's club. Not one lady showed up for the last meeting that was to be held at the doctor's home. Not one called his mother to tell her why she was not coming. Yousif was home when she rang up those who had telephones in their homes, only to be accused of condoning her husband's stubbornness.

Yousif watched his mother roll her eyes and bite her tongue as she listened to Imm Fahmi lecture her.

"Please don't get me started," Yasmin said, making a ball out of the silk kerchief in her hand. "What does our club have to do with arms and armaments? Don't you think he knows we're at war?

That night Yousif saw his scarlet-faced mother cry and berate her husband. One minute she'd accuse him of letting the situation get out of hand; the next minute she'd implore him to hire an attorney and stop them from "robbing" him of the hospital money. It was the first time in years that his parents had argued in front of him. For the rest of the evening his father played solitaire: scowling, grunting, but not budging.

Three days later the court ruled against his father. That same morning the hospital's bank deposit was transferred to the municipality's account. The news spread throughout Ardallah as though it were a national event. It reached Yousif at school, where he took it like an arrow in his heart. At least this time the students did not make fun of him or his father.

During lunch break Yousif ran to his father's clinic. The waiting room was empty. His father was out on a house call.

"You mean some people are still using him as a doctor?" Yousif asked Nurse Laila who was doing bookkeeping at her desk.

"Oh, they'll all come around," she said, sighing.

"How's he taking it?" he asked.

"He didn't say much, but I could tell he's bitter," she answered. "I don't blame him. After all he has done for this town."

"If I were him I'd feel sad, not bitter," he said, biting his own lips. "All they're doing is throwing that money away."

"I agree," she said, nodding. "But let's not be too hard on them. They can't get Deir Yasin out of their minds."

DR. SAFI CAME home with gifts for his wife: an expensive blue purse, a silk blouse, and a bottle of perfume. Having unwrapped the three boxes in the middle of the living room, Yasmin put everything on the round table and looked at her husband affectionately.

"Thank you," she said, smiling, as if to apologize for her own behavior.

But Yousif was not satisfied. "None of this bashful stuff," he said, pushing them toward each other, until they made up with a tender kiss.

Half an hour later, they were sitting by themselves drinking cocktails when the door bell rang. Yousif got up to answer it. At the door was Makram, the taxi-driver, carrying a tray of *kinafeh* and a kilo of tasty-smelling *shish kabab*.

"What's all this?" Yousif said, surprised.

"A delivery from Al-Karnak Restaurant," Makram answered, a boyish smile revealing his splendid teeth.

By that time his parents were standing behind him.

"Did you order this?" his wife asked, surprised. "What on earth for?"

"What do people do with food?" the doctor answered, tipping Makram.

"What am I going to do with the two pots of rice and *mlokhiyyeh* I just finished cooking?" she asked, leading them to the dining room.

"Don't worry," Yousif said, following both of them.

When they reached the dining room, Yousif waited for Fatima to place hot pads on the table. Then he uncovered and sampled the warm juicy kabab as if he hadn't had any in years.

As the sun slipped behind the far horizon, Yousif and his parents had a good, quiet meal together. They touched glasses and sipped red wine, not merely for pleasure but almost as a ritual. The wine seemed to bear for Yousif the significance of Eucharist, cleansing them of yesterday's "sins." A few rays streamed in, turning the window panes golden.

Yousif was happy to see his parents relaxed. In spite of the troubles outside, they appeared at peace with themselves and the world. Even without make-up his mother looked pretty. Her pale skin seemed to have recovered its softness. Yousif had been worried that the city's heavy-handed takeover of the money might crush his father. Now it was obvious that his father was sad, bitter—but somewhat relieved. His equanimity seemed to foretell refusal to retreat in a cave—or to hide behind a cocoon of hurt feelings. It also confirmed his tolerance of human folly.

Yousif wished that, one day, he and Salwa would be that understanding and forgiving.

FOR ALL THE twenty-five thousand pounds they had raised, Basim could purchase only two Enfield rifles, thirteen Bren guns, eighteen Sten sub-machine guns, three light Mortars, and ten boxes of ammunition. The total cost was no more than twelve thousand—the rest was to be saved until more guns could be found. But they were glad to get whatever they could. Basim was praised for acquiring the weapons so quickly and was empowered to look for more.

But the lack of sufficient guns did not deter the people of Ardallah from feeling exhilarated. A sense of pride swept every neighborhood, every shop, every cafe. Suddenly nobody was afraid. Everybody seemed gripped with a sense of mission: to save Ardallah. Another Deir Yasin it would never be. This Yousif could read in the women's faces as they shopped and bargained. He could see it in the way men talked and moved. He could see it in the manner children played hopscotch or flew their kites above the stunted houses, above the pine trees, and against Palestine's unblemished blue sky.

Amin's father was rejuvenated. With a crew of ten, he set out to build cement roadblocks at Ardallah's every entrance. And on top of each of the seven hills he proceeded to build modest watchtowers. He could have made a lot more money chiseling stones to build fine homes. But doing something on behalf of Palestine was his ultimate desire.

What also had the people cheering was that Basim had been able to grease a few palms and get the soccer players, Rassass and George Pinkley, released from prison. These two, who had been incarcerated over the "shoeshine incident," were now free, ready to help Ardallah in her hour of need.

When Yousif saw them again in the garden of Zahrawi's cafe, it was like witnessing the return of conquering heroes. The throngs around them were gleeful. Everyone was pressing to shake their hands, to offer his congratulations, to buy them drinks. Yousif could see Rassass and his pinkish companion, their bodies lithe and firm and their smiles broad and luminous. Breathing the air of freedom was making them giddy. Yousif was happy for them too.

During the third week of April, Basim set up a recruiting station in a grain merchant's shop not too far from the heart of town. Was this mobilization? Yousif thought. It struck him as too elementary to fight a war of destiny, but then he remembered who they were and how hard it had been for them to come that far. He watched as Basim, Rassass, and the hunter Aziz (for once without rabbits or partridges hung from his belt) manned three tables and took applications. Never had Yousif seen so many idlers leave their perpetual seats at the cafe, abandon their backgammon and pinochle games, and await their turn to serve. Yousif wondered if they had known there weren't enough guns to go around.

The same high morale was rampant at school. There was no doubt in Yousif's mind that all students were ready and willing to volunteer. All ustaz Hakim had to do was announce that those who would spend a night guarding the town would be excused from finals—and all of Yousif's classmates clapped for joy.

Yousif alone held back, determined not to compromise his principles. He was also still smarting from his classmates' animosity a week earlier. He wasn't about to do anything they were doing.

Nabeeh, the school's best runner, looked at him suspiciously.

"Still defiant?" Nabeeh asked, raising his voice to draw the others' attention.

"Let's not start that again," ustaz Hakim said, banging the desk with his fist. "Yousif is entitled to his reasons."

"If you ask me they're foolish reasons," Adnan said. "At least the doctor finally saw the light. Not Yousif."

"Yousif will do his share," the teacher defended his favorite student. "I can't believe what's happening to this class. You used to get along so well. You were all friends. Whatever happened to you? Has Yousif changed? Not that I can see. So get off his back, will you? We have a lot more important things to worry about."

Yousif bit his lips and nodded toward his teacher in gratitude. But deep down he was genuinely hurt. It bothered him that he was at odds with his friends. How could he expect Arabs and Jews to reconcile their differences when he couldn't reconcile his with his friends? He raised his hand.

"Perhaps," he said, looking around the room, "I'm responsible for some of the tension. If I have done anything wrong I want the whole class to know I'm sorry."

Silence hung over their heads. Everyone looked stunned. "Nabeeh," Yousif continued, "I apologize for saying it's none of your business. It is your business. And you Adnan, forgive me. I didn't mean to be so short with you. And you Amin, how I hate myself for putting you in awkward positions . . . for making you stand up for me. You are one of a kind."

Amin winked at him, saying, "One in a million."

"And you, ustaz Hakim," Yousif added. "Thank you for your confidence in me."

The teacher smiled. "See?" he joked, trying to mitigate the sentimentality.

"Above all," Yousif said, "I don't want us to go on quarreling with each other. When the time comes, I'll do my share as ustaz Hakim has said. I still don't believe war is the answer, but I intend to use my father's car to deliver food and medication to all the fighters on these hills. Someone should do it. Why not me?"

Adnan got out of his seat and extended his hand toward Yousif. "I'm sorry too," he said, blushing.

Then Yousif turned to Nabeeh and shook his hands. Adnan and Nabeeh shook Amin's hand. And for a minute arms were entangled and smiles were breaking out.

"That's the spirit," ustaz Hakim said, relieved. "All it takes is for someone to take the initiative. Yousif, we all thank you. Now let's open to page . . ."

They all turned to their books.

THIS TIME, convincing his father to let him use the Chrysler was easier than Yousif had expected. Whether it was the terror and bloodshed that were sweeping the country, whether it was the mellowing after defeat, he didn't know. But he did appreciate the fact that now he too could contribute to the war without having to apologize. And without having to carry a gun.

"Stop by the office," the doctor told him the following morning, as they were about to leave the house. "I'll give you some supplies."

"What kind of supplies?" Yousif asked.

"First Aid," the doctor said. "That's what you meant by medications, isn't it?"

"Yes, of course," Yousif remembered.

"And I'll give you a list of what I don't have. You can pick those up at the pharmacies in town. They ought to give them to you free. If they don't just tell them to send me the bill."

"What about the car? What time can I have it?"

"About five o'clock in the afternoon."

"I'll bring you home, then I'll take it if it's okay with you."

"Don't worry about me. I can always grab a taxi. But you need to check with Basim about getting the food. How do you plan to do it?"

"I guess I'll go around to the men's homes and pick up whatever their families have prepared for them."

"That's too much trouble. You're talking about fifty or sixty families every night. It's a lot easier to make arrangements with suppliers. You need to contact a couple of bakers, a couple of grocers, a couple of restaurants and let them all get things ready for you. Maybe Basim could get them to contribute their stuff, or sell them to you at cost. It needs a lot of coordination, but you can do it."

It was a bigger job than Yousif had anticipated. "Thanks for telling me all this," he said, looking at his watch. "Do you mind dropping me off at school? It's getting late."

They drove in silence. Yousif's head was buzzing with excitement.

From then on, his work was cut out for him. Every day, in the darkening light of dusk, Yousif would make the rounds to the several establishments he and Basim had arranged to supply the fighters. He'd pick up the breads and crates of vegetables and the cases of soft drinks and dozens of sandwiches, then head for the hills. Sometimes he would take Amin or Khalil or Adnan to help him. Most of the time he would do it alone.

ONE AFTERNOON Yousif drove Basim to four hills and five road entrances. What struck Yousif most at these posts were the men. They toted the guns with such enthusiasm, such pride. Looking at their laughing eyes, one would have thought they were getting ready for a wedding party. Among them was Adel Farhat, having a laugh with Rassass. Adel's gun looked puny compared to his powerful arms. Upon seeing Basim, both Adel and Rassass hastened to shake his hand. Yousif himself stayed several steps behind so as to discourage Adel from approaching him.

On his way back to Ardallah, Yousif was very quiet. Seeing Adel Farhat had depressed him. It also reminded him of how much he missed Salwa. While Basim rattled on about politics and guns and prices, he wondered about the engagement. When was she going to break it? Why wasn't he helping her? He shouldn't even let an impending war stand in the way. Maybe she was depending on him to make the next move. At one time he had thought of trying to intercede with her favorite teacher or the priest himself. Why hadn't he done it? Damn!

He dropped Basim off at the watchtower on the western hill and decided to do something. Enough was enough. Where was she now? What was she doing? What was she thinking? What plans were being hatched behind his back? He was anxious to know.

His first stop was at the house of the Greek Orthodox priest. The gray-bearded Father Samaan would be the one to marry Salwa and Adel Farhat, should she be forced to go ahead. Above all else, Yousif though, he must stave off that dreadful day.

The priest lived in one of the oldest and poorest parts of town, not far from Amin. There was a high stone wall built in front of the dust-colored two-room house, in the tradition of Muslims' homes—to protect the women from the eyes of strangers. The semi-circle in front was unpaved, and children were playing soccer or hide-and-seek. Yousif recognized many of them as the priest's grandchildren. He couldn't help but smile as he remembered this. As a Catholic, accustomed to celibate priests, he had a hard time adjusting to a married priest with five daughters and no less than eight grandchildren. He couldn't imagine a priest longing for a woman as he himself was longing for Salwa, then holding the Eucharist on Sunday morning. On the other hand, why not? Maybe it was more human than the Catholic tradition. Like everything else, he thought, there were no easy answers.

He felt awkward when he approached the enclosure and came across the priest's wife, crouching by an outside fire baking *shrak,* thin bread that looked like large doilies.

"Excuse me," he said. "I'm looking for Aboona Samaan."

The *khouriyyeh,* whose pale knees were showing, looked startled. She quickly turned her knees away from him and covered them with her elbows.

Yousif felt embarrassed. "I didn't mean to barge in on you like this," he apologized, backing out.

"Wait," she said, lifting the bread off the concave iron plate. She was wearing heavy-duty gloves. Smoke billowed all around her.

"He's not here," she said, getting up and smoothing her dress.

"Do you know when he'll be back?"

"He's out of town. If it's an emergency, you need to see Aboona Iskandar, his assistant."

"No, I need to see him personally. Perhaps later."

"Aren't you Dr. Safi's son?"

"Yes, I am. I'm sorry I didn't introduce myself. I'm Yousif Safi."

"Good to know you," she said. "No, son, I can't tell you when he'll be back. He had to go to Nazareth. There's no telling what might delay him."

"Is it safe? I mean traveling at a time like this?"

"I begged him not to," she answered, a faraway look in her eyes.

"Did he say when he'll be back?"

She shook her head. "What's today, Thursday?" she asked. "*Inshallah* in two or three days."

"It can wait. Again, I'm sorry."

"Think nothing of it. And give my regards to your mother."

"Thank you," Yousif told her, and walked back to his car.

NEXT, HE DROVE to a house behind the Lutheran church. Salwa's favorite teacher, Sitt Bahiyyeh, lived there. Lights were on, so he assumed she was home. He pulled the car over by the curb and sat with the engine running. He was thinking. Sitt Bahiyyeh was the one Salwa loved most. If any teacher could put in a good word for him, this was the one. But he was hesitant about approaching her on such a delicate matter. Why should she help him break off the engagement when she didn't even know him? Should he forget all about it and wait for the priest to get back? No, he finally said, the more help the better.

He turned off the engine, stepped out of the car, walked up to the front door on the second floor, and rang the bell.

When the tall, spinster teacher opened the door, Yousif felt tongue-tied. She seemed surprised to see him, and he didn't blame her. Only once in his life had he spoken to her, very briefly, at Arif's bookstore. But he had always liked her for her partiality to Salwa.

"Good evening," he eventually said.

"Good evening," she answered, her hazel eyes darkening.

They stood silent for a long moment. "I'd like to have a word with you. May I come in?"

She opened the door wider and then closed it behind him. She led him in, waddling in her usual way. Her patterned, blue dress shifted around her hefty hips.

"Who's there?" an old female voice asked from within.

"It's for me, Mother. Don't worry." Then turning to Yousif, Sitt Bahiyyeh said, "Ever since Deir Yasin, she hasn't been the same."

"I can imagine."

"Every time the door bell rings she turns white like a sheet, thinking the Zionists are coming to slaughter us."

"That bad?"

"When I leave in the morning to go to school, she locks the door and puts up the iron bar. Sometimes when I come back in the afternoon, it takes me five to ten minutes to convince her it's me before she'll open the door to let me in."

She motioned for him to sit. He sat in the nearest armchair and remained quiet. The heavily draped and carpeted room looked stuffy and gloomy. He watched her turn on a couple of lamps. The yellow light hardly dispelled the darkness.

"It's about Salwa," Yousif began, his throat dry.

"Salwa?"

"Salwa Taweel. You're her favorite teacher."

She smiled, sitting on a velvet sofa. "How do you know? You're not related, are you?"

"She told me," he answered, shaking his head. "I've always known."

"That's nice. But what about her?"

"She's engaged."

"I know."

"Well, that's it. I don't want her to be. She and I, that is, don't want her to be."

"She doesn't want to be engaged? That's news to me."

Yousif looked disappointed. He had expected Salwa to be wallowing in misery. He wanted her to let the whole world know she wanted *him*.

"We're in love," he confessed, his fingertips touching. "Have been for years."

Sitt Bahiyyeh laughed and crossed her arms around her big sagging bosom. "Been in love for years!" she repeated. "How old are you? Seventeen?"

Yousif wove his fingers and popped his knuckles. "Almost eighteen."

"I'm sorry. I didn't mean to laugh. At your age love can be excruciating. But it was charming. Go on."

Yousif spilled his heart out for her. Sitt Bahiyyeh was kind, listening attentively. A tapestry of the Last Supper loomed big over her head.

"How sad!" she told him, sighing. "What can I do?"

"She promised to break off the engagement. Will you find out what's taking her so long? Is she waiting on me to do something? I haven't been able to see her long enough to ask her myself. Will you tell her I still want her? My God, what am I saying? Tell her I can't live without her."

One of Sitt Bahiyyeh's hands cradled her face. "I don't know if I can do that."

"I know I'm asking much of you. But I need help. We both do."

"I'd hate for her father to find out I've been meddling in his family affairs. He wouldn't like it, I can tell you that. We try not to get involved with students' lives."

"Please help me. I'm in the dark. Am I hoping against hope?"

"How do your parents feel about all this? Are they for it? I'd hate to have two sets of parents accusing me of indiscretion."

"Don't worry about them. I'm my own man."

She smiled, her eyes growing misty. At that moment Yousif thought he had found an ally. A woman who had been jilted, perhaps because of a suitor's weakness or family pressure, would understand his deep concern.

"I'm glad to hear that," she said. "Very few men are, you know. But what about the war? People are worried about survival—and here you are making yourself sick over a girl."

"A very special girl," Yousif said, rising to leave. "I'd face the bombs better knowing she's mine."

"Tejri irriyaho bima la tash tehi issufunu. Sometimes the winds blow against the wish of the ships."

A shiver went down Yousif's spine. "Please don't say that."

"Breaking off an engagement is about as rare around here as a three-headed cat."

"There's always a first time. I've also been to see Father Samaan. With the help of you two . . ."

"Father Samaan?" she asked, standing. "Did he say he'd help you?"

Yousif looked startled. "No, he wasn't home. But I intend to see him when he comes back from out of town. What's wrong?"

"Father Samaan is Salwa's father's relative. Second or third cousin, I'm not sure. Anyway, he's not going to turn against his own kin. I wouldn't count on his help if I were you."

Yousif could feel his knees buckle under him. "I see," he said, sweating. "But isn't this a church matter? Would he marry her against her own free will? What do family ties have to do with it?"

She shook her head. "Blood runs thicker than you think."

Yousif looked at her straight in the eye. "That means you're my only hope. That means you've got to help me. Will you, please?"

"I'll see what I can do."

In the vestibule Yousif ran into Sitt Bahiyyeh's eighty-year-old mother. She looked like a ghost leaning on a cane. Her frightened eyes matched his.

21

Yousif decided to spend that night on the western hill. The sky was clear, the air nippy. The moon was full. A dozen men—a school teacher, a postman, a truck driver, a farmer, an electrical engineer, a bartender, a garbage collector, two former policemen, and a few shopkeepers—were sitting in a circle, all wishing the enemy would show up. They looked motley in their disparate clothing. At best, they were a long way from the steel-helmeted soldiers he had watched in movies, and from British soldiers he had grown up seeing in Palestine, all decked out in starched cotton khaki uniforms.

Was this what people referred to as the "front"? Where were the bunkers and the trenches? The watchtower Abu Amin had started was so far no more than six feet tall. Even when finished it wouldn't be more than a dingy closet. Was this war?

Soon a few men began to pace alone. One carried his rifle in his hand; others had them slung over their shoulders. It was getting cold and Yousif was fighting himself not to shiver in front of others.

"To do this job properly," Basim said, "we need at least two hundred guns and six hundred men. Maybe more."

"That many?" asked Omar Kilani, owner of the elegant variety store.

"Think about it," Basim said. "To protect each mountain you need three shifts, each consisting of thirty men. That means ninety men around the clock. Multiply that by seven (the number of mountains) and you'd need six hundred and thirty men. And don't forget another hundred men, at least, in the town itself—to guard the streets from a surprise attack."

"And Ardallah is a small town," Yousif observed. "What about big cities like Haifa and Jaffa? How many men do we need there?"

"Thousands," said Salah Shaaban, a public school teacher.

"Of course," Basim agreed. "And these cities have only recently begun buying some arms, just like us. We're totally unprepared. On the other hand, the Zionists have started taking their fighter planes out of the hangers that we must've mistaken for barns full of hay. They have a squadron of Messerschmidtt-109s from Czechoslovakia. Their American bombers include B-17s, C-46s, Constellations, Piper Cubs, Austers, Rapides. And what do we have?" He gestured lewdly with his middle finger.

"Damn the Arab armies," said the postman, Costa, his small eyes glistening in his apple-shaped face.

When they dispersed, Yousif heard Basim call out his name. He turned around and waited, not knowing what to expect. Suddenly, Basim threw a rifle at him.

"It's not loaded, is it?" Yousif asked, catching it.

"No," Basim replied, smiling. "You don't know much about guns, do you?"

"Nothing," Yousif replied, embarrassed.

"This is what you call an Enfield 303. British made. Had one like it in 1936—a gift from the Mufti."

Yousif didn't know one gun from another. Not even the difference between a gun and a rifle.

"What's a Mauser?" Yousif asked, for the sake of conversation. "I used to hear about it all the time."

"A clip-loaded German rifle," Basim told him. "A mighty good one, too."

"And the bazooka and the mortar?" Yousif asked. "What are they? Two names for the same thing?"

Basim grinned. "Boy, you are green," he said, lighting a cigarette. "They're not even close. The bazooka is carried on the shoulder. It's used for knocking out tanks and armored cars. I wish we had a few of those. The mortar is like that one over there. It sits on a base, has a long tube, and it takes two men to operate. One to feed it the shell, and one to adjust the angle of firing. Who knows, before the war is over you might know a thing or two about weapons."

The Enfield rifle felt heavy and cold in Yousif's hands. Again he was full of doubts. If he couldn't carry a gun, what was he doing here? He looked at the gun and then at Basim, feeling awkward.

"I might as well give you a lesson right now," Basim said, stepping closer.

In the moonlight Yousif could see his cousin's cunning grin. Yousif was inclined to tell him that he didn't want to learn how to use the gun, that he didn't believe in violence. But he kept quiet. This was neither the time nor the place. Besides, they both knew how the other felt.

Basim took the gun to demonstrate how it should be used. He removed the safety latch, cocked the firing mechanism, and showed Yousif how to aim. When he clicked it the other men were startled, but Basim quickly explained what he was doing.

"Hold it firm in your hands," Basim instructed him. "And support it with your shoulder. If you don't, it'll knock you down. I have no bullets to spare, but that's all you really have to know for now. Line the sight with the head of your enemy and shoot."

Yousif cringed. "Just like that? Shoot only to kill?"

"If that man is out to kill you, killing him first is easy," Basim said, the lines of his jaws firm. "Anyway, by the time you get a gun, the war might be over."

There was always that note of frustration, Yousif thought.

"Keep it for a while," Basim said, again handing him the gun. "You need to get used to it."

"It's so heavy," Yousif said, cradling it.

Basim nodded and went to talk to a couple of men about fifty feet away. They talked in whispers, as if afraid to make a noise. Basim was the only one who gestured. Then each went his way, passing Yousif in silence.

Far below, Yousif could see the lights of the international airport in Lydda. He could also see Jaffa, a town as Arab as London is British. Yet at its harbor, ship after ship had come full of Jewish refugees bent on making Jaffa their own. How could that be! It boggled his mind that the Jews could even think it possible. Palestine was theirs but not his? Ridiculous!

The mere mention of the word Palestine tingled his spine. The sound of it was music to his soul. Did the Jewish immigrants grow up in Palestine? Did they have an inalienable birthright to it but he didn't? What a travesty on logic! Did they play on these hills and in these valleys? When they were in Poland and Hungary and Germany and Russia and South Africa—did they pick almonds and figs and olives and oranges off the trees in the plush orchards that dotted the land of Palestine? Did they swim on the shores of Jaffa and Haifa and float on the salty waters of the Dead Sea? Did they smell the sweet open air, touch the soil, eat the fruits?

For thousands of years, the Palestinians had been here. And now the Jews want to come back and reclaim it? Just like that? How could they even think it?

Even if they did capture it, how long could they hold it? A generation or two—then what? What would they do when justice reared its head?

Yousif thought of the Palestinians who had sought their fortunes abroad but had always come back. He thought of the people of Ramallah and Bethlehem who had migrated to North and South America. They had gone, toiled for many years, but always returned to live and die in the homeland—Palestine. All the glitter and gold had not kept them away. Very few families, less than one tenth of one percent, had gone and stayed. Only Palestinian water could quench their thirst.

Yousif closed his eyes and took a deep breath, drinking in the soft cool air. The stillness enthralled him. The gun in his lap held no magic for him. He himself did not want to fight the Jews—only to warn them. Their dream would only turn to dust. They would be creating a bed of thorns for themselves and for their children and their children's children. A Jewish nation carved by the sword would never, never have peace. Simply because no Jew could possibly love the land of Palestine more than those who were born and raised on it could. Simply because in the Palestinian's veins ran the distillation of all his living on the hills of God.

The hours of the night crept away. At midnight Yousif heard the town clock chime its twelve lingering strokes. His ears became sharpened enough to hear distant sounds. The wailing of a fox sailed up the mountain like a note of despair. Yousif wondered what kept the fox awake. He got up and moved about, looking down at the twisting highway. The headlights of a passing car shone like two eyes above a black veil.

"It's brisk," said Omar Kilani, the most eligible bachelor in town. The suave forty-year-old man owned and operated the one store where every fashionable woman did her shopping. He was tall and dark with a smile that made Cary Grant's look like a frown. Rumors had it that Omar could steal any bride from her groom—even at the altar. What was he doing there with a gun in his hand? His cuff links and tie clip sparkled in the moonlight.

"Quite brisk," Yousif agreed, proud to be in such company.

The two stood on the cliff silently. Omar took out a package of cigarettes and offered him one. To Yousif, any gesture of acceptance was welcome. He hesitated a moment, then took one, hoping that Omar had not noticed his clumsiness. Both lit their cigarettes from Omar's gold-leafed lighter. Yousif relished the new experience. He appreciated the definite, purposeful movement of Omar's fingers, which flicked the lighter, cupped the flame, and then snapped it shut. Never had the act of lighting a cigarette seemed so meaningful, so artful. With his first cigarette dangling from the corner of his mouth, Yousif felt like an adult. But every now and then he would turn around to suppress a rising cough.

"They must know we're on guard," Yousif said. "That's why they're not coming."

Omar flashed a smile. "Sooner or later they'll be here."

"You think so?" Yousif asked, puffing.

"I'm sure."

Each resumed pacing.

Because the mountain was bare and the moon full, Yousif could see a long way down. He could see the vineyards, the olive orchards, and the gray stretches of barren land.

Moments later Yousif thought he saw a man coming up the mountain. The man was only a couple of fields down. Yousif assumed that he was someone from Ardallah, coming to help. Then he realized that the man was coming from the wrong direction.

"Who's there?" Yousif asked, tensing.

The man did not answer. A second later, the man made a quick movement and hid behind a stone wall. Yousif's suspicions were confirmed. Before he could turn to tell the others, they were already beside him.

"Behind that wall," Yousif said, pointing his finger.

"Are you sure?" Basim asked, taking the rifle from him and cocking it.

"I saw him."

"Let's wait," Basim whispered. "The moment he moves we'll see him. Go back to your places. We don't want to be an easy target."

The men dispersed.

"Watch out!" Basim called suddenly, throwing himself flat on the ground and pulling Yousif down with him. A hand grenade exploded about ten meters away. Had Basim not seen it coming, Yousif thought, they would have been both killed.

Yousif was still sprawled on the ground when Basim got up and sprinted to the lower field, chasing the man who had thrown the hand grenade. Yousif scrambled to watch. The man ran into a high stone wall which he could not jump over but started to climb. He reached the top and got ready to jump. Basim took deadly aim and a single shot echoed throughout the valley. Yousif heard a painful shriek, saw the man's hands fly away from his body which was plunging headlong.

They waited for few minutes before they went down to inspect his body.

"Eliyaho Slavinsky," Basim announced, reading the dead man's ID. "Look, here's another grenade."

"Is he by himself?" Yousif asked, his eyes searching the hills.

"I doubt it," Basim told him, removing a pistol and a bandoleer off the corpse. "They sent him to scout the area."

"I see," Yousif said. "Will they still come, now that they know the hill is guarded? They must've heard the shot."

"It depends on how strong they are," Basim explained. "If they think they can overtake us, they won't hesitate."

They started to walk up the hill, back to their positions.

"What about him?" Yousif asked, pointing to the corpse. The Zionist had been hit in the neck. His head was almost severed, flesh torn open and bleeding, tongue sticking out, eyes frozen. This was the kind of brutality Yousif had expected—had feared. He wanted to vomit.

"Let him rot," Basim answered, stomping on the dead soldier's fingers. "Here, take this. It's a Colt .45. Not as heavy as a rifle."

Yousif refused. "I can't believe you said that."

"What? That he should rot? Let me tell you something, big boy. He would've killed you in a second. And before he would've let you rot to hell, he would've beat the shit out of you, kicked your kidneys, and then sliced you up with his knife. Here, take this and start growing up."

Yousif accepted the dead man's revolver. But there was something still gnawing at Yousif's heart and he wanted to have it out with Basim. There was no sense holding a grudge.

"Killing this *yahudi* is one thing," Yousif told his cousin, "killing Isaac was something else, don't you think?"

Basim stopped abruptly and looked at Yousif, whose eyes were boring at him.

"I see no difference," Basim said. "An enemy is an enemy."

Yousif gnashed his teeth. "Isaac was a good *yahudi*. Not like the rest."

"Maybe," Basim said, walking again. "But anyone who comes after me with a gun in his hand cannot be trusted."

"I would've trusted Isaac with my life," Yousif said, walking behind him.

"You'll learn."

"He was like a brother to me. You could've saved him."

"Too late now."

"You let me down, Basim. You really did."

"You'll get over it."

"No, damn it. I won't."

Basim wheeled back and gazed at his younger cousin. "Listen, Yousif. A *yahudi* is a *yahudi* to the core. When it comes to Palestine, everyone of them is and will always be our enemy. Don't ever be fooled by their tears or their smiles."

Before they reached the top, more gunshots opened up from below. Basim and Yousif spun around.

"Damn!" Basim said, aghast. "Look at all those men. At least fifty."

Dark shadows of men were six or seven fields below. They would have been hard to recognize had they not moved. Quickly Basim hid behind a stone wall and started to fire back. So did the men on top of the hill. Yousif knelt down next to Basim. In the moment of danger he wanted to test whether or not he could shoot. But for the life of him he could not pull the trigger. Finally he gave up, knowing that it was not in him.

During a pause Basim ran to the hill top, followed by Yousif.

"Spread out," Basim told his men, moving. "And aim well. We don't have enough ammunition and this may be a long night. Also, look around the mountain slopes. Make sure we know all the directions they're coming from."

"What do you think they're after?" Costa asked.

"These two hills," he said, pointing, "control the road to the Jerusalem-Jaffa road. Maybe they're trying to cut us off from Lydda and Ramleh. We'll have to wait and see."

"Do you think they may be invading the other hill too?" Salah Shaaban asked.

"Maybe," Basim answered. "But Rassass and his men will do what we plan to do right here, give the bastards a lesson they'll never forget."

Like the men around him, Yousif cocked his ear to determine whether the opposite hill was being simultaneously invaded. Basim walked briskly, checking all sides of the mountain.

"Let me have the pistol," a bicycle repairman, wearing shorts, said to Yousif.

Yousif handed it to him gladly and stood by watching. Basim returned to where Yousif was standing. Basim crouched behind a stone wall, fired cautiously, took his clips out, loaded and fired again. It was hard for Yousif to determine whether anyone was hit. Then he heard someone below shriek.

"They're firing too much," Basim said, referring to his own men. "Damn it, tell them to take their time. Tell them to wait until they get closer. I don't care how many Jews there are. We can hold them."

Yousif carried his cousin's orders to all the fighters. "Basim says take your time," he told them.

The mountain turned metallic. Violence bloomed. Bullets flew all around Yousif as he returned to watch the invaders below. They were now only four fields away. His worst fears were fast becoming real. He was in the midst of a war. He couldn't run. He couldn't fight. What should he do? Anguished and confused, he relied on prayers.

"Lord," he murmured to himself, "I smell a plague. I hear the footsteps of the angel of Death echoing throughout the land. Rein him in, Lord. Stop him before he plunders, burns, and kills. Lift the evil spell off Your hills and restore peace, harmony, and contentment to the hearts of men. Make our enemies dream a different dream before we inflict so much pain on each other. On my knees, and in the name of Jesus, I beseech you, Lord, to stretch Your arms out and save *all* Your children."

The hand of God did not muzzle the firing guns. Within half an hour Basim and his men were running short of ammunition. The enemy was pounding relentlessly. With all the firework, Yousif wondered why the British army had not come to stop the fighting. Until the Mandate was over, keeping the peace was still their responsibility. No doubt they were busy packing. May 15 was less than a month away.

"They are spreading out," Omar hollered.

"I can see that," Basim answered, running around to inspect the four slopes, his gun at the ready.

Yousif could see the Zionists in constant motion. Red fire punctuated the darkness.

"We must prevent them from outflanking us," Basim commanded. "Omar, move that sub-machine gun fifty yards to your left. Jawad, move your Bren fifty yards to your right. Someone help them carry the stands. This way we'll catch them in crossfire. In the meantime, we'll keep the mortar in the center and I'll handle it myself. But I need someone with me. Costa, come over here."

"I don't know how," Costa whimpered.

"Never mind, I'll show you," Basim said.

Yousif was mortified. Ill-trained and ill-equipped, what saved them so far was the high ground. The whole mountain was rife with men anxious to kill each other. Movement below paralleled movement above. Bullets flashed and whizzed and echoed throughout the valley.

Yousif wished he could have another look at the dead soldier Basim had left to rot. Had he been in love with a girl like Salwa? How would she get the news? Would his family tell her or would she read it in the paper? Had the dead soldier's mother missed him for supper that night? Was she now sitting somewhere in Jerusalem or Tel Aviv wringing her hands? Or had she died in one of Hitler's camps, and her son had come to Palestine with fury in his heart? Yousif wished he could tell all mothers, Arab or Jewish, Kiss your husbands and children whenever they leave home.

When the two Bren sub-machine guns were in place, Basim ordered the gunners to open fire. Omar threw his fine blazer on a nearby stone wall and loosened his silk tie. Jawad rolled up his long sleeves and stomped his cigarette.

Both responded to Basim's command with relish. Yousif watched the impact of their onslaught on the Zionists four fields below. He could see them scampering in different directions. Some were leaping over stone walls, others falling to the ground.

Costa took out a pocketknife and gingerly opened a box full of bombs for the mortar. Yousif could see three rows of fours. They looked like cactus.

"Now what?" Costa asked.

Basim was busy adjusting the cross-leveling device and raising the barrel toward the sky. It seemed an odd angle for shooting downhill, Yousif thought.

"When I tell you, drop one in and get the hell out," Basim told Costa. "The minute it hits the bottom of the tube a pin will puncture it and ignite the dynamite inside the shell. There's no trigger to pull. The bomb will take off on its own. What I do is control the angle. Understand?"

"I guess," Costa said, hesitant.

"Come on, let's kill a few," Basim told him.

Yousif shook his head and watched Costa take out a bomb. Out of the box it looked more like a light bulb: broad at one end, narrow at the other.

"Ready?" Basim asked.

"Here it comes," Costa said, placing the bomb at the mouth of the barrel.

"No, no, no," Basim said, alarmed. "Turn it around."

Costa looked confused.

"It's not a light bulb you're screwing on," Basim instructed him. "Broad base first."

A bullet whizzed between Yousif and Basim. Had Yousif turned it would have caught him in the nose. It reminded him that they were not play-acting. Death had just whispered in his ear.

Basim didn't even seem to notice the bullet that had almost cut him down. "O.K.," he was telling Costa. "Drop it in and get out."

Yousif stepped back a few yards and watched. Seconds after Costa had dropped the bomb in, it shot out at a frightening speed. It went up about two hundred yards and then zoomed down behind a stone wall four fields below, exploding on impact. Its noise was thunderous. Yousif could hear rocks tumbling down. He couldn't tell if any Jews were killed, but he could see many of them running. A couple of them couldn't run fast enough, for they were indeed caught in the crossfire. The immediate area surrounding the blast was covered with white phosphorous smoke. Before the swirling smoke cleared, Basim sent another bomb hurling at the enemy below.

"I want the bastards never to come back," Basim said, gritting his teeth.

No sooner had he finished uttering the last word, than a bullet smashed into his right shoulder. Basim twitched but held onto the mortar with all his might. Yousif rushed closer to him, shocked. Death was inching closer and closer. But no bullet and no wound would stop Basim now. He went on angling the mortar, his shirt soaked with blood. His men saw him and tried to stop him, but he pushed them aside.

"Basim, you must stop," Yousif insisted. "You're bleeding."

"Never mind," Basim shot back like a man obsessed.

"But you must. You're losing too much blood."

"Then run along and get your father. I won't leave this hill."

Basim began giving orders, undaunted by his wound. From the looks of things, Yousif thought, Basim was losing too much blood. The least he could do was stop the bleeding until his father arrived.

Yousif rushed to the unfinished watchtower in which he had placed the First Aid kit, grabbed it, and went back to Basim.

"Didn't I tell you to go and get your father?" Basim said, his left hand pressing his right shoulder. The handkerchief he was applying was soaking wet.

"Just let me do one thing first," Yousif said.

Inside the kit were three bottles: iodine, alcohol, and peroxide. Yousif didn't know which one to use to wash the wound. He decided not to use any; he'd let his father take care of that. He piled up ten or fifteen cotton balls, each as large as a small egg, then wrapped them all up in a gauze. He hoped to God he was doing the right thing. The memory of old man Abu Khalil's mishandling of Amin's arm was too fresh on his mind.

"Please, Basim," Yousif said, "let me tape you and I'll be on my way."

A bullet whistled by a foot away from Yousif, and he belatedly ducked.

"See what I mean," Basim told him, "I don't have time to worry about a silly wound."

Yousif touched his cousin's shoulder. "It's not silly. You're losing too much blood."

While Basim was rearranging the angle of firing, Yousif managed to unbutton him to see for himself. The underwear shirt was torn and wet. His own fingers became messy. He was trying to stop Basim's bleeding, unfazed by the stickiness and smell. The bullet's point of entry was about five inches below the armpit, more to the front than to the side. But Yousif could feel no exit wound in Basim's side. The bullet was still trapped inside his body.

"Akhkhkhkhkh . . ." Basim hollered when Yousif accidentally touched the collar bone.

It felt fractured to Yousif's sensitive finger tips. But it also must have blocked the bullet.

"I'm sorry," Yousif said, removing his fingers swiftly. "But I think this broken collar bone saved your life."

"And you may be endangering it right now," Basim told him, "unless you get out of my way."

"Just one more minute," Yousif said, raising the T-shirt with one hand and applying the gauze and the cotton ball with the other. Only after he had finished taping him, did he realize what a hairy devil Basim was.

"How does it feel?" Yousif asked.

"O.K.," Basim grunted, turning the mortar halfway toward Omar.

"One more thing, please," Yousif said. "I need to bind you around the shoulder to cut the flow of blood."

"Hey, be careful there!" Basim said. "What are you trying to do, kill me?"

From his tone Yousif could tell that Basim was having luck lobbing bombs in the midst of the enemy. Yousif humored him long enough to arrest the bleeding by binding and twisting a bandage tightly under the arm and over the shoulder.

Raising and lowering and turning the mortar's barrel, Basim looked and acted as though he had never been hurt. "Get going," Basim told Yousif. Then looking at the clumsy binding Yousif had just finished, he added: "Jesus! An army of amateurs!"

WITH BULLETS whistling and flashing up and down the hill, Yousif ran down the other side of the hill to his car and sped to town. Most of the lights were out. The streets were deserted. He rushed home and found his parents as he had expected—waiting.

"Basim has been wounded," Yousif explained, excited.

"Good God!" his mother said, staring at his blood-stained fingers and shirt. "Are you wounded too?"

"Oh, no," Yousif told her. "I just finished taping him."

The doctor, who had been smoking his pipe and playing solitaire, dropped the cards and ran to get his jacket.

"Why didn't you bring him down with you?" the doctor asked. "It would help if I could see what I'm doing. We'd better check the flashlight in the glove compartment to make sure the batteries aren't dead."

In the meantime Yousif ran to the bathroom to wash his hands. He ended up washing his face too, for blood was splattered on his cheeks and forehead. But he didn't change clothes. There was no time.

"Hurry up, please," Yousif said, drying himself with a fluffy yellow towel. "And I want you to know that my hands weren't clean when I taped him. We don't want a repetition of what happened to Amin."

"I understand," his father replied. "Anybody else hurt?"

"I heard a few screams," Yousif answered, following him to the door. "I didn't bring them with me, because I knew you'd be going up the hill to see about Basim."

Dr. Safi still couldn't understand why Basim would not come down to the clinic. Yasmin followed them out on the balcony, urging Yousif not to stay out all night.

"Come back with your father," she called after him. "Do you hear me?"

"Mother!" Yousif replied, reproachful. "I'm not a child."

He left with his father, waving at his mother but not looking back.

They sped through town back to the hilltop. They found Basim alive, his spirits high. The enemy appeared to be retreating. The hill was going to be saved. But Basim had to be sure. He would not even stop for the doctor to examine him.

"If you can't help me while I'm firing," Basim told his uncle, "then you'll have to wait."

"Sit still for a moment and let me take a look at you," the doctor told him, raising his voice above the sound of shooting. "If you really want to save Ardallah, save yourself first. None of us will gain anything if you die. The way you're going you're a poor risk. Blood is still seeping through. We can't take chances."

He opened his handbag looking for something.

"No shots, Uncle," Basim warned.

"Come, come, Basim," the doctor said, impatient. "If you don't want to go to the clinic so I can take care of you properly, then lie down and let me see what I can do. I might be able to pull the bullet out without much trouble."

"I'll tell you what," Basim said, his face flushed with adrenaline. "A pain killer will do just fine."

Just then a Zionist ran toward them only two fields below.

"Basim, look," Yousif said.

But Omar must have also seen him, for he turned his Bren and riddled him with bullets. Yousif was horrified. This was going to be worse than the time the people of Ardallah had killed the seventeen boys, including Isaac. How would the Zionists retaliate? And how would the Arabs retaliate for the retaliation? Who would break the cycle of madness? The more he watched the more upset he became. It wasn't a pretty sight to see men blowing each other's brains out.

Basim was delighted. "Good for you, Omar," he shouted. "That's the way to shoot."

"You're mad," the doctor said. "Stop for a minute and let me take care of you. Life must be saved, even if it's wasted on those who have no respect for it."

Costa opened the third box of bombs and was ready to drop another one down the barrel.

"Out of my way, Uncle," Basim said, lowering the tube to no more than a forty-five degree angle.

"This is not a game, Basim," the doctor said, ducking his head.

"Look who's talking," Basim laughed, as the bomb shot high above the trees.

"There's no telling where the bullet will be in an hour," the doctor warned. "It might settle in so deep getting it out won't be that easy. It might even poison your whole system."

Basim was not convinced. "Look, Uncle," he said, "if you can't wait, then it's too bad. I will not leave."

Basim turned to his men and began firing orders. "Nicola, watch your target. And you, Ali. How much ammunition do you think we have?"

To Yousif's surprise, the enemy was now advancing again. Their firing was constant. Basim stopped handling the mortar in order to assess what was happening.

"Someone go to town and get us some help," Basim shouted.

"We can't leave," someone answered. It sounded like one of the former policemen.

"You will if I tell you," Basim barked, his fists at his hips. "Yousif, you go to town and ask for volunteers. See how many men are at the western entrance. There ought to be at least four. If there's no action there bring two back with you. Salem, take someone with you and run down the hill. Run to the cave by the spring fountain. You know the one I'm talking about?"

"I do," said Salem, a wiry bartender.

"You and Khaled take a few hand grenades with you. I think they're trying to cut us off from the road to town. Wait for them in ambush. As soon as you see them, fire from below. But don't shoot at us for Christsake."

Salem and Ali filled their pockets with hand grenades, slung their rifles over their shoulders, and hurried down the hill, taking the eastern route. Yousif had just turned on the motor of his car when suddenly a hand grenade fell a few yards from where he had left Basim and his father. By the time Costa hollered a warning it was too late. A flash of gunpowder rose and lit the sky. Darkness followed—then silence. Yousif turned the switch off and waited in his car. Many of the men were on the ground, covered with dust and smoke. Someone shrieked.

"What are you waiting for, another explosion?" Yousif could hear Basim thundering. "The doctor will treat the injured. No, I have a better idea. Let the doctor take them to his clinic. That's one way to get rid of him."

The men went back to their guns. In their frantic retreat Yousif could hear them asking about each other without pausing to find out. The enemy was blistering them; Basim was wounded; their lives were in danger. They had to keep moving.

"Husam, are you there?"

"Salah, are you all right?"

"Ahmad, I need help."

"My eye!"

"My leg!"

"Help, please help!"

Basim was still on the ground. It wasn't like him, Yousif thought. Yousif rushed to see if he was getting worse. All his fears were confirmed. Basim's shoulder was drooping and his face a picture of agony. But he would not admit it. His right hand clutched his chest, but he never stopped firing orders.

"Will you prop me up?" Basim asked. "If I can't fire at least I can watch."

Yousif did all he could for him and then started looking for his father. It was possible that Basim would listen to him now.

"Where's Dr. Safi? Have you seen my father? Look for the doctor."

"Hey, Yousif," a former policeman finally said. "Your father is here."

Yousif ran where the man was standing, next to the watchtower. His father was on the ground, his head leaning against the wall. He looked a mess: rumpled, covered with blood and dirt. Yousif's heart pounded. The doctor's eyes were closed. Yousif stiffened. He knelt near him, terrified.

"Father, can you hear me?"

The doctor's two hands were clutching his own chest. As the doctor inhaled, his chest would cave in rather than expand. It did not look normal.

The doctor opened his eyes with difficulty. Seeing his son beside him, he smiled. He had been hit in the stomach and chest. Yousif took off his shirt and covered the open wounds. He threw himself on his father's chest and, holding him tightly, began to sob. The doctor raised his right arm painfully, tapped his son on the shoulder and shook his head.

"I was on my way to take a piss inside the watchtower," the doctor said, clutching his chest and smiling a perverted smile. "Isn't that funny? My life for a piss!"

"We've got to carry you to the clinic," Yousif said, choking.

"What for?"

"What do you mean what for?"

"I can die here just as well."

"You're not going to die. Don't say that. You're not going to die." But deep in his heart Yousif knew he was dying.

"My lungs have collapsed," the doctor explained, gasping. "See how my chest compresses. I have what we call a sucking wound."

"A what?" Yousif asked.

The doctor bit his lower lip in a twisted smile. "A sucking wound . . ." he repeated, pressing both hands to his chest. "It sounds obscene, doesn't it?"

"Let me tape you then," Yousif suggested, rising to fetch the First Aid Kit.

"Don't waste your time," his father said. "That's not all that's wrong with me. I'd rather you stayed—"

The bullets continued to whistle and flash. The doctor closed his eyes and smiled. He seemed contented with the mystery dissolving between life and the unknown. He opened his eyes again, giving the impression of someone who had touched the bottom of the deep ocean and just come up for a last breath of air. Yousif grew tense.

"Samihni, Father," Yousif said, his voice catching. "Forgive me."

The doctor bit his lower lip. From the look on his face the pain must've been excruciating.

"Samihni, please, *samihni,* "Yousif pleaded.

"You've done nothing wrong," the doctor said, convulsing.

"Is there anything you want to tell me, Father?"

The doctor pressed two overlapping palms against his own blood-drenched chest. "Take care of your mother. Tell her to be brave. Get married and give her lots of grandchildren. She'd like that."

Yousif felt tears welling up in his eyes. The doctor's eyes widened. Questions, trivial and crucial, tumbled in Yousif's mind. But he remained silent. He squeezed his father's hand and stared at him—bewildered, afraid. His father squeezed back mightily, then his hand went limp. Something between them tore. Yousif was crushed.

As his father closed his eyes, Yousif felt total isolation. His father, he knew, was swimming into the unknown. He wanted to swim with him.

"Father, don't leave me."

The doctor forced a grin.

"Samihni, please, *samihni,* "Yousif murmured, touching his father's forehead.

The grin turned into a fragile, transcendent smile, signaling a retreat, a wading into a nameless void. "No need . . ."

With that the doctor's eyes closed forever. Yousif leaned forward and kissed his forehead. Then he looked at the face that was so familiar to him and now so strange. These brooding eyes would never see the light again. These silent lips were now wearing a gentle smile, a smile of contentment Yousif had never seen before.

Tears dried in his eyes.

Yousif sat for a long time, looking at his father. He thought about the things left undone, the things left unsaid. A mysterious new closeness seemed to bind them, and Yousif felt stronger. A strange feeling! Deep, calm, and comforting in the midst of chaos.

Suddenly, he was aroused out of his meditation.

"Maybe now he can appreciate what a gun can do," said Costa, the pudgy postman. "The town had to sue him for the hospital money."

Shocked, Yousif sprang to his feet and hit Costa in the stomach. Costa doubled up and Yousif hit him again.

Costa hollered, then fell to the ground. He tried to cock his rifle. But Yousif kicked it out of his hand, then grabbed it.

"Yousif?" Basim yelled. "Put that gun down. We just had our first victory, and now we're going to start fighting among ourselves? That's crazy. Put that gun down and listen to me."

"You listen to me," Yousif shouted. "This idiot is glad to see my father killed."

"Well . . ." Basim humored him, "what do you expect from an idiot?"

The lull expanded into deep silence. Moments passed, without a stir. Little by little, uneasy quiet returned to the mountain. More men gathered around: limping, wretched, grimy, pressing their wounds. Handsome and debonair Omar Kilani looked as haggard as a ploughman. But from the satisfied look on their faces Yousif could tell that they had struck a blow to the enemy, that they had chased them away. Yousif thought about the Zionists, who were still on their feet taking advantage of this moment and slipping into the black night. He wondered if they had carried their dead and wounded with them? He wondered if Eliyaho, the first soldier Basim had killed and left to rot, would be mourned tonight or next morning. Would his mother shriek as Yousif's own mother was sure to do before long?

"Basim," Yousif said, his voice softened. "You're not angry with me, are you?"

"I will be if you don't put it down."

They all waited. Yousif kept the gun pointed. The spasm had subsided.

"My father was a good man," Yousif said, choking.

"The best," Basim assured him. "At times difficult, but his heart was as big as this mountain."

"The hospital was his dream."

There was a long pause. Then Yousif collapsed, crying. He seemed drunk with shock. Drunk with love and hate. Drunk with faith and doubt.

"God," Yousif said, his head tilted heavenward.

Though absorbed, he could hear the men around him shifting their feet. His soft cry seemed to have a paralyzing effect.

"The boy is crazy," he heard one of them say.

"He's as innocent as the Lamb of God."

"What should it be, God?" Yousif cried, his eyes locked on the stars. "A church, a mosque, or a synagogue? You taught us to love each other, and we're doing just that. We love each other so much, we're killing each other. Isn't this love, God? And with our bones we're going to build a house of worship."

"Come on, now," Basim entreated.

"Hey, up there, are you listening to me or are you not? Why don't you answer me? Am I not your son too? Am I not your son, God?"

Yousif knelt near his father, his tears falling. Clutching his own shoulder, Basim stumbled forward. Then he knelt beside his uncle and cousin.

Dawn was now breaking. The enemy had vanished. The stillness of the hour was complete.

"Let's carry him home," Basim said to Yousif.

Slowly Yousif bent down and lifted his dead father to his shoulder. Basim and others tried to help, but he would not let them.

22

Kneeling in the back of the pickup truck with his father's warm body stretched on the floor beside him, Yousif caressed the dead man's forehead in disbelief. Too choked up to make a sound, his eyes swelled with tears and his body tensed. Then he threw himself over the corpse, sobbing.

When they reached the paved road on the western side of town, the driver shifted gears and sped down the street. He drove a few hundred yards, then abruptly pulled to the side of the road and stepped down. He asked Basim if they should drive directly to the doctor's house to inform his wife, or get some elderly relative to help them break the bad news. This was customary. Basim turned to look at Yousif and found him still crying.

"Yousif," Basim said, bending to touch the youth's shoulder. "What should we do? Who's going to tell your mother?"

Yousif hesitated, then said, "I am."

"It'll be hard on both of you," Basim cautioned. "Let's wake up Uncle Boulus. He could break it to her gently."

"No," Yousif said.

"I'd do it myself, except for all this blood from my own wounds. It might scare her."

Yousif shook his head. Convinced that Yousif would not change his mind, Basim motioned for the driver to move on.

On the way home, Yousif thought of that brief exchange. He had never before been consulted on such grave matters. These were adult people's decisions. But now he was an adult. Half an hour ago he had been the doctor's son; now, as the only male survivor, he was the head of the house. He began to understand death in realistic terms: the torch had been passed.

A new grief gripped Yousif when they reached his house. As they parked the pickup truck in the driveway, he could see his mother pacing in the living room and then hastily appearing at the window. The sound of the truck had startled her. Even at a distance Yousif could sense her state of mind. He climbed down, headed toward the house. She came out and stood on the veranda in the dark. He walked slowly toward her, suppressing the pain in his heart. Oh, God, how could he tell her? He saw his mother's hand go up to her mouth. She knew, he told himself. She walked down the steps like a phantom.

"Oh, no, no!" she murmured as they embraced, her face frightened.

Then she wailed, going limp in his arms. Basim put his un-injured arm around her waist. Both he and Yousif struggled to take her inside the house.

"Oh my God! Oh my God!" she kept screaming.

"Mother, Mother, let me hold you," Yousif consoled her, his chin trembling.

"How did it happen?" she cried, searching their faces. "He hasn't been gone an hour—"

On the veranda she beat her head against the marble column, shaking like a leaf.

Thunderstruck, Yousif looked at Basim for help.

"Let her get it out of her system," Basim said, his face grim.

"Did he suffer?" she cried, her eyes reflecting unimaginable terror. "Was he killed on the spot?"

"What's the use?" Yousif said. "He's gone."

"I want to know," she begged, clawing her face. "Were you beside him when he died? Did he say anything?"

Yousif broke into tears and couldn't answer. But Basim stood between them and led them inside.

Within minutes, the neighbors began to gather. Uncle Boulus and Aunt Hilaneh were the first to arrive. Then the barber and his wife, the widow seamstress, and the bus driver and his wife and middle-aged daughter.

"Before the house fills up," Basim said to Yousif, "you need to pick out a suit to put on him. He can't be buried like this."

True, Yousif thought, banging his head against the wall. Then he rushed to his parents' bedroom and opened the chifforobe. The birds in the adjacent room were in an uproar.

His father's large wardrobe of expensive suits stared at him like witnesses to a tragedy. Which one should he pick? Which silk shirt, which tie? What the hell did it matter, he said to himself. He grabbed the first one of each he could put his hands on and went back to the dining room, where his father's corpse was now laid on the table. Basim and Uncle Boulus were there, but no one else. Yasmin wanted to help, but the men would not let her.

"Just bring us some hot water and a few bath towels," Basim told her, "we'll do the rest."

The three men went to work, although Basim was handicapped. Uncle Boulus, his face yellow, stripped his brother-in-law naked. It was the first time Yousif had ever seen his father's genitals and he wished he had been spared the experience. It revolted him that his father's privacy was being violated. The doctor had always been prim, proper, decorous. Now, this! "Oh God!" Yousif said, crying. The doctor's chest and abdomen were covered with sticky blood and dirt.

They heard a knock on the door. Before they could open it Fatima stepped in with a large aluminum bowl full of steaming water. A load of towels draped her shoulder. Instinctively, Yousif threw his father's trousers over his genitals.

"Let me clean him up for you," she said, the sleeves of her ankle-length dress rolled up high on her white arms. The men looked at each other. But Fatima forced her way in and placed the water on the dining room table.

"Yousif," she said, "remove your father's watch and ring."

"No, no, no," Yousif protested, anger grabbing his throat. "I want them to go with him."

"What for?" Uncle Boulus agreed with Fatima. "You might as well wear them."

"I want him buried the way he always was: a dignified man," Yousif said, standing aside, pulling his hair.

"Things don't give dignity," Uncle Boulus reminded him, untying the black leather band.

"Keep the wedding band on him, that's all," Basim said, trying to remove the doctor's shoes with one hand.

Uncle Boulus handed the watch and black sapphire ring to Yousif. The water in the large bowl soon turned murky, like homemade red wine with sediment.

"Poor, poor Dr. Safi," Fatima lamented, scrubbing around the "sucking wound" that looked like a ripe black fig that had been torn open. "Who's going to make you Arabic coffee? Who's going to prepare the *nergileh* for you?"

Yousif moaned. "All that intelligence . . . all that nobility . . . food for worms," he said.

"Stop it now," Uncle Boulus told him, putting his arms around his shoulder. "It's not Christian."

"Food for worms," Yousif repeated, crying.

"Maybe you should go out. Fatima is doing all the work anyway."

Fifteen minutes later, Fatima helped the men carry the doctor's groomed body to the living room. He looked natural, Yousif thought, except his hair line was crooked and his striped red tie askew. The body was laid in a makeshift coffin: a mattress and a pillow in the middle of the room, covered with a white bed sheet. It radiated with goodness—in death as in life.

Time had been overturned. Night had become day. People came in droves. Each arrival sparked new misery. Amin and his parents, Jamal, even old man Abu Khalil, the bone fixer, were among those whose sleep had been disturbed. The house was soon filled with infernal noise. Neighbors and relatives continued to stream in, all with mouths creased, anxious, tearful.

Yousif collapsed on the sofa under the half-moon-shaped window, his arms around his mother. She buried her face in his chest. He tried to console her, but needed consolation himself. His hot tears fell on her head; she shook with sobbing. He was surrounded by a sea of agonized faces, not one wearing make-up. Aunt Hilaneh and Abla, cousin Salman's wife, tore the fronts of their dresses and beat their bosoms. The men had solemn faces; some even cried. Again and again Fatima howled. When Nurse Laila and her ramrod-straight husband arrived, the women went wild with dirges. Maha, Basim's wife, entered the house, her arms flailing. Salman threw himself over his uncle's body and cried like an old woman. Blow your trumpets, Cherubim! Yousif thought, as he glanced at winged angels embroidered on the draperies. Heavens, open your gates: one of God's noblest is on his way.

The dining room and one of the bedrooms were quickly transformed into sitting rooms. The furniture was removed and stacked elsewhere. Fouad Jubran noticed Basim standing in a corner on the eastern balcony with his left hand clutching his right shoulder. He had changed his blood-drenched shirt for one of Yousif's. But it too was now blotted. Basim was withdrawn, listening to bullets cracking and resonating in the distance. The rest of the men sat tensely quiet.

"My God, Basim," Fouad Jubran said, walking toward him. "You need help."

Basim shook his head. "What I need is someone to drive me back to the hill."

Yousif, who had been inside, appeared at the door. "Dr. Afifi is on his way," he said.

"Are you sure?" Basim asked, turning around.

"I just talked to him. He and Jihan will be here within ten minutes."

There was another burst of gunfire on a hill. Yousif was sure the Jews could not have returned to the same place. Basim perked his ears, then moved around the balcony, facing west. Others watched him and waited for some reaction.

"Hanna," Basim yelled.

The driver of the pickup truck jumped to his feet.

"Go back to the western hill," Basim told him, "and see what's going on. If things are quiet, bring the wounded for Dr. Afifi to take a look at them. We might as well let him make a night of it."

Several volunteered to go with Hanna, either to help him bring down the wounded or to stay as replacements. In the meantime, Dr. Jamil Safi's villa shook with grief, as more and more mourners arrived.

Basim was very quiet. "We need to double the number of men on every hill," he finally said.

Yousif moved closer to him. "But we beat them, didn't we?" Yousif whispered.

"Sure we did. But if we drove them away before they could pick up their casualties, they'd come back to get them. No good soldiers would leave their comrades behind."

Yousif gripped the railing, thinking. "Let's hope they weren't good soldiers," he said.

BY NOON, over a thousand people met at the doctor's house to bid him a last farewell. The cortege passed slowly through the town. Yousif walked by his mother's side, her arm entwined with his. He watched as men, including Amin and ustaz Hakim, took turns shouldering the coffin of their new martyr. Ardallah had better get used to such scenes, Yousif thought. The real war hadn't even started. Wait until the dead are counted by the hundreds.

The business district closed down for the funeral. The merchants who had their shops still open were seen rolling down their corrugated steel doors out of respect for the dead. The long column was headed by priests, ministers, Muslim religious leaders, the Arab District Commissioner, the mayor and the city council, and dignitaries of Ardallah and the neighboring towns and villages. Behind them was the open wooden casket held up high. Freckled twenty-year-old Mirwan, a distant cousin, walked behind them holding the cover. Following them were Basim and Yousif and their immediate family. The rest of the procession trailed behind.

The ceremony at St. George Catholic Church was brief. Yousif regretted that the patriarch or at least the bishop wasn't there for a proper send-off for his father. His father deserved the best. Father Mikhail gave what Yousif considered a short but dignified eulogy, praising the doctor's many virtues and citing examples of his dedication to Ardallah. Even the doctor's worst critics, he reminded them, must admit that the doctor had been a deeply religious man, a conscientious human being, and that the conflict that had erupted recently between him and the people of Ardallah was motivated by pure love.

"It's a reminder of the fallen state of mankind that this man of spirit, this beautiful soul, should have been considered too idealistic, too abstract for us ordinary people. Why isn't the world a fit place for such a good man? Because the world was capable of massacres like Deir Yasin."

Father Mikhail paused, lowered his voice and added, "The massacre of Deir Yasin gave rise to a cry that nearly tore him apart. His faith in the goodness of man was, to be sure, strained, shaken, shattered. But, it is a measure of his ultimate faith in humanity—that he did not succumb to utter despair. Till the very end he refused to believe that the grace of God would allow man to annihilate himself, but rather would lift him from the lower depths and would help him triumph and endure. Therefore, we must conclude that our departed brother, Dr. Jamil Safi, did not die a defeated man."

At the graveside, Yousif was ready to speak. He looked pale and distraught. He was afraid of breaking down and crying in public. To his surprise, the tears dried in his eyes. The crowd stood still, waiting for him to begin.

Basim was standing to his left, his shoulder heavily bandaged. Jamal's chin was trembling. Amin and all the teachers and classmates were there. His uncles and aunts were there—but not his grandparents and aunt Widad: they lived in Jerusalem and could not escape some raging battle in the Holy City. Ustaz Saadeh, was there; so was ustaz Rashad Hakim. So were hundreds of acquaintances and total strangers. So were Salwa and her parents. Yousif was sure Adel Farhat was there too, but he could not locate him. He wished Salwa could be at his side; he wished he had won her hand before his father's death. His mother was at his right, but he was afraid his emotions would fail him if he looked at her. Their eyes must not meet.

The hushed gathering, Yousif thought, bespoke of the town's eulogy to his father—a song of death composed of every moment he had lived.

He wanted to cry.

He wanted to cry because his father had left it all. And because his father had not touched every stone, embraced every tree, and kissed every face farewell.

He heard himself speaking. The words rolled out of his mouth. He listened to them as if they were uttered by someone else. After the opening sentences, he gained confidence. He was not choking with emotion; his voice was not failing him. The words were flowing as if he were reading a prepared speech. He glanced around; people were listening.

It was no secret, he told them, that his father had loved Ardallah and its people. Deep in his heart, the doctor had known that the feeling was mutual.

"With your help, his hospital will be built," Yousif declared. "It will stand—not in his memory only, but in the memory of those who share in his dream. But *built it will be.* If not this year, next year. If not next year, the year after. We will work on it as soon as this war, which we neither provoked nor instigated, is over and Palestine is made safe. But now that the war is upon us, it must be won. We all wish we had not been dragged into this fight. And should someone, even at this late stage, dare to wage *peace,* he shall find us ready to embrace it. Should someone challenge us with generosity of spirit, he shall not go wanting. For nothing will please us—nothing will more exalt my father's soul—than to see harmony return to Palestine, this holy, precious, tragic land."

The eyes of the near thousand mourners seemed to approve. His mother sniffled and dabbed her eyes. Salwa stared at him, her cheeks wet.

Yousif stood still for a long moment, feeling abandoned like Jesus at Gethsemane. If Jesus could not drink the cup of pain and sorrow, how could he? Then Yousif knelt by the open casket and kissed his father's forehead. It felt as hard and cold as a piece of marble. Its putrid taste lingered on his lips as several men converged on him and pulled him up.

"Control yourself," Salman told him, clutching his arm.

"Ma'a es salameh," Yousif said, gripped with emotion. "Go with peace."

As the grave diggers stepped forward to close the casket and lower it in the grave, the crowd began to disperse. Though tearful, Yousif was proud it was a befitting funeral. His father was honored in death. Many of his father's adversaries, including the lame councilman Ayoub Salameh and the stuttering Ghanem Jadallah—even the pudgy postman, Costa—were among those in attendance. Yousif was impressed but not surprised. Death occupied a special place among the Arabs. Whenever calamity struck, they all shared each other's sorrow and tended to forget and forgive.

"A man who left behind a son like you did not die," Jihan Afifi told Yousif. She hugged him and kissed him, but his eyes were on Salwa, who was standing at the other side of the grave. Finally, Salwa and her mother made their way to offer their condolences to him and his mother.

"Yislem rasak," Salwa told him, locking her eyes with his. "May you be safe."

"Oo rasik. And thank you for coming," Yousif told her, shaking and squeezing her hand.

Not only did she squeeze his back, but she patted it with her other hand.

It was a poignant moment. He took her warmth as a good signal. Her feelings for him were intact. It was enough to lift his spirit.

Salwa's mother was equally genuine. Her father, on the other hand, paid his respect to his mother and the rest of the family—but not to him. Yousif was sure it was a deliberate slight. It bothered him, not because he was ignored, but because it foretold trouble.

YOUSIF SKIPPED school for the rest of the week. Their house was full of people who continued to drop in at all hours to pay their respects. Relatives kept Yousif and his mother company—from morning till almost midnight. His mother never cooked or was allowed near the kitchen. Fatima showed Maha and Abla where everything was and these two relatives prepared all the food. On the third day, Yousif's grandparents and Aunt Widad and her family arrived from Jerusalem. Emotions erupted once again and the house trembled. After the situation had quieted down, the grief-stricken grandparents stayed with Yousif and his mother; Aunt Widad and Uncle Rasheed Ghattas and their three children stayed at Uncle Boulus's house, across the street.

When Yousif returned to school on Monday, wearing his father's gold wristwatch and black sapphire ring, he was touched by his teachers' and classmates' deference to him. No trace of ill will was left toward him or his deceased father. They all shook his hands, offered their condolences, and stood still around him as though his sorrow were theirs. A new bond seemed to pull them together. Yousif checked the tears in his eyes, but was grateful.

Despite the personal tragedy, Yousif never stopped thinking about politics. Now he was particularly encouraged by news that the Syrian military commander Fawzi al-Kawiqji and his thousand volunteers were engaging the enemy in battle near Beisan, in Galilee. Everybody else was encouraged too, except ustaz Hakim.

This morning they were in the school's basement, which had been converted into a simple gymnasium. The rectangular room had two ping pong tables, two punching bags, two dumbbells, and a set of gymnastic bars. All the students, including Yousif, wore blue shorts and white shirts and lined up against the walls, watching ustaz Hakim, who truly believed in the ideal of a fit mind in a fit body. Yousif felt guilty smiling at his teacher's antics on the bars, yet he couldn't help it. He marveled at seeing him swinging between the bars, flipping several times in mid-air to change directions, and then clutching the top bars without missing a beat. Yousif hated the comparison, but ustaz Hakim was as natural as a monkey on a tree.

"Skirmishes are not enough," ustaz Hakim said, his powerful hands gripping the top bars and his body swinging in the air. "It's an all-out war, and we're still twiddling our thumbs."

Yousif watched in awe as ustaz stood upside down between the bars, his biceps as big as oranges, then flipped backward with a flourish to land on his feet.

At least the teacher was doing his share, Yousif thought. Ustaz Hakim had spent the night before guarding Ardallah on top of one of the hills. At daybreak he went home, took a shower, changed clothes, and came straight to school.

Ustaz Hakim began sending the students up to perform for him, one at a time. Adnan was the best athlete in class and he got on first. Yousif could tell that Adnan intended to emulate his teacher, and Yousif feared for him. No one could be that accomplished without a natural talent and years of experience. For a while the students and teacher stopped talking politics and just watched. Adnan started out doing a few fancy tricks, the muscles of his biceps bulging—but not as big as the teacher's. He was skillful, but too eager to be in the master's class.

"What's the latest?" Amin asked the teacher.

"Don't you read the papers?" the ustaz chided him, his breathing even.

"We like to hear your opinion," Amin prodded.

"The United Nations," ustaz Hakim said, "is realizing that it has no actual power to enforce the partition. Now it's trying at Lake Success, in New York, to stop the fighting and create a trusteeship. We Arabs, or rather the heads of states, are meeting at Aley, Lebanon, and trying to stem the tide."

"And agreeing *not* to agree," said Yousif, repeating a popular sarcasm.

"Exactly," the ustaz said, mopping his face with a towel. "In the meantime, ships at Haifa and Jaffa harbors are still unloading thousands of Jewish immigrants and tons of ammunition."

Some of the students swore under their breath; others gathered around the teacher. Yousif folded his arms, wishing he could withdraw from the whole human race. A world that killed his father wasn't fit to live in. He glanced at his father's gold watch and rubbed his sapphire ring as though evoking him to reappear.

"King Abdullah seems to be our only hope," ustaz Hakim said. "His Arab Legion is the best trained and best equipped. But will he commit it seriously in total battle? An Englishman, Glubb Pasha, is commanding his army and Britain is financing his kingdom. Britain isn't about to let him have a free hand and deal the Zionists a blow. After all it was Balfour, another Englishman, who promised the Zionists a national home in Palestine."

Yousif and his classmates were all ears.

"Even if Britain permits the defeat of the Zionists," ustaz Hakim went on calmly, "will the United States stand idly by? This is an election year. Truman wants to live four more years at the White House."

"Fuck him," Adnan said, apparently keeping his ears tuned while swinging.

"Watch your tongue," the teacher continued. "Truman says he has more Jewish constituents than Arab, which is true. Therefore, he won't allow the Zionists to be defeated, because his election is much more important to him than a tiny distant country called Palestine could ever be. Personal tragedies don't concern him."

"Look at his record," Yousif said.

"Exactly. He's the only one to drop the atomic bomb. History will never forgive him for that, if nothing else."

Adnan jumped down and Radwan took his place. When Yousif's turn came he passed. He was more interested in politics than gymnastics. Could King Abdullah be trusted? Would he come to help and leave, or would he stay as an invader?

"My father says King Abdullah is a schemer," square-jawed Khaled said. "He says that if King Abdullah fights, he'll seize part of Palestine for himself. Do you agree?"

Ustaz Hakim smiled and threw the towel around his neck. "Abdullah is a shrewd, ambitious king," he told them. "No doubt about it. God knows what he and the British have in mind. Don't forget: he owes his throne to Churchill."

ON SATURDAY Yousif went out to Salman's shop to buy cannabis for his birds. When he returned home, he saw a green Buick parked in the driveway behind his father's green Chrysler. Whose was it?

Once inside, he immediately recognized its owners as the Haddad family from Haifa. The two families had known each other from years past when the Haddads had rented Yousif's next door neighbor's house for the summer. Yousif smiled when he saw them. Fond memories flooded his mind.

He remembered visiting them with his parents in Haifa. The Haddads lived in the Deir Mar Elias section of Mount Carmel, overlooking the splendid bay and the golden cupola of the Bahai Temple. Mr. Haddad owned a huge liquor business on the corner of El-Mulouk and Khayyat Streets and could afford a beautiful house, furnished with opulence typical of wealthy Arabs. And he was a prince in his house. Yousif's father had thought highly of him and always described his hospitality as *karam Araby* at its best. What Yousif had enjoyed most, he now recalled, were the magnificent ships at the harbor—especially at night.

The father, Abu Raji, was taller than most Arabs. His huge hands seemed to engulf Yousif's. Usually a well dressed man, Abu Raji today wore no jacket and no tie. He looked different, nervous. His wife was chubby and sweet. She hugged and kissed Yousif and told him how sorry she was to hear about his father's death. They had just arrived in town, taken a room at a hotel, and come to see the Nussrallah family in the middle of the block about renting their house again. Only then did they learn of the doctor's death. Mrs. Haddad apologized for her bright dress, looking at the other ladies in the room who wore black. On one side of the room were the Haddad's two sons, Raji and Munir. Raji was about fifteen and Munir twelve. They both looked taller than the summer before. Yousif shook their hands and sat next to them.

Abu Raji reached for his pack of cigarettes. Yousif felt he was failing as a host. He jumped to his feet, hastening to pick up a medium-sized silver tray full of cigarette packs and a box of Cuban cigars. It was a remnant of the week of the funeral when the house had been full of mourners. When Abu Raji reached for a cigarette from the tray Yousif was holding before him, Yousif insisted that he take a whole pack and a handful of cigars.

"Allah yirhamu," Abu Raji said, accepting only the pack of Players and praying for the doctor's soul.

"I didn't even bring a black dress with me," Imm Raji apologized. "We left in such haste . . . such haste."

"We couldn't help it," her husband interrupted, lighting a cigarette.

"He didn't give me time to pack," Imm Raji continued.

"Time, she says," her husband scoffed, crossing his legs.

Imm Raji took a deep breath. "I was in the kitchen washing dishes when the phone rang. All I could hear him say was, 'Get ready, get ready, we're leaving.' 'Leaving where?' I asked, trembling. 'Haifa,' he shouted back. He said he was on his way to pick up the boys from school and then we'd be leaving. In less than half an hour we closed the door and left everything behind us. Everything . . ." she said, wiping her eyes.

Yousif was disappointed that they had actually abandoned Haifa. Under no circumstance would he pick up and leave his home. No matter what the Zionists did or said, he would stay. He scanned the women around him, all looking like a flock of black crows, and found them attentive. He wondered where his grandfather and Uncle Rasheed were, but didn't ask.

"What happened to the resistance?" Yousif inquired.

"What resistance?" Abu Raji snapped. "How can the defenseless resist? Especially when they drop bombs all around you like hail and you don't have a damn thing . . ."

"I thought—" Yousif interrupted.

Imm Raji turned and looked at Yousif, anxious. "Don't forget the leaflets they were dropping from the sky," she added, "ordering us to leave. Either get out, they warned, or expect another Deir Yasin."

"Tell them about the loudspeakers, Mom," twelve-year-old Munir suggested.

"Yes," the mother remembered, gently pounding her bosom. "Day in and day out a car would tour the neighborhoods with someone blaring the same threat over and over: *leave or else.*"

The father looked offended. "It's easy to ask us, Why did you leave? Under the circumstances it was the only sensible thing to do."

The look of disapproval on Yousif's face was obvious.

"Oh," the father went on, "we raised a few thousand pounds the last few weeks and bought a few guns—"

"We did too," Yousif said.

"—and some of our boys did some sniping and some fist fighting. Some even attacked the Zionists from door to door. But what's the use? When the Zionists brought out the armored cars, the superior guns."

Yousif's mother sighed. "We know all about them," she recalled.

"You had one air raid, but we had dozens," the husband said, his face ashen. "With bombs falling over our heads and our streets turning into a Stalingrad, our morale went to pieces."

Aunt Hilaneh clucked, shaking her head.

"One time I was standing in front of the store when I heard a plane zooming above our heads," Abu Raji continued. "It looked like a Shell Oil tanker descending on us with the Star of David painted on its belly. Just before I ran inside, I happened to see one of its huge doors open and a pilot actually roll out a bomb as long as a large melon. When it exploded it took half the next block with it. Glass shattered miles away. What are you talking about?"

"The same thing in Jerusalem," Yousif's grandmother said.

"The things we can tell you," Aunt Widad concurred, lifting her one-year-old baby in her lap.

"Remember, we lived in Haifa," Abu Raji said, directing most of his words to Yousif. "Did you hear what the Haganah and Stern and Irgun did at Wadi Nisnas Street?"

Yousif shook his head and waited.

"Of course you didn't. Half of the atrocities are not reported. But they blocked the entrances of all the streets that led to Wadi Nisnas, trapped all who lived there, and butchered them in cold blood."

"Ya waili alayhom," Imm Raji lamented, wiping her own tears. "Two families who were our best friends were murdered in that incident."

Yousif watched the women around him. The expressions on their faces were a tangle of emotions.

"We saw ship after ship arrive," Abu Raji continued, "with all those Jewish immigrants who couldn't wait to turn their hatred for the Nazis against us. We saw the crates of ammunition being unloaded. At the same time, no Arab government was lifting a damn finger. We could read the handwriting on the wall."

"Up till now they've been warming up," Imm Raji explained. "Now it's war. Real war, believe me."

"If this is war, it's got to be the most lopsided in history," Yousif said, still worried about the implications of their flight.

"If someone tells you a hurricane is coming," Abu Raji argued, "will you stay put or will you run to the nearest shelter? That's exactly what we're doing. We're going to ride it out until the Arab armies arrive and then see what happens."

The baby in Aunt Widad's arms began to scream.

"We're ruined, ruined," Imm Raji complained, wiping the sweat on her face with her handkerchief. "We left everything behind: the store, the house, everything. We bought new furniture only last Christmas, and all I could do was to cover it with bed sheets and walk out. We're ruined, I tell you. Ruined."

"You speak as if you'd never go back," Yasmin said.

Imm Raji shook her head, smiling sadly. "I don't think we will. Even if we do, there'll be nothing left. Everything will have been looted."

"That's why I have to go back as soon as I can," her husband said, his left leg jerking.

"Oh, no, you don't," his wife insisted.

"I have to."

"Never."

"I've got to cement the front of the shop."

"And be killed like your neighbor Abu Ghassan?"

"It's a chance I've got to take."

Imm Raji then turned to Yousif's mother and said that it was perhaps wrong of her to mention what she was about to say, so soon after the doctor's death. But would she and Yousif consider renting part of their house to her sister and her husband?

"I'm sure they'll be arriving from Haifa today or tomorrow," Imm Raji explained.

Her sister was only seventeen years old and would want to live near her. The doctor's house was big, she went on to explain. Maybe they could spare a room for such a nice couple. Her sister had gotten married to their first cousin, a very nice young man, only a few years older than Yousif. They could get along well, she was sure. The groom was a graduate of the American University of Beirut, and had been teaching high school for less than a year. Hiyam, her sister, hadn't even finished secondary school. They weren't ready for marriage but had to rush it on account of the war. Quick marriages were the order of the day. Families were worried about their daughters.

She turned her head toward the women and spoke in a low confidential tone. "Girls are being raped left and right," she said. "And families with single girls are particularly worried, you know."

"Of course," Yousif's aunt Hilaneh agreed.

"Rape is worse than death," said the barber's wife, inhaling snuff.

"Especially virgins," Imm Raji whispered.

Yousif pretended not to have heard. All he could think of now was Salwa. Wasn't that the reason her engagement to Adel Farhat had been hurried? Where was she now? What was she doing? Was she in the company of her fiancé? The thought upset him. He hadn't checked with Sitt Bahiyyeh on account of his father's death. He couldn't wait to get back to her and see what she had learned for him.

"The situation is deteriorating," Abu Raji said, flicking ashes in his left palm until Yousif handed him an ashtray. "Maybe we should've gone to Lebanon, I don't know. Or at least to Ramallah. The central highlands, we figured, would be safer than the coastal cities. But then we decided to stay close by just in case we could slip back in and see about the house and store."

Yousif exhaled. "Let's hope you'll be able to go back soon."

"Allah yirham abook," the guest said, his voice dropping. "May God rest your father's soul. But what you saw here is nothing compared to what we saw. Believe me. It was hell."

There was a long pause. Everybody's mind seemed to wander.

"Some families headed for Trans-Jordan," Imm Raji interjected, her eyes red.

There was general agreement that that was not the thing to do.

"They might as well be going to a foreign country," Maha said, speaking for the first time.

"There's a big gap between Haifa and Amman," Yousif's mother added.

"My God," Imm Raji exclaimed, "Trans-Jordan is nothing but a desert."

"I wouldn't go to Jordan if they gave it to me," her husband said. "It would be a culture shock I'm not ready for."

"No, we couldn't do that," his wife agreed.

Yousif watched his mother and the other women wring their hands and pray to God for mercy. Fatima brought a tray of coffee, bitter on account of the mourning period. Imm Raji then spoke again to Yousif, hoping that he and his mother would agree to rent the room to her sister and brother-in-law. Again Yousif was being addressed as the man of the house. He felt bound to make a decision without further ado. Besides, if hundreds of families were to descend on Ardallah, the poor couple would need a place to stay.

"When they come we'll have a room for them," Yousif promised. "I'm sure mother agrees."

His mother looked at him, surprised. She seemed to think it was a hasty decision. But Imm Raji was quick to seal the agreement.

"Bless you," Imm Raji said. "You and Hiyam's husband will enjoy each other's company. He's twenty-two years old. Wonderful young man. You'll like him."

"What's his name?" Yousif asked.

"Izzat Hankash. Has a B.S. in chemistry. Very smart for his age."

Gloom deepened. Just before the guests got up to leave, Yousif's mother told them that next morning they would be having a Mass for the soul of the departed. Afterwards they'd visit the cemetery.

"Seventh Day Memorial," Yasmin explained, "and I thought you might like to know."

"Oh sure," Imm Raji said. "I'm glad you told us. What time?"

"Ten o'clock at St. George Catholic Church."

"We'll be there," Imm Raji said, looking at her husband, who was nodding.

Then they got up to leave, both husband and wife repeating *"Allah yirhamu."*

Yousif and his mother saw them to the door: the husband grim, the wife's eyes moist, their two gangling sons trailing behind.

WHILE THE WOMEN converged on the dining room to prepare the traditional Holy bread and boiled wheat to take to church, Yousif's head throbbed with confusion. The stories he had just heard about what was going on in Haifa electrified him. The runaway train was unstoppable. He wished his grandfather and Uncle Rasheed would hurry and come home. He was suffocating. He needed someone to take his father's place, to help him understand, to give him inner strength. He was told they had gone out to spend time with Uncle Boulus at his grain store, or to smoke a *nergileh* at one of the coffeehouses.

The pipe rack struck Yousif's fancy and he decided to pick up the habit. He got up to inspect the half-dozen pipes, finally selecting his father's favorite: a curved, brown Dunhill. He opened a drawer in the corner table and took out two pieces of Dunhill cloth, one yellow and the other gray, to polish the mouthpiece and bowl. His mind buzzing with fear and anxiety, he rubbed them both until they sparkled. Then he opened a blue can of Capstan tobacco and filled the bowl to the brim. He wasn't sure how tightly he should pack it. Well, he thought, there were a number of things in life he wasn't sure about. He sat in his father's armchair and struck a match. He pondered the red flame a long time before placing it squarely above the tobacco.

Yousif thought of Salwa. He wanted to go out and check with Sitt Bahiyyeh. But neither society nor his conscience would approve. It would be highly disrespectful of his father's memory to be thinking of love and marriage so soon after the tragedy. No, he should bide his time—and hope that Salwa's family would not push the issue on him. It scared him to death that marriages were being hurried on account of the war. Imm Raji's account of her sister's wedding gave him goose pimples.

He turned on the radio and switched the dial until he locked on a news broadcast.

"Nakrashi Pasha, Egypt's Prime Minister," the announcer was saying, "has declared against entering the war. But King Farouk has overruled him."

Damn both of them, Yousif thought. Suddenly he heard his maternal grandfather's and uncle's footsteps. He rose from his chair to greet them. He was glad to see them, especially his seventy-six-year-old grandfather, who had taken the death of his son-in-law badly. Yousif put his arm around him and led him to a chair, wishing his grandparents lived closer so he could look after them all the time.

Ever since he had his heart attack four years ago and had to close his specialty shop on Via Dolorosa, grandfather's health had been sliding. Yousif thought he looked thinner than ever—almost gaunt, fragile. Old age had made him susceptible to crying for the least provocation. And since he had come to Ardallah, four days ago, his eyelids were raw and the kerchief never left his hand.

Uncle Rasheed carried two newspapers under his arm. Yousif told them about the Haddads' visit.

"You should've heard what Abu and Imm Raji had to say," Yousif said, puffing on his pipe. "It's awful. The situation in Haifa is worse than we think."

The grandfather sniffled, wiped his own tears, and tapped his cane. But Uncle Rasheed opened two newspapers simultaneously, flashing two headlines.

"Take your pick," Uncle Rasheed said, his shoulders slumped. "Even these headlines may be too old."

One headline screamed, HAIFA IN PERIL. The other warned, HAIFA ABOUT TO FALL.

"Oh, God!" Yousif said, taking one of the newspapers from his uncle.

The newspaper spoke of tens of thousands of Haifa residents pushed out by the Jews. Many were being put on buses or trucks and driven to the Lebanese border in the north. Many were being put on boats. There were pockets of resistance, but unquestionably the situation for the Arabs looked grim—even hopeless.

Yousif wanted to crumble the newspaper, but two more items caught his eye. One was a report about an Arab League's meeting, where kings and presidents had flexed their muscles.

"Impotent!" Yousif said under his breath, turning the sheet.

The inside pages were full of poetry, some of it beautiful, ringing with memorable lines and inspired by the impending tragedy. The poets were exhorting the Arabs to defend their country and defy the aggressor. They likened Palestine to a lovely maiden about to be raped by the Zionists. In an obvious reference to the seven members of the Arab League, one of Yousif's favorite poets, Kamal Nasser, compared them to a cart with seven wheels—speedily running backward.

Sab'on aya qowmo min dowali
Tamshi lil khalfi ala ajali

Yousif loved poetry. But not now. Real drama was unfolding on the ground. People were being killed and mutilated. He had no patience for words or images. In the face of Deir Yasin and now Haifa, the most beautiful poetry in the world grated on his nerves. Gunshots were whistling and flashing in his mind.

23

"Sorry, not today," the baker said, standing in the pit in front of the open oven.

Yousif was dismayed. "And what am I to tell the men?" he asked.

"Tell them," the baker answered, "I wasn't counting on Haifa to fall. Tell them to come and protect *me* from the hungry mobs. They snatch the bread from my hand before I have a chance to put it on the counter."

Yousif sympathized with the baker, who looked dusty and exhausted. He watched him pick up the eight-foot wooden spatula and turn the loaves over. The oven glowed like the mouth of hell.

"What's the least you can give me?" Yousif asked. "They have to eat."

The short, middle-aged baker seemed to explode. "They have to eat. The poor bastards who lost their homes have to eat. What can I do? I used to pray for a few more customers. Now I'm expected to feed the whole country."

Yousif stood his ground. "The men won't like it."

"I have only two hands and twenty-four hours a day. Every now and then I have a stupid habit of collapsing. The whole town calls me Abul Banat already. *Haik nassibi.* What worse fate can I have? You tell me."

The baker's irritability was comical. The few women who had brought their dough to be baked cracked up laughing. The baker's nickname, they all knew, was in reference to his seven daughters. A man who could produce only girls was shamed like someone who was childless.

"I don't call you Abul Banat," Yousif said.

"Go ahead, I'm not stopping you. Even my brothers call me that."

Yousif waited until the merriment subsided. He was in a quandary. Nearly eighty men on seven hills depended on him for food tonight.

"What if I come back after I finish picking up the other stuff?" Yousif asked. "Will you have a few dozens for me then?"

"You can try but I can't promise."

Yousif stormed out of the darkened bakery, swearing. A new mob was rushing in to buy bread, pain and fatigue on their faces. Yousif stood on the crowded sidewalk, wondering whether to try other bakers or to make the rounds to each fighter's home to see if their families had any bread to spare.

Suddenly he heard incessant honking. He turned around. It was Makram, the taxi-driver with the pearly teeth, trying to get his attention. He had stopped and waved in the middle of a street jammed with cars and pedestrians.

"You know a man by the name of Odeh Haddad?" Makram asked, his hands cupping his mouth.

"You mean Abu Raji?" Yousif shouted back.

Makram checked with two passengers and nodded. "Yes. Abu Raji from Haifa. Do you know if they're renting anywhere?"

Yousif had a strong feeling who the passengers were. He braved his way through the traffic to find out.

"These two are looking for them," Makram explained.

Yousif leaned on the car's door and peered through the window. The young couple on the back seat fit the image he had in mind.

"You must be Izzat and Hiyam," Yousif said.

The couple looked at each other, then at Yousif, puzzled.

"You know us?" the young man asked.

"You are Izzat Hankash. And you are Hiyam, Imm Raji's sister. Believe it or not you're staying at my house."

"Hallelujah!" Makram crowed. "We've been looking for someone who knows something all over town."

For a second Yousif didn't know whether to direct them to where the Haddads were staying or to take them home himself. He was anxious about finding bread, yet he wanted to break the happy news to Imm and Abu Raji. For the last few days they had been worried sick over them.

"I'm parked a block away," Yousif said. "Follow me."

WHEN THE TWO cars stopped in front of the Nussrallah's house, where the Haddads were staying, about ten people rushed to the edge of the balcony to see who it was. The first sounding of Yousif's horn brought Imm and Abu Raji and their children running to the street. There were hugs and kisses and tears and a lot of noise. Izzat and Hiyam were among the last to be driven out of Haifa, and everyone wanted to hear the latest news. To Yousif they looked like two people who had fallen off a truck. All they carried with them was a tan leather scuffed suitcase.

Minutes later they were all settled on the Nussrallah's big balcony. Though she appeared dishevelled and distraught, Hiyam was a lovely girl with a charming pout and natural *kuhol* around her eyes. Yousif thought she was about two inches shorter than Salwa, but there was nothing small about her figure. She was ripe and rounded in all the right places. But she looked frightened, clinging to her young husband. Now nervous and unkempt, Izzat was tall, thin, and sported a mustache that covered his wide upper lip. It made him look older than twenty-two.

"What happened to your family, dear?" Yasmin asked Hiyam. "Are they alright?"

Yousif was surprised that his mother was actually out of her house at this time. Normally, a bereaved mother or wife would not venture out for forty days—sometimes even up to six months. But his mother must have felt that she and the Haddads were bonded by sorrow—that it was in keeping with her mourning to visit with them.

"I don't know," Hiyam answered, clutching Izzat's arm. "I haven't seen them in a week."

"Oh dear! You think they're still back there?" Yasmin inquired, immersed in black.

"Could be. But I doubt it. From what we could tell the Jews weren't allowing anybody to stay."

Abu Raji crossed his long legs, his lips turning bluish. "Only God knows where they'll end up. And you, Izzat. What about your family?"

Izzat, who looked dehydrated, asked for a glass of water. Margo, one of the Nusrallah daughters, rushed to the kitchen and returned with two, for him and his wife.

Izzat took a long sip. "When we first told my parents we were coming to Ardallah," he said, "they thought we were crazy. They didn't think any part of Palestine was safe. They themselves wanted to go to Lebanon. But we had already promised to join you and didn't want to change our plans or worry you more."

"It was terrible," Hiyam said, resting her head on her husband's shoulder.

"Mother wanted to come with us," Izzat continued, his finger circling the rim of the glass, "but when the time came my father was undecided. This angered the Jewish soldier. He pushed them with the butt of his gun, demanding they make up their minds."

"About what?" Mrs. Haddad asked, patting her sister's hand.

"He wanted them to either get on the boat to Lebanon or join us in the taxi. My father would take one step this way and another step that way. Finally the soldier slammed the door of the taxi shut and told the driver to go on." Izzat's chin looked wrinkled.

Listening to Izzat, Yousif remembered his own father's death. Agony swelled in him anew. He looked at his mother and feared that her porcelain skin would crack.

"And then?" Yousif asked, holding back the tears.

"Izzat turned around," Hiyam took over in the telling, "to wave goodbye to his parents. His father was already a heap on the ground."

"Aaaaaaaahhhhh," several shrieked.

The death scene on the hill top replayed itself in Yousif's mind. His father flat on his back, the sucking wound, the last words, the peace and contentment on his face.

"Did they kill him?" Abu Raji wanted to know. "Did you hear a shot?"

"Shots were going on all the time," Izzat answered, his eyes misty. "Whether they killed him or not we don't know. All I saw was my father stretched out on the ground. Maybe he was wounded, I don't know."

It was too much for Yousif to take. He wanted to leave. But out of respect for Izzat, he stayed.

"He's probably still alive, then," the widow seamstress presumed.

"I hope so," Izzat said, smoothing Hiyam's hair.

"Most likely they shot him in the leg," the bus driver's wife offered, her hands characteristically under the hem of her sweater.

"Allah ija zee hom," Mrs. Nusrallah prayed. "May God punish them."

The quiet on the balcony drowned the street traffic. Ardallah was filling up. A couple of cars full of anxious people stopped to ask for a room to rent. Housing was becoming a major problem. People were getting desperate.

"If you ask every one of these people," Abu Raji said, referring to those who'd just been turned away, "he'd tell you a horror story."

The silence was funereal. The end of Abu Raji's cigarette glowed like an evil eye. When Yousif left to feed the fighters, he did not know whether he was running away from death or toward it.

JAFFA'S FALL within a week after Haifa's sounded a clanging alarm in Yousif's head. He recalled Basim's prediction that when the Zionists finished with Haifa they would turn their attention either to Jaffa in the south or Acre in the north. After that they would start hitting towns such as Lydda and Ramleh. The recent attack on Ardallah must have been an advance for a major assault on the inland.

It was late in the afternoon when Yousif decided to check with Dr. Afifi about his father's office. What should they do with it now? Close it? Sell it? To whom? Ever since his father's death Yousif had not had the heart to set foot in it. He had even sent nurse Laila's salary through Uncle Boulus, telling her he would see her soon.

Dr. Afifi's office was in the old district, only a couple of miles or so away from Yousif's house. Yousif decided to go on foot rather than drive. As he walked through the town, he was astonished at the transformation. Refugees from Jaffa were arriving in large numbers. Truck after truck passed him, loaded with mattresses, pots and pans, chairs—all piled up on top of each other. Children were strapped on or held onto whatever they could. It was a grim procession of desperate people looking for a place to hide.

On his way to the clinic, Yousif saw people clustering around the new arrivals. Their stories of the Zionist invasion were shocking. The onslaught had been swift and devastating. People had been ordered to leave. One warned another, until the trickle had turned into an avalanche.

Listening to an unshaven fisherman wearing the baggy pants of his trade, Yousif lost his patience.

"But why did you all leave?" Yousif snapped.

Angry eyes pierced Yousif as though he were the enemy.

"Watch your tone, mister," a tall cross-eyed stranger threatened.

"I didn't mean it that way," Yousif said. "I'm sorry."

The fisherman was still stung. "Listen to him," he said. "When they come after you here in Ardallah, I hope I'll be around to watch you shake in your boots. There's no bravery in the face of the big guns, especially if you are as defenseless as we are."

"That's the truth," another refugee grunted.

"The odds were a hundred to one against us," the fisherman went on, staring at Yousif.

"I'm sorry," Yousif again apologized. He could hear Salwa lambasting him for being so insensitive. If he felt so strongly about Palestine, why didn't he fight? Why didn't he carry a gun?

"Before we left Jaffa," the weather-beaten man continued, now addressing the crowd, "I saw something I never thought possible. On top of Hassan Bey Mosque was a white and blue flag. I had never seen it before, but I just knew it had to belong to the Zionists."

"Oh!" groaned all those surrounding him.

"Disgusting!" said a stranger with two dimples.

"Just think," the fisherman murmured, "a Zionist flag on top of Hassan Bey Mosque!" He lowered his head in shame and clutched it with both hands.

Men buzzed like bees in a jar. They caucused here and there and spoke of one thing—Jaffa. They seemed to make a sharp distinction between Jaffa and Haifa. Haifa, they rationalized, had a sizeable Jewish majority; Jaffa, on the other hand, was close to one hundred per cent Arab. Even the UN had parceled it to the Arabs. Jaffa's fall to the enemy meant only one thing: the Zionists were grabbing more than they had been allotted. They were seizing all they could before the Arab armies arrived. Yousif could imagine how Salwa would feel if she were to hear all this.

Navigating his way through the crowds, Yousif began to acknowledge that the Arabs were losing round one. But, by God, round one only. His stomach began to churn. One day, he vowed, these people who were now pouring out their hearts on the sidewalks and in the streets—would galvanize the wrath of God. Those who scored first were not necessarily the ultimate victors. Out of desperation, he found himself quoting poetry:

Itha esha'bo yowman arada al-hayah
Fala budda an yestajeeba al-kaddar

If one day the people desire life
It's inevitable for fate to respond

Yousif climbed the narrow exterior steps to Dr. Afifi's office. He had never been there before. He found it weird that he, the son of the most prominent doctor in town, would be going to somebody else's clinic. Thank God he wasn't sick. On the other hand, he might as well get used to the vicissitudes of life. His father was dead. Should he and his mother—or even Salwa—need medical help from now on, there was no one better to see than Dr. Afifi.

After leafing through magazines in the waiting room for about five minutes, Yousif was ushered into Dr. Afifi's office. It was much smaller than his father's. And there was no human skull staring at him with piercing empty sockets. Short, heavy-lidded Dr. Afifi was friendly but nervous. He dropped the pen in his hand and walked around the cluttered desk to greet him. Yousif could have sworn that the doctor's hair had turned grayer in the last few weeks.

"Nothing is wrong with you, I hope," Dr. Afifi said, extending his hand.

"Not medically," Yousif said, shaking it.

They sat down. The noise on the street below lapped at the window like tongues of flame.

"Father's clinic," Yousif said, taking a deep breath. "What do we do with it?"

"I've been thinking about that myself," Dr. Afifi said, lighting a cigarette though the one in the ashtray was still long and burning. "Have you and your mother given it much thought?"

"Not really. I know we can't keep it closed."

"No, that wouldn't be proper. You need income and—"

"There aren't enough clinics to take care of all those people."

"Especially now. God knows we could use the hospital your father, *Allah yirhamu,* wanted to build."

Yousif remained silent.

"Let me check around," the doctor said, smoke billowing around his head. "Maybe one of the doctors from Jaffa or Haifa could operate it until they go back—if they go back. Maybe one of them can rent it from you outright, or give you a percentage. I'll just have to wait and see. I went to medical school with Ali Mehdi from Jaffa and Edward Tuffaha from Haifa. I don't know if they're here or not. If they are I need to look after them. My God, the rich and the poor are in the same boat nowadays."

Yousif got up to leave. "Thanks, Doctor. I'll be grateful for all your help."

"Don't mention it. Give my regards to your mother. Jihan and I will be coming to see you soon."

"We'd love to have you."

Before Yousif reached the door, the doctor called his name.

"Yousif . . . I don't know how you're set for money. But you know you can always count on us. You hear?"

"Thanks," Yousif replied, touched.

"I mean it. These are uncertain times. With the loss of your father and the loss of income and the troubles ahead, one can't be too sure."

"You'll be the first to know." Yousif closed the door and went out, a lump in his throat.

THE OMINOUS parting words followed Yousif like a bandit. Were they on the brink of yet another disaster? Might he and his mother need financial help?

Yousif knew that they still owned the old home, which was a source of rental income. His father had also owned a large stock in Cinema Firyal. The annual dividends from that investment alone came close to two thousand pounds a year, more than the annual income of ten teachers put together.

Yousif's father had been a saver. When Yousif had checked at al-Wattan Bank a week after his father's death, he discovered that they had sixteen hundred pounds in a savings account and seven hundred and fifty in a checking account. That was more money than Amin and his family had seen in their entire lives. And if Yousif and his mother lived sensibly it should last them several years without ever needing anyone's help.

But as Yousif hurried through hordes of refugees from Jaffa and Haifa swarming the streets, he knew that sooner or later they could be among the displaced. He was struck by other concerns. So what should he do about the money in the bank? Should he leave it there? Should he withdraw it to take with them if they too were expelled? Wouldn't that be dangerous? What if they were robbed? What if they left it in the bank and it became a frozen asset? What if the enemy confiscated it altogether? To top it all, he thought of Salwa. Good God, what if they were separated?

Yousif's mind and heart were in an uproar as he approached Sitt Bahiyyeh's quiet neighborhood. He climbed her stairs and rang the bell. By the time the door opened and he saw the teacher standing before him, the skin puffy under her eyes, he was convinced that drinking poison would be easier for him than relinquishing Salwa. If he couldn't save her from the clutch of domestic tyranny, how could he hope to save Palestine?

"Mother is taking a nap," Sitt Bahiyyeh whispered, gently closing the door behind her. "Let's talk out here."

Yousif looked around, out of customary precaution. Then he realized that he wasn't a thief, for God's sake, and he couldn't care less who might see him.

"I expected you sooner," she began.

"I couldn't—" Yousif replied.

"Well, of course," she said, extending her hand. *"Yislam rasak."*

"Oo rasik," he said, shaking it.

An eight-wheeled truck full of refugees was going up the steep hill. The chatter of the men, women, and children riding above the bedsprings and mattresses and bundles of clothing filled the neighborhood.

Sitt Bahiyyeh's bosom heaved as the homeless paraded before their eyes.

"There are a lot of sad people in this world," she said, holding the railing.

It was a bad omen, Yousif thought. The ending was embedded in the beginning. Was she preparing him for a blow?

"Tell me," he begged.

"What's there to tell?"

"Did you talk to Salwa? In person? What were her exact words?"

"My mind is cluttered these days," she said. "I can't even tell you what I had for breakfast. But I do remember her telling me that she did all she could on your behalf, but it was no use."

Yousif's heart stopped. A young boy riding a bicycle downhill seemed to have lost his brakes and was screaming at the top of his voice. A mob of youngsters were running behind him, those coming up rushing out of his way. But Yousif's eyes and ears were now glued on Sitt Bahiyyeh.

"She's getting married Sunday," Sitt Bahiyyeh said, pursing her lips.

"No, she's not," Yousif said, in disbelief.

"I'm afraid she is."

"This coming Sunday?"

Sitt Bahiyyeh nodded. "I'm afraid so."

"That's three days after my eighteenth birthday!"

"Ya haraam!" she said, shaking her head. "The scar will be reopened every year."

"What am I going to do?" Yousif moaned, kicking the wall.

"I wish I didn't have to tell you this, but you asked me and I'm not going to lie. That's what she told me Friday. I happened to be in the principal's office when she came and asked to be excused for the rest of the semester on account of the wedding."

Yousif was shocked. "That was the first time you talked to her? Didn't you two have a private conversation earlier? Didn't you tell her about my visit?"

Sitt Bahiyyeh's face contorted in sympathy. "Of course I did. I told her that the next day after you came. We had heart-to-heart discussions several times since. When I found out you weren't making things up, I bent my own rules and got involved. So I can tell you with all honesty she did try to break off the engagement. She even got her mother to lean toward you. But when her father got wind of what the two of them were up to, he made Adel Farhat rush the wedding date."

"The father did?" Yousif asked, astonished.

"I believe so," she said. Then as if reading his mind, she added: *"Masabbato iddini tasbihon bimatrahiha.* At certain times, cursing religion is as good as saying a prayer. The fact remains: she's getting married and there's nothing you can do about it. Take my advice. On that Sunday, go out of town. If you can't, get drunk, get a long night's sleep. When you wake up in the morning you won't feel any better, but at least it will all be behind you."

Yousif was in a daze. "Get drunk?"

"If I weren't supposed to be a lady, I'd say come over and we'll get drunk together."

"You would?" Yousif said, still in a trance.

"Why not? I am the expert around here on the pain that lingers." She said the last words with a twisted mouth that mocked the whole East. "But scandal at my age would kill my mother quicker than the Zionists. And it would ruin the rest of my already inglorious life. Go on Yousif. I'll be thinking of you while I'm tipping the glass in solitude."

Yousif's legs were weightless, yet he had no energy to lift them. Her raw wounds aroused in him memories of Jamal. The blind musician wasn't the only one who had not recovered from unrequited love. Wasn't he still suffering even though the girl he loved had been married for twenty years and had three children?

"I'll do two more things for you," Sitt Bahiyyeh promised.

Yousif waited, convinced that the bile in her system was surfacing. "I'm listening," he said.

"I'll compose a litany of curses for you—should you need them."

"And the other?"

"I will not attend Salwa's wedding—even though she is my favorite student."

Yousif began to thank her, then his mind blanked. A tidal wave had just crashed over him and he didn't know whether he was being thrown off to the shore or was about to be swallowed by the deep dark waters.

DARKNESS WAS beginning to fall. But no night could be as black as Yousif's heart at this moment. Between his personal losses and the Arabs' military defeats, he felt he was being sucked in by a vacuum. There was little he could do about the general situation in Palestine. But he swore to God and to all the angels and saints and demons who could hear him that Salwa's wedding to Adel Farhat would never, ever happen.

All the neighbors were in front of Uncle Boulus's house, including Yousif's mother. Some were sitting in the familiar semi-circle. Others were listening and leaning against the building. From a distance Yousif recognized the center of attention. It was Maria—the robust, red-headed neighbor's daughter. She was a nurse who had worked in Jaffa. Her white uniform and the little white cap above her carrot-red hair filled his childhood memories. When she had visited her family and strode through the neighborhood, her round body and genuine smile made her look like a lovable snowman. Maria and Yousif's mother were good friends, although Maria was many years younger.

"Several months ago," Maria was telling the group, "the British made me the head nurse at the hospital. I ran it as best I could. When they left they told me I was doing a wonderful job. Then one day this week, Dr. Ruttman told me that a ship was coming to take the Arab patients to Beirut. She's a Jewish lady and a long-time friend. I couldn't believe it. They're too sick to be moved, I argued. But it was no use. She said they were doing it for humanitarian reasons. There was no sense in keeping them in a war-torn city, she said, when they could get better care somewhere else. I asked her: 'Are you sending away the Jewish patients, too?'"

"Good question," Uncle Boulus said, flicking his *masbaha*.

"She stared at me and said, 'Just do as you're told.' But then I said, 'If you're scared being in an Arab town, don't worry. You and the patients will be safe. We will all look after you. There are plenty of Arab doctors and nurses who would take care of all patients. But no patient must be moved.' Dr. Ruttman would have none of it. I couldn't figure her out. Then it hit me. She was acting on someone else's orders. 'Get them out,' she said and walked away." Maria paused to catch her breath.

"Well, did you get the patients out?" Yousif asked again.

"We had to," Maria said. "She was chief-of-staff. Her word was final."

Here, too, Yousif was disturbed. He wanted to tell Maria that they did not have to leave just because a Jewish doctor told them to leave. The Arab nurses and doctors and orderlies and patients should have staged a rebellion and refused to let her push them around. Even if the Jewish soldiers had already occupied the hospital, the Arabs should not have let that woman intimidate them. What could the soldiers have done? Killed them? All of them? Were the Jews that bad? That strong? Then he remembered the massacre of Deir Yasin and realized that the Irgun or the Stern Gang might have slaughtered whoever resisted.

"We moved the patients outdoors until the garden was full," Maria continued, perspiring. "Some were put on stretchers. Others we sat in chairs. Many were dying and those we tried to keep in their rooms. But again Dr. Ruttman insisted that there would be no exceptions. 'Out' she repeated, pointing her finger to the door. How that woman changed. All of a sudden she became a different person. When the ship arrived, the whole thing turned out to be a hoax."

Yousif was puzzled. "What do you mean?" he asked.

"It wasn't a rescue ship at all," Maria explained. "It came full of Zionists from Europe. They wanted the hospital evacuated to make room for them."

"Aaaaaaahhhhh!!!!" many gasped.

The rest were stunned.

"They tricked you," Aunt Hilaneh finally said, her hands folded.

"That doctor knew all along the ship was full of Jewish immigrants," Uncle

Boulus added. "But what happened to the patients?"

"By the time we knew what was happening," Maria said, "things were moving pretty fast. When the Zionists occupied Al-Manshiyyeh and Hassan Bey Mosque we knew it was all over for us. Some of us wanted to stay and ride out the storm, others didn't. Two nurses and one patient had been raped the week before, and if that wasn't bad enough they remembered Deir Yasin. So we all pitched in. The Arab doctors and nurses and orderlies helped—even some of the British soldiers helped. We put the patients in ambulances and cars and sent them home. Some were even moved as far as Lydda and Ramleh. And now listen to this: in my confusion I forgot the payroll in my desk. No one has been paid. I don't know what to do."

"What can you do?" Yousif asked. "You might as well forget it."

"I'm thinking of going back just in case the money is still there. God knows we all need it, especially now."

"What makes you think they'd let you in?" Yousif's mother asked, looking very pale without make-up.

"You'd find Jaffa ringed with soldiers," said an old man disconsolately.

Maria's audience fell silent. They all seemed frightened. Helpless. The seamstress said she and her husband were seriously thinking of going to Amman. Aunt Hilaneh said that it had crossed their mind. Uncle Boulus squirmed. His sharp nose looked pinched and yellow at the same time.

As though to get them off the quarrelsome track, Yasmin said, "If you do decide to go to Amman, Yousif and I will go with you."

Yousif was shocked. "What makes you think I'd go?" he asked his mother. Without waiting for her to answer, he turned to the others, adding, "This kind of talk is irresponsible. What if we all left? Do we want the Zionists to walk right in? We might as well send them an invitation. I can't believe my ears. I thought you wanted the hospital money to buy arms and fight. Now I see that you're a bunch of quitters."

The fear of another Deir Yasin dominated the heated debate. All of them, except Yousif, were scared and did not mind admitting it. The Zionists were winning, they argued, and they would not put it past them to repeat the massacre wherever they went. What Yousif feared most, however, was losing Salwa. That was his biggest worry.

BY ENGLISH period the next day, Tuesday, when they were supposed to discuss Charles Dickens's *Tale of Two Cities,* Yousif's mind was in turmoil. He was thinking of what to do about Salwa, when the principal, ustaz Saadeh, announced that school would close a month earlier.

"That means," he added, "the graduation ceremony will be on April 29, not on May 25 as it was originally scheduled."

Like most students, Yousif began to count in his head. "You mean this coming Friday?" he asked. That was only two days before Salwa's wedding day.

"I mean five days from now," the principal informed them. "It will be held at Cinema Firyal, three o'clock in the afternoon. There's no time to print announcements, but each of you can invite ten people."

"Ten?" Nadeem objected. "There are eight in my immediate family. And I know I need a dozen more for my aunts and uncles."

"I do, too," Radwan concurred.

"This is only high school," the principal explained. "Not the university. Wait until you come back as doctors and lawyers and engineers. Then you can throw a big party and invite the whole town if you like."

"But that could be ages from now," Husam protested.

"Okay, okay," the principal said, waving his hand to calm them down. "I'll see what I can do. What we need to do now is decide on a valedictorian. According to school tradition, it's simply a matter of grades. The first in class is automatically chosen—unless there's a grave charge against him. I suspect there's no grave charge against Yousif."

There was a burst of applause. Yousif smiled and thanked the principal and his classmates for the honor.

Then Adnan raised his hand. "If Yousif had continued to behave the way he did after Isaac's death—"

"Or during the debate about the hospital money," Mousa interrupted, presumably reading Adnan's mind.

"—many of us would've opposed his selection. But he's okay now."

Caught by surprise, for his mind was on Salwa, Yousif bit his lip and nodded. "Let bygones be bygones."

NOW YOUSIF had two things to worry about: his speech and Salwa's wedding. Both lay heavy on his shoulders. He knew he could scribble something to please the crowd—but what about the wedding? His future with Salwa was slipping away from him. This turned his mind away from his graduation.

He tore up every draft he wrote. One approach was to attack Britain, Truman, and the Zionists. Another was to call for revenge against the murderers of Deir Yasin and the invaders of Haifa and Jaffa. The principal, ustaz Saadeh, found the draft Yousif finally showed him still unacceptable and asked him to go home and rewrite it.

"It's the same old platitudes and slogans we've been hearing for years," the principal told him, sitting behind his desk. "People are literally suffocating from all this rhetoric. It would be a nice change if someone would tell them the truth."

"And be ostracized like my father?" Yousif asked.

"That's the challenge," ustaz Saadeh said, "to please and offend at the same time—without getting killed."

Back in his room, Yousif discovered that the challenge was greater than he had realized. He could do it if his mind weren't so preoccupied with Salwa. But she consumed every minute of every wakeful hour, and sometimes invaded his dreams. How could he think straight when he was about to lose her forever? By the same token, what would he tell a people who had already lost half of their country before the war even began? What hope could he give them? How could he stir them up to action when thousands had become homeless while the rest were unarmed and on the verge of being stampeded? Where would his pitiable generation fit in such a leaderless, defeated society? How long, he asked himself, would it take them to pick up the pieces and face the uncertain future?

In these hours of desperation and loneliness, Yousif missed his father intensely.

THE GRADUATING class of twenty-two students sat on one side of the stage. The faculty on the other. There were no caps and gowns: only blue suits, white shirts, and red ties. Some of the clothes were new. Because of the hard times and short notice, most, however, were faded. Some were even borrowed. In the middle sat the principal and the main speaker, Raja Ballout, the famed journalist from Jaffa, and Father Mikhail representing the Catholic Church. The main auditorium was nearly full, which surprised Yousif. It was the same theater where Salwa had told him of Adel Farhat's intentions. Unconsciously winding the watch he had inherited from his father, he spotted the seats where they had had that heart-wrenching conversation. Too bad she was not there now. How he ached to see her. But none of her relatives or friends were graduating, and he could not have invited her.

His thoughts of Salwa were suddenly interrupted. The principal had just introduced him. Yousif walked to the rostrum and faced the audience. The nervousness he had felt at his father's graveside did not plague him now. His opening sentence was shocking, and he could not wait to deliver it.

"I'm looking for someone to arrest me," Yousif began.

Hushed silence descended on the audience.

"I'm looking for someone to handcuff me," he resumed, "and to throw me in jail—should I let my country down. Where is my jailer? Nay, where is my leader who beckoned and I refused to follow, who exhausted himself in search for peace and I opposed his quest? Where is my jailer, and the jailer of every graduating senior in Palestine who can look us in the eye and say we did not do our duty, that we have failed our motherland? Is there no leader to inspire and lead men to the trenches, to the roofs, and to the gates of the enemy? Is there no leader who, with wisdom and diplomacy and tenacity, is trying to clear our adversary's vision, to compel him to negotiate and compromise? Is there no leader who can charge us for having failed to commit ourselves and execute his master plan? No, there is no leader, no jailer, no charge—and no master plan."

The audience was deep in thought. Yousif's tirade, which he delivered without stridency, lasted only ten minutes. He complimented his people on their steadfastness in the face of tremendous odds, and berated them for having sat on their haunches for all those years.

"My generation and future generations *will* charge and *will* convict," he thundered in conclusion. "Woe to him who will be found to have trespassed against us. Woe to him, for the day of judgment is as inevitable to come as for the snow to thaw, as for the sun to rise from the depth of darkness."

The audience broke out in applause. They stood up, cheering. The lanky, pale commencement speaker, Raja Ballout, rose impulsively and shook Yousif's hand warmly. Yousif himself didn't think much of his own rhetoric. He thought even less of those who were so easily satisfied with words.

There was nothing he could do to change the outcome of the war. But there was something he could do to stop Salwa from slipping out of his hands. The loss of Salwa would be much more than either his heart or mind could bear. As he stood on the stage bowing in gratitude for the warm response he was getting, his mind was already on the personal battle ahead.

24

Sunday! The day Salwa was supposed to marry someone else. The day the earth would stop spinning around the dimming sun.

The night before, Yousif had not slept—thinking, brooding, worrying. He counted the hours, the minutes. He had not given a hint to anyone of the plan that was hatching in his mind, not even Amin. Instead, he had visited Jamal and talked only about his sense of loss. And he had met classmates who teased him about Salwa's wedding. Everywhere he went he heard people mention her name, as if to taunt him. He took it all in stride, until the coil within him became so tight it was ready to snap.

Long before dawn, he woke with a heavy heart.

For days Yousif had been imagining a crazy plan to confront Salwa's father in the church. He would leap up in the middle of the ceremony and tell the priest that Salwa was being forced into marriage. He would put everybody on the spot—including Salwa—and take his chances.

But what if his plan didn't work? Salwa would be gone, lost. Tonight she would be kissed and undressed. Tonight she would sleep in someone else's arms. Tonight she would be intimate with someone she did not love. The mere thought of this abomination outraged him.

He wondered what Salwa was thinking. He wondered if she had last-minute regrets. Had she forgotten him? Had she resigned herself to fate?

He pictured her house filling up early in the morning. There would be cleaning and cooking and crying; there would be a rush to heat the water tank for her shower; to spread on her bed all the fineries she would wear; to have a heart-to-heart talk with her mother. By eleven o'clock she would be chauffeured to a beauty salon, accompanied by a relative or two. She would skip lunch because she would be nervous, and because many of her girlfriends would surround her for last-minute endearments.

Yousif envisioned a woman's hands applying the bride's make-up. He pictured Salwa in her wedding dress, tears streaming down her cheeks and everybody fussing about her mascara. He saw her relatives around her, hugging, kissing, and wishing her well. All day long her two brothers, Akram and Zuhair, would be inconsolable.

Yousif also imagined what Adel Farhat would be going through. In keeping with tradition, the barber would come to the house to cut the groom's hair. Men and women would form a circle around the groom while he was being primed. Adel would be shaved, powdered, and doused with cologne to meet his beautiful bride. Lying in bed, Yousif heard the songs, saw the dances.

Relatives and guests would arrive at both houses. The groom and his party would form a procession to the church, then the party would split. A small group would stay with Adel outside the church. But a number of his relatives and guests of honor would go to Salwa's house to bring her out for him. There would be a touching, tearful moment as the bride kissed and bade her family farewell.

The image was too stirring for Yousif to remain lying down. He sat up in bed, choking with emotion. Sunlight filled the room. He heard his mother and Fatima going about their morning work. The town was waking. He could hear cars speeding by and pastry peddlers in the streets selling their *tamari.* Even the birds in their cage down the hall were still chirping. Life went on, oblivious to his fears. He wanted to freeze the morning. If a warrior could make the sun stand still—why couldn't a lover stop a wedding?

The Sunday morning routine must remain intact, Yousif told himself. Nothing must attract his mother's suspicion. He took a long hot bath, put on a white shirt and blue trousers—not a suit which he normally would wear to go to church. He ate his mother's special omelet and retired to the living room to hear the news.

There was one more item Yousif wished to discuss with his mother. How could he embark on matrimony or enter the world of adults if he remained in the dark? What he had in mind today related to inheritance in general and the money in the bank in particular. Whose was it now that his father was dead? His? Hers? Theirs? Could he transfer the money to his name? Specifically, could he draw on it to pay Adel Farhat? He knew that the Arab society was patriarchal. Every boy a treasure. Every man a prince. But how did that translate in financial life?

When his mother crossed the hallway, a dish towel in her hands, he asked her to join him.

"Anything wrong?" she asked, dressed in black.

"Sit down, will you?" he said. "I was just wondering—"

"About what?" she asked, sitting on the edge of the sofa.

"The money in the bank," he began, weighing his words.

She seemed disquieted. "Yes?"

"It's still in father's name. Shouldn't it be transferred?"

"Of course. Put it in your name. Next time you see Fouad Jubran, let him handle the paper work. He's our attorney, I suppose."

Yousif was quiet.

"Speak up," his mother said. "What's on your mind?"

"I was just thinking," Yousif said. "Legally—is it not yours?"

"No," she told him. "Legally it's yours—most of it anyway."

"Under which law?" Yousif asked. "Civil or religious?"

His mother had a confounded look. "I really don't know," she admitted. "Ask Fouad Jubran about that. He'll tell you."

"I will," Yousif said, determined to know everything.

"All I know is," his mother continued, "it's a man's world. I may be entitled to one-eighth or one-fourth, but what's the difference? What's mine is yours. I know you're not going to throw me out. You'll take care of me."

"Throw you out? Take care of you? My God! You're my mother."

"The Muslim inheritance law is even harder on females. If a man has only daughters, his nephews—mind you, not even his daughters—will inherit everything."

"No wonder Abul Banat has such a short temper."

"The baker? If anything happens to him, his nephews will inherit everything?"

"Are you sure?"

"That's what people say."

"Incredible! I thought the Qur'an provides security to the woman."

"Don't take my word. I'm just a lay person. Besides, it doesn't apply to us anyway."

"Interesting, though. But tell me, now that Father is gone—"

"Allah yirhamu."

"—this house, the two bank accounts, the cinema stock—"

"—and the old house and the clinic," his mother added. "They're all yours.

And that's the way I'd want it, too. You're the man of the house now."

Yousif was still not satisfied. "What if I turned out to be unworthy? What if I married a girl with a mean streak? What then? You'd be at her mercy."

His mother nodded. "I'll count on you to set her straight. *El faras hasab el faris.* A filly is as good as her rider. That's why your father and I did our best to raise you knowing right from wrong. From now on it's all up to you. But promise me one thing."

"I'll try."

"Think twice before you do anything. And be fair. Your father always said you have a good head on your shoulders."

"I promise. I hope I'll never fail you."

"Or your father. Remember, his spirit is still with us."

Yousif rose, kissed the top of his mother's head, and left—chagrined that he had struck such a promise. What would she think of him in the next few hours? Would she be understanding? Would she feel betrayed?

THE WEDDING was at three o'clock that afternoon. Yousif roamed the town, passing the *souk,* Salwa's school, and Cinema Firyal. For an hour he walked aimlessly around town. All he could think of was that Salwa would soon slip out of his hand like a ring off a soapy finger. The wholeness he felt with her would be lost forever; emptiness would become a way of life.

I'd be a fool to let it happen, Yousif thought. We're losing Palestine because we're not doing enough to save it. I'll lose Salwa too if I don't fight for her.

He had to act. He looked at his watch. 1:40. There was still more than an hour before the crowd arrived at the church. He felt hungry, and stopped at Abdeen's for a *shawirma* sandwich. Instead, he drank two glasses of *arak* and ate only a bite. That was a mistake, he soon realized. His head felt light, as if his skull were being lifted by the vapor of the alcohol. No, no, he must be careful. Drunkenness would not help matters; it would only jeopardize his scheme. He must walk and let his head clear up. But he must avoid people lest he betray his intentions.

Striking out in a new direction, he passed the cemetery. He thought of visiting his father's grave. But this was no time to be morbid or overly sentimental. He decided against it. Instead, he stomped on the sidewalk to shake the dust off his shoes, then propped his foot on a low stone wall and wiped each shoe with his neatly pressed handkerchief.

Yousif watched the church from a distance, careful not to be noticed. Single people and couples arrived and went through the gate. An elderly couple passed close by him. He retreated into a side street and pretended to be window shopping.

Few would have believed him, for the window he was staring at was a laundry shop. Yousif saw his reflection in the clear glass. By reflex his hand went up to smooth his disheveled hair. He gazed at his own image, as if to find himself.

The wedding procession was coming up the hill. First he could hear it, then he could see it. Rolling slowly between the men and singing women was the black Mercedes which he knew carried Salwa and her parents. A lump the size of a walnut rose in his throat. He leaned against a wall and watched, kicking the sidewalk. The procession drove past the outer gate. A minute later, he followed.

Walking briskly, Yousif was as purposeful as a crusader on behalf of all the mismatched couples in Ardallah. All the bright, beautiful, young women who had had to marry their cousins—simply because they were cousins. The unhappy girls who had been forced to marry old men—simply because they were rich. The wives who suffered in silence—simply because they were incompatible with their husbands. He could think of Amal Shalhoub who loved to write poetry but was married to a brute—gluttonous, drunken, and foul-mouthed. He could think of Ghada Antar, forced to marry at the point of a gun someone thirty years her senior and to bear five children before she was twenty-five.

Yousif sneaked inside the half-empty Greek Orthodox church. The walls of the two-hundred year-old sanctuary were covered with icons. Reds and browns and golds were the dominant colors. The small electric lights, two shafts of sunlight, and many candles all failed to dispel the shadows.

Women in modern dress wore hats or lacy handkerchiefs on their heads in lieu of scarves. Other women in the traditional native costumes looked like monarch butterflies. Their multi-colored, flowered, silk shawls radiated under the windows. Men's bald heads gleamed, as they stood with their hats and fezes in their hands.

Salwa was already at the altar, her tall, sculptured figure a vision of beauty. Yousif gasped and clutched the back of the seat before him. He was alone in his pew. No one had seen him. Even the elderly priest, Father Samaan, standing in the arched door to the altar and looking in his direction, did not seem to notice him.

Sitt Bahiyyeh had told him that the priest was Salwa's father's cousin, and that blood was thicker than one thought.

"Ordinarily," Father Samaan began, "we would announce the wedding banns for three consecutive Sundays before the wedding date. But due to the war, we will dispense with tradition. Should anyone, however, have a reason to believe that this marriage should *not* take place, let him speak now or forever hold his peace."

The short, plump, graying priest held the Bible in his two hands and waited. The congregation remained dead silent. A baby cried but his mother quickly cupped his mouth. Again, the priest scanned the audience. He was about to proceed with his ceremony when Yousif jumped to his feet.

"This wedding must be stopped," Yousif blurted. His voice was much louder than he had intended. The audience spun around to see who it was. Yousif heard them gasp . . . groan. He saw Shafiq, Salwa's cousin, begin to move suddenly in his direction. Yousif clenched his fists ready to fight, but there was no need. Three other men grabbed and held Shafiq in the aisle to restrain him.

"This is a very serious matter," Father Samaan cautioned. "I hope and pray you know what you're saying."

"I do," Yousif answered, sweating. His eyes focused on Salwa. She had also turned and was watching in disbelief, her right hand poised at her mouth. Their eyes met and held. Yousif had not warned her. He had no idea how she would react. But he had taken his chance. It was too late to stop now.

"Speak up, then," the priest commanded. "What compels you to make such a grave charge?"

"A simple reason," Yousif answered, now in better control of his nerves. "Salwa loves me and I love her. We want to marry each other. What she's going through here is against her will. Against her wishes."

Shafiq looked like a caged animal wanting to break loose. But the men held onto him and sat him down. Men and women traded glances and exchanged whispers. Others voiced their opinions for everyone to hear.

"Can you believe this?" asked the wife of the Lutheran minister.

"This is a first for me," her husband answered.

"Is this really happening or am I dreaming?" asked Shafiq's father.

"It's happening, all right," his skinny wife told him.

"Man ya'ish yara," a rosy-cheeked old relative said, shaking his head. "He who lives long enough will see everything."

Yousif heard every word and watched every pair of eyes that bore into him. The commotion intensified. The priest was trying hard to keep it down. The groom's old parents were so upset they rattled their disgust in plain Arabic.

"Don't listen to that boy," Salwa's father shouted at the priest. "Throw him out and let's get on with the ceremony. Throw him out." Anton Taweel gazed at Yousif, his eyes full of hate. "I'll deal with you later," he said ominously.

The groom, Adel Farhat, stepped off the dais before the altar and tried to calm Salwa's father. Meanwhile the priest held up both hands: one clutching the Bible, the other trying to quiet the uproar. Yousif saw the bridesmaid, Huda, put her arm around Salwa's waist in support. He only wished he were in her place.

"Quiet, quiet," the priest pleaded, pacing right and left. "This can't go on. We must have it settled. We're in the House of God. You must show respect."

Finally, the shocked congregation quieted down and listened. But there was tension in the air. Most were astonished. A few seemed amused. Some stared at Yousif the way they had stared at Isaac just before killing him. For a moment Yousif was afraid.

"Don't listen to that boy," Anton Taweel again told the priest, stepping into the aisle. His wife tried to restrain him, but he shoved her aside with his elbow.

"Anton," pleaded the agitated priest, "please give me a chance to find out what's going on. I beg of you." Then he turned to Salwa and addressed her in a louder voice so that everyone could hear. "Is what Yousif said true?"

Salwa seemed mortified and dumbstruck, staring at the priest. Even at a distance Yousif could tell her coloring was changing.

"It's essential that we know," the priest patiently explained. "There's nothing I can do until you give me your answer."

Hope shot through Yousif like an electric shock. He could feel the blood tingling in his veins. He was gratified that the priest had not dismissed his claim out of hand. The next minute would determine his whole future. The happiness of a lifetime rested on her tongue. He held the pew before him, closed his eyes and prayed. *Please, God, make it work. Please, please, God, grant me this wish.*

"Tell him it's not true," her father told her.

To Yousif it sounded more of a threat than advice. He held his breath and waited. What if the pressure were too much for Salwa? What if she stumbled, gave the wrong answer?

"Let her speak of her own free will," the priest told the irate father. "If there's any kind of pressure, I will not—"

"Good for you," Yousif shouted.

Anton Taweel flared up again. "I am *not* pressuring her," he protested. "I'm only telling her not to listen to that bastard."

"No, no, no," the priest said. "You mustn't use such language."

"Yes, you are pressuring her," Yousif shouted. "I told you how we felt about each other but you didn't listen."

Yousif was surrounded now by many people, including Fouad Jubran and his pregnant wife, who were trying to silence him.

"Quiet, quiet!" the priest demanded, scurrying in the aisle. "I'll do the talking. We must have the bride's answer."

Hushed silence followed. The eyes of the whole crowd focused on Salwa.

"Again I must ask you," the priest told Salwa, his voice shaking. "Is what Yousif said true? Are you being forced into this marriage? Are you and Yousif in love, and do you wish to marry each other?"

Yousif saw Salwa staring at him. She began to sob. His heart sank to his feet. She buried her head in her hands. Huda's arms held her steady. Salwa looked up at her parents, her tears glistening "I'm sorry, Father. I'm sorry, Mother. It is true."

"NO!" her father exploded, flailing his arms and moving toward her. "No daughter of mine is in love."

"Is it better that I lie to you?" Salwa pleaded.

Yousif wished he had wings. He wanted to fly and hug her and kiss her for the whole world to see. "Bless you, Salwa! Bless you!" he cried.

Once again, the crowd turned around and looked at him. Some of the tension was breaking out in smiles and giggles.

"Go on with the wedding," Anton Taweel demanded of the priest. "Don't listen to this childishness."

"I cannot," Father Samaan said.

"What do you mean you cannot?" the other man cried, furious. "I'm her father. I say go ahead and marry them."

"I cannot," the priest repeated, shutting the book in his hand. "She has spoken loud and clear. And the Church respects her wishes."

Yousif clapped his hands. But not all of the crowd seemed satisfied. Several urged the priest to go on with the questioning.

"All right then, one more question," the priest told Salwa, acquiescing to the crowd's demands. "Our dearest Salwa, please listen carefully. Do you or do you not want to go ahead with the wedding?"

Before Salwa could answer, someone in the crowd protested. The priest's interrogation was too broad. He exhorted him to be precise.

The old priest became more flustered. Holding his right hand to his mouth, he cleared his throat and waved his arm for everyone to be quiet. Then he turned to Salwa and said, "I'll repeat the question one more time. Our dearest Salwa, do you or do you not wish to take this man Adel Farhat as your lawful wedded husband? Think before you answer."

Yousif could hear the groom's mother cackling up front. Every now and then she would turn her head and swear at him. After a long and agonizing delay, Salwa said, "I do not."

The priest pushed her further. "You do not *what?* Make yourself absolutely clear."

The fire that Yousif knew was in Salwa returned to her eyes.

"Can't you all hear me?" she asked, her pitch high and her neck raised like a swan. "Can't you all understand? I do *not* wish to be married to the groom Adel Farhat who's standing beside me right here at the altar."

Sparks flew. Relatives on both sides were stunned, outraged. Some shook their heads, some frowned, some said what a shame, others began to leave.

"I'll break both of their necks," Anton Taweel threatened, rushing toward his daughter. He was stopped by the groom.

"No, you won't," Adel Farhat said, speaking up for the first time. Again people became quiet. They all seemed anxious to hear what the groom had to say.

"Any two people," Adel continued, loud and clear, "who have the nerve to go through what these two have—*deserve* each other. And they have my blessing. I had my suspicions, but I didn't realize it was this serious. I guess I should've looked into it more carefully. If that's how she feels, it's better to call it off right now than to live in misery." He turned to Salwa, and added ironically, "I thank you for sparing me the agony of a lifetime."

"Good for you!" Yousif shouted again.

Some people broke out in applause and praised Adel's decency. Others still seemed stunned. Yousif's heart fluttered with incredible joy. He felt like celebrating but knew it was the wrong time and wrong place. He looked at Salwa to see how she was savoring their victory. Their eyes met briefly. Then he saw her burst into tears and rush out, both hands lifting her long wedding dress. Her mother ran out after her. Huda, the bridesmaid, tried to catch up and pull up her train. And again Shafiq, Salwa's angry cousin, threatened to demolish Yousif.

"As for you, boy," Adel said, looking straight at Yousif, "I'm going to get you off the hook. My God, I could knock your teeth out and thrash you here and now—"

"Just try it!" Yousif warned.

"—but you're not worth it. All I want you to do is pay all my expenses—every bracelet, every handkerchief, every bottle of *arak,* every kilo of meat, every ounce of coffee—and you can have your so-called love."

"Her heart belongs to me," Yousif screamed. "Not you. *Me.*"

Yousif had not wanted to have such a hot exchange. He wished he had not lost his temper.

"They mustn't be allowed to get away with it," the butcher sneered. "Love is nonsense."

The crowd began to leave.

"I didn't think you had it in you," a young relative with a full head of curly hair told Yousif.

Many grumbled and gave him a nasty look.

"Disgusting."

"Bad precedent."

"The girl is worse than the boy. Can you imagine!"

The wife of a grocer who owned a shop next to Salman's, looked Yousif straight in the eye and said, "Spoiler."

Dalal Omran, a tall attractive woman had a frown on her face. Yousif feared her tongue. She approached him as if to lash at him, but in his ear she whispered, "Every woman in this town ought to give you a kiss." She squeezed his hand.

Yousif was beginning to enjoy his triumph, when he felt a blow on his back. He turned around to see who had struck him, when another searing blow landed on his mouth. It was the groom's cousin, Kareem, who seemed angrier than Shafiq. Kareem gnashed his teeth and called Yousif a dirty dog. Yousif tried to hit him back. But the aisle was too full. A freckled pharmacist separated the two, advising Yousif not to take any chances.

"Next time you want to do something like this," the pharmacist told him, "you need to get your relatives with you. You can't fight them all alone."

"I don't want to fight," Yousif said.

"Go on," the councilman with the wooden leg, Ayoub Salameh, told him. "You must've been born a troublemaker."

Yousif bristled. "I beg your pardon."

"After today marriages in this town will never be the same. Go on, before they kill you."

Throughout the turmoil Yousif kept his eyes on the area of the altar. He could see Salwa's parents arguing with each other. Then they were joined by the priest and other relatives, forming a knot. Yousif was dying to know what they were saying.

Soon Yousif found himself outside the church. Some congratulated him, slapping him on the shoulder, but most looked at him derisively. Yousif felt his upper lip swell. A few minutes later Salwa's father appeared at the doorway, looking as tall as Lucifer. Yousif could see his long face, flushed and bluish. He seemed angry, tormented, bewildered, vulnerable.

"Hey, boy," the father said in an anguished, loud voice that froze the pandemonium. Everyone turned and looked at him. "You've stopped the wedding. But here's a promise I make before man and God: I swear on my honor and the honor of my mother and father that unless you marry my daughter by next Sunday you will never, never, never marry her."

A new commotion broke out. Yousif didn't know what to think.

"It's better than going to the movies," said a woman standing behind Yousif.

"Can you believe all this?" her female companion asked.

Yousif felt his own skull hammered. He had not meant to humiliate this man and cause him such pain—or to put himself in such a predicament. His head was spinning. He didn't know whether to be happy or sad. His own father hadn't been dead for more than ten days—and they were still in mourning. How could he marry Salwa by next Sunday?

"If it were mmmmme," Ghanem Jadallah stuttered, "I'd make the son of bbbbbitch marry her hhhhhere and now."

"Poor Yousif can't do that," his wife said. "He has his mother to worry about. She's still in black."

"Pppppoor my aaaaass," Ghanem added, glaring at her. "That's his probbbbblem."

Others were less hostile. From the snatches of conversations Yousif could hear, he gathered that Salwa's father really had no other option. Some considered the ultimatum a wise move. Who would marry Salwa after today? they all asked. His daughter was more or less marked. No one in his right mind would touch her or come near her. Anton Taweel might as well swallow his pride and let her marry the one she wanted. What else could the poor fellow do?

Yousif could follow their argument—even agree with it. But the irony did not escape him. First he had to battle her father and now he would have to battle his own mother. Would she agree to a wedding so soon after his father's death? Yousif didn't think so, considering that such things were taboo. On the other hand, would he risk losing Salwa forever? It seemed he had no choice but to get married next Sunday. He couldn't humiliate her father twice in a week and make him delay the wedding date a few more months. People's tongues were bound to wag until the tie was knotted. Malicious gossip was what Anton Taweel was trying to avoid. Yousif felt dizzy. Unless he married Salwa by next Sunday—it was hard to predict what her father would do. Some fathers were known to turn violent. What if he harmed Salwa?

Yousif became even more worried when he saw Salwa's father clutch his own chest. What if the man had a sudden heart attack and died before next Sunday? What if he died angry at his daughter? Wouldn't he, Yousif, feel guilty for life? Wouldn't he be setting up a barrier between him and Salwa that might damage their happiness? In fact, was it not possible that Salwa might rebel against him now, to assuage her conscience? Stranger things had happened. What had he gained, Yousif asked himself, if he were to be denied Salwa forever? Arrows of desire and despair pierced his heart. What was he going to do now? Dizzily, he put his hand on his face. Both his mouth and nose were bleeding from the blows he had received inside. But what he dreaded most was what might be awaiting him at home.

25

The news of Yousif's shocking behavior had reached home before he did. From the driveway he could see many heads in the living room. Relatives, friends, and neighbors were probably with his mother, he thought—all enjoying an afternoon of juicy gossip. He hesitated at the wrought-iron gate, his heart constricted. He knew his mother would be embarrassed. In time he would convince her that what he had done was right. But would she agree to a quick wedding? This he did not know. Nor did he relish at the moment facing the music in his own home and in front of so many women.

"Sa'eedeh," he greeted everyone, standing at the entrance to the living room.

Everyone in the room responded hello—except his mother.

Yousif, who had not taken his eyes off her, felt shaken.

"Aren't you speaking to me, Mother?" he asked. "I said *sa'eedeh.*"

She glared at him, strands of hair falling on her forehead.

"Why are you so upset?" he asked.

There was a long pause. She looked crushed: her eyes enlarged, her skin sallow, her mouth twisted.

"What have you heard?" Yousif pressed.

"Enough," she said, mournful. "I'm glad your father isn't around."

"He would've been proud," Yousif boasted. "Many praised me. Some even called me a hero."

"The majority call you *majnoon,"* his mother cried. "And they are telling the truth. You *are* insane."

All the ladies in the living room seemed embarrassed by the confrontation. Looking guilty, they avoided Yousif's eyes. Some of them picked up their purses off the floor, pretending to be ready to leave.

Yousif was cut to the quick by his mother's remarks. "I'm not insane," he defended himself.

"Is this the respect you show your father's memory?" his mother wanted to know, anger rising in her voice. "Ten days after he's been killed, you go out and disgrace yourself in front of the whole town?"

Yousif could feel the sweat on his back turn icy. Out of respect for his mother, he bit his tongue and walked away. He went to the birds' cage. But his mother followed him.

"How can you do such a thing?" she cried, her eyes brimming with tears.

She might as well have fired a shotgun. The two hundred birds seemed terrified. They flew in all directions, clinging to the mesh-wire for their lives.

"I will not discuss it until you calm down," he said, reaching for a water pitcher to fill a tiny container.

"Calm down? How can I calm down when the apple of my eye makes a fool of himself? Is this the way you reward our trust in you? Is this how you do us proud?"

When he did not answer, she pounded a wooden stud. The birds flapped madly, colliding in the air.

"I warned Salwa's father, but he didn't listen."

"That entitles you to interfere with people's lives?"

"I couldn't lose Salwa. She means the world to me."

"You are selfish. A sore loser. A spoiler."

Yousif took a deep breath. "I never thought I'd hear you say this to me."

"Neither did I," she said. She buried her head in her hands and began sobbing.

Her agony was so genuine Yousif felt rotten. He opened the door and went toward her, stretching his arms.

"It's not as bad as all that," he said, enfolding her.

"Don't touch me," she said, pushing him away. "I wish God would strike me dead this second. It's a hundred times better than having to face the people, to answer all the questions—"

"Salwa's father doesn't want to answer questions, either," Yousif said. "That's why he's demanding that I marry her next week."

From the look on her face she seemed to know.

"I don't blame him," she said. "Who would marry his daughter after you've blackened her name?"

"I saved her from a lifetime of misery."

She glared at him. "Let me tell you something," she said. "If you decide to get married next Sunday, don't expect me to be there."

She walked off, crying. He stood among the birds—their twittering reflecting his confusion. Anton Taweel had put him up the tree and now his own mother was shooting at him.

Later that night, Yousif and his mother sat on the eastern balcony. The storm had subsided. They were now both drained, calm, reflective. With them were Aunt Hlianeh, Izzat and Hiyam, and cousin Salman and his wife, Abla. Uncle Boulus, whom Yousif desperately needed at the moment, had gone to Jerusalem to see about his parents and no one knew when to expect him.

All evening Hiyam had acted like a dutiful daughter-in-law, attending to their needs. Because they were still in mourning she did not have to serve any fruits or sweets, but she seemed attentive nevertheless. What she did most was empty the ashtray in front of Salman, serve water and bitter coffee, and look ready to do whatever was needed. At one point, not entirely jesting, Yousif remarked how nice it would be to have Salwa around the house to do what Hiyam was now doing. He tried to make his mother smile, but she wasn't amused. Nor did she cry or whimper. She just sat close to the railing, stoic, her hands clasped in her lap.

In a way, Yousif was glad Hiyam and Izzat were now living with them at the house. They were closer to his age and could empathize with him. On the other hand, seeing them together was torture. Every time he saw her smile at her husband and brush her long auburn hair against his cheek, they reminded him of what he was missing. Her satiny skin, seductive mouth, the tilt of her neck—her perfume, slippers, peignoir—all made him wish he were married to Salwa.

Next morning, Yousif woke with only one thing on his mind—Salwa. How was she feeling now? Was she remorseful? Did she miss him as much as he missed her? How was she coping with her father? Remembering yesterday's episode, Yousif felt electrified. The idea that he might—just might—be married to Salwa by next Sunday thrilled him. He tossed and turned, then bolted straight up—thinking. Had there been precedent to what he had done yesterday? Had any wedding been canceled on account of a jealous lover? Yousif could not recall exactly similar circumstances. But he had heard that brides and grooms were known to be switched at the last moment. Wasn't there a semblance of truth in the Arabic proverb, "Even at her own wedding ceremony a bride will never know who will receive her at the altar"? And what about the other proverb which said that a male cousin had the right to force his female cousin off a white horse as she rode, like a fully clothed Lady Godiva, on her way to her wedding? Meaning: should a male cousin choose to claim the bride for himself, he could do so even if it meant a last-minute rescue. But Yousif was not pleased with this reasoning. One, he was not Salwa's cousin. Two, such nonsense had taken place in olden times. No modern Arab would subscribe to it. Yousif was for free will in marriage. He was for liberating women—not for confining them to outmoded customs. He was for love.

What now? Yousif thought, still in bed. What amends could he make to salvage the situation?

The first step in the healing process, he thought, was to make a financial settlement with Adel Farhat. That would prove to the townspeople—and mainly to his mother—that he was mature, responsible. Maybe then they could begin to see him in a new light. But would that persuade his own mother to give him the green light? What would it take to gain her blessings?

Yousif put his blue robe on and went out looking for his mother. Yasmin was in her room making her bed.

"Good morning," he said, standing behind her and giving her an affectionate squeeze.

"Good morning," she answered, fluffing a pillow.

"Feel any better?" he asked.

She sighed but did not answer.

A few minutes later, they were alone in the living room drinking coffee. The room had a dream-like quality about it. Rays of sunshine cut it in half, casting the intricate design of the crocheted drapes all over the furniture. The floor and one of the walls looked like a leopard's skin. Izzat and Hiyam were still asleep. Speaking in a low voice, Yousif divulged his plans.

"What kind of money would Adel Farhat be asking for?" he asked her, sipping his coffee.

"It depends on how much he spent," she told him, putting her cup down. "Is he going to make you pay for everything?"

"I have no idea. I'll pay what's reasonable. But I won't let him gouge me."

There was a pause. Their hands were spotted with the soft pattern of the drapes. The radio was on. Abdel Aziz Mahmoud was singing one of Yousif's favorites. A song about patience.

"I can't wait for Boulus to come back," Yasmin said. "I want to hear what he thinks."

"I hope he'll say I was right standing up—"

"Breaking a man's heart is right?"

"Saving Salwa from a loveless marriage is right."

"You have no regrets?"

"No regrets. No repentance. Nothing. Just think. By now Salwa would've been a married woman. No way. Next Sunday she's going to be mine."

His mother pursed her lips. "We're still in mourning. Do you want me to come to your wedding decked in black?"

"It wasn't my idea to rush the wedding. If it were left up to me, I'd rather wait. At least until after the first anniversary of father's death. But Anton Taweel is pressuring me. If we can't budge him, will you go along with me?"

"You want me to be disrespectful to your father's memory?"

"God forbid. But these are abnormal times. We need to adapt. Are you with me?"

"My heart says yes and my head says no."

"Mother, there's no time. We're talking about next Sunday."

"Let's see what your uncle says. I see him coming."

Yousif jumped to his feet. He could see Uncle Boulus by the wrought-iron gate, headed their way. He dropped a cigarette on the ground and stepped on it.

Moments later Uncle Boulus was inside the living room. All the three did was nod and mumble good morning.

"When did you get in?" Yasmin asked her brother.

"After midnight," Boulus answered, taking a seat.

"Did you bring mother and father with you?" Yasmin asked, anxious.

"They wouldn't come," Boulus told her, lighting another cigarette. "East Jerusalem is relatively safe, or that's what they think. Besides, Widad and her family have moved in with them."

"They did?" Yasmin asked, brightening for the first time all morning. "I'm so glad."

Yousif hurried to the kitchen and brought back an empty demitasse cup. Yasmin took it from him, filled it with coffee, and handed it to her brother.

Uncle Boulus took a sip and a long drag on his cigarette. "What is this I hear about you?" he asked his nephew.

Yousif smiled nervously. "It's true."

"You've managed to get yourself trapped, haven't you?" Uncle Boulus continued. "It's a case of damned if you do and damned if you don't."

Silence was glacial.

"What about you, Yasmin?" Uncle Boulus asked. "Are you ready for a wedding?"

"What do you think?" Yasmin answered, dabbing her chin and forehead.

Yousif's heart skipped in anticipation.

"It seems to me," Uncle Boulus said, "we've reached a dead end. Let them get married and be done with."

Yasmin's face lost all its color. "Boulus, what are you saying?"

"I see no way out of it now," her brother told her.

"But the timing is so wrong."

"He imposed it on us," Yousif interrupted.

"That's because you imposed yourself on him," his mother corrected him. "If you didn't intrude in his affairs he wouldn't have bothered you in the least."

"Well, that's history. I had to do it."

To avoid his mother's glare, Yousif poured coffee in each cup.

"I'll agree to the wedding, only after a decent period of mourning," Yasmin said. "At least six months. And not a day sooner."

Uncle Boulus took out his *masbaha* and leaned on his elbow. "Listen, Yasmin," he said. "If your son doesn't marry Salwa he's going to blame you for the rest of his life. You know that as much as I do. Now he has a chance, let him grab it. One thing for sure, we can't take Anton Taweel for granted. Nor can we taunt him. If he takes umbrage again, as I'm sure he will, he can get nasty. He's liable to change his mind. I've known him to be more stubborn than a bull. We certainly don't want Yousif to lock horns with him. There's no telling what a proud, injured, scandalized man will do."

"Still, we're in mourning," Yasmin protested.

"I wouldn't want to cross him at this stage," her brother said. "I know how you feel and how he feels exactly. You want her, you can have her. But on my terms, not yours. That's what he's saying."

Yasmin began to wipe the sweat on her crimson face. "You must make him agree to an engagement for the time being."

"I won't even ask him," her brother advised. "It would be bucking him again. You can't turn his daughter's wedding into a fiasco and then force him to eat his own words."

"That's right, Mother," Yousif agreed. "We can't make him compromise twice in a row."

Yasmin looked at her son, disappointed. "You ought to be thinking of your father, whose body was laid in the middle of this floor only ten days ago."

Yousif swallowed hard. "Wherever he is, he'll understand . . ." he said, biting his lower lip.

"For your sake, I hope so," Yasmin said, looking weary.

For the next half-hour the three went round and round. Yousif mentioned that he had seen Anton Taweel clutch his own chest in front of the church. What if he died before Yousif and Salwa got married? Wouldn't that complicate matters? Might not Salwa become guilt ridden? Might she not even change her mind about Yousif altogether? Uncle Boulus agreed that anything was possible. Yasmin was in a dither. She rubbed her own temples. She just couldn't see how they could sing and dance and have wedding ceremonies while they were still in mourning. Wouldn't they be criticized? Wasn't Dr. Safi worthy of respect in death? Was she to be denied the opportunity to attend her only son's wedding—wearing bright colors and smiling?

Yousif's heart ached. He patted his mother's hand, trying to comfort her.

"Give to each his due," her brother counseled. "You gave Jamil all his rights when he died, now you give the living their rights."

Brother and sister traded looks that were full of despair and understanding. With a hand gesture, born out of resignation if not frustration, Uncle Boulus seemed to tell Yasmin, "Let him go."

There was a long pause.

"We're forgetting," Uncle Boulus said, his voice lowered, "that we're in the midst of war. Let's get this whole thing behind us and think about tomorrow. Bigger troubles are still ahead. Come to think of it, the wedding might not be a bad idea after all. If Anton Taweel is having chest pains, he might die. At least he'll have Yousif to look after his family. If you die, Yasmin—"

"God forbid," Yousif said.

"Well, these things happen," Uncle Boulus said, clicking his *masbaha* and waxing philosophical. "Especially in war. I might die, you might die . . . who knows. Well, if Yasmin dies, Salwa will look after you."

Yasmin sighed sharply. "All right, you can get married," she told her son, looking him straight in the eye. "But promise me one thing, let's keep it simple and dignified. No fanfare. No hoopla. You hear me, Yousif? Dignified."

"Sure, Mother," Yousif said, a prey of tangled emotions. "Whatever you wish."

At that moment, Fatima walked in the front door, a basket of groceries on her head. She had to stoop a little to enter. Then she unloaded herself, placing the basket next to the door. Her face was flushed.

"No one is talking about politics anymore," Fatima said, like a bubbling brook. "The whole town is talking about you, Yousif."

Yousif was curious. "What are they saying?"

"That you are another Majnoon Laila," Fatima answered, wiping her face.

Yousif knew what that meant. They were referring to the seventh-century poet who had gone mad for having loved and lost. Mad or not, Yousif was glad he had stopped the wedding.

"Majnoon Salwa," Yousif corrected her, smiling. "And proud of it."

"Don't you worry," Fatima said, sitting down on the edge of a chair and taking a deep breath. "I gave them a piece of my mind."

"Who's them?" Yousif asked.

"Everybody. At the butcher's shop. At the baker's. Throughout the *souk.*"

"What did you tell them?" Yousif prodded.

"I told them when the dust settles down Anton Taweel is going to be glad the way things turned out. He ought to be on his hands and knees, thanking God for what you did."

"You told them all that?" Yousif asked, amused.

"Sure did," Fatima boasted, the gap between her front teeth looking wide.

Then Yasmin told Fatima that they had decided to go ahead with the wedding. Fatima jumped to her feet, both her hands cupping her mouth as though she were ready to start ululating.

"No singing," Yasmin begged.

"No singing?" Fatima asked, crestfallen. "The doctor, *Allah yirhamu,* wouldn't have it any other way."

"Not now, please," Yasmin said, her eyes misty.

To change the mood, Yousif smiled at Fatima. "I may not be able to keep my promise," he teased her, "and buy you that embroidered dress so soon."

"Yes, you can," Fatima answered, bending down to pick up her basket. "I know a woman who has just the dress I want and she'd sell it to me in no time."

All smiled—except Yasmin. But even she finally looked as though a burden had been lifted off her shoulders. And Yousif was pleased.

"Come on, Yousif," Uncle Boulus said, rising and pocketing his *masbaha.* "Time is running short and we have a lot to do."

DURING THE DAY, Yousif and his uncle assembled relatives (such as Salman but not Basim, who could not be located) and a group of dignitaries (such as the mayor and Fouad Jubran and Dr. Fareed Afifi) to help them smoothe Anton Taweel's ruffled feathers and to officially ask him for Salwa's hand.

When they arrived at the Taweels' house, about seven o'clock, awaiting them was a similarly large group of relatives and prominent people, including Father Samaan, who had won Yousif's heart for having refused to be railroaded into marrying Salwa to Adel Farhat.

As the arriving party went around the large living room shaking hands with the men who had stood to greet them, Yousif's heart fluttered. He was apprehensive about shaking Anton Taweel's hand. Only yesterday, Yousif remembered, Anton had wanted to strangle him. Being the youngest of his group, Yousif was the last in line. As he shook other men's hands, he kept his eyes on Salwa's father, who looked like a man ready to receive condolences rather than the good wishes of those who wanted his daughter for one of their sons.

Before he knew it, Yousif had his hand in Anton Taweel's hand. It was a lukewarm handshake. Their lips barely parted. Yousif was undecided whether to simply say hello or to apologize. Nor could he tell what Salwa's father uttered when his lips moved. But Yousif didn't care. He was only glad it was all over with and he was now moving on to shake another man's hand.

For about five minutes the conversation centered on health, weather, and politics. They all agreed that the outcome of the war was anybody's guess. Yousif sat, his legs crossed at the ankles and his hands folded in his lap. Then he heard his Uncle Boulus clear his throat. The whole gathering simmered down.

"I'm honored," Uncle Boulus began, his voice raised so that everyone could hear, "to speak on behalf of my nephew and my sister and the whole Safi family—and to ask you, Anton Taweel, for your daughter Salwa's hand in marriage to our nephew Yousif. We hope he will be worthy of your acceptance. We also hope that in time he'll be a worthy addition to your family that you may regard him as your son. Nothing will gladden my heart and your heart more, I hope, than to see these two young innocent people, Salwa and Yousif, who seem fated for each other, and who come from two honorable families that have been bonded by friendship over the years—nothing will please us all, I must say, than to see them receive your blessings and all your good wishes."

Silence echoed. Anton Taweel looked rigid, haughty. Yousif was impressed by his uncle's impassioned plea on his behalf, although he regarded such flowery language and unabashed sentimentality a bit archaic. He couldn't help but wonder if the words had been premeditated or whether they just gushed out of his uncle spontaneously.

Salwa's father remained solemn, noncommittal—even though he was the one who had demanded an early wedding. Till the last second, Yousif thought, Anton was playing hard. But the mayor and the priest and other men were urging him to give his consent.

"Barek," a chorus of men said. "Go ahead. Give them your blessings."

Finally, Anton Taweel, black pouches under his eyes, looked around. *"Mabrook,"* he said, without enthusiasm. "May their wedding be blessed."

Men cheered. The word *mabrook* resounded around the room. Again before he knew it, Yousif was urged to get up and embrace his "new uncle" and kiss him on both cheeks and beg forgiveness. This Yousif did with exaggerated formality—glad that no one had asked him to kiss Salwa's father's hand out of respect and as an admission of having done him wrong. Yousif was determined to balk at such an obsequious gesture, should it be suggested, at the risk of alienating his future father-in-law one more time.

While other men recited platitudes such as "it will blow over" and "all's well that ends well," Yousif remained standing in the room, wanting to get Anton's attention.

"Excuse me," Yousif said, nervous, "may I have your permission to see Salwa . . . now that we're going to get married."

Men all around him guffawed. They said it was about time he saw her. They said the poor fellow had waited long enough. They said he couldn't believe his dream was coming true. Eventually, the good cheer infected the guarded Anton. On his face flickered a faint smile.

"I guess you may," Anton said, sitting down.

Yousif dashed out of the room as Father Samaan began telling a story about the man in Genesis who plowed his uncle's fields for seven years in order to win his daughter's hand—only to lose her to someone else and to start another seven years of hard labor.

Salwa was in the kitchen, leaning against the counter, her arms folded. Her mother was there too, tending two large brass pots of coffee. They seemed to have been expecting him.

"Welcome to the family," Imm Akram said, breaking into smiles and extending both arms.

"The honor is mine," Yousif said, embracing her and kissing her on both cheeks.

"Your persistence has certainly paid off. *Mabrook*."

"Thanks," Yousif said, then turned to Salwa.

There was a nervous pause. Salwa was blushing. Then the mother slipped out of the room.

For a moment Yousif and Salwa continued to stare at each other. Then he rushed to sweep her off her feet. There was a fraction of hesitation on her part, then she fell into his arms. Every cell in his body rejoiced. Salwa was a willing partner, letting him mould her to his body, smell and feel her hair, luxuriate in her warmth. But when he tried to kiss her, she turned her head away.

"After all we've been through," he whispered, "you deny me a kiss?"

"Not yet," she demurred. "Not here . . ."

"I've risked my life for this moment."

"Don't tempt your fate," she murmured, looking in his eyes.

"For you I'll tempt the gods," he muttered, their cheeks touching.

Suddenly Salwa succumbed and their lips brushed like feathers. He became intoxicated; she melted in his arms as the kiss deepened and continued. Their bodies fit so well, her mouth tasted so good, he wanted the moment to last. Never in his life had he felt any better. Or happier. Or more alive.

After they had disengaged, they just held hands. Heat waves were still ripping through Yousif's body.

"I love you," he said, looking at her eyes.

"Ih cha na," she answered, smiling.

Suddenly they both burst out laughing. Salwa had quoted from the story of a nitwit who was madly in love. When he met the object of his desires he poured his heart to her in the most "poetic" clichés he could muster. He compared her to the moon, to the sun. He called her dewy-eyed, lithe-limbed like a gazelle, tall and elegant like a palm tree. Her skin was like marble, her kisses sweet like honey. He was a harp and she was the finger which plucked and caressed the strings to make music. He loved her, he adored her, he worshiped her, he'd crawl to hell for her. To which the simple country girl answered: *ih cha na*—me too.

Yousif couldn't believe his luck. The most beautiful girl in the world was his. She was there laughing with him and holding his hand. He couldn't keep his eyes off her.

"I'm in a daze," Yousif said.

"You were so brave at the church," she told him. "When I heard your voice and turned around and saw you, I *knew* you were the one for me."

Yousif feigned disappointment. "Only then you knew?"

"I just hope I'll love you for the rest of my life as much as I loved you at that moment."

"You'll love me more. But just imagine! Now you're mine, mine."

"And you're my hero."

"Do you blame me for being in a daze?" he said, hugging her again.

"What I can't believe is my father's reversal," she confessed.

"Me, too," Yousif agreed. "I didn't know what to expect."

Her large eyes focused on him. "I'm glad you're so happy," she said.

"Tell me, where would you like to go on the honeymoon?"

"Honeymoon! Can you believe we're even discussing it? Right now I'm supposed to be on honeymoon with—"

"Sshhhh," he said, touching her lips. "Don't mention his name. He never existed."

"I promise. And I don't care where we go. I just want to be with you."

Again they fell into each other's arms. The coffee on the fire boiled over and hissed. But they didn't care. There was no shyness now. It was a kiss that resonated in the depth of their souls.

ON TUESDAY, Yousif had his father's bank accounts transferred to his name. On Wednesday morning, Adel Farhat came to Fouad Jubran's office bearing an invoice in his pocket. It was long and detailed. But one glance at the bottom line and Yousif knew that he would never pay it—even if he could.

The man must be crazy. Five hundred and eighty pounds!!! Yousif passed the sheet of paper to Uncle Boulus, who was sitting next to him. His uncle studied it carefully, but not one muscle in his face moved. Yousif waited for someone to speak. If it took till the end of eternity, he was not about to break the icy silence.

Big hulking Fouad Jubran, his jacket draped on the back of his chair, cleared his throat. "Figures can be adjusted," he said, opening a new pack of cigarettes. "A fair settlement can always be reached if the two parties want to settle their dispute. But what's at stake here is more important than money. I'd like for us to enter the negotiations in good faith and leave the room shaking hands. Ardallah is a small town. We're destined to live together for a long time—if this damn war lets us. I consider all of us one family."

"Life is too short to carry a grudge," Uncle Boulus said, taking out his *masbaha.*

"Absolutely," the attorney said, offering them cigarettes and ringing his bell for some coffee.

Yousif watched Adel Farhat's face. It looked like a slab of granite. The attorney might as well have been addressing people in another room.

"But it seems to me," Uncle Boulus said, "that this list here is a bit excessive, don't you think?"

"I can document every item," Adel Farhat protested, one leg tucked under the chair and the other one extended. "But I don't think I have to. My integrity should not be questioned."

"Of course not," the attorney hastened.

"No one is questioning your integrity," Uncle Boulus said. "I'm sure it cost you this much."

"Why is it excessive then?" Adel asked. "If you agree that it must have cost me this much, pay me and let me go."

"I meant excessive," Uncle Boulus explained, "in the sense that you expect Yousif to pay for the whole affair."

"He ruined the whole affair, didn't he?" Adel said, mocking.

There was another awkward silence. Yousif watched the other three, giving them a chance to air their views. They could argue all they wanted but he would pay what he thought was fair and not one piaster more. At the same time, deep in his heart he felt sorry for Adel. The man's humiliation was etched over his face like a scar across the firmament.

"Yousif, what do you think?" Fouad Jubran asked.

"First I want to apologize to Adel," Yousif said, his tone oozing with confidence.

"Tell him apologies not accepted," Adel said, his face turning red.

"I meant you no harm. It could've been anyone—"

"Tell him to get to the point," Adel demanded, his anger rising.

Yousif wanted to look in the man's eyes and tell him that it was nothing personal, that Adel just happened to be in his and Salwa's way. But, withdrawn and hostile, Adel Farhat never once looked at him. Finally, Fouad Jubran and Uncle Boulus told Yousif with looks and gestures to forget about the apologies and go on with the negotiations.

"From what I hear," Yousif said, "no wedding in this town ever cost this much. A few cost around five hundred pounds, the rest cost a whole lot less."

"See?" Adel Farhat said, with a pious smirk. "He's questioning my integrity."

"No, I'm not," Yousif said, anxious to get Adel's attention. "What I was trying to tell you is that I don't think I should pay for the gold watch, the bracelets, the crosses, the diamond ring . . ."

"What's he paying for then?" Adel said, looking at the attorney. "The wedding invitations and postage? Ridiculous."

"I didn't say that either," Yousif defended himself. "Stop putting words in my mouth."

"It seems to me you both have a point," the attorney said, like a true peacemaker, Yousif thought. "But the way I see it, the expenses can be divided into two columns: perishables and non-perishables. Used or not used."

Yousif jumped up and snatched the invoice off the desk. "He wants five hundred and eighty pounds," he said, ready to do some mental calculating. "Let's see now. Three hundred and forty of it went for a diamond ring and jewelry. It sounds like a lot, but that's OK. Another hundred and ten for topcoat, dresses, shoes, perfumes, underwear, etc. If we add all this together, we come up with four hundred and fifty pounds. And if we subract it from the total he's asking for, we end up with a hundred and thirty pounds. I don't know exactly for what, but I'm willing to pay it and forget about the whole mess."

"During the engagement period, she used some of it," Adel protested, rising to his feet. "Then there were the engagement and wedding expenses."

"That's why I'm willing to pay the hundred and thirty pounds. But that's all."

It was the first concrete offer and Yousif got the impression that the ball was now rolling.

"It's a good start," Fouad Jubran said, reaching for a pencil and a pad.

"It's not a start at all," Yousif corrected him. "It's all I'm willing to pay."

Adel rose in a huff. "Then I'll meet him in court," he threatened.

"With pleasure," Yousif said, unblinking. "Ten attorneys won't cost me as much as he wants me to pay. I'll show him how to tie up his money."

But after two rounds of coffee, three ashtrays full of cigarette butts, two huddles between Yousif and his uncle, and a room clouded with smoke, Fouad Jubran and Uncle Boulus ironed out an agreement whereby Adel Farhat would turn over every item on his list and Yousif would pay the entire bill. Adel Farhat was apparently glad to unload everything he had bought for Salwa. Such items, he must have rationalized, were jinxed and he wasn't interested in keeping any. Which was God-sent for Yousif. After all, a bride required a diamond ring, jewelry, and a trousseau from the groom. The deal they had just concluded was bound to save Yousif time.

Yousif whipped out a checkbook from his hip pocket and wrote a check for that amount. It was the first check he had ever written in his life and he signed it with a flourish. He was buying not only Salwa's freedom—but their wedding bliss.

"You bring the goods to Mr. Jubran," Yousif told Adel, "and he'll give you your money." Then he handed the check to the attorney.

Adel Farhat agreed and rose to leave. But he seemed to have something on his mind.

"What is it?" Yousif asked.

Adel ignored him. "I'll bring the items I have. Not the items already in Salwa's possession."

Yousif understood. Because Salwa had aborted the wedding to Adel Farhat, she was supposed to return to him everything he had given her. And because he had settled up with Yousif, he was in turn supposed to deliver everything to him. It would be a tangled affair.

"Oh, sure," the attorney agreed. "No need to bother with too many exchanges. Yousif and Salwa are going to be married to each other, you know."

Adel Farhat's coloring, which already had an unhealthy cast, turned bluish.

Yousif knew that Adel was aware that they were getting married. Yet hearing the news again must have upset him. It tugged at Yousif's heart that his rival was so unhappy. But, then, no one ever said losing Salwa was easy. It would crush anybody.

26

Saturday night—before the wedding—the house's sparkling lights belied the drama within its walls. Yousif stood on the balcony all alone. His eyes roamed over Ardallah's mountains, but his heart was full of pains and joys. Men were guarding the city against a possible Jewish attack, and look what he was doing! The need to do two different things and to be in two different places at the same time bothered him, as so many things had done lately. This was the night he had always hoped for—why did his pleasures have to be so dimmed? Tomorrow he would be wedded to Salwa—why should his celebration be tempered? Why did his happiness have to be so incomplete? Oh, how he missed his father. If only he had been living! And his mother inside—how pitiful she looked in her crosscurrents of loyalties! Women of her generation mourned for extended periods; some never left the house for six months, even a year. Some didn't put on lipstick or powder their noses. Some didn't make sweets or serve any to their guests. And here was his mother cutting her grief short—all on his account.

As Yousif held the railing, his mind traveled a few months back. He remembered other weddings—the kind his would have been like under different circumstances. Normally, hundreds of people would be at his house. Lights would be strung from tree to tree. Tables would be placed all over the garden. Inside the house a small Arabic band would be playing. Women would be singing and dancing. Every five or ten minutes there would be an ear-piercing ululation. The part Yousif had usually enjoyed most, was when twelve or fifteen men danced the *dabkeh* with one man in the middle—waving a cane or a sword or crouching or going down on his knees and bending backward until his head touched the floor. Then the dancer would spring up, leap to his feet, and begin to swirl. How much Yousif had enjoyed the *mal'ab,* when thirty or forty men lined up, often in the street in front of the house, and chanted and clapped and swayed, their voices robust and their movements rhythmic. What a spectacle! What a thrill for the dancers and singers as well as the crowd watching! Those were the days, Yousif thought, when Palestine was at peace and his father was still living. There was none of this excitement tonight, Yousif regretted, as he ambled in.

The house was crowded. There was his mother sitting on the sofa under one of the two half-moon-shaped windows. She was decked in black, trying, the poor woman, to put on a front. But deep in her heart, Yousif knew, she was crying. Aunts and uncles and cousins were around her, plus a few friends and neighbors, even though no one had been invited. Those came, he was sure, to be happy for him and to commiserate with his bereaved mother. Dr. Fareed Afifi was there with his beautiful wife, Jihan. Fouad Jubran was there with his wife, who looked as though she might have triplets. Amin and his parents were there, bringing to Yousif's mind the memories of the months his parents had spent building the little villa. Jamal was there, reminding him of Isaac and his *'oud* playing. Abla and Maha and Aunt Hilaneh were, the last he had seen them, busy in the kitchen preparing *maza.* Fatima and Hiyam were attending to the ladies. Amin and Izzat were looking after the men.

But Basim, of course, Yousif mused, was never around. What would happen tomorrow at the church? Basim had promised to be his best man. Who could count on it? Good thing Salman was willing to substitute, just in case Basim didn't show up. Yousif had wanted Amin, his best friend, to be his best man. But Amin was a Muslim.

About eight o'clock Salwa's parents and young brothers arrived, accompanied by three or four couples from their side of the family. Such a visit was traditional. Everyone in the room stood up, glad to see them. Yousif and Uncle Boulus and Salman hastened to receive them at the door and to offer them the best seats. Yousif went out of his way to speak to Anton Taweel, who, for a change, seemed relaxed and in good spirits.

"Ahlan wa sahlan," Yousif told them. "You are most welcome."

"Thank you," Anton said, smiling and patting him on the back.

As usual, Salwa's mother was vivacious. She and her daughter looked just alike, people commented. Yousif agreed to a point. No one, in his opinion, could compare to Salwa. To his dismay, but not surprise, Salwa herself was not with them. Tradition also dictated that the bride and groom must not see each other so close to the wedding. Next time they met it would be at the church.

No sooner had the guests arrived than, suddenly, Abla pulled out a flute she must've been carrying and handed it to Salman, her husband. Salman looked startled. He refused to touch his own instrument, cutting a quick glance at Yasmin for fear of criticism.

"Listen, Auntie," Abla said to Yasmin, "Yousif is not a widower. He's a young man and he's getting married only once. He deserves to have some celebration the night before his wedding."

The whole house seemed to tense. But Abla was not daunted.

"Some of you may think I'm talking out of line," Abla continued, "but I don't think so. The dead are dead and may God rest their souls. But life is for the living. Yousif deserves a song or two, a dance or two. Oh, my God, a stranger passing by would think this is a wake—not a *sahra.*"

All eyes shifted to Yasmin. She seemed to be thrown in a new dither.

"You think I want the wedding of my only son to be like this?" Yasmin lamented, gently pounding her chest with her fist. "But it can't be helped. It's his fate."

"I don't think so," Abla objected, like a fiery prosecutor. "Those who are our friends will understand. Those who are not our friends will talk. But who cares about them? Let them drink the ocean." She spun around, asking those in the room for moral support. "Tell me if I'm wrong. Please tell me if I'm being disrespectful to my uncle's memory, *Allah yirhamu.*"

"If you think I'm going to play the flute," Salman said, "you're crazy. Who told you you could bring it, anyway?"

"I brought it on my own," his wife told him, "because I knew you'd refuse. But I'm being practical. The best way to put misery behind is to bury it. *Haraam* Yousif," she added, her face full of pity. "What has he done to be denied some kind of celebration? Not a big one—but at least enough to make his wedding not look like a funeral. Abu Akram, what do you think?"

There was stony silence. She had addressed her remark to Anton Taweel, Salwa's father, who did not seem to think it was his place to take sides.

"I'm sorry . . ." he faltered, his eyebrows arching.

"I'm sorry too," Abla told him. "I don't mean to put you on the spot. It's just I respect your opinion. Perhaps—"

"I understand," Anton said, "but please leave me out of it. The doctor, *Allah yirhamu,* is yours; the groom is yours; the wedding is yours."

"Yours too," Abla reminded him.

"Oh, yes, of course," he told her, "but in your house we are guests. Whatever you do will be fine with us."

Everyone in the room seemed to agree. Many praised and even thanked Anton Taweel for his tact. Yousif was beginning to appreciate a side of Anton he had never suspected. But Abla pressed on.

"Please, Auntie," Abla said, cornering Yasmin. "Nobody is going to lift a finger or open his mouth unless you give your permission. Let us have some fun for Yousif's sake."

Yousif crossed the room and squeezed himself next to his mother. "It's not necessary," he said, putting his arm around his mother's shoulders. "I don't feel right about having a *sahra*." Ringing in his ears were his mother's words. "No fanfare, no hoopla," she had said. Any changes must come from her.

Abla's face contorted. "See there?" she pleaded with Yasmin. "See how sad he sounds? He needs a cheerful send-off. Uncle in his grave would insist on it."

Yasmin took a deep sigh and nodded her head. "Play, Salman, play. And may God forgive us."

Abla seized the moment, pushing for more concessions. "So we don't have to go through this again," she said to her aunt, "you won't mind brightening up the mood a bit more, would you? Everybody has such a long face."

Yasmin shook her head and dismissed Abla affectionately with the back of her hand. "Do what you want," she said, seemingly relieved not to be depriving her only son of what was his due.

With little coaxing, Salman took the flute and played. Men lit their cigarettes or put them out in anticipation. Silence prevailed as the old favorites seeped out of the flute like liquid gold. But Salman's tunes seemed to put the audience in a melancholy mood. Abla fussed at him, telling him to play something cheerful. In the meantime, Maha thrust a maroon-covered *'oud* in Jamal's lap. Yousif gasped. The *'oud* was Isaac's. Jamal himself must have realized it. Yousif saw him recoil, putting his arms behind him. Everyone in the room clapped and pleaded with Jamal to oblige them. Watching and hearing Jamal play, they all said, was a privilege in itself.

"I've never played in public," Jamal explained, his chin trembling.

"Well, it's about time," Abla prodded.

"Not tonight," Jamal apologized.

All eyes turned to Yasmin. She was the only who could convince him.

"Go on, Jamal," Yasmin said. "Your kind of music is good for the soul."

"See," Abla told Jamal, smiling. "Even Auntie agrees."

Jamal hesitated. Then he surprised everybody, particularly Yousif. Jamal asked to sit on a high-backed chair and Abu Amin was only glad to give him his. The room stood still. Jamal crossed his legs and cradled the *'oud* in his lap. The strumming of two or three notes reverberated throughout the house. Those who were not in the room seemed pulled in by magnet. The familiar songs, rendered expertly, cut deep in Yousif's heart and unlocked some painful memories. He swallowed hard as he recalled Isaac playing the very same instrument.

Bent on enlivening the party, Abla asked someone to dance. She pleaded with and cajoled a few women, but everyone apologized and remained seated. Finally, she herself had to step in the middle of the room. She had a nice figure and she moved gracefully. Men and woman began to clap. Yousif squeezed his mother and looked at her eyes. They were growing misty. Abla's cheeks were flushed but she seemed to be enjoying herself. Then she pulled up Amin and he danced with her, his stump showing from under his short sleeve.

"May we dance at your own wedding, *habibi* Amin," Yasmin told him.

"Inshallah," Amin's mother responded, clapping louder.

When Amin stopped, Abla reached for Jihan Afifi's hand and gently pulled her to the middle of the floor. She didn't know how, Jihan protested, but Abla would have none of it. The crowd got excited and wanted to see Jihan dance. Soon Jihan was unable to resist. Jamal's music reached a new height. Jihan blushed and then got in step with the beat of music. Putting a hand on her waist and raising the other above her head, she swayed and twirled a lace handkerchief. All eyes were on her. Abla let her dance solo, and joined the others clapping. Yousif was fascinated by Jihan's dancing. She seemed like the proverbial reed in motion. He wished Salwa were with him to watch.

"Get up and dance with me," Jihan told her husband, pulling his hand while still dancing.

Dr. Afifi looked aghast. "You must be kidding," he told her.

"No, I'm not," Jihan said. "You dance better than I do."

Pleased with the idea, men showered the doctor with encouragement. Soon Dr. Afifi found himself on the dance floor. Now Jihan was dancing with vigor. Suddenly Fatima hoisted a drum above the heads of the crowd for everyone to see. The crowd loosened up. Yasmin pushed a lock of hair in resignation. Fatima began to play: sometimes banging on the drum with her palms, sometimes with her fingers. Then she paused long enough to almost shake the room with a sudden burst of trilling. All the pent-up emotions seemed to have been rolled into one and were now pouring out of her lungs and throat.

Singing or dancing or clapping, everyone got involved. There seemed to be no stopping to the frenzy. The only two who did not join in the merriment were Anton Taweel and Yasmin. Anton was drinking; Yasmin was crying.

Half an hour later, everyone was exhausted. Those who had stood up from excitement, collapsed in their seats. Those who had come in late and couldn't find a place to sit, ended up sitting on the floor. All the time Jamal hadn't stopped playing as though all the sweetness and agonies of his unrequited love had surfaced.

Jamal could sense not only a need for a change of pace, but an insatiable hunger for ballads. The strings of his *'oud* hummed tenderly. The crowd hushed. Yousif watched Jamal fondle the strings like a man caressing the earlobes of a woman. The tune he was now strumming called for singing, but no one would volunteer. The music never ceased, but continued to flow, to yearn, to plead for linkage with a human voice. Soon Aunt Hilaneh responded, her voice warm and slithering like summertime water seeping out of a dark cave. Yousif could almost hear the hearts around him soaking up the feeling like a parched desert strip. A spring breeze from Ardallah's mountains seemed to drift into the room. Picturesque Ardallah flashed in Yousif's mind, with all its vineyards and all its greenness. Yousif could almost smell and taste its fruits and vegetables, and could almost hear his birds chirping. Ardallah lived for him—so did the whole of Palestine—and he could almost see the treetops moving and the rains pouring. If only Salwa were with him to share this Palestinian moment, as if she needed someone to remind her of what they were fighting for.

From the forlorn looks on the others' faces, Yousif could tell that their minds had been invaded. Aunt Hilaneh's supple voice continued to roll, bathing them like the warm waters of the Jordan River. But soon she ran out of verses. Others came to her assistance, reciting a line or singing a phrase. She managed a bit longer, but then ran out completely. The ballad was long, and Yousif knew most of the lines. But he would not sing, out of respect for his mother. Yasmin seemed not to mind the way the night had turned out, but he could see a cast of sadness on her face. Abu Amin sang. Imm Amin sang. Fouad Jubran's pregnant wife sang. The gentle song seemed to tickle the spine of all listeners. Amin and Izzat passed around more drinks. Hiyam and Maha brought out more *maza*.

Psyched and conditioned like the rest, Yasmin jolted one and all. She began to hum—then, in trepidation and yearning, she started to sing. Faces bunched up. Lips puckered. Eyes became tearful. Yousif felt a lump in his throat. He pressed his mother to his side and kissed her left cheek. If only Salwa were there to see her shedding her grief for their sake.

There wasn't a hint of nationalism in the song, yet it aroused in Yousif a Palestinian fervor. Strange, he thought. The night before his wedding he ought to be feeling romantic. Yet the pulsating music seemed to transport him —to other places, other times. As the other listeners, who, like him, seemed floodedwith nostalgia, hummed along with his mother, he found Salwa and Palestine sharing his passion. He envisioned his people battling to save the simple life his mother's song evoked. In his heart—in his marrow—he could feel the chill of a possible loss. The sights and sounds of Ardallah and Ramallah and Acre and Jaffa and Haifa and Gaza and Jerusalem and Jericho and Bethlehem and Bait Jala and Batoonia and Bireh and Birzeit and Baiteen and Lydda and Ramleh and Kufr Qasim and Karameh and Nablus and Tul Karim and Jineen and Kharbatha and Ni'leen and El-Khalil and Sarafand and Bisan and Shafa 'Amr and Tabariyya and Halhool and Deir Yasin and all the cities and towns and villages and hamlets in between, with all their olives and all their figs and all their cactuses and all their berries and all their grapes and all their oranges and all their lemons and all their barley and all their wheat and all their farmers and all their hewers and all their shepherds and all their sheep and all their quails and all their pigeons and all their rabbits and all their fishes and all their gazelles, all in one and one in all—throbbed in his veins and streamed out of his consciousness like a river of sacred waters.

ST. GEORGE Catholic Church was packed, for many had come uninvited. Yousif's valor a week earlier and his short but now-famous romance with Salwa must have caused the sensation, Yousif thought.

As he walked down the aisle, his mother at his arm and his chest puffed out, Yousif exuded youthful confidence. He considered himself the happiest of men, and he wished all lovers the fulfillment of their dreams. Turning and looking at both sides of the aisle, he could see people whispering and craning their necks. Many women, either in hats or shawls, were dabbing their eyes, seemingly in empathy with his mother. He could see, sitting up front, Salwa's mellowed cousin, Shafiq, who, only last Sunday, had threatened to tear him apart. He could also see Jamal next to ustaz Saadeh and his wife who were not far from the organ. To his right, Yousif could see Sitt Bahiyyeh, who was beaming at him. He nodded in her direction, making a mental note to invite her for dinner and to drink a toast for all her kindnesses. To his right, he could see his classmates, their eyes lit up with laughter and envy. In the middle of the church he could see Amin with his own parents, and next to them Fatima in her embroidered dress. How young and attractive she looked—and how happy. He could see the mayor (minus his cigar, for a change) and many council members. Even Ghanem Jadallah, the stutterer who had berated Yousif the week before, was there. Yousif could see acquaintances, strangers. Because Basim was not there, Salman had to substitute as the best man. Yousif snickered at seeing his sheepish cousin in suit and tie. Formal wear suited him like a bathing suit on a nun.

Then she appeared. Salwa was more dazzling than the flood of light which ushered her in from the front entrance. Yousif's heart pounded. Escorted by her father, she was a vision to behold. She was the only girl he knew whose breathtaking beauty was daily perfecting itself. He felt mystified, even now, at how much he loved her. His chest constricted when he realized how close he had come to losing her. That would have been tantamount to laying him in a casket. For a second he remembered visiting his father's grave that morning, and he was glad he had. How he wished his father were there to see him getting married.

Yousif glanced at his mother sitting in the front pew next to Uncle Boulus and Aunt Hilaneh. He appreciated her having exchanged her black shroud for a gray suit. The double strings of white pearls and white earrings seemed to soften her intense mourning. And the white carnation on her chest was, to him, the ultimate emblem of sacrifice. But, Mother, he wanted to tell her, look at Salwa! Wasn't she beautiful? Too bad their honeymoon would be just for one night in town at al-Rowda Hotel. He wished they were going to Lebanon or Egypt for a whole month. He wanted Salwa to occupy his time—his bed—as much as she had occupied his thoughts. But what was wrong with him? He should be rejoicing not complaining. Seeing Salwa walking down the aisle and getting closer, closer, he felt the luckiest and proudest man on earth. A goddess (what else would you call her?) was walking toward him. *Him.*

Two minutes later, Yousif and her father were staring at each other. A moment, charged with emotion, passed between them. Utter faithfulness, Anton's eyes seemed to demand. Absolutely, Yousif's eyes replied. What a watershed in their lives, Yousif thought. Yesterday's enemies were today's friends. As misty-eyed Anton Taweel handed Salwa over to him, Yousif shook his hand with undying gratitude and a silent promise to be worthy of his daughter. But when Salwa hugged her father and rapped his back fervently, Yousif could hear sniffling in the pews. He had to check his own tears.

Minutes into the ceremony, Father Mikhail asked Yousif if he would take Salwa as his wedded wife. Yousif's quick response, "I do," caused a good-natured ripple of laughter. After all poor Yousif had gone through to get Salwa, the laugh seemed to say, you ask him such a question? Yousif and Salwa held hands and traded looks full of love.

Much later, Father Mikhail was placing and switching on their heads two crowns. He did it three times. Then he led them and the best man, Salman, and the bridesmaid, Huda, into a procession around the altar. Yousif felt someone tugging at the bottom of his jacket. He turned around and looked. Aunt Hilaneh had gotten up from her seat and was now "stitching" his tails with a threadless needle. No one had told him she was going to do it.

"What is she doing?" Salwa whispered, surprised.

Yousif grinned. "Haven't you seen it before? It's an old tradition."

"Yes, but what does it mean?"

"I'll tell you later."

When the wedding ceremony was over, Salwa and Yousif delighted the guests, and especially themselves, with a long kiss. Then they both bent down to embrace and kiss their parents and immediate families and to receive their congratulations. Instantly, all the pity and love and joy and suffering of all those attending burst out in an unprecedented round of applause. The newlyweds strode out glowing like two mortals who had been ordained by God and crowned by the Church for common destiny.

For the next half hour, and in the shadow of the church, Yousif and Salwa stood in line with their parents and a few close people, to shake hands with the well-wishers. Most of the gifts were of money tucked inside wedding cards or plain envelopes. A few were loose bills. Abla stood behind the bride and groom with a large purse in which she stuffed all gifts. Maha, Basim's wife, handed out pieces of chocolate and sugar-coated almonds wrapped in twill and tied with a blue ribbon. Were things normal, Yousif thought, there would have been a fancy reception and a seated dinner at a hotel garden. Had his father been living and Palestine at peace, well . . .

"Mabrook," everyone said, shaking Yousif's hand.

Yousif thanked one and all. But he mainly thanked God—over and over again—that Salwa was his bride.

THAT NIGHT, Yousif and Salwa drank champagne, compliments of the owners of Al-Rowda Hotel. Al-Andalus Hotel was bigger and plusher, but Yousif deliberately avoided registering there. He didn't have the heart to check in a hotel managed by Adel Farhat.

Glasses in hand, Yousif and Salwa stood at a window on the third floor, looking down on the garden below. It was the scene where the fund-raising meeting had been held, where the bombs from the Jewish air raid had fallen. During that raid, Yousif now remembered, the proprietress's fiancé had been killed. Yousif did not mention it now. Neither did Salwa.

"That's where you were knocked down," Yousif told Salwa, pointing his finger.

"You mean where the branch almost crushed my back," Salwa said, smiling. "How can I forget! Especially your lying flat on top of me."

"Good thing I did," Yousif said, savoring the memory.

"How sweet," she teased him. "You were simply rescuing me, weren't you? Like you always do."

He put his arm around her. Once more they touched glasses. Once more they kissed, their lips barely open.

"Tell me about what your aunt Hilaneh was doing at the church," she reminded him. "What does a needle without a thread going in and out of a garment signify?"

Yousif smiled but avoided her eyes.

"Why are you smiling?"

"It's what you said. In and out."

Salwa looked confused. "I don't understand. It's not a religious symbol?"

"Not really," he answered.

"Don't be so coy. And tell me what it means."

"You really want to know?"

"Would I be asking if I didn't?"

"It symbolizes love-making."

Salwa blushed. "I don't believe it. You're making it up."

"No, I'm not. Imagine the act. Then compare it to the motion of a needle without a thread . . . going in and out . . ."

Salwa seemed to concentrate. "You're embarrassing me," she said, walking away from the window.

"I didn't mean to. The tradition simply says we wish you lots and lots of sex and lots and lots of children."

She put the glass down on the dresser and hurried toward the bathroom. On her way she picked up and carried with her a silk gown she had lain on the edge of the bed. Yousif laughed and poured himself another glass of champagne. They had hardly eaten their dinner, and he shouldn't be drinking on an empty stomach. But he needed something to steady his nerves. If Salwa only knew, he thought. He was as nervous as she was.

Then he began to undress, wondering what to do next. Should he keep his underclothing on and wait for her in the middle of the room? Should he get completely naked and wait for her in bed? Well, that depended on how long she would take getting prepared. He removed his shirt, shoes and socks and sat in a chair, contemplating his fortune. The sight of the mountains in the distance made him think of Basim and his men. What was Basim up to that he couldn't come to his cousin's wedding? Were they anticipating an attack on Ardallah? Thinking of war made Yousif again wonder how long tonight's happiness would last. The real honeymoon would have to wait until after the war. But he tried not to get depressed. After all, this was his wedding night. He shut the curtain and turned off the lights. Except one. If Salwa insisted he would turn it off later. But first he had to see her in all her glory.

He heard the bathroom door open and saw a light. He waited, transfixed. Salwa appeared, wearing a white silk nightgown. He felt a rush in his heart—an explosion of happiness. When he recovered his senses he put his glass down. One of her straps had fallen down her long arm (was it on purpose?) exposing a part of her he had never seen. Her eyes were full of the mystery of an older woman. Her wavy auburn hair was below her shoulder, her skin creamy. Yousif could only imagine how she smelled. He could only imagine how she must feel in his arms. Soon he would know, he kept telling himself. She was his for life. Quickly he shed his pants. He moved toward her like a pilgrim on holy ground. Slowly she dropped the other strap, unfolding before his eyes like Salome. Her breasts beckoned him, like two goblets full of milk and honey. Was he dreaming?

But when Yousif rose to the challenge and touched them, then drank to his fill, he knew that his mind and body were awake. He also knew that magic had touched his soul.

27

War had not been a respecter of Yousif's wedding. It had even gotten hotter while he and Salwa were on their brief honeymoon. But no progress for either side was discernible on the ground. The crunch was yet to come.

Eight days after he had been married, Yousif was on his way to Dr. Fareed Afifi's clinic to see about his father's clinic. But he ran into a distraction of major proportions. He had to see it, even though he didn't want to be late for the appointment. He stopped at the Saha, the five-point clearing at the entrance of town. Standing almost on the same spot where he, Amin, and Isaac had watched Jewish spies descend from a yellow bus, Yousif saw now a caravan of army jeeps and trucks overflowing with remnant British soldiers make its last exit from Ardallah.

Britain's gradual departure from Palestine had been unceremonial. Over the last few months they had been shutting down camps and transferring authority—almost always in favor of the Jews.

Now it was May 14—with nine hours left to the British Mandate. Some of the soldiers waved their hands wearily, but the people on the crowded sidewalk cafes paid little attention. Most ignored them, Yousif noticed, except for an elderly man who spat at the sight and a school boy who hurled a stone that fell short of its moving target. The incident caused Yousif to shift focus. Beyond his world was another world "out there" that was just as real, just as tragic.

Yousif wished Salwa were with him, not at home with his mother, to watch the momentous event unfolding before his eyes. This was the kind of moment they would be telling their children and grandchildren about. History was in the making; cataclysmic changes were in the offing. He was witnessing an end and a beginning—a death and rebirth. He looked up at the blue sky, wondering what the gods had in mind. The din of heavy traffic in his ears, Yousif crossed his fingers, closed his eyes, and offered a silent prayer.

"Go to hell," a man shouted, shaking his fist at a departing British wagon full of soldiers wearing shorts. He was a hollow-eyed shopkeeper standing on the sidewalk in front of his newspaper and magazine racks.

A pastry vendor passing by grunted, "What's the use!"

The shopkeeper viewed him angrily. "What did you say?"

"Shaking a fist now is a bit too late," the vendor answered, clanking his castanets to draw attention to his piping hot *hareeseh*.

"The sight of them makes me sick."

"Have no fear," the peddler said, smirking. "Our brethren Arabs will save the day."

"That's a laugh," the shopkeeper replied, walking toward his counter.

Yousif recognized the irony of the unobtrusive folding down and pulling out of the British. It contrasted dramatically with the end of World War I when they'd been welcomed as conquerors who helped the Arabs liberate their land from the hated Turks. Then Arab men and women had met them at the outskirts of towns—singing, dancing, throwing flowers. Yousif had heard about General Allenby's entry into Jerusalem—and of the Arabs' regard for him as a hero. People still talked about his humility and depth of faith. He had refused to enter Jerusalem on horseback and would not wave any sword like a conqueror.

Yousif could remember other happy days for the British in Palestine. How could he forget the mile after mile of British armored tanks passing through Ardallah during World War II when he was still in elementary school? Students had lined up for several days along the highways to watch the olive-colored tanks rumble past. Yousif smiled now as he recalled an Arab gamine, about thirteen years old, who had scandalized her family and the whole town for winning so many rides from soldiers only too eager to have her sit in their laps. Whatever happened to that family? Yousif now wondered.

Yousif also remembered the white horse on which young Princess Elizabeth—or was it Margaret?—had ridden in Ardallah during one of the Royal Family's visits. Oh, how the people had talked then of the splendor and majesty of this young girl who was in line to the British throne. They were particularly fond of a rumor—neither confirmed nor denied—that the teenage princess had fed her horse nothing but chocolate. Those days of British glory were eclipsed by the dismal present. Now Arabs shouted and swore openly at their former rulers. How times had changed, Yousif thought.

THE APPOINTMENT at Dr. Afifi's office was at 4:00 but Yousif was fifteen minutes early. He couldn't stand being late. Dr. Afifi was supposed to introduce him to Dr. Tuffaha, a classmate and now an exile from Haifa, to talk about the future of his father's clinic. Nurse Maria had promised to join them. To Yousif's surprise, all three were there waiting for him to arrive.

Dr. Tuffaha had bushy white hair and freckles that covered his hands and face. But what struck Yousif most about him was his heavy breathing. Even when he was silent he sounded like a *nergileh* being sucked on by an addict.

After the introduction, Yousif noticed something a bit unusual. Dr. Afifi's small radio had been set conspicuously in the middle of his desk. Also, it was a bit loud for background music. Even while they talked about terms and conditions for leasing the clinic, the radio continued to make its presence felt.

Yousif agreed to a month-to-month lease, at fifty pounds a month. Then he added one stipulation: the new management must keep Nurse Laila on the payroll.

"She's been with my father for over five years," Yousif said, "and I don't want her to start looking for a job now."

"We could probably use her," Dr. Tuffaha said, looking at Maria. "What do you think?"

"Most likely we'll need her," Maria said.

At that point the music got too loud and Dr. Afifi had to turn it down a little.

"We heard there's going to be an important announcement on the Jewish station," Dr. Afifi explained to Yousif, who seemed bewildered by the intrusion.

Yousif looked at his watch. It was 3:50. They all expected David Ben Gurion to declare the establishment of a Jewish state. But that was to happen soon after midnight—right after the British had left.

"What could it be?" Yousif wondered.

"Only the Devil knows what the Zionists are up to now," Maria commented, her purse in her lap.

"We'll soon find out," Dr. Tuffaha said, putting out one cigarette and lighting up another.

At four o'clock sharp they heard David Ben Gurion's first few words in Hebrew, then a translation of the Jewish Proclamation of Independence. "The Land of Israel was the birthplace of the Jewish people . . ."

"Israel?" Dr. Afifi said. "Is that what they're going to call it?"

"Could be," Dr. Tuffaha said, shrugging his shoulder.

"I was betting on Zion."

"They can call it Hell for all I care," Dr. Tuffaha said, pulling on his cigarette.

"But can they do that now?" Maria asked, looking at her watch. "Technically the British Mandate is still on."

It was Friday, Yousif remembered. The Jews were probably doing it eight hours early on account of their Sabbath. He tried to explain but was interrupted.

"Shh," Dr. Tuffaha said, leaning forward and listening.

"The recent holocaust," the translator continued, "which engulfed millions of Jews in Europe, proved anew the need to solve the problem of the homeless—"

"Oh sure," Dr. Afifi said, rolling his eyes, "you solve one problem by creating another one just like it. What are we going to do about our homeless?"

The screams of those at the cafe below reminded Yousif of the anger that had followed the decision to partition Palestine.

"Allahu Akbar," someone hollered.

A few bullets rang out and Yousif and all those with him rushed to the window. A tall, angry young man was standing in the middle of the clogged narrow street, pointing his revolver heavenward and still firing.

"Listen!" Yousif said, back to the radio.

"We hereby proclaim the establishment of the Jewish state in Palestine to be called Medinath Israel—The State of Israel—"

I-S-R-A-E-L!!!

The name scratched Yousif's body and soul like a steel brush on a tin sheet. It burned his ears like acid. The sweetest name on earth, Palestine, was to be replaced—at least in half the country—by a name so alien to him, so indigestible.

"In the midst of wanton aggression," the translator went on, "we yet call upon the Arab inhabitants of the State of Israel to preserve the ways of peace and play their part in the development of the State, on the basis of full and equal citizenship and due representation in all its bodies and institutions—provisional and permanent."

"WHAT A LIE!" Maria and Dr. Tuffaha said in unison.

"Tell it to the survivors of Deir Yasin," Yousif said.

"Even when they quote the Balfour Declaration they lie," the freckled doctor said, hissing like a punctured tube. "After it says 'His Majesty's Government views with favor the establishment in Palestine of a national home for the Jewish people,'" Dr. Tuffaha elaborated, "it goes on to say *'it being understood that nothing shall be done which may prejudice the civil and religious rights of the non-Jewish communities in Palestine . . .'* And what do our civilized, compassionate, moral, innocent, new Jewish neighbors do? They massacre a couple of villages and chase out tens of thousands from Jaffa and Haifa. That's what."

"God knows what else they have in store for us," Maria wondered.

Yousif wondered, too, feeling chilled.

NEXT DAY everybody was reading the newspapers. Yousif bought *Falastin* from old man Mussroor, who was carrying a big bundle of newspapers and shouting, "Last day of British Mandate . . . Last day of British Mandate." Izzat scurried with others and got *Ad-difaa'* from a younger peddler standing in front of Cinema Firyal screaming, "Earth-shaking events. Read all about them."

With hearts pumping, Yousif and Izzat sat at Zahrawi's Cafe and devoured the news. Yousif read about the Jewish meeting which had been held the day before at a museum on Dizengoff Street in Tel Aviv, where Ben Gurion had read the declaration for the establishment of a provisional government. He read about the British commissioner, Sir Alan Cunningham, who had left last night one hour before schedule. The reporter commented, "Instead of leaving at midnight, the commissioner miscalculated the time, bungled the last British act in Palestine, and left one hour early. It is a fitting close to a sorry mandate—one clouded with one mistake after another." He read about the Arab Armies which had begun to slip into Palestine during the night. He read about the Egyptians' raid on Tel Aviv. His heart pumped even faster, begrudgingly recalling an Arabic proverb, *in ma 'ikret ma sifyet,* meaning that things had to get worse before they got any better.

Yousif looked for statistics. He could find no new breakdown in numbers summing up Arab and Jewish strengths. The newspaper rustling in his hands, he recalled estimates that had left him unsettled. Whereas five Arab countries were lining up together in the fighting, each of them was willing to commit only a portion of her troops. These five Arab countries (Egypt, Jordan, Lebanon, Syria, and Iraq) would be engaging an army the Zionists had built under the eyes and nose of the British Mandate.

Yousif knew that Egypt was ruled by a corrupt playboy who cared more about his belly dancers than his armed forces. Lebanon was too tiny and fragile to make much of a contribution. The few hundred men she would post at her borders with northern Palestine would be only symbolic. Syria (like Lebanon) had only become independent from the French two years earlier. Her total armed forces were no more than three thousand men. The one battle-ready army that could make a difference was Jordan's Arab Legion. But how many of its ten thousand men would its British commander, Glubb Pasha, be willing to send to the front? That was the question most people asked. That was the question to which Yousif, and Salwa for sure, wanted an answer. Of all Arab regimes, Jordan and Iraq (ruled by the same Hashemites) were the "friendliest" to Britain. Would they oppose her policies? Could they even if they wanted to?

Bearing these facts in mind, Yousif felt uneasy as he turned over the pages of his newspaper. The Arabs were putting on a show the world would view as high drama. Egypt's Prime Minister, Mahmoud Nokrashy Pasha, had wanted to stay out of the war altogether. In reality the Arab regimes were rattling sabers to please the masses—but reluctant to fight. A case of a drum without sound. Or a sound without fury.

One item in particular caught Yousif's attention. It was Truman's swift recognition of the new Jewish State.

"Six minutes after Ben Gurion finished reading his speech. Can you believe it?" Yousif asked, putting down the paper.

"Even against the advice of his own State Department," Izzat answered.

"He wants to win reelection so bad he can taste it. What does he care about you and me?"

Similar sentiments were being expressed all around them. Men cursed. Others swore. One player shut the backgammon box with a bang.

Suddenly there was an excited roar and then the sound of gravel like bones being crushed under the feet of running men. Coming down the street before them was the first convoy of Jordanian soldiers, all of them wearing on their heads red and white *hattas.* They were riding in a score of Land Rovers and army trucks. Everyone, including Yousif, jumped to his feet and stood on a stone wall to watch the happiest sight in years. Palestinians clapped. Jordanian soldiers, mostly Bedouins—short, lean, dark, dressed in ankle-length desert robes, and wearing long hair or goatees—waved back. But where were the tanks and half-tracks, Yousif wondered? Where were the cannons?

"Ahlan . . . ahlan," Yousif heard the crowd cheering. "Most welcome."

"At long last!" Izzat screamed.

Yousif was uncertain. The prospect of a full-scale war did not thrill him. But he did hope it wasn't too late to recapture Haifa and Jaffa. Perhaps there would be no more Deir Yasins. Perhaps no more cities would fall. Yousif hoped for a quick solution; otherwise, it could get bloodier.

Izzat slapped him on the shoulder, grinning. Yousif was nervous, but he grinned back. Maybe there was something to cheer about, he thought. Soon the Syrians and Lebanese and Iraqis and Egyptians would enter. Maybe their arrival would sober up the Zionists. He couldn't wait for peaceful life to return to Ardallah. Then he and Salwa would live in a normal world.

THE FOLLOWING week, Yousif observed, was the most eventful in the history of the Arab-Jewish conflict. Now that the Arab armies were actually on the ground engaging the enemy, the Palestinians were buoyed by high hopes. Ben Gurion just might have to tear up that piece of paper and forget about Hertzl's cockeyed dream. But the optimism did not last long.

Seventy-six hours after the creation of Israel, Russia shocked Palestinians by recognizing Israel. The Arabs were trapped, Yousif heard people say. To make things worse, the fighting was not going well.

During the day, Yousif would spend his time reading, listening to the radio, and hearing people exchange information and rumors. Late in the afternoon, he would gather the provisions and head for the mountains to feed the watchmen. In the evening, he would visit his Uncle Boulus's house where the whole neighborhood would gather to rehash the news of the last twenty-four hours. Sometimes he and Salwa would hold court at his own house, as his parents had done. Izzat and Hiyam were always there, and so was Amin. Occasionally new arrivals from Haifa and Jaffa would join them—those who were now renting in the neighborhood.

"The Egyptians are really pushing," Izzat said, as they sat one starry night on the balcony. "They're about twenty-five miles south of Tel Aviv."

"The Iraqis are about to cut off Tel Aviv from Haifa," Hiyam added, clinging to her husband. "If they keep it up we should be all right."

Yousif was not convinced. "But the Lebanese and Syrians aren't doing much in the north."

"They captured Dajania in Galilee," Izzat argued. "And almost captured Acre. That's not bad."

"Not enough," Amin said. "And then the Jordanians? What have they done?"

"So far nothing," Yousif admitted.

"What do you mean nothing?" Hiyam said. "Glubb Pasha has his headquarters at Grand Hotel in Ramallah. He and his British commanders are drinking scotch and soda."

Several laughed. Yousif had not realized that Hiyam had a sense of humor.

"Hiyam and Amin are right," Salwa said. "When are they going to start? After all, the Arab Armies are all under King Abdullah's command. How can he order other armies around when he isn't committing his own?"

An uneasy silence hovered over the balcony. "He must have his reasons," Yousif offered. But deep down he knew that any excuse was a lame one.

SO FAR THE Jordanians themselves had not achieved any victories to speak of. But suddenly, a few days later, the Arab Legion began for the first time to unleash power that the so-called-Israelis had not seen before or even anticipated. The Arab masses, including Yousif, were elated. Yousif believed the quicker the victory the shorter the war. That meant fewer casualties on both sides.

The Jordanians' barrage terrified Jerusalem. Yousif and Salwa and their friends could not believe the sudden change. The whole of Arab Palestine was feverish with hope. Unexpectedly King Abdullah's Arab Legion tightened the grip on Jerusalem to the point of strangling its Jewish inhabitants. One newspaper account after another spoke of Jordanian artillery pounding Jewish strongholds. Photographs of Jordanian soldiers riding Jerusalem's ancient walls and aiming their guns on Jewish targets thrilled Arab readers. After a week of letting the Jews have their way, and leaving the defense of the Holy City to the Mufti's irregulars, the Jordanian army dealt the Zionists one blow after another. For a start they recaptured Mandelbaum Gate and Notre-Dame Hospice, then they seized kibbutz Kfar Etzion.

Now that the war was on, Yousif wanted to win. He followed the news with hunger. He read about the Jordanians who without the benefit of an air force were rendering the enemy helpless. From Shaykh Jarrah they blasted Jewish homes in Musrarah and convoys to Hadassah Hospital. From Mount Olive they hit the Jewish fortifications on the campus of Hebrew University on Mount Scopus. From the Muslim Quarter inside the old city they bombarded the Jewish Quarter. From Zion Gate they devastated Shamma'a. In many instances hand-to-hand fighting spread from street to street, from door to door. Soon the old walled city was well within the Jordanians' grasp.

Everywhere Yousif went he heard about new heroes. At the baker's shop where he picked up a hundred loaves of pita bread, he heard about Fawzi al-Qutub, born and raised in Jerusalem, the private citizen who with the help of a few friends blasted the *Jerusalem Post*, bombed Ben Yahuda Street, and leveled the Jewish Agency.

"Long live Fawzi al-Qutub," said the flour-covered Abul Banat.

At the grocery, where he picked up bushels of cucumbers, tomatoes, and apples, Yousif heard about Abdullah Tell, the Jordanian colonel, who was dealing havoc to the Jews of old Jerusalem.

"We need a few more like him," the grocer Abu Husni said, helping Yousif load up his car.

That night on one of the hilltops where Basim was staying, Yousif heard the men talk about the defenders not only of Jerusalem but of Latrun—where the Trappist monks had their monastery. But the Jordanian army was there, too, punching with all its military power.

Basim seemed to know many of the Jordanian officers. When he spoke of them his face was aglow. "Emile Jmai'an and Mahmoud al-Rousan repulsed the Jewish invaders three times," he boasted. "They are writing history with unbridled courage."

On another hill Yousif learned that Rassass and his British friend, George Pinkley, had gone to join Abdullah Tell in the attack on Jerusalem. Two days later they had been joined by ustaz Hakim. The hills of Ardallah were too quiet for those three.

But could the Arabs keep up the momentum, Yousif wondered? After all, Sarafand and its military camp had fallen into the hands of the Zionists, as had Acre after a long siege. Also, northern Palestine and the coastal areas were firmly held by the enemy.

DURING ONE of their walks, Yousif and Salwa crossed the marketplace. The little square was jammed with people, many more than usual. The newlyweds looked at each other, puzzled. What had happened? People were gathered in front of Darweesh Cafe listening to the radio. More people joined the crowd.

"Jordan's Legion Army has occupied East Jerusalem," the newscaster told them.

The crowd went crazy. Fists went up. Headdresses were thrown in the air.

"Shh," they told each other so they could listen.

"King Abdullah's valiant army has conquered the old city of Jerusalem. It has fiercely battled on the rooftops and in the blind alleys, and methodically destroyed the last pockets of Zionist resistance."

The crowd cheered. Even the announcer's voice became more ecstatic.

"Two rabbis were seen walking through the dust and smoke carrying the white flag of surrender. The Zionist remnants have been flushed out. Many of them have been seen fleeing outside the walls of the Old City. King Abdullah's brave army has cut off the supply lines to the Jewish underground in Jerusalem. The Tel Aviv-Jerusalem road has been blocked, making the Jewish surrender in the holy city of Al-Quds highly imminent. The leader of the Jewish Quarter himself, Rabbi Mordechai Weingarten, will sign the documents of surrender before *al-battal* Abdullah Tell."

The crowd cheered in unison. *"Al-battal Abdullah Tell . . . Al-battal Abdullah Tell,"* shook the valley.

"Wow!!!" Yousif said. "Abdullah Tell might pull us through."

"I always knew there's a god," Salwa said, squeezing his hand.

Suddenly, Yousif heard Basim's voice. But he could not see him. Momentarily, Yousif saw him being carried on the shoulders of four or five men. The crowd hushed in anticipation. The memory of Basim's speech on November 29, the year before, flooded Yousif's mind. On that black day, the United Nations had passed the resolution to partition Palestine.

"Hurray for the Arab Legion," Basim shouted, wobbling above the uneven shoulders of those carrying him.

The valley resounded with shouts of joy.

"This is the best news yet," Basim continued. "We need good news."

"YEEESSS," the crowd roared.

"Cheers for the brave," Basim shouted, his arms up in the air, "the liberators of Al-Quds—the Holy City."

Yousif could see his cousin was whipping up the crowd to a frenzy.

"But I have a question to ask," Basim continued, his mood now serious. "If the Arab Legion can occupy Old Jerusalem overnight, why has it been playing for the last two weeks? For the last two weeks both sides have been locked in a tug-of-war. Suddenly—boom—and Al-Quds is in our hands. What does this tell us?"

Like the rest of the five or six hundred men and women, Yousif waited in total suspense. Again, Salwa squeezed his hand.

"Two things. First, that someone has been holding back the valiant army from carrying out its sacred duty. Could it possibly be the one nicknamed Abu Honake, the Englishman who heads the Arab Legion? An Englishman commanding one of our armies is an abomination. Is Abu Honake taking orders from London itself? I smell a plot—a collusion. Someone is bargaining behind our back."

"For sure," Salwa screamed.

"Second," Basim went on above the sound of the crowd, "it should tell us that the Arab Legion is a strong army, capable of dealing the Zionists a heavy blow. Let it get on with its work. Let *al-battal* Abdullah Tell have a free hand. Let him lead his brave men and occupy the whole city—old *and* new. Don't you agree?"

Clenched fists went up in the air. "YEEESSS!" the crowd screamed.

Basim waved his arms for the crowd to settle down and hear him out. "The message we want to send to Amman is this: Victory can be ours. The great Arab Legion can win. Either stop playing politics or stop those who are. Whoever is playing games must stop. Don't hold back the army. For Allah's sake, for the sake of our national honor, and for the sake of our security—capture and hold all of Jerusalem."

"YEEESSS!" the crowd screamed again.

"And when the Jews start begging for a truce—for a lull in the fighting—don't listen."

"NO TRUCE," the crowd howled.

"Don't let the Jews trick us. Let their appeal to the United Nations for a halt in fighting go unanswered. Or better still, answer it with the sound of cannons. Pound them until they surrender."

"YEEESSS!" the crowd shouted.

"If we agree to a truce, they'll use the time as a breathing spell to retrench, to rearm, to come back at us with fury. And we're not *majaneen.* "

"No, we're not *majaneen,* " the crowd echoed. "We're not crazy."

"Go on winning," Basim exhorted, "until total victory is ours."

"YEEESSS!" the crowd responded as Basim got down and disappeared.

Holding Salwa's hand, Yousif pushed his way through the crowd trying to get hold of his cousin. There were things he wanted to discuss with him, things to tell him. But Basim had vanished.

28

The fighting raged on around Gaza, Galilee, and Jerusalem. But the truce Basim had alluded to did in fact turn out to be in the works. The United Nations' Count Folke Bernadotte was trying to arrange for a thirty-day cease-fire. The Arab masses were horrified. Yousif, however, was ambivalent. On the one hand, he was for a truce if it might lead to negotiations and peaceful solution. On the other hand, he could find no hint that the combatants would actually sit down and talk.

Day after day Yousif became more convinced that the Jews seemed poised to accept. The Arab leaders, however, were staunchly and—for once—unanimously opposed. News bulletins from Cairo, Baghdad, Amman, Beirut, Damascus, and all Arab capitals were shrill in warning against any kind of truce.

A week after Basim's oration in the marketplace, Yousif sat down to eat lunch. As he scooped a tablespoon of rice and *fassoolia,* one of the first meals his bride had attempted under the supervision of his mother, his eyes devoured the editorial page of *Al-Jihad* newspaper. He read:

> We will be the biggest fools on earth if we fall for a gimmick they are calling "truce." The so-called-Israelis are realizing that they have no staying power against our valiant soldiers. Now they want a "breathing spell."
>
> If we allow them to have it at this crucial time, we will be facing a

formidable enemy when the fighting is resumed. But if we continue to fight for a few more weeks, they will be hollering *"ya khali, ya 'ammi"*—as our man on the street would say.

Common sense will tell you that you do not take your foot off your enemy's neck until he "cries uncle." If we have patience, if we give our commanders and soldiers a free hand to fight in the tradition of our mighty warriors, we will savor victory.

And the Zionists will have learned never again to make the preposterous claim that Palestine is theirs but not ours.

But if we let the United Nations bamboozle us into accepting what they are tooting as a respite, we will *deserve* to be defeated. The fact that so-called Israel instigated the "truce" should tell us something. It should tell us that she is in trouble and we should not let her off the hook. Not until Palestine is free of her aggression.

Reject the truce we must. After all, who would want to listen to the counsel of the West, which is responsible for the Balfour Declaration? Who would want to dignify what the United Nations says—that body of ignoramuses who dared to partition our land?

Arabs everywhere, beware! Ring the alarm bells!

Leaders—are you listening? Say no to truce. Say yes to victory. Future generations will either bless you or curse you for what you do now. Let not the West—that unchallenged master of deceit—rob us of a victory that any blind man can see is within our grasp.

YOUSIF FINISHED gulping his lunch, anxious to get out. He needed to talk about the prospect of a truce with someone who knew more than he did. Besides, Salwa was busy with his mother, trying to learn how to be a homemaker.

Passing his high school, he decided to drop in on the principal, ustaz Saadeh. One of the best-informed men in town, the principal just might be able to explain the ramifications of the rumored truce.

"For us, it would be a colossal disaster," the principal predicted.

Ustaz Saadeh was watering the jasmine pot on the window sill of his office, overlooking the soccer field, when Yousif walked in. Now that he was through caring for his plant, he went back to his desk and sat down.

"What puzzles me is that the truce is not coupled with negotiations," Yousif said. "If they're going to talk about hammering out an agreement then it's okay. But—"

Ustaz Saadeh smiled a thin smile. "That's not what it's intended for."

"What then?" Yousif asked.

"To improve the Jews' chances," ustaz Saadeh answered, picking up his briefcase and putting it on his lap. "They still control Haifa and Jaffa, but on the whole the Jews aren't winning. They've been repulsed at Lydda and Ramleh. They've been repulsed at Latrun. They've lost Dejania in the north, not to mention Old Jerusalem. And don't forget that New Jerusalem, the largest Jewish population outside Tel Aviv, is still under siege. Their loudspeakers can be heard every day, begging for help. They seem to be running out of food and water. How long can this go on? If the war continues a few more weeks, Jerusalem is certain to fall. And so will the rest of Palestine. And it will all be ours."

Yousif waited for a different punch line. "So?" he said.

"It's not in the script, my boy," ustaz Saadeh said, emptying his brief case on his desk. "The script calls for the biggest plum in the pudding to go to the Jews. It's not happening. So stop the cameras and reshoot the scene."

"And we're going to fall for it?" Yousif asked. "If we continue to have the upper hand maybe the Jews will come to their senses and negotiate."

The principal shook his head, his smile as sunny as his office. "Yousif, listen to me. This piece of theater has been written over the last half century. Who gets what is preordained on paper. Now they must put it on the ground. No matter what it takes."

"You mean the Jews?"

"No, I mean the West. Listen, Yousif. Jews were murdered in Germany by the millions. Now Jews are vulnerable in Palestine. You think the world is going to sit by and let them lose?"

"The West persecuted the Jews. We didn't."

"Well, of course. And not only the Germans. The Russians, Spanish, French, and British before them. Britain threw them out for centuries. America won't even let them join her country clubs. Your father and I were in America and we know all about their gentlemen's agreement. Now they're all saints—lecturing us on how to behave. If rescuing the Jewish state means stopping the war and resupplying the Haganah with arms, under the guise of a truce, then there is going to be a truce."

"How phony," Yousif said.

"The whole world is phony," the principal said, growing solemn.

"But our leaders are against the truce," Yousif argued.

"So what?"

"The UN can't make us accept the truce if we don't want it."

"Then it will be imposed."

"We'll resist."

"Be realistic. We're in no position to do a damn thing. Remember, we're not fighting the Jews. The Jews we can handle. It's the big powers we have to worry about. They're strong and we're weak. For example: what can King Abdullah do when his government's entire budget comes from Britain? The salaries of his soldiers, his post office clerks, his teachers, his cabinet—all these salaries come in a package of twenty-five million pounds a year. And don't forget his army. All his guns and all his ammunition come from Britain. Even his top officers and the head of the army himself are British. Without this subsidy, the king will be running his kingdom on empty. If Britain wants him to have a truce—and it does—then he'll have a truce. As simple as that."

Yousif's throat went dry. "Then the Mandate isn't over," he said.

"The Mandate is over—but not Colonialism. Or even the Crusades. So-called-Israel will be the new European outpost."

"I thought it was the Jews who are using the West," Yousif said.

"Maybe they are. And maybe the West is using the Jews. Time will tell. What's clear is this: no matter who is using whom—we are being had. In plain Arabic, Palestine as we know it is doomed. Who knows—maybe one day a strong Arab will rise and unite us. Maybe then, and only then, will we be able to redeem ourselves."

Yousif was impatient. "We can't sit and wait. We have to organize."

The principal seemed to scrutinize his face. "Maybe we can—and I commend you for thinking that we should. But right now I'm afraid we're whistling in the wind."

Yousif's Adam's apple rose up and down. "Then you expect the truce to come about?"

"It's a given," ustaz Saadeh said. "I expect an announcement any day. But here's the rub: while we're sitting on our butts and gloating over our few minor successes, the Zionists will take advantage of the truce. They'll break the blockade of Jerusalem 'for humanitarian reasons.' And their European allies will send them one arms shipment after another."

Yousif felt jolted. "Maybe we're losing round one," he said, coming out of a mental fog. "There's still hope. Men like Basim and Abdullah Tell and Fawzi al-Qutub and Jmai'an and al-Rousan and ustaz Hakim aren't going to lie down and die. They'll find a way to fight back. Basim said so, and I believe him."

Ustaz Saadeh moved a piece of candy in his mouth, his round face ruddy. "It's not a matter of patriotism or courage. I'll put any Arab soldier, not just the ones you mentioned, against a dozen Jews any time. One on one the Jew doesn't have a chance. But there's a lot more to it than that. Our numerical superiority and our staying power will have no bearing on the outcome."

"Because of the international conspiracy?" Yousif asked.

"Which is nothing to sneeze at," the principal explained, nodding. "Important matters are being discussed behind the scenes—in chambers and corridors and across polished mahogany tables. The real battles have been fought and won in foreign capitals. Your father understood all this."

Suddenly Yousif was thrown back in time. He missed his father, who had fallen victim of such convictions.

No sunlight could penetrate the gloom that hovered over their heads.

"That's why I'm sorry you're not going abroad to complete your education," the principal said, reclining in his swivel chair.

"Why?" Yousif asked.

"Because you need to be ready for round two, to use your own words," his teacher told him, leaning on his elbow and chewing his lower lip. "Oh, I'm sure we're going to put up a resistance of some sort. But such things could go on for years. You need to get your education first. Then you can come back and fight the Zionists with your brain—not your muscle. Not your gun. That's how they fought us and that's how they're still fighting us. By using their brains."

Yousif rose to his feet. "You're beginning to sound like my father."

"Allah yirhamu," ustaz Saadeh said, his voice low. "One of the regrets of my life is having opposed him over the hospital money. He wasn't only good—he was wise."

Yousif smiled at his father's vindication. But as he left, his heart was heavy.

LATE THAT AFTERNOON, Yousif was telling his mother and Salwa and Jihan about his principal's dispassionate appraisal. While the three were enveloped in uncertainty, Izzat and Hiyam returned, their arms entwined. Yousif's heart leaped. But Izzat's face was paler than usual. Instead of greeting those in the house, Izzat stood at the door of the living room, looking like someone who had just lost his brother.

"What is it?" Yousif asked.

Izzat's lips twitched. "Both sides have accepted the truce."

Though expecting it, Yousif felt suddenly drained. "It really happened?" he asked, turning on the radio. "Where did you hear it?"

"On the news. The whole town is talking about it."

"Did they set a date?" Salwa asked, worried.

"June 11 through July 9," Izzat answered. "It starts this coming Friday at 10 o'clock."

"Jesus!" Yousif exclaimed.

"What did we do that for?" Jihan Afifi asked, her face blanched. "The Jews were losing. Now they could rearm."

"We didn't accept it just because we're foolish," Yousif's mother said. "God knows what threats and promises the big powers used to turn us around."

Jihan put out her cigarette and got up. Her husband would be very upset, she said. She picked up her navy-blue purse and left, as if her departure would ward off an oncoming disaster. Salwa saw her to the door, then returned, biting her fingernails. Yasmin stared out the window. Hiyam and Izzat sat on the sofa like two statues. The words of ustaz Saadeh rushed to Yousif's mind. Maybe they were watching a play. The curtain had just come down on Act I. The suspense during this intermission would be taut, chilling.

ON JUNE 11, both sides honored an agreement to stop fighting for thirty days. Long before Abdullah Tell signed for the Arabs and David Shlatiel for the Jews, the Arabs—including Yousif—were highly suspicious of each other's motives.

Again, Yousif read and heard about Arabs demonstrating against the truce. Again he began to read about unilateral violations by the so-called-Israelis.

One evening, two weeks later, Yousif and Salwa were sitting with Hiyam and Izzat on the balcony.

"What I want to know is this," Salwa said. "Since Israel is violating the truce, why do we have to honor it? Opening a new road and sending convoys to Jerusalem is clearly a violation. Why do we let them do it?"

Because that was not in the script, Yousif wanted to tell her. But he was too overwhelmed by the events to answer. His thoughts were interrupted by Izzat, who was turning the pages of a newspaper he was reading.

"The harbors of Haifa and Jaffa," Izzat read, "are buzzing with Zionists unloading arms shipments. They are not wasting a minute resupplying themselves. Loads and loads of mortars, machine guns, Sten guns are being shipped every day. Enough dynamite is being brought in to blow up Palestine over a hundred times."

Hiyam crossed her legs in anger. "In the meantime we're napping."

"Says who?" Yousif asked, sacrastic. "The Egyptians in Gaza are reading *al-baakooka*—the comic strips."

"Enough to make one puke," Salwa said.

Thirty days later, on July 9, the truce ended. It ended, Yousif knew, because Count Bernadotte's attempt at further mediation had failed. The Swede had drawn a new partition map which both sides rejected. The Arabs rejected it because partition by any other name was still a partition. To them the concept was unfair. The idea of establishing a Jewish state on Arab land was unthinkable. For their part, the Israelis rejected it because the count had parceled out the Negev and Jerusalem to the Arabs.

Now, Yousif knew, the Zionists were anxious to resume fighting. Why shouldn't they, he thought, now that they had tripled their strength? During the last month, they had enough time to train another army and to equip it with the best Europe and America had to offer. Within days, the Zionists broke through the blockade of Jerusalem. Now Ramleh and Lydda, two Arab strongholds near Jaffa—only fifteen miles west of Ardallah—were threatened.

One morning Yousif and Salwa sat in the living room listening to the news and drinking coffee.

"Before the truce," Yousif said, "the Arab Legion checked the Zionists' advances against Lydda and Ramleh. Now they're receiving fresh and deadlier attacks."

"Why not?" Salwa answered. "The Zionists have recovered their initiative. They're now much stronger and far more daring."

Yousif turned off the radio. "The rumors we heard about violations and illegal shipments during the truce all turned out to be true."

"It makes me sick."

AND THEN the refugees came—like a raging flood.

Early one morning in mid-July, Yousif opened the door to bring in the milk container and saw two women walking with huge bundles of clothing on their heads. He stopped and looked. A flood of other men and women followed, some carrying babies, others holding children's hands. They were coming from the west, from the direction of Lydda and Ramleh, which in the last few days had seen the worst fighting.

Yousif hurried inside and told Salwa and his mother. Salwa in turn knocked on Hiyam and Izzat's bedroom and woke them up. They all rushed out to see the street full of people filing past. Yousif walked toward the wrought-iron gate, followed by the others. The morning was quiet except for children crying and the ominous thud of a thousand feet. The long street down the hill was jammed with strangers. Men and women were carrying suitcases. Others were walking empty-handed. Many just sat anywhere they could, looking wide-eyed, tired, bewildered.

"My God," Salwa exclaimed, "there must be thousands of them."

A middle-aged woman carrying an infant dragged her feet toward them. "A glass of water, *ya khalti.*"

The misery in the woman's eyes broke Yousif's heart. He ran inside to get a pitcher and a few glasses. When he came out, he saw that some of the arrivals had turned in their driveway and were walking toward the house, dropping whatever they were carrying and collapsing. Cries for water rose from all directions as the strangers saw the tray of water in his hands. He filled the two glasses and handed them to those closest to him. A woman reached for the pitcher and took it from his hand. Yousif ran inside again to get more water. Yasmin and Salwa were right behind him.

"Salwa, *habibti,* start slicing some bread," his mother said, lighting the stove.

"How can we feed all these people?" Salwa fretted, reaching for a knife.

"We'll do all we can," Hiyam said, joining them.

"There must be at least a hundred in the front yard," Salwa said.

Izzat and Yousif took out all the glasses and pitchers they could find and filled them with water. But too many hands were outstretched. Too many eyes were begging. Yousif did not have enough drinking glasses to go around. The anguish on these faces appalled him. On his way back to the house, he saw Izzat energetically pumping the cistern. People were camping everywhere: in the driveway, on the Chrysler, on the doorsteps. Yousif could hardly make his way inside without stepping on someone.

From the balcony he could see that all the neighbors were faced with a similar situation. The street below his house was crowded. So was the street which led to the cemetery. Half an hour ago the refugees had arrived from one or two streets. Now they were converging from all directions. Ardallah was being overwhelmed with people. Everywhere he looked he saw streams of humanity. Because of their vast numbers, they seemed to stand still.

In less than fifteen minutes all the vegetables and fruits in their garden were consumed. Now they were short of groceries, so Salwa sent Yousif to the nearest store. He jumped off the balcony, crossed the neighbors' yard, and took shortcuts to avoid the crowds. Luckily he arrived at Salman's store early enough to get five dozen cans of sardines and Spam.

"Is it that bad?" Salman asked, beginning to feel the rush.

"You can't imagine," Yousif answered, hurrying out.

He carried the basket and went to another store for bread. He thought of the baker Abul Banat and decided to leave him alone. He'd probably be short of temper this morning. Everywhere Yousif went he was almost too late. The most he could get was a dozen loaves of pita bread. Fatima would have to bake more.

The avalanche of people continued. So did the steady stampede on groceries. Salwa had not asked him for any vegetables, but when he saw people reaching for everything in sight, he bought all the tomatoes and lettuce he could carry. Yousif carried the full basket and headed home. The streets were getting more congested by the minute.

All day Yousif worked in and out of the kitchen passing food and water. His mother took out the jars of cheese and olives and pickles she normally put up for winter and began to dish them out in plates and saucers. Salwa boiled eggs and potatoes. Hiyam sliced tomatoes and cucumbers and opened sardine cans. Yousif and Izzat delivered the food to the hungry crowds. Soon the people were in the house using the bathroom. There was a long waiting line. Yousif had to show them the out-house in the lower yard that served Fatima's family and the field workers.

At night they had to make room for some of the new arrivals to sleep in the house. Still they could not accommodate more than six or seven families. Yousif and Izzat moved furniture and spread extra mattresses around the floor. They spread carpets and rugs on the balcony and distributed pillows. Some had to bundle their jackets or sweaters or *abayas* under their heads. One man opened the car windows and put his two children to sleep on the front and back seats. Strange, Yousif thought, staring out the window. In the confusion he had not heard a single account of what had happened. All he could remember now was a woman saying they were lucky it was summer. Such an exodus in winter would have been hell.

It was a perfect cloudless night. Moonlight filled the bedroom. Before he went to bed, Yousif checked on his mother in the adjacent room. She had looked weary and he wanted to make sure she was all right.

He knocked, then opened the door. "Mother," he said, "have you taken your blood pressure pill?"

"No use," she said quietly.

Her voice was so low he had to strain his ears.

"Whoever thought Lydda and Ramleh would fall?" she asked. "That's the beginning of the end."

Yousif nodded. "Lydda's men are known for their courage. They wouldn't have left on their own."

"Absolutely not. They would've come out fighting. Not like this. Not like herded sheep."

Yousif couldn't say anything that would make her feel better. His mind wandered. It occurred to Yasmin that the doors of the house were open with so many strangers roaming around.

"Nearly everything we own is in this house," she whispered, "yet I'm not afraid. Maybe I should be, but for some reason I'm not."

A baby began to cry outside the bedroom door. Yousif could hear the mother trying to calm it. Muffled voices from outside came through the open window. Yousif looked out. The view was panoramic. The night sky had a soft, blue tone. Under the fruit and pine trees, the ground was strewn with sleeping bodies.

EARLY NEXT MORNING some of the people on Yousif's property began to leave. By noon half of them were gone. More victims were on the street, staggering. But now Yousif could see Jordanian army vehicles and private automobiles meeting the weary crowds at the edge of town and carrying them to open fields.

For Yousif, however, the day promised to be as hectic as the one before. A quick trip to the *souk* assured him there was no let-up in what had to be done. Mobs were bottlenecked in the narrow streets. The spacious court in front of the Greek Orthodox church was overflowing. Some families became separated from each other. Children were looking for their parents, parents for their children. The turmoil made the chances of their finding each other most difficult.

Here and there Yousif heard snatches of dialogue. They had been forced to travel up and down the rocky mountains on foot, a man was saying. They had been forbidden to use the highways because the enemy claimed to need them for military purposes. Several men were gathered around the husky unshaven young man who was telling his story. Yousif joined the listeners and heard the man describe the brutal march up and down the mountains.

"It was awful," the man recounted. "Guns behind our backs, guns over our heads. But the worst part about it was the heat. Simply unbearable. A drop of water was more precious than gold. Several people died from thirst."

Yousif's throat tightened. Others cursed and shook their heads.

"What did you do with the dead?" a cigar-smoker asked.

"Left them behind," the unshaven man answered. "What else could we have done? God knows what happened to them by now."

Yousif could only imagine the corpses in the heat. Food for worms, he thought, remembering his father. He chewed on his lower lip.

"Didn't the Jordanian army try to meet you?" a watermelon vendor asked.

The displaced man nodded sarcastically.

"Sure," he said. "On the outskirts of Ardallah. It was hot like hell and we'd been walking for more than twenty hours. The distance we crossed was about twenty miles, but it felt ten times longer because of the terrain. Up and down the mountains. Up and down. When we got to the highway, there was a prim and proper soldier standing by his jeep. He took one look at a woman and saw the hem of her dress raised above her knee and the front of her dress open. 'Have you no shame, woman?' he said gruffly. 'Cover up before you embarrass the men around you.'"

Like the rest of the men around the unshaven narrator, Yousif smiled cynically. He could only imagine the woman's reply.

"What did she say?" Yousif asked.

"She just looked at him with contempt," the narrator continued. "'Men, did you say?' she asked. 'I don't see any men. If there were men around we wouldn't be refugees. There are no men around here. You show me real men and I'll cover up. I wouldn't think of embarrassing them.'"

Yousif walked home thinking of the story he had just heard. He found Salwa and his mother and Hiyam sitting on the doorstep crying while trying to console a hysterical young woman. She was a bride of a few weeks, she sobbed, when Lydda had fallen. A little girl who had just climbed down a tree came and stood by her. She was her niece, a six-year-old girl with rosy cheeks and round black eyes full of wonder and light. Yousif thought she was the most adorable child he had ever seen.

"Two Israelis came to our house and told us to leave. They pointed their guns at us and we felt there was no sense in arguing with them. I told them I'd like to take a few things with us, but one of them put the muzzle of his gun up my face and said not to touch a thing. Just move."

"Damn them!" Salwa said.

"So we moved. We were almost outside the front gate when one of them shouted to wait. He came running behind us. He said he wanted to search us for jewelry. But my husband and I said we had no jewelry except our wedding bands. We took them off and handed them to the soldier, but he wanted to frisk us. While I was pleading with them to let us go, my husband tried to escape. He had all our jewelry hidden on his body and couldn't stand there and let them rob us. So he tried to run away. But as soon as he started to run, they shot him in the back."

"Aaaaaah!!!" the audience gasped.

"He fell to the ground and died on the spot," the young bride continued, wiping her tears. "They emptied his pockets and his shoes and took every piece of jewelry we owned and all the money he had on him."

"Tell them how he slapped you," the six-year-old girl prodded, her eyes shining.

"He slapped me on both sides," the bride said, combing the little girl's hair with her fingers.

"Ikassir idaih," the young girl said. "May his hands be broken."

Yousif's mother made the sign of the cross over the young girl's head and invoked God to protect her from the evil eye.

"Then he pushed me with the butt of his gun," the young woman continued.

"I threw myself on my husband's body and began to scream. But they picked me up and kept shoving me until I joined the rest of the crowd at the edge of town."

Her crying turned into intense sobbing. Yousif saw all the women's eyes fill up again with tears.

He turned to the little girl. "What's your name?"

"Zahra," she said, with confidence beyond her age.

"That's a pretty name," Yousif told her. "Tell me, Zahra. What are you going to do when you grow up?"

"I'm going to kick them in the shin," she said, demonstrating with her tiny foot.

No one laughed. Yousif wasn't sure who would start the inevitable revolution—the Arab forces that were being denied a victory or the Arab masses who were being victimized. If he were a betting man he'd bet on the Zahras of the future.

THAT EVENING, after all the refugees had left Yousif's ground, Yasmin could not wait for Izzat and Hiyam to leave the house. While they were getting ready to go out, Yousif could hear his mother and wife whispering and then opening and closing many drawers.

"What was the banging all about?" Yousif asked his mother as she came into the living room. "What are you two up to?"

"We were looking for these," Yasmin told him, holding a hammer and a chisel.

Yousif did not understand. He looked to Salwa for an explanation.

"She thinks we need to hide the jewelry," Salwa told him. "You heard what the people of Lydda and Ramleh said. The Zionists will rob us if they come."

Yousif put down the book he was reading. "Mother, the Zionists are not coming here."

His mother paid him no attention. "Don't bet on it," she said. "Come, let me show you."

Salwa went back to the kitchen. Yousif followed his mother into her bedroom. "Where do you think is the best place?" Yasmin asked.

"Under the chifforobe. But I don't think—"

Without giving him a chance to finish, she opened the chifforobe and began to empty it. First she took out her dresses and laid them on her bed. In the meantime, Yousif, resigned to what she was about to do, began taking out the bottom drawers and stacking them in the hallway.

"What are we going to do with your father's clothes?" she asked, breathing hard.

Yousif had a lump in his throat when he saw all his father's suits. "Put them on the other bed," he told her.

"I mean what are we going to do with them?" she asked again. "We can't keep them in the house forever."

"Let's not talk about it," he said, putting his shoulder to the chifforobe. It was a big tall closet with two long mirrors on front of it. But now that it was empty, he could move it inch by inch.

"Let me help you," she said.

"It's better if I do it alone," he told her.

After he had cleared a tile that was sitting right under the chifforobe, Yousif took the tools and crouched down. Very gently he went around the tile, chiseling and hammering and blowing the dust away until he loosened it. Then he put the chisel under one side and lifted it up. He was pleased he had done it without chipping or breaking the beautiful tile which bore Arabesque decorations in light blue. Then he began digging a hole which he knew would have to be at least five or six inches deep.

By the time he was through, his mother came into the room. Under her left arm she was carrying a bundle wrapped in a white and green scarf. He knew it was the jewelry. In her hand was a small tin can in which she was stirring a cement mix.

"Are you sure this is what you want to do?" he asked, taking the bundle from her.

"Why not?" she said, watching him unwrap it.

The gold bracelets, crosses and chains, and the diamond rings and broaches and watches were all there. In his hand was a little treasure. She had two diamond rings that were worth some money: one two karats and the other four karats. Even Salwa's diamond ring and bracelets were there. Even a bride wasn't allowed to show off her wedding treasures, he thought.

"What are you going to do every time either of you needs them? Dig them up?"

"I won't need them," she said, "until the war is over."

Yousif wasn't sure. "If you say so," he said, bending down to bury them under the ground and re-cement the tile.

After he had finished, Yousif washed his hands in the bathroom. Then the smell of cumin filled his nostrils and he went to watch his mother teach Salwa to cook. She was preparing *bamiyeh* with meat and a side dish of rice. The dried okra was tiny and browned just as he liked them.

"Do you think we should take our money out of the bank?" he asked, standing behind his mother.

Yasmin stirred the pine nuts in the skillet, thinking. "Maybe we should get some of it."

"The Zionists might steal it from us. But there's a chance we may be able to sneak out with some of it."

"Good thinking," Salwa told him, piling rice on a platter.

Yousif threw the towel over his shoulder. "I'll get to the bank early in the morning," He said.

AN HOUR LATER, Yousif saw his Uncle Boulus in the driveway walking toward the house. He looked paler and thinner than usual.

"Some Ardallah families are getting ready to leave," his uncle informed them, lighting a cigarette. "I can't really say I blame them."

Yousif and Salwa were disappointed; his mother was sympathetic.

"I can't blame them either," Yasmin said, placing an ashtray next to her brother. "Maybe we should go away ourselves."

"We just may," the uncle confided, crossing his legs. "If only for a few weeks or months until the storm passes over."

"That's running away," Yousif objected. "At least the people of Lydda and Ramleh were driven out. We haven't been."

His uncle seemed irritated. "The handwriting is on the wall," he lectured him.

There was a pause. What bothered Yousif most was the calm and finality with which his uncle brushed him aside. Yousif remained quiet and watched his uncle stare out the window. Beneath the surface, the older man's nerves seemed jangled.

Still, Yousif refused to give in. "I wish father were alive to see them running away like rabbits."

"That's what I say," Salwa said in a huff.

His uncle looked at them curiously. "I'm surprised at both of you. I'd like for you two to show understanding and compassion and not to be so quick condemning people and calling them names. Maybe you're not afraid. But most people are. The stories they hear from the refugees are scaring them. The enemy has consolidated its gains on the coast and is probably getting ready to go after central Palestine. Logic will tell you we'll be next. After all, how far are they from us now? No more than a twenty-minute drive. Who's going to stop them if they show up with their tanks and planes? The thirty or forty guns Basim bought?"

"We now have fifty-two guns and two mortars," Salwa explained. "And Basim keeps looking for more."

"By the time he finds any it may be too late. Besides, what will fifty-two guns and two mortars do in a full-scale war like this?"

"No kidding!" Yousif said. "That's what my father used to say when all of you ganged up on him."

"I didn't gang up on him. Besides, forget about your father and the hospital money. Your father is dead. If any of that money is left it can't be much. Be sensible. Look at things as they are. Whoever thought the Zionists would have the ability or audacity to raid Damascus, Amman, and Cairo? But they did."

"And what did the Arabs do?" his mother asked. "Nothing."

"The Syrians are still bogged down in the north," his uncle continued. "The Iraqis came close to cutting off Haifa from Tel Aviv. But you see, King Abdullah is the commander-in-chief of all Arab armies engaged in this war. Which is fine. The trouble is, Glubb Pasha heads his army. And what do you know! This damn Englishman objected to what the Iraqis were doing."

"They were messing up Britain's plans," Yousif said.

"He warned them to stop their push or he'd cut off all the ammunition."

"That's when they began saying *ako slah mako awamer,* "Salwa said. "We have the weapons but not the orders."

"Do you think that Glubb Pasha is working in our behalf? Or is he here to implement Britain's policies?"

Yousif remained unmoved.

"All right then," his uncle continued. "How can we fight a war with our hands tied behind our backs? It's all politics. Dirty politics at that."

Yousif remembered his conversation with his principal. "Ustaz Saadeh calls it a piece of theater."

"I call it a farce," Uncle Boulus said, lighting a cigarette.

Yasmin exhaled. "People are not stupid," she said. "They can read the signs."

Brother and sister seemed to be working in concert, Yousif thought.

"We all know," Uncle Boulus said, "that the other Arab governments can win if they put their mind to it. For some odd reason they don't seem to be doing it. The enemy is well-equipped and strong—especially after the truce. What do you expect unarmed people to do? Wait for a miracle?"

Yasmin got excited and began to fan herself with a handkerchief. "It's hopeless," she said, her face creased with worry. "What's the sense of denying it?"

Yousif knew that he had lost the argument, but could not accept the facts. "If Uncle leaves, you go with him. Salwa and I are staying."

"Absolutely," Salwa said, walking out.

"I will not budge without you two," Yasmin said. "What do you think I am—crazy?" She got up, looked out the window, then followed Salwa out of the room.

"Leaving isn't that easy either," the uncle reflected, flicking his worry beads. "It takes money. And that's something I'm short of at the moment."

What startled Yousif most about the confession was the sadness in his uncle's voice. He had always thought him to be financially comfortable, if not rich. He must have been living far beyond his means, Yousif surmised.

"Business hasn't been too good the last few months and I, uh, I lost what I had . . . at the poker table," the uncle explained. "I hit a losing streak that wouldn't stop. Every time I tried to recover my losses I sank deeper. Now I even have a mortgage on my house."

"You what?"

"Very few people know it. Not your mother, not even my wife."

His uncle's fingers clicked the *masbaha* nervously. And for the first time Yousif noticed the dark rings under his eyes.

"I'm sorry," Yousif said. "I really am."

For his proud uncle to admit such a secret to his young nephew, Yousif realized, was tantamount to stripping himself naked. A soul had just been shamed before his eyes.

"Whatever we have is yours," Yousif offered, fixing his uncle with a meaningful look. "You know that."

Emotion, unarticulated and genuine, passed between them.

29

Within a week, about ten thousand of the refugees who had come to Ardallah departed further inland to towns such as Ramallah and Nablus. Many left the country altogether, headed toward Jordan and Syria. The six or seven thousand who stayed behind were mostly the feeble or destitute who could neither afford to pay their way nor walk the distance.

Overnight, refugee camps sprouted all over Ardallah. The neighborhood playground was not spared. Yards belonging to churches, mosques, or schools were found ideal. Yousif's schoolyard was among the first to be converted. Some of the refugees tied the four corners of a green or yellow bedspread to a tree, a window or a post they stuck in the ground, and made it their shelter. Some had fought their way into the marketplace and managed to obtain a tent from a Jordanian army truck, which they raised in the middle of an empty field. Those, Yousif thought, were the lucky ones. Many simply camped out in the open air.

Just before dawn, Yousif was awakened by the sound of bombs exploding in the distance. Was it an air raid, he thought? Where was Basim?

He woke up Salwa. Then the two met Yasmin and the other couple in the dark corridor. They all rushed to the living room to determine the source. Yousif opened the window. Heavy firing was coming from behind the cemetery on the opposite hill. Yousif hurried to the west balcony, followed by the others. From there they could hear some distant screams and see many lights dotting the mountaintop.

"Oh no!" his mother cried, putting on the pink bed-jacket she was carrying. "It's an attack."

Sporadic firing increased. One car was heard screeching and shifting gears. The valley echoed shouts and incoherent cries, coming from all directions. On the balcony the four listened, mesmerized.

"It's a major attack," Izzat concluded. "The Israelis must've entered the town."

"What's happening on the hilltops?" Yousif asked. He was thinking of Basim.

"I won't be surprised if there were casualties already," Izzat said, putting his arm around Hiyam's shoulders.

"I'm going to find out," Yousif told them, rushing inside.

"Find out how?" his mother asked, alarmed. "Where are you going?"

"Our men need help," Yousif said, taking off the robe and reaching for yesterday's clothes that were piled on a chair in his room.

Salwa urged him to go; Yasmin begged him not to be hasty.

"Wait for me," Izzat said, from his room. "I'll go with you."

Yousif thought of the money that they might need. He realized now he had made a mistake not withdrawing all of it from the bank. He had left only ten pounds in the checking account but had not touched the savings.

"You're not listening," his mother complained, putting her hand on him.

"No, I'm not," Yousif said, buttoning his shirt and rushing into the corridor.

"Auntie!" Salwa protested. "You expect him to sit here while the town is being invaded?"

"What can he do?" Yasmin asked. "He can't even fire a gun."

"He'll learn," Salwa said, confident.

Hiyam was almost in tears. "I'm scared," she told her husband.

"You'll be all right," Izzat said, stuffing his shirt in his pants. "Just lock the door and keep each other company."

His car keys in hand, Yousif rushed out of the front door. Izzat was right behind him.

They got in the car in a hurry. Yousif turned the ignition and started to back out of the driveway. Izzat shouted at the women standing on the balcony to go inside and lock the door behind them.

But as Yousif tried to back out through the iron gate, a jeep suddenly pulled up and blocked their way. Two uniformed men wearing helmets jumped out, their guns at the ready.

One of the soldiers was tall and slender. The other was shorter, heavier, with a thick mustache. Yousif knew they were Israelis.

"Get out," the tall soldier demanded in English, pointing his gun through the open window. It was no more than inches from Yousif's temple.

Yousif froze. He cut off the engine, his mind racing. What could he do? He had no gun. Izzat was unarmed. The two soldiers were flanking them, nervous.

Yousif and Izzat glanced at each other.

"I said get out," the same soldier barked, touching Yousif's chin with his barrel.

"Oo inteh kaman," Yousif heard the burly soldier tell Izzat. "You too. *Inzal.*"

Yousif nodded, opening the door. He did not dare look at Izzat. But he could hear the other door opening and closing.

To Yousif, the walk between his car and the front door of his own house was torturous. All kinds of thoughts and fears went through his mind. The moment everyone had dreaded came true. The Zionists had invaded. They had beaten all of Ardallah's defenses and probably killed Basim. What were the invaders going to do now? Occupy Ardallah? Disarm the people, put them under curfew?

The darkness of the hour was soon criss-crossed by the headlights of several speeding cars. Yousif could hear tanks rumbling up the opposite mountain and on the street below. His mind flashed back to the summer before. He remembered the nine Jewish men and women who had descended the bus wearing short shorts and carrying duffle bags on their backs. The spade work of those spies, he thought now, was paying off.

"Iftah al-bab," the tall soldier ordered Yousif, nudging him with the tip of his gun. "Open the door."

Of course, Yousif thought. One of the attackers spoke Arabic like a native. Yousif tried the handle but the door was locked.

"Tell them to open up," the same soldier commanded.

As though in a nightmare, Yousif found himself knocking on his own door, hoping it would not open. He could imagine his mother and Salwa inside, clinging to each other, worried stiff.

"I'm warning you," the tall soldier said in English, clicking his gun. "If the door is not open in one minute I'll shoot."

"Mother, Salwa, open the door!" Yousif pleaded. "They'll kill us if you don't."

"Hiyam, hurry up," Izzat begged. "It's serious."

Yousif bit his lip, knocking louder and louder. He thought he heard Salwa's footsteps, but then the screams in the streets drowned the sound.

"Thirty seconds," the tall soldier said, the barrel of his gun resting on Yousif's shoulder.

The key clicked. The iron bar was unlatched. The handle was now moving.

The door opened. The two soldiers pushed Yousif and Izzat in front of them, using them as a shield. Yousif's mother looked like Mary at the foot of the Cross. Salwa was wide-eyed and stiff. Hiyam looked sickly, panic-stricken. She tried to run to her husband but one of the soldiers blocked her with his gun.

The short, burly, mustached soldier kept his gun on Izzat and Yousif. In the light Yousif could tell that his face was pock-marked. The tall soldier had a concave chest and odd way of walking. He seemed to throw his feet in front of him.

"Anyone else in the house?" the soldier barked, his blue eyes roaming all over the house. He seemed to be in charge. Yousif took him for an officer, even though he saw no stars or stripes on his earth-colored uniform.

Yousif and the other three occupants shook their heads.

"Out," the tall soldier said, pointing to the door with his gun.

Yousif thought they were crazy. Why did they bring him and Izzat in then? But his mind was in a riot. He couldn't worry about their idiocy. The main thing was to survive.

"Out where?" Yousif asked.

"Out of the house," the officer said. "And out of town. It's being occupied."

Hiyam and Yousif's mother began to cry, but not Salwa. Unable to reach their men, they clung to each other. For a moment, Yousif wanted to jump the invader and wrest his gun from him. But he soon felt the muzzle of the second gun in the narrow of his back.

"We just got here from Haifa," Izzat protested. "We can't be pushed out twice in a month."

"That's your problem," the soldier spoke again. "Out. And do it quickly."

"Bavakasha," Yousif's mother pleaded.

Like everyone in the room, Yousif looked at his mother—surprised. What was she saying?

"Haeem atta medaber Hebrew?" the officer asked. "You speak our language?"

"Lo," Yasmin answered, shaking her head. "Only a word or two. I used to know more when I lived in Jerusalem."

The officer studied her from head to toe. "It doesn't matter. Out," he grunted.

"Bavakasha," Yousif's mother again pleaded. "Please. Occupy the town, do what you want. But don't force us out. This is our home. We can't leave it. Where would we go?"

"Go to Abdullah," the burly soldier told her, stepping on her bare toe in his attempt to block her from going anywhere.

"Abdullah?" she cried, looking at her son.

"Abdullah?" Hiyam asked, bewildered. "Where's Abdullah?"

"He means King Abdullah," Salwa explained. "Trans-Jordan."

"Go to Abdullah. Go to Abdullah," the soldier repeated, anxious to get rid of them.

Through the door, Yousif could see his Uncle Boulus and his wife, Aunt Hilaneh, pushed out on the street. He could see the Haddad family, Hiyam's sister and husband and children, milling in the square. There were many mothers carrying children, and he could hear their crying.

But now Yousif felt powerless. And he hated himself because Salwa was there to see him in such a state. Only a few days ago he had been haranguing all those who were thinking of leaving. He had wanted them to stay and fight. Fight with what? he now asked himself. He wondered about Basim and the men on the hilltops. Were they fighting? Did many of them get killed? He thought of Amin and his family. What were they doing? And how was Maha, Basim's wife, handling the children?

Yousif looked at the two soldiers with machine guns. What could he do to defend his women? Nothing. His head buzzed. Obey. No. Defy. Obey. Defy. Defy. Obey. Shame filled his being.

He heard his mother speak.

"As you say," she said to the soldier, squeezing her son's hand. "Just give us time to put on some clothes and throw a few things in a suitcase."

"Are you crazy?" the burly pockmarked soldier said. "There's no time. What do you think this is? Move."

"Go out like this?" Salwa asked, shocked. "In our robes?"

"As you are," the same soldier commanded.

Izzat became furious. He looked at his wife in her flimsy gown and robe, put his arm around her protectively. "My wife is not going out like this," he said. "She's practically naked."

"Shut up," the tall soldier warned him.

"We're willing to cooperate," Izzat explained, "but you must give us a chance to put on some clothes."

"You want a chance, we'll give you a chance," the soldier said, reaching for Hiyam.

"Hey, wait a minute," Izzat protested, holding on to his wife. "What are you going to do?"

"We're going to give you a chance to watch her ass getting fucked," the soldier answered.

The arrival of two more soldiers on the balcony seemed to make the tall officer more cocky, for he confidently motioned with his head and spoke to the other soldier in Hebrew. Yousif watched their every movement. What he saw gave him a glint of hope, although he didn't know why. The two soldiers seemed to be arguing with each other. The tall soldier raised his voice and the shorter burly soldier shook his head and then stormed out of the house. Yousif looked at his mother for a clue, for she seemed to remember a few words of Hebrew. But she either didn't know what they were saying or was afraid to do any interpreting. But what they were arguing about soon became clear. The tall soldier handed his gun to one of the new arrivals and began to pull Hiyam from her husband. She screamed. Izzat enfolded her with both arms. Now the two new soldiers, one with a violet birthmark on his left cheek, the other with a scar above his right eyebrow, moved in on Izzat, hitting him with the butts of their guns.

Yousif sprang forward and tried to pull them away from Izzat. But the two men turned on him and flattened him against the wall with their fists. Stunned by the quick blows, Yousif saw the whole room spinning. He shook his head to recover his senses, and felt his cheeks burning.

The soldier who was now carrying two guns leaned one of them against the wall to better restrain Izzat, who was fighting like a cornered cat. In a split second Yousif saw his chance and dashed for the gun against the wall.

"Leave that girl alone or I'll shoot, so help me God," Yousif threatened, thankful for Basim's lesson in handling firearms, however brief.

He had them at a disadvantage and was determined to fire at the slightest provocation. Outraged by what they were about to do, he felt raw energy run through his veins, cleansing his system of any doubt or fear. Without his gun the tall soldier looked like a mouse, and the other two had their arms entangled with Izzat's. Yousif was the only one with the gun at the ready. And he was poised to blast them off, the barrel of his gun inching from one head to another.

"You asked us to leave and we said we would," Yousif protested. "What more do you want? Must you rape to be satisfied?"

The room stood still. Eyes became glazed. Silence reverberated.

"Don't move," a voice commanded.

Yousif's heart sank. He could recognize the voice as that of the burly soldier, who apparently had crept back from the balcony and was now standing behind him, his barrel inches from his neck. Salwa and Yasmin shrieked in unison.

As Yousif's gallantry evaporated, one of the soldiers stepped forward and took the gun from his hand. Yousif surrendered it without a whimper. Repossessing the gun, the mouse turned into a lion. He moved toward Yousif briskly, and slapped him on the face.

"One more stunt like that and I'll fuck you, too," he said, slapping Yousif on the other cheek. Then he walked away, motioning for the new arrivals to bring Hiyam to him.

The soldier with the birthmark and the one with the scar above his eyebrows pulled Hiyam from her husband's embrace and led her to the adjacent living room. Yousif's mother covered her eyes with her hands. Izzat turned around and buried his head in a corner, plugging his ears with his fingers. His cheeks still burning from the couple of slaps, Yousif fully understood the meaning of helplessness. His heart ached for Hiyam and her husband. What if they raped Salwa? Or his mother? But the house was bursting with motion and he was too dazed to think any further.

Yousif shifted his eyes from one room to the next. In the foyer where they were standing, the soldier with the scar on his eyebrow had returned and was now forcing Izzat to turn around and look. Then the soldier with the birthmark pulled Yasmin's hands from her eyes. By showing no sign of shame or anger, Salwa seemed to escape their attention. In the living room, the tall soldier put his helmet on the round table and threw Hiyam on the sofa, pushing her clothes above her waist. Hiyam tried to cover herself and flee, but the Zionist soldiers again overpowered her. Yousif heard the metallic tear of a zipper. He saw him force Hiyam's panties off and plunge himself between her naked thighs.

Izzat trembled and closed his eyes. The Zionist was pushing himself in and out of Hiyam, oblivious to her pitiful cries and her hands trying to push him away. Yousif saw his mother faint and fall. He bent over her to try and revive her. He patted her cheeks, still hearing the sofa's springs squeak rhythmically under the officer's thrusts. A moment later he heard the officer grunt and looked up to see him collapse on Hiyam's body.

Yousif and Izzat were forced to watch the soldier zip up his pants with a sickening smirk on his face, then pick up his helmet as though he had done nothing unusual. To Yousif, the humiliation was unbearable. Hiyam covered her face with a pillow and began to sob; Izzat stared, his eyes glazed and wild. His mother still lying on the floor unconscious. Yousif scanned the room for some water to sprinkle on her face. But before he could rise, the soldier with the birthmark reached for the vase by the mirror and dumped the water and the tulips on her face and neck. She looked like a corpse in a coffin ready to be buried. Yousif was outraged. But the splashing of water made her stir. Yousif was relieved to see her open her eyes.

"Now get some clothes on," the rapist soldier demanded, winking at his comrades.

"Todaraba," Yousif's mother said.

Yousif understood the Hebrew word. It meant thank you very much. Why in hell was his mother thanking the attackers? He looked at her and then at Salwa, shocked. But she looked pitiable. The poor woman, he realized, had lost her senses.

"You have less than a minute," the soldier said to Yousif, "or we'll fuck the rest, including you."

Yousif knew better than to argue. They threw clothes on their backs and were ready to leave. Their arms around each other, as if to hide their unspeakable shame, Izzat and Hiyam hurried out of the house. The crowd on the street was big and Yousif did not want to lose them. He wanted them to wait so they could journey together and look after each other. But Hiyam and Izzat seemed encapsulated in a world of hate and disgust. Yousif respected their wish to be alone. With more tears in his heart than in his eyes, he watched them reach the wrought-iron gate. As they merged with the flock of displaced people, he wondered if they would be able to catch up with them. In a flash of despair, he even wondered if he would ever see them again.

"The keys, Mother," Yousif said, searching his body. "The keys."

"What keys?" she asked, frantic.

"Salwa, where are the car keys? I put them down somewhere."

"Yes, find them," the officer said, glad they remembered.

Was there a shift in the soldier's attitude? Yousif wondered. First he had let them put on some clothes, and now he was anxious for them to find the car keys. When at last Yousif found them under a book on his dresser, the tall soldier snatched them from him.

"You can't have the car," the officer told them, pocketing the keys and pushing the four off the front veranda. "The military needs all the vehicles and all the highways. Hit the mountains."

"Look," Yousif protested, trembling. But the sight of the compact gun in the officer's hand made him stop.

The officer walked away, arrogance pouring out of his eyes. Suddenly, a thought crossed Yousif's mind. He remembered something he had to do. Yasmin and Salwa were standing in the yard, their arms loaded with dresses. The other young soldiers with the birthmark and scar were a few steps away, their guns at the ready. Yousif was alone with the short heavyset soldier.

"Listen," Yousif begged. "I've got to get back to the house."

"Absolutely not," the pudgy soldier objected.

"Please. It would only take a minute. Come with me if you like."

"There's no time. Move, I said."

"Here, take this. It's a gold watch. Take it, I don't mind. Just let me go in for a minute."

Yousif slipped off his wrist the watch that had once belonged to his father. The soldier took it and put it in his pocket without looking at it. The two regarded each other.

"If you try something foolish, I'll kill you," the soldier warned, his look deadly.

"Promise," Yousif said. Then he ran up the steps and entered the house.

The heavyset soldier was at his heels.

Yousif went directly to the aviary. Daylight was creeping in gently. The birds were up, their cheery chirping and singing filling the room. He entered it, his heart fluttering as much as the birds around him. The soldier with the gun stood at the door. Yousif walked to the east window. Without the slightest hesitation he opened it for the first time in a year. The birds began to fly out. He opened one chamber after another until all the birds became aware of the open window and sought the outdoors. The lattice iron slowed down their escape. Some of the openings were jammed with birds. Smiling at their hurry, Yousif walked to the window facing the balcony.

"You're taking too much time," the soldier snapped.

Yousif seemed unconscious of the remark. Nothing mattered now, he thought. The soldier and the whole rotten world could go to hell. With some effort, Yousif jarred the window loose and opened it. Again he watched the same rush repeated. In less than a minute the whole room was empty. Yousif stood in the middle of the room, as though his own soul had taken flight. He surveyed the cages with the moving swings and the food and water containers. Now they looked deserted—as Ardallah soon would be.

"You're crazy," the soldier told him. "And I'm crazy to stand here and let you do this."

Yousif appeared not to have heard. He looked outside and saw that some of the birds had not flown far. They were on the trees just outside the east window. He looked at the other side of the room and saw some of the birds on the balcony railing. They, too, were hovering close to the window. Then he heard a shot, followed simultaneously by a woman's sharp cry. The pock-marked soldier was on the balcony firing at the birds. Yousif saw one bird fall, stirring the rest to fly away in every direction. Most of them dipped and twisted and escaped the swift bullets which rang through the cool air of dawn. Yousif was relieved. But the cry which had come from outside was his mother's. He knew that she and Salwa were terrified for him. He ran down the dim hallway to reassure them.

"Waqqif willa battookh," the pock-marked soldier hollered after him. "Stop or I'll shoot."

Yousif stopped and turned. "I just wanted to let the women know—"

The pudgy soldier caught up with him, his eyes expanded.

"I wasn't running away," Yousif explained. "How can I possibly—?"

Silence crackled.

"A rifle is no good for bird hunting," the soldier said, standing inches from him. "But it's ideal for killing men like you."

"But not the human spirit," Yousif said, smelling cigarettes on the man's breath.

"You're a bastard," the soldier told him, grazing his throat with his gun.

Death was at hand. Yousif trembled inside and raised his hands to surrender.

"One false move," the soldier cautioned, "and I'll splatter your brain all over the wall. Move and keep your mouth shut."

Their faces white, Salwa and Yasmin were standing frozen on the steps. The officer and the other two soldiers were keeping them from re-entering the house. Where was Salwa's militancy now? Yousif couldn't help but think. He felt sorry for her, knowing that she knew what he was thinking.

"The shots—" Yasmin said, looking pathetic. "I thought he killed you."

"I should've," the pock-marked soldier said, pouting. "Now keep moving and don't stop."

But before they had descended the steps, Yousif heard the soldier call him. He stopped and slowly turned. Danger melted his bones.

"Here's your damn watch," the soldier said, throwing it at him.

Yousif caught it, glad to get it back. Their eyes met. But then the soldier looked past him, unwilling to show a trace of kindness.

"Keep moving," the soldier barked, pointing the gun.

Yousif and his wife and mother moved on command. But at the wrought-iron gate Yousif turned and looked back. The house, the little villa, loomed before his eyes. The bacchanal rang in Yousif's ears. The food, the drinks, the chanting. Where were Captain Malloy and his entourage who had then professed friendship? Where was Isaac, still alive when the house was being built? Salwa, shining like a golden star in her yellow dress? Amin's father, who supervised the chiseling of every stone? How many cups of coffee had Fatima served the stonecutters who had toiled and sweated in the sun for months on end?

This was the house that sat like a crown on one of the seven hills. Would he come home again? The flowers, the fruit trees—would he smell them, taste them again? He could see his father in his robe walking around the garden, bending to smell his roses, reaching to pluck one for his wife. Would an outsider from Europe now claim it? Live in it? Yousif choked up. "Whoever you may be," his soul cried, "take care of the house my parents built."

In front of his uncle's house, Yousif, Salwa, and Yasmin joined the long line of disinherited.

30

Like the tributaries of a mighty river, people first trickled, then poured into Ardallah's main street to form a gigantic procession, the biggest Yousif had ever seen. The hour of gathering was most unlikely. Night was lifting slowly, revealing a pale blue sky above the interlacing tree branches around the homes and between the high shadowy buildings in the business district.

Ironically the *muezzin* near the marketplace was circling his minaret as he had always done at this hour, calling man to pray. An Israeli soldier standing at the entrance of a dark alley shouted at him to stop. But the *muezzin* either did not hear him or did not heed his order. He went on chanting his Qur'anic verse. Yousif could see him in his black robe and white turban, his right hand cupping his right ear for harmony.

Swept along in the human flood, Yousif and his two women passed all the familiar places: Fardous Cafe, Salman's "apothecary," Nashwan's Ice Cream Parlor, and Arif's Bookstore. At the *saha,* four of the five streets were blocked by Israeli soldiers mounted on trucks that were parked sideways. The road to Ramallah, just north of Jerusalem, was blocked. The road to Jaffa was blocked. The road to Lydda and Ramleh was blocked. The road to Nablus, in the northeast, was blocked. The road on which they had just traveled was blocked by the thickening crowds. That left them shepherded on a back road leading to—where? Yousif had no idea.

Old residents and new arrivals were joined together in an exodus. Some had managed to bundle a few of their belongings in white bed sheets tied with brown twine and carried on their heads. Some were burdened with bulging suitcases and straw baskets which Yousif knew they would soon abandon.

They had not yet left Ardallah, but the fear of separation was already acute. Mothers were calling for children. Husbands were looking for their relatives. Where was Salwa's family? Where was Uncle Boulus? Where was Amin? He looked around and saw some of his classmates.

At the edge of town, the Israeli soldiers created another panic. They stopped and frisked every man and woman for weapons and valuables. Here the sight of young Jewish women in military uniform was startling. They wore berets and carried guns and looked as mean and threatening as their male counterparts.

To see young Jewish women frisking Arab men and ordering them around caused an ebb in Arab morale. To see young Jewish men frisking Arab women and ordering them around was the ultimate disgrace. But here the Arabs could not band together and resist as they had done when the British soldier tried to frisk Miriam in front of the church. Now it was different. The new occupying power was ready to open fire for the smallest provocation. They took their money, their diamonds, and their wedding rings and bands. They took their bracelets and their earrings, their crosses, and their watches.

"The bastards," Yousif said, gritting his teeth. "There's no end to their evil."

"Ssshhh," his mother begged, her eyes full of fear.

"Stealing our homes is not enough?" Salwa asked. "Now they have to rob us of everything else? It's criminal—even in wartime."

Men and women around them muttered in agreement.

"Will you two stop?" Yasmin begged, pulling Yousif's hand and staring at Salwa. "Do you want us killed?"

Burning with outrage, Yousif crouched and put his gold watch in his right sock, hiding it under his instep. His mother stuffed the money Yousif had taken out of the bank inside her brassiere.

"What about the other four hundred?" she asked.

"Didn't I give them to you to put away?" he asked.

"You did," she answered. "And I put them in the dresser's top drawer."

"So why do you think I had them?"

Her frightened eyes were still fixed on him. "I thought you got them when you went back to the house?"

Salwa looked sympathetic. "With the soldier right behind him? How could he?"

"Lehlehlehleh," Yasmin clucked, wringing her hands.

Yousif felt the twist of a knife. Yet he kept the dismay to himself.

"Well," Yousif said, "we just handed whoever opened that drawer a nice gift."

"Lehlehlehleh," Yasmin repeated. The line at the right corner of her mouth seemed to deepen.

"Don't hide everything," a man with a missing front tooth advised. "Leave them something to satisfy their greed."

It turned out to be good advice. The couple ahead of Yousif had no valuables on them. The man's pockets were turned out and found empty and his wife had no gold—not even a wedding band. Not believing them, the soldier insisted they open their suitcase. He put his hands through it and then dumped its contents on the flap of an army pickup truck. Still, he could find nothing of value.

"We left everything behind," the dark middle-aged man protested.

"Liar," the compact soldier with curly hair replied, going through all items piece by piece. The search continued unsuccessfully for several minutes.

"You're wasting your time," the Arab said, the muscles of his jaw rippling.

"I don't believe you," the soldier insisted. "Where did you put it?"

"Nowhere. We don't have anything."

"Liar."

The soldier rummaged through the whole suitcase, pulling out, to the couple's embarrassment, the man's shorts and woman's black lacy panties. Finally the soldier stumbled onto something. Apparently, the man had cut a hole under the armpits of his jacket and hidden the money inside the shoulder pads. The soldier ripped both sleeves with a knife and took out the bundle of money. He then set out to make an example of the couple.

"Because they lied," the soldier shouted, holding the jacket for everyone to see, "they can't even take their suitcase with them. Don't make their mistake. Turn in what gold or diamonds or money you have, or you'll lose everything."

Yousif and his mother exchanged furtive looks and debated what to do. Yousif wanted to turn in the cross around his neck but Salwa would not let him. It was bad luck, she told him, and made sure he listened. They were next in line. Yousif turned in his Parker pen set and all the change in his pocket. Both Yasmin and Salwa emptied their cluttered purses. The soldier picked up the two blue and red bills, and asked Yasmin to remove the gold-coin earrings from her ears. She handed them to the soldier.

"Next," the soldier said, snatching the gold from her hand.

Yousif could hear his mother breathe a sigh of relief. But Yousif looked around frantically. Where was Maha, Basim's wife? Where were Salwa's parents and brothers? And Hiyam and Izzat—where were they? What if the soldiers did one more humiliating thing to Hiyam? Would she lose her mind?

The crowd passed between two army vehicles full of soldiers. Young and old, rich and poor, they all walked under the muzzles of the guns.

"I'm already lost," one man said, looking about confused. "Where are we?"

"On your way to Abdullah," a soldier on the truck told him. "Go to Abdullah. King Abdullah."

The crowd muttered and continued to walk. They were out of the city limits now. The narrow road was no longer paved. To avoid a bottleneck, some people spilled over on both sides to cross empty fields. Yousif was determined that they should stay on the road, crowded as it was. Yasmin tried to help him carry some of the clothes, but he would not let her.

"Some of the dresses, at least," she insisted, taking part of the load in his arms.

"If we only had a suitcase," Salwa said, helping her mother-in-law.

The barren rocky field to their left was full of people huddling or walking or looking for a lost one. A few were striking out on their own, heading toward a shallow *wadi* as though they knew where they were going. A few small houses were nestled on the opposite mountain.

"This is the old Jericho road," Yasmin recognized. "Now I remember. It's supposed to be treacherous. Only last year a Ramallah bus rolled over and all the passengers were killed. Yousif, be careful."

"I didn't even know there was such a road," Salwa said, her ankle turning under her.

All kinds of thoughts flashed through Yousif's mind. Did Basim survive the attack? Who was killed? Did they resist to the last minute? To the last man? Did they cut their losses and run? He wished he knew. He wished he could've helped.

"We must get off this road," Yousif said, shifting the clothes in his arms. "When we get to Beir Zait or Deir Dibwan we must get off. Go to Ramallah, maybe. Or even Nablus."

"It's no use," his mother answered, looking tired already.

"They want us out of Palestine altogether," Salwa added. "Didn't you hear what the soldiers said? 'Go to Abdullah. Go to Abdullah.' They said it to the people of Lydda and Ramleh. They said it in our house. And they said it on the street. They must really mean it. It's Jericho they have in mind for us. And from there across the river to Jordan. No part of Palestine is safe now."

Yousif looked around, swearing. "We don't have to do what the bastards tell us." What about Jamal? Ustaz Sa'adeh? And Sitt Bahiyyeh? My God, what was she doing with her eighty-year old mother? He looked around, searching. He thought he saw the *khouriyyeh,* but wasn't sure. All he was sure of was a building headache. Seeing his mother wiping the sweat off her face, Yousif worried about her high blood pressure.

"Did you bring your pills?" he asked.

"Who had time to think?" Yasmin said, surprised.

They had walked a mile or so. The sun was now just above the horizon. They were on the highest mountain ridge in Palestine. The cool breeze felt refreshing. But should they proceed all the way to Jericho, Yousif thought, they would swelter from the heat. Jericho, a winter resort, would certainly give them a warm welcome.

"Damn!" Yousif said. "We don't even know where Maha is. She'll need help with the children."

Yasmin bit her lip and stared at him guiltily. "Basim would be very upset."

"If he's alive," Salwa told her.

"My God!" Yasmin exclaimed. "You think—"

"The explosions we heard early in the morning," Yousif reminded his mother. "He may have escaped death and he may not have. We can only speculate."

Yasmin's crimson color deepened. "Don't speculate in front of Maha," she said, biting her lip.

"First let's find her," Salwa said.

"But how can we?" Yasmin asked. "There are at least twenty thousand people on this road."

"We must, though," Yousif said. "She can't manage by herself. The baby is only two years old."

They were turning a corner. To make way for the crowd while they stopped, Yousif pulled Salwa against a stone wall and let the crowd go by. The sound of thousands of feet drowned the agonized human voices. It was the wrong place for them to stand. They had to continue walking, looking around. Most of the people within reach were strangers.

At the first clearing, Yousif and his two women stepped off the country road. They stood in the shade of an olive tree, watching the marchers. Others joined, equally lost and disturbed. Maha was not in sight. Yousif asked about his Uncle Boulus but no one knew where he was either. Suddenly Amin appeared, and they were happy to have found each other. No, he had not seen Maha.

"Listen, you don't have any water, do you?" Amin asked. "Silly question, I know, but my little brother is awfully thirsty."

"No," Yousif answered. "We're all going to be in trouble."

Amin nodded. Their eyes met. The sweat on Amin's forehead made his dark skin glisten.

"I'd better go," Amin said. He stepped back on the crowded narrow road and went ahead looking for water.

"Amin," Yousif called after him, but his voice was lost in the hubbub. "I wish I had asked him where they're headed."

"He couldn't have told you," his mother said, leaning against the tree. "We don't know where we're going either."

They waited for ten minutes. No one showed up who knew Maha's whereabouts. Yousif and company abandoned the road, but walked parallel to it. Some were already resting in the fields. Mothers were breast-feeding their babies. Three men were urinating against a tree, their backs to the road.

By noon they had passed the outskirts of Beir Zait and were getting close to Deir Dibwan.

"How far have we crossed?" his mother asked, her face smeared with dust and sweat.

"About twelve to fifteen miles," he answered.

"And Jericho?" she wanted to know. "How many more?"

A stone turned under Yousif's foot. "Thirty to forty miles," he answered. "I doubt we'll make it tonight."

"Tonight! Are you crazy?" Yasmin asked, stopping. "I can hardly breathe already. It'll probably take me a week the way I feel."

"Then you'll die on the road," he said. "We have nothing to eat or drink."

"I wish I had died with your father," she said.

"Father didn't die," he reminded her. "He was killed."

"Killed, died," she said. "What's the difference."

Some of the marchers broke away from the rest, heading toward Beir Zait or Deir Dibwan. Salwa looked concerned about her mother-in-law. She told Yousif she hoped Yasmin could make it.

"I'm worried about her, too," Yousif whispered. Then turning to his mother, he said. "Mother, do you think we should spend the night in one of the villages?"

"What villages?" Yasmin asked, lifting her feet with difficulty. "Beir Zait and Deir Dibwan are tiny villages. They can't absorb all these people. Not even for one night. We'll end up sleeping on the street."

"What about Taibeh or Jifna? They are just four or five miles away."

"No," his mother said. "I'd rather move on to safer grounds."

Yousif was not convinced. "But can you make it?"

"I'll have to. If I don't, just bury me and keep going."

"God forbid," Yousif said, making the sign of the cross.

Suddenly, they saw four planes zoom overhead and strafe the open space on both sides of the road about two hundred yards ahead.

"There's your answer," Yasmin said. "You still want to stop over?"

Yousif bit his lips. Many of the marchers stopped and looked. Within seconds they heard explosions and saw black pillars of smoke rising in the distance.

Yousif felt light-headed. Why were the Israelis bombing the countryside?

"They want to shake us up," Yousif told his mother. "Make us feel insecure."

The four planes streaked off against the blue sky. Everyone looked up. Some of the women clung to their husbands and sons. Children cried, wrapping their arms around their parents' necks.

"It looks like they own the sky," a money exchanger said, his dusty white shirt untucked.

"Who's to challenge them?" Salwa asked, catching Yasmin from falling.

"That's right," a stranger said. "Except for the Egyptians we have no air force to engage them."

"And the Egyptians are still bogged down near Gaza," Yasmin complained. "A lot of good that'll do us."

Yousif heard the word "engagement" and smiled wryly. It was not a war, only an engagement. Yet, here they were on the way to becoming refugees.

The four planes returned, flying very low above their heads. Their roar caused a new panic among the marchers. Yousif could see the Israeli blue-and-white flag painted below their bellies.

"Still chasing us?" one skinny old man said. "Damn the day we heard of them."

The planes swooped down on both sides of the long line of refugees. Then, Yousif saw bombs falling—luckily, away from the crowd.

The screams of the marchers were louder than the two explosions. In their rush, a few fell and scraped their arms and legs. Children's crying intensified.

Yousif turned and looked. Where was the rest of his family? Was he ever going to find any of them? Hiyam and Izzat had left the house only ten minutes before him and his mother. Where did Uncle Boulus and Aunt Hilaneh vanish? What about Fatima? Her husband was old and her children were young.

"They bombed the fields," a young *fellah* said, squinting his eyes.

"I can't tell from here," Yousif said, climbing a big rock. "Most likely they've strafed the highway."

"What the hell for?" a young stranger asked.

"To make it unfit for travel," Yousif speculated. "And to warn us not to turn right or left. Not to go to Ramallah or Nablus. They want us to keep on going straight—all the way to Jericho. And beyond."

"In short," Salwa said, "they're herding us out of Palestine."

Many of the marchers agreed. In his bones Yousif could feel the Israeli determination to evacuate the country of its Arab population.

Crossing a field with his mother and wife at his side, Yousif was too weak to carry the dresses. He discarded them one by one. Salwa threw off all the clothes she had, except one dress she flung over her shoulder. Groaning and complaining, Yasmin followed suit, thankful for the relief. Some women, she said, had more stamina than others or were more physically fit. Both Yousif and Salwa put their arms around Yasmin and guided her through the brush and rocks. The sun was beating down on them. The going was slow. Fortunately, Yousif thought, they were still traveling flat lands. After Deir Dibwan, the descent would be rapid. Jericho was literally the lowest spot on earth—two thousand feet below sea level. Any road to it had to be steep. Even the main road between Jerusalem and Jericho was perilous. It twisted and turned until pressure plugged one's ears.

They stopped by a stone quarry to rest on a large rock. Yousif could see many people squatting or stretching out. Ali, the watermelon vendor, was carrying his fragile eighty-year old father on his back. Yousif admired the son but wondered how long he could keep it up. Shibly, the tailor, passed Yousif, looking pathetic. He was a known diabetic and seemed to have shrunk to half his size since Yousif had last seen him a month or two earlier. Now he looked like a ghost, his teeth rotten and his belt wrapped around him twice. A woman in her ninth month passed them, her feet wobbling under the enormous weight. Her arms were at her sides, not only pushing away protectively but balancing her as if she were walking on a high tight wire. She seemed exhausted, ready to fall.

"Allahu Akbar," a man said, exasperated. "A woman in her condition should've been allowed to stay. But *awlad al-haraam* wouldn't let her."

"Allahu Akbar," another man cried in anguish.

A throng of people gathered around another man lying in the middle of the road. Elsewhere word spread that a child was dehydrating. Someone far off shouted back that he had a wet handkerchief which he had soaked in a spring by the road. Quickly Yousif saw the red handkerchief being passed reverentially above the people's heads like an Easter candle burning with holy fire.

"I feel faint," Yasmin gasped, her sweat streaming down her flushed face. "I can't take this heat."

"We'd better find you a place to rest," Yousif answered, worried.

"We made a mistake," she gasped again, fanning herself with a handkerchief. "We should've gone to Beir Zait."

"I told you so," Yousif reminded them.

"My heart won't slow down and my feet are killing me."

"You'll make it," Yousif assured her.

"I don't think so. I really don't."

The look in her eyes alarmed him and Salwa.

THE JULY SUN was now straight above their heads, pinning them down without mercy. The air was stifling. Shirts and dresses stuck to perspiring bodies. The red clay fields were barren, not fit for grazing sheep. They were the roaming sheep, Yousif thought—twenty thousand strong. Even the roaming was becoming more arduous with every new field to cross. Yousif opened his shirt and untucked its edges, hoping it would billow and create a cooling breeze. The shirt hung limply, giving him no comfort. Even Yasmin was not above unbuttoning the top of her dress. Some of the women villagers had already tucked the hems of their black ankle-length dresses under their red and gold sashes, exposing legs and flesh above knees never before seen outside their bedrooms.

They struggled on and on, stumbling here, catching their breath there, and holding hands whenever necessary. They stepped over open ditches. They walked around large boulders smoothed by the rains of the centuries. They came upon a corpse covered by someone's checkered *hatta*. Yousif could not tell the dead man's age, but he guessed it at forty. He motioned to Salwa with his eyes. She and Yasmin turned around and looked, and he had to console both as if the dead man were their relative. Tears filled Yasmin's eyes, and her face contorted. Others passed and shook their heads. Some made the sign of the cross. Others cried openly. Many tried to hide the scene from the eyes of their children.

"Ya waili 'alaih," Yasmin mourned. "They left him behind. Imagine!"

"Soon the animals will find him," Salwa added, her chin trembling.

Like a vortex, the terrain sucked them to the depth of the first canyon. The long, circular line of humanity on the road seemed hardly moving. As Yousif shuffled along, his feet swelled and his lips became dry. His tongue lay like a piece of wood stuck in his mouth for no purpose. He swirled it around for saliva but there was none. Even the sweat on his body had long evaporated, leaving him without any moisture. He feared for his mother: her face a deep crimson, with the sun and high blood pressure conspiring against her. He tried to put his arm around her waist again. She could not bear the touch. Their bodies were so scorched the light brush of a feather became hurtful. Yousif was so drained of energy, any act of kindness on his part became an exertion. Each walked alone, feet unsteady.

More bodies lay dead along the way. More wailing echoed through the *wadi*. Yousif saw and listened, his mind befuddled. Two bodies. Three bodies. He was becoming accustomed to tragedies, but not immune to them. A howl split the air. Yousif and Salwa looked up. A man had fallen. They saw him tumbling in mid-air, his death cry reverberating into silence.

The march went on. One more casualty, Yousif thought, worthy only of a look and, perhaps, a silent prayer. There would be more deaths—many more. He only wished he had a drop of water to wet his tongue. Only a drop.

"Drink your urine," an old rugged farmer told him. "But try not to piss too much. Save it for the road. It's a long stretch."

Yousif was horrified. He looked at the man, disgusted.

"Suit yourself," the old man said, taking long strides and looking ahead. "Bigger men than you have done it. It's a matter of life and death."

"You've done it?" Yousif asked.

"Yes, I have," the farmer admitted. "My wife, too."

Yousif looked at the old woman in disbelief. She nodded and told him there was no shame in the face of death. She had already discarded her shawl and headdress and was walking with the energy of a woman determined to overcome hardship. Compared to her, his mother seemed fragile.

The talk of drinking urine somehow made Yousif's thirst more acute. But he would never succumb to such bestial behavior, he vowed—not he who was so squeamish.

At two o'clock in the afternoon the march dwindled to a halt. People were panting and too weak to continue. Yasmin was spent, and collapsed under the nearest tree. Salwa tended to all her needs as though she were her own mother. Yousif loved her for it. In their immediate vicinity, there were a few trees and a few large rocks. Many of the marchers looked like a flock of crows resting in the shade of hanging cliffs on both sides of the valley. Little by little, the human machine in each of them had gradually shut down.

"I wish we had kept one or two of our dresses to cover our heads," Yasmin said, her breathing heavy. She felt the top of her head and added, "The sun will kill us."

Yasmin looked so wretched and puffy, Yousif forgot how tired he was. Her eyes closed from sheer fatigue. Her chest heaved rhythmically. Salwa wished she had something soft to put under her head and make her lie down. He got up and plodded about looking for a smooth rock. Soon he returned with one. He took off his shirt and piled it on top of the small rock and helped his mother stretch her rigid body. Then, with difficulty, on account of the swelling, he removed her shoes. Both he and Salwa sat down and watched her drift into instant sleep, worried about her condition.

A parade of stragglers tried to find a suitable spot to settle around them. An obese woman with ungainly layers of fat and a blue network of varicose veins jiggled past them. Yousif marveled at her ability to travel so far. Near her a man was clutching his right side and complaining of a gallbladder attack. Yousif saw him double up with pain. The man's wife and children circled around him and cried.

Then suddenly he saw Salman and his family.

"Salman!" Yousif shouted, springing to his feet. His cousin was crossing another field, unaware of their proximity. "Salman! Abla! We're here."

Salman and Abla stopped and looked around. Yousif and Salwa rushed to help them with their children. Salman was carrying a two-month-old baby. Abla was holding her three-year-old daughter's hand. They all hugged each other, overcome by emotion. Yousif led them to the tree under which his mother was sleeping. They all sat and looked at her, careful not to wake her.

"The babies," Yousif said, taking the baby from Abla's arms, "how did they manage?"

"It hasn't been easy," Abla said, expelling a deep breath.

"And how about you, Reem, darling?" Salwa asked, touching the little girl's face. "Have you been walking too? Aren't your little feet tired? Heh?"

Reem, the three-year-old daughter with the pony tail, buried her head in her mother's lap and went to sleep. Salman's look was glazed, his bald head sweaty. He sat speechless, staring into space. Abla spoke of the misery they had encountered.

"Luckily," Abla said, her hair stringy, "I'm still breast-feeding the baby. If it weren't for my milk I think the two kids would have died. I know they would've. I even wet my fingers with my own milk and passed it on to Salman. I'm sorry Yousif, I don't mean to embarrass you, but it's true. I squirted a few drops and passed them on to Salman. Then I licked my own palm."

Truly embarrassed, Yousif looked away. He remembered what the old woman had told him: "There's no shame in the face of death."

"Milk is better than urine," Yousif muttered, picking a pebble and throwing it.

Yasmin stirred, then opened her eyes. Seeing Salman and his family around her, she became flustered and tried to sit up.

"Oh, my God, you're here," Yasmin said, overcome with emotion. "How are you, darlings?"

"As expected," Abla told her, fiddling with her daughter's hair.

"Have you seen Maha?" Yasmin asked, anxious. "Or my brother Boulus?"

Abla shook her head. "But I saw your tenants. Is it true about the rape?"

Yousif nodded, rocking the baby in his arms. Salman's eyes were fixed on the far horizon.

"Pull yourself together," his wife admonished him. "You can't go on like this."

Salman toyed with his thumbs. "Two days ago," he said, breaking the silence, "I bought five hundred pounds' worth of goods. I stocked the shop up to the ceiling." There was a tremor in his voice.

"You didn't know this was going to happen," Abla consoled her husband. "And it's not as if we'll be gone forever. We'll be back."

Salman shook his head, looking glum.

"Sure we'll be back," Abla insisted. "My God, don't you think—?"

"Who's going to take us back?" Yousif sneered. "The Arab armies?"

"Why not?" Abla challenged him.

"Look at the evidence," Yousif said, casting his eyes on the multitude of displaced people.

"This is temporary," she explained.

Salman seemed to be in another world. "And all that cash under the mattress," he muttered. "I remembered it at the door. But the soldier wouldn't let me go back. I bet he found it."

"Allah will provide," his wife said, rubbing the length of his tense spine. "Let's be thankful we escaped the fate of Deir Yasin."

"That's the first thing that crossed my mind," Yasmin said. She then repeated how Hiyam had been raped. And for the third or fourth time, Yousif guessed, she related how he, Yousif, had gone inside to free his birds, how she heard two gunshots and thought he had been killed.

"Money isn't everything," Yasmin added. "Property isn't either. Thank God we're all safe. Thank God none of the children are hurt."

LATE THAT AFTERNOON, the sun began to set behind them. The shadows on the facing cliffs were getting long, promising relief from the heat. Yousif's mother was now breathing regularly. At least Salman was not sulking. They all felt hungry, but thirst was more of a problem. Yousif rose to look for some water. With luck he might find Maha—or Salwa's family. Suddenly he remembered Jamal and felt ashamed for not having thought of him earlier. Could a blind man possibly be forced to make such a journey? That *would* be cruel—but knowing the enemy, he put nothing past them.

"Stay right here," Yousif said to Salwa and the rest.

"Where are you going?" Salwa asked, anxious.

"To look around. Maybe I'll find someone we know. But if you move, we may get separated."

"I'll go with you," Salwa said, rising with new energy.

Standing up, Yousif surveyed the scene for landmarks. He chose to go backward, and began to climb the mountain he had earlier descended. Salwa followed him. He waited for her and let her drape her arm around his neck. The clusters of people here and there reminded him of the religious picnic of Sitna Miriam. Here, however, the mood was not festive. Children were not playing. Here were gloomy people, some in their pajamas and nightgowns. Those in traditional costumes blended best with the terrain. Yousif and Salwa explored the area carefully, wishing for as little as a puddle of dirty water or a blade of grass. There was none.

Those they met were equally desperate. Yousif saw a big rock to his right and was able to push it—looking for what, he didn't know. As it began to roll down the hill, he worried it might hurt someone—but soon it stopped. The brown dirt under it looked a bit damp. Amazed at his own excitement, he let go of Salwa's arm and bent down. He dug his fingers and scooped a handful. He looked to see if someone other than Salwa were watching. Then he raised his hand to his mouth and smeared the dirt on his lips. He hated doing it, regarding himself as a pig. His chafed lips welcomed the ointment, but he refused to eat dirt.

"What are you doing?" Salwa asked, bewildered.

"My lips are parched, anything will make them feel better. Here, try some."

"Are you crazy?" she asked, walking away.

Down and down the marchers went, while Yousif and Salwa struggled up in the opposite direction. Climbing the steep hill was hard. As they labored, he put his hand on his right knee and pushed down to propel himself. Then he would pull up Salwa. Whenever he could he would grasp at an undergrowth to pull both of them along. He recognized a few people, but they all looked drugged. Their leathery faces were tired, their widened eyes dull and empty. Arif, the bookseller, was among them, his shirt open and stained with sweat and his bald head glistening. The three waved to each other like strangers, each weak-kneed and engrossed in his or her own quest.

Unexpectedly, they had come upon Salwa's family. They were in an open field with nothing to shield them from the beating sun. Salwa's mother was the first to notice them. She stood up, waving her arm. But her husband and two sons remained lying on the ground.

"Look!" Yousif said, excited. He nudged Salwa and pointed his finger.

"Hurry!!!" Salwa screamed, wanting to run.

Yousif had to hold her, cautioning her about the heat.

Yousif didn't know what to think. Were they exhausted? Was Anton Taweel sick? Unable to restrain Salwa any further, Yousif let go of her and saw her make a dash. He picked up his pace and followed her, worried.

By the time Yousif reached them, Salwa had already hugged her mother and was on her knees next to her father. The whole atmosphere was charged.

"What's wrong?" Yousif asked, shaking Imm Akram's hand. Then seeing the fear on her face, he quickly bent down next to Salwa. His father-in-law looked ashen. Salwa's eyes were already clouded.

"How are you, Uncle?" Yousif asked.

Anton Taweel, now Uncle Anton, shook his head. "I had a terrible chest pain. Right here. In the middle of my chest. Right under the small bone of my rib cage."

Salwa clutched her father's hand. "What about your arm?" she asked. "Did you have a shooting pain?"

Her father nodded. "In my left arm. Like an electric bolt. They say that's the real sign of a heart attack."

Salwa began to whimper. Imm Akram woke up her children, who sat up alarmed. Yousif knew that the man was dying.

"It's the heat," Imm Akram said, wringing her hands. "And the long walk. May they never rest in peace."

Aware that tragedy was about to strike, Yousif was glad that he and Salwa's father were on good terms. What if the man were to die, he thought, still holding a grudge?

Against all odds, Yousif wanted to find a doctor, or a heart patient who might have a pill to spare. Yousif hadn't gone more than fifty meters when suddenly he heard Salwa shrieking. He spun around and ran back, his muscles aching.

Imm Akram was scratching her own face. Salwa was flung across her father's chest. Men and women were walking by, shaking their heads. Yousif was afraid he was too late. As he got closer, he could see Anton's eyes rolling, his mouth frothing. Yousif knelt beside Salwa and put his arm around her waist. Salwa's crying became louder.

"Uncle," Yousif said, "I want you to know I'm sorry for the pain I've caused you. I didn't mean to hurt you, I swear."

"Nor did I, Father," Salwa sobbed. "Tell us you forgive us. Tell us you're not mad at us."

Anton did not answer but looked at them intently. His eyes were bulging, their white now yellow.

"Please forgive us," Yousif pleaded, reaching to touch his hand. He squeezed it gently, hoping the man would squeeze his hand back. Anton did, looking like a man sinking in quicksand, begging for help.

A deep, harsh and strangling gurgle forced itself out of Anton's throat. "I forgive—" he started, but couldn't finish the sentence. His head dropped to the side and his arms went limp.

Salwa screamed and fell on her father's chest. Akram and Zuhair clung to their mother. She pressed them to her body, her face stained with tears. Yousif's chin began to tremble. Soon he too was crying. He put his hand on Salwa's back to console her. She sobbed convulsively. He could feel her whole body quivering.

"I'm sorry, darling," he told Salwa, tasting the salt of his own tears.

Salwa hugged Yousif and cried, resting her head on his shoulder. Then Yousif got up and went over to her mother. He kissed her on both cheeks, then pressed the young boys to his sides. He watched Salwa cradle her father's head in her arm and lean over him. She smoothed his hair, wiped the sweat on his forehead, and talked to him as though he were still alive.

"Is it too hot for you, Daddy?" she was saying. "You won't need someone to cover you up, will you, Daddy? What are you going to do when we leave? Will you be too lonely? Do you want me to stay with you? Who's going to keep you company?"

The death scene merged with Yousif's memory of his own father's death. And that of Isaac's. Yousif felt the lump in his throat grow bigger. He wanted to pull Salwa away. Then he decided that holding her back was not right. It was unnatural not to grieve.

Salwa's mother knelt beside her. "His eyes and mouth have to be closed before the body stiffens," she said.

"Don't say that!" Salwa cried. "I can't stand it."

"I'm sorry, *habibti,* but it's true," her mother told her. "And these things are his rights. Get away from him now and let me do what needs to be done."

Salwa's crying subsided. Yousif watched the mother resolutely set out to perform her duties. He stood between Zuhair and Akram, putting his arms around their shoulders. Gently, Mrs. Taweel closed her husband's eyelids and put her left palm under his chin and forced his mouth shut. She pressed the head between her two hands for a few minutes to ensure that the mouth would not reopen. Then she crossed his arms on his chest and pulled his legs straight.

"What difference does it make?" Salwa again sobbed, "if his legs are straight or not? He's dead, Mother, he's dead."

"Allah yirhamu," her mother replied, perfectly calm. "God rest his soul." She went about her business with dignity, paying no attention to her daughter's outbursts.

Yousif watched her with admiration and respect. The dead man's face looked like an Easter egg which had been dipped in many coloring cups. Was the dull mixture of green, yellow, and blue the ashen color of death? The two-day stubble of beard was mostly white. Yousif remarked to himself that Anton Taweel looked as impressive in death as he had in life.

Marchers filed by, pausing long enough to offer their condolences.

"God gave and God took."

"We came from dust, and to dust we return."

"We belong to God, and to Him we return."

They looked for a priest to say the last rites, but there was none to be found. The mother led in prayer. Yousif and her children knelt around the body. They said the Lord's Prayer; he said Hail Mary. Salwa's spasms had calmed down considerably. Her eyes had a faraway look, as if she were seeing a distant vision. But when the time came for them to resume their journey, her grief and anger were revived.

"We can't leave him like that," Salwa protested, her lips twitching. "How can we, Mother?"

"What else can we do?" her mother asked in return. "Who's going to haul him another twenty miles in this heat?"

"Maybe we can dig a grave," Yousif suggested.

"With what?" the mother asked, doubtful. "The ground is so hard."

Yousif had to agree with her. The mountain slope looked as though it had never been plowed. It occurred to him that perhaps they could cover the body with stones, but the rocky terrain was full of large boulders and small pebbles. Who was going to pile up enough stones to build a mound? And who, for God's sake, would dare put hard, hot stones on the man's face? Salwa would be outraged.

Then an old man offered his black *'abaa* as a cover. Yousif accepted it with gratitude and quickly unfolded it over the body. But Anton's body was too long and another man had to give up his white *hatta* to cover the legs. Then Yousif and the young boys gathered a few stones and placed them around the body. Not much of a burial, Yousif thought, but he kept it to himself.

"It's so cruel," Salwa whimpered, staring at the mound.

"God's will be done," her mother replied, her hands clasped in her lap.

"God? What God?" Salwa shouted.

Mrs. Taweel reproached her sharply, saying that she would not tolerate blasphemy. Again, Salwa's outbursts reminded Yousif of his own behavior at his father's death and at Isaac's. How could he blame her? Had he not gone berserk himself? He saw the mother bend down and kiss her husband's forehead, her face contorted. One by one, including Yousif, they all kissed the dead man farewell.

31

The sun seemed closer, whiter, meaner. The air seemed free of oxygen. The marchers moved like scarecrows. Death was their loyal companion.

Yousif knew he had to look after Salwa's mother and brothers. He couldn't allow them to drift off, especially now that they had no adult male to look after them. Putting his arms around Zuhair and Akram, Yousif felt they were now in his care. And in spite of the sad occasion, Yousif was gratified. How quickly fate had propelled him to a position of a caretaker! Looking after Salwa's family would be a duty. Under different circumstances it would have been a pleasure.

But Salwa was torn with grief. The minute they had walked away from her father's corpse, she buried her head in her hands and cried. Sometimes she'd let Yousif put his arm around her. Often, she'd strike out on her own, now pulling her hair, now wringing her hands. And always sobbing. Again and again, Yousif would leave the boys and try to calm her down.

"Control yourself," he said. "It's hard enough on all of us."

"Nothing will bring my father back," she said, crying.

"Allah yirhamu. But you need to be giving your mother strength."

Of course she would, Salwa said. But not right now. Yousif sensed that she was angry, not just sad. It bothered him that she might start blaming him for the death of her father. Tormented as she was, she must not make him a scapegoat.

"Look," he said, trying to catch up with her. "I hope you're not in any way blaming me, or yourself, for his death."

Salwa stopped in her track, gazing at him. "Did I say we were to blame?" she asked.

"The way you're looking at me—"

"I'm devastated," she said. "Right now, all I can think of is that he died and we left him in the wilderness."

Yousif watched his wife stand alone, bewildered, isolated: like a hollow tree stuck in the middle of the desert. Marchers streamed by like a flock of sheep. But she seemed unfazed by the din of highly-pitched cries mingled with a steady thud of footsteps. Slowly she began to move, like a woman crossing the borderline of a nightmare. She broke his heart. Then she walked briskly, unfettered by the harshness of the wilderness. Her mother was lagging behind her, aged by the tragedies of the last two days.

Suddenly the older woman stumbled and fell. Yousif rushed to help. She had fallen on her back, legs splayed. Yousif turned his head away, embarrassed for her. He gave her time to cover up.

"I'm so sorry," Yousif told her, lifting her up under the arms. "Are you all right?"

"Thank God nothing is broken," she said, apologizing. "You're kind."

"Maybe you ought to have the boys walk beside you," Yousif said.

"Good idea," she said, looking around for her children.

Yousif ran ahead to catch up with Salwa. He took her hand to help her cross some rough terrain.

THE MARCHERS were in the thousands and the going was so heavy, it took Yousif and the Taweel family almost an hour to reunite with his own family. He found them waiting for him in the vicinity of where he had left them. It was dusk. The red hot sun was ready to plunge behind the far horizon.

But Salwa's and her mother's pathetic condition must have shocked the waiting party. Yasmin jumped to her feet, dread registered all over her face.

"Salwa, why are you crying?" Yasmin asked, alarmed. "What's the matter, *habibti?*"

Yousif told his mother and the rest about Anton Taweel's death. Yasmin shrieked and hugged her daughter-in-law. Abla embraced the mother, Imm Akram, whose sobbing caused both of them to tremble. Salman turned white. Children cried. Marchers stopped to inquire. Again, pandemonium broke out. Tongues clucked. Heads shook. Questions tumbled. The sun turned bloody.

Sitting down on the dirt, they went over and over the details of Anton's death. Their shock, their sorrow seemed to deepen.

"And you left him behind?" Yasmin asked again and again.

"Without burial!" Abla said. "Can you imagine!"

"He's not the first or the last," Salman reminded them, wrapping his arms around his raised knees. "How many corpses did we pass along the way?"

"Lord have mercy on us," Yasmin said, making the sign of the Cross.

The dust of the marchers filled the air. Many were coughing.

Slowly Yasmin and Imm Akram began to hum. Other women marchers joined them and they all filled the night with dirges. The wake was made all the more bitter because of the wilderness. With each new arrival the chanting intensified. Tears flowed. Death was now on stage. Their drama had turned real, tragic.

Four more planes passed overhead. Yousif looked up to see their lights twinkling among the much brighter stars. It was too dark to identify them, but Yousif knew they could only be the enemy.

"God knows what's happening to him now," Imm Akram lamented, shaking her head. "And tomorrow the sun will be so hot, his body will decompose . . . and will start to smell."

The image was too strong for Salwa. She couldn't take it. She struck out on her own. Yousif got up and followed her. Thousands of marchers were strewn all over the mountain, covering its slopes like a human carpet. The night was still, except for crickets and crying babies.

Standing by a huge rock on the edge of a precipice, Salwa turned and looked at Yousif.

"Promise me one thing," she said, her eyes glistening.

Yousif feared what was coming. "I'll do my best," he said.

"Promise me to fight the Zionists as long as you live."

"That's the easy part," Yousif said, holding her hands.

"What's not so easy?"

"Knowing *how* to fight them."

"You'll find a way."

"We'll find it together."

"But promise me you'll fight them."

"I swear it on your father's and my father's graves," he said, wrapping his arm around her waist.

They leaned against the rock, deep in thought. New vistas of Palestinians on the run opened before their eyes. This was not a limited exodus out of Ardallah alone, they concluded. No, no. This was a general exodus out of Palestine altogether. The people from Galilee were trekking to Lebanon and Syria. People from Bethlehem were marching to Jordan. People from Gaza were headed for Egypt. The vision of hundreds of thousands of Palestinians being exiled made them forget for a moment about the death of Salwa's father. Palestine was being evacuated on a full scale. Tonight all Palestinians were isolated, trapped in a valley of death.

"Do you realize we're watching history in the making," Yousif reflected, remembering his tutoring days at his father's feet. "One day scholars will write books about all this. And here we are living the whole episode. It's a tale waiting for a teller to do it justice."

She looked at him quizzically. "When you talk like this you remind me of your father."

"I'm flattered," Yousif told her. "I wish I were half the man he was. He knew things, Salwa. And he understood as though he were connected to a different world."

"I like you the way you are," she said, expelling a deep breath.

Yousif turned her around. "You know," he said, "when I first saw the soldiers with guns in their hands I felt sorry for them. I really did. I was glad it wasn't me who was carrying the gun."

Salwa frowned. But she kept quiet, waiting for him to continue.

"At that point," he said, "I would've preferred getting killed myself than killing someone else."

"That's foolish," she said, not blinking.

"Like Khalil Gibran wrote, 'I'd rather be the deer and not the hunter, the anvil and not the hammer.' Or something like that."

"Still foolish."

"True, though. That's how I felt. Then I changed. Do you know at what precise moment I felt transformed? Not when they threw us out and robbed us at the outskirts of town. Not even when they raped Hiyam."

Salwa seemed at a loss.

"I know that it pales compared to what they're doing to us in general. And yet, the emotional impact of that moment shattered my senses."

"What are you talking about?" Salwa asked, curious.

"It's when that damn soldier stripped Hiyam," Yousif recalled, feeling a dryness in his mouth. "There she was—exposed, debased. When I saw her pubic hair flash before my eyes, I felt shame, anger, hate."

"Nothing could possibly be more humiliating," Salwa said, her eyes glazed.

"No, nothing."

"Imagine how she must've felt."

"Some men don't see that much of their wives even after they've had two or three children."

There was silence. Salwa looked reassured.

"I know you'll keep your promise," she said, reaching for his hand.

"So help me God," he vowed, looking her in the eye.

After a moment, Salwa added, "I wonder how many couples are making the same commitment."

"May their numbers multiply," Yousif said, wrapping her in his arms.

With the full silvery moon hanging over them like an eavesdropper, Yousif felt his heart pounding against Salwa's back.

THE NIGHT WAS clean and clear but not cool. Yousif had a hard time sleeping. Thirst was driving him crazy. Again, his tongue felt like a piece of chalk stuck in a dry hole in his head. The idea of urine occurred to him, but he felt repulsed. Even Abla's milk tantalized his palate. But how could he do it?

He lay awake, gazing at the solemnity of the silhouetted mountains. Every now and then he would smooth down Salwa's hair. The night was not as black as he had thought. He could see the outline of the hanging cliffs and the tops of the mounds below him. The mountain was steep. Descending it tomorrow would be hazardous. Salwa shifted in her sleep. Her head rested on her folded arms, her limbs stretched out uncovered. Yousif wanted her in his arms but knew that was impossible.

The multitude of refugees awoke long before dawn. Scattered over an area several miles wide, they seemed to pull each other by an invisible cord. The commotion resounded through the quiet valley. A shrill cry was heard, signifying another tragedy. Death had crept around during the night, Yousif knew. More hearts were broken. Other cries followed. Names of lost ones were called in anguish.

Yousif and his party gathered themselves up, beginning the second day's journey.

"The crowd seems to be getting bigger and bigger," Yasmin observed, strands of hair falling on her forehead.

Imm Akram nodded. "The worst thing that could happen to us now is to get separated."

"Let's all make sure we don't," Yousif said. "Hold each other's hands. Especially the children's. Don't strike out on your own. Salwa, are you listening?"

"I am," Salwa said, dusting off her dress.

"Should we get separated," Yousif continued, "let's all agree not to leave

Jordan. Stay in Jordan until we regroup and figure out what to do next. Agreed?"

Some said yes, but most of them nodded.

They resumed their journey, the dust of exile in their mouths. The canyons below looked foreboding.

THE SUN ROSE behind the inhospitable mountain, disclosing a vista of dull gray rocks and a sea of haggard faces. The stark Mount of Temptation looked majestic in the distance—a great divide between the wasteland they were crossing and the plush green fields of Jericho which lay beyond. To reach it was to survive; not to reach it was to be devoured by a callous, cavernous pit. A promise and a threat, Yousif thought, as he lugged little Reem on his back and trudged down the barren mountain. Salman, burdened with the baby in his arms, walked along grimly, followed by the rest.

"I'm hungry," Reem whimpered.

That was the moment they had all dreaded. The adults exchanged looks. No one answered the girl.

"I'm hungry," Reem repeated, crying.

Yousif patted her on the leg, saying they would soon have food. He lied and braced himself to lie even more. To get her mind off her hunger he began to tell a story. He told her about a nice family that lived on a nice street and was sleeping in a nice house when one stormy night a big bad wolf came knocking on the door. At first the wolf terrorized the mother and the children and bit the father in his leg until he couldn't walk. The children began to cry, worried to death about their father. But the father winked at them and they knew he was okay. Then the mother boiled some water and splashed it in the big bad wolf's face and the father ran to the kitchen and came back with a butcher's knife."

Suddenly baby Reem stopped sobbing. "Why?" she asked, sucking her thumb.

"To kill the big bad wolf, that's why. And by God he did."

"And what happened to the children? Were they scared?"

"Not after their father had dragged the body of the big bad wolf and thrown it outside where it belonged," Yousif told her. "Then he and the mother tucked them in their soft warm comfortable beds. And they went to sleep to dream nice dreams."

The ploy worked, but only for a brief moment. Soon Reem went back to crying for food.

Yasmin sighed and trudged weakly. "One doesn't know whether to cry for the dead or the living."

"I'm still hungry," Reem whimpered, kicking Yousif on the side.

Yousif put Reem down. Her mother held her hand. There was no stopping the little girl's crying. She wanted food and nothing would placate her. Abla tried to nurse her, but the girl refused. Her crying became intense. The adults rolled their eyes, bit their lips. What could they do? Yousif himself felt terribly thirsty. It was mid-morning, yet the intensity of the heat was already wearing him down.

"Wait, son, wait!" an old man cried.

Yousif looked up, his heart breaking. He saw an old man—bearded, shriveled. He tapped his cane, begging his son, the watermelon vendor, not to abandon him. Earlier, Yousif had seen the son carrying his fragile eighty-year-old father on his back. But after thirty or forty miles going up and down mountains, even the bag of bones must have felt heavy. Yousif watched in disbelief. He saw the old man's legs fail him. He saw him falter and fall, cutting himself on the forehead.

"I'll die, son," the old man pleaded, wiping his own blood.

"Forgive me, Father," the young man said, on the verge of tears, "but I can't wait here with you. We still have at least twenty miles to cross. I just can't do it."

Yousif was mystified. He waited for the little drama to end.

"For Allah's sake, don't leave me," the old man cried, his chin trembling. "Have mercy on your own father. Don't leave me. I'll die, son. I'll die . . ."

"I have young children to take care of," the son argued, visibly shaken. "You're my responsibility and they're my responsibility. What am I to do? I can't carry you on my back all the way to Jericho. We'd both die, and what will that do to the rest of the family? Who's going to take care of the little ones? Please understand. And *Allah isamihni*. May God forgive me."

Yousif watched the exchange, anguished, incredulous. The old man's frenzied cry did not deter his son. The young man walked ahead a few steps, determined not to look back, not to let sentiment or shame dissuade him.

All of Yousif's anxieties returned to nauseate him. His mother's face was flushed again. Salwa was consoling her mother. Little Reem's crying was unnerving. He himself could barely move his tongue. Yet now he felt a surge of energy.

"We're all doomed," Yousif cried, flailing his arms. "But we can't leave this old man behind to die in the wilderness. God may never forgive us such cruelty."

Salwa, obviously remembering the death of her father, burst in tears.

Many of the marchers stopped, curious. There was anguish in Yousif's voice. But he was reaching them. He jumped up on a high rock, motioning for them to listen.

Yasmin did not know what the devil he was up to. "Don't try to be a hero," she admonished him. "This problem is bigger than all of us. Get down."

Yousif ignored her pleas. Finally, the son came back, pointing a finger. "Are you accusing me of being cruel?" he asked.

"Of course not," Yousif said. "You're doing it because you think you have no choice. But we're going to help you."

Yousif turned and faced the small crowd. "We're going to help him carry this old father to safety."

"Do it, Yousif," Salwa told him, sobbing.

"Bravo," a strong young man said, stepping forward.

"If each and every able-bodied man," Yousif implored, "would carry *ha likhtyar* a hundred yards, we can save a human being. A burden that's shared is no burden at all. Let's all pitch in. I'll be the first. And you can be sure I'm just as tired as any of you. Come on. A human life is at stake."

Salwa threw him a kiss, her cheeks wet. Some of the marchers clapped. Many more smiled. Yousif was encouraged. Salman was shaking his head. Well, Yousif thought, Salman had his hands full. He didn't have to volunteer. But there were plenty of men who were ready.

Yousif walked to the old man and squatted before him. "Come on, Grandpa."

The old man hesitated. Yousif looked back. The old man was crying.

"No need for that," Yousif said. "Hop on."

The old man's son looked ashamed of himself. "I wasn't heartless," he said, sore and red-eyed.

"Who said you were?" Yousif asked. "Come on. We'll all take turns."

The son helped his father get on Yousif's back. The old man felt lighter than Yousif had expected. It must be the adrenaline, Yousif thought, walking briskly.

Yousif carried the scrawny old man for about a mile, stumbling, faltering. Now the old man would clutch his shoulders. Now he would clasp his bony hands around his neck. Then an Israeli bi-plane swooped down on them, as if dropping out of the blue. Yousif had been so engrossed with the old man that he didn't even hear it approaching. The marchers again panicked. They ran helter-skelter. Yousif crouched to let the old man off so that another man could carry him. Bombs did not explode, but they might have just as well. The stampede caused the dust to rise. Women and children screamed. An old man fell down and a dozen marchers stumbled all over him. Yousif looked around. He could see no trace of Salwa or his mother. It seemed as though the earth had split and swallowed her and everyone he knew.

"Ya Allah!" he exclaimed. Where did they go? Now what should he do? Where did they go? How could he find them among thirty thousand people? Must every horror be compounded?

THREE TORTUROUS hours later, Yousif could find no one. A song of doom began to echo in his head. Evil was laid bare before him. Its fullness seized him. He thought about where he was: in the shadow of the great mountain. Had not the devil tempted Jesus here? Whom was he tempting now? Whom was he stalking?

Now, Yousif felt that he himself was being tempted. He was hungry, thirsty, tired. And where was Salwa? Where was her family? He wanted to shout "Goddam! Goddam!" and shake his fist at the heavens, but he didn't. He hadn't lost his mind—yet. But how long, he asked, could one preserve his sanity in a situation like this, especially when the sun was penetrating his skin and drying every cell? "Drink your urine," a voice whispered within him. "Drink it. Humble yourself. Debase yourself. Know that you're weak. Know the limits of humiliation. The mountain says drink it. He who was tempted says drink it. Your lips and tongue demand it."

Yousif was too dehydrated and too foggy to question the inner voice. He veered off the beaten path, stood behind a pile of stones, and forced himself to leak a few drops. He collected them in the palm of his hand as if they were the elixir of life. He raised his hand up to his chin, closed his eyes. At first he hesitated, resisting the craving he suddenly felt. His mind was in turmoil. But then he weakened. The need for moisture burned his lips. Despite his revulsion, he found himself lowering his head into his palm.

He felt better—but too ashamed to tell others what he had done.

He wanted to walk fast, but his feet failed him. The eroded land was full of brush and stones. His ankles kept turning. His lips were dry again, his shoes tight. More important, there was still no sight of Salwa or his mother. Nor anybody from his family. He passed another baby's body, lying face down like a dead chicken. Death was becoming commonplace.

He stood on the edge of a high boulder, surveying the scene below. Thousands were descending at a slow pace. Many were meandering along with the terrain. The hills were rising and falling like the waves. He heard a voice call him. It was Adeeb, the rough classmate who had once fought Isaac.

"Have you seen Salwa or my mother?" Yousif asked.

"No," Adeeb answered, his arm in a sling.

"What happened to your arm?"

"I broke it this morning."

"Oh, no," Yousif said, remembering what had happened to Amin's broken arm. The two classmates now looked at each other, tormented. Adeeb's mother had already discarded her headdress. Her thinning, disheveled hair was solid grey. She stumbled along, lamenting her son's condition. She too remembered what had happened to Amin.

THE HINT OF a village in the distance acted as a magnet, pulling the marchers back together. There was a confluence as the scattered crowd began to head in one direction. Hope surged within Yousif as he hobbled along, too tired to feel the numbness of his feet. Standing on a high rock and watching the flat land below him and the outline of a community on the far horizon, he felt elated. He wanted to dance, too exhausted to feel the irony.

The village of El-Auja was, despite its dreariness, a welcome sight. Here the sea of marchers was met by inhabitants with jugs of water in their hands and by Jordanian soldiers with trucks and jeeps ready to transport them. Yousif was so beaten with fatigue he fell on his face, unable to rise. It flashed through his mind that here, at last, he would not be abandoned; here, at last, water was accessible. He lay there unseeing, unhearing, unfeeling. Voices clashed and receded in his ears. The earth spun around him.

Minutes later, he woke to an uproarious scene. The multitudes were still straggling into the village. The search for lost ones reached a peak. He rested on his elbows and watched a battered stream of refugees pass before him, all looking like millers—powdered with dust from head to toe. A farmer with a petrol can full of water passed him by. Yousif pulled at the man's garment begging with his eyes for a drink. The farmer obliged, helping Yousif place the punched hole in the corner to his mouth. Yousif hugged the can like a lost friend and drank with relish, taking brief pauses between lengthy, thirst-quenching gulps.

"Easy, easy," someone cautioned him. "It's not good to drink so fast."

"After such a long journey without water your lungs are too dry," another man added. "They'll crack if you're not careful."

Yousif was too thirsty to heed their advice. Having drunk enough, he cupped his hands and asked the farmer to pour him some more water. Yousif splashed the cool water across his warm, tense, dirty face. He enjoyed feeling it trickle down his throat and chest.

Suddenly Yousif leapt to his feet. Izzat and Hiyam were in sight.

"Izzat!" he cried. "You made it, you made it!"

Hiyam looked embarrassed, shy, crushed. Her hair had lost its sheen. Her forehead and long neck were bathed with sweat.

"Where's your family?" Izzat asked, holding Hiyam's hand. "Did Salwa and your mother make it all right?"

"I don't know," Yousif answered, feeling guilty.

"You don't know?" Izzat asked.

"We got separated. I was going to ask if you've seen them."

The young couple shook their heads in dismay. They were soon joined by

Hiyam's sister and brother-in-law: her hair unruly, his face unshaven. No, they had not seen Salwa or his mother, they said. Imm Raji sat on the grass-covered ground, exhausted. The others joined her. They formed a circle, enveloped by silence. Jordanian army trucks were lined up about fifty yards away. People were pleading, arguing for a ride.

"If I could only find them," Yousif said, his eyes searching.

He spent one more night outdoors on the outskirts of Jericho and the Dead Sea. The heat was unmerciful, the worry about his mother and Salwa unrelenting.

EARLY NEXT MORNING Yousif struck out on his own. His companions had decided to wait for a ride on account of the women. Jericho was around ten miles away. Yousif felt refreshed enough to attempt the short journey. The morning was cool. The grass and trees were wet with dew. But it was the flatness of the narrow paved road that impressed him most. Here were no boulders to climb over, no steep mountains to descend. Only green and brown plains stretched as far as his eyes could see.

The Mount of Temptation loomed large on Yousif's right. He remembered the monastery perched on one of the cliffs along the path to the top. He had been thirteen years old, but the impact of his visit there had remained with him. How deeply impressed he had been by the monks, by their seclusion and devotion to study and worship. The dark grotto, carved in the heart of the high mountain, lit only with candles, haunted him.

Yousif also remembered the lush fields and orchards of citrus fruits at the mountain's foot. How many times had he visited those same fields in his youth: running, tumbling and splashing water with children of his age and with his favorite cousin, nicknamed Abul Izz.

A few miles to the left was the excavation of Tel es-Sultan and the Hisham Palace, with its ancient but celebrated baths and colonnaded courts. He remembered his last visit there with his parents. He remembered the lesson he had learned from his father about Arab history. He could still see his father leaning against one of the columns, puffing on his pipe, and admiring the art and architecture of the seventh-century Ummayads. How could he forget The Tree of Life, which was considered the most beautiful mosaic in the world? Whatever happened to that snapshot of him and his father in front of the huge star in the main court?

As the sun glistened behind the palm and banana trees, a long line of weary marchers, like a dishonored army in retreat, fell into a rhythmic, grueling walk. Odd, Yousif thought, how most of the people around him were strangers and not from his hometown. Where was the mayor? Where was the principal, ustaz

Saadeh? He thought of Sitt Bahiyyeh and her shell of a mother. How did they manage? He wished Amin or Salman or Basim or Salwa or his mother were around.

"Did you know that at one time Antony gave Jericho to Cleopatra?" Yousif asked an old man wearing a battered fez and walking next to him.

The old man, apparently deep in thought, did not respond.

"That's right," Yousif went on, eager to share with someone the absurdities of history. "It was such a beautiful garden, he wanted his mistress to have it as a gift."

The old man looked at him quizzically. "Son," he said, "you're too young to be losing your mind."

Yousif was not affronted by the remark and let it stand. The idea that even Marc Antony had dared to give away what was not his appalled him. A tall slender Negress with a jug angled on her head appeared coming their way. When she saw the long line of marchers creeping toward her, she seemed puzzled and stepped off the road. Her jug of water was soon emptied as one marcher after another tipped it to his lips. If troubles came to Jericho, Yousif thought, this woman was going to wish she were back in Africa. For some reason most of those Ethiopians who had migrated to Palestine settled in Jericho. Except, of course, for the one or two peddlers of roasted peanuts who had often come to Ardallah during summer. Ardallah! He had been forced out of his hometown only a few days ago, yet it already seemed to recede into the past.

THE TWO-MILE road from Ain es-Sultan to the edge of Jericho's business district was teeming with displaced people who sat over their bundles in the shadows of the palm trees. Even the garden and front steps of the old two-story Ashour Hotel were overrun with people squatting from the pain of exertion. With difficulty, Yousif wove his way through the gate, down the narrow path, and up the flight of stairs—apologizing for stepping on a foot here or a hand there. If his mother or Salwa were to be found anywhere, surely he would find them here. For years, they had been friends with the hotel owners, Elias and Jean Ashour.

Yes! Yasmin was sitting at the far end of the balcony, next to the railing, her eyes searching. He saw her first, watched her wipe her crimson face with her limp handkerchief, then fan herself. Yousif called out her name. She looked up at him, her eyes beaming with unexpected joy. The balcony was congested. But that did not prevent both from elbowing their way toward each other.

"Yousif, *habibi,* I didn't see you coming," she said, breathing a sigh of relief, embracing him with all her might. "My eyes have been fixed on that gate for hours. How are you, *habibi?*"

"I'm fine," Yousif answered, hugging her warmly and kissing her on both cheeks. "How are *you?* Where's Salwa?"

"She's not with you?"

"I haven't seen her since yesterday."

"Oh, my God. Maybe she's with her mother and brothers."

"I hope so." The fact that they had promised each other to remain in Jordan should they get separated gave him little comfort. A number of things could go wrong and she might not be able to keep her promise. "When did you get here?" he asked.

"Early this morning. I was lucky to get a ride from El-Auja. How did you get here?"

"I walked."

"All the way from El-Auja?"

"No. All the way from Ardallah."

"How stupid of me," she remembered, hugging him again.

Feeling sharp pain in his legs, Yousif wanted to sit down. She turned around to offer him her chair, but it had already been taken. Inch by inch, they eased themselves inside the hotel.

"Ah, he's here," said Elias Ashour, the owner, smiling behind the front desk. "Welcome, Yousif, welcome. Your mother was so worried."

"I thought surely his bride would be with him," Yasmin said, wringing her hands.

"She's not?" Ashour said, frowning. "Well, sooner or later she'll show up."

"I hope so," Yousif said, letting his mother lean on him.

The smooth-faced, sun-tanned hotel owner motioned for them to leave the jammed lobby and join him in his office. Men and women were trying to register when there were no vacancies. Some were squatting on the marble floor.

But once Yousif and his mother were in Mr. Ashour's office, they collapsed on the soft armchairs. Each chair felt like a throne under them.

"Summer is our worst season," Elias Ashour said, his long sleeves rolled. His hazel-green eyes shone with anxiety.

"I can imagine," Yousif said, remembering Jericho as a winter resort. In summer months Jericho was like purgatory.

"From June through September, we usually keep a small staff," Elias Ashour continued, "just so we don't have to close down. Occasionally we have four or five guests who are in town on business. Otherwise it's dead. Look at the hotel now. It's bursting at the seams. I've never seen so many people in my life."

"This is nothing," Yousif said, edgy.

"No vacancies whatsoever," the hotel owner added, unmindful of what Yousif had said. "I just hope they don't tear down the hotel or mess up the garden. But what can I do?"

Yousif wanted to tell their host that there was something he could do: stop worrying about his silly hotel. Palestine was ravaged, people were homeless. The tall, heavy-set Elias Ashour, normally congenial, was becoming a chatterbox like his wife. But where was Mrs. Ashour—or Aunt Jean—as Yousif was used to calling her? And what was the business about no vacancies? Was it possible? The owner could not accommodate his best friends? Yousif's mother was on the verge of collapsing. Yousif felt grimy and in need of a hot bath in the worst way. And his feet were swollen and aching.

"Where's Aunt Jean?" Yousif asked, massaging his calf.

"In Greece," Elias Ashour answered. "She wanted to show the kids the Acropolis, of all things. As if we don't have enough ruins in Palestine."

"Especially in Jericho," Yousif's mother said, her face contorted.

"That's what I said," the man agreed. "Go ahead, I told her. I'm staying."

Yousif wondered if his wife had taken the children on vacation to sit out the war. But he didn't ask.

"Elias, may I use your phone?" Yasmin asked the hotel owner. "I'd like to call Jerusalem and check on my parents. They are old and sick and I have an awful feeling . . ."

Seeing that she was having difficulty rising out of her chair, Elias Ashour placed the telephone on the edge of the desk. "By all means," he said, "but you can't get through. All lines to most of Palestine have been cut off for days."

Yasmin was crestfallen. *"Oo ba'dain?"* she asked, helpless. "What's to become of them?"

No one answered.

"Listen," Elias Ashour said, leaning against the edge of his desk. "I've already assigned the kids' rooms to some other friends. You two can have our own bedroom."

"No, no," Yasmin objected. "We can't deprive you of your bed. Goodness! We are no better than the other people. We'll sleep where they sleep."

"Mustaheel," the hotel owner said. "Do you want me to be divorced? If Jean finds out you slept on a chair or on the floor, I'll never hear the end of it."

Yousif and his mother looked at each other. Yousif was dying for his mother to accept. He was not used to sleeping on anything except a bed. The same with her. What was wrong with being lucky and having such a friend? After all, what were friends for? Were it up to him, everyone would have a bed.

"Where would you sleep?" Yousif asked, addressing the hotel owner.

"Don't worry about me," Mr. Ashour told him. "The way things are, I don't need to sleep. And if I have to, I'll doze off right here in my office. How many times did I spend a whole night at the poker table with your father? *Allah yirhamu.*"

"May you live long," Yasmin said.

Elias Ashour sighed. "Gone are those days. But, what can we do? In the meantime, go up to the room and rest. Here's the key. Room 12. And I'll send you food with room service."

Yousif's mother looked flustered. "You're so kind."

Yousif was deeply touched. "We'll never forget you," he said.

The man's generosity made Yousif regret his earlier thoughts. One day he would repay the man—measure for measure.

"Maybe you can help us make up our mind," Yousif's mother said, wiping the sweat off her face. "Yousif and I haven't talked about it yet."

"We haven't seen each other, let alone talked," Yousif reminded her.

"That's what I meant," his mother explained. "Still, we have no plans? Give us your advice: should we stay in Jericho? Should we go to Amman? What do you think?"

Yousif was startled. "Mother, we promised each other to regroup in Jordan."

"Well," Yasmin said. "Suppose we find each other here in Jericho. We don't have to leave then, do we?"

The hotel owner did not hesitate. "Yes. Go to Jordan. That's what I would do if I were in your shoes. I can't conceive that any part of Palestine right now is out of danger. The damn truce tipped the scale in the Zionists' favor. When things settle down, you can always come back. But for the time being—keep going."

"I was afraid you'd say that," Yasmin said, pursing her lips. "Amman is only a hundred miles away. But there it's safe. Here it is not."

Silence hung in the air like an invisible shroud.

"Did you know my father-in-law, Anton Taweel?" Yousif asked.

"Was it Anton's daughter you married? I didn't know that. Good family. What about him?"

Yousif cringed. "He passed away."

Ashour was thunderstruck. "You mean died? How? Where?"

"Had a heart attack. About twenty miles from here."

"Jesus! What a shame!"

Yousif gave him the details, which sounded worse in the telling.

"Jesus!" Ashour repeated, his face turning bluish. "Left in the wilderness! What a tragedy! If he's not eaten already, his body will be bloated beyond recognition in this heat. Jesus!"

A dark shadow of sorrow and despair loomed on their faces. The three remained quiet, enveloped by memories, disturbed by uncertainties. The hubbub of the refugees was rising. The hotel's backyard was strewn with exhausted men and women—like a cemetery with open tombs.

TWO DAYS LATER Jericho was still swarming with people, but there was no hint of Salwa. Yousif and his mother waited in vain for a way out of the stifling city. But vehicles were rarer than snow in the desert. It seemed hopeless until, by a gift from heaven, Yousif ran into Makram, the taxi driver from Ardallah. Even then he and his mother had to wait two more days before Makram returned to pick them up. His dusty black Mercedes was already occupied by a couple and their three children when it arrived. But Yousif and his mother did not complain. They were luckier than most.

"What! No luggage?" the short, dark Makram jested as he moved swiftly around the car to open the doors.

"Funny," Yousif said. "Listen, Makram. Have you seen Salwa or any of her family?"

"No, I haven't."

"I can't believe this," Yousif said, frustrated. "Where did they go?"

The big man in the front seat got out and let Yousif squeeze in between him and the driver.

Abbas Bittar was a forty-eight-year-old business man from Jaffa. But his wife called him Abu Mamdouh, which made her Imm Mamdouh. Their three children were a son, Mamdouh, age ten; a daughter, Siham, age eight; and a baby, Azmi, age six months. Yousif judged them to be of comfortable means. They had about them the look and demeanor of those who knew, up till now, the good life. Imm Mamdouh was attractive, with flowing black hair. One of her upper teeth was turned sideways, and the whites of her eyes were conspicuously large. Yet neither distracted from her flaming sexiness. Looking at least fifteen years younger than her husband, she had a tendency to blabber. In comparison, Abu Mamdouh was taciturn.

The traffic was heavy. At the narrow, shaky Allenby Bridge over the Jordan River, the natural border between Palestine and Trans-Jordan, movement was imperceptible. Thousands of people were lined up alongside trucks and private cars, waiting to be checked and admitted into Trans-Jordan. Abu Mamdouh shook his head and cursed all those responsible for the tragedy. Yasmin sighed with impatience. The heat was so unbearable in the car, they had to open the four doors. But that brought no relief and proved a great nuisance to the pedestrians, so they had to close them again. The children in the car grew restless. Yousif's mother was sympathetic and commended them on their good behavior.

"God bless you, you've been angels," she told them, trying to take the baby from his mother's arms. The baby kicked her with his bare little feet and began to cry.

Bemused, Yousif watched his mother. Her flushed face worried him.

"I can't take much more of this," she complained, constantly fanning herself with her handkerchief. "Get out, son, and see what you can do. Tell them I'm sick. Do something. Makram, give someone five pounds. Get us out of here, please. I'm burning up."

"Mother!" Yousif said. "No one is privileged here. And stop talking about money. Where do you think you are?"

"The arrogance, the conceit of the Zionists is incredible," Abu Mamdouh reflected, smoldering like a chained lion. "They think they can come back after two thousand years and just take our homes, our farms?"

"And throw us out?" Yousif agreed.

"Especially," Abu Mamdouh added, "when we had nothing to do with their leaving in the first place."

Yasmin seemed in another world. "If we could only sit in the shade," she complained. "Look at all these people in the hot sun. Look at all the children. I don't see how they stand it."

Abu Mamdouh's bronze forehead glistened with sweat. He clasped and unclasped his hands over his enormous girth, saying it would be a long wait yet. For the first time, Yousif noticed the man's powerful hands: his fingers seemed as long and thick as cucumbers. Then Yousif thought he heard someone weeping. He turned around and looked. It was Imm Mamdouh. Baby Azmi was in her arms and clawing around her neck.

"Mortals are not supposed to question God's will," Yasmin said, wiping the sweat off her own forehead. "But I can't help feeling that He's been hard on us. It's not fair. It's not right."

"God knows we've never hurt a soul," Imm Mamdouh said, sniffling.

Everyone looked at her.

"You don't know us and we don't know you," Imm Mamdouh continued, pulling her baby from around her neck, and sitting him in her lap. "But let me tell you that my husband is one of the biggest orange exporters in Palestine."

"Stop bragging," Abu Mamdouh admonished her.

"I'm not bragging," his wife said.

"Of course you're not," Yousif's mother assured her.

"Now he's got nothing," Imm Mamdouh protested. "Do you blame him if he's speechless? Do you blame him if he's stunned by what the Jews did to us?"

"Some of them used to be my best friends," Abu Mamdouh said, looking straight ahead. "Did business together for years."

"May Allah topple their homes over their heads," Makram prayed, stretching his arms heavenward.

"He had over a hundred men and women working for him," Imm Mamdouh added. "And then he had to leave his orange groves, the chicken farm, the fifteen trucks, his fine home, his private car—and cross the country on foot. It's enough to make one curse."

"May God make all their wives widows," Makram prayed again at the top of his voice.

There was something comical about Makram's outbursts. But no one laughed.

Again the young mother's face contorted. Tears streamed down her cheeks. Baby Azmi scratched her neck. She pulled out her breast, pushing the nipple in his mouth. The temperature inside the car was oppressive. Yousif and Makram got out to stretch their legs. Abu Mamdouh remained in place, his eyes glazed.

Yousif walked around, looking at the Jordan River below. It was such a narrow "trickle" it hardly seemed to be an important international boundary. It twisted like an over-sized ditch, its banks covered with stones and scattered bushes. So shallow, had it been close to a village women would have washed their clothes in it. No, maybe not, for its water was murky.

How odd, Yousif thought, for God to have had His only son baptized in such a dreary place. God certainly did not do right by His own son, Yousif thought. Imagine! He even let him enter Jerusalem on a donkey. Not a fine carriage, not a white horse, not even a one-hump camel. A donkey—and probably a puny, scrawny one at that.

"Sorry, God," Yousif thought, looking at the deep blue sky. "If you would allow your own son to be nailed and stabbed, if you would let him die on the cross like a common criminal, you'd probably let our homes burn to the ground. If that's the way you'd treat your own son, to whom should we Palestinians turn for protection? You're acting as though we're not your children, as though you don't love us. You're treating us no better than our kings and presidents have been treating us. And you know what a disappointment they've turned out to be."

Soon, however, Yousif regretted his blasphemy and felt ashamed of himself. But he couldn't help his anger. Moments later, while no one was looking, he crossed himself, asking God for forgiveness.

32

As soon as they were finally ushered through the narrow gate of Allenby Bridge, the barren Jordanian terrain engulfed them. Only a bridge, a mythical boundary, and they were now in a different country. Long stretches of flat hot desert lay on both sides of the highway. Ahead was a caravan of countrymen, jammed in trucks, teetering on collapse. A greater number of people were braving the long journey on foot, once again like a tattered army in retreat.

Yousif felt disoriented. He looked back through the car window. His homeland was receding in the distance. Only a few minutes gone, and he was already feeling nostalgic. Gone was Palestine with its oranges and olives and balmy weather. Gone were the golden summer nights in Ardallah. Gone were the richly green thickets and leafy orchards of Jericho. Gone were the smells of mango and guava and the bitter taste of endive salad.

His eyes grew misty. And in his heart he could feel a growing hate.

A few miles away from Allenby bridge and the low lands of the Dead Sea, the terrain began to change. Spindly palm trees were scattered in the wide desert, like pillars of a lost civilization. Half an hour later, unfamiliar mountains and high cliffs hugged the road on both sides. Makram pushed on the gas. Yousif felt the heat wave rushing against his face through the open window.

Yousif was amazed how little he knew about Trans-Jordan, and how little contact existed between the people of these two neighboring states. He knew the name of King Abdullah; the names of the largest cities: Amman, Irbid, Jarash, Salt,

Zarqua; the name and the poetry of a rebel poet, Mustapha Wehby al-Tell; and the name of the attorney who had translated Dante's *The Human Comedy*. Above all, Yousif knew that Trans-Jordan was a vast desert inhabited by nomadic tribes. Arab history, particularly Arabic poetry, had instilled in him the love of the desert and the Bedu. He had always looked forward to the experience of knowing both. But not as an exile.

THE CITY OF Amman looked bleak and arid—like a large village spread out at random. Dust blew everywhere. The streets were narrow and mostly unpaved. Ugly white stone houses and mud-brick huts were strewn haphazardly on several hills. There were no curves to please the eye, no trees or flowers to enliven the drab scene or break the monotony.

The commotion that afternoon seemed incongruous in such a primitive and sleepy town. Buses and trucks and cars and pushcarts and camels and donkeys and pedestrians were thrown together, causing a pandemonium not unlike the one he had seen in Ardallah when the people of Lydda and Ramleh had first arrived. Drivers honked their horns, vendors shouted their wares, policemen whistled their directions, and Makram's taxi crawled to a halt. In the heart of town, congestion made movement impossible.

"You might as well forget about looking for a hotel room," Makram told them, waiting for the crowd to stop crossing the street. "Even King Abdullah couldn't get a room tonight."

"I bet," Yousif said.

"I mean it. It's that serious."

"You've been here and we haven't," Yasmin told him. "Just find us a place to spend the night. Tomorrow God will provide."

"Tomorrow will be more difficult," Makram advised. "Ten times more difficult."

"Well, what do you suggest?" inquired Abu Mamdouh.

"I say you ought to look for an apartment to rent for more than just one night. The sooner the better. If you're lucky your two families could share one. But that's up to you."

It was a long search. They knocked on fifteen or twenty doors only to be turned away because all the rooms had already been rented. Often there would be three or four families in line trying to negotiate with the landlord. Children cried. Tempers flared. Disappointment followed disappointment, but they persisted. They had no choice. They had to have a place to sleep. Everywhere they went, Yousif kept asking about Salwa. No one had seen her. It was getting dark, they were getting tired and hungry, but they took turns to knock. Frequently they would read the anguish on the faces of other apartment hunters and drive on. Once, as soon as Makram parked his car in front of a house that looked halfway decent, the owner looked out of the window and motioned for him and his group not to bother getting out.

But by eight o'clock that night luck smiled on them and they found a suitable place—a flat built on the roof of a grocery store. There was a small sitting room between the two bedrooms and a kitchen that led to a narrow balcony protruding above the narrow street below. Yousif and his mother took the bedroom on the left. The Bittar family occupied the one on the right. Behind the house, and hugging the slope, was a small patio shaded by an old, leaning tree. Except for the bedrooms, the two families had to share everything.

"This flat has never been lived in," the shriveled owner with a wrinkled white shirt and a sullen white *hatta* assured Yousif and his mother. "You can still smell the fresh paint."

"Yes, we can," Yasmin agreed, looking exhausted.

"May I crack the window?" Yousif asked. "It's a bit strong."

"Sure, go ahead. I don't mind. You're paying the rent, and you should feel at home. Frankly, I could've rented it for more than fifteen pounds a month. And I could've asked for a two-month deposit, like so many people are doing. But, I said to myself, no need adding to your misery."

"Thanks," Yousif replied, pulling hard to get the window unstuck.

"It's the fresh paint," the man explained.

Yousif rested against the window sill, and watched his mother wipe her forehead with her handkerchief. She seemed anxious for the man to leave, but he did not.

"Don't mind my saying so," the man said, fumbling in the pocket of his frayed blue pants with ugly wide stripes. He lit an off-brand cigarette and offered Yousif one, but Yousif declined. "You Palestinians live in better homes than we do, no question about that. I was in Jerusalem once, a long time ago, and I know what kind of homes you have. No one around here can afford that kind of luxury. But you're lucky to find a place. Any place. People around here are mostly poor. They build for themselves and no more. There are not many rooms to rent, believe me. Where are all those people going to stay I don't know."

"You've been kind to let us have the room," Yasmin said, walking around, craning her neck and rubbing its nape.

"You're welcome. I only wish it were better. Actually, I built it for me and my wife and our only son, Khalil. He's twenty-one. How old are you?"

"Eighteen," Yousif answered.

"He's three years older than you. I thought you looked a bit older than that. Anyway, he's a bachelor, and we thought maybe this summer we'd find him a wife."

"Inshallah," Yousif's mother said, standing by a wall and leaning her head against it.

"My wife and I planned to live in one room, and to let him and his bride have the other one. But, that's the way it goes." There was a touch of sadness in the voice of the thin-faced man.

"Who would've imagined," Yasmin said, pale and about to collapse.

Anxious about her health, Yousif walked to the door and opened it. "We're grateful to you," he told the man.

"Don't be grateful to me, son. Show all your gratitude, give all your thanks to Allah. We owe Him everything. I built these two rooms because Allah wanted me to have them. You found a place to stay because Allah wanted you to find it. Allah was, is, and will be everywhere. Allah did, does, and will do everything."

"Can He commit a sin?" Yousif asked, holding the door ajar.

The man's black beady eyes seemed not to understand. "Allah commit a sin?" he asked. "Heavenly Father. Son, you amaze me."

"I'm just wondering."

"That's a new one for me. Allah commit a sin? Amazing, I've never thought of that. Yet, if He's responsible for everything, and you're homeless, then it follows . . ." the man mumbled on his way out.

Yousif smiled and watched him go down the steps, shaken by the irreverence.

As soon as Yousif shut the door, Yasmin began to cry. She wailed for the first time since they had left Ardallah. Yousif watched her walk in a daze around the room, touch the white-washed walls with her fingertips, and bang her fist in agony. He heard her pray for the safety of Salwa and her family, her own parents, her sister Widad and her husband and children. He saw her put her forehead against the wall and cry fitfully.

"Have we come to this?" she moaned. "Have we come to this? Four walls, a bare floor, and not a mat to sit on? Oh, God, why? What have we done?"

Yousif was standing by the window watching the crossings of people and cars on the narrow, poorly-lit street below. He heard his mother sigh, and turned in time to see her collapse in a heap. He ran to her, and lifted her face gently off the mosaic floor. He sat beside her, holding her head close to his shoulder.

"Mother," he begged, "calm yourself, will you? As the man said, we're lucky."

She beat the bare floor with her fist, bursting out in tears.

"He's right," Yousif consoled her. "Where are all these people going to stay? You know what happened in Ardallah—they ended up in tents, remember? At least we have a roof over our heads. God knows where Salwa is. And Uncle Boulus and Aunt Hilaneh. And Maha and Salman and the rest. How are they managing? I get sick thinking about them."

His mother did not answer. Her mouth and chin continued to tremble.

Yousif racked his brain trying to say something to cheer her up. "The son is going to be furious," he said, "when he finds out his father has rented this place. Probably no room, no wedding. I'd be angry too."

Twenty minutes later, they heard a knock on the door. Yousif rose and opened it. A delivery boy wearing suspenders came in carrying a tray of food.

"Compliments of Abu Khalil," the delivery boy said, hesitating before putting the tray on the floor.

Yousif tipped him two shillings instead of one, and the boy seemed pleasantly surprised.

"Where did the food come from?" Yousif asked.

"From Abu Khalil. He owns the building and the grocery store below."

"I meant where did he order it from?"

"A small cafe next door. I work there."

"Is it possible to borrow a few chairs, until we get some furniture?'

"I don't know. We're awfully busy. But I'll see what I can do."

"Will you?"

On the aluminum tray were several *falafel* sandwiches, two dishes of pickles, four dishes of *hummus,* and several loaves of pita bread. That much food, Yousif realized, was meant for the two families.

Yousif took some of the food next door and returned to find his mother still crying. He did not know how to console her. There was a second knock on the door, and he was glad for the intrusion. The delivery boy had returned, carrying two low straw-bottomed chairs by each hand.

"You're so kind," Yousif told him, accepting two chairs.

At midnight, Yousif stretched out on the cold bare floor. He rolled over several times trying to sleep. His mother sat motionless by the window, staring outside. He shut his eyes, but his restless mind kept him awake. He folded his arms under his head and stared at the stark opposite wall. He must have pressed a nerve in his temple for the throb in his head swung like an invisible pendulum. He rolled on his back and stared at the ceiling, thinking of Salwa and the promise to stay in Jordan. Why hadn't they specified Amman in particular? How big was Jordan—how many cities would he have to go to? He must look for her in the morning, he told himself. Someone was bound to know where she was. His back ached. He rolled to his left side and then to his right. It was his most comfortable position, but he couldn't sleep.

"Lift up, oh God, this evil off your land," Yasmin prayed. "Save our children and protect our homes. Our enemies are Your enemies for they know not Your face."

Yousif opened his eyes. His mother was silhouetted against the moonlight, framed by the open window. She looked troubled, withdrawn. He closed his eyes again lest he intrude on her privacy.

"Why did You let them, my God, my Savior," she continued, "trespass so brutally against the innocent? They have come with unwarranted hostility in their hearts. They have uprooted people who have done them no harm. They bode us ill, oh Lord. Remove the storm from their hearts so that we may all see Your glory, so that, in Thy name, we may all live in peace."

When she began to sob, Yousif sat up fully awake. "You can't go on like this," he told her. "Think of your blood pressure."

"Blood pressure? Who cares? We're ruined. We're ruined."

She beat on her chest and then buried her head in her hands. Strands of hair fell to the side of her face.

"You ought to lie down," Yousif suggested. "It's not the softest bed but it's better than sitting up all night on this stool."

"If I sleep on this floor," she said, blowing her nose, "tomorrow morning my back will be stiff as a board. I'll never be able to get up."

"It's a hard floor," he admitted, resting on his elbows.

"God will deny them His blessings. I'm only glad your father isn't here to see all this."

Yousif's mind drifted back. "He's better off," he muttered, thinking.

"Wherever he is, he's watching."

"How much money do we have? At fifteen pounds a month for rent, it won't last long. Not to mention the cost of food."

"Here, count it."

She handed him a small bundle she had lifted from inside her bodice. The bills were wrapped in a lacy handkerchief. He unwrapped them and began to count.

"Sixty, seventy, eighty, some people wish they have this much, ninety—"

"Masakeen," she said, pursing her lips. "What's to become of them? How will they live? Thank God it's summer. What will happen when winter comes? We're all *masakeen.*"

"—hundred and ninety . . . two hundred . . . two hundred and ten—"

"If we only had the jewelry."

"—two hundred and forty, two hundred and fifty—"

"Yousif, what if they find it? Listen, son, what if they discover—?"

"Two hundred and eighty-five pounds. Plus the two in my pocket. And that's it. That's all we have to our names."

He folded the money and handed it to her, but she motioned for him to keep it. Yousif caught the anxiety in her eyes. "What's the matter?"

"On top of the jewelry—mine and Salwa's—we had to leave them four hundred pounds. An icing on the cake."

"To hell with it. Besides, there isn't a chance they'll find the jewelry."

"Why?"

"Because it's hidden."

"What if they move the furniture around? What if they notice something peculiar about that one tile?"

"Not a chance."

"I want to believe it, but I can't."

"Believe me, we'll be back before Christmas," he lied.

"Oh, sure."

"You don't think so?"

"Not for a moment. Every bone in my body tells me we'll never see our home again."

"Nonsense."

"You wait and see. Everything we own is gone: the two homes, stock, clinic, savings, jewelry, the cash."

Yousif was equally disturbed, but he wouldn't admit it. Both lapsed into silence.

"Go to sleep, will you?"

"Listen to him. Go to sleep, he says. And if we're lucky to go back, what will we find? Not a stick of furniture. Not a table, not a chair, not a dish, not a spoon."

"Everything is replaceable," Yousif said, rolling on the floor trying to sleep. "You yourself have said money and property aren't everything. Remember?"

She remained upright in her chair. He closed his eyes, welcoming the feel of a soft breeze. He hoped it would lull his senses. His mother was probably right. Going home would be next to impossible. Thoughts of Basim, Salman, Uncle Boulus, and their families crossed his mind. Above all, he thought of Salwa. Where was she? Wherever she was, he hoped she had a bed. Was she sleeping on the floor like him? He wondered how long it would take to find her. What if it took him a week? Or a month? First thing in the morning, he would start looking for her.

He rolled to his side, his left leg straight and his right leg curled to his stomach. His cheek rested on the floor. The cool, smooth surface pleased him. But he could not sleep, could not succumb for an hour—if only for an hour—of rest. Reluctantly, he opened his right eye, peeking at his mother. She was still rigid in her place by the window, her hands clasped in her lap, and her eyes staring into the silvery night.

A wave of delicious sleep crept over him, and he yearned to float away with it. But it passed, leaving him awake. A bird fluttered in his head, dipping and flying over a vista of hurts and concerns. His nerves were too strained for him to concentrate. He wished the bird would disappear. Yet the bird hovered over the same wound, unmindful of his wishes.

The stillness of the night was deafening. It belied the havoc and turmoil Yousif felt inside. From the little he knew about the history of Zionism, this was not meant to be a temporary exile. The Zionist soldiers had not pushed them out at gunpoint to welcome them back before Christmas. He and his people were driven out—to stay out. Was violating the land of Canaan and terrorizing all its inhabitants the Jewish way of keeping the Ten Commandments? Where was Moses to see what they were doing—raping, murdering, and throwing people into the wilderness?

He must do something to expedite their return. Which course should he follow? Should he become a politician and lobby on behalf of his people around the capitals of the world? Perhaps he could carry the fight all the way to the United Nations. Did the outside world know what had happened to the Palestinians? Or should he become a writer, a filmmaker, a journalist and tell the world how they were uprooted and forced into the wilderness? For Yousif, the memory of that journey was indelible. The good people around the globe should know about it. They would sympathize, they would understand.

But to what end? Would they help him recover Ardallah? Would they send him home again? Not likely. What then must he do? It was a Herculean task that required the work of governments. Would people listen to him? Would his classmates go along with his plans? What plans? Where would the money come from?

Yousif tossed and turned in despair. The floor was hard under him. But his thoughts kept racing. Was Salwa agonizing as he was? He felt responsible for her and her mother and brothers, especially now that her father was dead. He must find her.

Yousif's head buzzed with anguish. Maybe Salwa had stayed in Jericho, looking for him. My God! She didn't have any money on her. What if she were separated from her family? What then? Some of the refugees who had not been able to find an apartment that afternoon had spoken of leaving for other cities, maybe even to Syria or Lebanon where the influx of refugees was perhaps less acute. The thought that Yousif might not find Salwa soon intensified his misery. His fingernails dug deep in his palm.

He thought of Basim and the men on the hilltops. Had they fallen victims? Had they paid for their birthright with their blood? When would he find out if they were dead? God, he hoped no ill had come to any of them—especially Basim. He was a leader one could trust. Yousif also hoped nothing bad had happened to ustaz Hakim. Or ustaz Saadeh. Or Izzat and Amin. How soon could they all organize—at least politically? What would their first order of business be? Surely to negotiate a return for all these masses before Israel had a chance to demolish their villages and obliterate any trace of their existence. But would the Arab regimes give a handful of zealous Palestinians a free hand? Not likely. Not soon anyway. Would Israel recognize such a group as a negotiating partner? Israel had not bled them only to resurrect them. It had meant for them to vanish. Even if lightning struck and Israel had a change of heart, what price would it exact?

Again Yousif heard his mother's voice.

"How true Arabic proverbs are," she reflected.

Yousif looked up. She was still sitting by the window, as though wary of closing her eyes.

"Which one do you have in mind?" he asked, his eyes drowsy.

"Niyyal illi binam bham 'ateek. Lucky is he who sleeps with an old worry. How very true! An old worry is over something that has already passed. A new worry is over something yet to come."

Bitter years ahead, as implied in his mother's words, did not frighten him. He lay on the floor, letting the phantoms of the future take shape in his mind. But when he heard her cry, an electric shock tore through him. He sprang to his feet and held her close to his body. Her sobbing was like distant rumbling before the apocalypse. He could feel her trembling, and his blood began to simmer.

He stared out the window. He could see the bare outlines of a few makeshift tents. The full moon hovered over them like a caretaker.

"Don't cry, Mother," Yousif said, massaging her shoulders. "I swear to you on my father's grave, and on the graves of all the martyrs, that we will return."

Yasmin tightened her grip around his waist and buried her head in his chest, sobbing.

"Don't worry," he said, his heart in his mouth. "It will all come to pass."

Slowly, his mother withdrew from him. "He that believeth will make no haste," she quoted, doom pouring out of her eyes. "Make no promises you cannot keep."

"No, no," he said, holding her hands, words gushing out of him like a spring fountain. The promise he had made to Salwa two nights earlier rang in his ears. "You must understand. The conscience of the world must be pricked, awakened. And we will do it. This is *not* an idle promise. And it's *not* made in haste. We *shall* return. I promise you this on your honor and the honor of every mother weeping tonight. I promise you this for the sake of all of us who have been dispossessed—the families that have been denied their birthright and are now separated, the children who can't sleep because they're hungry, the babies who journeyed and died from thirst, the dead we left along the trail. Let this moon, which is staring at us like a grave one-eyed God, be my witness: we *shall* be delivered. We *shall* return."

About the Author

IBRAHIM FAWAL was born in Ramallah, Palestine. He moved to the United States to pursue his education, receiving a master's degree in Film from UCLA. He worked with renowned director David Lean as the "Jordanian" first assistant director on the classic *Lawrence of Arabia*. Fawal lives in Birmingham, Alabama, where he taught film and literature at Birmingham-Southern College and the University of Alabama at Birmingham. He recently earned his Ph.D. from Oxford University, where his concentration was an examination of Arab culture through the cinema of Youssef Chahine, the foremost film director of the Arab world. His dissertation, *Youssef Chahine,* has been published by the British Film Institute. *On the Hills of God* is Fawal's first novel. It won the PEN-Oakland Award for Excellence in Literature and has been translated into Arabic and German.